in print at
$16.95

PENGUIN BOOKS

THE PORTABLE EMERSON

Each volume in The Viking Portable Library either presents a representative selection from the works of a single outstanding writer or offers a comprehensive anthology on a special subject. Averaging 700 pages in length and designed for compactness and readability, these books fill a need not met by other compilations. All are edited by distinguished authorities, who have written introductory essays and included much other helpful material.

"The Viking Portables have done more for good reading and good writers than anything that has come along since I can remember."

— Arthur Mizener

Carl Bode teaches American literature and American studies at the University of Maryland. Founder and first president of the American Studies Association, he is also past president of the Popular Culture Association and the Mencken Society. His books include *The American Lyceum, Antebellum Culture,* and *Mencken.* He has edited *The Portable Thoreau, Collected Poems of Henry Thoreau,* and *The Best of Thoreau's Journals* and has co-edited *The Correspondence of Henry David Thoreau.*

Malcolm Cowley's books include *Exile's Return: A Literary Odyssey of the 1920s; The Faulkner-Cowley File: Letters and Memories, 1944–1962; A Second Flowering: Works and Days of the Lost Generation;* and *—And I Worked at the Writer's Trade: Chapters of Literary History, 1918–1978* (all published by Penguin Books). He was also the editor of *The Portable Faulkner* and *The Portable Hawthorne.* Malcolm Cowley died in 1989.

THE PORTABLE

EMERSON

New Edition

Edited by Carl Bode
in Collaboration with
Malcolm Cowley

PENGUIN BOOKS

PENGUIN BOOKS
Published by the Penguin Group
Viking Penguin Inc., 40 West 23rd Street, New York, New York 10010, U.S.A.
Penguin Books Ltd, 27 Wrights Lane, London W8 5TZ, England
Penguin Books Australia Ltd, Ringwood, Victoria, Australia
Penguin Books Canada Ltd, 2801 John Street,
Markham, Ontario, Canada L3R 1B4
Penguin Books (N.Z.) Ltd, 182–190 Wairau Road,
Auckland 10, New Zealand

Penguin Books Ltd, Registered Offices:
Harmondsworth, Middlesex, England

First published in the United States of America by
Viking Penguin Inc. 1946
Paperbound edition published 1957
Reprinted 1959, 1960, 1962, 1963, 1965 (twice), 1967, 1968,
1969 (twice), 1970, 1971, 1972, 1973, 1974, 1975, 1976
Published in Penguin Books 1977
Reprinted 1978, 1979, 1980
New Edition published 1981

10

LIBRARY OF CONGRESS CATALOGING IN PUBLICATION DATA
Emerson, Ralph Waldo, 1803–1882.
The portable Emerson.
(The Viking portable library)
Bibliography: p.
1. Bode, Carl, 1911– . II. Cowley, Malcolm,
1898–1989. III. Title.
[PS1603.B6 1981b] 813'.3 81-4047
ISBN 0 14 015 094 3   AACR2

Printed in the United States of America
Set in CRT Janson

The text of "Thoreau" is reprinted from *Studies in the American
Renaissance 1979* (Boston: Twayne Publishers, 1979) by permission.
Copyright © Ralph Waldo Emerson Memorial Association, 1979.

CONTENTS

INTRODUCTION
BY CARL BODE

~~~~~~~~~~~~~~~~~~~~~~~~~~~~

Approaching Emerson. Today we encounter an altered Emerson. We are able to benefit from fresh insights, in good part because of the full and definitive edition of his writing now being issued in Cambridge, where he himself once studied. The uncensored journals are especially valuable. By their light—usually steady, but at times flickering, at other times fierce—we can glimpse an Emerson only hinted at before, as well as recognize the familiar lineaments of the author and lecturer. We discover a more human Emerson, who occasionally jeers at his pretensions or doubts his mission and who periodically worries about the decline in his energy, not least as it enfeebles his emotional life. At rare intervals we see a private Emerson whose depths no one has plumbed. This is the man who, in the most haunting sentence in all his journals, reports about the only woman he really loved, "I visited Ellen's tomb & opened the coffin."

Far more frequently we find a comprehensible man, with abundant energy to cope with his world. This is the courageous minister who, impelled by conscience, gives up his Unitarian pulpit without any assurance that he will ever be employed again. This is the man who proceeds to make himself a poet-prophet and, through his efforts during four decades, surely does more than anyone else to raise the spiritual level of his countrymen.

The published works, now being re-edited, are naturally our richest resource for Emerson the author. Yet here too the journals are valuable. They are what he mined for his lectures and essays, for they became more than diaries; they became anthologies of his vast reading. He established a system. He would mark the book at hand, copy the most attractive passages into the current journal, digest them in his mind, and set down his reflections about them. Then from these he drafted the lectures and essays. The system worked, and a good many times throughout his long career the results were memorable.

The life that generated the writing. We might start with college, Harvard of course, where earlier Emersons had gone. He was a poor boy whose widowed mother supported him and her four other sons, one retarded, by taking in boarders. He was also a gifted boy. He passed the entrance examination nicely and entered Harvard in September 1817, barely fourteen years old, with the promise of a part-time job from the president.

His classmates learned to like the quiet stripling. Although he seldom took part in their coltish recreations, which included throwing furniture out of the window, he was discovered to have an unobtrusive sense of humor. In his studies he had an uneven freshman year and then improved markedly. However, he never quite won the top awards. An essay of his placed second in the Bowdoin Prize competition; he failed to make Phi Beta Kappa; and he was named class poet only, it was rumored, after half a dozen classmates declined.

Yet the four years at Harvard were significant. While several of his veteran professors lectured as if stuffed with straw, some newer ones proved genuinely exciting. Listening to Edward Everett's eloquence on Greece, Emerson resolved to give his own Greek studies "long & serious attention." Erudite George Ticknor introduced him to European literature, French especially; he learned a little about Montaigne, who would become a permanent favorite. Edward Tyrrell Channing taught him the art of orderly composition and persuasively preached the doctrine of the plain style rather than the fancy.

In philosophy he was not so fortunate in his professors, but the subject itself commanded his attention. He studied John Locke's theory that nearly everything we learn comes through our senses, as well as Dugald Stewart's theory that there are important things we know through a "common sense" beyond the five senses Locke depended on. He studied William Paley, whose ethical doctrine was highlighted by his debatable dictum "Whatever is expedient, is right." That he studied these philosophers is not to say that he agreed with them, except tentatively with Stewart. But, as the saying goes, they made him think.

Most important—so he asserted in after years—were the amount and range of the reading he did. Already enamored of print when he began his first journal in January 1820, he appropriately entitled it "Wide World." In June 1821 he compiled a list of books to be read as subject matter for themes and another of books he owned and had lent to friends. The first list was made up mainly of literature, biography, and travel; but it included Humphrey Davy's *Elements of Chemical Philosophy* and Richard Price's textbook on morals. The theme topics looked enterprising; one was the influence of weather on intellectual temperament. The second list was mainly literary, with Sir Walter Scott the favorite author.

Graduation arrived in August 1821. It was of course a rite of passage. Perhaps anticipating it, he had announced the year before that he wished to be called Waldo, not Ralph: a new persona, probably, to accompany a new life. If so, we can deduce from his journal that he was not quite sure what persona; he was engaged in finding himself.

Halfheartedly he tried teaching at his brother William's school for girls. He began to entertain some thoughts about the ministry, especially as the new Unitarianism was opening it up. And he read and wrote. The journals reveal that moral problems were already a prime interest, something that his college exercises had previously hinted at. Is virtue based on civilization? he wondered, for instance. He prepared embryo essays on such subjects as sympathy, human nature, and providence. He had been penning verses for years but now they improved, looking less starchy than before.

Leaning further toward the ministry, he supplemented his sporadic teaching with studies at the Harvard Divinity School. He survived a dire threat to any career he might like. It was blindness: for half a year he came close to losing his sight. Once he recovered he began to be plagued by lung trouble. Notwithstanding, he went ahead with his ministerial courses. In October 1826 his local ministers' association granted him his license to preach, a preliminary step to ordination. The quality of the sermons he gave from place to place soon marked him as having exceptional promise. Congregations found his words and ideas thought-provoking, never ordinary. As the prospects for a permanent post drew closer, he realized what he wanted. After declining invitations from several different churches, he accepted a call to the junior pastorate of Boston's famous Second Church. With it went the prospect of the senior pastorate when its currently ill incumbent resigned. His talents were increasingly recognized, in the pulpit and out. He was soon chosen chaplain of the Massachusetts State Senate and then elected to the Boston School Committee. He was on the way to being a public figure.

His personal life for a time looked as promising as his professional one; for he fell in love with and successfully wooed Ellen Louisa Tucker of Concord, New Hampshire. They met when he journeyed to Concord to preach in December 1827. A decade later he still remembered her first smile to him. She proved to be devout, affectionate, and—despite an ominous lung affliction—spirited. All our evidence indicates that this was the one time in his life he felt a genuine passion. When they became engaged it made him so happy that he was apprehensive. They married in September 1829, when he was twenty-six and she seventeen. "Oh Ellen, I do dearly love you," he exclaimed in his journal.

It was a good marriage. They enriched each other's emotional and religious life, but all too briefly. The consumption which everyone hoped would heal grew worse. In spite of temporary remissions Ellen died in February 1831. "O willingly, my wife, I would lie down in your tomb," Emerson wrote in agony.

Many a morning during the next months people met him walking to or from that tomb. It was in March 1832 that he wrote in his journal, without any explanation, "I visited Ellen's tomb & opened the coffin." The line could come from Poe. Many students of Emerson have debated it, one or two arguing that it was merely a dream. If so, the dream was formidable. My guess is that the line was a metaphor to remind him starkly that life was for the living, not the dead. Perhaps he thought that seeing the ruin of the body, literally or figuratively, would strengthen his belief in the immortality of the soul. But perhaps not. As he slowly recovered from Ellen's loss he started to formulate his own faith; and immortality found little place in it.

For more than a year after her death he plunged into his ministerial duties, partly for relief. He gave long thought to his sermons at the Second Church. Culling from his religious and nonreligious reading both, he planted the seeds of Transcendentalism in those sermons. He avoided the supernatural in favor of the moral and ethical. He began to develop the idea of compensation. There is a Christian compensation, he told himself and his hearers, for many afflictions in life including the loss of a loved one. He expounded the idea of self-trust. Though he preached that self-reliance was God-reliance, there was as much self as God in it.

The journals show that despite months of effort his ministry lost its meaning for him. Finally even the few rites of Unitarianism palled. The only one the Second Church insisted on was the Lord's Supper. When he felt that he could no longer administer it with an untroubled conscience, he resigned his post in September 1832.

Sorrowing for Ellen, uncertain how to live, he decided

to try to escape by traveling to Europe. After a sojourn in Italy he went to Great Britain and visited with the three writers who were influencing him most. The emphasis on nature and the individual in the already famous Romantic poets Wordsworth and Coleridge had struck a resounding chord in him, as had Coleridge's exaltation of what he called Reason over Understanding, of intuition over tuition. Emerson's encounter with those two Englishmen proved disappointing, but his day with the Scottish Transcendentalist Thomas Carlyle was magnificent. Emerson liked many of the places in the British Isles which he journeyed to, though he was no lisping anglophile who loved whatever he saw. About London he observed, for example, "Immense city. Very dull city."

The trip was tonic. On the way home, while still aboard ship, he probably laid plans for his first book. He had survived the traumas associated with Ellen and with the ministry, and now his ideas were ripening. Preacher that he remained, he yearned to share them with the world. Thanks to a legacy from Ellen, he could try to make his way as an author of inspirational books. In addition, through pure chance, the opportunity arose for him to become a lecturer.

The newborn lyceum system was spreading throughout New England and the Middle Atlantic States and even into the Midwest. Many a town or village was setting up a series of lectures each winter, paying the visiting lecturer a modest fee. The audiences believed that they wanted education; naturally enough they wanted entertainment also. No one ever accused Emerson of entertaining, but he soon proved himself the most impressive of educational lecturers—and this despite the fact that what he gave was as much inspiration as education. After the mid-1830s he earned a substantial part of his living by his lectures and did so with a minimum of compromise. Even then, being Emerson, he could scold himself in his journal, "Do, dear, when you come to write Lyceum lectures, remember that you are not to say, What must be said in a Lyceum?" He need not have been concerned. He gave his best, and sincerest, to his lectures; and after he had read, reread, and revised them they would become his printed essays.

He began in the lyceum by lecturing on science, but it was science humanized and broadly conceived. For instance, in January 1834 he chose the subject "The Relation of Man to the Globe." Because his vision was invariably wide, he attempted to give his hearers not only interesting information about human and natural life but the principles he thought underlay the information. These, he insisted, were moral principles. As he would announce in his first book, titled simply but grandly *Nature*, "Every natural process is a version of a moral sentence." For example, we see that a fractured bone which heals well becomes stronger than before. The preacher in him growing paramount, Emerson urged his hearers to adopt the principles he had formulated. And the language he used became increasingly emotive. It became the language not only of preaching but of poetry; although it was hard for people to see at the time, he was making himself into a poet-prophet. In fact he publicly suggested that.

Like many a poet he matured before middle age. The second half of the 1830s proved to be his peak period. It was in 1836 that he issued *Nature*; it would become the bible of Transcendentalism. In 1837 he gave the Phi Beta Kappa oration at Harvard, later called "The American Scholar." Printed as a pamphlet, its first edition of 500 sold out promptly, and the piece was soon hailed as America's literary Declaration of Independence. In 1838 he gave the Divinity School Address to Harvard's ministerial graduates. In it he attacked the formalities of religion, even the modest ones of Unitarianism. Boston's leading Unitarians reddened with rage, but others were stirred by its ringing accents.

As the 1830s approached their end, the journals show that he worked hard, with results much more brilliant than he realized, on the manuscript of his second book. He gave this one a simple title too: *Essays*. It appeared in 1841 and has long been acknowledged as an American classic. In 1844 he published *Essays: Second Series,* which proved to be nearly as impressive. He made a selection of his poetry, issuing it in book form in 1846; it gave off a shower of Transcendental sparks.

Thanks to his writing and lecturing his fame spread steadily. Though he begrudged acting as a public man, three major issues developed during his prime about which he felt he had to speak out: the expulsion of the Cherokees from Georgia, the war against Mexico, and of course slavery. Of all Indian tribes the Cherokees had worked hardest to conform to American mores. They had even devised a constitution and published a newspaper, *The Cherokee Phoenix.* Their reward was exile. Federal troops drove them across the Mississippi, and a quarter of the tribe died during the move. In April 1838 Emerson penned a bitter public letter—he called it a scream of protest—about the Cherokees to President Martin Van Buren. The Mexican War of 1846 he stigmatized as rank imperialism. "Behold the famous States / Harrying Mexico / With rifle and with knife!" he wrote scornfully in one of his poems.

The evils of slavery aroused him most. His indignation swelled into outrage as the Civil War neared. Yet, though he came to sympathize with the most fiery foes of slavery, the activists William Lloyd Garrison and Wendell Phillips and the fanatic John Brown, he remained Emerson. His outstanding speech against slavery opened with his apology as a scholar for meddling with politics. He made the speech in New York on March 7, 1854, the fourth anniversary of Daniel Webster's crucial oration on behalf of the bill to make everyone, North or South, assist in returning fugitive slaves to their masters. The first half is Emerson's stern indictment of Webster, the second a sterner indictment of slavery. Though he had seldom said harsher things, he kept his dignity.

Despite occasional controversies about what he said, his goodness shone so clearly that he became almost an untouchable. No public figure escapes criticism, but no one questioned the integrity of the man, however irregular his ideas or attitudes. When politics replaced religion as the most sensitive of subjects, he found himself, a few times, facing an audience openly hostile to his antislavery convictions. But only a few. In the North even the extremists, pro or anti, hesitated to attack him; in the South even the fire-eaters let him largely alone. After the Civil War he encountered a new, coarser America but the honors accorded him only increased. His lectures brought higher fees than before; his books sold more copies.

We might guess that as a result the journals would show us a sanguine Emerson from the outset, a man who grew more sanguine decade by decade, thanks to the acclaim he received, a man nearly as confident in private as in public. How could he make his stirring pronouncements without the conviction that he was right? A doubtful, hesitating poet-prophet would be an anomaly. The fact is that the journals show us an often divided man, with conflicting responses to inner and outer events. His reaction to the reception of the Divinity School Address is a striking early instance. To the world at large he promptly announced that he had said what he meant and that it was, for him at least, beyond argument. To himself he admitted in the journals that those critics who had called him evil or foolish were all too right. Two months later in the conclusion of a lecture entitled "The Protest," he maintained that every earnest man would encounter some painful crisis but that it should not alarm or confound him. After all, a man like that was a favorite of the universe.

Taking a long view of Emerson's journals we find that the cosmic optimist of the lectures and essays dominates. The optimism was not a pose. Yet periodically we perceive a pessimist, aging much before his time, who writes in August 1835, when only thirty-two, "After thirty a man wakes up sad every morning excepting perhaps five or six until the day of his death." The leading cause for this sadness was the onset of old age, even this early for

Emerson. The leading effect of old age was the diminishing of his vital energy, his "animal spirits," as he put it, of which he never had enough to satisfy himself or others. The lack was manifest in an emotional coolness, which he regretted acutely but could not abolish by an act of will. Not even—his journals suggest—in bed with Lidian.

Lidian was his second wife. They met in Plymouth in 1834 when Emerson visited the town to preach and lecture. She was the daughter of an affluent family, the Jacksons, and eight months older than he. Pale-skinned, dark-haired, charming, at times almost fey, she proved easy to court. From the beginning he fascinated her, and she even dreamt that they would marry. When she traveled to Concord to meet his family and friends, they agreed after talking with her that, though plain in appearance, she was interesting and attractive. She looked up to him as Ellen never had; his love for her lacked the flush of passion he had felt for Ellen. "This is a very sober joy," he reported to his brother William.

They married in September 1835. He brought her to the home he had recently purchased in Concord, where they would stay the rest of their lives. Local opinion was that they made a happy couple. Presumably he no longer woke up sad each morning. He had assured Lidian that he relished the homelier pleasures of nature, obviously including sex. Yet, over the years, it grew clear that his basic coolness had not vanished. At intervals he brooded about his deficiency, alternately decrying and defending it. With the passing of time he defended it more readily than he decried it. He observed in his journal for, probably, mid-June 1845, "I have organs also & delight in pleasure, but I have experience also that this pleasure is the bait of a trap." The trap for him lay in the fact that he had become convinced that all his energy flowed from the same font. If he spent any in sexual pleasure, he had less to give his writing. An orgasm was an extravagance.

This view surfaced increasingly in his lectures and essays. It brought about a certain bloodlessness, a more than Victorian caution, in the treatment of sex. Although as a cosmic optimist he long celebrated the sexuality of nature, he showed himself less than enthusiastic about it in humankind. Late in 1860 he published *The Conduct of Life*. One of the main threads connecting the chapters is the issue of continence vs. incontinence, of discipline vs. unrestraint. In addressing his readers Emerson, now near sixty, admitted the need for balancing both; but he stressed the value of discipline. Man should spend himself in "spiritual creation & not in begetting animals," he warned in a journal passage later incorporated in the book.

Before *The Conduct of Life* two other books of prose appeared, along with the *Poems*, but they were tangential to his Transcendentalism. *Representative Men*, issued in 1850, was basically biographical. It expatiated on the characters of half a dozen great men who interested him, ranging from Plato to, surprisingly, Napoleon. *English Traits*, issued in 1856, proved to be the least Emersonian of his books, with no poetry and scant philosophy in it. But it rested firmly on thoughtful observation and insight, with the gratifying if unexpected result that it became the best book on England written by an American during the nineteenth century. Incidentally, *English Traits* can remind us that Emerson was more than a stargazer, that he showed a realism about individuals which was both clear-sighted and compassionate. We also see this sort of realism superbly illustrated in his eulogy of Henry David Thoreau.

After *The Conduct of Life* several more books were published prior to his death in 1882, but for practical purposes his life as an author ended with that book. The crumbling creativity he had long worried over became a grim fact. He published two more volumes of poetry but they were mostly poetry of the past. A decade after *The Conduct of Life* he produced *Society and Solitude*, warmed-over Emerson with nothing special to distinguish it. His devoted daughter Ellen and a friend of his, James

Elliot Cabot, assembled the materials for *Letters and Social Aims,* published in 1875. It was a farewell volume. And when Emerson penned the final pages of his journal, they included a piece he entitled "Old Man," never finished.

Inventing a religion. In the crucial years after the death of his first wife and his resignation from the ministry, what Emerson did, perhaps half-consciously, was to formulate a new religion and make himself its prophet and law-giver.

He deeply needed such a religion and he became convinced that the public needed it also. He recognized from the start what he did not want. He rejected Judaism as austere, Buddhism as esoteric, Christianity as fossilized. Gradually he clarified what he did want. The essentials were simple: a kindly God, a kindly universe, and a few universal laws.

For inspiration he turned inevitably to his reading and, less than inevitably, to observation of the life going on around him. In the reading his guides ranged from Plato to the Scandinavian mystic Emanuel Swedenborg, from Goethe to Darwin. He spent many of the months among his books in the cloudy uplands where theology and philosophy merged with natural history. Natural history fascinated him as a nonscientist, as a humanist who considered it quaint. He wrote that by itself it had scant value, "but marry it to human history, & it is poetry."

As he settled down to compose his lectures and essays (the books would characteristically be clusters of essays), he searched his reading for two things. These were, first, what he came to call "lustres" or illuminating incidents, metaphors, or phrases; and, second, the universal laws which the lustres might exemplify. What did a natural fact mean? In his eagerness he sometimes strained for a meaning. After noting in his journal that the housefly, though as untamable as the jaguar, finally learns that he cannot penetrate a windowpane, Emerson went on to say that the soul of man, just as obdurate, finally learns that it cannot violate a universal law.

As he shaped the tenets of his creed his hope grew for its success. Fortunately, this was the best time in American history for new creeds, fresh faiths, to appear. Dozens did so, with Mormonism providing the most notable and durable example. We know that his hope was realized. Year after year he drew converts to him. Enthralled by his earnestness, uplifted by his ideas, moved by his prose poetry, they attended his lectures and read his essays, religiously. Of course we cannot tell how much his words affected their thoughts or actions. Yet even if they seldom understood all that he was saying, there can be no doubt that they took him seriously. The very newspaper reporters assigned to cover his lectures showed respect in what they wrote, if not outright admiration or a touch of awe. We can see that decade by decade their respect increased, as did the nation's. To begin with we have a New England prophet whose New England neighbors gave him a mixed reception; at the end a seer whose goodness and purity, along with a mellowing of his doctrines, brought him worldwide homage.

Though there were at least two bars to belief in Emerson's religion, neither was as forbidding as we might expect. One was the oddity of some of the tenets. For instance, the idea—a favorite of his from a favorite field, unscientific science—that the great globe we live on is reproduced in miniature, down to the tiniest detail, in a drop of dew. However, this was no more curious than, say, the Hindu idea that the world rests on the back of a tortoise.

The other obstacle lay in the contradictions which characterized his faith. As his moods shifted, so did some of his beliefs. But the main problem was that he proved to have a habit of mind which almost automatically saw two sides to everything, though one might be vastly more significant than the other. As we noted earlier, this is a grave flaw in a prophet. Aware of that himself, he tried as a rule to conceal it from outsiders. When he could not hide it he attempted to deal with it in other ways. He might say sardonically, "I am a very wicked man and . . . consistency is no wise to be expected from me." Or he might announce in lordly tones that a foolish consistency was the hobgoblin of little minds. But the contradictions were there and some were vital. The most daunting concerned the problem of evil. He devoted a key essay, "Compensation," in his first published series, to assuring us that God had created a benign universe and that in the long run all was for the best. However, halfway through the essay he conceded sadly, "There is a crack in every thing God has made."

Even this discrepancy, though it was more often noticed than any other, failed to deter the faithful. They fastened on the gleaming promises in Emerson's religion, and plainly many a man and woman found them good. They may have regretted that there was no provision for an afterlife, but probably that lack was balanced by the richness of the possibilities he revealed to them in this life.

At no time was the effectiveness of his preachments more widely agreed on than directly after his death. We would expect the eulogies to be lavish with their praise, but the point lay in the kind of praise. Essentially he was lauded either as the prophet of a new faith or as the almost saintly vitalizer of an old one. Whether he was eulogized in newspapers, magazines, or books, the view was much the same. *The Transcript*, most eminent of Boston papers, judged that he had been "the teacher, the inspirer, almost the conscience of thousands of Americans." *The Atlantic Monthly*, most eminent of magazines, printed a paean by the philosopher W. T. Harris in which he predicted that Emerson would be best remembered as a seer and lawgiver. Books were slower in appearing but their burden was similar. In his *Ralph Waldo Emerson*, issued in 1885, the sprightly and ordinarily irreverent Oliver Wendell Holmes couched his praise in the highest of religious terms. What was the mission on which Emerson visited our earth? Holmes asked. The answer was that he came to preach his gospel to us.

Tenets of the faith. In his first two books, the 1836 *Nature* and the 1841 *Essays*, Emerson did gladly what any nineteenth-century American prophet had to do. He preached a religion radiant with hope. *Nature* opened and closed with the assurance that we had no questions to ask which could not be answered, presumably with Emerson's assistance. He established the principle that nature had signal importance for us, and not in one way only. Indeed, it constituted half of life. In the course of the book he foreshadowed most of the principles he would contribute to Transcendentalism. Among them were the split of the cosmos into nature and the individual soul; the material world as an inferior copy of the spiritual; alternation as a basic fact of existence; and Reason as the proper label for intuition.

In the 1841 *Essays* his Transcendental religion came to full flower. The form it took there was the one we permanently associate with him. However, half hidden in it lay the contradictions which later made it lose some of its bloom. By the time he published *The Conduct of Life* the realities of his experience had made the contradictions all too clear, with the result that the optimism shrank even if it never vanished. And hope subsided somewhat as man's prospects narrowed. But that was nearly two decades later.

Meanwhile, the prime fact in the structure of Emerson's starry universe was that everything was double although he yearned to have it single. No matter whether the doubleness was physical or conceptual, he tried to wish it away. He loved the one, for example, at the expense of the many. Especially as a young man he exhorted his hearers and readers as individuals, rarely as a group. Considering the masses a calamity, and calling them just that, he pined for a universe peopled with individuals. For them he created his God, which he christened the Over-Soul and whose relation to the individual was one to one. And he insisted that this sacred relationship would be profaned by the interposition of such supposed aids as ministers or churches.

The trouble was, the masses declined to disappear. And not the masses only. As Emerson grew older he observed more doubleness around him rather than less. At times he complained about it in the privacy of his journal. However, in his lectures and essays he developed a central principle which he hoped would take care of the problem. It stemmed from alternation. He called the principle Polarity, using the word to indicate pairings, either of opposites or complements. The claims he made for it were breathtaking: he announced that the fact of two poles, two forces, was universal. He elaborated on the idea in the essay "Compensation." "An inevitable dualism bisects nature, so that each thing is a half, and suggests another thing to make it whole; as, spirit, matter; man, woman; odd, even; subjective, objective; in, out; upper, under; motion, rest." Even: good, bad.

Unlike many an exhorter, with or without a pulpit, Emerson envisioned a smiling universe in which evil played a trivial part. Yet evil could not be wished away any more than could the masses. He had only to glance around him to see everything from individual cruelty to national shame, from a poor woman's being beaten in Concord to Negro slavery's being protected throughout the United States. But Polarity helped to gloss over much of this. "Every sweet hath its sour," he said, "every evil its good." He insisted that people responded to the suffering inflicted on them by becoming better persons. He put Polarity to practical use by applying it in the guise of Compensation, in the essay of that name and elsewhere. For instance, if we were blinded, our hearing would grow marvelously acute. If we went bankrupt, we would realize the worthlessness of possessions. He adapted Compensation to make it a leveler. For anything we gained we would lose something. "The President has paid dear for his White House. It has commonly cost him all his peace, and the best of his manly attributes." Every sweet had indeed its sour.

The other guise of doubleness in his universe he labeled Correspondence. It was almost as important a principle as Polarity, though I see it as an aspect of Polarity. However, the two parts in Correspondence were not different and complementary, as they were in Polarity; they were alike in structure and different in some other way, for example in size. To Emerson the prime instance of Correspondence was the relation between the world of spirit and the world of nature. It was his preoccupation in *Nature.* There he construed nature as a material copy of spirit. Because a literal copy was impossible it had to be a metaphorical one. As he said, "Nature is the symbol of spirit." So Mount Katahdin, for example, stands for a noble thought. The laws of nature, vital though they were, proved to be merely applications of moral laws; "the axioms of physics translate into the laws of ethics." But making this translation demanded an intuitive leap on the part of the translator. It could not be taught and had to be accompanied, Emerson felt, by the conviction that the universe meant well.

Massively supporting Polarity and Correspondence stood the two-tiered universe, for a reconciled Emerson the ultimate doubleness. Within it two realities existed, spirit and matter; and naturally spirit transcended matter. Two ways of knowing likewise existed, intuition and tuition; and intuition naturally transcended tuition. Tuition taught us about the material world through our senses, while intuition illuminated the spiritual world for us in flashes of lightning. Borrowing from Coleridge, we recall, Emerson dubbed the instrument of intuition the Reason and that of tuition the Understanding. Reason assured us that the Over-Soul existed; the Understanding reported that our barn was red.

The deity that created the two-tiered universe made its

most extended appearance in the first book of essays, where Emerson devoted an entire chapter to the Over-Soul. However, in defining the indefinable he was no more successful than some other prophets, so he resorted to metaphors and manifestations. The Over-Soul was the Eternal One, which held each individual's being; it was the common heart; it was the overpowering reality; the universal presence; the divine mind; the holy spirit. But he broke off early in the chapter. "My words," he admitted, "fall short and cold." Notwithstanding, he proceeded to preach a luminous sermon in the chapter, with as its message the idea that if we join our soul to the Over-Soul we will benefit beyond any imagining.

Emerson could happily create a God for his cosmos, but he declined to create an Anti-God. Though he coped with most of the evidences of evil in the world through Compensation, some remained and he knew it. The fact forced him to make a single but significant concession: that the Over-Soul was an imperfect creator. We recall the bleak line in the essay "Compensation," that there was a crack in everything God had made. Most students of Emerson take that to mean that every unit the Over-Soul creates has a flaw. I think we should go further. I wonder whether we should not construe the crack as a crevasse, separating everything from everything else? The key word in the Over-Soul essay was unity, yet Emerson privately considered it unattainable. By their nature all things were antagonistic as well as divided. Nothing could ever unite for long, not even the individual soul with the Over-Soul, certainly not husband with wife. So Emerson thought in his darkest hours, as the journals show. A few times he admitted it in public, most notably in his essay "Experience." There he confessed that we could not even see one another clearly, let alone keep hold on one another to unite.

The buoyance in *Nature* and the initial book of essays was splendid but not all-encompassing. And the second book of essays contained a striking portent of things to come, the essay on experience just mentioned. In that essay, on what we learn about the world through our senses, the sureness with which he had previously pronounced on great issues was absent. Self-doubt had replaced self-trust. And free will had become a myth. "I would gladly allow the most to the will of man," he said in all candor, "but I have set my heart on honesty in this chapter, and I can see nothing at last, in success or failure, than more or less of the vital force supplied by the Eternal."

Instead of prompting us to plumb the depths and search the skies, Emerson declared in "Experience" that we existed among surfaces and should learn to skate smoothly over them. We needed to adjust to the fact that we could not come to grips with anything in its absolute state, either good or bad. We lived our life in a middling condition—and that was proper, for even good qualities became noxious when unmixed. Our consolation was that, though we could never be utterly happy, we could never be utterly sad. Emerson felt that sorrow had taught him only that it was shallow. "In the death of my son, now more than two years ago, I seem to have lost a beautiful estate—no more." Near the end of the essay he tried to rouse himself. "Up again, old heart," he cried in his final sentence. But the cry sounded hollow.

Of course we should not exaggerate the difference between the two volumes of essays. The second kept much of his optimism and nobility of tone; it reaffirmed the chief tenets of the creed. Yet in retrospect it looked more like a work of the Understanding than of the Reason. It predicted the bias that appeared years later in *The Conduct of Life*.

The *Essays: First Series,* above any other volume, gave his readers the youthful, triumphant Emerson; *The Conduct of Life* gave them the sober, experienced Emerson— a sadder and a wiser man, to quote Wordsworth. Though still disturbed because he could see two sides to everything, and by now opposing sides, he managed in this book to make a virtue of necessity. He now taught that the art of living lay in keeping contradictions ceaselessly suspended in the mind. This was a major concession, bringing with it several minor ones; what they had in common was that he was writing as an elderly man for aging readers. "In the conduct of life," he had counseled presciently some years before, "let us ... decently withdraw ourselves into modest & solitary resignation & rest."

The essence of the book lay in the first and fullest chapter. In it he named Fate as the most potent force to affect us, reducing the Over-Soul to a benign shadow. But he urged us to believe in free will. "If we must accept Fate we are not less compelled to affirm liberty," he said in his second paragraph. Both were real so we had to cope with both. How? By learning to maintain, in his phrase, a "double consciousness."

To give grandeur to Fate he had to take it from something else—in this case particularly, from Nature. As he had once said in "Compensation," "To empty here, you must condense there." Now Nature, in whose arms we used to rest content, had turned into a stern parent who brought us disasters as well as delights. Her earthquakes could kill by the hundred thousands. Emerson simply called her disasters acts of Providence. Nature was also responsible for our heredity, and Emerson granted an importance to heredity he had not granted before. "How shall a man escape from his ancestors?" he asked rhetorically. We had long thought that believing affirmatively would yield us limitless results; such was the power of positive thinking. Not anymore. Now Nature acting as circumstance assigned us not only our heredity, the keen brain or the dull one, but half the conditions of our daily life. Our fortunes were determined by our character, and our character was determined by our genes.

A resigned writer made these concessions in the early pages of the chapter but then recovered something of his old optimism. After all, he himself was trying to keep opposites in suspension. So he declared that Fate could help us as well as harm us. And to combat Fate we possessed two potent allies, thought and moral sentiment. Thought could turn the chaos of circumstance into order; moral sentiment could make us godlike. He ended the chapter by exhorting us to erect an altar to Beautiful Necessity. And another to Blessed Unity, which—somehow—"holds nature and souls in perfect solution."

Such was the final form of Emerson's creed. He lived more than twenty years longer but lacked either the energy or the will to make further changes.

The appeal of Emerson's ideas and art. Our impression of America during the two troubled decades before the Civil War is of a country charged with feverish energy. But in Emerson's eyes the energy was intermittent and useless; lethargy was far more frequent. One day in 1847 he lamented to his journal, "Alas for America. . . . The air is loaded with poppy, with imbecility, with dispersions, & sloth." He continued to feel, despite his periods of self-doubt, that the nation needed him. From lectern after lectern, in essay after essay, he tried to wake this sleeping, scatterbrained giant and urge him on to spiritual greatness. He dedicated his career—as he phrased it from the start, in *Nature*—to announcing "undiscovered regions of thought, and so communicating, through hope, new activity to the torpid spirit." In today's terms he offered his hearers and readers an alternative life-style, purposeful and inspired.

In its basics his message was simple and persuasive. There was no limit to what we could do; thanks to the Over-Soul we could do it without leaning on any human being; and in what we could do, the spiritual was vastly more significant than the material. We could scale the sheerest cliff alone, knowing that fulfillment awaited us at the top. To these inspiring essentials Emerson soberly added a caution toward the end of his career. It was that we had to keep in mind the hard fact that the opposite of this inspiring message had a truth of its own.

Ordinarily a writer has little chance to hear how his work sounds. But lecturing in the lyceum gave Emerson a golden opportunity to test his effectiveness. He could read his lectures aloud repeatedly before revising them for print. From the platform he could see what his audiences responded to, both in ideas and in expression. He could preserve what made them sit up and omit what made them yawn. Not that he would censor himself, but he could retain his most telling phrases for the essays. In addition his style benefited because he could revise away jolting rhythms or awkward sounds. Practice made him perfect; he himself more than once remarked dryly, quoting a folk saying, "The barber learns his trade on the orphan's chin." Over all, he could make the flow of energy in the essays stronger and smoother because of the lectures. His readers got more than their money's worth.

His readers had another advantage over his hearers. With his text before them, they could reflect on what they read. His best essays doubtless grew on them as they do on us. True, the contradictions as well as the complexities of his ideas became more apparent; and yet if his readers met him on his own terms, they found an intrinsic harmony in the essays. He himself believed that he thought in circles or spirals rather than straight lines and that his essays had a large logic if not a small. One way to test this is for us to switch his paragraphs around. If we do, we find that the order cannot be tampered with. It is a little like trying to regularize Emily Dickinson's poetry.

Regardless, it was not for the logical ordering of ideas that people read him. Nor was it for the universal laws he propounded. I doubt that people took even Correspondence very seriously. They could hardly believe that the universe was miniaturized in a drop of dew or that God reappeared "with all his parts in every moss and cobweb." With all his parts! What they read for primarily was what he wished them to read for: inspiration.

The inspiration surely came even more from the literary art with which he expressed his ideas than from the ideas themselves. He proved to be a magnificent rhetorician, with the power to communicate feelings even better than ideas. His skill showed in everything from single, happily chosen words to scintillating paragraphs. He was at his peak with sentences, as, for instance, when he demanded, "Trust thyself: every heart vibrates to that iron string." Our current quotation books are studded with such sentences from Emerson.

Much rarer but remarkably impressive are the paragraphs he composed when rising to an occasion. For example, the opening paragraph of the Divinity School Address, with its lush description of summer, or the closing paragraph of "Self-Reliance." In that paragraph he adroitly orchestrates a warning with a striking pronouncement. In gradually lengthening sentences with touches of biblical phrasing to them, he warns us not to depend on, but only to use, good luck; and not to interpret a piece of good fortune as an omen. Then he ends the paragraph with three incisive sentences. The turn in the first of these, "Do not believe it," is pure elegance. Here is the final part of the paragraph: "A political victory, a rise of rents, the recovery of your sick, or the return of your absent friend or some other favorable event, raises your spirit, and you think good days are preparing for you. Do not believe it. Nothing can bring you peace but yourself. Nothing can bring you peace but the triumph of principles."

But Emerson's appeal lies not only in his often splendid rhetoric and sometimes stirring ideas; it lies in something in between, which we might call his mode. He could take a perfectly straightforward sentence, with no embellishment to it, and curve it in such a way that it captured the attention. If we look closely, we can see that he thought not only in circles but in segments of circles. To show what I mean by his curving a sentence, let me cite one instance among a thousand, although an unusually ingenious one. It opens "Self-Reliance," to take that essay again: "I read the other day some verses written by an em-

inent painter, which were original and not conventional."
Despite its casual air the sentence holds three lures for us,
three catches to make us read. The first lies in the fact that
it is a painter—an eminent one, moreover—who has composed the verses. Why a painter instead of a poet? The
second is that the verses, as Emerson describes them, must
certainly be worth our reading. The third is that, after describing the verses, Emerson omits to quote them. We
turn the pages in the essay waiting for them to appear but
they never do.

Just as he was given to curving his sentences, he was
given to curving his paragraphs and, as I suggested before,
whole essays. Emerson always loved a crescent. He confessed in explaining Compensation that he was happy if he
could "draw the smallest arc" of its vast circle for us. . . .

Draw it and draw others too, he could and still can, for
our pleasure and instruction both.

A NOTE ON
THE SELECTIONS
BY MALCOLM COWLEY

This volume aims to present the essential Emerson, selected from the essays and poems he prepared for publication. It starts with his first book, *Nature* (1836), and it ends (except for the poems) with "Carlyle," his tribute to a friend of half a century that was printed in 1881, the year before Emerson died. His mind was failing then, and most of that lively tribute was copied from letters written long before. The intervening selections lay stress on the earlier and more vigorous essays. To make space for them I had to omit the correspondence and extracts from Emerson's fascinating Journals. There is only so much that a single volume can include.

This is not a revision of the original *Portable Emerson* but a new undertaking. The earlier *Portable* was edited by Mark Van Doren, an admirable scholar and a good friend, but not by temperament an Emersonian. He said in his Introduction—which, like everything he wrote, is a pleasure to read—that opinions differ as to why Emerson's work will survive. "The opinions are mainly two," he added: "his ideas were good, his writing was good. . . . the present selection tends to express the second opinion." Van Doren proposed "to show the writer in Emerson, not the philosopher." That was of course his privilege. His ability to recognize good writing was shown in his selection of poems, which I have followed here except for adding five others that I felt to be needed. But it seemed to me when using his book—as I did in two or three courses— that there was something almost perverse in his refusal to include those famous essays in which Emerson came closest to stating his philosophy. I felt their absence even more because those essays contain much of his best writing. It is in "The Poet" that we read:

> I look in vain for the poet whom I describe. . . . Our log-rolling, our stumps and their politics, our fisheries, our Negroes and Indians, our boasts and our repudiations, the wrath of rogues and the pusillanimity of honest men, the northern trade, the southern planting, the western clearing, Oregon and Texas, are yet unsung. Yet America is a poem in our eyes; its ample geography dazzles the imagination, and it will not wait long for metres.

We know that those lines inspired Whitman, and probably Thoreau as well, but Van Doren shows no sign of being moved by them. He says of "The Poet" that when Emerson "puts on robes to discuss poetry he rarefies the subject." Accordingly he omitted the essay, as he also omitted *Nature*, "Self-Reliance," "Compensation," "The Over-Soul," and "Experience." Without them it is hard to understand or explain what Emerson believed.

It isn't what most of us believe today. For all his influence in shaping the American mind, we now find it hard to accept his often uncompromising idealism or his absolute trust in the future, not to mention his notion that each of us can find the laws of the universe by searching his heart. The fact remains that his structure of thought was more complete and consistent than most of his critics have been willing to concede. In large part it derived from the Neoplatonists of the later Roman Empire, and theirs has proved to be a lasting tradition. Even when we reject Emerson's metaphysics, we are likely to be swayed by the psychological force of his beliefs (which are, by the way, easy to rephrase in more recent terms; for example, his Over-Soul often seems close to the Jungian notion of a collective unconscious).

Without the major essays, each as firmly constructed as

a speech by Cicero, each marching ahead from exordium to peroration, one misses something essential in Emerson. Without them one is tempted to believe, as Van Doren was not the first to assert, that he is best in separate sentences, but didn't really fit them together into essays or even into paragraphs. Emerson did write vivid and forthright sentences that have embedded themselves in our memories. "In every work of genius we recognize our own rejected thoughts; they come back to us with a certain alienated majesty." "I would write on the lintels of the door-post, *Whim.*" "Nothing is at last sacred but the integrity of your own mind." All those statements, and many others in the same essay, "Self-Reliance," are "sentences" in the Latin meaning of the word; they are ideas briefly and pungently expressed as axioms. They are what chiefly impress us at a first reading. But if we read the essay again, this time more carefully, we see that each sentence belongs in its context, occurs at the inevitable moment, and contributes to the total effect that Emerson planned. Because he disdained to use "therefores" and "howevers," we miss the logical connections, but they exist. The language cannot be treated merely as an ornament or ever be separated from the ideas.

Accordingly I have included the major essays in which Emerson presented those ideas, as well as a number of others in which he came down from the mountain and spoke in an angry or lightly humorous voice as a member of a New England community. The text, except in one instance, is that of the Centenary Edition, prepared in 1903 by Emerson's only surviving son. I admit to a fondness for that text, which isn't universally admired. Edward W. Emerson was a modest editor, hardworking and full of familial piety, but he took a few liberties with his father's prose, notably by modernizing the spelling and punctuation (as of 1903); also, he changed a very few archaic words. The result of his efforts was a reader's text, not a bibliographer's, with, after eighty years, a slight but not at all unpleasant air of venerability.

   In one case I followed a different authority. For the tribute to Thoreau I had the permission of a distinguished
Emersonian, Joel Myerson of the University of South
Carolina, to use the text of a manuscript in Emerson's
hand that he found in the Huntington Library and faithfully transcribed. It reproduces that admirable tribute as
Emerson prepared it for the printer, with all the commas
where he wanted them and no intervention by a copy editor. I owe a debt to Professor Myerson, as I owe another to
Gay Wilson Allen for his detailed and accurate *Waldo
Emerson*.

EMERSON'S ANNALS

1803   May 25, born in Boston.

1811   His father, the Reverend William Emerson, dies.

1812–17 Studies at Boston Public Latin School.

1817   Enrolls at Harvard College.

1821   Graduates with A.B degree.

1821–25 Works as reluctant schoolmaster, mostly in brother William's school in Boston.

1825   Enrolls at Harvard Divinity School.

1826   Receives approval to preach from county ministerial association.

1826–27 Travels as far south as St. Augustine to strengthen health and rid himself of lung trouble.

1827   Receives M.A. degree from Harvard Divinity School.

1828   Becomes engaged to Ellen Tucker.

1829   Becomes junior pastor at Second Church, Boston; marries Ellen.

1831   Ellen dies.

1832   Resigns pastorate; sails for Europe.

1833   Visits Italy, France, England, and Scotland; meets Wordsworth, Coleridge, and Carlyle.

1834   Begins long and noteworthy career as lyceum lecturer.

1835   Marries Lydia Jackson.

1836   Publishes first book, *Nature*; son Waldo born.

1837   Delivers oration at Harvard later called "The American Scholar."

1838   Delivers Divinity School Address at Harvard and is assailed by conservatives.

1841   Publishes first volume of *Essays*.

1842   Waldo dies; Emerson follows Margaret Fuller as editor of Transcendentalist magazine, *The Dial*.

1844   Publishes *Essays: Second Series*.

1845   Lets Thoreau use land by Walden Pond as site for cabin.

1846   Publishes *Poems*.

1847–48 Makes triumphal lecture tour of England and Scotland, with side trip to France; renews friendship with Carlyle.

1849   Besides lecturing widely, publishes *Nature, Addresses, and Lectures*.

1850   Publishes *Representative Men*.

1852   Reaches new high in lecturing popularity, with eighty-two engagements, some in Midwest.

1854   Attacks Fugitive Slave Law in widely heralded New York address.

1856   Publishes *English Traits*; is increasingly involved in antislavery movement; speaks on behalf of Charles Sumner, who had been assaulted in Senate.

1860   Publishes *The Conduct of Life*; speaks in memory of John Brown.

1862   Reads eulogy at Thoreau's funeral.

1862–65 Continues lecturing in North, though on reduced scale because of war.

1867   Publishes *May-Day and Other Poems*, which includes "Terminus," his farewell to the creative life.

1870   Publishes *Society and Solitude*; visits California.

1872   His house burns; to recover from that blow and also to improve his health, undertakes tour with daughter Ellen of England, France, Italy, and Egypt.

1873   Comes back to Concord invigorated, to find house restored by friends.

1875   His faculties failing, he publishes *Letters and Social Aims* with aid of Ellen and friend James Elliot Cabot.

1876   Publishes *Selected Poems* with Ellen's and Cabot's guidance.

1882   Dies of pneumonia April 27, after lengthy decline.

C.B.

The
Transcendentalist

Editor's Note

For us Emerson's first book remains the hardest. *Nature* is shot through with insights but many portions are murky. When writing it Emerson was in the process of formulating his ideas and amalgamating them with his omnivorous reading. The insights are worth our trouble, though. Take his theory of signs, which foreshadows some of today's semiotics. He tells us that, because certain words are signs of natural facts, moral ideas stem from material appearances. "Right" originally meant "straight," while "wrong" originally meant "twisted." His main lines of thought emerge clearly enough from among the obscurities. Nature is our guide, mentor, and woodland god. But nature isn't spirit, that indefinable flame which we share with the Eternal. Spirit is so strong that it can make us doubt that nature exists.

Emerson announced these views with a look of confidence which was so convincing that the book quickly attracted a number of New Englanders who dissented from current thought and were trying to find the proper shape for their dissent. Some of the most promising happily grouped themselves around Emerson. They agreed that there was a knowledge transcending sense, that it was of prime importance, and that Emerson was its prime exponent in New England. A modest volume of ninety-five pages, *Nature* was issued in September 1836 in an edition of one thousand copies, paid for by the author, who left his name off the title page. However, the authorship was an open secret. Reviewers who discussed the book knew whose it was as well as did the emerging young Transcendentalists. The reviews were evenly divided between derision and enthusiasm.

With "The American Scholar" Emerson took a giant step forward. The swirl of ideas was settling down. He spoke both clearly and brilliantly—he was giving an oration—though not always clearly enough for every member of Phi Beta Kappa who sat listening on August 31, 1837. Yet the consensus surely must have been that his call for America's intellectual independence was memorable. Later that year the piece was published, in pamphlet form. Emerson republished it with minor revisions and the added title "The American Scholar" in *Nature, Addresses, and Lectures* in 1849.

Who could quarrel with a call for intellectual independence? But a call for theological independence was something different, especially when sounded at a theological school. In itself Emerson's second great oration, delivered to the graduating class and its friends at Harvard Divinity School on July 15, 1838, displayed the same power and urgency that animated "The American Scholar" even though the subject was more vague. However, this oration struck at the roots of his hearers' belief system because he was telling them that the ministry as an institution had proved itself not merely useless but harmful. The true communication between the individual and the deity was direct. The Unitarian establishment took wrathful notice of what this meant and never fully forgave him. The address was printed as a pamphlet in 1838 and did well enough to show that controversy sold books. Emerson published it with minor revisions in *Nature, Addresses, and Lectures.*

Though churches were largely closed to him after the Divinity School Address, the lecture platform was not. Taking advantage of the burgeoning lyceum, he began as early as 1835 to organize and offer courses of public lectures for a fee. During the winter of 1841–42 he gave eight "Lectures on the Times" to Boston audiences and afterward printed several of them in the new Transcendental journal, *The Dial.* They attested that he had resolved most of the obscurities in his book *Nature* and had moved beyond some of the partisanship of his two great orations. From this time on he would see two sides to nearly everything, though he naturally favored one. To balance his lecture on "The Transcendentalist," he preceded it with "The Conservative." He allowed little doubt, however, about where his heart was. For he defined the Conservatives as the party of the past and of philosophic materialism, while the Transcendentalists were the party of the future, of reform, and of philosophic idealism. He read "The Transcendentalist" in Boston on December 23, 1841, and, after revising and polishing it, printed it in *The Dial* of January 1843. Like "The American Scholar" and the Divinity School Address, its first publication as part of a book came in *Nature, Addresses, and Lectures.*

C.B.

NATURE

A subtle chain of countless rings
The next unto the farthest brings;
The eye reads omens where it goes,
And speaks all languages the rose;
And, striving to be man, the worm
Mounts through all the spires of form.

Introduction

Our age is retrospective. It builds the sepulchres of the fathers. It writes biographies, histories, and criticism. The foregoing generations beheld God and nature face to face; we, through their eyes. Why should not we also enjoy an original relation to the universe? Why should not we have a poetry and philosophy of insight and not of tradition, and a religion by revelation to us, and not the history of theirs? Embosomed for a season in nature, whose floods of life stream around and through us, and invite us, by the powers they supply, to action proportioned to nature, why should we grope among the dry bones of the past, or put the living generation into masquerade out of its faded wardrobe? The sun shines to-day also. There is more wool and flax in the fields. There are new lands, new men, new thoughts. Let us demand our own works and laws and worship.

Undoubtedly we have no questions to ask which are unanswerable. We must trust the perfection of the creation so far as to believe that whatever curiosity the order of things has awakened in our minds, the order of things can satisfy. Every man's condition is a solution in hieroglyphic to those inquiries he would put. He acts it as life, before he apprehends it as truth. In like manner, nature is already, in its forms and tendencies, describing its own design. Let us interrogate the great apparition that shines so peacefully around us. Let us inquire, to what end is nature?

All science has one aim, namely, to find a theory of nature. We have theories of races and of functions, but scarcely yet a remote approach to an idea of creation. We are now so far from the road to truth, that religious teachers dispute and hate each other, and speculative men are esteemed unsound and frivolous. But to a sound judgment, the most abstract truth is the most practical. Whenever a true theory appears, it will be its own evidence. Its test is, that it will explain all phenomena. Now many are thought not only unexplained but inexplicable; as language, sleep, madness, dreams, beasts, sex.

Philosophically considered, the universe is composed of Nature and the Soul. Strictly speaking, therefore, all that is separate from us, all which Philosophy distinguishes as the NOT ME, that is, both nature and art, all other men and my own body, must be ranked under this name, NATURE. In enumerating the values of nature and casting up their sum, I shall use the word in both senses;—in its common and in its philosophical import. In inquiries so general as our present one, the inaccuracy is not material; no confusion of thought will occur. *Nature*, in the common sense, refers to essences unchanged by man; space, the air, the river, the leaf. *Art* is applied to the mixture of his will with the same things, as in a house, a canal, a statue, a picture. But his operations taken together are so insignificant, a little chipping, baking, patching, and washing, that in an impression so grand as that of the world on the human mind, they do not vary the result.

I

To go into solitude, a man needs to retire as much from his chamber as from society. I am not solitary whilst I read and write, though nobody is with me. But if a man would be alone, let him look at the stars. The rays that come from those heavenly worlds will separate between him and what he touches. One might think the atmosphere was made transparent with this design, to give man, in the heavenly bodies, the perpetual presence of the sublime. Seen in the streets of cities, how great they are! If the stars should appear one night in a thousand years, how would men believe and adore; and preserve for many generations the remembrance of the city of God which had been shown! But every night come out these envoys of beauty, and light the universe with their admonishing smile.

The stars awaken a certain reverence, because though always present, they are inaccessible; but all natural objects make a kindred impression, when the mind is open to their influence. Nature never wears a mean appearance. Neither does the wisest man extort her secret, and lose his curiosity by finding out all her perfection. Nature never became a toy to a wise spirit. The flowers, the animals, the mountains, reflected the wisdom of his best hour, as much as they had delighted the simplicity of his childhood.

When we speak of nature in this manner, we have a distinct but most poetical sense in the mind. We mean the integrity of impression made by manifold natural objects. It is this which distinguishes the stick of timber of the wood-cutter from the tree of the poet. The charming landscape which I saw this morning is indubitably made up of some twenty or thirty farms. Miller owns this field, Locke that, and Manning the woodland beyond. But none of them owns the landscape. There is a property in the horizon which no man has but he whose eye can integrate all the parts, that is, the poet. This is the best part of these men's farms, yet to this their warranty-deeds give no title.

To speak truly, few adult persons can see nature. Most persons do not see the sun. At least they have a very superficial seeing. The sun illuminates only the eye of the man, but shines into the eye and the heart of the child. The lover of nature is he whose inward and outward senses are still truly adjusted to each other; who has retained the spirit of infancy even into the era of manhood. His intercourse with heaven and earth becomes part of his daily food. In the presence of nature a wild delight runs through the man, in spite of real sorrows. Nature says,— he is my creature, and maugre all his impertinent griefs, he shall be glad with me. Not the sun or the summer alone, but every hour and season yields its tribute of delight; for every hour and change corresponds to and authorizes a different state of the mind, from breathless noon to grimmest midnight. Nature is a setting that fits equally well a comic or a mourning piece. In good health, the air is a cordial of incredible virtue. Crossing a bare common, in snow puddles, at twilight, under a clouded sky, without having in my thoughts any occurrence of special good fortune, I have enjoyed a perfect exhilaration. I am glad to the brink of fear. In the woods, too, a man casts off his years, as the snake his slough, and at what period soever of life is always a child. In the woods is perpetual youth. Within these plantations of God, a decorum and sanctity reign, a perennial festival is dressed, and the guest sees not

how he should tire of them in a thousand years. In the
woods, we return to reason and faith. There I feel that
nothing can befall me in life,—no disgrace, no calamity
(leaving me my eyes), which nature cannot repair.
Standing on the bare ground,—my head bathed by the
blithe air and uplifted into infinite space,—all mean egotism vanishes. I become a transparent eyeball; I am nothing; I see all; the currents of the Universal Being circulate
through me; I am part or parcel of God. The name of the
nearest friend sounds then foreign and accidental: to be
brothers, to be acquaintances, master or servant, is then
a trifle and a disturbance. I am the lover of uncontained
and immortal beauty. In the wilderness, I find something
more dear and connate than in streets or villages. In the
tranquil landscape, and especially in the distant line of
the horizon, man beholds somewhat as beautiful as his
own nature.

The greatest delight which the fields and woods minister is the suggestion of an occult relation between man and
the vegetable. I am not alone and unacknowledged. They
nod to me, and I to them. The waving of the boughs in the
storm is new to me and old. It takes me by surprise, and
yet is not unknown. Its effect is like that of a higher
thought or a better emotion coming over me, when I
deemed I was thinking justly or doing right.

Yet it is certain that the power to produce this delight
does not reside in nature, but in man, or in a harmony of
both. It is necessary to use these pleasures with great temperance. For nature is not always tricked in holiday attire,
but the same scene which yesterday breathed perfume
and glittered as for the frolic of the nymphs is overspread
with melancholy to-day. Nature always wears the colors
of the spirit. To a man laboring under calamity, the heat
of his own fire hath sadness in it. Then there is a kind of
contempt of the landscape felt by him who has just lost by
death a dear friend. The sky is less grand as it shuts down
over less worth in the population.

II
Commodity

Whoever considers the final cause of the world will discern a multitude of uses that enter as parts into that result. They all admit of being thrown into one of the following classes: Commodity; Beauty; Language; and Discipline.

Under the general name of commodity, I rank all those advantages which our senses owe to nature. This, of course, is a benefit which is temporary and mediate, not ultimate, like its service to the soul. Yet although low, it is perfect in its kind, and is the only use of nature which all men apprehend. The misery of man appears like childish petulance, when we explore the steady and prodigal provision that has been made for his support and delight on this green ball which floats him through the heavens. What angels invented these splendid ornaments, these rich conveniences, this ocean of air above, this ocean of water beneath, this firmament of earth between? this zodiac of lights, this tent of dropping clouds, this striped coat of climates, this fourfold year? Beasts, fire, water, stones, and corn serve him. The field is at once his floor, his work-yard, his play-ground, his garden, and his bed.

> "More servants wait on man
> Than he'll take notice of."

Nature, in its ministry to man, is not only the material, but is also the process and the result. All the parts incessantly work into each other's hands for the profit of man. The wind sows the seed; the sun evaporates the sea; the wind blows the vapor to the field; the ice, on the other side of the planet, condenses rain on this; the rain feeds the plant; the plant feeds the animal; and thus the endless circulations of the divine charity nourish man.

The useful arts are reproductions or new combinations by the wit of man, of the same natural benefactors. He no longer waits for favoring gales, but by means of steam, he realizes the fable of Aeolus's bag, and carries the two and thirty winds in the boiler of his boat. To diminish friction, he paves the road with iron bars, and, mounting a coach with a ship-load of men, animals, and merchandise behind him, he darts through the country, from town to town, like an eagle or a swallow through the air. By the aggregate of these aids, how is the face of the world changed, from the era of Noah to that of Napoleon! The private poor man hath cities, ships, canals, bridges, built for him. He goes to the post-office, and the human race run on his errands; to the book-shop, and the human race read and write of all that happens, for him; to the court-house, and nations repair his wrongs. He sets his house upon the road, and the human race go forth every morning, and shovel out the snow, and cut a path for him.

But there is no need of specifying particulars in this class of uses. The catalogue is endless, and the examples so obvious, that I shall leave them to the reader's reflection, with the general remark, that this mercenary benefit is one which has respect to a farther good. A man is fed, not that he may be fed, but that he may work.

III
Beauty

A nobler want of man is served by nature, namely, the love of Beauty.

The ancient Greeks called the world κόσμος, beauty. Such is the constitution of all things, or such the plastic power of the human eye, that the primary forms, as the sky, the mountain, the tree, the animal, give us a delight *in and for themselves;* a pleasure arising from outline, color, motion, and grouping. This seems partly owing to the eye itself. The eye is the best of artists. By the mutual action of its structure and of the laws of light, perspective is produced, which integrates every mass of objects, of what character soever, into a well colored and shaded globe, so that where the particular objects are mean and unaffect-

ing, the landscape which they compose is round and symmetrical. And as the eye is the best composer, so light is
the first of painters. There is no object so foul that intense
light will not make beautiful. And the stimulus it affords
to the sense, and a sort of infinitude which it hath, like
space and time, make all matter gay. Even the corpse has
its own beauty. But besides this general grace diffused
over nature, almost all the individual forms are agreeable
to the eye, as is proved by our endless imitations of some
of them, as the acorn, the grape, the pine-cone, the wheat-
ear, the egg, the wings and forms of most birds, the lion's
claw, the serpent, the butterfly, sea-shells, flames, clouds,
buds, leaves, and the forms of many trees, as the palm.

For better consideration, we may distribute the aspects
of Beauty in a threefold manner.

1. First, the simple perception of natural forms is a delight. The influence of the forms and actions in nature is
so needful to man, that, in its lowest functions, it seems to
lie on the confines of commodity and beauty. To the body
and mind which have been cramped by noxious work or
company, nature is medicinal and restores their tone. The
tradesman, the attorney comes out of the din and craft of
the street and sees the sky and the woods, and is a man
again. In their eternal calm, he finds himself. The health of
the eye seems to demand a horizon. We are never tired, so
long as we can see far enough.

But in other hours, Nature satisfies by its loveliness,
and without any mixture of corporeal benefit. I see the
spectacle of morning from the hilltop over against my
house, from daybreak to sunrise, with emotions which an
angel might share. The long slender bars of cloud float like
fishes in the sea of crimson light. From the earth, as a
shore, I look out into that silent sea. I seem to partake its
rapid transformations; the active enchantment reaches my
dust, and I dilate and conspire with the morning wind.
How does Nature deify us with a few and cheap elements!
Give me health and a day, and I will make the pomp of
emperors ridiculous. The dawn is my Assyria; the sunset

and moonrise my Paphos, and unimaginable realms of faerie; broad noon shall be my England of the senses and the understanding; the night shall be my Germany of mystic philosophy and dreams.

Not less excellent, except for our less susceptibility in the afternoon, was the charm, last evening, of a January sunset. The western clouds divided and subdivided themselves into pink flakes modulated with tints of unspeakable softness, and the air had so much life and sweetness that it was a pain to come within doors. What was it that nature would say? Was there no meaning in the live repose of the valley behind the mill, and which Homer or Shakspeare could not re-form for me in words? The leafless trees become spires of flame in the sunset, with the blue east for their background, and the stars of the dead calices of flowers, and every withered stem and stubble rimed with frost, contribute something to the mute music.

The inhabitants of cities suppose that the country landscape is pleasant only half the year. I please myself with the graces of the winter scenery, and believe that we are as much touched by it as by the genial influences of summer. To the attentive eye, each moment of the year has its own beauty, and in the same field, it beholds, every hour, a picture which was never seen before, and which shall never be seen again. The heavens change every moment, and reflect their glory or gloom on the plains beneath. The state of the crop in the surrounding farms alters the expression of the earth from week to week. The succession of native plants in the pastures and roadsides, which makes the silent clock by which time tells the summer hours, will make even the divisions of the day sensible to a keen observer. The tribes of birds and insects, like the plants punctual to their time, follow each other, and the year has room for all. By watercourses, the variety is greater. In July, the blue pontederia or pickerel-weed blooms in large beds in the shallow parts of our pleasant river, and swarms with yellow butterflies in continual motion. Art cannot rival this pomp of purple and gold.

Indeed the river is a perpetual gala, and boasts each month a new ornament.

But this beauty of Nature which is seen and felt as beauty, is the least part. The shows of day, the dewy morning, the rainbow, mountains, orchards in blossom, stars, moonlight, shadows in still water, and the like, if too eagerly hunted, become shows merely, and mock us with their unreality. Go out of the house to see the moon, and 't is mere tinsel; it will not please as when its light shines upon your necessary journey. The beauty that shimmers in the yellow afternoons of October, who ever could clutch it? Go forth to find it, and it is gone; 't is only a mirage as you look from the windows of diligence.

2. The presence of a higher, namely, of the spiritual element is essential to its perfection. The high and divine beauty which can be loved without effeminacy, is that which is found in combination with the human will. Beauty is the mark God sets upon virtue. Every natural action is graceful. Every heroic act is also decent, and causes the place and the bystanders to shine. We are taught by great actions that the universe is the property of every individual in it. Every rational creature has all nature for his dowry and estate. It is his, if he will. He may divest himself of it; he may creep into a corner, and abdicate his kingdom, as most men do, but he is entitled to the world by his constitution. In proportion to the energy of his thought and will, he takes up the world into himself. "All those things for which men plough, build, or sail, obey virtue;" said Sallust. "The winds and waves," said Gibbon, "are always on the side of the ablest navigators." So are the sun and moon and all the stars of heaven. When a noble act is done,—perchance in a scene of great natural beauty; when Leonidas and his three hundred martyrs consume one day in dying, and the sun and moon come each and look at them once in the steep defile of Thermopylae; when Arnold Winkelried, in the high Alps, under the shadow of the avalanche, gathers in his side a sheaf of Austrian spears to break the line for his comrades;

are not these heroes entitled to add the beauty of the scene to the beauty of the deed? When the bark of Columbus nears the shore of America;—before it the beach lined with savages, fleeing out of all their huts of cane; the sea behind; and the purple mountains of the Indian Archipelago around, can we separate the man from the living picture? Does not the New World clothe his form with her palm-groves and savannahs as fit drapery? Ever does natural beauty steal in like air, and envelope great actions. When Sir Harry Vane was dragged up the Tower-hill, sitting on a sled, to suffer death as the champion of the English laws, one of the multitude cried out to him, "You never sate on so glorious a seat!" Charles II., to intimidate the citizens of London, caused the patriot Lord Russell to be drawn in an open coach through the principal streets of the city on his way to the scaffold. "But," his biographer says, "the multitude imagined they saw liberty and virtue sitting by his side." In private places, among sordid objects, an act of truth or heroism seems at once to draw to itself the sky as its temple, the sun as its candle. Nature stretches out her arms to embrace man, only let his thoughts be of equal greatness. Willingly does she follow his steps with the rose and the violet, and bend her lines of grandeur and grace to the decoration of her darling child. Only let his thoughts be of equal scope, and the frame will suit the picture. A virtuous man is in unison with her works, and makes the central figure of the visible sphere. Homer, Pindar, Socrates, Phocion, associate themselves fitly in our memory with the geography and climate of Greece. The visible heavens and earth sympathize with Jesus. And in common life whosoever has seen a person of powerful character and happy genius, will have remarked how easily he took all things along with him,—the persons, the opinions, and the day, and nature became ancillary to a man.

3. There is still another aspect under which the beauty of the world may be viewed, namely, as it becomes an object of the intellect. Beside the relation of things to virtue,

they have a relation to thought. The intellect searches out
the absolute order of things as they stand in the mind of
God, and without the colors of affection. The intellectual
and the active powers seem to succeed each other, and the
exclusive activity of the one generates the exclusive activity of the other. There is something unfriendly in each to
the other, but they are like the alternate periods of feeding
and working in animals; each prepares and will be followed by the other. Therefore does beauty, which, in relation to actions, as we have seen, comes unsought, and
comes because it is unsought, remain for the apprehension
and pursuit of the intellect; and then again, in its turn, of
the active power. Nothing divine dies. All good is eternally reproductive. The beauty of nature re-forms itself in
the mind, and not for barren contemplation, but for new
creation.

All men are in some degree impressed by the face of the
world; some men even to delight. This love of beauty is
Taste. Others have the same love in such excess, that, not
content with admiring, they seem to embody it in new
forms. The creation of beauty is Art.

The production of a work of art throws a light upon the
mystery of humanity. A work of art is an abstract or epitome of the world. It is the result or expression of nature,
in miniature. For although the works of nature are innumerable and all different, the result or the expression of
them all is similar and single. Nature is a sea of forms radically alike and even unique. A leaf, a sunbeam, a landscape, the ocean, make an analogous impression on the
mind. What is common to them all,—that perfectness and
harmony, is beauty. The standard of beauty is the entire
circuit of natural forms,—the totality of nature; which the
Italians expressed by defining beauty "il più nell' uno."
Nothing is quite beautiful alone; nothing but is beautiful
in the whole. A single object is only so far beautiful as it
suggests this universal grace. The poet, the painter, the
sculptor, the musician, the architect, seek each to concentrate this radiance of the world on one point, and each in

his several work to satisfy the love of beauty which stimu-
lates him to produce. Thus is Art a nature passed through
the alembic of man. Thus in art does Nature work
through the will of a man filled with the beauty of her first
works.

The world thus exists to the soul to satisfy the desire of
beauty. This element I call an ultimate end. No reason can
be asked or given why the soul seeks beauty. Beauty, in its
largest and profoundest sense, is one expression for the
universe. God is the all-fair. Truth, and goodness, and
beauty, are but different faces of the same All. But beauty
in nature is not ultimate. It is the herald of inward and
eternal beauty, and is not alone a solid and satisfactory
good. It must stand as a part, and not as yet the last or
highest expression of the final cause of Nature.

IV
Language

Language is a third use which Nature subserves to man.
Nature is the vehicle of thought, and in a simple, double,
and three-fold degree.

1. Words are signs of natural facts.
2. Particular natural facts are symbols of particular
   spiritual facts.
3. Nature is the symbol of spirit.

1. Words are signs of natural facts. The use of natural
history is to give us aid in supernatural history; the use of
the outer creation, to give us language for the beings and
changes of the inward creation. Every word which is used
to express a moral or intellectual fact, if traced to its root,
is found to be borrowed from some material appearance.
Right means *straight*; *wrong* means *twisted*. *Spirit* primarily means *wind*; *transgression*, the crossing of a *line*;
supercilious, the *raising of the eyebrow*. We say the *heart*
to express emotion, the *head* to denote thought; and
thought and *emotion* are words borrowed from sensible
things, and now appropriated to spiritual nature. Most of

the process by which this transformation is made, is hidden from us in the remote time when language was framed; but the same tendency may be daily observed in children. Children and savages use only nouns or names of things, which they convert into verbs, and apply to analogous mental acts.

2. But this origin of all words that convey a spiritual import,—so conspicuous a fact in the history of language,—is our least debt to nature. It is not words only that are emblematic; it is things which are emblematic. Every natural fact is a symbol of some spiritual fact. Every appearance in nature corresponds to some state of the mind, and that state of the mind can only be described by presenting that natural appearance as its picture. An enraged man is a lion, a cunning man is a fox, a firm man is a rock, a learned man is a torch. A lamb is innocence; a snake is subtle spite; flowers express to us the delicate affections. Light and darkness are our familiar expression for knowledge and ignorance; and heat for love. Visible distance behind and before us, is respectively our image of memory and hope.

Who looks upon a river in a meditative hour and is not reminded of the flux of all things? Throw a stone into the stream, and the circles that propagate themselves are the beautiful type of all influence. Man is conscious of a universal soul within or behind his individual life, wherein, as in a firmament, the natures of Justice, Truth, Love, Freedom, arise and shine. This universal soul he calls Reason: it is not mine, or thine, or his, but we are its; we are its property and men. And the blue sky in which the private earth is buried, the sky with its eternal calm, and full of everlasting orbs, is the type of Reason. That which intellectually considered we call Reason, considered in relation to nature, we call Spirit. Spirit is the Creator. Spirit hath life in itself. And man in all ages and countries embodies it in his language as the FATHER.

It is easily seen that there is nothing lucky or capricious in these analogies, but that they are constant, and pervade nature. These are not the dreams of a few poets, here and there, but man is an analogist, and studies relations in all objects. He is placed in the centre of beings, and a ray of relation passes from every other being to him. And neither can man be understood without these objects, nor these objects without man. All the facts in natural history taken by themselves, have no value, but are barren, like a single sex. But marry it to human history, and it is full of life. Whole floras, all Linnæus' and Buffon's volumes, are dry catalogues of facts; but the most trivial of these facts, the habit of a plant, the organs, or work, or noise of an insect, applied to the illustration of a fact in intellectual philosophy, or in any way associated to human nature, affects us in the most lively and agreeable manner. The seed of a plant,—to what affecting analogies in the nature of man is that little fruit made use of, in all discourse, up to the voice of Paul, who calls the human corpse a seed,—"It is sown a natural body; it is raised a spiritual body." The motion of the earth round its axis and round the sun, makes the day and the year. These are certain amounts of brute light and heat. But is there no intent of an analogy between man's life and the seasons? And do the seasons gain no grandeur or pathos from that analogy? The instincts of the ant are very unimportant considered as the ant's; but the moment a ray of relation is seen to extend from it to man, and the little drudge is seen to be a monitor, a little body with a mighty heart, then all its habits, even that said to be recently observed, that it never sleeps, become sublime.

Because of this radical correspondence between visible things and human thoughts, savages, who have only what is necessary, converse in figures. As we go back in history, language becomes more picturesque, until its infancy, when it is all poetry; or all spiritual facts are represented by natural symbols. The same symbols are found to make the original elements of all languages. It has moreover been observed, that the idioms of all languages approach each other in passages of the greatest eloquence and power. And as this is the first language, so is it the last.

This immediate dependence of language upon nature, this conversion of an outward phenomenon into a type of somewhat in human life, never loses its power to affect us. It is this which gives that piquancy to the conversation of a strong-natured farmer or backwoodsman, which all men relish.

A man's power to connect his thought with its proper symbol, and so to utter it, depends on the simplicity of his character, that is, upon his love of truth and his desire to communicate it without loss. The corruption of man is followed by the corruption of language. When simplicity of character and the sovereignty of ideas is broken up by the prevalence of secondary desires,—the desire of riches, of pleasure, of power, and of praise,—and duplicity and falsehood take place of simplicity and truth, the power over nature as an interpreter of the will is in a degree lost; new imagery ceases to be created, and old words are perverted to stand for things which are not; a paper currency is employed, when there is no bullion in the vaults. In due time the fraud is manifest, and words lose all power to stimulate the understanding or the affections. Hundreds of writers may be found in every long-civilized nation who for a short time believe and make others believe that they see and utter truths, who do not of themselves clothe one thought in its natural garment, but who feed unconsciously on the language created by the primary writers of the country, those, namely, who hold primarily on nature.

But wise men pierce this rotten diction and fasten words again to visible things; so that picturesque language is at once a commanding certificate that he who employs it is a man in alliance with truth and God. The moment our discourse rises above the ground line of familiar facts and is inflamed with passion or exalted by thought, it clothes itself in images. A man conversing in earnest, if he watch his intellectual processes, will find that a material image more or less luminous arises in his mind, contemporaneous with every thought, which furnishes the vestment of the thought. Hence, good writing and brilliant discourse are perpetual allegories. This imagery is spontaneous. It is the blending of experience with the present action of the mind. It is proper creation. It is the working of the Original Cause through the instruments he has already made.

These facts may suggest the advantage which the country-life possesses, for a powerful mind, over the artificial and curtailed life of cities. We know more from nature than we can at will communicate. Its light flows into the mind evermore, and we forget its presence. The poet, the orator, bred in the woods, whose senses have been nourished by their fair and appeasing changes, year after year, without design and without heed,—shall not lose their lesson altogether, in the roar of cities or the broil of politics. Long hereafter, amidst agitation and terror in national councils,—in the hour of revolution,—these solemn images shall reappear in their morning lustre, as fit symbols and words of the thoughts which the passing events shall awaken. At the call of a noble sentiment, again the woods wave, the pines murmur, the river rolls and shines, and the cattle low upon the mountains, as he saw and heard them in his infancy. And with these forms, the spells of persuasion, the keys of power are put into his hands.

3. We are thus assisted by natural objects in the expression of particular meanings. But how great a language to convey such pepper-corn informations! Did it need such noble races of creatures, this profusion of forms, this host of orbs in heaven, to furnish man with the dictionary and grammar of his municipal speech? Whilst we use this grand cipher to expedite the affairs of our pot and kettle, we feel that we have not yet put it to its use, neither are able. We are like travellers using the cinders of a volcano to roast their eggs. Whilst we see that it always stands ready to clothe what we would say, we cannot avoid the question whether the characters are not significant of themselves. Have mountains, and waves, and skies, no significance but what we consciously give them when we employ them as emblems of our thoughts? The world is

emblematic. Parts of speech are metaphors, because the whole of nature is a metaphor of the human mind. The laws of moral nature answer to those of matter as face to face in a glass. "The visible world and the relation of its parts, is the dial plate of the invisible." The axioms of physics translate the laws of ethics. Thus, "the whole is greater than its part;" "reaction is equal to action;" "the smallest weight may be made to lift the greatest, the difference of weight being compensated by time;" and many the like propositions, which have an ethical as well as physical sense. These propositions have a much more extensive and universal sense when applied to human life, than when confined to technical use.

In like manner, the memorable words of history and the proverbs of nations consist usually of a natural fact, selected as a picture or parable of a moral truth. Thus; A rolling stone gathers no moss; A bird in the hand is worth two in the bush; A cripple in the right way will beat a racer in the wrong; Make hay while the sun shines; 'T is hard to carry a full cup even; Vinegar is the son of wine; The last ounce broke the camel's back; Long-lived trees make roots first;—and the like. In their primary sense these are trivial facts, but we repeat them for the value of their analogical import. What is true of proverbs, is true of all fables, parables, and allegories.

This relation between the mind and matter is not fancied by some poet, but stands in the will of God, and so is free to be known by all men. It appears to men, or it does not appear. When in fortunate hours we ponder this miracle, the wise man doubts if at all other times he is not blind and deaf;

> "Can such things be,
> And overcome us like a summer's cloud,
> Without our special wonder?"

for the universe becomes transparent, and the light of higher laws than its own shines through it. It is the standing problem which has exercised the wonder and the study of every fine genius since the world began; from the era of the Egyptians and the Brahmins to that of Pythagoras, of Plato, of Bacon, of Leibnitz, of Swedenborg. There sits the Sphinx at the road-side, and from age to age, as each prophet comes by, he tries his fortune at reading her riddle. There seems to be a necessity in spirit to manifest itself in material forms; and day and night, river and storm, beast and bird, acid and alkali, preëxist in necessary Ideas in the mind of God, and are what they are by virtue of preceding affections in the world of spirit. A Fact is the end or last issue of spirit. The visible creation is the terminus or the circumference of the invisible world. "Material objects," said a French philosopher, "are necessarily kinds of *scoriae* of the substantial thoughts of the Creator, which must always preserve an exact relation to their first origin; in other words, visible nature must have a spiritual and moral side."

This doctrine is abstruse, and though the images of "garment," "scoriae," "mirror," etc., may stimulate the fancy, we must summon the aid of subtler and more vital expositors to make it plain. "Every scripture is to be interpreted by the same spirit which gave it forth,"—is the fundamental law of criticism. A life in harmony with Nature, the love of truth and of virtue, will purge the eyes to understand her text. By degrees we may come to know the primitive sense of the permanent objects of nature, so that the world shall be to us an open book, and every form significant of its hidden life and final cause.

A new interest surprises us, whilst, under the view now suggested, we contemplate the fearful extent and multitude of objects; since "every object rightly seen, unlocks a new faculty of the soul." That which was unconscious truth, becomes, when interpreted and defined in an object, a part of the domain of knowledge,—a new weapon in the magazine of power.

V
Discipline

In view of the significance of nature, we arrive at once at a
new fact, that nature is a discipline. This use of the world
includes the preceding uses, as parts of itself.

Space, time, society, labor, climate, food, locomotion,
the animals, the mechanical forces, give us sincerest lessons, day by day, whose meaning is unlimited. They educate both the Understanding and the Reason. Every
property of matter is a school for the understanding,—its
solidity or resistance, its inertia, its extension, its figure, its
divisibility. The understanding adds, divides, combines,
measures, and finds nutriment and room for its activity in
this worthy scene. Meantime, Reason transfers all these
lessons into its own world of thought, by perceiving the
analogy that marries Matter and Mind.

1. Nature is a discipline of the understanding in intellectual truths. Our dealing with sensible objects is a constant exercise in the necessary lessons of difference, of
likeness, of order, of being and seeming, of progressive arrangement; of ascent from particular to general; of combination to one end of manifold forces. Proportioned to the
importance of the organ to be formed, is the extreme care
with which its tuition is provided,—a care pretermitted in
no single case. What tedious training, day after day, year
after year, never ending, to form the common sense; what
continual reproduction of annoyances, inconveniences,
dilemmas; what rejoicing over us of little men; what dis-
puting of prices, what reckonings of interest,—and all
to form the Hand of the mind;—to instruct us that "good
thoughts are no better than good dreams, unless they be
executed!"

The same good office is performed by Property and its
filial systems of debt and credit. Debt, grinding debt,
whose iron face the widow, the orphan, and the sons of genius fear and hate;—debt, which consumes so much time,
which so cripples and disheartens a great spirit with cares

that seem so base, is a preceptor whose lessons cannot be foregone, and is needed most by those who suffer from it most. Moreover, property, which has been well compared to snow,—"if it fall level to-day, it will be blown into drifts to-morrow,"—is the surface action of internal machinery, like the index on the face of a clock. Whilst now it is the gymnastics of the understanding, it is hiving, in the foresight of the spirit, experience in profounder laws.

The whole character and fortune of the individual are affected by the least inequalities in the culture of the understanding; for example, in the perception of differences. Therefore is Space, and therefore Time, that man may know that things are not huddled and lumped, but sundered and individual. A bell and a plough have each their use, and neither can do the office of the other. Water is good to drink, coal to burn, wool to wear; but wool cannot be drunk, nor water spun, nor coal eaten. The wise man shows his wisdom in separation, in gradation, and his scale of creatures and of merits is as wide as nature. The foolish have no range in their scale, but suppose every man is as every other man. What is not good they call the worst, and what is not hateful, they call the best.

In like manner, what good heed Nature forms in us! She pardons no mistakes. Her yea is yea, and her nay, nay.

The first steps in Agriculture, Astronomy, Zoölogy (those first steps which the farmer, the hunter, and the sailor take), teach that Nature's dice are always loaded; that in her heaps and rubbish are concealed sure and useful results.

How calmly and genially the mind apprehends one after another the laws of physics! What noble emotions dilate the mortal as he enters into the councils of the creation, and feels by knowledge the privilege to BE! His insight refines him. The beauty of nature shines in his own breast. Man is greater that he can see this, and the universe less, because Time and Space relations vanish as laws are known.

Here again we are impressed and even daunted by the

immense Universe to be explored. "What we know is a point to what we do not know." Open any recent journal of science, and weigh the problems suggested concerning Light, Heat, Electricity, Magnetism, Physiology, Geology, and judge whether the interest of natural science is likely to be soon exhausted.

Passing by many particulars of the discipline of nature, we must not omit to specify two.

The exercise of the Will, or the lesson of power, is taught in every event. From the child's successive possession of his several senses up to the hour when he saith, "Thy will be done!" he is learning the secret that he can reduce under his will not only particular events but great classes, nay, the whole series of events, and so conform all facts to his character. Nature is thoroughly mediate. It is made to serve. It receives the dominion of man as meekly as the ass on which the Saviour rode. It offers all its kingdoms to man as the raw material which he may mould into what is useful. Man is never weary of working it up. He forges the subtile and delicate air into wise and melodious words, and gives them wing as angels of persuasion and command. One after another his victorious thought comes up with and reduces all things, until the world becomes at last only a realized will,—the double of the man.

2. Sensible objects conform to the premonitions of Reason and reflect the conscience. All things are moral; and in their boundless changes have an unceasing reference to spiritual nature. Therefore is nature glorious with form, color, and motion; that every globe in the remotest heaven, every chemical change from the rudest crystal up to the laws of life, every change of vegetation from the first principle of growth in the eye of a leaf, to the tropical forest and antediluvian coal-mine, every animal function from the sponge up to Hercules, shall hint or thunder to man the laws of right and wrong, and echo the Ten Commandments. Therefore is Nature ever the ally of Religion: lends all her pomp and riches to the religious sentiment. Prophet and priest, David, Isaiah, Jesus, have drawn

deeply from this source. This ethical character so penetrates the bone and marrow of nature, as to seem the end for which it was made. Whatever private purpose is answered by any member or part, this is its public and universal function, and is never omitted. Nothing in nature is exhausted in its first use. When a thing has served an end to the uttermost, it is wholly new for an ulterior service. In God, every end is converted into a new means. Thus the use of commodity, regarded by itself, is mean and squalid. But it is to the mind an education in the doctrine of Use, namely, that a thing is good only so far as it serves; that a conspiring of parts and efforts to the production of an end is essential to any being. The first and gross manifestation of this truth is our inevitable and hated training in values and wants, in corn and meat.

It has already been illustrated, that every natural process is a version of a moral sentence. The moral law lies at the centre of nature and radiates to the circumference. It is the pith and marrow of every substance, every relation, and every process. All things with which we deal, preach to us. What is a farm but a mute gospel? The chaff and the wheat, weeds and plants, blight, rain, insects, sun,—it is a sacred emblem from the first furrow of spring to the last stack which the snow of winter overtakes in the fields. But the sailor, the shepherd, the miner, the merchant, in their several resorts, have each an experience precisely parallel, and leading to the same conclusion: because all organizations are radically alike. Nor can it be doubted that this moral sentiment which thus scents the air, grows in the grain, and impregnates the waters of the world, is caught by man and sinks into his soul. The moral influence of nature upon every individual is that amount of truth which it illustrates to him. Who can estimate this? Who can guess how much firmness the sea-beaten rock has taught the fisherman? how much tranquillity has been reflected to man from the azure sky, over whose unspotted deeps the winds forevermore drive flocks of stormy clouds, and leave no wrinkle or stain? how much industry and providence and affection we have caught from the pantomime of brutes? What a searching preacher of self-command is the varying phenomenon of Health!

Herein is especially apprehended the unity of Nature,—the unity in variety,—which meets us everywhere. All the endless variety of things make an identical impression. Xenophanes complained in his old age, that, look where he would, all things hastened back to Unity. He was weary of seeing the same entity in the tedious variety of forms. The fable of Proteus has a cordial truth. A leaf, a drop, a crystal, a moment of time, is related to the whole, and partakes of the perfection of the whole. Each particle is a microcosm, and faithfully renders the likeness of the world.

Not only resemblances exist in things whose analogy is obvious, as when we detect the type of the human hand in the flipper of the fossil saurus, but also in objects wherein there is great superficial unlikeness. Thus architecture is called "frozen music," by De Staël and Goethe. Vitruvius thought an architect should be a musician. "A Gothic church," said Coleridge, "is a petrified religion." Michael Angelo maintained, that, to an architect, a knowledge of anatomy is essential. In Haydn's oratorios, the notes present to the imagination not only motions, as of the snake, the stag, and the elephant, but colors also; as the green grass. The law of harmonic sounds reappears in the harmonic colors. The granite is differenced in its laws only by the more or less of heat from the river that wears it away. The river, as it flows, resembles the air that flows over it; the air resembles the light which traverses it with more subtile currents; the light resembles the heat which rides with it through Space. Each creature is only a modification of the other; the likeness in them is more than the difference, and their radical law is one and the same. A rule of one art, or a law of one organization, holds true throughout nature. So intimate is this Unity, that, it is easily seen, it lies under the undermost garment of Nature, and betrays its source in Universal Spirit. For it per-

vades Thought also. Every universal truth which we
express in words, implies or supposes every other truth.
Omne verum vero consonat. It is like a great circle on a
sphere, comprising all possible circles; which, however,
may be drawn and comprise it in like manner. Every such
truth is the absolute Ens seen from one side. But it has innumerable sides.

The central Unity is still more conspicuous in actions.
Words are finite organs of the infinite mind. They cannot
cover the dimensions of what is in truth. They break,
chop, and impoverish it. An action is the perfection and
publication of thought. A right action seems to fill the eye,
and to be related to all nature. "The wise man, in doing
one thing, does all; or, in the one thing he does rightly, he
sees the likeness of all which is done rightly."

Words and actions are not the attributes of brute nature. They introduce us to the human form, of which all
other organizations appear to be degradations. When this
appears among so many that surround it, the spirit prefers
it to all others. It says, "From such as this have I drawn
joy and knowledge; in such as this have I found and beheld myself; I will speak to it; it can speak again; it can
yield me thought already formed and alive." In fact, the
eye,—the mind,—is always accompanied by these forms,
male and female; and these are incomparably the richest
informations of the power and order that lie at the heart of
things. Unfortunately every one of them bears the marks
as of some injury; is marred and superficially defective.
Nevertheless, far different from the deaf and dumb nature
around them, these all rest like fountain-pipes on the un-
fathomed sea of thought and virtue whereto they alone, of
all organizations, are the entrances.

It were a pleasant inquiry to follow into detail their
ministry to our education, but where would it stop? We
are associated in adolescent and adult life with some
friends, who, like skies and waters, are coextensive with
our idea; who, answering each to a certain affection of the
soul, satisfy our desire on that side; whom we lack power

to put at such focal distance from us, that we can mend or even analyze them. We cannot choose but love them. When much intercourse with a friend has supplied us with a standard of excellence, and has increased our respect for the resources of God who thus sends a real person to outgo our ideal; when he has, moreover, become an object of thought, and, whilst his character retains all its unconscious effect, is converted in the mind into solid and sweet wisdom,—it is a sign to us that his office is closing, and he is commonly withdrawn from our sight in a short time.

VI
Idealism

Thus is the unspeakable but intelligible and practicable meaning of the world conveyed to man, the immortal pupil, in every object of sense. To this one end of Discipline, all parts of nature conspire.

A noble doubt perpetually suggests itself,—whether this end be not the Final Cause of the Universe; and whether nature outwardly exists. It is a sufficient account of that Appearance we call the World, that God will teach a human mind, and so makes it the receiver of a certain number of congruent sensations, which we call sun and moon, man and woman, house and trade. In my utter impotence to test the authenticity of the report of my senses, to know whether the impressions they make on me correspond with outlying objects, what difference does it make, whether Orion is up there in heaven, or some god paints the image in the firmament of the soul? The relations of parts and the end of the whole remaining the same, what is the difference, whether land and sea interact, and worlds revolve and intermingle without number or end,— deep yawning under deep, and galaxy balancing galaxy, throughout absolute space,—or whether, without relations of time and space, the same appearances are inscribed in the constant faith of man? Whether nature enjoy a substantial existence without, or is only in the apocalypse of the mind, it is alike useful and alike venerable to me. Be it what it may, it is ideal to me so long as I cannot try the accuracy of my senses.

The frivolous make themselves merry with the Ideal theory, as if its consequences were burlesque; as if it affected the stability of nature. It surely does not. God never jests with us, and will not compromise the end of nature by permitting any inconsequence in its procession. Any distrust of the permanence of laws would paralyze the faculties of man. Their permanence is sacredly respected, and his faith therein is perfect. The wheels and springs of man are all set to the hypothesis of the permanence of nature. We are not built like a ship to be tossed, but like a house to stand. It is a natural consequence of this structure, that so long as the active powers predominate over the reflective, we resist with indignation any hint that nature is more short-lived or mutable than spirit. The broker, the wheelwright, the carpenter, the tollman, are much displeased at the intimation.

But whilst we acquiesce entirely in the permanence of natural laws, the question of the absolute existence of nature still remains open. It is the uniform effect of culture on the human mind, not to shake our faith in the stability of particular phenomena, as of heat, water, azote; but to lead us to regard nature as phenomenon, not a substance; to attribute necessary existence to spirit; to esteem nature as an accident and an effect.

To the senses and the unrenewed understanding, belongs a sort of instinctive belief in the absolute existence of nature. In their view man and nature are indissolubly joined. Things are ultimates, and they never look beyond their sphere. The presence of Reason mars this faith. The first effort of thought tends to relax this despotism of the senses which binds us to nature as if we were a part of it, and shows us nature aloof, and, as it were, afloat. Until this higher agency intervened, the animal eye sees, with wonderful accuracy, sharp outlines and colored surfaces. When the eye of Reason opens, to outline and surface are at once added grace and expression. These proceed from imagination and affection, and abate somewhat of the angular distinctness of objects. If the Reason be stimulated to more earnest vision, outlines and surfaces become transparent, and are no longer seen; causes and spirits are seen through them. The best moments of life are these delicious awakenings of the higher powers, and the reverential withdrawing of nature before its God.

Let us proceed to indicate the effects of culture.

1. Our first institution in the Ideal philosophy is a hint from Nature herself.

Nature is made to conspire with spirit to emancipate us. Certain mechanical changes, a small alteration in our local position, apprizes us of a dualism. We are strangely affected by seeing the shore from a moving ship, from a balloon, or through the tints of an unusual sky. The least change in our point of view gives the whole world a pictorial air. A man who seldom rides, needs only to get into a coach and traverse his own town, to turn the street into a puppet-show. The men, the women,—talking, running, bartering, fighting,—the earnest mechanic, the lounger, the beggar, the boys, the dogs, are unrealized at once, or, at least, wholly detached from all relation to the observer, and seen as apparent, not substantial beings. What new thoughts are suggested by seeing a face of country quite familiar, in the rapid movement of the railroad car! Nay, the most wonted objects, (make a very slight change in the point of vision,) please us most. In a camera obscura, the butcher's cart, and the figure of one of our own family amuse us. So a portrait of a well-known face gratifies us. Turn the eyes upside down, by looking at the landscape through your legs, and how agreeable is the picture, though you have seen it any time these twenty years!

In these cases, by mechanical means, is suggested the

difference between the observer and the spectacle—between man and nature. Hence arises a pleasure mixed with awe; I may say, a low degree of the sublime is felt, from the fact, probably, that man is hereby apprized that whilst the world is a spectacle, something in himself is stable.

2. In a higher manner the poet communicates the same pleasure. By a few strokes he delineates, as on air, the sun, the mountain, the camp, the city, the hero, the maiden, not different from what we know them, but only lifted from the ground and afloat before the eye. He unfixes the land and the sea, makes them revolve around the axis of his primary thought, and disposes them anew. Possessed himself by a heroic passion, he uses matter as symbols of it. The sensual man conforms thoughts to things; the poet conforms things to his thoughts. The one esteems nature as rooted and fast; the other, as fluid, and impresses his being thereon. To him, the refractory world is ductile and flexible; he invests dust and stones with humanity, and makes them the words of the Reason. The Imagination may be defined to be the use which the Reason makes of the material world. Shakspeare possesses the power of subordinating nature for the purposes of expression, beyond all poets. His imperial muse tosses the creation like a bauble from hand to hand, and uses it to embody any caprice of thought that is uppermost in his mind. The remotest spaces of nature are visited, and the farthest sundered things are brought together, by a subtile spiritual connection. We are made aware that magnitude of material things is relative, and all objects shrink and expand to serve the passion of the poet. Thus in his sonnets, the lays of birds, the scents and dyes of flowers he finds to be the *shadow* of his beloved; time, which keeps her from him, is his *chest;* the suspicion she has awakened, is her *ornament;*

The ornament of beauty is Suspect,
A crow which flies in heaven's sweetest air.

His passion is not the fruit of chance; it swells, as he speaks, to a city, or a state.

> No, it was builded far from accident;
> It suffers not in smiling pomp, nor falls
> Under the brow of thralling discontent;
> It fears not policy, that heretic,
> That works on leases of short numbered hours,
> But all alone stands hugely politic.

In the strength of his constancy, the Pyramids seem to him recent and transitory. The freshness of youth and love dazzles him with its resemblance to morning;

> Take those lips away
> Which so sweetly were forsworn;
> And those eyes,—the break of day,
> Lights that do mislead the morn.

The wild beauty of this hyperbole, I may say in passing, it would not be easy to match in literature.

This transfiguration which all material objects undergo through the passion of the poet,—this power which he exerts to dwarf the great, to magnify the small,—might be illustrated by a thousand examples from his Plays. I have before me the Tempest, and will cite only these few lines.

> ARIEL. The strong based promontory
> Have I made shake, and by the spurs plucked up
> The pine and cedar.

Prospero calls for music to soothe the frantic Alonzo, and his companions;

> A solemn air, and the best comforter
> To an unsettled fancy, cure thy brains
> Now useless, boiled within thy skull.

Again;

> The charm dissolves apace,
> And, as the morning steals upon the night,
> Melting the darkness, so their rising senses
> Begin to chase the ignorant fumes that mantle
> Their clearer reason.
> Their understanding
> Begins to swell: and the approaching tide
> Will shortly fill the reasonable shores
> That now lie foul and muddy.

The perception of real affinities between events (that is to say, of *ideal* affinities, for those only are real), enables the poet thus to make free with the most imposing forms and phenomena of the world, and to assert the predominance of the soul.

3. Whilst thus the poet animates nature with his own thoughts, he differs from the philosopher only herein, that the one proposes Beauty as his main end; the other Truth. But the philosopher, not less than the poet, postpones the apparent order and relations of things to the empire of thought. "The problem of philosophy," according to Plato, "is, for all that exists conditionally, to find a ground unconditioned and absolute." It proceeds on the faith that a law determines all phenomena, which being known, the phenomena can be predicted. That law, when in the mind, is an idea. Its beauty is infinite. The true philosopher and the true poet are one, and a beauty, which is truth, and a truth, which is beauty, is the aim of both. Is not the charm of one of Plato's or Aristotle's definitions strictly like that of the Antigone of Sophocles? It is, in both cases, that a spiritual life has been imparted to nature; that the solid seeming block of matter has been pervaded and dissolved by a thought; that this feeble human being has penetrated the vast masses of nature with an informing soul, and recognized itself in their harmony, that is, seized their law. In

physics, when this is attained, the memory disburthens itself of its cumbrous catalogues of particulars, and carries
centuries of observation in a single formula.

Thus even in physics, the material is degraded before
the spiritual. The astronomer, the geometer, rely on their
irrefragable analysis, and disdain the results of observation. The sublime remark of Euler on his law of arches,
"This will be found contrary to all experience, yet is
true;" had already transferred nature into the mind, and
left matter like an outcast corpse.

4. Intellectual science has been observed to beget invariably a doubt of the existence of matter. Turgot said,
"He that has never doubted the existence of matter, may
be assured he has no aptitude for metaphysical inquiries."
It fastens the attention upon immortal necessary un-
created natures, that is, upon Ideas; and in their presence
we feel that the outward circumstance is a dream and a
shade. Whilst we wait in this Olympus of gods, we think
of nature as an appendix to the soul. We ascend into their
region, and know that these are the thoughts of the Supreme Being. "These are they who were set up from everlasting, from the beginning, or ever the earth was. When
he prepared the heavens, they were there; when he established the clouds above, when he strengthened the fountains of the deep. Then they were by him, as one brought
up with him. Of them took he counsel."

Their influence is proportionate. As objects of science
they are accessible to few men. Yet all men are capable of
being raised by piety or by passion, into their region. And
no man touches these divine natures, without becoming,
in some degree, himself divine. Like a new soul, they
renew the body. We become physically nimble and light-
some; we tread on air; life is no longer irksome, and we
think it will never be so. No man fears age or misfortune
or death in their serene company, for he is transported out
of the district of change. Whilst we behold unveiled the
nature of Justice and Truth, we learn the difference be-

tween the absolute and the conditional or relative. We apprehend the absolute. As it were, for the first time, *we
exist*. We become immortal, for we learn that time and
space are relations of matter; that with a perception of
truth or a virtuous will they have no affinity.

5. Finally, religion and ethics, which may be fitly called
the practice of ideas, or the introduction of ideas into
life, have an analogous effect with all lower culture, in
degrading nature and suggesting its dependence on spirit.
Ethics and religion differ herein; that the one is the system
of human duties commencing from man; the other, from
God. Religion includes the personality of God; Ethics
does not. They are one to our present design. They both
put nature under foot. The first and last lesson of religion
is, "The things that are seen, are temporal; the things that
are unseen, are eternal." It puts an affront upon nature. It
does that for the unschooled, which philosophy does for
Berkeley and Viasa. The uniform language that may be
heard in the churches of the most ignorant sects is,—
"Contemn the unsubstantial shows of the world; they are
vanities, dreams, shadows, unrealities; seek the realities of
religion." The devotee flouts nature. Some theosophists
have arrived at a certain hostility and indignation towards
matter, as the Manichean and Plotinus. They distrusted
in themselves any looking back to these flesh-pots of
Egypt. Plotinus was ashamed of his body. In short, they
might all say of matter, what Michael Angelo said
of external beauty, "It is the frail and weary weed,
in which God dresses the soul which he has called into
time."

It appears that motion, poetry, physical and intellectual
science, and religion, all tend to affect our convictions of
the reality of the external world. But I own there is something ungrateful in expanding too curiously the particulars of the general proposition, that all culture tends to
imbue us with idealism. I have no hostility to nature, but a
child's love to it. I expand and live in the warm day like

corn and melons. Let us speak her fair. I do not wish to fling stones at my beautiful mother, nor soil my gentle nest. I only wish to indicate the true position of nature in regard to man, wherein to establish man all right education tends; as the ground which to attain is the object of human life, that is, of man's connection with nature. Culture inverts the vulgar views of nature, and brings the mind to call that apparent which it uses to call real, and that real which it uses to call visionary. Children, it is true, believe in the external world. The belief that it appears only, is an afterthought, but with culture this faith will as surely arise on the mind as did the first.

The advantage of the ideal theory over the popular faith is this, that it presents the world in precisely that view which is most desirable to the mind. It is, in fact, the view which Reason, both speculative and practical, that is, philosophy and virtue, take. For seen in the light of thought, the world always is phenomenal; and virtue subordinates it to the mind. Idealism sees the world in God. It beholds the whole circle of persons and things, of actions and events, of country and religion, not as painfully accumulated, atom after atom, act after act, in an aged creeping Past, but as one vast picture which God paints on the instant eternity for the contemplation of the soul. Therefore the soul holds itself off from a too trivial and microscopic study of the universal tablet. It respects the end too much to immerse itself in the means. It sees something more important in Christianity than the scandals of ecclesiastical history or the niceties of criticism; and, very incurious concerning persons or miracles, and not at all disturbed by chasms of historical evidence, it accepts from God the phenomenon, as it finds it, as the pure and awful form of religion in the world. It is not hot and passionate at the appearance of what it calls its own good or bad fortune, at the union or opposition of other persons. No man is its enemy. It accepts whatsoever befalls, as part of its lesson. It is a watcher more than a doer, and it is a doer, only that it may the better watch.

VII
Spirit

It is essential to a true theory of nature and of man, that it should contain somewhat progressive. Uses that are exhausted or that may be, and facts that end in the statement, cannot be all that is true of this brave lodging wherein man is harbored, and wherein all his faculties find appropriate and endless exercise. And all the uses of nature admit of being summed in one, which yields the activity of man an infinite scope. Through all its kingdoms, to the suburbs and outskirts of things, it is faithful to the cause whence it had its origin. It always speaks of Spirit. It suggests the absolute. It is a perpetual effect. It is a great shadow pointing always to the sun behind us.

The aspect of Nature is devout. Like the figure of Jesus, she stands with bended head, and hands folded upon the breast. The happiest man is he who learns from nature the lesson of worship.

Of that ineffable essence which we call Spirit, he that thinks most, will say least. We can foresee God in the coarse, and, as it were, distant phenomena of matter; but when we try to define and describe himself, both language and thought desert us, and we are as helpless as fools and savages. That essence refuses to be recorded in propositions, but when man has worshipped him intellectually, the noblest ministry of nature is to stand as the apparition of God. It is the organ through which the universal spirit speaks to the individual, and strives to lead back the individual to it.

When we consider Spirit, we see that the views already presented do not include the whole circumference of man. We must add some related thoughts.

Three problems are put by nature to the mind: What is matter? Whence is it? and Whereto? The first of these questions only, the ideal theory answers. Idealism saith: matter is a phenomenon, not a substance. Idealism acquaints us with the total disparity between the evidence of our own being and the evidence of the world's being. The one is perfect; the other, incapable of any assurance; the mind is a part of the nature of things; the world is a divine dream, from which we may presently awake to the glories and certainties of day. Idealism is a hypothesis to account for nature by other principles than those of carpentry and chemistry. Yet, if it only deny the existence of matter, it does not satisfy the demands of the spirit. It leaves God out of me. It leaves me in the splendid labyrinth of my perceptions, to wander without end. Then the heart resists it, because it balks the affections in denying substantive being to men and women. Nature is so pervaded with human life that there is something of humanity in all and in every particular. But this theory makes nature foreign to me, and does not account for that consanguinity which we acknowledge to it.

Let it stand then, in the present state of our knowledge, merely as a useful introductory hypothesis, serving to apprize us of the eternal distinction between the soul and the world.

But when, following the invisible steps of thought, we come to inquire, Whence is matter? and Whereto? many truths arise to us out of the recesses of consciousness. We learn that the highest is present to the soul of man; that the dread universal essence, which is not wisdom, or love, or beauty, or power, but all in one, and each entirely, is that for which all things exist, and that by which they are; that spirit creates; that behind nature, throughout nature, spirit is present; one and not compound it does not act upon us from without, that is, in space and time, but spiritually, or through ourselves: therefore, that spirit, that is, the Supreme Being, does not build up nature around us, but puts it forth through us, as the life of the tree puts forth new branches and leaves through the pores of the old. As a plant upon the earth, so a man rests upon the bosom of God; he is nourished by unfailing fountains, and draws at his need inexhaustible power. Who can set bounds to the possibilities of man? Once inhale the upper air, being admitted to behold the absolute natures of justice and truth, and we learn that man has access to the entire mind of the Creator, is himself the creator in the finite. This view, which admonishes me where the sources of wisdom and power lie, and points to virtue as to

> "The golden key
> Which opes the palace of eternity,"

carries upon its face the highest certificate of truth, because it animates me to create my own world through the purification of my soul.

The world proceeds from the same spirit as the body of man. It is a remoter and inferior incarnation of God, a projection of God in the unconscious. But it differs from the body in one important respect. It is not, like that, now subjected to the human will. Its serene order is inviolable by us. It is, therefore, to us, the present expositor of the divine mind. It is a fixed point whereby we may measure our departure. As we degenerate, the contrast between us and our house is more evident. We are as much strangers in nature as we are aliens from God. We do not understand the notes of birds. The fox and the deer run away from us; the bear and tiger rend us. We do not know the uses of more than a few plants, as corn and the apple, the potato and the vine. Is not the landscape, every glimpse of which hath a grandeur, a face of him? Yet this may show us what discord is between man and nature, for you cannot freely admire a noble landscape if laborers are digging in the field hard by. The poet finds something ridiculous in his delight until he is out of the sight of men.

VIII
Prospects

In inquiries respecting the laws of the world and the frame of things, the highest reason is always the truest. That which seems faintly possible, it is so refined, is often

faint and dim because it is deepest seated in the mind
among the eternal verities. Empirical science is apt to
cloud the sight, and by the very knowledge of functions
and processes to bereave the student of the manly contemplation of the whole. The savant becomes unpoetic.
But the best read naturalist who lends an entire and devout attention to truth, will see that there remains much to
learn of his relation to the world, and that it is not to be
learned by any addition or subtraction or other comparison of known quantities, but is arrived at by untaught sallies of the spirit, by a continual self-recovery, and by
entire humility. He will perceive that there are far more
excellent qualities in the student than preciseness and in-
fallibility; that a guess is often more fruitful than an indisputable affirmation, and that a dream may let us deeper
into the secret of nature than a hundred concerted experiments.

For the problems to be solved are precisely those which
the physiologist and the naturalist omit to state. It is not
so pertinent to man to know all the individuals of the animal kingdom, as it is to know whence and whereto is this
tyrannizing unity in his constitution, which evermore sep-
arates and classifies things, endeavoring to reduce the
most diverse to one form. When I behold a rich landscape,
it is less to my purpose to recite correctly the order and
superposition of the strata, than to know why all thought
of multitude is lost in a tranquil sense of unity. I cannot
greatly honor minuteness in details, so long as there is no
hint to explain the relation between things and thoughts;
no ray upon the *metaphysics* of conchology, of botany, of
the arts, to show the relation of the forms of flowers,
shells, animals, architecture, to the mind, and build science upon ideas. In a cabinet of natural history, we become sensible of a certain occult recognition and
sympathy in regard to the most unwieldy and eccentric
forms of beast, fish, and insect. The American who has
been confined, in his own country, to the sight of buildings designed after foreign models, is surprised on enter-

ing York Minster or St. Peter's at Rome, by the feeling that these structures are imitations also,—faint copies of an invisible archetype. Nor has science sufficient humanity, so long as the naturalist overlooks that wonderful congruity which subsists between man and the world; of which he is lord, not because he is the most subtile inhabitant, but because he is its head and heart, and finds something of himself in every great and small thing, in every mountain stratum, in every new law of color, fact of astronomy, or atmospheric influence which observation or analysis lays open. A perception of this mystery inspires the muse of George Herbert, the beautiful psalmist of the seventeenth century. The following lines are part of his little poem on Man.

> Man is all symmetry,
> Full of proportions, one limb to another,
> And all to all the world besides.
> Each part may call the farthest, brother;
> For head with foot hath private amity,
> And both with moons and tides.
>
> Nothing hath got so far
> But man hath caught and kept it as his prey;
> His eyes dismount the highest star:
> He is in little all the sphere.
> Herbs gladly cure our flesh, because that they
> Find their acquaintance there.
>
> For us, the winds do blow,
> The earth doth rest, heaven move, and fountains flow;
> Nothing we see, but means our good,
> As our delight, or as our treasure;
> The whole is either our cupboard of food,
> Or cabinet of pleasure.
>
> The stars have us to bed:
> Night draws the curtain; which the sun withdraws.
> Music and light attend our head.
> All things unto our flesh are kind,

In their descent and being; to our mind,
    In their ascent and cause.

    More servants wait on man
Than he'll take notice of. In every path,
    He treads down that which doth befriend him
    When sickness makes him pale and wan.
Oh mighty love! Man is one world, and hath
    Another to attend him.

The perception of this class of truths makes the attraction which draws men to science, but the end is lost sight of in attention to the means. In view of this half-sight of science, we accept the sentence of Plato, that "poetry comes nearer to vital truth than history." Every surmise and vaticination of the mind is entitled to a certain respect, and we learn to prefer imperfect theories, and sentences which contain glimpses of truth, to digested systems which have no one valuable suggestion. A wise writer will feel that the ends of study and composition are best answered by announcing undiscovered regions of thought, and so communicating, through hope, new activity to the torpid spirit.

I shall therefore conclude this essay with some traditions of man and nature, which a certain poet sang to me; and which, as they have always been in the world, and perhaps reappear to every bard, may be both history and prophecy.

'The foundations of man are not in matter, but in spirit. But the element of spirit is eternity. To it, therefore, the longest series of events, the oldest chronologies are young and recent. In the cycle of the universal man, from whom the known individuals proceed, centuries are points, and all history is but the epoch of one degradation.

'We distrust and deny inwardly our sympathy with nature. We own and disown our relation to it, by turns. We are like Nebuchadnezzar, dethroned, bereft of reason, and eating grass like an ox. But who can set limits to the remedial force of spirit?

'A man is a god in ruins. When men are innocent, life shall be longer, and shall pass into the immortal as gently as we awake from dreams. Now, the world would be insane and rabid, if these disorganizations should last for hundreds of years. It is kept in check by death and infancy. Infancy is the perpetual Messiah, which comes into the arms of fallen men, and pleads with them to return to paradise.

'Man is the dwarf of himself. Once he was permeated and dissolved by spirit. He filled nature with his overflowing currents. Out from him sprang the sun and moon; from man the sun, from woman the moon. The laws of his mind, the periods of his actions externized themselves into day and night, into the year and the seasons. But, having made for himself this huge shell, his waters retired; he no longer fills the veins and veinlets; he is shrunk to a drop. He sees that the structure still fits him, but fits him colossally. Say, rather, once it fitted him, now it corresponds to him from far and on high. He adores timidly his own work. Now is man the follower of the sun, and woman the follower of the moon. Yet sometimes he starts in his slumber, and wonders at himself and his house, and muses strangely at the resemblance betwixt him and it. He perceives that if his law is still paramount, if still he have elemental power, if his word is sterling yet in nature, it is not conscious power, it is not inferior but superior to his will. It is instinct.' Thus my Orphic poet sang.

At present, man applies to nature but half his force. He works on the world with his understanding alone. He lives in it and masters it by a penny-wisdom; and he that works most in it is but a half-man, and whilst his arms are strong and his digestion good, his mind is imbruted, and he is a selfish savage. His relation to nature, his power over it, is through the understanding, as by manure; the economic use of fire, wind, water, and the mariner's needle; steam, coal, chemical agriculture; the repairs of the human body by the dentist and the surgeon. This is such a resumption of power as if a banished king should buy his territories

inch by inch, instead of vaulting at once into his throne.
Meantime, in the thick darkness, there are not wanting
gleams of a better light,—occasional examples of the action of man upon nature with his entire force,—with reason as well as understanding. Such examples are, the
traditions of miracles in the earliest antiquity of all nations; the history of Jesus Christ; the achievements of a
principle, as in religious and political revolutions, and in
the abolition of the slave-trade; the miracles of enthusiasm, as those reported of Swedenborg, Hohenlohe, and
the Shakers; many obscure and yet contested facts, now
arranged under the name of Animal Magnetism; prayer;
eloquence; self-healing; and the wisdom of children.
These are examples of Reason's momentary grasp of the
sceptre; the exertions of a power which exists not in time
or space, but an instantaneous in-streaming causing
power. The difference between the actual and the ideal
force of man is happily figured by the schoolmen, in saying, that the knowledge of man is an evening knowledge,
vespertina cognitio, but that of God is a morning knowledge, *matutina cognitio*.

The problem of restoring to the world original and
eternal beauty is solved by the redemption of the soul.
The ruin or the blank that we see when we look at nature,
is in our own eye. The axis of vision is not coincident with
the axis of things, and so they appear not transparent but
opaque. The reason why the world lacks unity, and lies
broken and in heaps, is because man is disunited with
himself. He cannot be a naturalist until he satisfies all the
demands of the spirit. Love is as much its demand as perception. Indeed, neither can be perfect without the other.
In the uttermost meaning of the words, thought is devout,
and devotion is thought. Deep calls unto deep. But in actual life, the marriage is not celebrated. There are innocent men who worship God after the tradition of their
fathers, but their sense of duty has not yet extended to the
use of all their faculties. And there are patient naturalists,
but they freeze their subject under the wintry light of the

understanding. Is not prayer also a study of truth,—a sally of the soul into the unfound infinite? No man ever prayed heartily without learning something. But when a faithful thinker, resolute to detach every object from personal relations and see it in the light of thought, shall, at the same time, kindle science with the fire of the holiest affections, then will God go forth anew into the creation.

It will not need, when the mind is prepared for study, to search for objects. The invariable mark of wisdom is to see the miraculous in the common. What is a day? What is a year? What is summer? What is woman? What is a child? What is sleep? To our blindness, these things seem unaffecting. We make fables to hide the baldness of the fact and conform it, as we say, to the higher law of the mind. But when the fact is seen under the light of an idea, the gaudy fable fades and shrivels. We behold the real higher law. To the wise, therefore, a fact is true poetry, and the most beautiful of fables. These wonders are brought to our own door. You also are a man. Man and woman and their social life, poverty, labor, sleep, fear, fortune, are known to you. Learn that none of these things is superficial, but that each phenomenon has its roots in the faculties and affections of the mind. Whilst the abstract question occupies your intellect, nature brings it in the concrete to be solved by your hands. It were a wise inquiry for the closet, to compare, point by point, especially at remarkable crises in life, our daily history with the rise and progress of ideas in the mind.

So shall we come to look at the world with new eyes. It shall answer the endless inquiry of the intellect,—What is truth? and of the affections,—What is good? by yielding itself passive to the educated Will. Then shall come to pass what my poet said: 'Nature is not fixed but fluid. Spirit alters, moulds, makes it. The immobility or bruteness of nature is the absence of spirit; to pure spirit it is fluid, it is volatile, it is obedient. Every spirit builds itself a house, and beyond its house a world, and beyond its world a heaven. Know then that the world exists for you. For you

is the phenomenon perfect. What we are, that only can we
see. All that Adam had, all that Caesar could, you have
and can do. Adam called his house, heaven and earth;
Caesar called his house, Rome; you perhaps call yours, a
cobbler's trade; a hundred acres of ploughed land; or a
scholar's garret. Yet line for line and point for point your
dominion is as great as theirs, though without fine names.
Build therefore your own world. As fast as you conform
your life to the pure idea in your mind, that will unfold its
great proportions. A correspondent revolution in things
will attend the influx of the spirit. So fast will disagreeable
appearances, swine, spiders, snakes, pests, mad-houses,
prisons, enemies, vanish; they are temporary and shall be
no more seen. The sordor and filths of nature, the sun
shall dry up and the wind exhale. As when the summer
comes from the south the snow-banks melt and the face of
the earth becomes green before it, so shall the advancing
spirit create its ornaments along its path, and carry with it
the beauty it visits and the song which enchants it; it shall
draw beautiful faces, warm hearts, wise discourse, and heroic acts, around its way, until evil is no more seen. The
kingdom of man over nature, which cometh not with observation,—a dominion such as now is beyond his dream
of God,—he shall enter without more wonder than the
blind man feels who is gradually restored to perfect sight.'

THE AMERICAN
SCHOLAR

~~~~~~

*An Oration Delivered before the Phi Beta
Kappa Society, at Cambridge, August 31, 1837*

MR. PRESIDENT AND GENTLEMEN:

I greet you on the recommencement of our literary
year. Our anniversary is one of hope, and, perhaps, not
enough of labor. We do not meet for games of strength or
skill, for the recitation of histories, tragedies, and odes, like
the ancient Greeks; for parliaments of love and poesy,
like the Troubadours; nor for the advancement of science, like our contemporaries in the British and European
capitals. Thus far, our holiday has been simply a friendly
sign of the survival of the love of letters amongst a people
too busy to give to letters any more. As such it is precious
as the sign of an indestructible instinct. Perhaps the time
is already come when it ought to be, and will be, something else; when the sluggard intellect of this continent
will look from under its iron lids and fill the postponed
expectation of the world with something better than the
exertions of mechanical skill. Our day of dependence, our
long apprenticeship to the learning of other lands, draws
to a close. The millions that around us are rushing into
life, cannot always be fed on the sere remains of foreign
harvests. Events, actions arise, that must be sung, that will
sing themselves. Who can doubt that poetry will revive
and lead in a new age, as the star in the constellation Harp,
which now flames in our zenith, astronomers announce,
shall one day be the pole-star for a thousand years?

In this hope I accept the topic which not only usage but the nature of our association seem to prescribe to this day,—the AMERICAN SCHOLAR. Year by year we come up hither to read one more chapter of his biography. Let us inquire what light new days and events have thrown on his character and his hopes.

It is one of those fables which out of an unknown antiquity convey an unlooked-for wisdom, that the gods, in the beginning, divided Man into men, that he might be more helpful to himself; just as the hand was divided into fingers, the better to answer its end.

The old fable covers a doctrine ever new and sublime; that there is One Man,—present to all particular men only partially, or through one faculty; and that you must take the whole society to find the whole man. Man is not a farmer, or a professor, or an engineer, but he is all. Man is priest, and scholar, and statesman, and producer, and soldier. In the *divided* or social state these functions are parcelled out to individuals, each of whom aims to do his stint of the joint work, whilst each other performs his. The fable implies that the individual, to possess himself, must sometimes return from his own labor to embrace all the other laborers. But, unfortunately, this original unit, this fountain of power, has been so distributed to multitudes, has been so minutely subdivided and peddled out, that it is spilled into drops, and cannot be gathered. The state of society is one in which the members have suffered amputation from the trunk, and strut about so many walking monsters,—a good finger, a neck, a stomach, an elbow, but never a man.

Man is thus metamorphosed into a thing, into many things. The planter, who is Man sent out into the field to gather food, is seldom cheered by any idea of the true dignity of his ministry. He sees his bushel and his cart, and nothing beyond, and sinks into the farmer, instead of Man on the farm. The tradesman scarcely ever gives an ideal worth to his work, but is ridden by the routine of his craft, and the soul is subject to dollars. The priest becomes a form; the attorney a statute-book; the mechanic a machine; the sailor a rope of the ship.

In this distribution of functions the scholar is the delegated intellect. In the right state he is *Man Thinking.* In the degenerate state, when the victim of society, he tends to become a mere thinker, or still worse, the parrot of other men's thinking.

In this view of him, as Man Thinking, the theory of his office is contained. Him Nature solicits with all her placid, all her monitory pictures; him the past instructs; him the future invites. Is not indeed every man a student, and do not all things exist for the student's behoof? And, finally, is not the true scholar the only true master? But the old oracle said, "All things have two handles: beware of the wrong one." In life, too often, the scholar errs with mankind and forfeits his privilege. Let us see him in his school, and consider him in reference to the main influences he receives.

I. The first in time and the first in importance of the influences upon the mind is that of nature. Every day, the sun; and, after sunset, Night and her stars. Ever the winds blow; ever the grass grows. Every day, men and women, conversing—beholding and beholden. The scholar is he of all men whom this spectacle most engages. He must settle its value in his mind. What is nature to him? There is never a beginning, there is never an end, to the inexplicable continuity of this web of God, but always circular power returning into itself. Therein it resembles his own spirit, whose beginning, whose ending, he never can find,—so entire, so boundless. Far too as her splendors shine, system on system shooting like rays, upward, downward, without centre, without circumference,—in the mass and in the particle, Nature hastens to render account of herself to the mind. Classification begins. To the young mind every thing is individual, stands by itself. By and by, it finds how to join two things and see in them one nature; then three, then three thousand; and so, tyrannized over by its own unifying instinct, it goes on tying things together, diminishing anomalies, discovering roots running under ground whereby contrary and remote things cohere and flower out from one stem. It presently learns that since the dawn of history there has been a constant accumulation and classifying of facts. But what is classification but the perceiving that these objects are not chaotic, and are not foreign, but have a law which is also a law of the human mind? The astronomer discovers that geometry, a pure abstraction of the human mind, is the measure of planetary motion. The chemist finds proportions and intelligible method throughout matter; and science is nothing but the finding of analogy, identity, in the most remote parts. The ambitious soul sits down before each refractory fact; one after another reduces all strange constitutions, all new powers, to their class and their law, and goes on forever to animate the last fibre of organization, the outskirts of nature, by insight.

Thus to him, to this schoolboy under the bending dome of day, is suggested that he and it proceed from one root; one is leaf and one is flower; relation, sympathy, stirring in every vein. And what is that root? Is not that the soul of his soul? A thought too bold; a dream too wild. Yet when this spiritual light shall have revealed the law of more earthly natures,—when he has learned to worship the soul, and to see that the natural philosophy that now is, is only the first gropings of its gigantic hand, he shall look forward to an ever expanding knowledge as to a becoming creator. He shall see that nature is the opposite of the soul, answering to it part for part. One is seal and one is print. Its beauty is the beauty of his own mind. Its laws are the laws of his own mind. Nature then becomes to him the measure of his attainments. So much of nature as he is ignorant of, so much of his own mind does he not yet possess. And, in fine, the ancient precept, "Know thyself," and the modern precept, "Study nature," become at last one maxim.

II. The next great influence into the spirit of the scholar

is the mind of the Past,—in whatever form, whether of literature, of art, of institutions, that mind is inscribed. Books are the best type of the influence of the past, and perhaps we shall get at the truth,—learn the amount of this influence more conveniently,—by considering their value alone.

The theory of books is noble. The scholar of the first age received into him the world around; brooded thereon; gave it the new arrangement of his own mind, and uttered it again. It came into him life; it went out from him truth. It came to him short-lived actions; it went out from him immortal thoughts. It came to him business; it went from him poetry. It was dead fact; now, it is quick thought. It can stand, and it can go. It now endures, it now flies, it now inspires. Precisely in proportion to the depth of mind from which it issued, so high does it soar, so long does it sing.

Or, I might say, it depends on how far the process had gone, of transmuting life into truth. In proportion to the completeness of the distillation, so will the purity and imperishableness of the product be. But none is quite perfect. As no air-pump can by any means make a perfect vacuum, so neither can any artist entirely exclude the conventional, the local, the perishable from his book, or write a book of pure thought, that shall be as efficient, in all respects, to a remote posterity, as to contemporaries, or rather to the second age. Each age, it is found, must write its own books; or rather, each generation for the next succeeding. The books of an older period will not fit this.

Yet hence arises a grave mischief. The sacredness which attaches to the act of creation, the act of thought, is transferred to the record. The poet chanting was felt to be a divine man: henceforth the chant is divine also. The writer was a just and wise spirit: henceforward it is settled the book is perfect; as love of the hero corrupts into worship of his statue. Instantly the book becomes noxious: the guide is a tyrant. The sluggish and perverted mind of the multitude, slow to open to the incursions of Reason, hav-

ing once so opened, having once received this book, stands
upon it, and makes an outcry if it is disparaged. Colleges
are built on it. Books are written on it by thinkers, not by
Man Thinking; by men of talent, that is, who start wrong,
who set out from accepted dogmas, not from their own
sight of principles. Meek young men grow up in libraries,
believing it their duty to accept the views which Cicero,
which Locke, which Bacon, have given; forgetful that Cicero, Locke, and Bacon were only young men in libraries
when they wrote these books.

Hence, instead of Man Thinking, we have the book-
worm. Hence the book-learned class, who value books, as
such; not as related to nature and the human constitution,
but as making a sort of Third Estate with the world and
the soul. Hence the restorers of readings, the emendators,
the bibliomaniacs of all degrees.

Books are the best of things, well used; abused, among
the worst. What is the right use? What is the one end
which all means go to effect? They are for nothing but to
inspire. I had better never see a book than to be warped by
its attraction clean out of my own orbit, and made a satel-
lite instead of a system. The one thing in the world, of
value, is the active soul. This every man is entitled to; this
every man contains within him, although in almost all
men obstructed and as yet unborn. The soul active sees
absolute truth and utters truth, or creates. In this action it
is genius; not the privilege of here and there a favorite, but
the sound estate of every man. In its essence it is
progressive. The book, the college, the school of art, the
institution of any kind, stop with some past utterance of
genius. This is good, say they,—let us hold by this. They
pin me down. They look backward and not forward. But
genius looks forward: the eyes of man are set in his forehead, not in his hindhead: man hopes: genius creates.
Whatever talents may be, if the man create not, the pure
efflux of the Deity is not his;—cinders and smoke there
may be, but not yet flame. There are creative manners,
there are creative actions, and creative words; manners,

actions, words, that is, indicative of no custom or authority, but springing spontaneous from the mind's own sense of good and fair.

On the other part, instead of being its own seer, let it receive from another mind its truth, though it were in torrents of light, without periods of solitude, inquest, and self-recovery, and a fatal disservice is done. Genius is always sufficiently the enemy of genius by over-influence. The literature of every nation bears me witness. The English dramatic poets have Shakspearized now for two hundred years.

Undoubtedly there is a right way of reading, so it be sternly subordinated. Man Thinking must not be subdued by his instruments. Books are for the scholar's idle times. When he can read God directly, the hour is too precious to be wasted in other men's transcripts of their readings. But when the intervals of darkness come, as come they must,—when the sun is hid and the stars withdraw their shining,—we repair to the lamps which were kindled by their ray, to guide our steps to the East again, where the dawn is. We hear, that we may speak. The Arabian proverb says, "A fig tree, looking on a fig tree, becometh fruitful."

It is remarkable, the character of the pleasure we derive from the best books. They impress us with the conviction that one nature wrote and the same reads. We read the verses of one of the great English poets, of Chaucer, of Marvell, of Dryden, with the most modern joy,—with a pleasure, I mean, which is in great part caused by the abstraction of all *time* from their verses. There is some awe mixed with the joy of our surprise, when this poet, who lived in some past world, two or three hundred years ago, says that which lies close to my own soul, that which I also had well-nigh thought and said. But for the evidence thence afforded to the philosophical doctrine of the identity of all minds, we should suppose some preëstablished harmony, some foresight of souls that were to be, and some preparation of stores for their future wants, like the fact observed in insects, who lay up food before death for the young grub they shall never see.

I would not be hurried by any love of system, by any exaggeration of instincts, to underrate the Book. We all know, that as the human body can be nourished on any food, though it were boiled grass and the broth of shoes, so the human mind can be fed by any knowledge. And great and heroic men have existed who had almost no other information than by the printed page. I only would say that it needs a strong head to bear that diet. One must be an inventor to read well. As the proverb says, "He that would bring home the wealth of the Indies, must carry out the wealth of the Indies." There is then creative reading as well as creative writing. When the mind is braced by labor and invention, the page of whatever book we read becomes luminous with manifold allusion. Every sentence is doubly significant, and the sense of our author is as broad as the world. We then see, what is always true, that as the seer's hour of vision is short and rare among heavy days and months, so is its record, perchance, the least part of his volume. The discerning will read, in his Plato or Shakspeare, only that least part,—only the authentic utterances of the oracle;—all the rest he rejects, were it never so many times Plato's and Shakspeare's.

Of course there is a portion of reading quite indispensable to a wise man. History and exact science he must learn by laborious reading. Colleges, in like manner, have their indispensable office,—to teach elements. But they can only highly serve us when they aim not to drill, but to create; when they gather from far every ray of various genius to their hospitable halls, and by the concentrated fires, set the hearts of their youth on flame. Thought and knowledge are natures in which apparatus and pretension avail nothing. Gowns and pecuniary foundations, though of towns of gold, can never countervail the least sentence or syllable of wit. Forget this, and our American colleges will recede in their public importance, whilst they grow richer every year.

III. There goes in the world a notion that the scholar should be a recluse, a valetudinarian,—as unfit for any handiwork or public labor as a penknife for an axe. The so-called "practical men" sneer at speculative men, as if, because they speculate or *see*, they could do nothing. I have heard it said that the clergy,—who are always, more universally than any other class, the scholars of their day,—are addressed as women; that the rough, spontaneous conversation of men they do not hear, but only a mincing and diluted speech. They are often virtually disfranchised; and indeed there are advocates for their celibacy. As far as this is true of the studious classes, it is not just and wise. Action is with the scholar subordinate, but it is essential. Without it he is not yet man. Without it thought can never ripen into truth. Whilst the world hangs before the eye as a cloud of beauty, we cannot even see its beauty. Inaction is cowardice, but there can be no scholar without the heroic mind. The preamble of thought, the transition through which it passes from the unconscious to the conscious, is action. Only so much do I know, as I have lived. Instantly we know whose words are loaded with life, and whose not.

The world,—this shadow of the soul, or *other me*,—lies wide around. Its attractions are the keys which unlock my thoughts and make me acquainted with myself. I run eagerly into this resounding tumult. I grasp the hands of those next me, and take my place in the ring to suffer and to work, taught by an instinct that so shall the dumb abyss be vocal with speech. I pierce its order; I dissipate its fear; I dispose of it within the circuit of my expanding life. So much only of life as I know by experience, so much of the wilderness have I vanquished and planted, or so far have I extended my being, my dominion. I do not see how any man can afford, for the sake of his nerves and his nap, to spare any action in which he can partake. It is pearls and rubies to his discourse. Drudgery, calamity, exasperation, want, are instructors in eloquence and wisdom. The true scholar grudges every opportunity of action past by, as a loss of power. It is the raw material out of which the intellect moulds her splendid products. A strange process too, this by which experience is converted into thought, as a mulberry leaf is converted into satin. The manufacture goes forward at all hours.

The actions and events of our childhood and youth are now matters of calmest observation. They lie like fair pictures in the air. Not so with our recent actions,—with the business which we now have in hand. On this we are quite unable to speculate. Our affections as yet circulate through it. We no more feel or know it than we feel the feet, or the hand, or the brain of our body. The new deed is yet a part of life,—remains for a time immersed in our unconscious life. In some contemplative hour it detaches itself from the life like a ripe fruit, to become a thought of the mind. Instantly it is raised, transfigured; the corruptible has put on incorruption. Henceforth it is an object of beauty, however base its origin and neighborhood. Observe too the impossibility of antedating this act. In its grub state, it cannot fly, it cannot shine, it is a dull grub. But suddenly, without observation, the selfsame thing unfurls beautiful wings, and is an angel of wisdom. So is there no fact, no event, in our private history, which shall not, sooner or later, lose its adhesive, inert form, and astonish us by soaring from our body into the empyrean. Cradle and infancy, school and playground, the fear of boys, and dogs, and ferules, the love of little maids and berries, and many another fact that once filled the whole sky, are gone already; friend and relative, profession and party, town and country, nation and world, must also soar and sing.

Of course, he who has put forth his total strength in fit actions has the richest return of wisdom. I will not shut myself out of this globe of action, and transplant an oak into a flowerpot, there to hunger and pine; nor trust the revenue of some single faculty, and exhaust one vein of thought, much like those Savoyards, who, getting their livelihood by carving shepherds, shepherdesses, and smoking Dutchmen, for all Europe, went out one day to the mountain to find stock, and discovered that they had whittled up the last of their pine trees. Authors we have, in numbers, who have written out their vein, and who, moved by a commendable prudence, sail for Greece or Palestine, follow the trapper into the prairie, or ramble round Algiers, to replenish their merchantable stock.

If it were only for a vocabulary, the scholar would be covetous of action. Life is our dictionary. Years are well spent in country labors; in town; in the insight into trades and manufactures; in frank intercourse with many men and women; in science; in art; to the one end of mastering in all their facts a language by which to illustrate and embody our perceptions. I learn immediately from any speaker how much he has already lived, through the poverty or the splendor of his speech. Life lies behind us as the quarry from whence we get tiles and copestones for the masonry of to-day. This is the way to learn grammar. Colleges and books only copy the language which the field and the work-yard made.

But the final value of action, like that of books, and better than books, is that it is a resource. That great principle of Undulation in nature, that shows itself in the inspiring and expiring of the breath; in desire and satiety; in the ebb and flow of the sea; in day and night; in heat and cold; and, as yet more deeply ingrained in every atom and every fluid, is known to us under the name of Polarity,—these "fits of easy transmission and reflection," as Newton called them, are the law of nature because they are the law of spirit.

The mind now thinks, now acts, and each fit reproduces the other. When the artist has exhausted his materials, when the fancy no longer paints, when thoughts are no longer apprehended and books are a weariness,—he has always the resource *to live*. Character is higher than intellect. Thinking is the function. Living is the functionary. The stream retreats to its source. A great soul will be strong to live, as well as strong to think. Does he lack

organ or medium to impart his truths? He can still fall
back on this elemental force of living them. This is a total
act. Thinking is a partial act. Let the grandeur of justice
shine in his affairs. Let the beauty of affection cheer his
lowly roof. Those "far from fame," who dwell and act
with him, will feel the force of his constitution in the doings and passages of the day better than it can be measured by any public and designed display. Time shall
teach him that the scholar loses no hour which the man
lives. Herein he unfolds the sacred germ of his instinct,
screened from influence. What is lost in seemliness is
gained in strength. Not out of those on whom systems of
education have exhausted their culture, comes the helpful
giant to destroy the old or to build the new, but out of un-
handselled savage nature; out of terrible Druids and Ber-
serkers come at last Alfred and Shakspeare.

I hear therefore with joy whatever is beginning to be
said of the dignity and necessity of labor to every citizen.
There is virtue yet in the hoe and the spade, for learned as
well as for unlearned hands. And labor is everywhere
welcome; always we are invited to work; only be this limitation observed, that a man shall not for the sake of wider
activity sacrifice any opinion to the popular judgments
and modes of action.

I have now spoken of the education of the scholar by
nature, by books, and by action. It remains to say somewhat of his duties.

They are such as become Man Thinking. They may all
be comprised in self-trust. The office of the scholar is to
cheer, to raise, and to guide men by showing them facts
amidst appearances. He plies the slow, unhonored, and
unpaid task of observation. Flamsteed and Herschel, in
their glazed observatories, may catalogue the stars with
the praise of all men, and the results being splendid and
useful, honor is sure. But he, in his private observatory,
cataloguing obscure and nebulous stars of the human
mind, which as yet no man has thought of as such,—

watching days and months sometimes for a few facts; correcting still his old records;—must relinquish display and immediate fame. In the long period of his preparation he must betray often an ignorance and shiftlessness in popular arts, incurring the disdain of the able who shoulder him aside. Long he must stammer in his speech; often forego the living for the dead. Worse yet, he must accept—how often!—poverty and solitude. For the ease and pleasure of treading the old road, accepting the fashions, the education, the religion of society, he takes the cross of making his own, and, of course, the self-accusation, the faint heart, the frequent uncertainty and loss of time, which are the nettles and tangling vines in the way of the self-relying and self-directed; and the state of virtual hostility in which he seems to stand to society, and especially to educated society. For all this loss and scorn, what offset? He is to find consolation in exercising the highest functions of human nature. He is one who raises himself from private considerations and breathes and lives on public and illustrious thoughts. He is the world's eye. He is the world's heart. He is to resist the vulgar prosperity that retrogrades ever to barbarism, by preserving and communicating heroic sentiments, noble biographies, melodious verse, and the conclusions of history. Whatsoever oracles the human heart, in all emergencies, in all solemn hours, has uttered as its commentary on the world of actions,—these he shall receive and impart. And whatsoever new verdict Reason from her inviolable seat pronounces on the passing men and events of to-day,—this he shall hear and promulgate.

These being his functions, it becomes him to feel all confidence in himself, and to defer never to the popular cry. He and he only knows the world. The world of any moment is the merest appearance. Some great decorum, some fetish of a government, some ephemeral trade, or war, or man, is cried up by half mankind and cried down by the other half, as if all depended on this particular up or down. The odds are that the whole question is not worth the poorest thought which the scholar has lost in listening to the controversy. Let him not quit his belief that a popgun is a popgun, though the ancient and honorable of the earth affirm it to be the crack of doom. In silence, in steadiness, in severe abstraction, let him hold by himself; add observation to observation, patient of neglect, patient of reproach, and bide his own time,—happy enough if he can satisfy himself alone that this day he has seen something truly. Success treads on every right step. For the instinct is sure, that prompts him to tell his brother what he thinks. He then learns that in going down into the secrets of his own mind he has descended into the secrets of all minds. He learns that he who has mastered any law in his private thoughts, is master to that extent of all men whose language he speaks, and of all into whose language his own can be translated. The poet, in utter solitude remembering his spontaneous thoughts and recording them, is found to have recorded that which men in crowded cities find true for them also. The orator distrusts at first the fitness of his frank confessions, his want of knowledge of the persons he addresses, until he finds that he is the complement of his hearers;—that they drink his words because he fulfils for them their own nature; the deeper he dives into his privatest, secretest presentiment, to his wonder he finds this is the most acceptable, most public, and universally true. The people delight in it; the better part of every man feels, This is my music; this is myself.

In self-trust all the virtues are comprehended. Free should the scholar be,—free and brave. Free even to the definition of freedom, "without any hindrance that does not arise out of his own constitution." Brave; for fear is a thing which a scholar by his very function puts behind him. Fear always springs from ignorance. It is a shame to him if his tranquillity, amid dangerous times, arise from the presumption that like children and women his is a protected class; or if he seek a temporary peace by the diversion of his thoughts from politics or vexed questions, hiding his head like an ostrich in the flowering bushes, peeping into microscopes, and turning rhymes, as a boy whistles to keep his courage up. So is the danger a danger still; so is the fear worse. Manlike let him turn and face it. Let him look into its eye and search its nature, inspect its origin,—see the whelping of this lion,—which lies no great way back; he will then find in himself a perfect comprehension of its nature and extent; he will have made his hands meet on the other side, and can henceforth defy it and pass on superior. The world is his who can see through its pretension. What deafness, what stone-blind custom, what overgrown error you behold is there only by sufferance,—by your sufferance. See it to be a lie, and you have already dealt it its mortal blow.

Yes, we are the cowed,—we the trustless. It is a mischievous notion that we are come late into nature; that the world was finished a long time ago. As the world was plastic and fluid in the hands of God, so it is ever to so much of his attributes as we bring to it. To ignorance and sin, it is flint. They adapt themselves to it as they may; but in proportion as a man has any thing in him divine, the firmament flows before him and takes his signet and form. Not he is great who can alter matter, but he who can alter my state of mind. They are the kings of the world who give the color of their present thought to all nature and all art, and persuade men by the cheerful serenity of their carrying the matter, that this thing which they do is the apple which the ages have desired to pluck, now at last ripe, and inviting nations to the harvest. The great man makes the great thing. Wherever Macdonald sits, there is the head of the table. Linnæus makes botany the most alluring of studies, and wins it from the farmer and the herb-woman; Davy, chemistry; and Cuvier, fossils. The day is always his who works in it with serenity and great aims. The unstable estimates of men crowd to him whose mind is filled with a truth, as the heaped waves of the Atlantic follow the moon.

For this self-trust, the reason is deeper than can be

fathomed,—darker than can be enlightened. I might not
carry with me the feeling of my audience in stating my
own belief. But I have already shown the ground of my
hope, in adverting to the doctrine that man is one. I believe man has been wronged; he has wronged himself. He
has almost lost the light that can lead him back to his pre-
rogatives. Men are become of no account. Men in history,
men in the world of to-day, are bugs, are spawn, and are
called "the mass" and "the herd." In a century, in a millennium, one or two men; that is to say, one or two ap-
proximations to the right state of every man. All the rest
behold in the hero or the poet their own green and crude
being,—ripened; yes, and are content to be less, so *that*
may attain to its full stature. What a testimony, full of
grandeur, full of pity, is borne to the demands of his own
nature, by the poor clansman, the poor partisan, who rejoices in the glory of his chief. The poor and the low find
some amends to their immense moral capacity, for their
acquiescence in a political and social inferiority. They are
content to be brushed like flies from the path of a great
person, so that justice shall be done by him to that common nature which it is the dearest desire of all to see enlarged and glorified. They sun themselves in the great
man's light, and feel it to be their own element. They cast
the dignity of man from their downtrod selves upon the
shoulders of a hero, and will perish to add one drop of
blood to make that great heart beat, those giant sinews
combat and conquer. He lives for us, and we live in him.

Men, such as they are, very naturally seek money or
power; and power because it is as good as money,—the
"spoils," so called, "of office." And why not? for they aspire to the highest, and this, in their sleep-walking, they
dream is highest. Wake them and they shall quit the false
good and leap to the true, and leave governments to clerks
and desks. This revolution is to be wrought by the gradual
domestication of the idea of Culture. The main enterprise
of the world for splendor, for extent, is the upbuilding of a
man. Here are the materials strewn along the ground. The

private life of one man shall be a more illustrious monarchy, more formidable to its enemy, more sweet and serene in its influence to its friend, than any kingdom in
history. For a man, rightly viewed, comprehendeth the
particular natures of all men. Each philosopher, each bard,
each actor has only done for me, as by a delegate, what
one day I can do for myself. The books which once we
valued more than the apple of the eye, we have quite exhausted. What is that but saying that we have come up
with the point of view which the universal mind took
through the eyes of one scribe; we have been that man,
and have passed on. First, one, then another, we drain all
cisterns, and waxing greater by all these supplies, we
crave a better and more abundant food. The man has
never lived that can feed us ever. The human mind cannot
be enshrined in a person who shall set a barrier on any one
side to this unbounded, unboundable empire. It is one
central fire, which, flaming now out of the lips of Etna,
lightens the capes of Sicily, and now out of the throat of
Vesuvius, illuminates the towers and vineyards of Naples.
It is one light which beams out of a thousand stars. It is
one soul which animates all men.

But I have dwelt perhaps tediously upon this abstraction of the Scholar. I ought not to delay longer to add
what I have to say of nearer reference to the time and to
this country.

Historically, there is thought to be a difference in the
ideas which predominate over successive epochs, and
there are data for marking the genius of the Classic, of the
Romantic, and now of the Reflective or Philosophical age.
With the views I have intimated of the oneness or the
identity of the mind through all individuals, I do not
much dwell on these differences. In fact, I believe each individual passes through all three. The boy is a Greek; the
youth, romantic; the adult, reflective. I deny not, however,
that a revolution in the leading idea may be distinctly
enough traced.

Our age is bewailed as the age of Introversion. Must that needs be evil? We, it seems, are critical; we are embarrassed with second thoughts; we cannot enjoy any thing for hankering to know whereof the pleasure consists; we are lined with eyes; we see with our feet; the time is infected with Hamlet's unhappiness, —

"Sicklied o'er with the pale cast of thought."

It is so bad then? Sight is the last thing to be pitied. Would we be blind? Do we fear lest we should outsee nature and God, and drink truth dry? I look upon the discontent of the literary class as a mere announcement of the fact that they find themselves not in the state of mind of their fathers, and regret the coming state as untried; as a boy dreads the water before he has learned that he can swim. If there is any period one would desire to be born in, is it not the age of Revolution; when the old and the new stand side by side and admit of being compared; when the energies of all men are searched by fear and by hope; when the historic glories of the old can be compensated by the rich possibilities of the new era? This time, like all times, is a very good one, if we but know what to do with it.

I read with some joy of the auspicious signs of the coming days, as they glimmer already through poetry and art, through philosophy and science, through church and state.

One of these signs is the fact that the same movement which effected the elevation of what was called the lowest class in the state, assumed in literature a very marked and as benign an aspect. Instead of the sublime and beautiful, the near, the low, the common, was explored and poetized. That which had been negligently trodden under foot by those who were harnessing and provisioning themselves for long journeys into far countries, is suddenly found to be richer than all foreign parts. The literature of the poor, the feelings of the child, the philosophy of the street, the meaning of household life, are the topics of the time. It is a great stride. It is a sign—is it not?—of new vigor when the extremities are made active, when currents of warm life run into the hands and the feet. I ask not for the great, the remote, the romantic; what is doing in Italy or Arabia; what is Greek art, or Provençal minstrelsy; I embrace the common, I explore and sit at the feet of the familiar, the low. Give me insight into to-day, and you may have the antique and future worlds. What would we really know the meaning of? The meal in the firkin; the milk in the pan; the ballad in the street; the news of the boat; the glance of the eye; the form and the gait of the body;— show me the ultimate reason of these matters; show me the sublime presence of the highest spiritual cause lurking, as always it does lurk, in these suburbs and extremities of nature; let me see every trifle bristling with the polarity that ranges it instantly on an eternal law; and the shop, the plough, and the ledger referred to the like cause by which light undulates and poets sing;—and the world lies no longer a dull miscellany and lumber-room, but has form and order; there is no trifle, there is no puzzle, but one design unites and animates the farthest pinnacle and the lowest trench.

This idea has inspired the genius of Goldsmith, Burns, Cowper, and, in a newer time, of Goethe, Wordsworth, and Carlyle. This idea they have differently followed and with various success. In contrast with their writing, the style of Pope, of Johnson, of Gibbon, looks cold and pedantic. This writing is blood-warm. Man is surprised to find that things near are not less beautiful and wondrous than things remote. The near explains the far. The drop is a small ocean. A man is related to all nature. This perception of the worth of the vulgar is fruitful in discoveries. Goethe, in this very thing the most modern of the moderns, has shown us, as none ever did, the genius of the ancients.

There is one man of genius who has done much for this philosophy of life, whose literary value has never yet been rightly estimated;—I mean Emanuel Swedenborg. The most imaginative of men, yet writing with the precision of a mathematician, he endeavored to engraft a purely philosophical Ethics on the popular Christianity of his time. Such an attempt of course must have difficulty which no genius could surmount. But he saw and showed the connection between nature and the affections of the soul. He pierced the emblematic or spiritual character of the visible, audible, tangible world. Especially did his shade-loving muse hover over and interpret the lower parts of nature; he showed the mysterious bond that allies moral evil to the foul material forms, and has given in epical parables a theory of insanity, of beasts, of unclean and fearful things.

Another sign of our times, also marked by an analogous political movement, is the new importance given to the single person. Every thing that tends to insulate the individual,—to surround him with barriers of natural respect, so that each man shall feel the world is his, and man shall treat with man as a sovereign state with a sovereign state,—tends to true union as well as greatness. "I learned," said the melancholy Pestalozzi, "that no man in God's wide earth is either willing or able to help any other man." Help must come from the bosom alone. The scholar is that man who must take up into himself all the ability of the time, all the contributions of the past, all the hopes of the future. He must be an university of knowledges. If there be one lesson more than another which should pierce his ear, it is, The world is nothing, the man is all; in yourself is the law of all nature, and you know not yet how a globule of sap ascends; in yourself slumbers the whole of Reason; it is for you to know all; it is for you to dare all. Mr. President and Gentlemen, this confidence in the unsearched might of man belongs, by all motives, by all prophecy, by all preparation, to the American Scholar. We have listened too long to the courtly muses of Europe. The spirit of the American freeman is already suspected to be timid, imitative, tame. Public and private avarice make the air we breathe thick and fat. The scholar is decent, indolent, complaisant. See already the tragic consequence. The mind of this country, taught to aim at low objects, eats upon itself. There is no work for any but the decorous and the complaisant. Young men of the fairest promise, who begin life upon our shores, inflated by the mountain winds, shined upon by all the stars of God, find the earth below not in unison with these, but are hindered from action by the disgust which the principles on which business is managed inspire, and turn drudges, or die of disgust, some of them suicides. What is the remedy? They did not yet see, and thousands of young men as hopeful now crowding to the barriers for the career do not yet see, that if the single man plant himself indomitably on his instincts, and there abide, the huge world will come round to him. Patience,—patience; with the shades of all the good and great for company; and for solace the perspective of your own infinite life; and for work the study and the communication of principles, the making those instincts prevalent, the conversion of the world. Is it not the chief disgrace in the world, not to be an unit;—not to be reckoned one character;—not to yield that peculiar fruit which each man was created to bear, but to be reckoned in the gross, in the hundred, or the thousand, of the party, the section, to which we belong; and our opinion predicted geographically, as the north, or the south? Not so, brothers and friends—please God, ours shall not be so. We will walk on our own feet; we will work with our own hands; we will speak our own minds. The study of letters shall be no longer a name for pity, for doubt, and for sensual indulgence. The dread of man and the love of man shall be a wall of defence and a wreath of joy around all. A nation of men will for the first time exist, because each believes himself inspired by the Divine Soul which also inspires all men.

ADDRESS

~~~~~~~~~~~~~~~~~~~~~~~~~~~~~~~~~~

Delivered before the Senior Class in Divinity College, Cambridge, Sunday evening, July 15, 1838

In this refulgent summer, it has been a luxury to draw the breath of life. The grass grows, the buds burst, the meadow is spotted with fire and gold in the tint of flowers. The air is full of birds, and sweet with the breath of the pine, the balm-of-Gilead, and the new hay. Night brings no gloom to the heart with its welcome shade. Through the transparent darkness the stars pour their almost spiritual rays. Man under them seems a young child, and his huge globe a toy. The cool night bathes the world as with a river, and prepares his eyes again for the crimson dawn. The mystery of nature was never displayed more happily. The corn and the wine have been freely dealt to all creatures, and the never-broken silence with which the old bounty goes forward has not yielded yet one word of explanation. One is constrained to respect the perfection of this world in which our senses converse. How wide; how rich; what invitation from every property it gives to every faculty of man! In its fruitful soils; in its navigable sea; in its mountains of metal and stone; in its forests of all woods; in its animals; in its chemical ingredients; in the powers and path of light, heat, attraction and life, it is well worth the pith and heart of great men to subdue and enjoy it. The planters, the mechanics, the inventors, the astronomers, the builders of cities, and the captains, history delights to honor.

But when the mind opens and reveals the laws which traverse the universe and make things what they are, then shrinks the great world at once into a mere illustration and fable of this mind. What am I? and What is? asks the human spirit with a curiosity new-kindled, but never to be quenched. Behold these outrunning laws, which our imperfect apprehension can see tend this way and that, but not come full circle. Behold these infinite relations, so like, so unlike; many, yet one. I would study, I would know, I would admire forever. These works of thought have been the entertainments of the human spirit in all ages.

A more secret, sweet, and overpowering beauty appears to man when his heart and mind open to the sentiment of virtue. Then he is instructed in what is above him. He learns that his being is without bound; that to the good, to the perfect, he is born, low as he now lies in evil and weakness. That which he venerates is still his own, though he has not realized it yet. *He ought.* He knows the sense of that grand word, though his analysis fails to render account of it. When in innocency or when by intellectual perception he attains to say,—"I love the Right; Truth is beautiful within and without for evermore. Virtue, I am thine; save me; use me; thee will I serve, day and night, in great, in small, that I may be not virtuous, but virtue;"— then is the end of the creation answered, and God is well pleased.

The sentiment of virtue is a reverence and delight in the presence of certain divine laws. It perceives that this homely game of life we play, covers, under what seem foolish details, principles that astonish. The child amidst his baubles is learning the action of light, motion, gravity, muscular force; and in the game of human life, love, fear, justice, appetite, man, and God, interact. These laws refuse to be adequately stated. They will not be written out on paper, or spoken by the tongue. They elude our persevering thought; yet we read them hourly in each other's faces, in each other's actions, in our own remorse. The moral traits which are all globed into every virtuous act and thought,—in speech we must sever, and describe or suggest by painful enumeration of many particulars. Yet, as this sentiment is the essence of all religion, let me guide your eye to the precise objects of the sentiment, by an enumeration of some of those classes of facts in which this element is conspicuous.

The intuition of the moral sentiment is an insight of the perfection of the laws of the soul. These laws execute themselves. They are out of time, out of space, and not subject to circumstance. Thus in the soul of man there is a justice whose retributions are instant and entire. He who does a good deed is instantly ennobled. He who does a mean deed is by the action itself contracted. He who puts off impurity, thereby puts on purity. If a man is at heart just, then in so far is he God; the safety of God, the immortality of God, the majesty of God do enter into that man with justice. If a man dissemble, deceive, he deceives himself, and goes out of acquaintance with his own being. A man in the view of absolute goodness, adores, with total humility. Every step so downward, is a step upward. The man who renounces himself, comes to himself.

See how this rapid intrinsic energy worketh everywhere, righting wrongs, correcting appearances, and bringing up facts to a harmony with thoughts. Its operation in life, though slow to the senses, is at last as sure as in the soul. By it a man is made the Providence to himself, dispensing good to his goodness, and evil to his sin. Character is always known. Thefts never enrich; alms never impoverish; murder will speak out of stone walls. The least admixture of a lie,—for example, the taint of vanity, any attempt to make a good impression, a favorable appearance,—will instantly vitiate the effect. But speak the truth, and all nature and all spirits help you with unexpected furtherance. Speak the truth, and all things alive or brute are vouchers, and the very roots of the grass underground there do seem to stir and move to bear you witness. See again the perfection of the Law as it applies itself to the affections, and becomes the law of society. As we are, so we associate. The good, by affinity, seek the good; the vile, by affinity, the vile. Thus of their own volition, souls proceed into heaven, into hell.

These facts have always suggested to man the sublime creed that the world is not the product of manifold power, but of one will, of one mind; and that one mind is everywhere active, in each ray of the star, in each wavelet of the pool; and whatever opposes that will is everywhere balked and baffled, because things are made so, and not otherwise. Good is positive. Evil is merely privative, not absolute: it is like cold, which is the privation of heat. All evil is so much death or nonentity. Benevolence is absolute and real. So much benevolence as a man hath, so much life hath he. For all things proceed out of this same spirit, which is differently named love, justice, temperance, in its different applications, just as the ocean receives different names on the several shores which it washes. All things proceed out of the same spirit, and all things conspire with it. Whilst a man seeks good ends, he is strong by the whole strength of nature. In so far as he roves from these ends, he bereaves himself of power, or auxiliaries; his being shrinks out of all remote channels, he becomes less and less, a mote, a point, until absolute badness is absolute death.

The perception of this law of laws awakens in the mind a sentiment which we call the religious sentiment, and which makes our highest happiness. Wonderful is its power to charm and to command. It is a mountain air. It is the embalmer of the world. It is myrrh and storax, and chlorine and rosemary. It makes the sky and the hills sublime, and the silent song of the stars is it. By it is the universe made safe and habitable, not by science or power. Thought may work cold and intransitive in things, and find no end or unity; but the dawn of the sentiment of virtue on the heart, gives and is the assurance that Law is sovereign over all natures; and the worlds, time, space, eternity, do seem to break out into joy.

This sentiment is divine and deifying. It is the beatitude

of man. It makes him illimitable. Through it, the soul first knows itself. It corrects the capital mistake of the infant man, who seeks to be great by following the great, and hopes to derive advantages *from another*,—by showing the fountain of all good to be in himself, and that he, equally with every man, is an inlet into the deeps of Reason. When he says, "I ought;" when love warms him; when he chooses, warned from on high, the good and great deed; then, deep melodies wander through his soul from Supreme Wisdom.—Then he can worship, and be enlarged by his worship; for he can never go behind this sentiment. In the sublimest flights of the soul, rectitude is never surmounted, love is never outgrown.

This sentiment lies at the foundation of society, and successively creates all forms of worship. The principle of veneration never dies out. Man fallen into superstition, into sensuality, is never quite without the visions of the moral sentiment. In like manner, all the expressions of this sentiment are sacred and permanent in proportion to their purity. The expressions of this sentiment affect us more than all other compositons. The sentences of the oldest time, which ejaculate this piety, are still fresh and fragrant. This thought dwelled always deepest in the minds of men in the devout and contemplative East; not alone in Palestine, where it reached its purest expression, but in Egypt, in Persia, in India, in China. Europe has always owed to oriental genius its divine impulses. What these holy bards said, all sane men found agreeable and true. And the unique impression of Jesus upon mankind, whose name is not so much written as ploughed into the history of this world, is proof of the subtle virtue of this infusion.

Meantime, whilst the doors of the temple stand open, night and day, before every man, and the oracles of this truth cease never, it is guarded by one stern condition; this, namely; it is an intuition. It cannot be received at second hand. Truly speaking, it is not instruction, but provocation, that I can receive from another soul. What he announces, I must find true in me, or reject; and on his word, or as his second, be he who he may, I can accept nothing. On the contrary, the absence of this primary faith is the presence of degradation. As is the flood, so is the ebb. Let this faith depart, and the very words it spake and the things it made become false and hurtful. Then falls the church, the state, art, letters, life. The doctrine of the divine nature being forgotten, a sickness infects and dwarfs the constitution. Once man was all; now he is an appendage, a nuisance. And because the indwelling Supreme Spirit cannot wholly be got rid of, the doctrine of it suffers this perversion, that the divine nature is attributed to one or two persons, and denied to all the rest, and denied with fury. The doctrine of inspiration is lost; the base doctrine of the majority of voices usurps the place of the doctrine of the soul. Miracles, prophecy, poetry, the ideal life, the holy life, exist as ancient history merely; they are not in the belief, nor in the aspiration of society; but, when suggested, seem ridiculous. Life is comic or pitiful as soon as the high ends of being fade out of sight, and man becomes near-sighted, and can only attend to what addresses the senses.

These general views, which, whilst they are general, none will contest, find abundant illustration in the history of religion, and especially in the history of the Christian church. In that, all of us have had our birth and nurture. The truth contained in that, you, my young friends, are now setting forth to teach. As the Cultus, or established worship of the civilized world, it has great historical interest for us. Of its blessed words, which have been the consolation of humanity, you need not that I should speak. I shall endeavor to discharge my duty to you on this occasion, by pointing out two errors in its administration, which daily appear more gross from the point of view we have just now taken.

Jesus Christ belonged to the true race of prophets. He saw with open eye the mystery of the soul. Drawn by its severe harmony, ravished with its beauty, he lived in it, and had his being there. Alone in all history he estimated the greatness of man. One man was true to what is in you and me. He saw that God incarnates himself in man, and evermore goes forth anew to take possession of his World. He said, in this jubilee of sublime emotion, 'I am divine. Through me, God acts; through me, speaks. Would you see God, see me; or see thee, when thou also thinkest as I now think.' But what a distortion did his doctrine and memory suffer in the same, in the next, and the following ages! There is no doctrine of the Reason which will bear to be taught by the Understanding. The understanding caught this high chant from the poet's lips, and said, in the next age, 'This was Jehovah come down out of heaven. I will kill you, if you say he was a man.' The idioms of his language and the figures of his rhetoric have usurped the place of his truth; and churches are not built on his principles, but on his tropes. Christianity became a Mythus, as the poetic teaching of Greece and of Egypt, before. He spoke of miracles; for he felt that man's life was a miracle, and all that man doth, and he knew that this daily miracle shines as the character ascends. But the word Miracle, as pronounced by Christian churches, gives a false impression; it is Monster. It is not one with the blowing clover and the falling rain.

He felt respect for Moses and the prophets, but no unfit tenderness at postponing their initial revelations to the hour and the man that now is; to the eternal revelation in the heart. Thus was he a true man. Having seen that the law in us is commanding, he would not suffer it to be commanded. Boldly, with hand, and heart, and life, he declared it was God. Thus is he, as I think, the only soul in history who has appreciated the worth of man.

1. In this point of view we become sensible of the first defect of historical Christianity. Historical Christianity has fallen into the error that corrupts all attempts to communicate religion. As it appears to us, and as it has appeared for ages, it is not the doctrine of the soul, but an exaggeration of the personal, the positive, the ritual. It has dwelt, it dwells, with noxious exaggeration about the *per-*

son of Jesus. The soul knows no persons. It invites every man to expand to the full circle of the universe, and will have no preferences but those of spontaneous love. But by this eastern monarchy of a Christianity, which indolence and fear have built, the friend of man is made the injurer of man. The manner in which his name is surrounded with expressions which were once sallies of admiration and love, but are now petrified into official titles, kills all generous sympathy and liking. All who hear me, feel that the language that describes Christ to Europe and America is not the style of friendship and enthusiasm to a good and noble heart, but is appropriated and formal,—paints a demigod, as the Orientals or the Greeks would describe Osiris or Apollo. Accept the injurious impositions of our early catechetical instruction, and even honesty and self-denial were but splendid sins, if they did not wear the Christian name. One would rather be

> "A pagan, suckled in a creed outworn,"

than to be defrauded of his manly right in coming into nature and finding not names and places, not land and professions, but even virtue and truth foreclosed and monopolized. You shall not be a man even. You shall not own the world; you shall not dare and live after the infinite Law that is in you, and in company with the infinite Beauty which heaven and earth reflect to you in all lovely forms; but you must subordinate your nature to Christ's nature; you must accept our interpretations, and take his portrait as the vulgar draw it.

That is always best which gives me to myself. The sublime is excited in me by the great stoical doctrine, Obey thyself. That which shows God in me, fortifies me. That which shows God out of me, makes me a wart and a wen. There is no longer a necessary reason for my being. Already the long shadows of untimely oblivion creep over me, and I shall decease forever.

The divine bards are the friends of my virtue, of my intellect, of my strength. They admonish me that the gleams which flash across my mind are not mine, but God's; that they had the like, and were not disobedient to the heavenly vision. So I love them. Noble provocations go out from them, inviting me to resist evil; to subdue the world; and to Be. And thus, by his holy thoughts, Jesus serves us, and thus only. To aim to convert a man by miracles is a profanation of the soul. A true conversion, a true Christ, is now, as always, to be made by the reception of beautiful sentiments. It is true that a great and rich soul, like his, falling among the simple, does so preponderate, that, as his did, it names the world. The world seems to them to exist for him, and they have not yet drunk so deeply of his sense as to see that only by coming again to themselves, or to God in themselves, can they grow forevermore. It is a low benefit to give me something; it is a high benefit to enable me to do somewhat of myself. The time is coming when all men will see that the gift of God to the soul is not a vaunting, overpowering, excluding sanctity, but a sweet, natural goodness, a goodness like thine and mine, and that so invites thine and mine to be and to grow.

The injustice of the vulgar tone of preaching is not less flagrant to Jesus than to the souls which it profanes. The preachers do not see that they make his gospel not glad, and shear him of the locks of beauty and the attributes of heaven. When I see a majestic Epaminondas, or Washington; when I see among my contemporaries a true orator, an upright judge, a dear friend; when I vibrate to the melody and fancy of a poem; I see beauty that is to be desired. And so lovely, and with yet more entire consent of my human being, sounds in my ear the severe music of the bards that have sung of the true God in all ages. Now do not degrade the life and dialogues of Christ out of the circle of this charm, by insulation and peculiarity. Let them lie as they befell, alive and warm, part of human life and of the landscape and of the cheerful day.

2. The second defect of the traditionary and limited way of using the mind of Christ is a consequence of the

first; this, namely; that the Moral Nature, that Law of laws whose revelations introduce greatness—yea, God himself—into the open soul, is not explored as the fountain of the established teaching in society. Men have come to speak of the revelation as somewhat long ago given and done, as if God were dead. The injury to faith throttles the preacher; and the goodliest of institutions becomes an uncertain and inarticulate voice.

It is very certain that it is the effect of conversation with the beauty of the soul, to beget a desire and need to impart to others the same knowledge and love. If utterance is denied, the thought lies like a burden on the man. Always the seer is a sayer. Somehow his dream is told; somehow he publishes it with solemn joy: sometimes with pencil on canvas, sometimes with chisel on stone, sometimes in towers and aisles of granite, his soul's worship is builded; sometimes in anthems of indefinite music; but clearest and most permanent, in words.

The man enamored of this excellency becomes its priest or poet. The office is coeval with the world. But observe the condition, the spiritual limitation of the office. The spirit only can teach. Not any profane man, not any sensual, not any liar, not any slave can teach, but only he can give, who has; he only can create, who is. The man on whom the soul descends, through whom the soul speaks, alone can teach. Courage, piety, love, wisdom, can teach; and every man can open his door to these angels, and they shall bring him the gift of tongues. But the man who aims to speak as books enable, as synods use, as the fashion guides, and as interest commands, babbles. Let him hush.

To this holy office you propose to devote yourselves. I wish you may feel your call in throbs of desire and hope. The office is the first in the world. It is of that reality that it cannot suffer the deduction of any falsehood. And it is my duty to say to you that the need was never greater of new revelation than now. From the views I have already expressed, you will infer the sad conviction, which I share,

I believe, with numbers, of the universal decay and now
almost death of faith in society. The soul is not preached.
The Church seems to totter to its fall, almost all life extinct. On this occasion, any complaisance would be criminal which told you, whose hope and commission it is
to preach the faith of Christ, that the faith of Christ is
preached.

It is time that this ill-suppressed murmur of all
thoughtful men against the famine of our churches;—this
moaning of the heart because it is bereaved of the consolation, the hope, the grandeur that come alone out of the
culture of the moral nature,—should be heard through the
sleep of indolence, and over the din of routine. This great
and perpetual office of the preacher is not discharged.
Preaching is the expression of the moral sentiment in application to the duties of life. In how many churches, by
how many prophets, tell me, is man made sensible that he
is an infinite Soul; that the earth and heavens are passing
into his mind; that he is drinking forever the soul of God?
Where now sounds the persuasion, that by its very melody imparadises my heart, and so affirms its own origin in
heaven? Where shall I hear words such as in elder ages
drew men to leave all and follow,—father and mother,
house and land, wife and child? Where shall I hear these
august laws of moral being so pronounced as to fill my ear,
and I feel ennobled by the offer of my uttermost action
and passion? The test of the true faith, certainly, should
be its power to charm and command the soul, as the laws
of nature control the activity of the hands,—so commanding that we find pleasure and honor in obeying. The faith
should blend with the light of rising and of setting suns,
with the flying cloud, the singing bird, and the breath of
flowers. But now the priest's Sabbath has lost the splendor
of nature; it is unlovely; we are glad when it is done; we
can make, we do make, even sitting in our pews, a far better, holier, sweeter, for ourselves.

Whenever the pulpit is usurped by a formalist, then is
the worshipper defrauded and disconsolate. We shrink as

soon as the prayers begin, which do not uplift, but smite and offend us. We are fain to wrap our cloaks about us, and secure, as best we can, a solitude that hears not. I once heard a preacher who sorely tempted me to say I would go to church no more. Men go, thought I, where they are wont to go, else had no soul entered the temple in the afternoon. A snow-storm was falling around us. The snow-storm was real, the preacher merely spectral, and the eye felt the sad contrast in looking at him, and then out of the window behind him into the beautiful meteor of the snow. He had lived in vain. He had no one word intimating that he had laughed or wept, was married or in love, had been commended, or cheated, or chagrined. If he had ever lived and acted, we were none the wiser for it. The capital secret of his profession, namely, to convert life into truth, he had not learned. Not one fact in all his experience had he yet imported into his doctrine. This man had ploughed and planted and talked and bought and sold; he had read books; he had eaten and drunken; his head aches, his heart throbs; he smiles and suffers; yet was there not a surmise, a hint, in all the discourse, that he had ever lived at all. Not a line did he draw out of real history. The true preacher can be known by this, that he deals out to the people his life,—life passed through the fire of thought. But of the bad preacher, it could not be told from his sermon what age of the world he fell in; whether he had a father or a child; whether he was a freeholder or a pauper; whether he was a citizen or a countryman; or any other fact of his biography. It seemed strange that the people should come to church. It seemed as if their houses were very unentertaining, that they should prefer this thought-less clamor. It shows that there is a commanding attraction in the moral sentiment, that can lend a faint tint of light to dulness and ignorance coming in its name and place. The good hearer is sure he has been touched sometimes; is sure there is somewhat to be reached, and some word that can reach it. When he listens to these vain words, he comforts himself by their relation to his remembrance of better hours, and so they clatter and echo unchallenged.

I am not ignorant that when we preach unworthily, it is not always quite in vain. There is a good ear, in some men, that draws supplies to virtue out of very indifferent nutriment. There is poetic truth concealed in all the commonplaces of prayer and of sermons, and though foolishly spoken, they may be wisely heard; for each is some select expression that broke out in a moment of piety from some stricken or jubilant soul, and its excellency made it remembered. The prayers and even the dogmas of our church are like the zodiac of Denderah and the astronomical monuments of the Hindoos, wholly insulated from anything now extant in the life and business of the people. They mark the height to which the waters once rose. But this docility is a check upon the mischief from the good and devout. In a large portion of the community, the religious service gives rise to quite other thoughts and emotions. We need not chide the negligent servant. We are struck with pity, rather, at the swift retribution of his sloth. Alas for the unhappy man that is called to stand in the pulpit, and *not* give bread of life. Everything that befalls, accuses him. Would he ask contributions for the missions, foreign or domestic? Instantly his face is suffused with shame, to propose to his parish that they should send money a hundred or a thousand miles, to furnish such poor fare as they have at home and would do well to go the hundred or the thousand miles to escape. Would he urge people to a godly way of living;—and can he ask a fellow-creature to come to Sabbath meetings, when he and they all know what is the poor uttermost they can hope for therein? Will he invite them privately to the Lord's Supper? He dares not. If no heart warm this rite, the hollow, dry, creaking formality is too plain, than that he can face a man of wit and energy and put the invitation without terror. In the street, what has he to say to the bold village blasphemer? The village blasphemer sees fear in the face, form, and gait of the minister.

Let me not taint the sincerity of this plea by any over-sight of the claims of good men. I know and honor the pu-rity and strict conscience of numbers of the clergy. What life the public worship retains, it owes to the scattered company of pious men, who minister here and there in the churches, and who, sometimes accepting with too great tenderness the tenet of the elders, have not accepted from others, but from their own heart, the genuine impulses of virtue, and so still command our love and awe, to the sanctity of character. Moreover, the exceptions are not so much to be found in a few eminent preachers, as in the better hours, the truer inspirations of all,—nay, in the sin-cere moments of every man. But, with whatever excep-tion, it is still true that tradition characterizes the preaching of this country; that it comes out of the mem-ory, and not out of the soul; that it aims at what is usual, and not at what is necessary and eternal; that thus histori-cal Christianity destroys the power of preaching, by withdrawing it from the exploration of the moral nature of man; where the sublime is, where are the resources of as-tonishment and power. What a cruel injustice it is to that Law, the joy of the whole earth, which alone can make thought dear and rich; that Law whose fatal sureness the astronomical orbits poorly emulate;—that it is travestied and depreciated, that it is behooted and behowled, and not a trait, not a word of it articulated. The pulpit in losing sight of this Law, loses its reason, and gropes after it knows not what. And for want of this culture the soul of the community is sick and faithless. It wants nothing so much as a stern, high, stoical, Christian discipline, to make it know itself and the divinity that speaks through it. Now man is ashamed of himself; he skulks and sneaks through the world, to be tolerated, to be pitied, and scarcely in a thousand years does any man dare to be wise and good, and so draw after him the tears and blessings of his kind.

Certainly there have been periods when, from the inac-tivity of the intellect on certain truths, a greater faith was possible in names and persons. The Puritans in England

and America found in the Christ of the Catholic Church and in the dogmas inherited from Rome, scope for their austere piety and their longings for civil freedom. But their creed is passing away, and none arises in its room. I think no man can go with his thoughts about him into one of our churches, without feeling that what hold the public worship had on men is gone, or going. It has lost its grasp on the affection of the good and the fear of the bad. In the country, neighborhoods, half parishes are *signing off*, to use the local term. It is already beginning to indicate character and religion to withdraw from the religious meetings. I have heard a devout person, who prized the Sabbath, say in bitterness of heart, "On Sundays, it seems wicked to go to church." And the motive that holds the best there is now only a hope and a waiting. What was once a mere circumstance, that the best and the worst men in the parish, the poor and the rich, the learned and the ignorant, young and old, should meet one day as fellows in one house, in sign of an equal right in the soul, has come to be a paramount motive for going thither.

My friends, in these two errors, I think, I find the causes of a decaying church and a wasting unbelief. And what greater calamity can fall upon a nation than the loss of worship? Then all things go to decay. Genius leaves the temple to haunt the senate or the market. Literature becomes frivolous. Science is cold. The eye of youth is not lighted by the hope of other worlds, and age is without honor. Society lives to trifles, and when men die we do not mention them.

And now, my brothers, you will ask, What in these desponding days can be done by us? The remedy is already declared in the ground of our complaint of the Church. We have contrasted the Church with the Soul. In the soul then let the redemption be sought. Wherever a man comes, there comes revolution. The old is for slaves. When a man comes, all books are legible, all things transparent, all religions are forms. He is religious. Man is the wonder-worker. He is seen amid miracles. All men bless and curse. He saith yea and nay, only. The stationariness of religion; the assumption that the age of inspiration is past, that the Bible is closed; the fear of degrading the character of Jesus by representing him as a man;—indicate with sufficient clearness the falsehood of our theology. It is the office of a true teacher to show us that God is, not was; that He speaketh, not spake. The true Christianity,—a faith like Christ's in the infinitude of man,—is lost. None believeth in the soul of man, but only in some man or person old and departed. Ah me! no man goeth alone. All men go in flocks to this saint or that poet, avoiding the God who seeth in secret. They cannot see in secret; they love to be blind in public. They think society wiser than their soul, and know not that one soul, and their soul, is wiser than the whole world. See how nations and races flit by on the sea of time and leave no ripple to tell where they floated or sunk, and one good soul shall make the name of Moses, or of Zeno, or of Zoroaster, reverend forever. None assayeth the stern ambition to be the Self of the nation and of nature, but each would be an easy secondary to some Christian scheme, or sectarian connection, or some eminent man. Once leave your own knowledge of God, your own sentiment, and take secondary knowledge, as St. Paul's, or George Fox's, or Swedenborg's, and you get wide from God with every year this secondary form lasts, and if, as now, for centuries,—the chasm yawns to that breadth, that men can scarcely be convinced there is in them anything divine.

Let me admonish you, first of all, to go alone; to refuse the good models, even those which are sacred in the imagination of men, and dare to love God without mediator or veil. Friends enough you shall find who will hold up to your emulation Wesleys and Oberlins, Saints and Prophets. Thank God for these good men, but say, 'I also am a man.' Imitation cannot go above its model. The imitator dooms himself to hopeless mediocrity. The inventor did it because it was natural to him, and so in him it has a charm. In the imitator something else is natural, and he bereaves himself of his own beauty, to come short of another man's.

Yourself a newborn bard of the Holy Ghost, cast behind you all conformity, and acquaint men at first hand with Deity. Look to it first and only, that fashion, custom, authority, pleasure, and money, are nothing to you,—are not bandages over your eyes, that you cannot see,—but live with the privilege of the immeasurable mind. Not too anxious to visit periodically all families and each family in your parish connection,—when you meet one of these men or women, be to them a divine man; be to them thought and virtue; let their timid aspirations find in you a friend; let their trampled instincts be genially tempted out in your atmosphere; let their doubts know that you have doubted, and their wonder feel that you have wondered. By trusting your own heart, you shall gain more confidence in other men. For all our penny-wisdom, for all our soul-destroying slavery to habit, it is not to be doubted that all men have sublime thoughts; that all men value the few real hours of life; they love to be heard; they love to be caught up into the vision of principles. We mark with light in the memory the few interviews we have had, in the dreary years of routine and of sin, with souls that made our souls wiser; that spoke what we thought; that told us what we knew; that gave us leave to be what we inly were. Discharge to men the priestly office, and, present or absent, you shall be followed with their love as by an angel.

And, to this end, let us not aim at common degrees of merit. Can we not leave, to such as love it, the virtue that glitters for the commendation of society, and ourselves pierce the deep solitudes of absolute ability and worth? We easily come up to the standard of goodness in society. Society's praise can be cheaply secured, and almost all men are content with those easy merits; but the instant effect of conversing with God will be to put them away. There are persons who are not actors, not speakers, but influences; persons too great for fame, for display; who disdain eloquence; to whom all we call art and artist, seems too nearly allied to show and by-ends, to the exaggeration of the finite and selfish, and loss of the universal. The orators, the poets, the commanders encroach on us only as fair women do, by our allowance and homage. Slight them by preoccupation of mind, slight them, as you can well afford to do, by high and universal aims, and they instantly feel that you have right, and that it is in lower places that they must shine. They also feel your right; for they with you are open to the influx of the all-knowing Spirit, which annihilates before its broad noon the little shades and gradations of intelligence in the compositions we call wiser and wisest.

In such high communion let us study the grand strokes of rectitude: a bold benevolence, an independence of friends, so that not the unjust wishes of those who love us shall impair our freedom, but we shall resist for truth's sake the freest flow of kindness, and appeal to sympathies far in advance; and,—what is the highest form in which we know this beautiful element,—a certain solidity of merit, that has nothing to do with opinion, and which is so essentially and manifestly virtue, that it is taken for granted that the right, the brave, the generous step will be taken by it, and nobody thinks of commending it. You would compliment a coxcomb doing a good act, but you would not praise an angel. The silence that accepts merit as the most natural thing in the world, is the highest applause. Such souls, when they appear, are the Imperial Guard of Virtue, the perpetual reserve, the dictators of fortune. One needs not praise their courage,—they are the heart and soul of nature. O my friends, there are resources in us on which we have not drawn. There are men who rise refreshed on hearing a threat; men to whom a crisis which intimidates and paralyzes the majority,—demanding not the faculties of prudence and thrift, but comprehension, immovableness, the readiness of sacrifice,—comes graceful and beloved as a bride. Napoleon said of Massena, that he was not himself until the battle began to go against him; then, when the dead began to fall in ranks

around him, awoke his powers of combination, and he put
on terror and victory as a robe. So it is in rugged crises, in
unweariable endurance, and in aims which put sympathy
out of question, that the angel is shown. But these are
heights that we can scarce remember and look up to without contrition and shame. Let us thank God that such
things exist.

And now let us do what we can to rekindle the smoul-
dering, nigh quenched fire on the altar. The evils of the
church that now is are manifest. The question returns,
What shall we do? I confess, all attempts to project and
establish a Cultus with new rites and forms, seem to me
vain. Faith makes us, and not we it, and faith makes its
own forms. All attempts to contrive a system are as cold as
the new worship introduced by the French to the goddess
of Reason,—to-day, pasteboard and filigree, and ending
to-morrow in madness and murder. Rather let the breath
of new life be breathed by you through the forms already
existing. For if once you are alive, you shall find they shall
become plastic and new. The remedy to their deformity is
first, soul, and second, soul, and evermore, soul. A whole
popedom of forms one pulsation of virtue can uplift and
vivify. Two inestimable advantages Christianity has given
us; first the Sabbath, the jubilee of the whole world,
whose light dawns welcome alike into the closet of the
philosopher, into the garret of toil, and into prison-cells,
and everywhere suggests, even to the vile, the dignity of
spiritual being. Let it stand forevermore, a temple, which
new love, new faith, new sight shall restore to more than
its first splendor to mankind. And secondly, the institution of preaching,—the speech of man to men,—essentially the most flexible of all organs, of all forms. What
hinders that now, everywhere, in pulpits, in lecture-
rooms, in houses, in fields, wherever the invitation of men
or your own occasions lead you, you speak the very truth,
as your life and conscience teach it, and cheer the waiting,
fainting hearts of men with new hope and new revelation?

I look for the hour when that supreme Beauty which

ravished the souls of those Eastern men, and chiefly of those Hebrews, and through their lips spoke oracles to all time, shall speak in the West also. The Hebrew and Greek Scriptures contain immortal sentences, that have been bread of life to millions. But they have no epical integrity; are fragmentary; are not shown in their order to the intellect. I look for the new Teacher that shall follow so far those shining laws that he shall see them come full circle; shall see their rounding complete grace; shall see the world to be the mirror of the soul; shall see the identity of the law of gravitation with purity of heart; and shall show that the Ought, that Duty, is one thing with Science, with Beauty, and with Joy.

THE TRANSCENDENTALIST

The first thing we have to say respecting what are called *new views* here in New England, at the present time, is, that they are not new, but the very oldest of thoughts cast into the mould of these new times. The light is always identical in its composition, but it falls on a great variety of objects, and by so falling is first revealed to us, not in its own form, for it is formless, but in theirs; in like manner, thought only appears in the objects it classifies. What is popularly called Transcendentalism among us, is Idealism; Idealism as it appears in 1842. As thinkers, mankind have ever divided into two sects, Materialists and Idealists; the first class founding on experience, the second on consciousness; the first class beginning to think from the data of the senses, the second class perceive that the senses are not final, and say, The senses give us representations of things, but what are the things themselves, they cannot tell. The materialist insists on facts, on history, on the force of circumstances and the animal wants of man; the idealist on the power of Thought and of Will, on inspiration, on miracle, on individual culture. These two modes of thinking are both natural, but the idealist contends that his way of thinking is in higher nature. He concedes all that the other affirms, admits the impressions of sense, admits their coherency, their use and beauty, and then asks the materialist for his grounds of assurance that things are as his senses represent them. But I, he says, affirm facts not affected by the illusions of sense, facts which are of the same nature as the faculty which reports them, and not liable to doubt; facts which in their first appearance to us assume a native superiority to material facts, degrading these into a language by which the first are to be spoken; facts which it only needs a retirement from the senses to discern. Every materialist will be an idealist; but an idealist can never go backward to be a materialist.

The idealist, in speaking of events, sees them as spirits. He does not deny the sensuous fact: by no means; but he will not see that alone. He does not deny the presence of this table, this chair, and the walls of this room, but he looks at these things as the reverse side of the tapestry, as the *other end*, each being a sequel or completion of a spiritual fact which nearly concerns him. This manner of looking at things transfers every object in nature from an independent and anomalous position without there, into the consciousness. Even the materialist Condillac, perhaps the most logical expounder of materialism, was constrained to say, "Though we should soar into the heavens, though we should sink into the abyss, we never go out of ourselves; it is always our own thought that we preceive." What more could an idealist say?

The materialist, secure in the certainty of sensation, mocks at fine-spun theories, at star-gazers and dreamers, and believes that his life is solid, that he at least takes nothing for granted, but knows where he stands, and what he does. Yet how easy it is to show him that he also is a phantom walking and working amid phantoms, and that he need only ask a question or two beyond his daily questions to find his solid universe growing dim and impalpable before his sense. The sturdy capitalist, no matter how deep and square on blocks of Quincy granite he lays the foundations of his banking-house or Exchange, must set it, at last, not on a cube corresponding to the angles of his structure, but on a mass of unknown materials and solidity, red-hot or white-hot perhaps at the core, which rounds off to an almost perfect sphericity, and lies floating in soft air, and goes spinning away, dragging bank and banker with it at a rate of thousands of miles the hour, he knows not whither,—a bit of bullet, now glimmering, now darkling through a small cubic space on the edge of an unimaginable pit of emptiness. And this wild balloon, in which his whole venture is embarked, is a just symbol of his whole state and faculty. One thing at least, he says, is certain, and does not give me the headache, that figures do not lie; the multiplication table has been hitherto found unimpeachable truth; and, moreover, if I put a gold eagle in my safe, I find it again to-morrow;—but for these thoughts, I know not whence they are. They change and pass away. But ask him why he believes that an uniform experience will continue uniform, or on what grounds he founds his faith in his figures, and he will perceive that his mental fabric is built up on just as strange and quaking foundations as his proud edifice of stone.

In the order of thought, the materialist takes his departure from the external world, and esteems a man as one product of that. The idealist takes his departure from his consciousness, and reckons the world an appearance. The materialist respects sensible masses, Society, Government, social art and luxury, every establishment, every mass, whether majority of numbers, or extent of space, or amount of objects, every social action. The idealist has another measure, which is metaphysical, namely the *rank* which things themselves take in his consciousness; not at all the size or appearance. Mind is the only reality, of which men and all other natures are better or worse reflectors. Nature, literature, history, are only subjective phenomena. Although in his action overpowered by the laws of action, and so, warmly cooperating with men, even preferring them to himself, yet when he speaks scientifically, or after the order of thought, he is constrained to degrade persons into representatives of truths. He does not respect labor, or the products of labor, namely property, otherwise than as a manifold symbol, illustrating with wonderful fidelity of details the laws of being; he does not respect government, except as far as it reiterates the law of his mind; nor the church, nor charities, nor arts, for themselves; but hears, as at a vast distance, what they say, as if his consciousness would speak to him through a pantomimic scene. His thought,—that is the Universe. His experience inclines him to behold the procession of facts you call the world, as flowing perpetually outward from an invisible, unsounded centre in himself, centre alike of him and of them, and necessitating him to regard all things as having a subjective or relative existence, relative to that aforesaid Unknown Centre of him.

From this transfer of the world into the consciousness, this beholding of all things in the mind, follow easily his whole ethics. It is simpler to be self-dependent. The height, the deity of man is to be self-sustained, to need no gift, no foreign force. Society is good when it does not violate me, but best when it is likest to solitude. Everything real is self-existent. Everything divine shares the self-existence of Deity. All that you call the world is the shadow of that substance which you are, the perpetual creation of the powers of thought, of those that are dependent and of those that are independent of your will. Do not cumber yourself with fruitless pains to mend and remedy remote effects; let the soul be erect, and all things will go well. You think me the child of my circumstances: I make my circumstance. Let any thought or motive of mine be different from that they are, the difference will transform my condition and economy. I—this thought which is called I—is the mould into which the world is poured like melted wax. The mould is invisible, but the world betrays the shape of the mould. You call it the power of circumstance, but it is the power of me. Am I in harmony with myself? my position will seem to you just and commanding. Am I vicious and insane? my fortunes will seem to you obscure and descending. As I am, so shall I associate, and so shall I act; Cæsar's history will paint out Cæsar. Jesus acted so, because he thought so. I do not wish to overlook or to gainsay any reality; I say I make my circumstance; but if you ask me, Whence am I? I feel like other men my relation to that Fact which cannot be spoken, or defined, nor even thought, but which exists, and will exist.

The Transcendentalist adopts the whole connection of spiritual doctrine. He believes in miracle, in the perpetual openness of the human mind to new influx of light and power; he believes in inspiration, and in ecstasy. He wishes that the spiritual principle should be suffered to demonstrate itself to the end, in all possible applications to the state of man, without the admission of anything unspiritual; that is, anything positive, dogmatic, personal. Thus the spiritual measure of inspiration is the depth of the thought, and never, who said it? And so he resists all attempts to palm other rules and measures on the spirit than its own.

In action he easily incurs the charge of anti-nomianism by his avowal that he, who has the Law-giver, may with safety not only neglect, but even contravene every written commandment. In the play of Othello, the expiring Desdemona absolves her husband of the murder, to her attendant Emilia. Afterwards, when Emilia charges him with the crime, Othello exclaims,

"You heard her say herself it was not I."

Emilia replies,

"The more angel she, and thou the blacker devil."

Of this fine incident, Jacobi, the Transcendental moralist, makes use, with other parallel instances, in his reply to Fichte. Jacobi, refusing all measure of right and wrong except the determinations of the private spirit, remarks that there is no crime but has sometimes been a virtue. "I," he says, "am that atheist, that godless person who, in opposition to an imaginary doctrine of calculation, would lie as the dying Desdemona lied; would lie and deceive, as Pylades when he personated Orestes; would assassinate like Timoleon; would perjure myself like Epaminondas and

John de Witt; I would resolve on suicide like Cato; I would commit sacrilege with David; yea, and pluck ears of corn on the Sabbath, for no other reason than that I was fainting for lack of food. For I have assurance in myself that in pardoning these faults according to the letter, man exerts the sovereign right which the majesty of his being confers on him; he sets the seal of his divine nature to the grace he accords."

In like manner, if there is anything grand and daring in human thought or virtue, any reliance on the vast, the unknown; any presentiment, any extravagance of faith, the spiritualist adopts it as most in nature. The oriental mind has always tended to this largeness. Buddhism is an expression of it. The Buddhist, who thanks no man, who says, "Do not flatter your benefactors," but who, in his conviction that every good deed can by no possibility escape its reward, will not deceive the benefactor by pretending that he has done more than he should, is a Transcendentalist.

You will see by this sketch that there is no such thing as a Transcendental *party;* that there is no pure Transcendentalist; that we know of none but prophets and heralds of such a philosophy; that all who by strong bias of nature have leaned to the spiritual side in doctrine, have stopped short of their goal. We have had many harbingers and forerunners; but of a purely spiritual life, history has afforded no example. I mean we have yet no man who has leaned entirely on his character, and eaten angels' food; who, trusting to his sentiments, found life made of miracles; who, working for universal aims, found himself fed, he knew not how; clothed, sheltered, and weaponed, he knew not how, and yet it was done by his own hands. Only in the instinct of the lower animals we find the suggestion of the methods of it, and something higher than our understanding. The squirrel hoards nuts and the bee gathers honey, without knowing what they do, and they are thus provided for without selfishness or disgrace.

Shall we say then that Transcendentalism is the Satur-

nalia or excess of Faith; the presentiment of a faith proper
to man in his integrity, excessive only when his imperfect
obedience hinders the satisfaction of his wish? Nature is
transcendental, exists primarily, necessarily, ever works
and advances, yet takes no thought for the morrow. Man
owns the dignity of the life which throbs around him, in
chemistry, and tree, and animal, and in the involuntary
functions of his own body; yet he is balked when he tries
to fling himself into this enchanted circle, where all is
done without degradation. Yet genius and virtue predict
in man the same absence of private ends and of conde-
scension to circumstances, united with every trait and talent of beauty and power.

This way of thinking, falling on Roman times, made
Stoic philosophers; falling on despotic times, made patriot
Catos and Brutuses; falling on superstitious times, made
prophets and apostles; on popish times, made protestants
and ascetic monks, preachers of Faith against the preachers of Works; on prelatical times, made Puritans and
Quakers; and falling on Unitarian and commercial times,
makes the peculiar shades of Idealism which we know.

It is well known to most of my audience that the Idealism of the present day acquired the name of Transcendental from the use of that term by Immanuel Kant, of
Königsberg, who replied to the skeptical philosophy of
Locke, which insisted that there was nothing in the intellect which was not previously in the experience of the
senses, by showing that there was a very important class
of ideas or imperative forms, which did not come by experience, but through which experience was acquired; that
these were intuitions of the mind itself; and he denomi-
nated them *Transcendental* forms. The extraordinary
profoundness and precision of that man's thinking have
given vogue to his nomenclature, in Europe and America,
to that extent that whatever belongs to the class of intuitive thought is popularly called at the present day *Transcendental.*

Although, as we have said, there is no pure Transcendentalist, yet the tendency to respect the intuitions and to give them, at least in our creed, all authority over our experience, has deeply colored the conversation and poetry of the present day; and the history of genius and of religion in these times, though impure, and as yet not incarnated in any powerful individual, will be the history of this tendency.

It is a sign of our times, conspicuous to the coarsest observer, that many intelligent and religious persons withdraw themselves from the common labors and competitions of the market and the caucus, and betake themselves to a certain solitary and critical way of living, from which no solid fruit has yet appeared to justify their separation. They hold themselves aloof: they feel the disproportion between their faculties and the work offered them, and they prefer to ramble in the country and perish of ennui, to the degradation of such charities and such ambitions as the city can propose to them. They are striking work, and crying out for somewhat worthy to do! What they do is done only because they are overpowered by the humanities that speak on all sides; and they consent to such labor as is open to them, though to their lofty dream the writing of Iliads or Hamlets, or the building of cities or empires seems drudgery.

Now every one must do after his kind, be he asp or angel, and these must. The question which a wise man and a student of modern history will ask, is, what that kind is? And truly, as in ecclesiastical history we take so much pains to know what the Gnostics, what the Essenes, what the Manichees, and what the Reformers believed, it would not misbecome us to inquire nearer home, what these companions and contemporaries of ours think and do, at least so far as these thoughts and actions appear to be not accidental and personal, but common to many, and the inevitable flower of the Tree of Time. Our American literature and spiritual history are, we confess, in the optative mood; but whoso knows these seething brains, these admirable radicals, these unsocial worshippers, these talkers who talk the sun and moon away, will believe that this heresy cannot pass away without leaving its mark.

They are lonely; the spirit of their writing and conversation is lonely; they repel influences; they shun general society; they incline to shut themselves in their chamber in the house, to live in the country rather than in the town, and to find their tasks and amusements in solitude. Society, to be sure, does not like this very well; it saith, Whoso goes to walk alone, accuses the whole world; he declares all to be unfit to be his companions; it is very uncivil, nay, insulting; Society will retaliate. Meantime, this retirement does not proceed from any whim on the part of these separators; but if any one will take pains to talk with them, he will find that this part is chosen both from temperament and from principle; with some unwillingness too, and as a choice of the less of two evils; for these persons are not by nature melancholy, sour, and unsocial,— they are not stockish or brute,—but joyous, susceptible, affectionate; they have even more than others a great wish to be loved. Like the young Mozart, they are rather ready to cry ten times a day, "But are you sure you love me?" Nay, if they tell you their whole thought, they will own that love seems to them the last and highest gift of nature; that there are persons whom in their hearts they daily thank for existing,—persons whose faces are perhaps unknown to them, but whose fame and spirit have penetrated their solitude,—and for whose sake they wish to exist. To behold the beauty of another character, which inspires a new interest in our own; to behold the beauty lodged in a human being, with such vivacity of apprehension that I am instantly forced home to inquire if I am not deformity itself; to behold in another the expression of a love so high that it assures itself,—assures itself also to me against every possible casualty except my unworthiness;—these are degrees on the scale of human happiness to which they have ascended; and it is a fidelity to this sentiment which has made common association distasteful to them. They wish a just and even fellowship, or none.

They cannot gossip with you, and they do not wish, as they are sincere and religious, to gratify any mere curiosity which you may entertain. Like fairies, they do not wish to be spoken of. Love me, they say, but do not ask who is my cousin and my uncle. If you do not need to hear my thought, because you can read it in my face and behavior, then I will tell it you from sunrise to sunset. If you cannot divine it, you would not understand what I say. I will not molest myself for you. I do not wish to be profaned.

And yet, it seems as if this loneliness, and not this love, would prevail in their circumstances, because of the extravagant demand they make on human nature. That, indeed, constitutes a new feature in their portrait, that they are the most exacting and extortionate critics. Their quarrel with every man they meet is not with his kind, but with his degree. There is not enough of him,—that is the only fault. They prolong their privilege of childhood in this wise; of doing nothing, but making immense demands on all the gladiators in the lists of action and fame. They make us feel the strange disappointment which overcasts every human youth. So many promising youths, and never a finished man! The profound nature will have a savage rudeness; the delicate one will be shallow, or the victim of sensibility; the richly accomplished will have some capital absurdity; and so every piece has a crack. 'T is strange, but this masterpiece is the result of such an extreme delicacy that the most unobserved flaw in the boy will neutralize the most aspiring genius, and spoil the work. Talk with a seaman of the hazards to life in his profession and he will ask you, 'Where are the old sailors? Do you not see that all are young men?' And we, on this sea of human thought, in like manner inquire, Where are the old idealists? where are they who represented to the last generation that extravagant hope which a few happy aspirants suggest to ours? In looking at the class of counsel, and power, and wealth, and at the matronage of the land, amidst all the prudence and all the triviality, one asks,

Where are they who represented genius, virtue, the invisible and heavenly world, to these? Are they dead,—taken in early ripeness to the gods,—as ancient wisdom foretold their fate? Or did the high idea die out of them, and leave their unperfumed body as its tomb and tablet, announcing to all that the celestial inhabitant, who once gave them beauty, had departed? Will it be better with the new generation? We easily predict a fair future to each new candidate who enters the lists, but we are frivolous and volatile, and by low aims and ill example do what we can to defeat this hope. Then these youths bring us a rough but effectual aid. By their unconcealed dissatisfaction they expose our poverty and the insignificance of man to man. A man is a poor limitary benefactor. He ought to be a shower of benefits—a great influence, which should never let his brother go, but should refresh old merits continually with new ones; so that though absent he should never be out of my mind, his name never far from my lips; but if the earth should open at my side, or my last hour were come, his name should be the prayer I should utter to the Universe. But in our experience, man is cheap and friendship wants its deep sense. We affect to dwell with our friends in their absence, but we do not; when deed, word, or letter comes not, they let us go. These exacting children advertise us of our wants. There is no compliment, no smooth speech with them; they pay you only this one compliment, of insatiable expectation; they aspire, they severely exact, and if they only stand fast in this watch-tower, and persist in demanding unto the end, and without end, then are they terrible friends, whereof poet and priest cannot choose but stand in awe; and what if they eat clouds, and drink wind, they have not been without service to the race of man.

With this passion for what is great and extraordinary, it cannot be wondered at that they are repelled by vulgarity and frivolity in people. They say to themselves, It is better to be alone than in bad company. And it is really a wish to be met,—the wish to find society for their hope and religion,—which prompts them to shun what is called society. They feel that they are never so fit for friendship as when they have quitted mankind and taken themselves to friend. A picture, a book, a favorite spot in the hills or the woods which they can people with the fair and worthy creation of the fancy, can give them often forms so vivid that these for the time shall seem real, and society the illusion.

But their solitary and fastidious manners not only withdraw them from the conversation, but from the labors of the world; they are not good citizens, not good members of society; unwillingly they bear their part of the public and private burdens; they do not willingly share in the public charities, in the public religious rites, in the enterprises of education, of missions foreign and domestic, in the abolition of the slave-trade, or in the temperance society. They do not even like to vote. The philanthropists inquire whether Transcendentalism does not mean sloth: they had as lief hear that their friend is dead, as that he is a Transcendentalist; for then is he paralyzed, and can never do anything for humanity. What right, cries the good world, has the man of genius to retreat from work, and indulge himself? The popular literary creed seems to be, 'I am a sublime genius; I ought not therefore to labor.' But genius is the power to labor better and more availably. Deserve thy genius: exalt it. The good, the illuminated, sit apart from the rest, censuring their dulness and vices, as if they thought that by sitting very grand in their chairs, the very brokers, attorneys, and congressmen would see the error of their ways, and flock to them. But the good and wise must learn to act, and carry salvation to the combatants and demagogues in the dusty arena below.

On the part of these children it is replied that life and their faculty seem to them gifts too rich to be squandered on such trifles as you propose to them. What you call your fundamental institutions, your great and holy causes, seem to them great abuses, and, when nearly seen, paltry matters. Each 'cause' as it is called,—say Abolition, Temperance, say Calvinism, or Unitarianism,—becomes speedily a little shop, where the article, let it have been at first never so subtle and ethereal, is now made up into portable and convenient cakes, and retailed in small quantities to suit purchasers. You make very free use of these words 'great' and 'holy,' but few things appear to them such. Few persons have any magnificence of nature to inspire enthusiasm, and the philanthropies and charities have a certain air of quackery. As to the general course of living, and the daily employments of men, they cannot see much virtue in these, since they are parts of this vicious circle; and as no great ends are answered by the men, there is nothing noble in the arts by which they are maintained. Nay, they have made the experiment and found that from the liberal professions to the coarsest manual labor, and from the courtesies of the academy and the college to the conventions of the cotillon-room and the morning call, there is a spirit of cowardly compromise and seeming which intimates a frightful skepticism, a life without love, and an activity without an aim.

Unless the action is necessary, unless it is adequate, I do not wish to perform it. I do not wish to do one thing but once. I do not love routine. Once possessed of the principle, it is equally easy to make four or forty thousand applications of it. A great man will be content to have indicated in any the slightest manner his perception of the reigning Idea of his time, and will leave to those who like it the multiplication of examples. When he has hit the white, the rest may shatter the target. Every thing admonishes us how needlessly long life is. Every moment of a hero so raises and cheers us that a twelvemonth is an age. All that the brave Xanthus brings home from his wars is the recollection that at the storming of Samos, "in the heat of the battle, Pericles smiled on me, and passed on to another detachment." It is the quality of the moment, not the number of days, of events, or of actors, that imports.

New, we confess, and by no means happy, is our condition: if you want the aid of our labor, we ourselves stand in greater want of the labor. We are miserable with inaction. We perish of rest and rust: but we do not like your work.

'Then,' says the world, 'show me your own.'

'We have none.'

'What will you do, then?' cries the world.

'We will wait.'

'How long?'

'Until the Universe beckons and calls us to work.'

'But whilst you wait, you grow old and useless.'

'Be it so: I can sit in a corner and *perish* (as you call it), but I will not move until I have the highest command. If no call should come for years, for centuries, then I know that the want of the Universe is the attestation of faith by my abstinence. Your virtuous projects, so called, do not cheer me. I know that which shall come will cheer me. If I cannot work, at least I need not lie. All that is clearly due to-day is not to lie. In other places other men have encountered sharp trials, and have behaved themselves well. The martyrs were sawn asunder, or hung alive on meat-hooks. Cannot we screw our courage to patience and truth, and without complaint, or even with good-humor, await our turn of action in the Infinite Counsels?'

But to come a little closer to the secret of these persons, we must say that to them it seems a very easy matter to answer the objections of the man of the world, but not so easy to dispose of the doubts and objections that occur to themselves. They are exercised in their own spirit with queries which acquaint them with all adversity, and with the trials of the bravest heroes. When I asked them concerning their private experience, they answered somewhat in this wise: It is not to be denied that there must be some wide difference between my faith and other faith; and mine is a certain brief experience, which surprised me in the highway or in the market, in some place, at some time,—whether in the body or out of the body, God knoweth,—and made me aware that I had played the fool with fools all this time, but that law existed for me and for all; that to me belonged trust, a child's trust and obedi-

ence, and the worship of ideas, and I should never be fool
more. Well, in the space of an hour probably, I was let
down from this height; I was at my old tricks, the selfish
member of a selfish society. My life is superficial, takes no
root in the deep world; I ask, When shall I die and be relieved of the responsibility of seeing an Universe which I
do not use? I wish to exchange this flash-of-lightning faith
for continuous daylight, this fever-glow for a benign climate.

These two states of thought diverge every moment, and
stand in wild contrast. To him who looks at his life from
these moments of illumination, it will seem that he skulks
and plays a mean, shiftless and subaltern part in the
world. That is to be done which he has not skill to do, or
to be said which others can say better, and he lies by, or
occupies his hands with some plaything, until his hour
comes again. Much of our reading, much of our labor,
seems mere waiting: it was not that we were born for. Any
other could do it as well or better. So little skill enters into
these works, so little do they mix with the divine life, that
it really signifies little what we do, whether we turn a
grindstone, or ride, or run, or make fortune, or govern the
state. The worst feature of this double consciousness is,
that the two lives, of the understanding and of the soul,
which we lead, really show very little relation to each
other; never meet and measure each other: one prevails
now, all buzz and din; and the other prevails then, all infinitude and paradise; and, with the progress of life, the
two discover no greater disposition to reconcile themselves. Yet, what is my faith? What am I? What but a
thought of serenity and independence, an abode in the
deep blue sky? Presently the clouds shut down again; yet
we retain the belief that this petty web we weave will at
last be overshot and reticulated with veins of the blue, and
that the moments will characterize the days. Patience,
then, is for us, is it not? Patience, and still patience. When
we pass, as presently we shall, into some new infinitude,
out of this Iceland of negations, it will please us to reflect

that though we had few virtues or consolations, we bore with our indigence, nor once strove to repair it with hypocrisy or false heat of any kind.

But this class are not sufficiently characterized if we omit to add that they are lovers and worshippers of Beauty. In the eternal trinity of Truth, Goodness, and Beauty, each in its perfection including the three, they prefer to make Beauty the sign and head. Something of the same taste is observable in all the moral movements of the time, in the religious and benevolent enterprises. They have a liberal, even an æsthetic spirit. A reference to Beauty in action sounds, to be sure, a little hollow and ridiculous in the ears of the old church. In politics, it has often sufficed, when they treated of justice, if they kept the bounds of selfish calculation. If they granted restitution, it was prudence which granted it. But the justice which is now claimed for the black, and the pauper, and the drunkard, is for Beauty,—is for a necessity to the soul of the agent, not of the beneficiary. I say this is the tendency, not yet the realization. Our virtue totters and trips, does not yet walk firmly. Its representatives are austere; they preach and denounce; their rectitude is not yet a grace. They are still liable to that slight taint of burlesque which in our strange world attaches to the zealot. A saint should be as dear as the apple of the eye. Yet we are tempted to smile, and we flee from the working to the speculative reformer, to escape that same slight ridicule. Alas for these days of derision and criticism! We call the Beautiful the highest, because it appears to us the golden mean, escaping the dowdiness of the good and the heartlessness of the true. They are lovers of nature also, and find an indemnity in the inviolable order of the world for the violated order and grace of man.

There is, no doubt, a great deal of well-founded objection to be spoken or felt against the sayings and doings of this class, some of whose traits we have selected; no doubt they will lay themselves open to criticism and to lampoons, and as ridiculous stories will be to be told of them as of any. There will be cant and pretension; there will be subtilty and moonshine. These persons are of unequal strength, and do not all prosper. They complain that everything around them must be denied; and if feeble, it takes all their strength to deny, before they can begin to lead their own life. Grave seniors insist on their respect to this institution and that usage; to an obsolete history; to some vocation, or college, or etiquette, or beneficiary, or charity, or morning or evening call, which they resist as what does not concern them. But it costs such sleepless nights, alienations and misgivings,—they have so many moods about it; these old guardians never change *their* minds; they have but one mood on the subject, namely, that Antony is very perverse,—that it is quite as much as Antony can do to assert his rights, abstain from what he thinks foolish, and keep his temper. He cannot help the re-action of this injustice in his own mind. He is braced-up and stilted; all freedom and flowing genius, all sallies of wit and frolic nature are quite out of the question; it is well if he can keep from lying, injustice, and suicide. This is no time for gaiety and grace. His strength and spirits are wasted in rejection. But the strong spirits overpower those around them without effort. Their thought and emotion comes in like a flood, quite withdraws them from all notice of these carping critics; they surrender themselves with glad heart to the heavenly guide, and only by implication reject the clamorous nonsense of the hour. Grave seniors talk to the deaf,—church and old book mumble and ritualize to an unheeding, preoccupied and advancing mind, and thus they by happiness of greater momentum lose no time, but take the right road at first.

But all these of whom I speak are not proficients; they are novices; they only show the road in which man should travel, when the soul has greater health and prowess. Yet let them feel the dignity of their charge, and deserve a larger power. Their heart is the ark in which the fire is concealed which shall burn in a broader and universal flame. Let them obey the Genius then most when his impulse is wildest; then most when he seems to lead to uninhabitable deserts of thought and life; for the path which the hero travels alone is the highway of health and benefit to mankind. What is the privilege and nobility of our nature but its persistency, through its power to attach itself to what is permanent?

Society also has its duties in reference to this class, and must behold them with what charity it can. Possibly some benefit may yet accrue from them to the state. In our Mechanics' Fair, there must be not only bridges, ploughs, carpenters' planes, and baking troughs, but also some few finer instruments,—rain-gauges, thermometers, and telescopes; and in society, besides farmers, sailors, and weavers, there must be a few persons of purer fire kept specially as gauges and meters of character; persons of a fine, detecting instinct, who note the smallest accumulations of wit and feeling in the bystander. Perhaps too there might be room for the exciters and monitors; collectors of the heavenly spark, with power to convey the electricity to others. Or, as the storm-tossed vessel at sea speaks the frigate or 'line packet' to learn its longitude, so it may not be without its advantage that we should now and then encounter rare and gifted men, to compare the points of our spiritual compass, and verify our bearings from superior chronometers.

Amidst the downward tendency and proneness of things, when every voice is raised for a new road or another statute or a subscription of stock; for an improvement in dress, or in dentistry; for a new house or a larger business; for a political party, or the division of an estate;—will you not tolerate one or two solitary voices in the land, speaking for thoughts and principles not marketable or perishable? Soon these improvements and mechanical inventions will be superseded; these modes of living lost out of memory; these cities rotted, ruined by war, by new inventions, by new seats of trade, or the geologic changes:—all gone, like the shells which sprinkle the sea-beach with a white colony to-day, forever renewed to be forever destroyed. But the thoughts which these few hermits strove to proclaim by silence as well as by speech, not only by what they did, but by what they forbore to do, shall abide in beauty and strength, to reorganize themselves in nature, to invest themselves anew in other, perhaps higher endowed and happier mixed clay than ours, in fuller union with the surrounding system.

Essays:
First and Second
Series

Editor's Note

Given a chance, Emerson's initial volume of essays can make a remarkable impression on us. Its ideas can still invigorate; its tone can inspire; its writing can glow. Yet while Emerson was preparing these essays in 1839 and 1840, he was suffering from the ambivalence which handicapped him during much of his career. He noted with dismay in the journal for October 7, 1840, "The poor work has looked poorer daily as I strove to end it." However, by the time he was correcting the proofs he was, if not optimistic, at least determined to do as well as possible. On the day he sent the manuscript to the publisher, January 1, 1841, he made a New Year's resolution to add the remaining touches to his text with "as much grandeur of spirit" as he could command.

When the book came out in March it enchanted Emerson's friends and admirers, but they constituted a minority. Most of the reviewers were cool, for Emerson had become a controversial figure and his Transcendentalism seemed to them either vain or subversive. Emerson himself predicted that he would "one day write something better." In spite of its mixed reception the book quickly made a place for itself. The so-called second edition came out in September 1847, but two other small printings had sold out before it.

Emerson had failed to finish one piece for his 1841 collection, an essay on Nature. He used it as the centerpiece for his second collection. Sufficiently encouraged by the interest the first had aroused in the United States and pleasantly surprised by its success in Great Britain, he

went ahead with the preparation of *Essays: Second Series.*
He worked at it during the winter of 1843–44. Though in-
spiriting, the collection proved to be more sober than the
prior one. For two years around the turn of the decade
things had gone well for him privately as well as professionally, despite his psychological ups and downs. But the
death of his little son in January 1842 from scarlet fever
shook his confidence in the cosmos. He claimed that he recovered it entirely, but we can wonder on reading the
essay which Emerson entitled "Experience." *Essays: Second Series* came out in October 1844, to be greeted by various voices but none of them, by this time, disrespectful.
Emerson was now a man to be taken seriously; he was
achieving national and international recognition. The first
edition ran to 2000 copies, and other editions followed.

                                                    C.B.

HISTORY

~~~~~~~~~~~~~~~~~~~~~~~~~~~~

There is no great and no small
To the Soul that maketh all:
And where it cometh, all things are;
And it cometh everywhere

I am the owner of the sphere,
Of the seven stars and the solar year,
Of Cæsar's hand, and Plato's brain,
Of Lord Christ's heart, and Shakspeare's strain.

There is one mind common to all individual men. Every man is an inlet to the same and to all of the same. He that is once admitted to the right of reason is made a freeman of the whole estate. What Plato has thought, he may think; what a saint has felt, he may feel; what at any time has befallen any man, he can understand. Who hath access to this universal mind is a party to all that is or can be done, for this is the only and sovereign agent.

Of the works of this mind history is the record. Its genius is illustrated by the entire series of days. Man is explicable by nothing less than all his history. Without hurry, without rest, the human spirit goes forth from the beginning to embody every faculty, every thought, every emotion which belongs to it, in appropriate events. But the thought is always prior to the fact; all the facts of history preëxist in the mind as laws. Each law in turn is made by circumstances predominant, and the limits of nature give power to but one at a time. A man is the whole encyclopædia of facts. The creation of a thousand forests is in

one acorn, and Egypt, Greece, Rome, Gaul, Britain,
America, lie folded already in the first man. Epoch after
epoch, camp, kingdom, empire, republic, democracy, are
merely the application of his manifold spirit to the manifold world.

This human mind wrote history, and this must read it.
The Sphinx must solve her own riddle. If the whole of
history is in one man, it is all to be explained from individual experience. There is a relation between the hours of
our life and the centuries of time. As the air I breathe is
drawn from the great repositories of nature, as the light on
my book is yielded by a star a hundred millions of miles
distant, as the poise of my body depends on the equilib-
rium of centrifugal and centripetal forces, so the hours
should be instructed by the ages and the ages explained by
the hours. Of the universal mind each individual man is
one more incarnation. All its properties consist in him.
Each new fact in his private experience flashes a light on
what great bodies of men have done, and the crises of his
life refer to national crises. Every revolution was first a
thought in one man's mind, and when the same thought
occurs to another man, it is the key to that era. Every reform was once a private opinion, and when it shall be a
private opinion again it will solve the problem of the age.
The fact narrated must correspond to something in me to
be credible or intelligible. We, as we read, must become
Greeks, Romans, Turks, priest and king, martyr and executioner; must fasten these images to some reality in our
secret experience, or we shall learn nothing rightly. What
befell Asdrubal or Cæsar Borgia is as much as illustration
of the mind's powers and depravations as what has befallen us. Each new law and political movement has a
meaning for you. Stand before each of its tablets and say,
'Under this mask did my Proteus nature hide itself.' This
remedies the defect of our too great nearness to ourselves.
This throws our actions into perspective,—and as crabs,
goats, scorpions, the balance and the waterpot lose their
meanness when hung as signs in the zodiac, so I can see

my own vices without heat in the distant persons of Solomon, Alcibiades, and Catiline.

It is the universal nature which gives worth to particular men and things. Human life, as containing this, is mysterious and inviolable, and we hedge it round with penalties and laws. All laws derive hence their ultimate reason; all express more or less distinctly some command of this supreme, illimitable essence. Property also holds of the soul, covers great spiritual facts, and instinctively we at first hold to it with swords and laws and wide and complex combinations. The obscure consciousness of this fact is the light of all our day, the claim of claims; the plea for education, for justice, for charity; the foundation of friendship and love and of the heroism and grandeur which belong to acts of self-reliance. It is remarkable that involuntarily we always read as superior beings. Universal history, the poets, the romancers, do not in their stateliest pictures,—in the sacerdotal, the imperial palaces, in the triumphs of will or of genius,—anywhere lose our ear, anywhere make us feel that we intrude, that this is for better men; but rather is it true that in their grandest strokes we feel most at home. All that Shakspeare says of the king, yonder slip of a boy that reads in the corner feels to be true of himself. We sympathize in the great moments of history, in the great discoveries, the great resistances, the great prosperities of men;—because there law was enacted, the sea was searched, the land was found, or the blow was struck, *for us,* as we ourselves in that place would have done or applauded.

We have the same interest in condition and character. We honor the rich because they have externally the freedom, power, and grace which we feel to be proper to man, proper to us. So all that is said of the wise man by Stoic or Oriental or modern essayist, describes to each reader his own idea, describes his unattained but attainable self. All literature writes the character of the wise man. Books, monuments, pictures, conversation, are portraits in which he finds the lineaments he is forming. The silent and the

eloquent praise him and accost him, and he is stimulated
wherever he moves, as by personal allusions. A true aspirant therefore, never needs look for allusions personal and
laudatory in discourse. He hears the commendation, not
of himself, but, more sweet, of that character he seeks, in
every word that is said concerning character, yea further
in every fact and circumstance,—in the running river and
the rustling corn. Praise is looked, homage tendered, love
flows, from mute nature, from the mountains and the
lights of the firmament.

These hints, dropped as it were from sleep and night,
let us use in broad day. The student is to read history actively and not passively; to esteem his own life the text,
and books the commentary. Thus compelled, the Muse of
history will utter oracles, as never to those who do not respect themselves. I have no expectation that any man will
read history aright who thinks that what was done in a remote age, by men whose names have resounded far, has
any deeper sense than what he is doing to-day.

The world exists for the education of each man. There
is no age or state of society or mode of action in history to
which there is not somewhat corresponding in his life.
Every thing tends in a wonderful manner to abbreviate itself and yield its own virtue to him. He should see that he
can live all history in his own person. He must sit solidly
at home, and not suffer himself to be bullied by kings or
empires, but know that he is greater than all the geography and all the government of the world; he must transfer
the point of view from which history is commonly read,
from Rome and Athens and London, to himself, and not
deny his conviction that he is the court, and if England or
Egypt have anything to say to him he will try the case; if
not, let them forever be silent. He must attain and maintain that lofty sight where facts yield their secret sense,
and poetry and annals are alike. The instinct of the mind,
the purpose of nature, betrays itself in the use we make of
the signal narrations of history. Time dissipates to shining
ether the solid angularity of facts. No anchor, no cable, no

fences avail to keep a fact a fact. Babylon, Troy, Tyre, Palestine, and even early Rome are passing already into fiction. The Garden of Eden, the sun standing still in Gibeon, is poetry thenceforward to all nations. Who cares what the fact was, when we have made a constellation of it to hang in heaven an immortal sign? London and Paris and New York must go the same way. "What is history," said Napoleon, "but a fable agreed upon?" This life of ours is stuck round with Egypt, Greece, Gaul, England, War, Colonization, Church, Court and Commerce, as with so many flowers and wild ornaments grave and gay. I will not make more account of them. I believe in Eternity. I can find Greece, Asia, Italy, Spain and the Islands,—the genius and creative principle of each and of all eras, in my own mind.

We are always coming up with the emphatic facts of history in our private experience and verifying them here. All history becomes subjective; in other words there is properly no history, only biography. Every mind must know the whole lesson for itself,—must go over the whole ground. What it does not see, what it does not live, it will not know. What the former age has epitomized into a formula or rule for manipular convenience, it will lose all the good of verifying for itself, by means of the wall of that rule. Somewhere, sometime, it will demand and find compensation for that loss, by doing the work itself. Ferguson discovered many things in astronomy which had long been known. The better for him.

History must be this or it is nothing. Every law which the state enacts indicates a fact in human nature; that is all. We must in ourselves see the necessary reason of every fact,—see how it could and must be. So stand before every public and private work; before an oration of Burke, before a victory of Napoleon, before a martyrdom of Sir Thomas More, of Sidney, of Marmaduke Robinson; before a French Reign of Terror, and a Salem hanging of witches; before a fanatic Revival and the Animal Magnetism in Paris, or in Providence. We assume that we under like influence should be alike affected, and should achieve the like; and we aim to master intellectually the steps and reach the same height or the same degradation that our fellow, our proxy has done.

All inquiry into antiquity, all curiosity respecting the Pyramids, the excavated cities, Stonehenge, the Ohio Circles, Mexico, Memphis,—is the desire to do away this wild, savage, and preposterous There or Then, and introduce in its place the Here and the Now. Belzoni digs and measures in the mummy-pits and pyramids of Thebes until he can see the end of the difference between the monstrous work and himself. When he has satisfied himself, in general and in detail, that it was made by such a person as he, so armed and so motived, and to ends to which he himself should also have worked, the problem is solved; his thought lives along the whole line of temples and sphinxes and catacombs, passes through them all with satisfaction, and they live again to the mind, or are *now*.

A Gothic cathedral affirms that it was done by us and not done by us. Surely it was by man, but we find it not in our man. But we apply ourselves to the history of its production. We put ourselves into the place and state of the builder. We remember the forest-dwellers, the first temples, the adherence to the first type, and the decoration of it as the wealth of the nation increased; the value which is given to wood by carving led to the carving over the whole mountain of stone of a cathedral. When we have gone through this process, and added thereto the Catholic Church, its cross, its music, its processions, its Saints' days and image-worship, we have as it were been the man that made the minster; we have seen how it could and must be. We have the sufficient reason.

The difference between men is in their principle of association. Some men classify objects by color and size and other accidents of appearance; others by intrinsic likeness, or by the relation of cause and effect. The progress of the intellect is to the clearer vision of causes, which neglects surface differences. To the poet, to the philosopher, to the saint, all things are friendly and sacred, all events profitable, all days holy, all men divine. For the eye is fastened on the life, and slights the circumstance. Every chemical substance, every plant, every animal in its growth, teaches the unity of cause, the variety of appearance.

Upborne and surrounded as we are by this all-creating nature, soft and fluid as a cloud or the air, why should we be such hard pedants, and magnify a few forms? Why should we make account of time, or of magnitude, or of figure? The soul knows them not, and genius, obeying its law, knows how to play with them as a young child plays with graybeards and in churches. Genius studies the causal thought, and far back in the womb of things sees the rays parting from one orb, that diverge, ere they fall, by infinite diameters. Genius watches the monad through all his masks as he performs the metempsychosis of nature. Genius detects through the fly, through the caterpillar, through the grub, through the egg, the constant individual; through countless individuals the fixed species; through many species the genus; through all genera the steadfast type; through all the kingdoms of organized life the eternal unity. Nature is a mutable cloud which is always and never the same. She casts the same thought into troops of forms, as a poet makes twenty fables with one moral. Through the bruteness and toughness of matter, a subtle spirit bends all things to its own will. The adamant streams into soft but precise form before it, and whilst I look at it its outline and texture are changed again. Nothing is so fleeting as form; yet never does it quite deny itself. In man we still trace the remains or hints of all that we esteem badges of servitude in the lower races; yet in him they enhance his nobleness and grace; as Io, in Æschylus, transformed to a cow, offends the imagination; but how changed when as Isis in Egypt she meets Osiris-Jove, a beautiful woman with nothing of the metamorphosis left but the lunar horns as the splendid ornament of her brows!

The identity of history is equally intrinsic, the diversity

equally obvious. There is, at the surface, infinite variety of things; at the centre there is simplicity of cause. How many are the acts of one man in which we recognize the same character! Observe the sources of our information in respect to the Greek genius. We have the *civil history* of that people, as Herodotus, Thucydides, Xenophon, and Plutarch have given it; a very sufficient account of what manner of persons they were and what they did. We have the same national mind expressed for us again in their *literature*, in epic and lyric poems, drama, and philosophy; a very complete form. Then we have it once more in their *architecture*, a beauty as of temperance itself, limited to the straight line and the square,—a builded geometry. Then we have it once again in *sculpture*, the "tongue on the balance of expression," a multitude of forms in the utmost freedom of action and never transgressing the ideal serenity; like votaries performing some religious dance before the gods, and, though in convulsive pain or mortal combat, never daring to break the figure and decorum of their dance. Thus of the genius of one remarkable people we have a fourfold representation: and to the senses what more unlike than an ode of Pindar, a marble centaur, the peristyle of the Parthenon, and the last actions of Phocion?

Every one must have observed faces and forms which, without any resembling feature, make a like impression on the beholder. A particular picture or copy of verses, if it do not awaken the same train of images, will yet superinduce the same sentiment as some wild mountain walk, although the resemblance is nowise obvious to the senses, but is occult and out of the reach of the understanding. Nature is an endless combination and repetition of a very few laws. She hums the old well-known air through innumerable variations.

Nature is full of a sublime family likeness throughout her works, and delights in startling us with resemblances in the most unexpected quarters. I have seen the head of an old sachem of the forest which at once reminded the eye of a bald mountain summit, and the furrows of the brow suggested the strata of the rock. There are men whose manners have the same essential splendor as the simple and awful sculpture on the friezes of the Parthenon and the remains of the earliest Greek art. And there are compositions of the same strain to be found in the books of all ages. What is Guido's Rospigliosi Aurora but a morning thought, as the horses in it are only a morning cloud? If any one will but take pains to observe the variety of actions to which he is equally inclined in certain moods of mind, and those to which he is averse, he will see how deep is the chain of affinity.

A painter told me that nobody could draw a tree without in some sort becoming a tree; or draw a child by studying the outlines of its form merely,—but by watching for a time his motions and plays, the painter enters into his nature and can then draw him at will in every attitude. So Roos "entered into the inmost nature of a sheep." I knew a draughtsman employed in a public survey who found that he could not sketch the rocks until their geological structure was first explained to him. In a certain state of thought is the common origin of very diverse works. It is the spirit and not the fact that is identical. By a deeper apprehension, and not primarily by a painful acquisition of many manual skills, the artist attains the power of awakening other souls to a given activity.

It has been said that "common souls pay with what they do, nobler souls with that which they are." And why? Because a profound nature awakens in us by its actions and words, by its very looks and manners, the same power and beauty that a gallery of sculpture or of pictures addresses.

Civil and natural history, the history of art and of literature, must be explained from individual history, or must remain words. There is nothing but is related to us, nothing that does not interest us,—kingdom, college, tree, horse, or iron shoe,—the roots of all things are in man. Santa Croce and the Dome of St. Peter's are lame copies

after a divine model. Strasburg Cathedral is a material
counterpart of the soul of Erwin of Steinbach. The true
poem is the poet's mind; the true ship is the ship-builder.
In the man, could we lay him open, we should see the reason for the last flourish and tendril of his work; as every
spine and tint in the sea-shell preëxists in the secreting
organs of the fish. The whole of heraldry and of chivalry is
in courtesy. A man of fine manners shall pronounce your
name with all the ornament that titles of nobility could
ever add.

The trivial experience of every day is always verifying
some old prediction to us and converting into things the
words and signs which we had heard and seen without
heed. A lady with whom I was riding in the forest said to
me that the woods always seemed to her *to wait*, as if the
genii who inhabit them suspended their deeds until the
wayfarer had passed onward; a thought which poetry has
celebrated in the dance of the fairies, which breaks off on
the approach of human feet. The man who has seen the
rising moon break out of the clouds at midnight, has been
present like an archangel at the creation of light and of the
world. I remember one summer day in the fields my companion pointed out to me a broad cloud, which might extend a quarter of a mile parallel to the horizon, quite
accurately in the form of a cherub as painted over
churches,—a round block in the centre, which it was easy
to animate with eyes and mouth, supported on either side
by wide-stretched symmetrical wings. What appears once
in the atmosphere may appear often, and it was undoubtedly the archetype of that familiar ornament. I have seen
in the sky a chain of summer lightning which at once
showed to me that the Greeks drew from nature when
they painted the thunderbolt in the hand of Jove. I have
seen a snow-drift along the sides of the stone wall which
obviously gave the idea of the common architectural scroll
to abut a tower.

By surrounding ourselves with the original circumstances we invent anew the orders and the ornaments of

architecture, as we see how each people merely decorated its primitive abodes. The Doric temple preserves the semblance of the wooden cabin in which the Dorian dwelt. The Chinese pagoda is plainly a Tartar tent. The Indian and Egyptian temples still betray the mounds and subterranean houses of their forefathers. "The custom of making houses and tombs in the living rock," says Heeren in his Researches on the Ethiopians, "determined very naturally the principal character of the Nubian Egyptian architecture to the colossal form which it assumed. In these caverns, already prepared by nature, the eye was accustomed to dwell on huge shapes and masses, so that when art came to the assistance of nature it could not move on a small scale without degrading itself. What would statues of the usual size, or neat porches and wings have been, associated with those gigantic halls before which only Colossi could sit as watchmen or lean on the pillars of the interior?"

The Gothic church plainly originated in a rude adaptation of the forest trees, with all their boughs, to a festal or solemn arcade; as the bands about the cleft pillars still indicate the green withes that tied them. No one can walk in a road cut through pine woods, without being struck with the architectural appearance of the grove, especially in winter, when the barrenness of all other trees shows the low arch of the Saxons. In the woods in a winter afternoon one will see as readily the origin of the stained glass window, with which the Gothic cathedrals are adorned, in the colors of the western sky seen through the bare and crossing branches of the forest. Nor can any lover of nature enter the old piles of Oxford and the English cathedrals, without feeling that the forest overpowered the mind of the builder, and that his chisel, his saw and plane still reproduced its ferns, its spikes of flowers, its locust, elm, oak, pine, fir and spruce.

The Gothic cathedral is a blossoming in stone subdued by the insatiable demand of harmony in man. The mountain of granite blooms into an eternal flower, with the

lightness and delicate finish as well as the aerial proportions and perspective of vegetable beauty.

In like manner all public facts are to be individualized,
all private facts are to be generalized. Then at once History becomes fluid and true, and Biography deep and
sublime. As the Persian imitated in the slender shafts and
capitals of his architecture the stem and flower of the lotus
and palm, so the Persian court in its magnificent era never
gave over the nomadism of its barbarous tribes, but travelled from Ecbatana, where the spring was spent, to Susa
in summer and to Babylon for the winter.

In the early history of Asia and Africa, Nomadism and
Agriculture are the two antagonist facts. The geography
of Asia and of Africa necessitated a nomadic life. But the
nomads were the terror of all those whom the soil or the
advantages of a market had induced to build towns. Agriculture therefore was a religious injunction, because of the
perils of the state from nomadism. And in these late and
civil countries of England and America these propensities
still fight out the old battle, in the nation and in the individual. The nomads of Africa were constrained to wander,
by the attacks of the gad-fly, which drives the cattle mad,
and so compels the tribe to emigrate in the rainy season
and to drive off the cattle to the higher sandy regions. The
nomads of Asia follow the pasturage from month to
month. In America and Europe the nomadism is of trade
and curiosity; a progress, certainly, from the gad-fly of
Astaboras to the Anglo and Italomania of Boston Bay. Sacred cities, to which a periodical religious pilgrimage was
enjoined, or stringent laws and customs tending to invigorate the national bond, were the check on the old rovers;
and the cumulative values of long residence are the re-
straints on the itinerancy of the present day. The antagonism of the two tendencies is not less active in individuals,
as the love of adventure or the love of repose happens to
predominate. A man of rude health and flowing spirits has
the faculty of rapid domestication, lives in his wagon and
roams through all latitudes as easily as a Calmuc. At sea,

or in the forest, or in the snow, he sleeps as warm, dines with as good appetite, and associates as happily as beside his own chimneys. Or perhaps his facility is deeper seated, in the increased range of his faculties of observation, which yield him points of interest wherever fresh objects meet his eyes. The pastoral nations were needy and hungry to desperation; and this intellectual nomadism, in its excess, bankrupts the mind through the dissipation of power on a miscellany of objects. The home-keeping wit, on the other hand, is that continence or content which finds all the elements of life in its own soil; and which has its own perils of monotony and deterioration, if not stimulated by foreign infusions.

Every thing the individual sees without him corresponds to his states of mind, and every thing is in turn intelligible to him, as his onward thinking leads him into the truth to which that fact or series belongs.

The primeval world,—the Fore-World, as the Germans say,—I can dive to it in myself as well as grope for it with researching fingers in catacombs, libraries, and the broken reliefs and torsos of ruined villas.

What is the foundation of that interest all men feel in Greek history, letters, art and poetry, in all its periods from the Heroic or Homeric age down to the domestic life of the Athenians and Spartans, four or five centuries later? What but this, that every man passes personally through a Grecian period. The Grecian state is the era of the bodily nature, the perfection of the senses,—of the spiritual nature unfolded in strict unity with the body. In it existed those human forms which supplied the sculptor with his models of Hercules, Phœbus, and Jove; not like the forms abounding in the streets of modern cities, wherein the face is a confused blur of features, but composed of incorrupt, sharply defined and symmetrical features, whose eye-sockets are so formed that it would be impossible for such eyes to squint and take furtive glances on this side and on that, but they must turn the whole head. The manners of that period are plain and fierce. The reverence exhibited is for personal qualities; courage, address, self-command, justice, strength, swiftness, a loud voice, a broad chest. Luxury and elegance are not known. A sparse population and want make every man his own valet, cook, butcher and soldier, and the habit of supplying his own needs educates the body to wonderful performances. Such are the Agamemnon and Diomed of Homer, and not far different is the picture Xenophon gives of himself and his compatriots in the Retreat of the Ten Thousand. "After the army had crossed the river Teleboas in Armenia, there fell much snow, and the troops lay miserably on the ground covered with it. But Xenophon arose naked, and taking an axe, began to split wood; whereupon others rose and did the like." Throughout his army exists a boundless liberty of speech. They quarrel for plunder, they wrangle with the generals on each new order, and Xenophon is as sharp-tongued as any and sharper-tongued than most, and so gives as good as he gets. Who does not see that this is a gang of great boys, with such a code of honor and such lax discipline as great boys have?

The costly charm of the ancient tragedy, and indeed of all the old literature, is that the persons speak simply,— speak as persons who have great good sense without knowing it, before yet the reflective habit has become the predominant habit of the mind. Our admiration of the antique is not admiration of the old, but of the natural. The Greeks are not reflective, but perfect in their senses and in their health, with the finest physical organization in the world. Adults acted with the simplicity and grace of children. They made vases, tragedies and statues, such as healthy senses should,—that is, in good taste. Such things have continued to be made in all ages, and are now, wherever a healthy physique exists; but, as a class, from their superior organization, they have surpassed all. They combine the energy of manhood with the engaging unconsciousness of childhood. The attraction of these manners is that they belong to man, and are known to every man in virtue of his being once a child; besides that there are always individuals who retain these characteristics. A person of childlike genius and inborn energy is still a Greek, and revives our love of the Muse of Hellas. I admire the love of nature in the Philoctetes. In reading those fine apostrophes to sleep, to the stars, rocks, mountains and waves, I feel time passing away as an ebbing sea. I feel the eternity of man, the identity of his thought. The Greek had, it seems, the same fellow-beings as I. The sun and moon, water and fire, met his heart precisely as they meet mine. Then the vaunted distinction between Greek and English, between Classic and Romantic schools, seems superficial and pedantic. When a thought of Plato becomes a thought to me,—when a truth that fired the soul of Pindar fires mine, time is no more. When I feel that we two meet in a perception, that our two souls are tinged with the same hue, and do as it were run into one, why should I measure degrees of latitude, why should I count Egyptian years?

The student interprets the age of chivalry by his own age of chivalry, and the days of maritime adventure and circumnavigation by quite parallel miniature experiences of his own. To the sacred history of the world he has the same key. When the voice of a prophet out of the deeps of antiquity merely echoes to him a sentiment of his infancy, a prayer of his youth, he then pierces to the truth through all the confusion of tradition and the caricature of institutions.

Rare, extravagant spirits come by us at intervals, who disclose to us new facts in nature. I see that men of God have from time to time walked among men and made their commission felt in the heart and soul of the commonest hearer. Hence evidently the tripod, the priest, the priestess inspired by the divine afflatus.

Jesus astonishes and overpowers sensual people. They cannot unite him to history, or reconcile him with themselves. As they come to revere their intuitions and aspire to live holily, their own piety explains every fact, every word.

How easily these old worships of Moses, of Zoroaster, of Menu, of Socrates, domesticate themselves in the mind. I cannot find any antiquity in them. They are mine as much as theirs.

I have seen the first monks and anchorets, without crossing seas or centuries. More than once some individual has appeared to me with such negligence of labor and such commanding contemplation, a haughty beneficiary begging in the name of God, as made good to the nineteenth century Simeon the Stylite, the Thebais, and the first Capuchins.

The priestcraft of the East and West, of the Magian, Brahmin, Druid, and Inca, is expounded in the individual's private life. The cramping influence of a hard formalist on a young child, in repressing his spirits and courage, paralyzing the understanding, and that without producing indignation, but only fear and obedience, and even much sympathy with the tyranny,—is a familiar fact, explained to the child when he becomes a man, only by seeing that the oppressor of his youth is himself a child tyrannized over by those names and words and forms of whose influence he was merely the organ to the youth. The fact teaches him how Belus was worshipped and how the Pyramids were built, better than the discovery by Champollion of the names of all the workmen and the cost of every tile. He finds Assyria and the Mounds of Cholula at his door, and himself has laid the courses.

Again, in that protest which each considerate person makes against the superstition of his times, he repeats step for step the part of old reformers, and in the search after truth finds, like them, new perils to virtue. He learns again what moral vigor is needed to supply the girdle of a superstition. A great licentiousness treads on the heels of a reformation. How many times in the history of the world has the Luther of the day had to lament the decay of piety in his own household! "Doctor," said his wife to Martin Luther, one day, "how is it that whilst subject to papacy we prayed so often and with such fervor, whilst now we pray with the utmost coldness and very seldom?"

The advancing man discovers how deep a property he has in literature,—in all fable as well as in all history. He finds that the poet was no odd fellow who described strange and impossible situations, but that universal man wrote by his pen a confession true for one and true for all. His own secret biography he finds in lines wonderfully intelligible to him, dotted down before he was born. One after another he comes up in his private adventures with every fable of Æsop, of Homer, of Hafiz, of Ariosto, of Chaucer, of Scott, and verifies them with his own head and hands.

The beautiful fables of the Greeks, being proper creations of the imagination and not of the fancy, are universal verities. What a range of meanings and what perpetual pertinence has the story of Prometheus! Beside its primary value as the first chapter of the history of Europe, (the mythology thinly veiling authentic facts, the invention of the mechanic arts and the migration of colonies,) it gives the history of religion, with some closeness to the faith of later ages. Prometheus is the Jesus of the old mythology. He is the friend of man; stands between the unjust "justice" of the Eternal Father and the race of mortals, and readily suffers all things on their account. But where it departs from the Calvinistic Christianity and exhibits him as the defier of Jove, it represents a state of mind which readily appears wherever the doctrine of Theism is taught in a crude, objective form, and which seems the self-defence of man against this untruth, namely a discontent with the believed fact that a God exists, and a feeling that the obligation of reverence is onerous. It would steal if it could the fire of the Creator, and live apart from him and independent of him. The Prometheus Vinctus is the romance of skepticism. Not less true to all time are the details of that stately apologue. Apollo kept the flocks of Admetus, said the poets. When the gods come

among men, they are not known. Jesus was not; Socrates
and Shakspeare were not. Antæus was suffocated by the
gripe of Hercules, but every time he touched his mother-
earth his strength was renewed. Man is the broken giant,
and in all his weakness both his body and his mind are invigorated by habits of conversation with nature. The
power of music, the power of poetry, to unfix and as it
were clap wings to solid nature, interprets the riddle
of Orpheus. The philosophical perception of identity
through endless mutations of form makes him know the
Proteus. What else am I who laughed or wept yesterday,
who slept last night like a corpse, and this morning stood
and ran? And what see I on any side but the transmigra-
tions of Proteus? I can symbolize my thought by using the
name of any creature, of any fact, because every creature
is man agent or patient. Tantalus is but a name for you
and me. Tantalus means the impossibility of drinking the
waters of thought which are always gleaming and waving within sight of the soul. The transmigration of souls is
no fable. I would it were; but men and women are only
half human. Every animal of the barn-yard, the field and
the forest, of the earth and of the waters that are under the
earth, has contrived to get a footing and to leave the print
of its features and form in some one or other of these upright, heaven-facing speakers. Ah! brother, stop the ebb of
thy soul,—ebbing downward into the forms into whose
habits thou hast now for many years slid. As near and
proper to us is also that old fable of the Sphinx, who was
said to sit in the road-side and put riddles to every passenger. If the man could not answer, she swallowed him alive.
If he could solve the riddle, the Sphinx was slain. What is
our life but an endless flight of winged facts or events? In
splendid variety these changes come, all putting questions
to the human spirit. Those men who cannot answer by a
superior wisdom these facts or questions of time, serve
them. Facts encumber them, tyrannize over them, and
make the men of routine, the men of *sense*, in whom a literal obedience to facts has extinguished every spark of

that light by which man is truly man. But if the man is true to his better instincts or sentiments, and refuses the dominion of facts, as one that comes of a higher race; remains fast by the soul and sees the principle, then the facts fall aptly and supple into their places; they know their master, and the meanest of them glorifies him.

See in Goethe's Helena the same desire that every word should be a thing. These figures, he would say, these Chirons, Griffins, Phorkyas, Helen and Leda, are somewhat, and do exert a specific influence on the mind. So far then are they eternal entities, as real to-day as in the first Olympiad. Much revolving them he writes out freely his humor, and gives them body to his own imagination. And although that poem be as vague and fantastic as a dream, yet is it much more attractive than the more regular dramatic pieces of the same author, for the reason that it operates a wonderful relief to the mind from the routine of customary images,—awakens the reader's invention and fancy by the wild freedom of the design, and by the unceasing succession of brisk shocks of surprise.

The universal nature, too strong for the petty nature of the bard, sits on his neck and writes through his hand; so that when he seems to vent a mere caprice and wild romance, the issue is an exact allegory. Hence Plato said that "poets utter great and wise things which they do not themselves understand." All the fictions of the Middle Age explain themselves as a masked or frolic expression of that which in grave earnest the mind of that period toiled to achieve. Magic and all that is ascribed to it is a deep presentiment of the powers of science. The shoes of swiftness, the sword of sharpness, the power of subduing the elements, of using the secret virtues of minerals, of understanding the voices of birds, are the obscure efforts of the mind in a right direction. The preternatural prowess of the hero, the gift of perpetual youth, and the like, are alike the endeavor of the human spirit "to bend the shows of things to the desires of the mind."

In Perceforest and Amadis de Gaul a garland and a rose

bloom on the head of her who is faithful, and fade on the
brow of the inconstant. In the story of the Boy and the
Mantle even a mature reader may be surprised with a
glow of virtuous pleasure at the triumph of the gentle
Genelas; and indeed all the postulates of elfin annals,—
that the fairies do not like to be named; that their gifts are
capricious and not to be trusted; that who seeks a treasure
must not speak; and the like,—I find true in Concord,
however they might be in Cornwall or Bretagne.

Is it otherwise in the newest romance? I read the Bride
of Lammermoor. Sir William Ashton is a mask for a vulgar temptation, Ravenswood Castle a fine name for proud
poverty, and the foreign mission of state only a Bunyan
disguise for honest industry. We may all shoot a wild bull
that would toss the good and beautiful, by fighting down
the unjust and sensual. Lucy Ashton is another name for
fidelity, which is always beautiful and always liable to calamity in this world.

But along with the civil and metaphysical history of
man, another history goes daily forward,—that of the external world,—in which he is not less strictly implicated.
He is the compend of time; he is also the correlative of nature. His power consists in the multitude of his affinities,
in the fact that his life is intertwined with the whole chain
of organic and inorganic being. In old Rome the public
roads beginning at the Forum proceeded north, south,
east, west, to the centre of every province of the empire,
making each market-town of Persia, Spain and Britain
pervious to the soldiers of the capital: so out of the human
heart go as it were highways to the heart of every object in
nature, to reduce it under the dominion of man. A man is a
bundle of relations, a knot of roots, whose flower and
fruitage is the world. His faculties refer to natures out of
him and predict the world he is to inhabit, as the fins of
the fish foreshow that water exists, or the wings of an
eagle in the egg presuppose air. He cannot live without a
world. Put Napoleon in an island prison, let his faculties
find no men to act on, no Alps to climb, no stake to play

for, and he would beat the air, and appear stupid. Transport him to large countries, dense population, complex interests and antagonist power, and you shall see that the man Napoleon, bounded that is by such a profile and outline, is not the virtual Napoleon. This is but Talbot's shadow;—

> "His substance is not here.
> For what you see is but the smallest part
> And least proportion of humanity;
> But were the whole frame here,
> It is of such a spacious, lofty pitch,
> Your roof were not sufficient to contain it."

Columbus needs a planet to shape his course upon. Newton and Laplace need myriads of age and thick-strewn celestial areas. One may say a gravitating solar system is already prophesied in the nature of Newton's mind. Not less does the brain of Davy or of Gay-Lussac, from childhood exploring the affinities and repulsions of particles, anticipate the laws of organization. Does not the eye of the human embryo predict the light? the ear of Handel predict the witchcraft of harmonic sound? Do not the constructive fingers of Watt, Fulton, Whittemore, Arkwright, predict the fusible, hard, and temperable texture of metals, the properties of stone, water, and wood? Do not the lovely attributes of the maiden child predict the refinements and decorations of civil society? Here also we are reminded of the action of man on man. A mind might ponder its thoughts for ages and not gain so much self-knowledge as the passion of love shall teach it in a day. Who knows himself before he has been thrilled with indignation at an outrage, or has heard an eloquent tongue, or has shared the throb of thousands in a national exultation or alarm? No man can antedate his experience, or guess what faculty or feeling a new object shall unlock, any more than he can draw to-day the face of a person whom he shall see to-morrow for the first time.

I will not now go behind the general statement to explore the reason of this correspondency. Let it suffice that in the light of these two facts, namely, that the mind is One, and that nature is its correlative, history is to be read and written.

Thus in all ways does the soul concentrate and reproduce its treasures for each pupil. He too shall pass through the whole cycle of experience. He shall collect into a focus the rays of nature. History no longer shall be a dull book. It shall walk incarnate in every just and wise man. You shall not tell me by languages and titles a catalogue of the volumes you have read. You shall make me feel what periods you have lived. A man shall be the Temple of Fame. He shall walk, as the poets have described that goddess, in a robe painted all over with wonderful events and experiences;—his own form and features by their exalted intelligence shall be that variegated vest. I shall find in him the Foreworld; in his childhood the Age of Gold, the Apples of Knowledge, the Argonautic Expedition, the calling of Abraham, the building of the Temple, the Advent of Christ, Dark Ages, the Revival of Letters, the Reformation, the discovery of new lands, the opening of new sciences and new regions in man. He shall be the priest of Pan, and bring with him into humble cottages the blessing of the morning stars, and all the recorded benefits of heaven and earth.

Is there somewhat overweening in this claim? Then I reject all I have written, for what is the use of pretending to know what we know not? But it is the fault of our rhetoric that we cannot strongly state one fact without seeming to belie some other. I hold our actual knowledge very cheap. Hear the rats in the wall, see the lizard on the fence, the fungus under foot, the lichen on the log. What do I know sympathetically, morally, of either of these worlds of life? As old as the Caucasian man,—perhaps older,—these creatures have kept their counsel beside him, and there is no record of any word or sign that has passed from one to the other. What connection do the

books show between the fifty or sixty chemical elements
and the historical eras? Nay, what does history yet record
of the metaphysical annals of man? What light does it
shed on those mysteries which we hide under the names
Death and Immortality? Yet every history should be
written in a wisdom which divined the range of our affinities and looked at facts as symbols. I am ashamed to see
what a shallow village tale our so-called History is. How
many times we must say Rome, and Paris, and Constantinople! What does Rome know of rat and lizard? What
are Olympiads and Consulates to these neighboring systems of being? Nay, what food or experience or succor
have they for the Esquimaux seal-hunter, for the Kanàka
in his canoe, for the fisherman, the stevedore, the porter?

Broader and deeper we must write our annals,—from
an ethical reformation, from an influx of the ever new,
ever sanative conscience,—if we would trulier express our
central and wide-related nature, instead of this old chronology of selfishness and pride to which we have too long
lent our eyes. Already that day exists for us, shines in on
us at unawares, but the path of science and of letters is not
the way into nature. The idiot, the Indian, the child and
unschooled farmer's boy stand nearer to the light by
which nature is to be read, than the dissector or the antiquary.

SELF-RELIANCE

~~~~~~~~~~~~~~~~~~~~~~~~~~~~~~~~~~~~~~

"Ne te quæsiveris extra."

Man is his own star; and the soul that can
Render an honest and a perfect man,
Commands all light, all influence, all fate;
Nothing to him falls early or too late.
Our acts our angels are, or good or ill,
Our fatal shadows that walk by us still.

Epilogue to Beaumont and Fletcher's
Honest Man's Fortune

Cast the bantling on the rocks,
Suckle him with the she-wolf's teat,
Wintered with the hawk and fox,
Power and speed be hands and feet.

I read the other day some verses written by an eminent painter which were original and not conventional. The soul always hears an admonition in such lines, let the subject be what it may. The sentiment they instil is of more value than any thought they may contain. To believe your own thought, to believe that what is true for you in your private heart is true for all men,—that is genius. Speak your latent conviction, and it shall be the universal sense; for the inmost in due time becomes the outmost, and our first thought is rendered back to us by the trumpets of the Last Judgment. Familiar as the voice of the mind is to each, the highest merit we ascribe to Moses, Plato and Milton is that they set at naught books and traditions, and spoke not what men, but what *they* thought. A man should learn to detect and watch that gleam of light which flashes across his mind from within, more than the lustre of the firmament of bards and sages. Yet he dismisses without notice his thought, because it is his. In every work of genius we recognize our own rejected thoughts; they come back to us with a certain alienated majesty. Great works of art have no more affecting lesson for us than this. They teach us to abide by our spontaneous impression with good-humored inflexibility then most when the whole cry of voices is on the other side. Else to-morrow a stranger will say with masterly good sense precisely what we have thought and felt all the time, and we shall be forced to take with shame our own opinion from another.

There is a time in every man's education when he arrives at the conviction that envy is ignorance; that imitation is suicide; that he must take himself for better for worse as his portion; that though the wide universe is full of good, no kernel of nourishing corn can come to him but through his toil bestowed on that plot of ground which is given to him to till. The power which resides in him is new in nature, and none but he knows what that is which he can do, nor does he know until he has tried. Not for nothing one face, one character, one fact, makes much impression on him, and another none. This sculpture in the memory is not without preëstablished harmony. The eye was placed where one ray should fall, that it might testify of that particular ray. We but half express ourselves, and are ashamed of that divine idea which each of us represents. It may be safely trusted as proportionate and of good issues, so it be faithfully imparted, but God will not have his work made manifest by cowards. A man is relieved and gay when he has put his heart into his work and done his best; but what he has said or done otherwise shall give him no peace. It is a deliverance which does not deliver. In the attempt his genius deserts him; no muse befriends; no invention, no hope.

Trust thyself: every heart vibrates to that iron string.

Accept the place the divine providence has found for you, the society of your contemporaries, the connection of events. Great men have always done so, and confided themselves childlike to the genius of their age, betraying their perception that the absolutely trustworthy was seated at their heart, working through their hands, predominating in all their being. And we are now men, and must accept in the highest mind the same transcendent destiny; and not minors and invalids in a protected corner, not cowards fleeing before a revolution, but guides, redeemers and benefactors, obeying the Almighty effort and advancing on Chaos and the Dark.

What pretty oracles nature yields us on this text in the face and behavior of children, babes, and even brutes! That divided and rebel mind, that distrust of a sentiment because our arithmetic has computed the strength and means opposed to our purpose, these have not. Their mind being whole, their eye is as yet unconquered, and when we look in their faces we are disconcerted. Infancy conforms to nobody; all conform to it; so that one babe commonly makes four or five out of the adults who prattle and play to it. So God has armed youth and puberty and manhood no less with its own piquancy and charm, and made it enviable and gracious and its claims not to be put by, if it will stand by itself. Do not think the youth has no force, because he cannot speak to you and me. Hark! in the next room his voice is sufficiently clear and emphatic. It seems he knows how to speak to his contemporaries. Bashful or bold then, he will know how to make us seniors very unnecessary.

The nonchalance of boys who are sure of a dinner, and would disdain as much as a lord to do or say aught to conciliate one, is the healthy attitude of human nature. A boy is in the parlor what the pit is in the playhouse; independent, irresponsible, looking out from his corner on such people and facts as pass by, he tries and sentences them on their merits, in the swift, summary way of boys, as good, bad, interesting, silly, eloquent, troublesome. He cumbers himself never about consequences, about interests; he gives an independent, genuine verdict. You must court him; he does not court you. But the man is as it were clapped into jail by his consciousness. As soon as he has once acted or spoken with *éclat* he is a committed person, watched by the sympathy or the hatred of hundreds, whose affections must now enter into his account. There is no Lethe for this. Ah, that he could pass again into his neutrality! Who can thus avoid all pledges and, having observed, observe again from the same unaffected, unbiased, unbribable, unaffrighted innocence,—must always be formidable. He would utter opinions on all passing affairs, which being seen to be not private but necessary, would sink like darts into the ear of men and put them in fear.

These are the voices which we hear in solitude, but they grow faint and inaudible as we enter into the world. Society everywhere is in conspiracy against the manhood of every one of its members. Society is a joint-stock company, in which the members agree, for the better securing of his bread to each shareholder, to surrender the liberty and culture of the eater. The virtue in most request is conformity. Self-reliance is its aversion. It loves not realities and creators, but names and customs.

Whoso would be a man, must be a nonconformist. He who would gather immortal palms must not be hindered by the name of goodness, but must explore if it be goodness. Nothing is at last sacred but the integrity of your own mind. Absolve you to yourself, and you shall have the suffrage of the world. I remember an answer which when quite young I was prompted to make to a valued adviser who was wont to importune me with the dear old doctrines of the church. On my saying, "What have I to do with the sacredness of traditions, if I live wholly from within?" my friend suggested,—"But these impulses may be from below, not from above." I replied, "They do not seem to me to be such; but if I am the Devil's child, I will live then from the Devil." No law can be sacred to me but

that of my nature. Good and bad are but names very readily transferable to that or this; the only right is what is
after my constitution; the only wrong what is against it. A
man is to carry himself in the presence of all opposition as
if every thing were titular and ephemeral but he. I am
ashamed to think how easily we capitulate to badges and
names, to large societies and dead institutions. Every decent and well-spoken individual affects and sways me
more than is right. I ought to go upright and vital, and
speak the rude truth in all ways. If malice and vanity wear
the coat of philanthropy, shall that pass? If an angry bigot
assumes this bountiful cause of Abolition, and comes to
me with his last news from Barbadoes, why should I not
say to him, 'Go love thy infant; love thy wood-chopper; be
good-natured and modest; have that grace; and never varnish your hard, uncharitable ambition with this incredible
tenderness for black folk a thousand miles off. Thy love
afar is spite at home.' Rough and graceless would be such
greeting, but truth is handsomer than the affectation of
love. Your goodness must have some edge to it,—else it is
none. The doctrine of hatred must be preached, as the
counteraction of the doctrine of love, when that pules and
whines. I shun father and mother and wife and brother
when my genius calls me. I would write on the lintels of
the door-post, *Whim*. I hope it is somewhat better than
whim at last, but we cannot spend the day in explanation.
Expect me not to show cause why I seek or why I exclude
company. Then again, do not tell me, as a good man did
to-day, of my obligation to put all poor men in good situations. Are they *my* poor? I tell thee, thou foolish philan-
thropist, that I grudge the dollar, the dime, the cent I give
to such men as do not belong to me and to whom I do not
belong. There is a class of persons to whom by all spiritual
affinity I am bought and sold; for them I will go to prison
if need be; but your miscellaneous popular charities; the
education at college of fools; the building of meeting-
houses to the vain end to which many now stand; alms to
sots, and the thousand-fold Relief Societies;—though I

confess with shame I sometimes succumb and give the dollar, it is a wicked dollar, which by and by I shall have the manhood to withhold.

Virtues are, in the popular estimate, rather the exception than the rule. There is the man *and* his virtues. Men do what is called a good action, as some piece of courage or charity, much as they would pay a fine in expiation of daily non-appearance on parade. Their works are done as an apology or extenuation of their living in the world,—as invalids and the insane pay a high board. Their virtues are penances. I do not wish to expiate, but to live. My life is for itself and not for a spectacle. I much prefer that it should be of a lower strain, so it be genuine and equal, than that it should be glittering and unsteady. I wish it to be sound and sweet, and not to need diet and bleeding. I ask primary evidence that you are a man, and refuse this appeal from the man to his actions. I know that for myself it makes no difference whether I do or forbear those actions which are reckoned excellent. I cannot consent to pay for a privilege where I have intrinsic right. Few and mean as my gifts may be, I actually am, and do not need for my own assurance or the assurance of my fellows any secondary testimony.

What I must do is all that concerns me, not what the people think. This rule, equally arduous in actual and in intellectual life, may serve for the whole distinction between greatness and meanness. It is the harder because you will always find those who think they know what is your duty better than you know it. It is easy in the world to live after the world's opinion; it is easy in solitude to live after our own; but the great man is he who in the midst of the crowd keeps with perfect sweetness the independence of solitude.

The objection to conforming to usages that have become dead to you is that it scatters your force. It loses your time and blurs the impression of your character. If you maintain a dead church, contribute to a dead Bible-society, vote with a great party either for the government

or against it, spread your table like base housekeepers,—
under all these screens I have difficulty to detect the precise man you are: and of course so much force is withdrawn from your proper life. But do your work, and I
shall know you. Do your work, and you shall reinforce
yourself. A man must consider what a blind-man's-buff is
this game of conformity. If I know your sect I anticipate
your argument. I hear a preacher announce for his text
and topic the expediency of one of the institutions of his
church. Do I not know beforehand that not possibly can
he say a new and spontaneous word? Do I not know that
with all this ostentation of examining the grounds of the
institution he will do no such thing? Do I not know that
he is pledged to himself not to look but at one side, the
permitted side, not as a man, but as a parish minister? He
is a retained attorney, and these airs of the bench are the
emptiest affectation. Well, most men have bound their
eyes with one or another handkerchief, and attached
themselves to some one of these communities of opinion.
This conformity makes them not false in a few particulars,
authors of a few lies, but false in all particulars. Their
every truth is not quite true. Their two is not the real two,
their four not the real four; so that every word they say
chagrins us and we know not where to begin to set them
right. Meantime nature is not slow to equip us in the
prison-uniform of the party to which we adhere. We come
to wear one cut of face and figure, and acquire by degrees
the gentlest asinine expression. There is a mortifying experience in particular, which does not fail to wreak itself
also in the general history; I mean "the foolish face of
praise," the forced smile which we put on in company
where we do not feel at ease, in answer to conversation
which does not interest us. The muscles, not spontane-
ously moved but moved by a low usurping wilfulness,
grow tight about the outline of the face, with the most disagreeable sensation.

For nonconformity the world whips you with its displeasure. And therefore a man must know how to estimate

a sour face. The by-standers look askance on him in the public street or in the friend's parlor. If this aversion had its origin in contempt and resistance like his own he might well go home with a sad countenance; but the sour faces of the multitude, like their sweet faces, have no deep cause, but are put on and off as the wind blows and a newspaper directs. Yet is the discontent of the multitude more formidable than that of the senate and the college. It is easy enough for a firm man who knows the world to brook the rage of the cultivated classes. Their rage is decorous and prudent, for they are timid, as being very vulnerable themselves. But when to their feminine rage the indignation of the people is added, when the ignorant and the poor are aroused, when the unintelligent brute force that lies at the bottom of society is made to growl and mow, it needs the habit of magnanimity and religion to treat it godlike as a trifle of no concernment.

The other terror that scares us from self-trust is our consistency; a reverence for our past act or word because the eyes of others have no other data for computing our orbit than our past acts, and we are loth to disappoint them.

But why should you keep your head over your shoulder? Why drag about this corpse of your memory, lest you contradict somewhat you have stated in this or that public place? Suppose you should contradict yourself; what then? It seems to be a rule of wisdom never to rely on your memory alone, scarcely even in acts of pure memory, but to bring the past for judgment into the thousand-eyed present, and live ever in a new day. In your metaphysics you have denied personality to the Deity, yet when the devout motions of the soul come, yield to them heart and life, though they should clothe God with shape and color. Leave your theory, as Joseph his coat in the hand of the harlot, and flee.

A foolish consistency is the hobgoblin of little minds, adored by little statesmen and philosophers and divines. With consistency a great soul has simply nothing to do.

He may as well concern himself with his shadow on the wall. Speak what you think now in hard words and to-morrow speak what to-morrow thinks in hard words again, though it contradict every thing you said to-day.— 'Ah, so you shall be sure to be misunderstood.'—Is it so bad then to be misunderstood? Pythagoras was misunderstood, and Socrates, and Jesus, and Luther, and Copernicus, and Galileo, and Newton, and every pure and wise spirit that ever took flesh. To be great is to be misunderstood.

I suppose no man can violate his nature. All the sallies of his will are rounded in by the law of his being, as the inequalities of Andes and Himmaleh are insignificant in the curve of the sphere. Nor does it matter how you gauge and try him. A character is like an acrostic or Alexandrian stanza;—read it forward, backward, or across, it still spells the same thing. In this pleasing contrite wood-life which God allows me, let me record day by day my honest thought without prospect or retrospect, and, I cannot doubt, it will be found symmetrical, though I mean it not and see it not. My book should smell of pines and resound with the hum of insects. The swallow over my window should interweave that thread or straw he carries in his bill into my web also. We pass for what we are. Character teaches above our wills. Men imagine that they communicate their virtue or vice only by overt actions, and do not see that virtue or vice emit a breath every moment.

There will be an agreement in whatever variety of actions, so they be each honest and natural in their hour. For of one will, the actions will be harmonious, however unlike they seem. These varieties are lost sight of at a little distance, at a little height of thought. One tendency unites them all. The voyage of the best ship is a zigzag line of a hundred tacks. See the line from a sufficient distance, and it straightens itself to the average tendency. Your genuine action will explain itself and will explain your other genuine actions. Your conformity explains nothing. Act singly, and what you have already done singly will justify you now. Greatness appeals to the future. If I can be firm enough to-day to do right and scorn eyes, I must have done so much right before as to defend me now. Be it how it will, do right now. Always scorn appearances and you always may. The force of character is cumulative. All the foregone days of virtue work their health into this. What makes the majesty of the heroes of the senate and the field, which so fills the imagination? The consciousness of a train of great days and victories behind. They shed a united light on the advancing actor. He is attended as by a visible escort of angels. That is it which throws thunder into Chatham's voice, and dignity into Washington's port, and America into Adams's eye. Honor is venerable to us because it is no ephemera. It is always ancient virtue. We worship it to-day because it is not of to-day. We love it and pay it homage because it is not a trap for our love and homage, but is self-dependent, self-derived, and therefore of an old immaculate pedigree, even if shown in a young person.

I hope in these days we have heard the last of conformity and consistency. Let the words be gazetted and ridiculous henceforward. Instead of the gong for dinner, let us hear a whistle from the Spartan fife. Let us never bow and apologize more. A great man is coming to eat at my house. I do not wish to please him; I wish that he should wish to please me. I will stand here for humanity, and though I would make it kind, I would make it true. Let us affront and reprimand the smooth mediocrity and squalid contentment of the times, and hurl in the face of custom and trade and office, the fact which is the upshot of all history, that there is a great responsible Thinker and Actor working wherever a man works; that a true man belongs to no other time or place, but is the centre of things. Where he is, there is nature. He measures you and all men and all events. Ordinarily, every body in society reminds us of somewhat else, or of some other person. Character, reality, reminds you of nothing else; it takes place of the whole creation. The man must be so much that he must

make all circumstances indifferent. Every true man is a
cause, a country, and an age; requires infinite spaces and
numbers and time fully to accomplish his design;—and
posterity seem to follow his steps as a train of clients. A
man Cæsar is born, and for ages after we have a Roman
Empire. Christ is born, and millions of minds so grow and
cleave to his genius that he is confounded with virtue and
the possible of man. An institution is the lengthened
shadow of one man; as, Monachism, of the Hermit Antony; the Reformation, of Luther; Quakerism, of Fox;
Methodism, of Wesley; Abolition, of Clarkson. Scipio,
Milton called "the height of Rome;" and all history resolves itself very easily into the biography of a few stout
and earnest persons.

Let a man then know his worth, and keep things under
his feet. Let him not peep or steal, or skulk up and down
with the air of a charity-boy, a bastard, or an interloper in
the world which exists for him. But the man in the street,
finding no worth in himself which corresponds to the
force which built a tower or sculptured a marble god, feels
poor when he looks on these. To him a palace, a statue, or
a costly book have an alien and forbidding air, much like a
gay equipage, and seem to say like that, "Who are you,
Sir?" Yet they all are his, suitors for his notice, petitioners
to his faculties that they will come out and take possession. The picture waits for my verdict; it is not to command me, but I am to settle its claims to praise. That
popular fable of the sot who was picked up dead-drunk in
the street, carried to the duke's house, washed and dressed
and laid in the duke's bed, and, on his waking, treated
with all obsequious ceremony like the duke, and assured
that he had been insane, owes its popularity to the fact
that it symbolizes so well the state of man, who is in the
world a sort of sot, but now and then wakes up, exercises
his reason and finds himself a true prince.

Our reading is mendicant and sycophantic. In history
our imagination plays us false. Kingdom and lordship,
power and estate, are a gaudier vocabulary than private

John and Edward in a small house and common day's work; but the things of life are the same to both; the sum total of both is the same. Why all this deference to Alfred and Scanderbeg and Gustavus? Suppose they were virtuous; did they wear out virtue? As great a stake depends on your private act to-day as followed their public and renowned steps. When private men shall act with original views, the lustre will be transferred from the actions of kings to those of gentlemen.

The world has been instructed by its kings, who have so magnetized the eyes of nations. It has been taught by this colossal symbol the mutual reverence that is due from man to man. The joyful loyalty with which men have everywhere suffered the king, the noble, or the great proprietor to walk among them by a law of his own, make his own scale of men and things and reverse theirs, pay for benefits not with money but with honor, and represent the law in his person, was the hieroglyphic by which they obscurely signified their consciousness of their own right and comeliness, the right of every man.

The magnetism which all original action exerts is explained when we inquire the reason of self-trust. Who is the Trustee? What is the aboriginal Self, on which a universal reliance may be grounded? What is the nature and power of that science-baffling star, without parallax, without calculable elements, which shoots a ray of beauty even into trivial and impure actions, if the least mark of independence appear? The inquiry leads us to that source, at once the essence of genius, of virtue, and of life, which we call Spontaneity or Instinct. We denote this primary wisdom as Intuition, whilst all later teachings are tuitions. In that deep force, the last fact behind which analysis cannot go, all things find their common origin. For the sense of being which in calm hours rises, we know not how, in the soul, is not diverse from things, from space, from light, from time, from man, but one with them and proceeds obviously from the same source whence their life and being also proceed. We first share the life by which things exist and afterwards see them as appearances in nature and forget that we have shared their cause. Here is the fountain of action and of thought. Here are the lungs of that inspiration which giveth man wisdom and which cannot be denied without impiety and atheism. We lie in the lap of immense intelligence, which makes us receivers of its truth and organs of its activity. When we discern justice, when we discern truth, we do nothing of ourselves, but allow a passage to its beams. If we ask whence this comes, if we seek to pry into the soul that causes, all philosophy is at fault. Its presence or its absence is all we can affirm. Every man discriminates between the voluntary acts of his mind and his involuntary perceptions, and knows that to his involuntary perceptions a perfect faith is due. He may err in the expression of them, but he knows that these things are so, like day and night, not to be disputed. My wilful actions and acquisitions are but roving;—the idlest reverie, the faintest native emotion, command my curiosity and respect. Thoughtless people contradict as readily the statement of perceptions as of opinions, or rather much more readily; for they do not distinguish between perception and notion. They fancy that I choose to see this or that thing. But perception is not whimsical, but fatal. If I see a trait, my children will see it after me, and in course of time all mankind,—although it may chance that no one has seen it before me. For my perception of it is as much a fact as the sun.

The relations of the soul to the divine spirit are so pure that it is profane to seek to interpose helps. It must be that when God speaketh he should communicate, not one thing, but all things; should fill the world with his voice; should scatter forth light, nature, time, souls, from the centre of the present thought; and new date and new create the whole. Whenever a mind is simple and receives a divine wisdom, old things pass away,—means, teachers, texts, temples fall; it lives now, and absorbs past and future into the present hour. All things are made sacred by relation to it,—one as much as another. All things are dissolved to their centre by their cause, and in the universal miracle petty and particular miracles disappear. If therefore a man claims to know and speak of God and carries you backward to the phraseology of some old mouldered nation in another country, in another world, believe him not. Is the acorn better than the oak which is its fulness and completion? Is the parent better than the child into whom he has cast his ripened being? Whence then this worship of the past? The centuries are conspirators against the sanity and authority of the soul. Time and space are but physiological colors which the eye makes, but the soul is light: where it is, is day; where it was, is night; and history is an impertinence and an injury if it be any thing more than a cheerful apologue or parable of my being and becoming.

Man is timid and apologetic; he is no longer upright; he dares not say 'I think,' 'I am,' but quotes some saint or sage. He is ashamed before the blade of grass or the blowing rose. These roses under my window make no reference to former roses or to better ones; they are for what they are; they exist with God to-day. There is no time to them. There is simply the rose; it is perfect in every moment of its existence. Before a leaf-bud has burst, its whole life acts; in the full-blown flower there is no more; in the leafless root there is no less. Its nature is satisfied and it satisfies nature in all moments alike. But man postpones or remembers; he does not live in the present, but with reverted eye laments the past, or, heedless of the riches that surround him, stands on tiptoe to foresee the future. He cannot be happy and strong until he too lives with nature in the present, above time.

This should be plain enough. Yet see what strong intellects dare not yet hear God himself unless he speak the phraseology of I know not what David, or Jeremiah, or Paul. We shall not always set so great a price on a few texts, on a few lives. We are like children who repeat by rote the sentences of grandames and tutors, and, as they grow older, of the men of talents and character they chance to see,—painfully recollecting the exact words they spoke; afterwards, when they come into the point of view which those had who uttered these sayings, they understand them and are willing to let the words go; for at any time they can use words as good when occasion comes. If we live truly, we shall see truly. It is as easy for the strong man to be strong, as it is for the weak to be weak. When we have new perception, we shall gladly disburden the memory of its hoarded treasures as old rubbish. When a man lives with God, his voice shall be as sweet as the murmur of the brook and the rustle of the corn.

And now at last the highest truth on this subject remains unsaid; probably cannot be said; for all that we say is the far-off remembering of the intuition. That thought by what I can now nearest approach to say it, is this. When good is near you, when you have life in yourself, it is not by any known or accustomed way; you shall not discern the footprints of any other; you shall not see the face of man; you shall not hear any name;—the way, the thought, the good, shall be wholly strange and new. It shall exclude example and experience. You take the way from man, not to man. All persons that ever existed are its forgotten ministers. Fear and hope are alike beneath it. There is somewhat low even in hope. In the hour of vision there is nothing that can be called gratitude, nor properly joy. The soul raised over passion beholds identity and eternal causation, perceives the self-existence of Truth and Right, and calms itself with knowing that all things go well. Vast spaces of nature, the Atlantic Ocean, the South Sea; long intervals of time, years, centuries, are of no account. This which I think and feel underlay every former state of life and circumstances, as it does underlie my present, and what is called life and what is called death.

Life only avails, not the having lived. Power ceases in the instant of repose; it resides in the moment of transition from a past to a new state, in the shooting of the gulf, in the darting to an aim. This one fact the world hates; that the soul *becomes;* for that forever degrades the past, turns all riches to poverty, all reputation to a shame, confounds the saint with the rogue, shoves Jesus and Judas equally aside. Why then do we prate of self-reliance? Inasmuch as the soul is present there will be power not confident but agent. To talk of reliance is a poor external way of speaking. Speak rather of that which relies because it works and is. Who has more obedience than I masters me, though he should not raise his finger. Round him I must revolve by the gravitation of spirits. We fancy it rhetoric when we speak of eminent virtue. We do not yet see that virtue is Height, and that a man or a company of men, plastic and permeable to principles, by the law of nature must overpower and ride all cities, nations, kings, rich men, poets, who are not.

This is the ultimate fact which we so quickly reach on this, as on every topic, the resolution of all into the everblessed ONE. Self-existence is the attribute of the Supreme Cause, and it constitutes the measure of good by the degree in which it enters into all lower forms. All things real are so by so much virtue as they contain. Commerce, husbandry, hunting, whaling, war, eloquence, personal weight, are somewhat, and engage my respect as examples of its presence and impure action. I see the same law working in nature for conservation and growth. Power is, in nature, the essential measure of right. Nature suffers nothing to remain in her kingdoms which cannot help itself. The genesis and maturation of a planet, its poise and orbit, the bended tree recovering itself from the strong wind, the vital resources of every animal and vegetable, are demonstrations of the self-sufficing and therefore self-relying soul.

Thus all concentrates: let us not rove; let us sit at home with the cause. Let us stun and astonish the intruding rabble of men and books and institutions by a simple declaration of the divine fact. Bid the invaders take the shoes from off their feet, for God is here within. Let our simplicity judge them, and our docility to our own law demonstrate the poverty of nature and fortune beside our native riches.

But now we are a mob. Man does not stand in awe of man, nor is his genius admonished to stay at home, to put itself in communication with the internal ocean, but it goes abroad to beg a cup of water of the urns of other men. We must go alone. I like the silent church before the service begins, better than any preaching. How far off, how cool, how chaste the persons look, begirt each one with a precinct or sanctuary! So let us always sit. Why should we assume the faults of our friend, or wife, or father, or child, because they sit around our hearth, or are said to have the same blood? All men have my blood and I all men's. Not for that will I adopt their petulance or folly, even to the extent of being ashamed of it. But your isolation must not be mechanical, but spiritual, that is, must be elevation. At times the whole world seems to be in conspiracy to importune you with emphatic trifles. Friend, client, child, sickness, fear, want, charity, all knock at once at thy closet door and say,—'Come out unto us.' But keep thy state; come not into their confusion. The power men possess to annoy me I give them by a weak curiosity. No man can come near me but through my act. "What we love that we have, but by desire we bereave ourselves of the love."

If we cannot at once rise to the sanctities of obedience and faith, let us at least resist our temptations; let us enter into the state of war and wake Thor and Woden, courage and constancy, in our Saxon breasts. This is to be done in our smooth times by speaking the truth. Check this lying hospitality and lying affection. Live no longer to the expectation of these deceived and deceiving people with whom we converse. Say to them, 'O father, O mother, O wife, O brother, O friend, I have lived with you after appearances hitherto. Henceforward I am the truth's. Be it known unto you that henceforward I obey no law less than the eternal law. I will have no covenants but proximities. I shall endeavor to nourish my parents, to support my family, to be the chaste husband of one wife,—but these relations I must fill after a new and unprecedented way. I appeal from your customs. I must be myself. I cannot break myself any longer for you, or you. If you can love me for what I am, we shall be the happier. If you cannot, I will still seek to deserve that you should. I will not hide my tastes or aversions. I will so trust that what is deep is holy, that I will do strongly before the sun and moon whatever inly rejoices me and the heart appoints. If you are noble, I will love you; if you are not, I will not hurt you and myself by hypocritical attentions. If you are true, but not in the same truth with me, cleave to your companions; I will seek my own. I do this not selfishly but humbly and truly. It is alike your interest, and mine, and all men's, however long we have dwelt in lies, to live in truth. Does this sound harsh to-day? You will soon love what is dictated by your nature as well as mine, and if we follow the truth it will bring us out safe at last.'—But so may you give these friends pain. Yes, but I cannot sell my liberty and my power, to save their sensibility. Besides, all persons have their moments of reason, when they look out into the region of absolute truth; then will they justify me and do the same thing.

The populace think that your rejection of popular standards is a rejection of all standard, and mere antinomianism; and the bold sensualist will use the name of philosophy to gild his crimes. But the law of consciousness abides. There are two confessionals, in one or the other of which we must be shriven. You may fulfil your round of duties by clearing yourself in the *direct*, or in the *reflex* way. Consider whether you have satisfied your relations to father, mother, cousin, neighbor, town, cat and dog—whether any of these can upbraid you. But I may also neglect this reflex standard and absolve me to myself. I have my own stern claims and perfect circle. It denies the name of duty to many offices that are called duties. But if I can discharge its debts it enables me to dispense with the popular code. If any one imagines that this law is lax, let him keep its commandment one day.

And truly it demands something godlike in him who has cast off the common motives of humanity and has ventured to trust himself for a taskmaster. High be his heart, faithful his will, clear his sight, that he may in good earnest be doctrine, society, law, to himself, that a simple purpose may be to him as strong as iron necessity is to others!

If any man consider the present aspects of what is called by distinction *society*, he will see the need of these ethics. The sinew and heart of man seem to be drawn out, and we are become timorous, desponding whimperers. We are afraid of truth, afraid of fortune, afraid of death, and afraid of each other. Our age yields no great and perfect persons. We want men and women who shall renovate life and our social state, but we see that most natures are insolvent, cannot satisfy their own wants, have an ambition out of all proportion to their practical force and do lean and beg day and night continually. Our housekeeping is mendicant, our arts, our occupations, our marriages, our religion we have not chosen, but society has chosen for us. We are parlor soldiers. We shun the rugged battle of fate, where strength is born.

If our young men miscarry in their first enterprises they lose all heart. If the young merchant fails, men say he is *ruined*. If the finest genius studies at one of our colleges and is not installed in an office within one year afterwards in the cities or suburbs of Boston or New York, it seems to his friends and to himself that he is right in being disheartened and in complaining the rest of his life. A sturdy lad from New Hampshire or Vermont, who in turn tries all the professions, who *teams it, farms it, peddles*, keeps a school, preaches, edits a newspaper, goes to Congress, buys a township, and so forth, in successive years, and always like a cat falls on his feet, is worth a hundred of these city dolls. He walks abreast with his days and feels no shame in not 'studying a profession,' for he does not postpone his life, but lives already. He has not one chance, but a hundred chances. Let a Stoic open the resources of man and tell men they are not leaning willows, but can and must detach themselves; that with the exercise of self-trust, new powers shall appear; that a man is the word made flesh, born to shed healing to the nations; that he should be ashamed of our compassion, and that the moment he acts from himself, tossing the laws, the books, idolatries and customs out of the window, we pity him no more but thank and revere him;—and that teacher shall restore the life of man to splendor and make his name dear to all history.

It is easy to see that a greater self-reliance must work a revolution in all the offices and relations of men; in their religion; in their education; in their pursuits; their modes of living; their association; in their property; in their speculative views.

1. In what prayers do men allow themselves! That which they call a holy office is not so much as brave and manly. Prayer looks abroad and asks for some foreign addition to come through some foreign virtue, and loses itself in endless mazes of natural and supernatural, and mediatorial and miraculous. Prayer that craves a particular commodity, anything less than all good, is vicious. Prayer is the contemplation of the facts of life from the highest point of view. It is the soliloquy of a beholding and jubilant soul. It is the spirit of God pronouncing his works good. But prayer as a means to effect a private end is meanness and theft. It supposes dualism and not unity in nature and consciousness. As soon as the man is at one with God, he will not beg. He will then see prayer in all action. The prayer of the farmer kneeling in his field to weed it, the prayer of the rower kneeling with the stroke of his oar, are true prayers heard throughout nature, though for cheap ends. Caratach, in Fletcher's "Bonduca," when admonished to inquire the mind of the god Audate, replies,—

His hidden meaning lies in our endeavors;
Our valors are our best gods.

Another sort of false prayers are our regrets. Discontent is the want of self-reliance: it is infirmity of will. Regret calamities if you can thereby help the sufferer; if not, attend your own work and already the evil begins to be repaired. Our sympathy is just as base. We come to them who weep foolishly and sit down and cry for company, instead of imparting to them truth and health in rough electric shocks, putting them once more in communication with their own reason. The secret of fortune is joy in our hands. Welcome evermore to gods and men is the self-helping man. For him all doors are flung wide; him all tongues greet, all honors crown, all eyes follow with desire. Our love goes out to him and embraces him because he did not need it. We solicitously and apologetically caress and celebrate him because he held on his way and scorned our disapprobation. The gods love him because men hated him. "To the persevering mortal," said Zoroaster, "the blessed Immortals are swift."

As men's prayers are a disease of the will, so are their creeds a disease of the intellect. They say with those foolish Israelites, 'Let not God speak to us, lest we die. Speak thou, speak any man with us, and we will obey.' Everywhere I am hindered of meeting God in my brother, because he has shut his own temple doors and recites fables merely of his brother's, or his brother's brother's God. Every new mind is a new classification. If it prove a mind of uncommon activity and power, a Locke, a Lavoisier, a Hutton, a Bentham, a Fourier, it imposes its classification on other men, and lo! a new system. In proportion to the depth of the thought, and so to the number of the objects it touches and brings within reach of the pupil, is his complacency. But chiefly is this apparent in creeds and churches, which are also classifications of some powerful mind acting on the elemental thought of duty and man's relation to the Highest. Such is Calvinism, Quakerism, Swedenborgism. The pupil takes the same delight in subordinating every thing to the new terminology as a girl who has just learned botany in seeing a new earth and new seasons thereby. It will happen for a time that the pupil will find his intellectual power has grown by the study of his master's mind. But in all unbalanced minds the classification is idolized, passes for the end and not for a speedily exhaustible means, so that the walls of the system blend to their eye in the remote horizon with the walls of the universe; the luminaries of heaven seem to them hung on the arch their master built. They cannot imagine how you aliens have any right to see,—how you can see; 'It must be somehow that you stole the light from us.' They do not yet perceive that light, unsystematic, indomitable, will break into any cabin, even into theirs. Let them chirp awhile and call it their own. If they are honest and do well, presently their neat new pinfold will be too strait and low, will crack, will lean, will rot and vanish, and the immortal light, all young and joyful, million-orbed, million-colored, will beam over the universe as on the first morning.

2. It is for want of self-culture that the superstition of Travelling, whose idols are Italy, England, Egypt, retains its fascination for all educated Americans. They who made England, Italy, or Greece venerable in the imagination, did so by sticking fast where they were, like an axis of the earth. In manly hours we feel that duty is our place. The soul is no traveller; the wise man stays at home, and when his necessities, his duties, on any occasion call him from his house, or into foreign lands, he is at home still and shall make men sensible by the expression of his countenance that he goes, the missionary of wisdom and virtue, and visits cities and men like a sovereign and not like an interloper or a valet.

I have no churlish objection to the circumnavigation of the globe for the purposes of art, of study, and benevolence, so that the man is first domesticated, or does not go abroad with the hope of finding somewhat greater than he knows. He who travels to be amused, or to get somewhat which he does not carry, travels away from himself, and grows old even in youth among old things. In Thebes, in

Palmyra, his will and mind have become old and dilapidated as they. He carries ruins to ruins.

Travelling is a fool's paradise. Our first journeys discover to us the indifference of places. At home I dream that at Naples, at Rome, I can be intoxicated with beauty and lose my sadness. I pack my trunk, embrace my friends, embark on the sea, and at last wake up in Naples, and there beside me is the stern fact, the sad self, unrelenting, identical, that I fled from. I seek the Vatican and the palaces. I affect to be intoxicated with sights and suggestions, but I am not intoxicated. My giant goes with me wherever I go.

3. But the rage of travelling is a symptom of a deeper unsoundness affecting the whole intellectual action. The intellect is vagabond, and our system of education fosters restlessness. Our minds travel when our bodies are forced to stay at home. We imitate; and what is imitation but the travelling of the mind? Our houses are built with foreign taste; our shelves are garnished with foreign ornaments; our opinions, our tastes, our faculties, lean, and follow the Past and the Distant. The soul created the arts wherever they have flourished. It was in his own mind that the artist sought his model. It was an application of his own thought to the thing to be done and the conditions to be observed. And why need we copy the Doric or the Gothic model? Beauty, convenience, grandeur of thought and quaint expression are as near to us as to any, and if the American artist will study with hope and love the precise thing to be done by him, considering the climate, the soil, the length of the day, the wants of the people, the habit and form of the government, he will create a house in which all these will find themselves fitted, and taste and sentiment will be satisfied also.

Insist on yourself; never imitate. Your own gift you can present every moment with the cumulative force of a whole life's cultivation; but of the adopted talent of another you have only an extemporaneous half possession. That which each can do best, none but his Maker can teach him. No man yet knows what it is, nor can, till that person has exhibited it. Where is the master who could have taught Shakspeare? Where is the master who could have instructed Franklin, or Washington, or Bacon, or Newton? Every great man is a unique. The Scipionism of Scipio is precisely that part he could not borrow. Shakspeare will never be made by the study of Shakspeare. Do that which is assigned you, and you cannot hope too much or dare too much. There is at this moment for you an utterance brave and grand as that of the colossal chisel of Phidias, or trowel of the Egyptians, or the pen of Moses or Dante, but different from all these. Not possibly will the soul, all rich, all eloquent, with thousand-cloven tongue, deign to repeat itself; but if you can hear what these patriarchs say, surely you can reply to them in the same pitch of voice; for the ear and the tongue are two organs of one nature. Abide in the simple and noble regions of thy life, obey thy heart, and thou shalt reproduce the Foreworld again.

4. As our Religion, our Education, our Art look abroad, so does our spirit of society. All men plume themselves on the improvement of society, and no man improves.

Society never advances. It recedes as fast on one side as it gains on the other. It undergoes continual changes; it is barbarous, it is civilized, it is christianized, it is rich, it is scientific; but this change is not amelioration. For every thing that is given something is taken. Society acquires new arts and loses old instincts. What a contrast between the well-clad, reading, writing, thinking American, with a watch, a pencil and a bill of exchange in his pocket, and the naked New Zealander, whose property is a club, a spear, a mat and an undivided twentieth of a shed to sleep under! But compare the health of the two men and you shall see that the white man has lost his aboriginal strength. If the traveller tell us truly, strike the savage with a broad-axe and in a day or two the flesh shall unite and heal as if you struck the blow into soft pitch, and the same blow shall send the white to his grave.

The civilized man has built a coach, but has lost the use of his feet. He is supported on crutches, but lacks so much support of muscle. He has a fine Geneva watch, but he fails of the skill to tell the hour by the sun. A Greenwich nautical almanac he has, and so being sure of the information when he wants it, the man in the street does not know a star in the sky. The solstice he does not observe; the equinox he knows as little; and the whole bright calendar of the year is without a dial in his mind. His note-books impair his memory; his libraries overload his wit; the insurance-office increases the number of accidents; and it may be a question whether machinery does not encumber; whether we have not lost by refinement some energy, by a Christianity, entrenched in establishments and forms, some vigor of wild virtue. For every Stoic was a Stoic; but in Christendom where is the Christian?

There is no more deviation in the moral standard than in the standard of height or bulk. No greater men are now than ever were. A singular equality may be observed between the great men of the first and of the last ages; nor can all the science, art, religion, and philosophy of the nineteenth century avail to educate greater men than Plutarch's heroes, three or four and twenty centuries ago. Not in time is the race progressive. Phocion, Socrates, Anaxagoras, Diogenes, are great men, but they leave no class. He who is really of their class will not be called by their name, but will be his own man, and in his turn the founder of a sect. The arts and inventions of each period are only its costume and do not invigorate men. The harm of the improved machinery may compensate its good. Hudson and Behring accomplished so much in their fishing-boats as to astonish Parry and Franklin, whose equipment exhausted the resources of science and art. Galileo, with an opera-glass, discovered a more splendid series of celestial phenomena than any one since. Columbus found the New World in an undecked boat. It is curious to see the periodical disuse and perishing of means and machinery which were introduced with loud laudation a few years or centuries before. The great genius returns to essential man. We reckoned the improvements of the art of war among the triumphs of science, and yet Napoleon conquered Europe by the bivouac, which consisted of falling back on naked valor and disencumbering it of all aids. The Emperor held it impossible to make a perfect army, says Las Casas, "without abolishing our arms, magazines, commissaries and carriages, until, in imitation of the Roman custom, the soldier should receive his supply of corn, grind it in his hand-mill and bake his bread himself."

Society is a wave. The wave moves onward, but the water of which it is composed does not. The same particle does not rise from the valley to the ridge. Its unity is only phenomenal. The persons who make up a nation to-day, next year die, and their experience dies with them.

And so the reliance on Property, including the reliance on governments which protect it, is the want of self-reliance. Men have looked away from themselves and at things so long that they have come to esteem the religious, learned and civil institutions as guards of property, and they deprecate assaults on these, because they feel them to be assaults on property. They measure their esteem of each other by what each has, and not by what each is. But a cultivated man becomes ashamed of his property, out of new respect for his nature. Especially he hates what he has if he see that it is accidental,—came to him by inheritance, or gift, or crime; then he feels that it is not having; it does not belong to him, has no root in him and merely lies there because no revolution or no robber takes it away. But that which a man is, does always by necessity acquire; and what the man acquires, is living property, which does not wait the beck of rulers, or mobs, or revolutions, or fire, or storm or bankruptcies, but perpetually renews itself wherever the man breathes. "Thy lot or portion of life," said the Caliph Ali, "is seeking after thee; therefore be at rest from seeking after it." Our dependence on these foreign goods leads us to our slavish respect for numbers. The political parties meet in numerous conventions; the greater the concourse and with each new uproar of announcement, The delegation from Essex! The Democrats from New Hampshire! The Whigs of Maine! the young patriot feels himself stronger than before by a new thousand of eyes and arms. In like manner the reformers summon conventions and vote and resolve in multitude. Not so, O friends! will the God deign to enter and inhabit you, but by a method precisely the reverse. It is only as a man puts off all foreign support and stands alone that I see him to be strong and to prevail. He is weaker by every recruit to his banner. Is not a man better than a town? Ask nothing of men, and, in the endless mutation, thou only firm column must presently appear the upholder of all that surrounds thee. He who knows that power is inborn, that he is weak because he has looked for good out of him and elsewhere, and, so perceiving, throws himself unhesitatingly on his thought, instantly rights himself, stands in the erect position, commands his limbs, works miracles; just as a man who stands on his feet is stronger than a man who stands on his head.

So use all that is called Fortune. Most men gamble with her, and gain all, and lose all, as her wheel rolls. But do thou leave as unlawful these winnings, and deal with Cause and Effect, the chancellors of God. In the Will work and acquire, and thou hast chained the wheel of Chance, and shall sit hereafter out of fear from her rotations. A political victory, a rise of rents, the recovery of your sick or the return of your absent friend, or some other favorable event raises your spirits, and you think good days are preparing for you. Do not believe it. Nothing can bring you peace but yourself. Nothing can bring you peace but the triumph of principles.

COMPENSATION

The wings of Time are black and white,
Pied with morning and with night.
Mountain tall and ocean deep
Trembling balance duly keep.
In changing moon, in tidal wave,
Glows the feud of Want and Have.
Gauge of more and less through space
Electric star and pencil plays.
The lonely Earth amid the balls
That hurry through the eternal halls,
A makeweight flying to the void,
Supplemental asteroid,
Or compensatory spark,
Shoots across the neutral Dark.

Man's the elm, and Wealth the vine,
Stanch and strong the tendrils twine:
Though the frail ringlets thee deceive,
None from its stock that vine can reave.
Fear not, then, thou child infirm,
There's no god dare wrong a worm.
Laurel crowns cleave to deserts
And power to him who power exerts;
Hast not thy share? On wingèd feet,
Lo! it rushes thee to meet;
And all that Nature made thy own,
Floating in air or pent in stone,
Will rive the hills and swim the sea
And, like thy shadow, follow thee.

Ever since I was a boy I have wished to write a discourse on Compensation; for it seemed to me when very young that on this subject life was ahead of theology and the people knew more than the preachers taught. The documents too from which the doctrine is to be drawn, charmed my fancy by their endless variety, and lay always before me, even in sleep; for they are the tools in our hands, the bread in our basket, the transactions of the street, the farm and the dwelling-house; greetings, relations, debts and credits, the influence of character, the nature and endowment of all men. It seemed to me also that in it might be shown men a ray of divinity, the present action of the soul of this world, clean from all vestige of tradition; and so the heart of man might be bathed by an inundation of eternal love, conversing with that which he knows was always and always must be, because it really is now. It appeared moreover that if this doctrine could be stated in terms with any resemblance to those bright intuitions in which this truth is sometimes revealed to us, it would be a star in many dark hours and crooked passages in our journey, that would not suffer us to lose our way.

I was lately confirmed in these desires by hearing a sermon at church. The preacher, a man esteemed for his orthodoxy, unfolded in the ordinary manner the doctrine of the Last Judgment. He assumed that judgment is not executed in this world; that the wicked are successful; that the good are miserable; and then urged from reason and from Scripture a compensation to be made to both parties in the next life. No offence appeared to be taken by the congregation at this doctrine. As far as I could observe when the meeting broke up they separated without remark on the sermon.

Yet what was the import of this teaching? What did the preacher mean by saying that the good are miserable in the present life? Was it that houses and lands, offices, wine, horses, dress, luxury, are had by unprincipled men, whilst the saints are poor and despised; and that a compensation is to be made to these last hereafter, by giving them the like gratifications another day,—bank-stock and doubloons, venison and champagne? This must be the compensation intended; for what else? Is it that they are to have leave to pray and praise? to love and serve men? Why, that they can do now. The legitimate inference the disciple would draw was,—'We are to have *such* a good time as the sinners have now;'—or, to push it to its extreme import,—'You sin now, we shall sin by and by; we would sin now, if we could; not being successful we expect our revenge to-morrow.'

The fallacy lay in the immense concession that the bad are successful; that justice is not done now. The blindness of the preacher consisted in deferring to the base estimate of the market of what constitutes a manly success, instead of confronting and convicting the world from the truth; announcing the presence of the soul; the omnipotence of the will; and so establishing the standard of good and ill, of success and falsehood.

I find a similar base tone in the popular religious works of the day and the same doctrines assumed by the literary men when occasionally they treat the related topics. I think that our popular theology has gained in decorum, and not in principle, over the superstitions it has displaced. But men are better than their theology. Their daily life gives it the lie. Every ingenuous and aspiring soul leaves the doctrine behind him in his own experience, and all men feel sometimes the falsehood which they cannot demonstrate. For men are wiser than they know. That which they hear in schools and pulpits without afterthought, if said in conversation would probably be questioned in silence. If a man dogmatize in a mixed company on Providence and the divine laws, he is answered by a silence which conveys well enough to an observer the dissatisfaction of the hearer, but his incapacity to make his own statement.

I shall attempt in this and the following chapter ["Spir-

itual Laws"] to record some facts that indicate the path of
the law of Compensation; happy beyond my expectation
if I shall truly draw the smallest arc of this circle.

Polarity, or action and reaction, we meet in every part
of nature; in darkness and light; in heat and cold; in the
ebb and flow of waters; in male and female; in the inspiration and expiration of plants and animals; in the equation
of quantity and quality in the fluids of the animal body; in
the systole and diastole of the heart; in the undulations of
fluids and of sound; in the centrifugal and centripetal
gravity; in electricity, galvanism, and chemical affinity.
Superinduce magnetism at one end of a needle, the opposite magnetism takes place at the other end. If the south
attracts, the north repels. To empty here, you must condense there. An inevitable dualism bisects nature, so that
each thing is a half, and suggests another thing to make it
whole; as, spirit, matter; man, woman; odd, even; subjective, objective; in, out; upper, under; motion, rest; yea,
nay.

Whilst the world is thus dual, so is every one of its
parts. The entire system of things gets represented in
every particle. There is somewhat that resembles the ebb
and flow of the sea, day and night, man and woman, in a
single needle of the pine, in a kernel of corn, in each individual of every animal tribe. The reaction, so grand in the
elements, is repeated within these small boundaries. For
example, in the animal kingdom the physiologist has
observed that no creatures are favorites, but a certain
compensation balances every gift and every defect. A sur-
plusage given to one part is paid out of a reduction from
another part of the same creature. If the head and neck are
enlarged, the trunk and extremities are cut short.

The theory of the mechanic forces is another example.
What we gain in power is lost in time, and the converse.
The periodic or compensating errors of the planets is another instance. The influences of climate and soil in political history is another. The cold climate invigorates. The

barren soil does not breed fevers, crocodiles, tigers or scorpions.

The same dualism underlies the nature and condition of man. Every excess causes a defect; every defect an excess. Every sweet hath its sour; every evil its good. Every faculty which is a receiver of pleasure has an equal penalty put on its abuse. It is to answer for its moderation with its life. For every grain of wit there is a grain of folly. For every thing you have missed, you have gained something else; and for every thing you gain, you lose something. If riches increase, they are increased that use them. If the gatherer gathers too much, Nature takes out of the man what she puts into his chest; swells the estate, but kills the owner. Nature hates monopolies and exceptions. The waves of the sea do not more speedily seek a level from their loftiest tossing than the varieties of condition tend to equalize themselves. There is always some levelling circumstance that puts down the overbearing, the strong, the rich, the fortunate, substantially on the same ground with all others. Is a man too strong and fierce for society and by temper and position a bad citizen,—a morose ruffian, with a dash of the pirate in him?—Nature sends him a troop of pretty sons and daughters who are getting along in the dame's classes at the village school, and love and fear for them smooths his grim scowl to courtesy. Thus she contrives to intenerate the granite and felspar, takes the boar out and puts the lamb in and keeps her balance true.

The farmer imagines power and place are fine things. But the President has paid dear for his White House. It has commonly cost him all his peace, and the best of his manly attributes. To preserve for a short time so conspicuous an appearance before the world, he is content to eat dust before the real masters who stand erect behind the throne. Or do men desire the more substantial and permanent grandeur of genius? Neither has this an immunity. He who by force of will or of thought is great and overlooks thousands, has the charges of that eminence. With every influx of light comes new danger. Has he light? he must bear witness to the light, and always outrun that sympathy which gives him such keen satisfaction, by his fidelity to new revelations of the incessant soul. He must hate father and mother, wife and child. Has he all that the world loves and admires and covets?—he must cast behind him their admiration and afflict them by faithfulness to his truth and become a byword and a hissing.

This law writes the laws of cities and nations. It is in vain to build or plot or combine against it. Things refuse to be mismanaged long. *Res nolunt diu male administrari.* Though no checks to a new evil appear, the checks exist and will appear. If the government is cruel, the governor's life is not safe. If you tax too high, the revenue will yield nothing. If you make the criminal code sanguinary, juries will not convict. If the law is too mild, private vengeance comes in. If the government is a terrific democracy, the pressure is resisted by an over-charge of energy in the citizen, and life glows with a fiercer flame. The true life and satisfactions of man seem to elude the utmost rigors or felicities of condition and to establish themselves with great indifferency under all varieties of circumstances. Under all governments the influence of character remains the same,—in Turkey and in New England about alike. Under the primeval despots of Egypt, history honestly confesses that man must have been as free as culture could make him.

These appearances indicate the fact that the universe is represented in every one of its particles. Every thing in nature contains all the powers of nature. Every thing is made of one hidden stuff; as the naturalist sees one type under every metamorphosis, and regards a horse as a running man, a fish as a swimming man, a bird as a flying man, a tree as a rooted man. Each new form repeats not only the main character of the type, but part for part all the details, all the aims, furtherances, hindrances, energies and whole system of every other. Every occupation, trade, art, transaction, is a compend of the world and a correlative of every other. Each one is an entire emblem of human life; of its good and ill, its trials, its enemies, its course and its end. And each one must somehow accommodate the whole man and recite all his destiny.

The world globes itself in a drop of dew. The microscope cannot find the animalcule which is less perfect for being little. Eyes, ears, taste, smell, motion, resistance, appetite, and organs of reproduction that take hold on eternity,—all find room to consist in the small creature. So do we put our life into every act. The true doctrine of omnipresence is that God reappears with all his parts in every moss and cobweb. The value of the universe contrives to throw itself into every point. If the good is there, so is the evil; if the affinity, so the repulsion; if the force, so the limitation.

Thus is the universe alive. All things are moral. That soul which within us is a sentiment, outside of us is a law. We feel its inspiration; but there in history we can see its fatal strength. "It is in the world, and the world was made by it." Justice is not postponed. A perfect equity adjusts its balance in all parts of life. Ἀεὶ γὰρ εὖ πίπτουσιν οἱ Διὸς κύβοι,—The dice of God are always loaded. The world looks like a multiplication-table, or a mathematical equation, which, turn it how you will, balances itself. Take what figure you will, its exact value, nor more nor less, still returns to you. Every secret is told, every crime is punished, every virtue rewarded, every wrong redressed, in silence and certainty. What we call retribution is the universal necessity by which the whole appears wherever a part appears. If you see smoke, there must be fire. If you see a hand or a limb, you know that the trunk to which it belongs is there behind.

Every act rewards itself, or in other words integrates itself, in a twofold manner; first in the thing, or in real nature; and secondly in the circumstance, or in apparent nature. Men call the circumstance the retribution. The causal retribution is in the thing and is seen by the soul. The retribution in the circumstance is seen by the understanding; it is inseparable from the thing, but is often spread over a long time and so does not become distinct until after many years. The specific stripes may follow late after the offence, but they follow because they accompany it. Crime and punishment grow out of one stem. Punishment is a fruit that unsuspected ripens within the flower of the pleasure which concealed it. Cause and effect, means and ends, seed and fruit, cannot be servered; for the effect already blooms in the cause, the end preëxists in the means, the fruit in the seed.

Whilst thus the world will be whole and refuses to be disparted, we seek to act partially, to sunder, to appropriate; for example,—to gratify the senses we sever the pleasure of the senses from the needs of the character. The ingenuity of man has always been dedicated to the solution of one problem,—how to detach the sensual sweet, the sensual strong, the sensual bright, etc., from the moral sweet, the moral deep, the moral fair; that is, again, to contrive to cut clean off this upper surface so thin as to leave it bottomless; to get a *one end*, without an *other end*. The soul says, 'Eat;' the body would feast. The soul says, 'The man and woman shall be one flesh and one soul;' the body would join the flesh only. The soul says, 'Have dominion over all things to the ends of virtue;' the body would have the power over things to its own ends.

The soul strives amain to live and work through all things. It would be the only fact. All things shall be added unto it,—power, pleasure, knowledge, beauty. The particular man aims to be somebody; to set up for himself; to truck and higgle for a private good; and, in particulars, to ride that he may ride; to dress that he may be dressed; to eat that he may eat; and to govern, that he may be seen. Men seek to be great; they would have offices, wealth, power, and fame. They think that to be great is to possess one side of nature,—the sweet, without the other side, the bitter.

This dividing and detaching is steadily counteracted. Up to this day it must be owned no projector has had the smallest success. The parted water reunites behind our hand. Pleasure is taken out of pleasant things, profit out of profitable things, power out of strong things, as soon as we seek to separate them from the whole. We can no more halve things and get the sensual good, by itself, than we can get an inside that shall have no outside, or a light without a shadow. "Drive out Nature with a fork, she comes running back."

Life invests itself with inevitable conditions, which the unwise seek to dodge, which one and another brags that he does not know, that they do not touch him;—but the brag is on his lips, the conditions are in his soul. If he escapes them in one part they attack him in another more vital part. If he has escaped them in form and in the appearance, it is because he has resisted his life and fled from himself, and the retribution is so much death. So signal is the failure of all attempts to make this separation of the good from the tax, that the experiment would not be tried,—since to try it is to be mad,—but for the circumstance that when the disease began in the will, of rebellion and separation, the intellect is at once infected, so that the man ceases to see God whole in each object, but is able to see the sensual allurement of an object and not see the sensual hurt; he sees the mermaid's head but not the dragon's tail and thinks he can cut off that which he would have from that which he would not have. "How secret art thou who dwellest in the highest heavens in silence, O thou only great God, sprinkling with an unwearied providence certain penal blindnesses upon such as have unbridled desires!"

The human soul is true to these facts in the painting of fable, of history, of law, of proverbs, of conversation. It finds a tongue in literature unawares. Thus the Greeks called Jupiter, Supreme Mind; but having traditionally ascribed to him many base actions, they involuntarily made amends to reason by tying up the hands of so bad a god. He is made as helpless as a king of England. Prometheus knows one secret which Jove must bargain for;

Minerva, another. He cannot get his own thunders; Minerva keeps the key of them:—

> "Of all the gods, I only know the keys
> That ope the solid doors within whose vaults
> His thunders sleep."

A plain confession of the in-working of the All and of its moral aim. The Indian mythology ends in the same ethics; and it would seem impossible for any fable to be invented and get any currency which was not moral. Aurora forgot to ask youth for her lover, and though Tithonus is immortal, he is old. Achilles is not quite invulnerable; the sacred waters did not wash the heel by which Thetis held him. Siegfried, in the Nibelungen, is not quite immortal, for a leaf fell on his back whilst he was bathing in the dragon's blood, and that spot which it covered is mortal. And so it must be. There is a crack in every thing God has made. It would seem there is always this vindictive circumstance stealing in at unawares even into the wild poesy in which the human fancy attempted to make bold holiday and to shake itself free of the old laws,—this back-stroke, this kick of the gun, certifying that the law is fatal; that in nature nothing can be given, all things are sold.

This is that ancient doctrine of Nemesis, who keeps watch in the universe and lets no offence go unchastised. The Furies, they said, are attendants on justice, and if the sun in heaven should transgress his path they would punish him. The poets related that stone walls and iron swords and leathern thongs had an occult sympathy with the wrongs of their owners; that the belt which Ajax gave Hector dragged the Trojan hero over the field at the wheels of the car of Achilles, and the sword which Hector gave Ajax was that on whose point Ajax fell. They recorded that when the Thasians erected a statue to Theagenes, a victor in the games, one of his rivals went to it by night and endeavored to throw it down by repeated blows, until at last he moved it from its pedestal and was crushed to death beneath its fall.

This voice of fable has in it somewhat divine. It came from thought above the will of the writer. That is the best part of each writer which has nothing private in it; that which he does not know; that which flowed out of his constitution and not from his too active invention; that which in the study of a single artist you might not easily find, but in the study of many you would abstract as the spirit of them all. Phidias it is not, but the work of man in that early Hellenic world that I would know. The name and circumstance of Phidias, however convenient for history, embarrass when we come to the highest criticism. We are to see that which man was tending to do in a given period, and was hindered, or, if you will, modified in doing, by the interfering volitions of Phidias, of Dante, of Shakspeare, the organ whereby man at the moment wrought.

Still more striking is the expression of this fact in the proverbs of all nations, which are always the literature of reason, or the statements of an absolute truth without qualification. Proverbs, like the sacred books of each nation, are the sanctuary of the intuitions. That which the droning world, chained to appearances, will not allow the realist to say in his own words, it will suffer him to say in proverbs without contradiction. And this law of laws, which the pulpit, the senate and the college deny, is hourly preached in all markets and workshops by flights of proverbs, whose teaching is as true and as omnipresent as that of birds and flies.

All things are double, one against another.—Tit for tat; an eye for an eye; a tooth for a tooth; blood for blood; measure for measure; love for love.—Give, and it shall be given you.—He that watereth shall be watered himself.—What will you have? quoth God; pay for it and take it.—Nothing venture, nothing have.—Thou shalt be paid exactly for what thou hast done, no more, no less.—Who doth not work shall not eat.—Harm watch, harm catch.—

Curses always recoil on the head of him who imprecates them.—If you put a chain around the neck of a slave, the other end fastens itself around your own.—Bad counsel confounds the adviser.—The Devil is an ass.

It is thus written, because it is thus in life. Our action is overmastered and characterized above our will by the law of nature. We aim at a petty end quite aside from the public good, but our act arranges itself by irresistible magnetism in a line with the poles of the world.

A man cannot speak but he judges himself. With his will or against his will he draws his portrait to the eye of his companions by every word. Every opinion reacts on him who utters it. It is a thread-ball thrown at a mark, but the other end remains in the thrower's bag. Or rather it is a harpoon hurled at the whale, unwinding, as it flies, a coil of cord in the boat, and, if the harpoon is not good, or not well thrown, it will go nigh to cut the steersman in twain or to sink the boat.

You cannot do wrong without suffering wrong. "No man had ever a point of pride that was not injurious to him," said Burke. The exclusive in fashionable life does not see that he excludes himself from enjoyment, in the attempt to appropriate it. The exclusionist in religion does not see that he shuts the door of heaven on himself in striving to shut out others. Treat men as pawns and nine-pins and you shall suffer as well as they. If you leave out their heart, you shall lose your own. The senses would make things of all persons; of women, of children, of the poor. The vulgar proverb, "I will get it from his purse or get it from his skin," is sound philosophy.

All infractions of love and equity in our social relations are speedily punished. They are punished by fear. Whilst I stand in simple relations to my fellow-man, I have no displeasure in meeting him. We meet as water meets water, or as two currents of air mix, with perfect diffusion and interpenetration of nature. But as soon as there is any departure from simplicity and attempt at halfness, or good for me that is not good for him, my neighbor feels the wrong; he shrinks from me as far as I have shrunk from him; his eyes no longer seek mine; there is war between us; there is hate in him and fear in me.

All the old abuses in society, universal and particular, all unjust accumulations of property and power, are avenged in the same manner. Fear is an instructor of great sagacity and the herald of all revolutions. One thing he teaches, that there is rottenness where he appears. He is a carrion crow, and though you see not well what he hovers for, there is death somewhere. Our property is timid, our laws are timid, our cultivated classes are timid. Fear for ages has boded and mowed and gibbered over government and property. That obscene bird is not there for nothing. He indicates great wrongs which must be revised.

Of the like nature is that expectation of change which instantly follows the suspension of our voluntary activity. The terror of cloudless noon, the emerald of Polycrates, the awe of prosperity, the instinct which leads every generous soul to impose on itself tasks of a noble asceticism and vicarious virtue, are the tremblings of the balance of justice through the heart and mind of man.

Experienced men of the world know very well that it is best to pay scot and lot as they go along, and that a man often pays dear for a small frugality. The borrower runs in his own debt. Has a man gained any thing who has received a hundred favors and rendered none? Has he gained by borrowing, through indolence or cunning, his neighbor's wares, or horses, or money? There arises on the deed the instant acknowledgment of benefit on the one part and of debt on the other; that is, of superiority and inferiority. The transaction remains in the memory of himself and his neighbor; and every new transaction alters according to its nature their relation to each other. He may soon come to see that he had better have broken his own bones than to have ridden in his neighbor's coach, and that "the highest price he can pay for a thing is to ask for it."

A wise man will extend this lesson to all parts of life,

and know that it is the part of prudence to face every claimant and pay every just demand on your time, your talents, or your heart. Always pay; for first or last you must pay your entire debt. Persons and events may stand for a time between you and justice, but it is only a postponement. You must pay at last your own debt. If you are wise you will dread a prosperity which only loads you with more. Benefit is the end of nature. But for every benefit which you receive, a tax is levied. He is great who confers the most benefits. He is base,—and that is the one base thing in the universe,—to receive favors and render none. In the order of nature we cannot render benefits to those from whom we receive them, or only seldom. But the benefit we receive must be rendered again, line for line, deed for deed, cent for cent, to somebody. Beware of too much good staying in your hand. It will fast corrupt and worm worms. Pay it away quickly in some sort.

Labor is watched over by the same pitiless laws. Cheapest, say the prudent, is the dearest labor. What we buy in a broom, a mat, a wagon, a knife, is some application of good sense to a common want. It is best to pay in your land a skilful gardener, or to buy good sense applied to gardening; in your sailor, good sense applied to navigation; in the house, good sense applied to cooking, sewing, serving; in your agent, good sense applied to accounts and affairs. So do you multiply your presence, or spread yourself throughout your estate. But because of the dual constitution of things, in labor as in life there can be no cheating. The thief steals from himself. The swindler swindles himself. For the real price of labor is knowledge and virtue, whereof wealth and credit are signs. These signs, like paper money, may be counterfeited or stolen, but that which they represent, namely, knowledge and virtue, cannot be counterfeited or stolen. These ends of labor cannot be answered but by real exertions of the mind, and in obedience to pure motives. The cheat, the defaulter, the gambler, cannot extort the knowledge of material and moral nature which his honest care and pains yield to the operative. The law of nature is, Do the thing, and you shall have the power; but they who do not the thing have not the power.

Human labor, through all its forms, from the sharpening of a stake to the construction of a city or an epic, is one immense illustration of the perfect compensation of the universe. The absolute balance of Give and Take, the doctrine that every thing has its price,—and if that price is not paid, not that thing but something else is obtained, and that it is impossible to get anything without its price,—is not less sublime in the columns of a ledger than in the budgets of states, in the laws of light and darkness, in all the action and reaction of nature. I cannot doubt that the high laws which each man sees implicated in those processes with which he is conversant, the stern ethics which sparkle on his chisel-edge, which are measured out by his plumb and foot-rule, which stand as manifest in the footing of the shop-bill as in the history of a state,—do recommend to him his trade, and though seldom named, exalt his business to his imagination.

The league between virtue and nature engages all things to assume a hostile front to vice. The beautiful laws and substances of the world persecute and whip the traitor. He finds that things are arranged for truth and benefit, but there is no den in the wide world to hide a rogue. Commit a crime, and the earth is made of glass. Commit a crime, and it seems as if a coat of snow fell on the ground, such as reveals in the woods the track of every partridge and fox and squirrel and mole. You cannot recall the spoken word, you cannot wipe out the foot-track, you cannot draw up the ladder, so as to leave no inlet or clew. Some damning circumstance always transpires. The laws and substances of nature,—water, snow, wind, gravitation,—become penalties to the thief.

On the other hand the law holds with equal sureness for all right action. Love, and you shall be loved. All love is mathematically just, as much as the two sides of an algebraic equation. The good man has absolute good, which

like fire turns every thing to its own nature, so that you
cannot do him any harm; but as the royal armies sent
against Napoleon, when he approached cast down their
colors and from enemies became friends, so disasters of all
kinds, as sickness, offence, poverty, prove benefactors:—

>   "Winds blow and waters roll
>   Strength to the brave and power and deity,
>   Yet in themselves are nothing."

The good are befriended even by weakness and defect.
As no man had ever a point of pride that was not injurious
to him, so no man had ever a defect that was not somewhere made useful to him. The stag in the fable admired
his horns and blamed his feet, but when the hunter
came, his feet saved him, and afterwards, caught in the
thicket, his horns destroyed him. Every man in his lifetime needs to thank his faults. As no man thoroughly understands a truth until he has contended against it, so no
man has a thorough acquaintance with the hindrances or
talents of men until he has suffered from the one and seen
the triumph of the other over his own want of the same.
Has he a defect of temper that unfits him to live in society? Thereby he is driven to entertain himself alone and
acquire habits of self-help; and thus, like the wounded
oyster, he mends his shell with pearl.

Our strength grows out of our weakness. The indignation which arms itself with secret forces does not awaken
until we are pricked and stung and sorely assailed. A great
man is always willing to be little. Whilst he sits on the
cushion of advantages, he goes to sleep. When he is
pushed, tormented, defeated, he has a chance to learn
something; he has been put on his wits, on his manhood;
he has gained facts; learns his ignorance; is cured of the
insanity of conceit; has got moderation and real skill. The
wise man throws himself on the side of his assailants. It is
more his interest than it is theirs to find his weak point.
The wound cicatrizes and falls off from him like a dead

skin, and when they would triumph, lo! he has passed on invulnerable. Blame is safer than praise. I hate to be defended in a newspaper. As long as all that is said is said against me, I feel a certain assurance of success. But as soon as honeyed words of praise are spoken for me I feel as one that lies unprotected before his enemies. In general, every evil to which we do not succumb is a benefactor. As the Sandwich Islander believes that the strength and valor of the enemy he kills passes into himself, so we gain the strength of the temptation we resist.

The same guards which protect us from disaster, defect and enmity, defend us, if we will, from selfishness and fraud. Bolts and bars are not the best of our institutions, nor is shrewdness in trade a mark of wisdom. Men suffer all their life long under the foolish superstition that they can be cheated. But it is as impossible for a man to be cheated by any one but himself, as for a thing to be and not to be at the same time. There is a third silent party to all our bargains. The nature and soul of things takes on itself the guaranty of the fulfilment of every contract, so that honest service cannot come to loss. If you serve an ungrateful master, serve him the more. Put God in your debt. Every stroke shall be repaid. The longer the payment is withholden, the better for you; for compound interest on compound interest is the rate and usage of this exchequer.

The history of persecution is a history of endeavors to cheat nature, to make water run up hill, to twist a rope of sand. It makes no difference whether the actors be many or one, a tyrant or a mob. A mob is a society of bodies voluntarily bereaving themselves of reason and traversing its work. The mob is man voluntarily descending to the nature of the beast. Its fit hour of activity is night. Its actions are insane, like its whole constitution. It persecutes a principle; it would whip a right; it would tar and feather justice, by inflicting fire and outrage upon the houses and persons of those who have these. It resembles the prank of boys, who run with fire-engines to put out the ruddy au-

rora streaming to the stars. The inviolate spirit turns their
spite against the wrongdoers. The martyr cannot be dishonored. Every lash inflicted is a tongue of fame; every
prison a more illustrious abode; every burned book or
house enlightens the world; every suppressed or expunged
word reverberates through the earth from side to side.
Hours of sanity and consideration are always arriving to
communities, as to individuals, when the truth is seen and
the martyrs are justified.

Thus do all things preach the indifferency of circumstances. The man is all. Every thing has two sides, a good
and an evil. Every advantage has its tax. I learn to be content. But the doctrine of compensation is not the doctrine
of indifferency. The thoughtless say, on hearing these representations,—What boots it to do well? there is one event
to good and evil; if I gain any good I must pay for it; if I
lose any good I gain some other; all actions are indifferent.

There is a deeper fact in the soul than compensation, to
wit, its own nature. The soul is not a compensation, but a
life. The soul *is*. Under all this running sea of circumstance, whose waters ebb and flow with perfect balance,
lies the aboriginal abyss of real Being. Essence, or God, is
not a relation or a part, but the whole. Being is the vast affirmative, excluding negation, self-balanced, and swallow-
ing up all relations, parts and times within itself. Nature,
truth, virtue, are the influx from thence. Vice is the absence or departure of the same. Nothing, Falsehood, may
indeed stand as the great Night or shade on which as a
background the living universe paints itself forth, but no
fact is begotten by it; it cannot work, for it is not. It cannot
work any good; it cannot work any harm. It is harm inasmuch as it is worse not to be than to be.

We feel defrauded of the retribution due to evil acts,
because the criminal adheres to his vice and contumacy
and does not come to a crisis or judgment anywhere in visible nature. There is no stunning confutation of his nonsense before men and angels. Has he therefore outwitted

the law? Inasmuch as he carries the malignity and the lie with him he so far deceases from nature. In some manner there will be a demonstration of the wrong to the understanding also; but, should we not see it, this deadly deduction makes square the eternal account.

Neither can it be said, on the other hand, that the gain of rectitude must be bought by any loss. There is no penalty to virtue; no penalty to wisdom; they are proper additions of being. In a virtuous action I properly *am;* in a virtuous act I add to the world; I plant into deserts conquered from Chaos and Nothing and see the darkness receding on the limits of the horizon. There can be no excess to love, none to knowledge, none to beauty, when these attributes are considered in the purest sense. The soul refuses limits, and always affirms an Optimism, never a Pessimism.

His life is a progress, and not a station. His instinct is trust. Our instinct uses "more" and "less" in application to man, of the *presence of the soul,* and not of its absence; the brave man is greater than the coward; the true, the benevolent, the wise, is more a man and not less, than the fool and knave. There is no tax on the good of virtue, for that is the incoming of God himself, or absolute existence, without any comparative. Material good has its tax, and if it came without desert or sweat, has no root in me, and the next wind will blow it away. But all the good of nature is the soul's, and may be had if paid for in nature's lawful coin, that is, by labor which the heart and the head allow. I no longer wish to meet a good I do not earn, for example to find a pot of buried gold, knowing that it brings with it new burdens. I do not wish more external goods,—neither possessions, nor honors, nor powers, nor persons. The gain is apparent; the tax is certain. But there is no tax on the knowledge that the compensation exists and that it is not desirable to dig up treasure. Herein I rejoice with a serene eternal peace. I contract the boundaries of possible mischief. I learn the wisdom of St. Bernard,—"Nothing

can work me damage except myself; the harm that I sustain I carry about with me, and never am a real sufferer but by my own fault."

In the nature of the soul is the compensation for the inequalities of condition. The radical tragedy of nature seems to be the distinction of More and Less. How can Less not feel the pain; how not feel indignation or malevolence towards More? Look at those who have less faculty, and one feels sad and knows not well what to make of it. He almost shuns their eye; he fears they will upbraid God. What should they do? It seems a great injustice. But see the facts nearly and these mountainous inequalities vanish. Love reduces them as the sun melts the iceberg in the sea. The heart and soul of all men being one, this bitterness of *His* and *Mine* ceases. His is mine. I am my brother and my brother is me. If I feel overshadowed and outdone by great neighbors, I can yet love; I can still receive; and he that loveth maketh his own the grandeur he loves. Thereby I make the discovery that my brother is my guardian, acting for me with the friendliest designs, and the estate I so admired and envied is my own. It is the nature of the soul to appropriate all things. Jesus and Shakspeare are fragments of the soul, and by love I conquer and incorporate them in my own conscious domain. His virtue,—is not that mine? His wit,—if it cannot be made mine, it is not wit.

Such also is the natural history of calamity. The changes which break up at short intervals the prosperity of men are advertisements of a nature whose law is growth. Every soul is by this intrinsic necessity quitting its whole system of things, its friends and home and laws and faith, as the shell-fish crawls out of its beautiful but stony case, because it no longer admits of its growth, and slowly forms a new house. In proportion to the vigor of the individual these revolutions are frequent, until in some happier mind they are incessant and all worldly relations hang very loosely about him, becoming as it were a transparent fluid membrane through which the living form is

seen, and not, as in most men, an indurated heterogeneous fabric of many dates and of no settled character, in which the man is imprisoned. Then there can be enlargement, and the man of to-day scarcely recognizes the man of yesterday. And such should be the outward biography of man in time, a putting off of dead circumstances day by day, as he renews his raiment day by day. But to us, in our lapsed estate, resting, not advancing, resisting, not coöperating with the divine expansion, this growth comes by shocks.

We cannot part with our friends. We cannot let our angels go. We do not see that they only go out that archangels may come in. We are idolaters of the old. We do not believe in the riches of the soul, in its proper eternity and omnipresence. We do not believe there is any force in to-day to rival or recreate that beautiful yesterday. We linger in the ruins of the old tent where once we had bread and shelter and organs, nor believe that the spirit can feed, cover, and nerve us again. We cannot again find aught so dear, so sweet, so graceful. But we sit and weep in vain. The voice of the Almighty saith, 'Up and onward for evermore!' We cannot stay amid the ruins. Neither will we rely on the new; and so we walk ever with reverted eyes, like those monsters who look backwards.

And yet the compensations of calamity are made apparent to the understanding also, after long intervals of time. A fever, a mutilation, a cruel disappointment, a loss of wealth, a loss of friends, seems at the moment unpaid loss, and unpayable. But the sure years reveal the deep remedial force that underlies all facts. The death of a dear friend, wife, brother, lover, which seemed nothing but privation, somewhat later assumes the aspect of a guide or genius; for it commonly operates revolutions in our way of life, terminates an epoch of infancy or of youth which was waiting to be closed, breaks up a wonted occupation, or a household, or style of living, and allows the formation of new ones more friendly to the growth of character. It permits or constrains the formation of new acquaintances and

the reception of new influences that prove of the first importance to the next years; and the man or woman who
would have remained a sunny garden-flower, with no
room for its roots and too much sunshine for its head, by
the falling of the walls and the neglect of the gardener is
made the banian of the forest, yielding shade and fruit to
wide neighborhoods of men.

SPIRITUAL LAWS

The living Heaven thy prayers respect,
House at once and architect,
Quarrying man's rejected hours,
Builds there with eternal towers;
Sole and self-commanded works,
Fears not undermining days,
Grows by decays,
And, by the famous might that lurks
In reaction and recoil,
Makes flame to freeze and ice to boil;
Forging, through swart arms of Offence,
The silver seat of Innocence.

When the act of reflection takes place in the mind, when
we look at ourselves in the light of thought, we discover
that our life is embosomed in beauty. Behind us, as we go,
all things assume pleasing forms, as clouds do far off. Not
only things familiar and stale, but even the tragic and terrible are comely as they take their place in the pictures of
memory. The river-bank, the weed at the water-side, the
old house, the foolish person, however neglected in the
passing, have a grace in the past. Even the corpse that has
lain in the chambers has added a solemn ornament to the
house. The soul will not know either deformity or pain. If
in the hours of clear reason we should speak the severest
truth, we should say that we had never made a sacrifice. In
these hours the mind seems so great that nothing can be
taken from us that seems much. All loss, all pain, is partic-

ular; the universe remains to the heart unhurt. Neither vexations nor calamities abate our trust. No man ever stated his griefs as lightly as he might. Allow for exaggeration in the most patient and sorely ridden hack that ever was driven. For it is only the finite that has wrought and suffered; the infinite lies stretched in smiling repose.

The intellectual life may be kept clean and healthful if man will live the life of nature and not import into his mind difficulties which are none of his. No man need be perplexed in his speculations. Let him do and say what strictly belongs to him, and though very ignorant of books, his nature shall not yield him any intellectual obstructions and doubts. Our young people are diseased with the theological problems of original sin, origin of evil, predestination and the like. These never presented a practical difficulty to any man,—never darkened across any man's road who did not go out of his way to seek them. These are the soul's mumps and measles and whooping-coughs, and those who have not caught them cannot describe their health or prescribe the cure. A simple mind will not know these enemies. It is quite another thing that he should be able to give account of his faith and expound to another the theory of his self-union and freedom. This requires rare gifts. Yet without this self-knowledge there may be a sylvan strength and integrity in that which he is. "A few strong instincts and a few plain rules" suffice us.

My will never gave the images in my mind the rank they now take. The regular course of studies, the years of academical and professional education have not yielded me better facts than some idle books under the bench at the Latin School. What we do not call education is more precious than that which we call so. We form no guess, at the time of receiving a thought, of its comparative value. And education often wastes its effort in attempts to thwart and balk this natural magnetism, which is sure to select what belongs to it.

In like manner our moral nature is vitiated by any interference of our will. People represent virtue as a struggle, and take to themselves great airs upon their attainments, and the question is everywhere vexed when a noble nature is commended, whether the man is not better who strives with temptation. But there is no merit in the matter. Either God is there or he is not there. We love characters in proportion as they are impulsive and spontaneous. The less a man thinks or knows about his virtues the better we like him. Timoleon's victories are the best victories, which ran and flowed like Homer's verses, Plutarch said. When we see a soul whose acts are all regal, graceful and pleasant as roses, we must thank God that such things can be and are, and not turn sourly on the angel and say 'Crump is a better man with his grunting resistance to all his native devils.'

Not less conspicuous is the preponderance of nature over will in all practical life. There is less intention in history than we ascribe to it. We impute deep-laid far-sighted plans to Cæsar and Napoleon; but the best of their power was in nature, not in them. Men of an extraordinary success, in their honest moments, have always sung 'Not unto us, not unto us.' According to the faith of their times they have built altars to Fortune, or to Destiny, or to St. Julian. Their success lay in their parallelism to the course of thought, which found in them an unobstructed channel; and the wonders of which they were the visible conductors seemed to the eye their deed. Did the wires generate the galvanism? It is even true that there was less in them on which they could reflect than in another; as the virtue of a pipe is to be smooth and hollow. That which externally seemed will and immovableness was willingness and self-annihilation. Could Shakspeare give a theory of Shakspeare? Could ever a man of prodigious mathematical genius convey to others any insight into his methods? If he could communicate that secret it would instantly lose its exaggerated value, blending with the daylight and the vital energy the power to stand and to go.

The lesson is forcibly taught by these observations that our life might be much easier and simpler than we make it;

that the world might be a happier place than it is; that there is no need of struggles, convulsions, and despairs, of the wringing of the hands and the gnashing of the teeth; that we miscreate our own evils. We interfere with the optimism of nature; for whenever we get this vantage-ground of the past, or of a wiser mind in the present, we are able to discern that we are begirt with laws which execute themselves.

The face of external nature teaches the same lesson. Nature will not have us fret and fume. She does not like our benevolence or our learning much better than she likes our frauds and wars. When we come out of the caucus, or the bank, or the Abolition-convention, or the Temperance-meeting, or the Transcendental club into the fields and woods, she says to us, 'So hot? my little Sir.'

We are full of mechanical actions. We must needs intermeddle and have things in our own way, until the sacrifices and virtues of society are odious. Love should make joy; but our benevolence is unhappy. Our Sunday-schools and churches and pauper-societies are yokes to the neck. We pain ourselves to please nobody. There are natural ways of arriving at the same ends at which these aim, but do not arrive. Why should all virtue work in one and the same way? Why should all give dollars? It is very inconvenient to us country folk, and we do not think any good will come of it. We have not dollars, merchants have; let them give them. Farmers will give corn; poets will sing; women will sew; laborers will lend a hand; the children will bring flowers. And why drag this dead weight of a Sunday-school over the whole Christendom? It is natural and beautiful that childhood should inquire and maturity should teach; but it is time enough to answer questions when they are asked. Do not shut up the young people against their will in a pew and force the children to ask them questions for an hour against their will.

If we look wider, things are all alike; laws and letters and creeds and modes of living seem a travesty of truth.

Our society is encumbered by ponderous machinery, which resembles the endless aqueducts which the Romans built over hill and dale and which are superseded by the discovery of the law that water rises to the level of its source. It is a Chinese wall which any nimble Tartar can leap over. It is a standing army, not so good as a peace. It is a graduated, titled, richly appointed empire, quite superfluous when town-meetings are found to answer just as well.

Let us draw a lesson from nature, which always works by short ways. When the fruit is ripe, it falls. When the fruit is despatched, the leaf falls. The circuit of the waters is mere falling. The walking of man and all animals is a falling forward. All our manual labor and works of strength, as prying, splitting, digging, rowing and so forth, are done by dint of continual falling, and the globe, earth, moon, comet, sun, star, fall for ever and ever.

The simplicity of the universe is very different from the simplicity of a machine. He who sees moral nature out and out and thoroughly knows how knowledge is acquired and character formed, is a pedant. The simplicity of nature is not that which may easily be read, but is inexhaustible. The last analysis can no wise be made. We judge of a man's wisdom by his hope, knowing that the perception of the inexhaustibleness of nature is an immortal youth. The wild fertility of nature is felt in comparing our rigid names and reputations with our fluid consciousness. We pass in the world for sects and schools, for erudition and piety, and we are all the time jejune babes. One sees very well how Pyrrhonism grew up. Every man sees that he is that middle point whereof every thing may be affirmed and denied with equal reason. He is old, he is young, he is very wise, he is altogether ignorant. He hears and feels what you say of the seraphim, and of the tin-peddler. There is no permanent wise man except in the figment of the Stoics. We side with the hero, as we read or paint, against the coward and the robber; but we have been ourselves that coward and robber, and shall be again,—not in the low circumstance, but in comparison with the grandeurs possible to the soul.

A little consideration of what takes place around us every day would show us that a higher law than that of our will regulates events; that our painful labors are unnecessary and fruitless; that only in our easy, simple, spontaneous action are we strong, and by contenting ourselves with obedience we become divine. Belief and love,—a believing love will relieve us of a vast load of care. O my brothers, God exists. There is a soul at the centre of nature and over the will of every man, so that none of us can wrong the universe. It has so infused its strong enchantment into nature that we prosper when we accept its advice, and when we struggle to wound its creatures our hands are glued to our sides, or they beat our own breasts. The whole course of things goes to teach us faith. We need only obey. There is guidance for each of us, and by lowly listening we shall hear the right word. Why need you choose so painfully your place and occupation and associates and modes of action and of entertainment? Certainly there is a possible right for you that precludes the need of balance and wilful election. For you there is a reality, a fit place and congenial duties. Place yourself in the middle of the stream of power and wisdom which animates all whom it floats, and you are without effort impelled to truth, to right and a perfect contentment. Then you put all gainsayers in the wrong. Then you are the world, the measure of right, of truth, of beauty. If we would not be mar-plots with our miserable interferences, the work, the society, letters, arts, science, religion of men would go on far better than now, and the heaven predicted from the beginning of the world, and still predicted from the bottom of the heart, would organize itself, as do now the rose and the air and the sun.

I say, *do not choose;* but that is a figure of speech by which I would distinguish what is commonly called *choice* among men, and which is a partial act, the choice of the hands, of the eyes, of the appetites, and not a whole act of the man. But that which I call right or goodness, is the choice of my constitution; and that which I call heaven, and inwardly aspire after, is the state or circumstance desirable to my constitution; and the action which I in all my years tend to do, is the work for my faculties. We must hold a man amenable to reason for the choice of his daily craft or profession. It is not an excuse any longer for his deeds that they are the custom of his trade. What business has he with an evil trade? Has he not a *calling* in his character?

Each man has his own vocation. The talent is the call. There is one direction in which all space is open to him. He has faculties silently inviting him thither to endless exertion. He is like a ship in a river; he runs against obstructions on every side but one, on that side all obstruction is taken away and he sweeps serenely over a deepening channel into an infinite sea. This talent and this call depend on his organization, or the mode in which the general soul incarnates itself in him. He inclines to do something which is easy to him and good when it is done, but which no other man can do. He has no rival. For the more truly he consults his own powers, the more difference will his work exhibit from the work of any other. His ambition is exactly proportioned to his powers. The height of the pinnacle is determined by the breadth of the base. Every man has this call of the power to do somewhat unique, and no man has any other call. The pretence that he has another call, a summons by name and personal election and outward "signs that mark him extraordinary and not in the roll of common men," is fanaticism, and betrays obtuseness to perceive that there is one mind in all the individuals, and no respect of persons therein.

By doing his work he makes the need felt which he can supply, and creates the taste by which he is enjoyed. By doing his own work he unfolds himself. It is the vice of our public speaking that it has not abandonment. Somewhere, not only every orator but every man should let out

all the length of all the reins; should find or make a frank
and hearty expression of what force and meaning is in
him. The common experience is that the man fits himself
as well as he can to the customary details of that work or
trade he falls into, and tends it as a dog turns a spit. Then
is he a part of the machine he moves; the man is lost. Until
he can manage to communicate himself to others in his
full stature and proportion, he does not yet find his vocation. He must find in that an outlet for his character, so
that he may justify his work to their eyes. If the labor is
mean, let him by his thinking and character make it liberal. Whatever he knows and thinks, whatever in his apprehension is worth doing, that let him communicate, or
men will never know and honor him aright. Foolish,
whenever you take the meanness and formality of that
thing you do, instead of converting it into the obedient
spiracle of your character and aims.

We like only such actions as have already long had the
praise of men, and do not perceive that any thing man can
do may be divinely done. We think greatness entailed or
organized in some places or duties, in certain offices or occasions, and do not see that Paganini can extract rapture
from a catgut, and Eulenstein from a jews-harp, and a
nimble-fingered lad out of shreds of paper with his scis-
sors, and Landseer out of swine, and the hero out of the
pitiful habitation and company in which he was hidden.
What we call obscure condition or vulgar society is that
condition and society whose poetry is not yet written, but
which you shall presently make as enviable and renowned
as any. In our estimates let us take a lesson from kings.
The parts of hospitality, the connection of families, the
impressiveness of death, and a thousand other things, royalty makes its own estimate of, and a royal mind will. To
make habitually a new estimate,—that is elevation.

What a man does, that he has. What has he to do with
hope or fear? In himself is his might. Let him regard no
good as solid but that which is in his nature and which
must grow out of him as long as he exists. The goods of

fortune may come and go like summer leaves; let him scatter them on every wind as the momentary signs of his infinite productiveness.

He may have his own. A man's genius, the quality that differences him from every other, the susceptibility to one class of influences, the selection of what is fit for him, the rejection of what is unfit, determines for him the character of the universe. A man is a method, a progressive arrangement; a selecting principle, gathering his like to him wherever he goes. He takes only his own out of the multiplicity that sweeps and circles round him. He is like one of those booms which are set out from the shore on rivers to catch drift-wood, or like the loadstone amongst splinters of steel. Those facts, words, persons, which dwell in his memory without his being able to say why, remain because they have a relation to him not less real for being as yet unapprehended. They are symbols of value to him as they can interpret parts of his consciousness which he would vainly seek words for in the conventional images of books and other minds. What attracts my attention shall have it, as I will go to the man who knocks at my door, whilst a thousand persons as worthy go by it, to whom I give no regard. It is enough that these particulars speak to me. A few anecdotes, a few traits of character, manners, face, a few incidents, have an emphasis in your memory out of all proportion to their apparent significance if you measure them by the ordinary standards. They relate to your gift. Let them have their weight, and do not reject them and cast about for illustration and facts more usual in literature. What your heart thinks great, is great. The soul's emphasis is always right.

Over all things that are agreeable to his nature and genius the man has the highest right. Everywhere he may take what belongs to his spiritual estate, nor can he take anything else though all doors were open, nor can all the force of men hinder him from taking so much. It is vain to attempt to keep a secret from one who has a right to know it. It will tell itself. That mood into which a friend can

bring us is his dominion over us. To the thoughts of that
state of mind he has a right. All the secrets of that state of
mind he can compel. This is a law which statesmen use in
practice. All the terrors of the French Republic, which
held Austria in awe, were unable to command her diplo-
macy. But Napoleon sent to Vienna M. de Narbonne, one
of the old noblesse, with the morals, manners and name of
that interest, saying that it was indispensable to send to
the old aristocracy of Europe men of the same connection,
which in fact constitutes a sort of free-masonry. M. de
Narbonne in less than a fortnight penetrated all the secrets of the imperial cabinet.

Nothing seems so easy as to speak and to be understood. Yet a man may come to find *that* the strongest of
defences and of ties,—that he has been understood; and he
who has received an opinion may come to find it the most
inconvenient of bonds.

If a teacher have any opinion which he wishes to conceal, his pupils will become as fully indoctrinated into that
as into any which he publishes. If you pour water into a
vessel twisted into coils and angles, it is vain to say, I will
pour it only into this or that;—it will find its level in all.
Men feel and act the consequences of your doctrine without being able to show how they follow. Show us an arc of
the curve, and a good mathematician will find out the
whole figure. We are always reasoning from the seen to
the unseen. Hence the perfect intelligence that subsists
between wise men of remote ages. A man cannot bury his
meanings so deep in his book but time and like-minded
men will find them. Plato had a secret doctrine, had he?
What secret can he conceal from the eyes of Bacon? of
Montaigne? of Kant? Therefore Aristotle said of his
works, "They are published and not published."

No man can learn what he has not preparation for
learning, however near to his eyes is the object. A chemist
may tell his most precious secrets to a carpenter, and he
shall be never the wiser,—the secrets he would not utter
to a chemist for an estate. God screens us evermore from

premature ideas. Our eyes are holden that we cannot see things that stare us in the face, until the hour arrives when the mind is ripened; then we behold them, and the time when we saw them not is like a dream.

Not in nature but in man is all the beauty and worth he sees. The world is very empty, and is indebted to this gilding, exalting soul for all its pride. "Earth fills her lap with splendors" *not* her own. The vale of Tempe, Tivoli and Rome are earth and water, rocks and sky. There are as good earth and water in a thousand places, yet how unaffecting!

People are not the better for the sun and moon, the horizon and the trees; as it is not observed that the keepers of Roman galleries or the valets of painters have any elevation of thought, or that librarians are wiser men than others. There are graces in the demeanor of a polished and noble person which are lost upon the eye of a churl. These are like the stars whose light has not yet reached us.

He may see what he maketh. Our dreams are the sequel of our waking knowledge. The visions of the night bear some proportion to the visions of the day. Hideous dreams are exaggerations of the sins of the day. We see our evil affections embodied in bad physiognomies. On the Alps the traveller sometimes beholds his own shadow magnified to a giant, so that every gesture of his hand is terrific. "My children," said an old man to his boys scared by a figure in the dark entry, "my children, you will never see anything worse than yourselves." As in dreams, so in the scarcely less fluid events of the world every man sees himself in colossal, without knowing that it is himself. The good, compared to the evil which he sees, is as his own good to his own evil. Every quality of his mind is magnified in some one acquaintance, and every emotion of his heart in some one. He is like a quincunx of trees, which counts five,—east, west, north, or south; or an initial, medial, and terminal acrostic. And why not? He cleaves to one person and avoids another, according to their likeness or unlikeness to himself, truly seeking himself in his associates and moreover in his trade and habits and gestures and meats and drinks, and comes at last to be faithfully represented by every view you take of his circumstances.

He may read what he writes. What can we see or acquire but what we are? You have observed a skilful man reading Virgil. Well, that author is a thousand books to a thousand persons. Take the book into your two hands and read your eyes out, you will never find what I find. If any ingenious reader would have a monopoly of the wisdom or delight he gets, he is as secure now the book is Englished, as if it were imprisoned in the Pelews' tongue. It is with a good book as it is with good company. Introduce a base person among gentlemen, it is all to no purpose; he is not their fellow. Every society protects itself. The company is perfectly safe, and he is not one of them, though his body is in the room.

What avails it to fight with the eternal laws of mind, which adjust the relation of all persons to each other by the mathematical measure of their havings and beings? Gertrude is enamored of Guy; how high, how aristocratic, how Roman his mien and manners! to live with him were life indeed, and no purchase is too great; and heaven and earth are moved to that end. Well, Gertrude has Guy; but what now avails how high, how aristocratic, how Roman his mien and manners, if his heart and aims are in the senate, in the theatre and in the billiard-room, and she has no aims, no conversation that can enchant her graceful lord?

He shall have his own society. We can love nothing but nature. The most wonderful talents, the most meritorious exertions really avail very little with us; but nearness or likeness of nature,—how beautiful is the ease of its victory! Persons approach us, famous for their beauty, for their accomplishments, worthy of all wonder for their charms and gifts; they dedicate their whole skill to the hour and the company,—with very imperfect result. To be sure it would be ungrateful in us not to praise them loudly. Then, when all is done, a person of related mind, a brother or sister by nature, comes to us so softly and easily, so nearly and intimately, as if it were the blood in our proper veins, that we feel as if some one was gone, instead of another having come; we are utterly relieved and refreshed; it is a sort of joyful solitude. We foolishly think in our days of sin that we must court friends by compliance to the customs of society, to its dress, its breeding, and its estimates. But only that soul can be my friend which I encounter on the line of my own march, that soul to which I do not decline and which does not decline to me, but, native of the same celestial latitude, repeats in its own all my experience. The scholar forgets himself and apes the customs and costumes of the man of the world to deserve the smile of beauty, and follows some giddy girl, not yet taught by religious passion to know the noble woman with all that is serene, oracular and beautiful in her soul. Let him be great, and love shall follow him. Nothing is more deeply punished than the neglect of the affinities by which alone society should be formed, and the insane levity of choosing associates by others' eyes.

He may set his own rate. It is a maxim worthy of all acceptation that a man may have that allowance he takes. Take the place and attitude which belong to you, and all men acquiesce. The world must be just. It leaves every man, with profound unconcern, to set his own rate. Hero or driveller, it meddles not in the matter. It will certainly accept your own measure of your doing and being, whether you sneak about and deny your own name, or whether you see your work produced to the concave sphere of the heavens, one with the revolution of the stars.

The same reality pervades all teaching. The man may teach by doing, and not otherwise. If he can communicate himself he can teach, but not by words. He teaches who gives, and he learns who receives. There is no teaching until the pupil is brought into the same state or principle in which you are; a transfusion takes place; he is you and you are he; then is a teaching, and by no unfriendly chance or bad company can he ever quite lose the benefit. But your propositions run out of one ear as they ran in at

the other. We see it advertised that Mr. Grand will deliver
an oration on the Fourth of July, and Mr. Hand before the
Mechanics' Association, and we do not go thither, because
we know that these gentlemen will not communicate their
own character and experience to the company. If we had
reason to expect such a confidence we should go through
all inconvenience and opposition. The sick would be carried in litters. But a public oration is an escapade, a non-
committal, an apology, a gag, and not a communication,
not a speech, not a man.

A like Nemesis presides over all intellectual works. We
have yet to learn that the thing uttered in words is not
therefore affirmed. It must affirm itself, or no forms of
logic or of oath can give it evidence. The sentence must
also contain its own apology for being spoken.

The effect of any writing on the public mind is mathematically measurable by its depth of thought. How much
water does it draw? If it awaken you to think, if it lift you
from your feet with the great voice of eloquence, then the
effect is to be wide, slow, permanent, over the minds of
men; if the pages instruct you not, they will die like flies in
the hour. The way to speak and write what shall not go
out of fashion is to speak and write sincerely. The argument which has not power to reach my own practice, I
may well doubt will fail to reach yours. But take Sidney's
maxim:—"Look in thy heart, and write." He that writes
to himself writes to an eternal public. That statement only
is fit to be made public which you have come at in attempting to satisfy your own curiosity. The writer who
takes his subject from his ear and not from his heart,
should know that he has lost as much as he seems to have
gained, and when the empty book has gathered all its
praise, and half the people say, 'What poetry! what genius!' it still needs fuel to make fire. That only profits
which is profitable. Life alone can impart life; and though
we should burst we can only be valued as we make ourselves valuable. There is no luck in literary reputation.
They who make up the final verdict upon every book are

not the partial and noisy readers of the hour when it appears, but a court as of angels, a public not to be bribed, not to be entreated and not to be overawed, decides upon every man's title to fame. Only those books come down which deserve to last. Gilt edges, vellum and morocco, and presentation-copies to all the libraries will not preserve a book in circulation beyond its intrinsic date. It must go with all Walpole's Noble and Royal Authors to its fate. Blackmore, Kotzebue or Pollok may endure for a night, but Moses and Homer stand for ever. There are not in the world at any one time more than a dozen persons who read and understand Plato,—never enough to pay for an edition of his works; yet to every generation these come duly down, for the sake of those few persons, as if God brought them in his hand. "No book," said Bentley, "was ever written down by any but itself." The permanence of all books is fixed by no effort, friendly or hostile, but by their own specific gravity, or the intrinsic importance of their contents to the constant mind of man. "Do not trouble yourself too much about the light on your statue," said Michel Angelo to the young sculptor; "the light of the public square will test its value."

In like manner the effect of every action is measured by the depth of the sentiment from which it proceeds. The great man knew not that he was great. It took a century or two for that fact to appear. What he did, he did because he must; it was the most natural thing in the world, and grew out of the circumstances of the moment. But now, every thing he did, even to the lifting of his finger or the eating of bread, looks large, all-related, and is called an institution.

These are the demonstrations in a few particulars of the genius of nature; they show the direction of the stream. But the stream is blood; every drop is alive. Truth has not single victories; all things are its organs,—not only dust and stones, but errors and lies. The laws of disease, physicians say, are as beautiful as the laws of health. Our philosophy is affirmative and readily accepts the testimony of negative facts, as every shadow points to the sun. By a divine necessity every fact in nature is constrained to offer its testimony.

Human character evermore publishes itself. The most fugitive deed and word, the mere air of doing a thing, the intimated purpose, expresses character. If you act you show character; if you sit still, if you sleep, you show it. You think because you have spoken nothing when others spoke, and have given no opinion on the times, on the church, on slavery, on marriage, on socialism, on secret societies, on the college, on parties and persons, that your verdict is still expected with curiosity as a reserved wisdom. Far otherwise; your silence answers very loud. You have no oracle to utter, and your fellow-men have learned that you cannot help them; for oracles speak. Doth not Wisdom cry and Understanding put forth her voice?

Dreadful limits are set in nature to the powers of dissimulation. Truth tyrannizes over the unwilling members of the body. Faces never lie, it is said. No man need be deceived who will study the changes of expression. When a man speaks the truth in the spirit of truth, his eye is as clear as the heavens. When he has base ends and speaks falsely, the eye is muddy and sometimes asquint.

I have heard an experienced counsellor say that he never feared the effect upon a jury of a lawyer who does not believe in his heart that his client ought to have a verdict. If he does not believe it his unbelief will appear to the jury, despite all his protestations, and will become their unbelief. This is that law whereby a work of art, of whatever kind, sets us in the same state of mind wherein the artist was when he made it. That which we do not believe we cannot adequately say, though we may repeat the words never so often. It was this conviction which Swedenborg expressed when he described a group of persons in the spiritual world endeavoring in vain to articulate a proposition which they did not believe; but they could not, though they twisted and folded their lips even to indignation.

A man passes for that he is worth. Very idle is all curiosity concerning other people's estimate of us, and all fear of remaining unknown is not less so. If a man know that he can do any thing,—that he can do it better than any one else,—he has a pledge of the acknowledgment of that fact by all persons. The world is full of judgment-days, and into every assembly that a man enters, in every action he attempts, he is gauged and stamped. In every troop of boys that whoop and run in each yard and square, a newcomer is as well and accurately weighed in the course of a few days and stamped with his right number, as if he had undergone a formal trial of his strength, speed and temper. A stranger comes from a distant school, with better dress, with trinkets in his pockets, with airs and pretensions; an older boy says to himself, 'It's of no use; we shall find him out to-morrow.' 'What has he done?' is the divine question which searches men and transpierces every false reputation. A fop may sit in any chair of the world nor be distinguished for his hour from Homer and Washington; but there need never be any doubt concerning the respective ability of human beings. Pretension may sit still, but cannot act. Pretension never feigned an act of real greatness. Pretension never wrote an Iliad, nor drove back Xerxes, nor christianized the world, nor abolished slavery.

As much virtue as there is, so much appears; as much goodness as there is, so much reverence it commands. All the devils respect virtue. The high, the generous, the self-devoted sect will always instruct and command mankind. Never was a sincere word utterly lost. Never a magnanimity fell to the ground, but there is some heart to greet and accept it unexpectedly. A man passes for that he is worth. What he is engraves itself on his face, on his form, on his fortunes, in letters of light. Concealment avails him nothing, boasting nothing. There is confession in the glances of our eyes, in our smiles, in salutations, and the grasp of hands. His sin bedaubs him, mars all his good impression. Men know not why they do not trust him, but they do not trust him. His vice glasses his eye, cuts lines of mean ex-

pression in his cheek, pinches the nose, sets the mark of
the beast on the back of the head, and writes O fool! fool!
on the forehead of a king.

If you would not be known to do any thing, never do it.
A man may play the fool in the drifts of a desert, but
every grain of sand shall seem to see. He may be a solitary
eater, but he cannot keep his foolish counsel. A broken
complexion, a swinish look, ungenerous acts and the want
of due knowledge,—all blab. Can a cook, a Chiffinch, an
Iachimo be mistaken for Zeno or Paul? Confucius exclaimed,—"How can a man be concealed? How can a man
be concealed?"

On the other hand, the hero fears not that if he withhold the avowal of a just and brave act it will go unwit-
nessed and unloved. One knows it,—himself,—and is
pledged by it to sweetness of peace and to nobleness of
aim which will prove in the end a better proclamation of it
than the relating of the incident. Virtue is the adherence
in action to the nature of things and the nature of things
makes it prevalent. It consists in a perpetual substitution
of being for seeming, and with sublime propriety God is
described as saying, I AM.

The lesson which these observations convey is, Be, and
not seem. Let us acquiesce. Let us take our bloated noth-
ingness out of the path of the divine circuits. Let us un-
learn our wisdom of the world. Let us lie low in the Lord's
power and learn that truth alone makes rich and great.

If you visit your friend, why need you apologize for not
having visited him, and waste his time and deface your
own act? Visit him now. Let him feel that the highest love
has come to see him, in thee its lowest organ. Or why need
you torment yourself and friend by secret self-reproaches
that you have not assisted him or complimented him with
gifts and salutations heretofore? Be a gift and a benedic-
tion. Shine with real light and not with the borrowed reflection of gifts. Common men are apologies for men; they
bow the head, excuse themselves with prolix reasons, and
accumulate appearances because the substance is not.

We are full of these superstitions of sense, the worship of magnitude. We call the poet inactive, because he is not a president, a merchant, or a porter. We adore an institution, and do not see that it is founded on a thought which we have. But real action is in silent moments. The epochs of our life are not in the visible facts of our choice of a calling, our marriage, our acquisition of an office, and the like, but in a silent thought by the wayside as we walk; in a thought which revises our entire manner of life and says,—'Thus hast thou done, but it were better thus.' And all our after years, like menials, serve and wait on this, and according to their ability execute its will. This revisal or correction is a constant force, which, as a tendency, reaches through our lifetime. The object of the man, the aim of these moments, is to make daylight shine through him, to suffer the law to traverse his whole being without obstruction, so that on what point soever of his doing your eye falls it shall report truly of his character, whether it be his diet, his house, his religious forms, his society, his mirth, his vote, his opposition. Now he is not homogeneous, but heterogeneous, and the ray does not traverse; there are no thorough lights, but the eye of the beholder is puzzled, detecting many unlike tendencies and a life not yet at one.

Why should we make it a point with our false modesty to disparage that man we are and that form of being assigned to us? A good man is contented. I love and honor Epaminondas, but I do not wish to be Epaminondas. I hold it more just to love the world of this hour than the world of his hour. Nor can you, if I am true, excite me to the least uneasiness by saying, 'He acted and thou sittest still.' I see action to be good, when the need is, and sitting still to be also good. Epaminondas, if he was the man I take him for, would have sat still with joy and peace, if his lot had been mine. Heaven is large, and affords space for all modes of love and fortitude. Why should we be busy-bodies and superserviceable? Action and inaction are alike to the true. One piece of the tree is cut for a weathercock and one for the sleeper of a bridge; the virtue of the wood is apparent in both.

I desire not to disgrace the soul. The fact that I am here certainly shows me that the soul had need of an organ here. Shall I not assume the post? Shall I skulk and dodge and duck with my unseasonable apologies and vain modesty and imagine my being here impertinent? less pertinent than Epaminondas or Homer being there? and that the soul did not know its own needs? Besides, without any reasoning on the matter, I have no discontent. The good soul nourishes me and unlocks new magazines of power and enjoyment to me every day. I will not meanly decline the immensity of good, because I have heard that it has come to others in another shape.

Besides, why should we be cowed by the name of Action? 'T is a trick of the senses,—no more. We know that the ancestor of every action is a thought. The poor mind does not seem to itself to be any thing unless it have an outside badge,—some Gentoo diet, or Quaker coat, or Calvinistic prayer-meeting, or philanthropic society, or a great donation, or a high office, or, any how, some wild contrasting action to testify that it is somewhat. The rich mind lies in the sun and sleeps, and is Nature. To think is to act.

Let us, if we must have great actions, make our own so. All action is of an infinite elasticity, and the least admits of being inflated with the celestial air until it eclipses the sun and moon. Let us seek *one* peace by fidelity. Let me heed my duties. Why need I go gadding into the scenes and philosophy of Greek and Italian history before I have justified myself to my benefactors? How dare I read Washington's campaigns when I have not answered the letters of my own correspondents? Is not that a just objection to much of our reading? It is a pusillanimous desertion of our work to gaze after our neighbors. It is peeping. Byron says of Jack Bunting,—

He knew not what to say, and so he swore.

I may say it of our preposterous use of books,—He knew not what to do, and so *he read*. I can think of nothing to fill my time with, and I find the Life of Brant. It is a very extravagant compliment to pay to Brant, or to General Schuyler, or to General Washington. My time should be as good as their time,—my facts, my net of relations, as good as theirs, or either of theirs. Rather let me do my work so well that other idlers if they choose may compare my texture with the texture of these and find it identical with the best.

This over-estimate of the possibilities of Paul and Pericles, this under-estimate of our own, comes from a neglect of the fact of an identical nature. Bonaparte knew but one merit, and rewarded in one and the same way the good soldier, the good astronomer, the good poet, the good player. The poet uses the names of Cæsar, of Tamerlane, of Bonduca, of Belisarius; the painter uses the conventional story of the Virgin Mary, of Paul, of Peter. He does not therefore defer to the nature of these accidental men, of these stock heroes. If the poet write a true drama, then he is Cæsar, and not the player of Cæsar; then the self-same strain of thought, emotion as pure, wit as subtle, motions as swift, mounting, extravagant, and a heart as great, self-sufficing, dauntless, which on the waves of its love and hope can uplift all that is reckoned solid and precious in the world,—palaces, gardens, money, navies, kingdoms,—marking its own incomparable worth by the slight it casts on these gauds of men;—these all are his, and by the power of these he rouses the nations. Let a man believe in God, and not in names and places and persons. Let the great soul incarnated in some woman's form, poor and sad and single, in some Dolly or Joan, go out to service and sweep chambers and scour floors, and its effulgent daybeams cannot be muffled or hid, but to sweep and scour will instantly appear supreme and beautiful actions, the top and radiance of human life, and all people will get mops and brooms; until, lo! suddenly the great soul has enshrined itself in some other form and done some other deed, and that is now the flower and head of all living nature.

We are the photometers, we the irritable goldleaf and tinfoil that measure the accumulations of the subtle element. We know the authentic effects of the true fire through every one of its million disguises.

THE OVER-SOUL

"But souls that of his own good life partake,
   He loves as his own self; dear as his eye
   They are to Him: He'll never them forsake:
   When they shall die, then God himself shall die:
   They live, they live in blest eternity."

Henry More

Space is ample, east and west,
But two cannot go abreast,
Cannot travel in it two:
Yonder masterful cuckoo
Crowds every egg out of the nest,
Quick or dead, except its own;
A spell is laid on sod and stone,
Night and Day 've been tampered with,
Every quality and pith
Surcharged and sultry with a power
That works its will on age and hour.

There is a difference between one and another hour of life
in their authority and subsequent effect. Our faith comes
in moments; our vice is habitual. Yet there is a depth in
those brief moments which constrains us to ascribe more
reality to them than to all other experiences. For this reason the argument which is always forthcoming to silence
those who conceive extraordinary hopes of man, namely
the appeal to experience, is for ever invalid and vain. We
give up the past to the objector, and yet we hope. He must
explain this hope. We grant that human life is mean,
but how did we find out that it was mean? What is

the ground of this uneasiness of ours; of this old discontent? What is the universal sense of want and ignorance, but the fine innuendo by which the soul makes its enormous claim? Why do men feel that the natural history of man has never been written, but he is always leaving behind what you have said of him, and it becomes old, and books of metaphysics worthless? The philosophy of six thousand years has not searched the chambers and magazines of the soul. In its experiments there has always remained, in the last analysis, a residuum it could not resolve. Man is a stream whose source is hidden. Our being is descending into us from we know not whence. The most exact calculator has no prescience that somewhat incalculable may not balk the very next moment. I am constrained every moment to acknowledge a higher origin for events than the will I call mine.

As with events, so is it with thoughts. When I watch that flowing river, which, out of regions I see not, pours for a season its streams into me, I see that I am a pensioner; not a cause but a surprised spectator of this ethereal water; that I desire and look up and put myself in the attitude of reception, but from some alien energy the visions come.

The Supreme Critic on the errors of the past and the present, and the only prophet of that which must be, is that great nature in which we rest as the earth lies in the soft arms of the atmosphere; that Unity, that Over-Soul, within which every man's particular being is contained and made one with all other; that common heart of which all sincere conversation is the worship, to which all right action is submission; that overpowering reality which confutes our tricks and talents, and constrains every one to pass for what he is, and to speak from his character and not from his tongue, and which evermore tends to pass into our thought and hand and become wisdom and virtue and power and beauty. We live in succession, in division, in parts, in particles. Meantime within man is the soul of the whole; the wise silence; the universal beauty, to which

ready on a platform that commands the sciences and arts, speech and poetry, action and grace. For whoso dwells in this moral beatitude already anticipates those special powers which men prize so highly. The lover has no talent, no skill, which passes for quite nothing with his enamored maiden, however little she may possess of related faculty; and the heart which abandons itself to the Supreme Mind finds itself related to all its works, and will travel a royal road to particular knowledges and powers. In ascending to this primary and aboriginal sentiment we have come from our remote station on the circumference instantaneously to the centre of the world, where, as in the closet of God, we see causes, and anticipate the universe, which is but a slow effect.

One mode of the divine teaching is the incarnation of the spirit in a form,—in forms, like my own. I live in society; with persons who answer to thoughts in my own mind, or express a certain obedience to the great instincts to which I live. I see its presence to them. I am certified of a common nature; and these other souls, these separated selves, draw me as nothing else can. They stir in me the new emotions we call passion; of love, hatred, fear, admiration, pity; thence come conversation, competition, persuasion, cities and war. Persons are supplementary to the primary teaching of the soul. In youth we are mad for persons. Childhood and youth see all the world in them. But the larger experience of man discovers the identical nature appearing through them all. Persons themselves acquaint us with the impersonal. In all conversation between two persons tacit reference is made, as to a third party, to a common nature. That third party or common nature is not social; it is impersonal; is God. And so in groups where debate is earnest, and especially on high questions, the company become aware that the thought rises to an equal level in all bosoms, that all have a spiritual property in what was said, as well as the sayer. They all become wiser than they were. It arches over them like a temple, this unity of thought in which every heart beats

with nobler sense of power and duty, and thinks and acts
with unusual solemnity. All are conscious of attaining to a
higher self-possession. It shines for all. There is a certain
wisdom of humanity which is common to the greatest
men with the lowest, and which our ordinary education
often labors to silence and obstruct. The mind is one, and
the best minds, who love truth for its own sake, think
much less of property in truth. They accept it thankfully
everywhere, and do not label or stamp it with any man's
name, for it is theirs long beforehand, and from eternity.
The learned and the studious of thought have no monopoly of wisdom. Their violence of direction in some degree
disqualifies them to think truly. We owe many valuable
observations to people who are not very acute or profound, and who say the thing without effort which we
want and have long been hunting in vain. The action of
the soul is oftener in that which is felt and left unsaid than
in that which is said in any conversation. It broods over
every society, and they unconsciously seek for it in each
other. We know better than we do. We do not yet possess
ourselves, and we know at the same time that we are much
more. I feel the same truth how often in my trivial conversation with my neighbors, that somewhat higher in
each of us overlooks this by-play, and Jove nods to Jove
from behind each of us.

Men descend to meet. In their habitual and mean service to the world, for which they forsake their native nobleness, they resemble those Arabian sheiks who dwell in
mean houses and affect an external poverty, to escape the
rapacity of the Pacha, and reserve all their display of
wealth for their interior and guarded retirements.

As it is present in all persons, so it is in every period of
life. It is adult already in the infant man. In my dealing
with my child, my Latin and Greek, my accomplishments
and my money stead me nothing; but as much soul as I
have avails. If I am wilful, he sets his will against mine,
one for one, and leaves me, if I please, the degradation of
beating him by my superiority of strength. But if I re-

nounce my will and act for the soul, setting that up as umpire between us two, out of his young eyes looks the same soul; he reveres and loves with me.

The soul is the perceiver and revealer of truth. We know truth when we see it, let sceptic and scoffer say what they choose. Foolish people ask you, when you have spoken what they do not wish to hear, 'How do you know it is truth, and not an error of your own?' We know truth when we see it, from opinion, as we know when we are awake that we are awake. It was a grand sentence of Emanuel Swedenborg, which would alone indicate the greatness of that man's perception,—"It is no proof of a man's understanding to be able to affirm whatever he pleases; but to be able to discern that what is true is true, and that what is false is false,—this is the mark and character of intelligence." In the book I read, the good thought returns to me, as every truth will, the image of the whole soul. To the bad thought which I find in it, the same soul becomes a discerning, separating sword, and lops it away. We are wiser than we know. If we will not interfere with our thought, but will act entirely, or see how the thing stands in God, we know the particular thing, and every thing, and every man. For the Maker of all things and all persons stands behind us and casts his dread omniscience through us over things.

But beyond this recognition of its own in particular passages of the individual's experience, it also reveals truth. And here we should seek to reinforce ourselves by its very presence, and to speak with a worthier, loftier strain of that advent. For the soul's communication of truth is the highest event in nature, since it then does not give somewhat from itself, but it gives itself, or passes into and becomes that man whom it enlightens; or in proportion to that truth he receives, it takes him to itself.

We distinguish the announcements of the soul, its manifestations of its own nature, by the term *Revelation*. These are always attended by the emotion of the sublime. For this communication is an influx of the Divine mind

into our mind. It is an ebb of the individual rivulet before
the flowing surges of the sea of life. Every distinct apprehension of this central commandment agitates men with
awe and delight. A thrill passes through all men at the reception of new truth, or at the performance of a great action, which comes out of the heart of nature. In these
communications the power to see is not separated from
the will to do, but the insight proceeds from obedience,
and the obedience proceeds from a joyful perception.
Every moment when the individual feels himself invaded
by it is memorable. By the necessity of our constitution a
certain enthusiasm attends the individual's consciousness
of that divine presence. The character and duration of this
enthusiasm vary with the state of the individual, from an
ecstasy and trance and prophetic inspiration,—which is its
rarer appearance,—to the faintest glow of virtuous emotion, in which form it warms, like our household fires, all
the families and associations of men, and makes society
possible. A certain tendency to insanity has always attended the opening of the religious sense in men, as if they
had been "blasted with excess of light." The trances of
Socrates, the "union" of Plotinus, the vision of Porphyry,
the conversion of Paul, the aurora of Behmen, the convulsions of George Fox and his Quakers, the illumination of
Swedenborg, are of this kind. What was in the case of
these remarkable persons a ravishment, has, in innumerable instances in common life, been exhibited in less striking manner. Everywhere the history of religion betrays a
tendency to enthusiasm. The rapture of the Moravian and
Quietist; the opening of the eternal sense of the Word, in
the language of the New Jerusalem Church; the *revival* of
the Calvinistic churches; the *experiences* of the Methodists, are varying forms of that shudder of awe and delight
with which the individual soul always mingles with the
universal soul.

The nature of these revelations is the same; they are
perceptions of the absolute law. They are solutions of the
soul's own questions. They do not answer the questions

which the understanding asks. The soul answers never by words, but by the thing itself that is inquired after.

Revelation is the disclosure of the soul. The popular notion of a revelation is that it is a telling of fortunes. In past oracles of the soul the understanding seeks to find answers to sensual questions, and undertakes to tell from God how long men shall exist, what their hands shall do and who shall be their company, adding names and dates and places. But we must pick no locks. We must check this low curiosity. An answer in words is delusive; it is really no answer to the questions you ask. Do not require a description of the countries towards which you sail. The description does not describe them to you, and to-morrow you arrive there and know them by inhabiting them. Men ask concerning the immortality of the soul, the employments of heaven, the state of the sinner, and so forth. They even dream that Jesus has left replies to precisely these interrogatories. Never a moment did that sublime spirit speak in their *patois*. To truth, justice, love, the attributes of the soul, the idea of immutableness is essentially associated. Jesus, living in these moral sentiments, heedless of sensual fortunes, heeding only the manifestations of these, never made the separation of the idea of duration from the essence of these attributes, nor uttered a syllable concerning the duration of the soul. It was left to his disciples to sever duration from the moral elements, and to teach the immortality of the soul as a doctrine, and maintain it by evidences. The moment the doctrine of the immortality is separately taught, man is already fallen. In the flowing of love, in the adoration of humility, there is no question of continuance. No inspired man ever asks this question or condescends to these evidences. For the soul is true to itself, and the man in whom it is shed abroad cannot wander from the present, which is infinite, to a future which would be finite.

These questions which we lust to ask about the future are a confession of sin. God has no answer for them. No answer in words can reply to a question of things. It is not in an arbitrary "decree of God," but in the nature of man, that a veil shuts down on the facts of to-morrow; for the soul will not have us read any other cipher than that of cause and effect. By this veil which curtains events it instructs the children of men to live in to-day. The only mode of obtaining an answer to these questions of the senses is to forego all low curiosity, and, accepting the tide of being which floats us into the secret of nature, work and live, work and live, and all unawares the advancing soul has built and forged for itself a new condition, and the question and the answer are one.

By the same fire, vital, consecrating, celestial, which burns until it shall dissolve all things into the waves and surges of an ocean of light, we see and know each other, and what spirit each is of. Who can tell the grounds of his knowledge of the character of the several individuals in his circle of friends? No man. Yet their acts and words do not disappoint him. In that man, though he knew no ill of him, he put no trust. In that other, though they had seldom met, authentic signs had yet passed, to signify that he might be trusted as one who had an interest in his own character. We know each other very well,—which of us has been just to himself and whether that which we teach or behold is only an inspiration or is our honest effort also.

We are all discerners of spirits. That diagnosis lies aloft in our life or unconscious power. The intercourse of society, its trade, its religion, its friendships, its quarrels, is one wide judicial investigation of character. In full court, or in small committee, or confronted face to face, accuser and accused, men offer themselves to be judged. Against their will they exhibit those decisive trifles by which character is read. But who judges? and what? Not our understanding. We do not read them by learning or craft. No; the wisdom of the wise man consists herein, that he does not judge them; he lets them judge themselves and merely reads and records their own verdict.

By virtue of this inevitable nature, private will is overpowered, and, maugre our efforts or our imperfections, your genius will speak from you, and mine from me. That which we are, we shall teach, not voluntarily but involuntarily. Thoughts come into our minds by avenues which we never left open, and thoughts go out of our minds through avenues which we never voluntarily opened. Character teaches over our head. The infallible index of true progress is found in the tone the man takes. Neither his age, nor his breeding, nor company, nor books, nor actions, nor talents, nor all together can hinder him from being deferential to a higher spirit than his own. If he have not found his home in God, his manners, his forms of speech, the turn of his sentences, the build, shall I say, of all his opinions will involuntarily confess it, let him brave it out how he will. If he have found his centre, the Deity will shine through him, through all the disguises of ignorance, of ungenial temperament, of unfavorable circumstance. The tone of seeking is one, and the tone of having is another.

The great distinction between teachers sacred or literary,—between poets like Herbert, and poets like Pope,—between philosophers like Spinoza, Kant and Coleridge, and philosophers like Locke, Paley, Mackintosh and Stewart,—between men of the world who are reckoned accomplished talkers, and here and there a fervent mystic, prophesying half insane under the infinitude of his thought,—is that one class speak *from within,* or from experience, as parties and possessors of the fact; and the other class *from without,* as spectators merely, or perhaps as acquainted with the fact on the evidence of third persons. It is of no use to preach to me from without. I can do that too easily myself. Jesus speaks always from within, and in a degree that transcends all others. In that is the miracle. I believe beforehand that it ought so to be. All men stand continually in the expectation of the appearance of such a teacher. But if a man do not speak from within the veil, where the word is one with that it tells of, let him lowly confess it.

The same Omniscience flows into the intellect and

makes what we call genius. Much of the wisdom of the
world is not wisdom, and the most illuminated class of
men are no doubt superior to literary fame, and are not
writers. Among the multitude of scholars and authors we
feel no hallowing presence; we are sensible of a knack and
skill rather than of inspiration; they have a light and know
not whence it comes and call it their own; their talent is
some exaggerated faculty, some overgrown member, so
that their strength is a disease. In these instances the intellectual gifts do not make the impression of virtue, but
almost of vice; and we feel that a man's talents stand in the
way of his advancement in truth. But genius is religious. It
is a larger imbibing of the common heart. It is not anomalous, but more like and not less like other men. There is in
all great poets a wisdom of humanity which is superior to
any talents they exercise. The author, the wit, the partisan, the fine gentleman, does not take place of the man.
Humanity shines in Homer, in Chaucer, in Spenser, in
Shakspeare, in Milton. They are content with truth. They
use the positive degree. They seem frigid and phlegmatic
to those who have been spiced with the frantic passion and
violent coloring of inferior but popular writers. For they
are poets by the free course which they allow to the informing soul, which through their eyes beholds again and
blesses the things which it hath made. The soul is superior
to its knowledge, wiser than any of its works. The great
poet makes us feel our own wealth, and then we think less
of his compositions. His best communication to our mind
is to teach us to despise all he has done. Shakspeare carries
us to such a lofty strain of intelligent activity as to suggest
a wealth which beggars his own; and we then feel that the
splendid works which he has created, and which in other
hours we extol as a sort of self-existent poetry, take no
stronger hold of real nature than the shadow of a passing
traveller on the rock. The inspiration which uttered itself
in Hamlet and Lear could utter things as good from day to
day for ever. Why then should I make account of Hamlet

and Lear, as if we had not the soul from which they fell as syllables from the tongue?

This energy does not descend into individual life on any other condition than entire possession. It comes to the lowly and simple; it comes to whomsoever will put off what is foreign and proud; it comes as insight; it comes as serenity and grandeur. When we see those whom it inhabits, we are apprised of new degrees of greatness. From that inspiration the man comes back with a changed tone. He does not talk with men with an eye to their opinion. He tries them. It requires of us to be plain and true. The vain traveller attempts to embellish his life by quoting my lord and the prince and the countess, who thus said or did to *him*. The ambitious vulgar show you their spoons and brooches and rings, and preserve their cards and compliments. The more cultivated, in their account of their own experience, cull out the pleasing, poetic circumstance,—the visit to Rome, the man of genius they saw, the brilliant friend they know; still further on perhaps the gorgeous landscape, the mountain lights, the mountain thoughts they enjoyed yesterday,—and so seek to throw a romantic color over their life. But the soul that ascends to worship the great God is plain and true; has no rose-color, no fine friends, no chivalry, no adventures; does not want admiration; dwells in the hour that now is, in the earnest experience of the common day,—by reason of the present moment and the mere trifle having become porous to thought and bilulous of the sea of light.

Converse with a mind that is grandly simple, and literature looks like word-catching. The simplest utterances are worthiest to be written, yet are they so cheap and so things of course, that in the infinite riches of the soul it is like gathering a few pebbles off the ground, or bottling a little air in a phial, when the whole earth and the whole atmosphere are ours. Nothing can pass there, or make you one of the circle, but the casting aside your trappings and dealing man to man in naked truth, plain confession and omniscient affirmation.

Souls such as these treat you as gods would, walk as gods in the earth, accepting without any admiration your wit, your bounty, your virtue even,—say rather your act of duty, for your virtue they own as their proper blood, royal as themselves, and over-royal, and the father of the gods. But what rebuke their plain fraternal bearing casts on the mutual flattery with which authors solace each other and wound themselves! These flatter not. I do not wonder that these men go to see Cromwell and Christina and Charles the Second and James the First and the Grand Turk. For they are, in their own elevation, the fellows of kings, and must feel the servile tone of conversation in the world. They must always be a godsend to princes, for they confront them, a king to a king, without ducking or concession, and give a high nature the refreshment and satisfaction of resistance, of plain humanity, of even companionship and of new ideas. They leave them wiser and superior men. Souls like these make us feel that sincerity is more excellent than flattery. Deal so plainly with man and woman as to constrain the utmost sincerity and destroy all hope of trifling with you. It is the highest compliment you can pay. Their "highest praising," said Milton, "is not flattery, and their plainest advice is a kind of praising."

Ineffable is the union of man and God in every act of the soul. The simplest person who in his integrity worships God, becomes God; yet for ever and ever the influx of this better and universal self is new and unsearchable. It inspires awe and astonishment. How dear, how soothing to man, arises the idea of God, peopling the lonely place, effacing the scars of our mistakes and disappointments! When we have broken our god of tradition and ceased from our god of rhetoric, then may God fire the heart with his presence. It is the doubling of the heart itself, nay, the infinite enlargement of the heart with a power of growth to a new infinity on every side. It inspires in man an infallible trust. He has not the conviction, but the sight, that the best is the true, and may in that thought easily dismiss all particular uncertainties and fears, and adjourn to the sure revelation of time the solution of his private riddles. He is sure that his welfare is dear to the heart of being. In the presence of law to his mind he is overflowed with a reliance so universal that it sweeps away all cherished hopes and the most stable projects of mortal condition in its flood. He believes that he cannot escape from his good. The things that are really for thee gravitate to thee. You are running to seek your friend. Let your feet run, but your mind need not. If you do not find him, will you not acquiesce that it is best you should not find him? for there is a power, which, as it is in you, is in him also, and could therefore very well bring you together, if it were for the best. You are preparing with eagerness to go and render a service to which your talent and your taste invite you, the love of men and the hope of fame. Has it not occurred to you that you have no right to go, unless you are equally willing to be prevented from going? O, believe, as thou livest, that every sound that is spoken over the round world, which thou oughtest to hear, will vibrate on thine ear! Every proverb, every book, every byword that belongs to thee for aid or comfort, shall surely come home through open or winding passages. Every friend whom not thy fantastic will but the great and tender heart in thee craveth, shall lock thee in his embrace. And this because the heart in thee is the heart of all; not a valve, not a wall, not an intersection is there anywhere in nature, but one blood rolls uninterruptedly an endless circulation through all men, as the water of the globe is all one sea, and, truly seen, its tide is one.

Let man then learn the revelation of all nature and all thought to his heart; this, namely; that the Highest dwells with him; that the sources of nature are in his own mind, if the sentiment of duty is there. But if he would know what the great God speaketh, he must 'go into his closet and shut the door,' as Jesus said. God will not make himself manifest to cowards. He must greatly listen to himself, withdrawing himself from all the accents of other men's devotion. Even their prayers are hurtful to him, until he have made his own. Our religion vulgarly stands on numbers of believers. Whenever the appeal is made,— no matter how indirectly,—to numbers, proclamation is then and there made that religion is not. He that finds God a sweet enveloping thought to him never counts his company. When I sit in that presence, who shall dare to come in? When I rest in perfect humility, when I burn with pure love, what can Calvin or Swedenborg say?

It makes no difference whether the appeal is to numbers or to one. The faith that stands on authority is not faith. The reliance on authority measures the decline of religion, the withdrawal of the soul. The position men have given to Jesus, now for many centuries of history, is a position of authority. It characterizes themselves. It cannot alter the eternal facts. Great is the soul, and plain. It is no flatterer, it is no follower; it never appeals from itself. It believes in itself. Before the immense possibilities of man all mere experience, all past biography, however spotless and sainted, shrinks away. Before that heaven which our presentiments foreshow us, we cannot easily praise any form of life we have seen or read of. We not only affirm that we have few great men, but, absolutely speaking, that we have none; that we have no history, no record of any character or mode of living that entirely contents us. The saints and demigods whom history worships we are constrained to accept with a grain of allowance. Though in our lonely hours we draw a new strength out of their memory, yet, pressed on our attention, as they are by the thoughtless and customary, they fatigue and invade. The soul gives itself, alone, original and pure, to the Lonely, Original and Pure, who, on that condition, gladly inhabits, leads and speaks through it. Then is it glad, young and nimble. It is not wise, but it sees through all things. It is not called religious, but it is innocent. It calls the light its own, and feels that the grass grows and the stone falls by a law inferior to, and dependent on, its nature. Behold, it saith, I am born into the great, the universal mind. I, the imperfect, adore my own Perfect. I am somehow receptive of the great soul, and thereby I do overlook the sun and the stars and feel them to be the fair accidents and effects which change and pass. More and more the surges of everlasting nature enter into me, and I become public and human in my regards and actions. So come I to live in thoughts and act with energies which are immortal. Thus revering the soul, and learning, as the ancient said, that "its beauty is immense," man will come to see that the world is the perennial miracle which the soul worketh, and be less astonished at particular wonders; he will learn that there is no profane history; that all history is sacred; that the universe is represented in an atom, in a moment of time. He will weave no longer a spotted life of shreds and patches, but he will live with a divine unity. He will cease from what is base and frivolous in his life and be content with all places and with any service he can render. He will calmly front the morrow in the negligency of that trust which carries God with it and so hath already the whole future in the bottom of the heart.

CIRCLES

Nature centres into balls,
And her proud ephemerals,
Fast to surface and outside,
Scan the profile of the sphere;
Knew they what that signified,
A new genesis were here.

The eye is the first circle; the horizon which it forms is the second; and throughout nature this primary figure is repeated without end. It is the highest emblem in the cipher of the world. St. Augustine described the nature of God as a circle whose centre was everywhere and its circumference nowhere. We are all our lifetime reading the copious sense of this first of forms. One moral we have already deduced in considering the circular or compensatory character of every human action. Another analogy we shall now trace, that every action admits of being outdone. Our life is an apprenticeship to the truth that around every circle another can be drawn; that there is no end in nature, but every end is a beginning; that there is always another dawn risen on mid-noon, and under every deep a lower deep opens.

This fact, as far as it symbolizes the moral fact of the Unattainable, the flying Perfect, around which the hands of man can never meet, at once the inspirer and the condemner of every success, may conveniently serve us to connect many illustrations of human power in every department.

There are no fixtures in nature. The universe is fluid and volatile. Permanence is but a word of degrees. Our globe seen by God is a transparent law, not a mass of facts. The law dissolves the fact and holds it fluid. Our culture is the predominance of an idea which draws after it this train of cities and institutions. Let us rise into another idea; they will disappear. The Greek sculpture is all melted away, as if it had been statues of ice; here and there a solitary figure or fragment remaining, as we see flecks and scraps of snow left in cold dells and mountain clefts in June and July. For the genius that created it creates now somewhat else. The Greek letters last a little longer, but are already passing under the same sentence and tumbling into the inevitable pit which the creation of new thought opens for all that is old. The new continents are built out of the ruins of an old planet; the new races fed out of the decomposition of the foregoing. New arts destroy the old. See the investment of capital in aqueducts, made useless by hydraulics; fortifications, by gun-powder; roads and canals, by railways; sails, by steam; steam by electricity.

You admire this tower of granite, weathering the hurts of so many ages. Yet a little waving hand built this huge wall, and that which builds is better than that which is built. The hand that built can topple it down much faster. Better than the hand and nimbler was the invisible thought which wrought through it; and thus ever, behind the coarse effect, is a fine cause, which, being narrowly seen, is itself the effect of a finer cause. Everything looks permanent until its secret is known. A rich estate appears to women a firm and lasting fact; to a merchant, one easily created out of any materials, and easily lost. An orchard, good tillage, good grounds, seem a fixture, like a gold mine, or a river, to a citizen; but to a large farmer, not much more fixed than the state of the crop. Nature looks provokingly stable and secular, but it has a cause like all the rest; and when once I comprehend that, will these fields stretch so immovably wide, these leaves hang so individually considerable? Permanence is a word of de-

grees. Every thing is medial. Moons are no more bounds
to spiritual power than bat-balls.

The key to every man is his thought. Sturdy and defying though he look, he has a helm which he obeys, which
is the idea after which all his facts are classified. He can
only be reformed by showing him a new idea which commands his own. The life of man is a self-evolving circle,
which, from a ring imperceptibly small, rushes on all sides
outwards to new and larger circles, and that without end.
The extent to which this generation of circles, wheel
without wheel, will go, depends on the force or truth of
the individual soul. For it is the inert effort of each
thought, having formed itself into a circular wave of circumstance,—as for instance an empire, rules of an art, a
local usage, a religious rite,—to heap itself on that ridge
and to solidify and hem in the life. But if the soul is quick
and strong it bursts over that boundary on all sides and
expands another orbit on the great deep, which also runs
up into a high wave, with attempt again to stop and to
bind. But the heart refuses to be imprisoned; in its first
and narrowest pulses it already tends outward with a vast
force and to immense and innumerable expansions.

Every ultimate fact is only the first of a new series.
Every general law only a particular fact of some more general law presently to disclose itself. There is no outside, no
inclosing wall, no circumference to us. The man finishes
his story,—how good! how final! how it puts a new face on
all things! He fills the sky. Lo! on the other side rises also a
man and draws a circle around the circle we had just pronounced the outline of the sphere. Then already is our
first speaker not man, but only a first speaker. His only redress is forthwith to draw a circle outside of his antagonist. And so men do by themselves. The result of to-day,
which haunts the mind and cannot be escaped, will presently be abridged into a word, and the principle that
seemed to explain nature will itself be included as one example of a bolder generalization. In the thought of to-
morrow there is a power to upheave all thy creed, all the

creeds, all the literatures of the nations, and marshal thee to a heaven which no epic dream has yet depicted. Every man is not so much a workman in the world as he is a suggestion of that he should be. Men walk as prophecies of the next age.

Step by step we scale this mysterious ladder; the steps are actions, the new prospect is power. Every several result is threatened and judged by that which follows. Every one seems to be contradicted by the new; it is only limited by the new. The new statement is always hated by the old, and, to those dwelling in the old, comes like an abyss of scepticism. But the eye soon gets wonted to it, for the eye and it are effects of one cause; then its innocency and benefit appear, and presently, all its energy spent, it pales and dwindles before the revelation of the new hour.

Fear not the new generalization. Does the fact look crass and material, threatening to degrade thy theory of spirit? Resist it not; it goes to refine and raise thy theory of matter just as much.

There are no fixtures to men, if we appeal to consciousness. Every man supposes himself not to be fully understood; and if there is any truth in him, if he rests at last on the divine soul, I see not how it can be otherwise. The last chamber, the last closet, he must feel was never opened; there is always a residuum unknown, unanalyzable. That is, every man believes that he has a greater possibility.

Our moods do not believe in each other. To-day I am full of thoughts and can write what I please. I see no reason why I should not have the same thought, the same power of expression, to-morrow. What I write, whilst I write it, seems the most natural thing in the world; but yesterday I saw a dreary vacuity in this direction in which now I see so much; and a month hence, I doubt not, I shall wonder who he was that wrote so many continuous pages. Alas for this infirm faith, this will not strenuous, this vast ebb of a vast flow! I am God in nature; I am a weed by the wall.

The continual effort to raise himself above himself, to

work a pitch above his last height, betrays itself in a man's relations. We thirst for approbation, yet cannot forgive the approver. The sweet of nature is love; yet if I have a friend I am tormented by my imperfections. The love of me accuses the other party. If he were high enough to slight me, then could I love him, and rise by my affection to new heights. A man's growth is seen in the successive choirs of his friends. For every friend whom he loses for truth, he gains a better. I thought as I walked in the woods and mused on my friends, why should I play with them this game of idolatry? I know and see too well, when not voluntarily blind, the speedy limits of persons called high and worthy. Rich, noble and great they are by the liberality of our speech, but truth is sad. O blessed Spirit, whom I forsake for these, they are not thou! Every personal consideration that we allow costs us heavenly state. We sell the thrones of angels for a short and turbulent pleasure.

How often must we learn this lesson? Men cease to interest us when we find their limitations. The only sin is limitation. As soon as you once come up with a man's limitations, it is all over with him. Has he talents? has he enterprise? has he knowledge? It boots not. Infinitely alluring and attractive was he to you yesterday, a great hope, a sea to swim in; now, you have found his shores, found it a pond, and you care not if you never see it again.

Each new step we take in thought reconciles twenty seemingly discordant facts, as expressions of one law. Aristotle and Plato are reckoned the respective heads of two schools. A wise man will see that Aristotle platonizes. By going one step farther back in thought, discordant opinions are reconciled by being seen to be two extremes of one principle, and we can never go so far back as to preclude a still higher vision.

Beware when the great God lets loose a thinker on this planet. Then all things are at risk. It is as when a conflagration has broken out in a great city, and no man knows what is safe, or where it will end. There is not a piece of science but its flank may be turned to-morrow; there is not any literary reputation, not the so-called eternal names of fame, that may not be revised and condemned. The very hopes of man, the thoughts of his heart, the religion of nations, the manners and morals of mankind are all at the mercy of a new generalization. Generalization is always a new influx of the divinity into the mind. Hence the thrill that attends it.

Valor consists in the power of self-recovery, so that a man cannot have his flank turned, cannot be out-generalled, but put him where you will, he stands. This can only be by his preferring truth to his past apprehension of truth, and his alert acceptance of it from whatever quarter; the intrepid conviction that his laws, his relations to society, his Christianity, his world, may at any time be superseded and decease.

There are degrees in idealism. We learn first to play with it academically, as the magnet was once a toy. Then we see in the heyday of youth and poetry that it may be true, that it is true in gleams and fragments. Then its countenance waxes stern and grand, and we see that it must be true. It now shows itself ethical and practical. We learn that God IS; that he is in me; and that all things are shadows of him. The idealism of Berkeley is only a crude statement of the idealism of Jesus, and that again is a crude statement of the fact that all nature is the rapid efflux of goodness executing and organizing itself. Much more obviously is history and the state of the world at any one time directly dependent on the intellectual classification then existing in the minds of men. The things which are dear to men at this hour are so on account of the ideas which have emerged on their mental horizon, and which cause the present order of things, as a tree bears its apples. A new degree of culture would instantly revolutionize the entire system of human pursuits.

Conversation is a game of circles. In conversation we pluck up the *termini* which bound the common of silence on every side. The parties are not to be judged by the

spirit they partake and even express under this Pentecost.
To-morrow they will have receded from this high-water
mark. To-morrow you shall find them stooping under the
old pack-saddles. Yet let us enjoy the cloven flame whilst
it glows on our walls. When each new speaker strikes a
new light, emancipates us from the oppression of the last
speaker to oppress us with the greatness and exclusiveness
of his own thought, then yields us to another redeemer,
we seem to recover our rights, to become men. O, what
truths profound and executable only in ages and orbs, are
supposed in the announcement of every truth! In common
hours, society sits cold and statuesque. We all stand waiting, empty,—knowing, possibly, that we can be full, surrounded by mighty symbols which are not symbols to us,
but prose and trivial toys. Then cometh the god and converts the statues into fiery men, and by a flash of his eye
burns up the veil which shrouded all things, and the
meaning of the very furniture, of cup and saucer, of chair
and clock and tester, is manifest. The facts which loomed
so large in the fogs of yesterday,—property, climate,
breeding, personal beauty and the like, have strangely
changed their proportions. All that we reckoned settled
shakes and rattles; and literatures, cities, climates, religions, leave their foundations and dance before our eyes.
And yet here again see the swift circumscription! Good as
is discourse, silence is better, and shames it. The length of
the discourse indicates the distance of thought betwixt the
speaker and the hearer. If they were at a perfect understanding in any part, no words would be necessary
thereon. If at one in all parts, no words would be suffered.

Literature is a point outside of our hodiernal circle
through which a new one may be described. The use of
literature is to afford us a platform whence we may command a view of our present life, a purchase by which we
may move it. We fill ourselves with ancient learning, in-
stall ourselves the best we can in Greek, in Punic, in
Roman houses, only that we may wiselier see French,
English and American houses and modes of living. In like

manner we see literature best from the midst of wild nature, or from the din of affairs, or from a high religion. The field cannot be well seen from within the field. The astronomer must have his diameter of the earth's orbit as a base to find the parallax of any star.

Therefore we value the poet. All the argument and all the wisdom is not in the encyclopædia, or the treatise on metaphysics, or the Body of Divinity, but in the sonnet or the play. In my daily work I incline to repeat my old steps, and do not believe in remedial force, in the power of change and reform. But some Petrarch or Ariosto, filled with the new wine of his imagination, writes me an ode or a brisk romance, full of daring thought and action. He smites and arouses me with his shrill tones, breaks up my whole chain of habits, and I open my eye on my own possibilities. He claps wings to the sides of all the solid old lumber of the world, and I am capable once more of choosing a straight path in theory and practice.

We have the same need to command a view of the religion of the world. We can never see Christianity from the catechism:—from the pastures, from a boat in the pond, from amidst the songs of wood-birds we possibly may. Cleansed by the elemental light and wind, steeped in the sea of beautiful forms which the field offers us, we may chance to cast a right glance back upon biography. Christianity is rightly dear to the best of mankind; yet was there never a young philosopher whose breeding had fallen into the Christian church by whom that brave text of Paul's was not specially prized: "Then shall also the Son be subject unto Him who put all things under him, that God may be all in all." Let the claims and virtues of persons be never so great and welcome, the instinct of man presses eagerly onward to the impersonal and illimitable, and gladly arms itself against the dogmatism of bigots with this generous word out of the book itself.

The natural world may be conceived of as a system of concentric circles, and we now and then detect in nature slight dislocations which apprise us that this surface on which we now stand is not fixed, but sliding. These manifold tenacious qualities, this chemistry and vegetation, these metals and animals, which seem to stand there for their own sake, are means and methods only,—are words of God, and as fugitive as other words. Has the naturalist or chemist learned his craft, who has explored the gravity of atoms and the elective affinities, who has not yet discerned the deeper law whereof this is only a partial or approximate statement, namely that like draws to like, and that the goods which belong to you gravitate to you and need not be pursued with pains and cost? Yet is that statement approximate also, and not final. Omnipresence is a higher fact. Not through subtle subterranean channels need friend and fact be drawn to their counterpart, but, rightly considered, these things proceed from the eternal generation of the soul. Cause and effect are two sides of one fact.

The same law of eternal procession ranges all that we call the virtues, and extinguishes each in the light of a better. The great man will not be prudent in the popular sense; all his prudence will be so much deduction from his grandeur. But it behooves each to see, when he sacrifices prudence, to what god he devotes it; if to ease and pleasure, he had better be prudent still; if to a great trust, he can well spare his mule and panniers who has a winged chariot instead. Geoffrey draws on his boots to go through the woods, that his feet may be safer from the bite of snakes; Aaron never thinks of such a peril. In many years neither is harmed by such an accident. Yet it seems to me that with every precaution you take against such an evil you put yourself into the power of the evil. I suppose that the highest prudence is the lowest prudence. Is this too sudden a rushing from the centre to the verge of our orbit? Think how many times we shall fall back into pitiful calculations before we take up our rest in the great sentiment, or make the verge of to-day the new centre. Besides, your bravest sentiment is familiar to the humblest men. The poor and the low have their way of expressing the last facts of philosophy as well as you. "Blessed be nothing" and "The worse things are, the better they are" are proverbs which express the transcendentalism of common life.

One man's justice is another's injustice; one man's beauty another's ugliness; one man's wisdom another's folly; as one beholds the same objects from a higher point. One man thinks justice consists in paying debts, and has no measure in his abhorrence of another who is very remiss in this duty and makes the creditor wait tediously. But that second man has his own way of looking at things; asks himself Which debt must I pay first, the debt to the rich, or the debt to the poor? the debt of money, or the debt of thought to mankind, of genius to nature? For you, O broker, there is no other principle but arithmetic. For me, commerce is of trivial import; love, faith, truth of character, the aspiration of man, these are sacred; nor can I detach one duty, like you, from all other duties, and concentrate my forces mechanically on the payment of moneys. Let me live onward; you shall find that, though slower, the progress of my character will liquidate all these debts without injustice to higher claims. If a man should dedicate himself to the payment of notes, would not this be injustice? Does he owe no debt but money? And are all claims on him to be postponed to a landlord's or a banker's?

There is no virtue which is final; all are initial. The virtues of society are vices of the saint. The terror of reform is the discovery that we must castaway our virtues, or what we have always esteemed such, into the same pit that has consumed our grosser vices:—

> "Forgive his crimes, forgive his virtues too,
>   Those smaller faults, half converts to the right."

It is the highest power of divine moments that they abolish our contritions also. I accuse myself of sloth and unprofitableness day by day; but when these waves of God flow into me I no longer reckon lost time. I no longer poorly compute my possible achievement by what remains to me of the month or the year; for these moments confer a sort of omnipresence and omnipotence which asks nothing of duration, but sees that the energy of the mind is commensurate with the work to be done, without time.

And thus, O circular philosopher, I hear some reader exclaim, you have arrived at a fine Pyrrhonism, at an equivalence and indifferency of all actions, and would fain teach us that *if we are true*, forsooth, our crimes may be lively stones out of which we shall construct the temple of the true God!

I am not careful to justify myself. I own I am gladdened by seeing the predominance of the saccharine principle throughout vegetable nature, and not less by beholding in morals that unrestrained inundation of the principle of good into every chink and hole that selfishness has left open, yea into selfishness and sin itself; so that no evil is pure, nor hell itself without its extreme satisfactions. But lest I should mislead any when I have my own head and obey my whims, let me remind the reader that I am only an experimenter. Do not set the least value on what I do, or the least discredit on what I do not, as if I pretended to settle any thing as true or false. I unsettle all things. No facts are to me sacred; none are profane; I simply experiment, an endless seeker with no Past at my back.

Yet this incessant movement and progression which all things partake could never become sensible to us but by contrast to some principle of fixture or stability in the soul. Whilst the eternal generation of circles proceeds, the eternal generator abides. That central life is somewhat superior to creation, superior to knowledge and thought, and contains all its circles. Forever it labors to create a life and thought as large and excellent as itself, but in vain, for that which is made instructs how to make a better.

Thus there is no sleep, no pause, no preservation, but all things renew, germinate and spring. Why should we import rags and relics into the new hour? Nature abhors the old, and old age seems the only disease; all others run into this one. We call it by many names,—fever, intemperance, insanity, stupidity and crime; they are all forms of old age; they are rest, conservatism, appropriation, inertia; not newness, not the way onward. We grizzle every day. I see no need of it. Whilst we converse with what is above us, we do not grow old, but grow young. Infancy, youth, receptive, aspiring, with religious eye looking upward, counts itself nothing and abandons itself to the instruction flowing from all sides. But the man and woman of seventy assume to know all, they have outlived their hope, they renounce aspiration, accept the actual for the necessary and talk down to the young. Let them then become organs of the Holy Ghost; let them be lovers; let them behold truth; and their eyes are uplifted, their wrinkles smoothed, they are perfumed again with hope and power. This old age ought not to creep on a human mind. In nature every moment is new; the past is always swallowed and forgotten; the coming only is sacred. Nothing is secure but life, transition, the energizing spirit. No love can be bound by oath or covenant to secure it against a higher love. No truth so sublime but it may be trivial to-morrow in the light of new thoughts. People wish to be settled; only as far as they are unsettled is there any hope for them.

Life is a series of surprises. We do not guess to-day the mood, the pleasure, the power of to-morrow, when we are building up our being. Of lower states, of acts of routine and sense, we can tell somewhat; but the masterpieces of God, the total growths and universal movements of the soul, he hideth; they are incalculable. I can know that truth is divine and helpful; but how it shall help me I can have no guess, for *so to be* is the sole inlet of *so to know.* The new position of the advancing man has all the powers of the old, yet has them all new. It carries in its bosom all the energies of the past, yet is itself an exhalation of the morning. I cast away in this new moment all my once hoarded knowledge, as vacant and vain. Now for the first time seem I to know any thing rightly. The simplest words,—we do not know what they mean except when we love and aspire.

The difference between talents and character is adroitness to keep the old and trodden round, and power and courage to make a new road to new and better goals. Character makes an overpowering present; a cheerful, determined hour, which fortifies all the company by making them see that much is possible and excellent that was not thought of. Character dulls the impression of particular events. When we see the conqueror we do not think much of any one battle or success. We see that we had exaggerated the difficulty. It was easy to him. The great man is not convulsible or tormentable; events pass over him without much impression. People say sometimes, 'See what I have overcome; see how cheerful I am; see how completely I have triumphed over these black events.' Not if they still remind me of the black event. True conquest is the causing the calamity to fade and disappear as an early cloud of insignificant result in a history so large and advancing.

The one thing which we seek with insatiable desire is to forget ourselves, to be surprised out of our propriety, to lose our sempiternal memory and to do something without knowing how or why; in short to draw a new circle. Nothing great was ever achieved without enthusiasm. The way of life is wonderful; it is by abandonment. The great moments of history are the facilities of performance through the strength of ideas, as the works of genius and religion. "A man," said Oliver Cromwell, "never rises so high as when he knows not whither he is going." Dreams and drunkenness, the use of opium and alcohol are the semblance and counterfeit of this oracular genius, and hence their dangerous attraction for men. For the like reason they ask the aid of wild passions, as in gaming and war, to ape in some manner these flames and generosities of the heart.

THE POET

A moody child and wildly wise
Pursued the game with joyful eyes,
Which chose, like meteors, their way,
And rived the dark with private ray:
They overleapt the horizon's edge,
Searched with Apollo's privilege;
Through man, and woman, and sea, and star
Saw the dance of nature forward far;
Through worlds, and races, and terms, and times
Saw musical order, and pairing rhymes.

Olympian bards who sung
Divine ideas below,
Which always find us young,
And always keep us so.

Those who are esteemed umpires of taste are often persons who have acquired some knowledge of admired pictures or sculptures, and have an inclination for whatever is elegant; but if you inquire whether they are beautiful souls, and whether their own acts are like fair pictures, you learn that they are selfish and sensual. Their cultivation is local, as if you should rub a log of dry wood in one spot to produce fire, all the rest remaining cold. Their knowledge of the fine arts is some study of rules and particulars, or some limited judgment of color or form, which is exercised for amusement or for show. It is a proof of the shallowness of the doctrine of beauty as it lies in the minds of our amateurs, that men seem to have lost the per-

ception of the instant dependence of form upon soul.
There is no doctrine of forms in our philosophy. We were
put into our bodies, as fire is put into a pan to be carried
about; but there is no accurate adjustment between the
spirit and the organ, much less is the latter the germina-
tion of the former. So in regard to other forms, the intellectual men do not believe in any essential dependence of
the material world on thought and volition. Theologians
think it a pretty air-castle to talk of the spiritual meaning
of a ship or a cloud, of a city or a contract, but they prefer
to come again to the solid ground of historical evidence;
and even the poets are contented with a civil and con-
formed manner of living, and to write poems from the
fancy, at a safe distance from their own experience. But
the highest minds of the world have never ceased to explore the double meaning, or shall I say the quadruple or
the centuple or much more manifold meaning, of every
sensuous fact; Orpheus, Empedocles, Heraclitus, Plato,
Plutarch, Dante, Swedenborg, and the masters of sculpture, picture and poetry. For we are not pans and barrows,
nor even porters of the fire and torch-bearers, but children
of the fire, made of it, and only the same divinity trans-
muted and at two or three removes, when we know least
about it. And this hidden truth, that the fountains whence
all this river of Time and its creatures floweth are intrin-
sically ideal and beautiful, draws us to the consideration
of the nature and functions of the Poet, or the man of
Beauty; to the means and materials he uses, and to the
general aspect of the art in the present time.

The breadth of the problem is great, for the poet is representative. He stands among partial men for the complete
man, and apprises us not of his wealth, but of the common
wealth. The young man reveres men of genius, because, to
speak truly, they are more himself than he is. They receive of the soul as he also receives, but they more. Nature
enhances her beauty, to the eye of loving men, from their
belief that the poet is beholding her shows at the same

time. He is isolated among his contemporaries by truth and by his art, but with this consolation in his pursuits, that they will draw all men sooner or later. For all men live by truth and stand in need of expression. In love, in art, in avarice, in politics, in labor, in games, we study to utter our painful secret. The man is only half himself, the other half is his expression.

Notwithstanding this necessity to be published, adequate expression is rare. I know not how it is that we need an interpreter, but the great majority of men seem to be minors, who have not yet come into possession of their own, or mutes, who cannot report the conversation they have had with nature. There is no man who does not anticipate a supersensual utility in the sun and stars, earth and water. These stand and wait to render him a peculiar service. But there is some obstruction or some excess of phlegm in our constitution, which does not suffer them to yield the due effect. Too feeble fall the impressions of nature on us to make us artists. Every touch should thrill. Every man should be so much an artist that he could report in conversation what had befallen him. Yet, in our experience, the rays or appulses have sufficient force to arrive at the senses, but not enough to reach the quick and compel the reproduction of themselves in speech. The poet is the person in whom these powers are in balance, the man without impediment, who sees and handles that which others dream of, traverses the whole scale of experience, and is representative of man, in virtue of being the largest power to receive and to impart.

For the Universe has three children, born at one time, which reappear under different names in every system of thought, whether they be called cause, operation and effect; or, more poetically, Jove, Pluto, Neptune; or, theologically, the Father, the Spirit and the Son; but which we will call here the Knower, the Doer and the Sayer. These stand respectively for the love of truth, for the love of good, and for the love of beauty. These three are equal.

Each is that which he is, essentially, so that he cannot be surmounted or analyzed, and each of these three has the power of the others latent in him and his own, patent.

The poet is the sayer, the namer, and represents beauty. He is a sovereign, and stands on the centre. For the world is not painted or adorned, but is from the beginning beautiful; and God has not made some beautiful things, but Beauty is the creator of the universe. Therefore the poet is not any permissive potentate, but is emperor in his own right. Criticism is infested with a cant of materialism, which assumes that manual skill and activity is the first merit of all men, and disparages such as say and do not, overlooking the fact that some men, namely poets, are natural sayers, sent into the world to the end of expression, and confounds them with those whose province is action but who quit it to imitate the sayers. But Homer's words are as costly and admirable to Homer as Agamemnon's victories are to Agamemnon. The poet does not wait for the hero or the sage, but, as they act and think primarily, so he writes primarily what will and must be spoken, reckoning the others, though primaries also, yet, in respect to him, secondaries and servants; as sitters or models in the studio of a painter, or as assistants who bring building-materials to an architect.

For poetry was all written before time was, and whenever we are so finely organized that we can penetrate into that region where the air is music, we hear those primal warblings and attempt to write them down, but we lose ever and anon a word or a verse and substitute something of our own, and thus miswrite the poem. The men of more delicate ear write down these cadences more faithfully, and these transcripts, though imperfect, become the songs of the nations. For nature is as truly beautiful as it is good, or as it is reasonable, and must as much appear as it must be done, or be known. Words and deeds are quite indifferent modes of the divine energy. Words are also actions, and actions are a kind of words.

The sign and credentials of the poet are that he announces that which no man foretold. He is the true and only doctor; he knows and tells; he is the only teller of news, for he was present and privy to the appearance which he describes. He is a beholder of ideas and an utterer of the necessary and causal. For we do not speak now of men of poetical talents, or of industry and skill in metre, but of the true poet. I took part in a conversation the other day concerning a recent writer of lyrics, a man of subtle mind, whose head appeared to be a music-box of delicate tunes and rhythms, and whose skill and command of language we could not sufficiently praise. But when the question arose whether he was not only a lyrist but a poet, we were obliged to confess that he is plainly a contemporary, not an eternal man. He does not stand out of our low limitations, like a Chimborazo under the line, running up from a torrid base through all the climates of the globe, with belts of the herbage of every latitude on its high and mottled sides; but this genius is the landscape-garden of a modern house, adorned with fountains and statues, with well-bred men and women standing and sitting in the walks and terraces. We hear, through all the varied music, the ground-tone of conventional life. Our poets are men of talents who sing, and not the children of music. The argument is secondary, the finish of the verses is primary.

For it is not metres, but a metre-making argument that makes a poem,—a thought so passionate and alive that like the spirit of a plant or an animal it has an architecture of its own, and adorns nature with a new thing. The thought and the form are equal in the order of time, but in the order of genesis the thought is prior to the form. The poet has a new thought; he has a whole new experience to unfold; he will tell us how it was with him, and all men will be the richer in his fortune. For the experience of each new age requires a new confession, and the world seems always waiting for its poet. I remember when I was young how much I was moved one morning by tidings that genius had appeared in a youth who sat near me at table. He had left his work and gone rambling none knew whither, and had written hundreds of lines, but could not tell whether that which was in him was therein told; he could tell nothing but that all was changed,—man, beast, heaven, earth and sea. How gladly we listened! how credulous! Society seemed to be compromised. We sat in the aurora of a sunrise which was to put out all the stars. Boston seemed to be at twice the distance it had the night before, or was much farther than that. Rome,—what was Rome? Plutarch and Shakspeare were in the yellow leaf, and Homer no more should be heard of. It is much to know that poetry has been written this very day, under this very roof, by your side. What! that wonderful spirit has not expired! These stony moments are still sparkling and animated! I had fancied that the oracles were all silent, and nature had spent her fires; and behold! all night, from every pore, these fine auroras have been streaming. Every one has some interest in the advent of the poet, and no one knows how much it may concern him. We know that the secret of the world is profound, but who or what shall be our interpreter, we know not. A mountain ramble, a new style of face, a new person, may put the key into our hands. Of course the value of genius to us is in the veracity of its report. Talent may frolic and juggle; genius realizes and adds. Mankind in good earnest have availed so far in understanding themselves and their work, that the foremost watchman on the peak announces his news. It is the truest word ever spoken, and the phrase will be the fittest, most musical, and the unerring voice of the world for that time.

All that we call sacred history attests that the birth of a poet is the principal event in chronology. Man, never so often deceived, still watches for the arrival of a brother who can hold him steady to a truth until he has made it his own. With what joy I begin to read a poem which I confide in as an inspiration? And now my chains are to be broken; I shall mount above these clouds and opaque airs in which I live,—opaque, though they seem transparent,—and from the heaven of truth I shall see and com-

prehend my relations. That will reconcile me to life and
renovate nature, to see trifles animated by a tendency, and
to know what I am doing. Life will no more be a noise;
now I shall see men and women, and know the signs by
which they may be discerned from fools and satans. This
day shall be better than my birthday: then I became an animal; now I am invited into the science of the real. Such is
the hope, but the fruition is postponed. Oftener it falls
that this winged man, who will carry me into the heaven,
whirls me into mists, then leaps and frisks about with me
as it were from cloud to cloud, still affirming that he is
bound heavenward; and I, being myself a novice, am slow
in perceiving that he does not know the way into the heavens, and is merely bent that I should admire his skill to
rise like a fowl or a flying fish, a little way from the ground
or the water; but the all-piercing, all-feeding and ocular air
of heaven that man shall never inhabit. I tumble down
again soon into my old nooks, and lead the life of exaggerations as before, and have lost my faith in the possibility
of any guide who can lead me thither where I would
be.

But, leaving these victims of vanity, let us, with new
hope, observe how nature, by worthier impulses, has in-
sured the poet's fidelity to his office of announcement and
affirming, namely by the beauty of things, which becomes
a new and higher beauty when expressed. Nature offers
all her creatures to him as a picture-language. Being used
as a type, a second wonderful value appears in the object,
far better than its old value; as the carpenter's stretched
cord, if you hold your ear close enough, is musical in the
breeze. "Things more excellent than every image," says
Jamblichus, "are expressed through images." Things
admit of being used as symbols because nature is a symbol, in the whole, and in every part. Every line we can
draw in the sand has expression; and there is no body
without its spirit or genius. All form is an effect of character; all condition, of the quality of the life; all harmony, of
health; and for this reason a perception of beauty should

be sympathetic, or proper only to the good. The beautiful
rests on the foundations of the necessary. The soul makes
the body, as the wise Spenser teaches:—

> "So every spirit, as it is more pure,
>   And hath in it the more of heavenly light,
> So it the fairer body doth procure
>   To habit in, and it more fairly dight,
>   With cheerful grace and amiable sight.
> For, of the soul, the body form doth take,
> For soul is form, and doth the body make."

Here we find ourselves suddenly not in a critical speculation but in a holy place, and should go very warily
and reverently. We stand before the secret of the world,
there where Being passes into Appearance and Unity into
Variety.

The Universe is the externization of the soul. Wherever
the life is, that bursts into appearance around it. Our science is sensual, and therefore superficial. The earth and
the heavenly bodies, physics and chemistry, we sensually
treat, as if they were self-existent; but these are the retinue
of that Being we have. "The mighty heaven," said Proclus, "exhibits, in its transfigurations, clear images of the
splendor of intellectual perceptions; being moved in con-
junction with the unapparent periods of intellectual natures." Therefore science always goes abreast with the
just elevation of the man, keeping step with religion and
metaphysics; or the state of science is an index of our self-
knowledge. Since every thing in nature answers to a moral
power, if any phenomenon remains brute and dark it is
because the corresponding faculty in the observer is not
yet active.

No wonder then, if these waters be so deep, that we
hover over them with a religious regard. The beauty of the
fable proves the importance of the sense; to the poet, and
to all others; or, if you please, every man is so far a poet as
to be susceptible of these enchantments of nature; for all

men have the thoughts whereof the universe is the celebration. I find that the fascination resides in the symbol. Who loves nature? Who does not? Is it only poets, and men of leisure and cultivation, who live with her? No; but also hunters, farmers, grooms and butchers, though they express their affection in their choice of life and not in their choice of words. The writer wonders what the coachman or the hunter values in riding, in horses and dogs. It is not superficial qualities. When you talk with him he holds these at as slight a rate as you. His worship is sympathetic; he has no definitions, but he is commanded in nature by the living power which he feels to be there present. No imitation or playing of these things would content him; he loves the earnest of the north wind, of rain, of stone and wood and iron. A beauty not explicable is dearer than a beauty which we can see to the end of. It is nature the symbol, nature certifying the supernatural, body overflowed by life which he worships with coarse but sincere rites.

The inwardness and mystery of this attachment drive men of every class to the use of emblems. The schools of poets and philosophers are not more intoxicated with their symbols than the populace with theirs. In our political parties, compute the power of badges and emblems. See the great ball which they roll from Baltimore to Bunker Hill! In the political processions, Lowell goes in a loom, and Lynn in a shoe, and Salem in a ship. Witness the cider-barrel, the log-cabin, the hickory-stick, the palmetto, and all the cognizances of party. See the power of national emblems. Some stars, lilies, leopards, a crescent, a lion, an eagle, or other figure which came into credit God knows how, on an old rag of bunting, blowing in the wind on a fort at the ends of the earth, shall make the blood tingle under the rudest or the most conventional exterior. The people fancy they hate poetry, and they are all poets and mystics!

Beyond this universality of the symbolic language, we are apprised of the divineness of this superior use of things, whereby the world is a temple whose walls are covered with emblems, pictures and commandments of the Deity,—in this, that there is no fact in nature which does not carry the whole sense of nature; and the distinctions which we make in events and in affairs, of low and high, honest and base, disappear when nature is used as a symbol. Thought makes everything fit for use. The vocabulary of an omniscient man would embrace words and images excluded from polite conversation. What would be base, or even obscene, to the obscene, becomes illustrious, spoken in a new connection of thought. The piety of the Hebrew prophets purges their grossness. The circumcision is an example of the power of poetry to raise the low and offensive. Small and mean things serve as well as great symbols. The meaner the type by which a law is expressed, the more pungent it is, and the more lasting in the memories of men; just as we choose the smallest box or case in which any needful utensil can be carried. Bare lists of words are found suggestive to an imaginative and excited mind; as it is related of Lord Chatham that he was accustomed to read in Bailey's Dictionary when he was preparing to speak in Parliament. The poorest experience is rich enough for all the purposes of expressing thought. Why covet a knowledge of new facts? Day and night, house and garden, a few books, a few actions, serve us as well as would all trades and all spectacles. We are far from having exhausted the significance of the few symbols we use. We can come to use them yet with a terrible simplicity. It does not need that a poem should be long. Every word was once a poem. Every new relation is a new word. Also we use defects and deformities to a sacred purpose, so expressing our sense that the evils of the world are such only to the evil eye. In the old mythology, mythologists observe, defects are ascribed to divine natures, as lameness to Vulcan, blindness to Cupid, and the like,—to signify exuberances.

For as it is dislocation and detachment from the life of God that makes things ugly, the poet, who re-attaches things to nature and the Whole,—re-attaching even artificial things and violation of nature, to nature, by a deeper insight,—disposes very easily of the most disagreeable facts. Readers of poetry see the factory-village and the railway, and fancy that the poetry of the landscape is broken up by these; for these works of art are not yet consecrated in their reading; but the poet sees them fall within the great Order not less than the beehive or the spider's geometrical web. Nature adopts them very fast into her vital circles, and the gliding train of cars she loves like her own. Besides, in a centred mind, it signifies nothing how many mechanical inventions you exhibit. Though you add millions, and never so surprising, the fact of mechanics has not gained a grain's weight. The spiritual fact remains unalterable, by many or by few particulars; as no mountain is of any appreciable height to break the curve of the sphere. A shrewd country-boy goes to the city for the first time, and the complacent citizen is not satisfied with his little wonder. It is not that he does not see all the fine houses and know that he never saw such before, but he disposes of them as easily as the poet finds place for the railway. The chief value of the new fact is to enhance the great and constant fact of Life, which can dwarf any and every circumstance, and to which the belt of wampum and the commerce of America are alike.

The world being thus put under the mind for verb and noun, the poet is he who can articulate it. For though life is great, and fascinates and absorbs; and though all men are intelligent of the symbols through which it is named; yet they cannot originally use them. We are symbols and inhabit symbols; workmen, work, and tools, words and things, birth and death, all are emblems; but we sympathize with the symbols, and being infatuated with the economical uses of things, we do not know that they are thoughts. The poet, by an ulterior intellectual perception, gives them a power which makes their old use forgotten, and puts eyes and a tongue into every dumb and inanimate object. He perceives the independence of the thought on the symbol, the stability of the thought, the accidency and fugacity of the symbol. As the eyes of Lyncæus were said to see through the earth, so the poet turns the world to glass, and shows us all things in their right series and procession. For through that better perception he stands one step nearer to things, and sees the flowing or metamorphosis; perceives that thought is multiform; that within the form of every creature is a force impelling it to ascend into a higher form; and following with his eyes the life, uses the forms which express that life, and so his speech flows with the flowing of nature. All the facts of the animal economy, sex, nutriment, gestation, birth, growth, are symbols of the passage of the world into the soul of man, to suffer there a change and reappear a new and higher fact. He uses forms according to the life, and not according to the form. This is true science. The poet alone knows astronomy, chemistry, vegetation and animation, for he does not stop at these facts, but employs them as signs. He knows why the plain or meadow of space was strown with these flowers we call suns and moons and stars; why the great deep is adorned with animals, with men, and gods; for in every word he speaks he rides on them as the horses of thought.

By virtue of this science the poet is the Namer or Language-maker, naming things sometimes after their appearance, sometimes after their essence, and giving to every one its own name and not another's, thereby rejoicing the intellect, which delights in detachment or boundary. The poets made all the words, and therefore language is the archives of history, and, if we must say it, a sort of tomb of the muses. For though the origin of most of our words is forgotten, each word was at first a stroke of genius, and obtained currency because for the moment it symbolized the world to the first speaker and to the hearer. The etymologist finds the deadest word to have been once a brilliant picture. Language is fossil poetry. As the limestone of the continent consists of infinite masses of the shells of animalcules, so language is made up of images or tropes, which now, in their secondary use, have long ceased to remind us of their poetic origin. But the poet names the thing because he sees it, or comes one step nearer to it than any other. This expression or naming is not art, but a second nature, grown out of the first, as a leaf out of a tree. What we call nature is a certain self-regulated motion or change; and nature does all things by her own hands, and does not leave another to baptize her but baptizes herself; and this through the metamorphosis again. I remember that a certain poet described it to me thus:—

Genius is the activity which repairs the decays of things, whether wholly or partly of a material and finite kind. Nature, through all her kingdoms, insures herself. Nobody cares for planting the poor fungus; so she shakes down from the gills of one agaric countless spores, any one of which, being preserved, transmits new billions of spores to-morrow or next day. The new agaric of this hour has a chance which the old one had not. This atom of seed is thrown into a new place, not subject to the accidents which destroyed its parent two rods off. She makes a man; and having brought him to ripe age, she will no longer run the risk of losing this wonder at a blow, but she detaches from him a new self, that the kind may be safe from accidents to which the individual is exposed. So when the soul of the poet has come to ripeness of thought, she detaches and sends away from it its poems or songs,—a fearless, sleepless, deathless progeny, which is not exposed to the accidents of the weary kingdom of time; a fearless, vivacious offspring, clad with wings (such was the virtue of the soul out of which they came) which carry them fast and far, and infix them irrecoverably into the hearts of men. These wings are the beauty of the poet's soul. The songs, thus flying immortal from their mortal parent, are pursued by clamorous flights of censures, which swarm in far greater numbers and threaten to devour them; but these last are not winged. At the end of a very short leap they fall plump down and rot, having received from the

souls out of which they came no beautifull wings. But
the melodies of the poet ascend and leap and pierce
into the deeps of infinite time.

So far the bard taught me, using his freer speech. But
nature has a higher end, in the production of new individuals, than security, namely *ascension,* or the passage of
the soul into higher forms. I knew in my younger days the
sculptor who made the statue of the youth which stands in
the public garden. He was, as I remember, unable to tell
directly what made him happy or unhappy, but by wonderful indirections he could tell. He rose one day, according to his habit, before the dawn, and saw the morning
break, grand as the eternity out of which it came, and for
many days after, he strove to express this tranquillity, and
lo! his chisel had fashioned out of marble the form of a
beautiful youth, Phosphorus, whose aspect is such that it
is said all persons who look on it become silent. The poet
also resigns himself to his mood, and that thought which
agitated him is expressed, but *alter idem,* in a manner totally new. The expression is organic, or the new type
which things themselves take when liberated. As, in the
sun, objects paint their images on the retina of the eye, so
they, sharing the aspiration of the whole universe, tend to
paint a far more delicate copy of their essence in his mind.
Like the metamorphosis of things into higher organic
forms is their change into melodies. Over everything
stands its dæmon or soul, and, as the form of the thing is
reflected by the eye, so the soul of the thing is reflected by
a melody. The sea, the mountain-ridge, Niagara, and
every flower-bed, pre-exist, or super-exist, in pre-canta-
tions, which sail like odors in the air, and when any man
goes by with an ear sufficiently fine, he overhears them
and endeavors to write down the notes without diluting or
depraving them. And herein is the legitimation of criticism, in the mind's faith that the poems are a corrupt version of some text in nature with which they ought to be
made to tally. A rhyme in one of our sonnets should not

be less pleasinig than the iterated nodes of a seashell, or the resembling difference of a group of flowers. The pairing of the birds in an idyl, not tedious as our idyls are; a tempest is a rough ode, without falsehood or rant; a summer, with its harvest sown, reaped and stored, is an epic song, subordinating how many admirably executed parts. Why should not the symmetry and truth that modulate these, glide into our spirits, and we participate the invention of nature?

This insight, which expresses itself by what is called Imagination, is a very high sort of seeing, which does not come by study, but by the intellect being where and what it sees; by sharing the path or circuit of things through forms, and so making them translucid to others. The path of things is silent. Will they suffer a speaker to go with them? A spy they will not suffer; a lover, a poet, is the transcendency of their own nature,—him they will suffer. The condition of true naming, on the poet's part, is his resigning himself to the divine *aura* which breathes through forms, and accompanying that.

It is a secret which every intellectual man quickly learns, that beyond the energy of his possessed and conscious intellect he is capable of a new energy (as of an intellect doubled on itself), by abandonment to the nature of things; that beside his privacy of power as an individual man, there is a great public power on which he can draw, by unlocking, at all risks, his human doors, and suffering the ethereal tides to roll and circulate through him; then he is caught up into the life of the Universe, his speech is thunder, his thought is law, and his words are universally intelligible as the plants and animals. The poet knows that he speaks adequately then only when he speaks somewhat wildly, or "with the flower of the mind;" not with the intellect used as an organ, but with the intellect released from all service and suffered to take its direction from its celestial life; or as the ancients were wont to express themselves, not with intellect alone but with the intellect inebriated by nectar. As the traveller who has lost his way throws his reins on his horse's neck and trusts to the instinct of the animal to find his road, so must we do with the divine animal who carries us through this world. For if in any manner we can stimulate this instinct, new passages are opened for us into nature; the mind flows into and through things hardest and highest, and the metamorphosis is possible.

This is the reason why bards love wine, mead, narcotics, coffee, tea, opium, the fumes of sandalwood and tobacco, or whatever other procurers of animal exhilaration. All men avail themselves of such means as they can, to add this extraordinary power to their normal powers; and to this end they prize conversation, music, pictures, sculpture, dancing, theatres, travelling, war, mobs, fires, gaming, politics, or love, or science, or animal intoxication, —which are several coarser or finer *quasi*-mechanical substitutes for the true nectar, which is the ravishment of the intellect by coming nearer to the fact. These are auxiliaries to the centrifugal tendency of a man, to his passage out into free space, and they help him to escape the custody of that body in which he is pent up, and of that jail-yard of individual relations in which he is enclosed. Hence a great number of such as were professionally expressers of Beauty, as painters, poets, musicians and actors, have been more than others wont to lead a life of pleasure and indulgence; all but the few who received the true nectar; and, as it was a spurious mode of attaining freedom, as it was an emancipation not into the heavens but into the freedom of baser places, they were punished for that advantage they won, by a dissipation and deterioration. But never can any advantage be taken of nature by a trick. The spirit of the world, the great calm presence of the Creator, comes not forth to the sorceries of opium or of wine. The sublime vision comes to the pure and simple soul in a clean and chaste body. This is not an inspiration, which we owe to narcotics, but some counterfeit excitement and fury. Milton says that the lyric poet may drink wine and live generously, but the epic poet, he who shall sing of the

gods and their descent unto men, must drink water out of
a wooden bowl. For poetry is not 'Devil's wine,' but God's
wine. It is with this as it is with toys. We fill the hands and
nurseries of our children with all manner of dolls, drums
and horses; withdrawing their eyes from the plain face
and sufficing objects of nature, the sun and moon, the animals, the water and stones, which should be their toys. So
the poet's habit of living should be set on a key so low that
the common influences should delight him. His cheerfulness should be the gift of the sunlight; the air should suffice for his inspiration, and he should be tipsy with water.
That spirit which suffices quiet hearts, which seems to
come forth to such from every dry knoll of sere grass,
from every pine stump and half-imbedded stone on which
the dull March sun shines, comes forth to the poor and
hungry, and such as are of simple taste. If thou fill thy
brain with Boston and New York, with fashion and covet-
ousness, and wilt stimulate thy jaded senses with wine
and French coffee, thou shalt find no radiance of wisdom
in the lonely waste of the pine woods.

If the imagination intoxicates the poet, it is not inactive
in other men. The metamorphosis excites in the beholder
an emotion of joy. The use of symbols has a certain power
of emancipation and exhilaration for all men. We seem to
be touched by a wand which makes us dance and run
about happily, like children. We are like persons who
come out of a cave or cellar into the open air. This is the
effect on us of tropes, fables, oracles and all poetic forms.
Poets are thus liberating gods. Men have really got a new
sense, and found within their world another world, or nest
of worlds; for, the metamorphosis once seen, we divine
that it does not stop. I will not now consider how much
this makes the charm of algebra and the mathematics,
which also have their tropes, but it is felt in every definition; as when Aristotle defines *space* to be an immovable
vessel in which things are contained;—or when Plato defines a *line* to be a flowing point; or *figure* to be a bound of
solid; and many the like. What a joyful sense of freedom

we have when Vitruvius announces the old opinion of artists that no architect can build any house well who does
not know something of anatomy. When Socrates, in
Charmides, tells us that the soul is cured of its maladies by
certain incantations, and that these incantations are beautiful reasons, from which temperance is generated in
souls; when Plato calls the world an animal, and Timæus
affirms that the plants also are animals; or affirms a man to
be a heavenly tree, growing with his root, which is his
head, upward; and, as George Chapman, following him,
writes,

> "So in our tree of man, whose nervie root
> Springs in his top;"—

when Orpheus speaks of hoariness as "that white flower
which marks extreme old age;" when Proclus calls the universe the statue of the intellect; when Chaucer, in his
praise of 'Gentilesse,' compares good blood in mean condition to fire, which, though carried to the darkest house
betwixt this and the mount of Caucasus, will yet hold its
natural office and burn as bright as if twenty thousand
men did it behold; when John saw, in the Apocalypse, the
ruin of the world through evil, and the stars fall from
heaven as the fig tree casteth her untimely fruit; when
Æsop reports the whole catalogue of common daily relations through the masquerade of birds and beasts;—we
take the cheerful hint of the immortality of our essence
and its versatile habit and escapes, as when the gypsies say
of themselves "it is in vain to hang them, they cannot die."

The poets are thus liberating gods. The ancient British
bards had for the title of their order, "Those who are free
throughout the world." They are free, and they make free.
An imaginative book renders us much more service at
first, by stimulating us through its tropes, than afterward
when we arrive at the precise sense of the author. I think
nothing is of any value in books excepting the transcendental and extraordinary. If a man is inflamed and carried

away by his thought, to that degree that he forgets the authors and the public and heeds only this one dream which holds him like an insanity, let me read his paper, and you may have all the arguments and histories and criticism. All the value which attaches to Pythagoras, Paracelsus, Cornelius Agrippa, Cardan, Kepler, Swedenborg, Schelling, Oken, or any other who introduces questionable facts into his cosmogony, as angels, devils, magic, astrology, palmistry, mesmerism, and so on, is the certificate we have of departure from routine, and that here is a new witness. That also is the best success in conversation, the magic of liberty, which puts the world like a ball in our hands. How cheap even the liberty then seems; how mean to study, when an emotion communicates to the intellect the power to sap and upheave nature; how great the perspective! nations, times, systems, enter and disappear like threads in tapestry of large figure and many colors; dream delivers us to dream, and while the drunkenness lasts we will sell our bed, our philosophy, our religion, in our opulence.

There is good reason why we should prize this liberation. The fate of the poor shepherd, who, blinded and lost in the snow-storm, perishes in a drift within a few feet of his cottage door, is an emblem of the state of man. On the brink of the waters of life and truth, we are miserably dying. The inaccessibleness of every thought but that we are in, is wonderful. What if you come near to it; you are as remote when you are nearest as when you are farthest. Every thought is also a prison; every heaven is also a prison. Therefore we love the poet, the inventor, who in any form, whether in an ode or in an action or in looks and behavior, has yielded us a new thought. He unlocks our chains and admits us to a new scene.

This emancipation is dear to all men, and the power to impart it, as it must come from greater depth and scope of thought, is a measure of intellect. Therefore all books of the imagination endure, all which ascend to that truth that the writer sees nature beneath him, and uses it as his exponent. Every verse or sentence possessing this virtue will take care of its own immortality. The religions of the world are the ejaculations of a few imaginative men.

But the quality of the imagination is to flow, and not to freeze. The poet did not stop at the color or the form, but read their meaning; neither may he rest in this meaning, but he makes the same objects exponents of his new thought. Here is the difference betwixt the poet and the mystic, that the last nails a symbol to one sense, which was a true sense for a moment, but soon becomes old and false. For all symbols are fluxional; all language is vehicular and transitive, and is good, as ferries and horses are, for conveyance, not as farms and houses are, for homestead. Mysticism consists in the mistake of an accidental and individual symbol for an universal one. The morning-redness happens to be the favorite meteor to the eyes of Jacob Behmen, and comes to stand to him for truth and faith; and, he believes, should stand for the same realities to every reader. But the first reader prefers as naturally the symbol of a mother and child, or a gardener and his bulb, or a jeweller polishing a gem. Either of these, or of a myriad more, are equally good to the person to whom they are significant. Only they must be held lightly, and be very willlingly translated into the equivalent terms which others use. And the mystic must be steadily told,—All that you say is just as true without the tedious use of that symbol as with it. Let us have a little algebra, instead of this trite rhetoric,—universal signs, instead of these village symbols,—and we shall both be gainers. The history of hierarchies seems to show that all religious error consisted in making the symbol too stark and solid, and was at last nothing but an excess of the organ of language.

Swedenborg, of all men in the recent ages, stands eminently for the translator of nature into thought. I do not know the man in history to whom things stood so uniformly for words. Before him the metamorphosis continually plays. Everything on which his eye rests, obeys the impulses of moral nature. The figs become grapes whilst he eats them. When some of his angels affirmed a truth, the laurel twig which they held blossomed in their hands. The noise which at a distance appeared like gnashing and thumping, on coming nearer was found to be the voice of disputants. The men in one of his visions, seen in heavenly light, appeared like dragons, and seemed in darkness; but to each other they appeared as men, and when the light from heaven shone into their cabin, they complained of the darkness, and were compelled to shut the window that they might see.

There was this perception in him which makes the poet or seer an object of awe and terror, namely that the same man or society of men may wear one aspect to themselves and their companions, and a different aspect to higher intelligences. Certain priests, whom he describes as conversing very learnedly together, appeared to the children who were at some distance, like dead horses; and many the like misappearances. And instantly the mind inquires whether these fishes under the bridge, yonder oxen in the pasture, those dogs in the yard, are immutably fishes, oxen and dogs, or only so appear to me, and perchance to themselves appear upright men; and whether I appear as a man to all eyes. The Brahmins and Pythagoras propounded the same question, and if any poet has witnessed the transformation he doubtless found it in harmony with various experiences. We have all seen changes as considerable in wheat and caterpillars. He is the poet and shall draw us with love and terror, who sees through the flowing vest the firm nature, and can declare it.

I look in vain for the poet whom I describe. We do not with sufficient plainness or sufficient profoundness address ourselves to life, nor dare we chaunt our own times and social circumstance. If we filled the day with bravery, we should not shrink from celebrating it. Time and nature yield us many gifts, but not yet the timely man, the new religion, the reconciler, whom all things await. Dante's praise is that he dared to write his autobiography in colossal cipher, or into universality. We have yet had no genius in America, with tyrannous eye, which knew the value of our incomparable materials, and saw, in the barbarism and materialism of the times, another carnival of the same gods whose picture he so much admires in Homer; then in the Middle Age; then in Calvinism. Banks and tariffs, the newspaper and caucus, Methodism and Unitarianism, are flat and dull to dull people, but rest on the same foundations of wonder as the town of Troy and the temple of Delphi, and are as swiftly passing away. Our log-rolling, our stumps and their politics, our fisheries, our Negroes and Indians, our boasts and our repudiations, the wrath of rogues and the pusillanimity of honest men, the northern trade, the southern planting, the western clearing, Oregon and Texas, are yet unsung. Yet America is a poem in our eyes; its ample geography dazzles the imagination, and it will not wait long for metres. If I have not found that excellent combination of gifts in my countrymen which I seek, neither could I aid myself to fix the idea of the poet by reading now and then in Chalmers's collection of five centuries of English poets. These are wits more than poets, though there have been poets among them. But when we adhere to the ideal of the poet, we have our difficulties even with Milton and Homer. Milton is too literary, and Homer too literal and historical.

But I am not wise enough for a national criticism, and must use the old largeness a little longer, to discharge my errand from the muse to the poet concerning his art.

Art is the path of the creator to his work. The paths or methods are ideal and eternal, though few men ever see them; not the artist himself for years, or for a lifetime, unless he come into the conditions. The painter, the sculptor, the composer, the epic rhapsodist, the orator, all partake one desire, namely to express themselves symmetrically and abundantly, not dwarfishly and fragmentarily. They found or put themselves in certain conditions, as, the painter and sculptor before some impressive human figures; the orator into the assembly of the people; and the others in such scenes as each has found exciting to his intellect; and each presently feels the new desire. He hears a voice, he sees a beckoning. Then he is apprised, with wonder, what herds of dæmons hem him in. He can no more rest; he says, with the old painter, "By God it is in me and must go forth of me." He pursues a beauty, half seen, which flies before him. The poet pours out verses in every solitude. Most of the things he says are conventional, no doubt; but by and by he says something which is original and beautiful. That charms him. He would say nothing else but such things. In our way of talking we say 'That is yours, this is mine;' but the poet knows well that it is not his; that it is as strange and beautiful to him as to you; he would fain hear the like eloquence at length. Once having tasted this immortal ichor, he cannot have enough of it, and as an admirable creative power exists in these intellections, it is of the last importance that these things get spoken. What a little of all we know is said! What drops of all the sea of our science are baled up! and by what accident it is that these are exposed, when so many secrets sleep in nature! Hence the necessity of speech and song; hence these throbs and heart-beatings in the orator, at the door of the assembly, to the end namely that thought may be ejaculated as Logos, or Word.

Doubt not, O poet, but persist. Say 'It is in me, and shall out.' Stand there, balked and dumb, stuttering and stammering, hissed and hooted, stand and strive, until at last rage draw out of thee that *dream*-power which every night shows thee is thine own; a power transcending all limit and privacy, and by virtue of which a man is the conductor of the whole river of electricity. Nothing walks, or creeps, or grows, or exists, which must not in turn arise and walk before him as exponent of his meaning. Comes he to that power, his genius is no longer exhaustible. All the creatures by pairs and by tribes pour into his mind as into a Noah's ark, to come forth again to people a new world. This is like the stock of air for our respiration or for the combustion of our fireplace; not a measure of gallons, but the entire atmosphere if wanted. And therefore the rich poets, as Homer, Chaucer, Shakspeare, and Raphael, have obviously no limits to their works except the limits of their lifetime, and resemble a mirror carried through the street, ready to render an image of every created thing.

O poet! a new nobility is conferred in groves and pastures, and not in castles or by the swordblade any longer. The conditions are hard, but equal. Thou shalt leave the world, and know the muse only. Thou shalt not know any longer the times, customs, graces, politics, or opinions of men, but shalt take all from the muse. For the time of towns is tolled from the world by funereal chimes, but in nature the universal hours are counted by succeeding tribes of animals and plants, and by growth of joy on joy. God wills also that thou abdicate a manifold and duplex life, and that thou be content that others speak for thee. Others shall be thy gentlemen and shall represent all courtesy and worldly life for thee; others shall do the great and resounding actions also. Thou shalt lie close hid with nature, and canst not be afforded to the Capitol or the Exchange. The world is full of renunciations and apprenticeships, and this is thine; thou must pass for a fool and a churl for a long season. This is the screen and sheath in which Pan has protected his well-beloved flower, and thou shalt be known only to thine own, and they shall console thee with tenderest love. And thou shalt not be able to rehearse the names of thy friends in thy verse, for an old shame before the holy ideal. And this is the reward; that the ideal shall be real to thee, and the impressions of the actual world shall fall like summer rain, copious, but not troublesome to thy invulnerable essence. Thou shalt have the whole land for thy park and manor, the sea for thy bath and navigation, without tax and without envy; the woods and the rivers thou shalt own, and thou shalt possess that wherein others are only tenants and boarders. Thou true land-lord! sea-lord! air-lord! Wherever snow falls or water flows or birds fly, wherever day and night meet in twilight, wherever the blue heaven is hung by clouds or sown with stars, wherever are forms with transparent boundaries, wherever are outlets into celestial space, wherever is danger, and awe, and love,—there is Beauty, plenteous as rain, shed for thee, and though thou shouldst walk the world over, thou shalt not be able to find a condition inopportune or ignoble.

EXPERIENCE

~~~~~~

> The lords of life, the lords of life,—
> I saw them pass,
> In their own guise,
> Like and unlike,
> Portly and grim,
> Use and Surprise,
> Surface and Dream,
> Succession swift, and spectral Wrong,
> Temperament without a tongue,
> And the inventor of the game
> Omnipresent without name;—
> Some to see, some to be guessed,
> They marched from east to west:
> Little man, least of all,
> Among the legs of his guardians tall,
> Walked about with puzzled look:—
> Him by the hand dear Nature took;
> Dearest Nature, strong and kind,
> Whispered, 'Darling, never mind!
> To-morrow they will wear another face,
> The founder thou! these are thy race!'

Where do we find ourselves? In a series of which we do not know the extremes, and believe that it has none. We wake and find ourselves on a stair; there are stairs below us, which we seem to have ascended; there are stairs above us, many a one, which go upward and out of sight. But the Genius which according to the old belief stands at the door by which we enter, and gives us the lethe to drink,

that we may tell no tales, mixed the cup too strongly, and
we cannot shake off the lethargy now at noonday. Sleep
lingers all our lifetime about our eyes, as night hovers all
day in the boughs of the fir-tree. All things swim and glitter. Our life is not so much threatened as our perception.
Ghostlike we glide through nature, and should not know
our place again. Did our birth fall in some fit of indigence
and frugality in nature, that she was so sparing of her fire
and so liberal of her earth that it appears to us that we lack
the affirmative principle, and though we have health and
reason, yet we have no superfluity of spirit for new creation? We have enough to live and bring the year about,
but not an ounce to impart or to invest. Ah that our Genius were a little more of a genius! We are like millers on
the lower levels of a stream, when the factories above
them have exhausted the water. We too fancy that the
upper people must have raised their dams.

If any of us knew what we were doing, or where we are
going, then when we think we best know! We do not know
to-day whether we are busy or idle. In times when we
thought ourselves indolent, we have afterwards discovered
that much was accomplished and much was begun in us.
All our days are so unprofitable while they pass, that 't is
wonderful where or when we ever got anything of this
which we call wisdom, poetry, virtue. We never got it on
any dated calendar day. Some heavenly days must have
been intercalated somewhere, like those that Hermes won
with dice of the Moon, that Osiris might be born. It is said
all martyrdoms looked mean when they were suffered.
Every ship is a romantic object, except that we sail in.
Embark, and the romance quits our vessel and hangs on
every other sail in the horizon. Our life looks trivial, and
we shun to record it. Men seem to have learned of the
horizon the art of perpetual retreating and reference.
'Yonder uplands are rich pasturage, and my neighbor has
fertile meadow, but my field,' says the querulous farmer,
'only holds the world together.' I quote another man's
saying; unluckily that other withdraws himself in the

same way, and quotes me. 'T is the trick of nature thus to
degrade to-day; a good deal of buzz, and somewhere a result slipped magically in. Every roof is agreeable to the
eye until it is lifted; then we find tragedy and moaning
women and hard-eyed husbands and deluges of lethe, and
the men ask, 'What's the news?' as if the old were so bad.
How many individuals can we count in society? how
many actions? how many opinions? So much of our time
is preparation, so much is routine, and so much retrospect,
that the pith of each man's genius contracts itself to a very
few hours. The history of literature—take the net result of
Tiraboschi, Warton, or Schlegel—is a sum of very few
ideas and of very few original tales; all the rest being
variation of these. So in this great society wide lying
around us, a critical analysis would find very few spontaneous actions. It is almost all custom and gross sense.
There are even few opinions, and these seem organic in
the speakers, and do not disturb the universal necessity.

What opium is instilled into all disaster! It shows formidable as we approach it, but there is at last no rough rasp-
ing friction, but the most slippery sliding surfaces; we fall
soft on a thought; *Ate Dea* is gentle,—

> "Over men's heads walking aloft,
>   With tender feet treading so soft."

People grieve and bemoan themselves, but it is not half so
bad with them as they say. There are moods in which we
court suffering, in the hope that here at least we shall find
reality, sharp peaks and edges of truth. But it turns out to
be scene-painting and counterfeit. The only thing grief
has taught me is to know how shallow it is. That, like all
the rest, plays about the surface, and never introduces me
into the reality, for contact with which we would even pay
the costly price of sons and lovers. Was it Boscovich who
found out that bodies never come in contact? Well, souls
never touch their objects. An innavigable sea washes with
silent waves between us and the things we aim at and

converse with. Grief too will make us idealists. In the death of my son, now more than two years ago, I seem to have lost a beautiful estate,—no more. I cannot get it nearer to me. If to-morrow I should be informed of the bankruptcy of my principal debtors, the loss of my property would be a great inconvenience to me, perhaps, for many years; but it would leave me as it found me,—neither better nor worse. So is it with this calamity; it does not touch me; something which I fancied was a part of me, which could not be torn away without tearing me nor enlarged without enriching me, falls off from me and leaves no scar. It was caducous. I grieve that grief can teach me nothing, nor carry me one step into real nature. The Indian who was laid under a curse that the wind should not blow on him, nor water flow to him, nor fire burn him, is a type of us all. The dearest events are summer-rain, and we the Para coats that shed every drop. Nothing is left us now but death. We look to that with a grim satisfaction, saying, There at least is reality that will not dodge us.

I take this evanescence and lubricity of all objects, which lets them slip through our fingers then when we clutch hardest, to be the most unhandsome part of our condition. Nature does not like to be observed, and likes that we should be her fools and playmates. We may have the sphere for our cricket-ball, but not a berry for our philosophy. Direct strokes she never gave us power to make; all our blows glance, all our hits are accidents. Our relations to each other are oblique and casual.

Dream delivers us to dream, and there is no end to illusion. Life is a train of moods like a string of beads, and as we pass through them they prove to be many-colored lenses which paint the world their own hue, and each shows only what lies in its focus. From the mountain you see the mountain. We animate what we can, and we see only what we animate. Nature and books belong to the eyes that see them. It depends on the mood of the man whether he shall see the sunset or the fine poem. There are always sunsets, and there is always genius; but only a few hours so serene that we can relish nature or criticism. The more or less depends on structure or temperament. Temperament is the iron wire on which the beads are strung. Of what use is fortune or talent to a cold and defective nature? Who cares what sensibility or discrimination a man has at some time shown, if he falls asleep in his chair? or if he laugh and giggle? or if he apologize? or is infected with egotism? or thinks of his dollar? or cannot go by food? or has gotten a child in his boyhood? Of what use is genius, if the organ is too convex or too concave and cannot find a focal distance within the actual horizon of human life? Of what use, if the brain is too cold or too hot, and the man does not care enough for results to stimulate him to experiment, and hold him up in it? or if the web is too finely woven, too irritable by pleasure and pain, so that life stagnates from too much reception without due outlet? Of what use to make heroic vows of amendment, if the same old law-breaker is to keep them? What cheer can the religious sentiment yield, when that is suspected to be secretly dependent on the seasons of the year and the state of the blood? I knew a witty physician who found the creed in the biliary duct, and used to affirm that if there was disease in the liver, the man became a Calvinist, and if that organ was sound, he became a Unitarian. Very mortifying is the reluctant experience that some unfriendly excess or imbecility neutralizes the promise of genius. We see young men who owe us a new world, so readily and lavishly they promise, but they never acquit the debt; they die young and dodge the account; or if they live they lose themselves in the crowd.

Temperament also enters fully into the system of illusions and shuts us in a prison of glass which we cannot see. There is an optical illusion about every person we meet. In truth they are all creatures of given temperament, which will appear in a given character, whose boundaries they will never pass; but we look at them, they seem alive, and we presume there is impulse in them. In the moment it seems impulse; in the year, in the lifetime, it turns out to be a certain uniform tune which the revolving barrel of the music-box must play. Men resist the conclusion in the morning, but adopt it as the evening wears on, that temper prevails over everything of time, place and condition, and is inconsumable in the flames of religion. Some modifications the moral sentiment avails to impose, but the individual texture holds its dominion, if not to bias the moral judgments, yet to fix the measure of activity and of enjoyment.

I thus express the law as it is read from the platform of ordinary life, but must not leave it without noticing the capital exception. For temperament is a power which no man willingly hears any one praise but himself. On the platform of physics we cannot resist the contracting influences of so-called science. Temperament puts all divinity to rout. I know the mental proclivity of physicians. I hear the chuckle of the phrenologists. Theoretic kidnappers and slave-drivers, they esteem each man the victim of another, who winds him round his finger by knowing the law of his being; and, by such cheap signboards as the color of his beard or the slope of his occiput, reads the inventory of his fortunes and character. The grossest ignorance does not disgust like this impudent knowingness. The physicians say they are not materialists; but they are:—Spirit is matter reduced to an extreme thinness: O *so* thin!—But the definition of *spiritual* should be, *that which is its own evidence*. What notions do they attach to love! what to religion! One would not willingly pronounce these words in their hearing, and give them the occasion to profane them. I saw a gracious gentleman who adapts his conversation to the form of the head of the man he talks with! I had fancied that the value of life lay in its inscrutable possibilities; in the fact that I never know, in addressing myself to a new individual, what may befall me. I carry the keys of my castle in my hand, ready to throw them at the feet of my lord, whenever and in what disguise soever he shall appear. I know he is in the neighborhood, hidden among vagabonds. Shall I preclude my future by taking a high seat and kindly adapting my conversation to the shape of heads? When I come to that, the doctors shall buy me for a cent.—'But, sir, medical history; the report to the Institute; the proven facts!'—I distrust the facts and the inferences. Temperament is the veto or limitation-power in the constitution, very justly applied to restrain an opposite excess in the constitution, but absurdly offered as a bar to original equity. When virtue is in presence, all subordinate powers sleep. On its own level, or in view of nature, temperament is final. I see not, if one be once caught in this trap of so-called sciences, any escape for the man from the links of the chain of physical necessity. Given such an embryo, such a history must follow. On this platform one lives in a sty of sensualism, and would soon come to suicide. But it is impossible that the creative power should exclude itself. Into every intelligence there is a door which is never closed, through which the creator passes. The intellect, seeker of absolute truth, or the heart, lover of absolute good, intervenes for our succor, and at one whisper of these high powers we awake from ineffectual struggles with this nightmare. We hurl it into its own hell, and cannot again contract ourselves to so base a state.

The secret of the illusoriness is in the necessity of a succession of moods or objects. Gladly we would anchor, but the anchorage is quicksand. This onward trick of nature is too strong for us: *Pero si muove.* When at night I look at the moon and stars, I seem stationary, and they to hurry. Our love of the real draws us to permanence, but health of body consists in circulation, and sanity of mind in variety or facility of association. We need change of objects. Dedication to one thought is quickly odious. We house with the insane, and must humor them; then conversation dies out. Once I took such delight in Montaigne that I thought I should not need any other book; before that, in Shakspeare; then in Plutarch; then in Plotinus; at one time in

Bacon; afterwards in Goethe; even in Bettine; but now I turn the pages of either of them languidly, whilst I still cherish their genius. So with pictures; each will bear an emphasis of attention once, which it cannot retain, though we fain would continue to be pleased in that manner. How strongly I have felt of pictures that when you have seen one well, you must take your leave of it; you shall never see it again. I have had good lessons from pictures which I have since seen without emotion or remark. A deduction must be made from the opinion which even the wise express on a new book or occurrence. Their opinion gives me tidings of their mood, and some vague guess at the new fact, but is nowise to be trusted as the lasting relation between that intellect and that thing. The child asks, 'Mamma, why don't I like the story as well as when you told it me yesterday?' Alas! child, it is even so with the oldest cherubim of knowledge. But will it answer thy question to say, Because thou wert born to a whole and this story is a particular? The reason of the pain this discovery causes us (and we make it late in respect to works of art and intellect) is the plaint of tragedy which murmurs from it in regard to persons, to friendship and love.

That immobility and absence of elasticity which we find in the arts, we find with more pain in the artist. There is no power of expansion in men. Our friends early appear to us as representatives of certain ideas which they never pass or exceed. They stand on the brink of the ocean of thought and power, but they never take the single step that would bring them there. A man is like a bit of Labrador spar, which has no lustre as you turn it in your hand until you come to a particular angle; then it shows deep and beautiful colors. There is no adaptation or universal applicability in men, but each has his special talent, and the mastery of successful men consists in adroitly keeping themselves where and when that turn shall be oftenest to be practised. We do what we must, and call it by the best names we can, and would fain have the praise of having intended the result which ensues. I cannot recall any form of man who is not superfluous sometimes. But is not this pitiful? Life is not worth the taking, to do tricks in.

Of course it needs the whole society to give the symmetry we seek. The party-colored wheel must revolve very fast to appear white. Something is earned too by conversing with so much folly and defect. In fine, whoever loses, we are always of the gaining party. Divinity is behind our failures and follies also. The plays of children are nonsense, but very educative nonsense. So it is with the largest and solemnest things, with commerce, government, church, marriage, and so with the history of every man's bread, and the ways by which he is to come by it. Like a bird which alights nowhere, but hops perpetually from bough to bough, is the Power which abides in no man and in no woman, but for a moment speaks from this one, and for another moment from that one.

But what help from these fineries or pedantries? What help from thought? Life is not dialectics. We, I think, in these times, have had lessons enough of the futility of criticism. Our young people have thought and written much on labor and reform, and for all that they have written, neither the world nor themselves have got on a step. Intellectual tasting of life will not supersede muscular activity. If a man should consider the nicety of the passage of a piece of bread down his throat, he would starve. At Education Farm the noblest theory of life sat on the noblest figures of young men and maidens, quite powerless and melancholy. It would not rake or pitch a ton of hay; it would not rub down a horse; and the men and maidens it left pale and hungry. A political orator wittily compared our party promises to western roads, which opened stately enough, with planted trees on either side to tempt the traveller, but soon became narrow and narrower and ended in a squirrel-track and ran up a tree. So does culture with us; it ends in headache. Unspeakably sad and barren does life look to those who a few months ago were dazzled with the splendor of the promise of the times. "There is now no longer any right course of action nor any self-devotion left among the Iranis." Objections and criticism we have had our fill of. There are objections to every course of life and action, and the practical wisdom infers an indifferency, from the omnipresence of objection. The whole frame of things preaches indifference. Do not craze yourself with thinking, but go about your business anywhere. Life is not intellectual or critical, but sturdy. Its chief good is for well-mixed people who can enjoy what they find, without question. Nature hates peeping, and our mothers speak her very sense when they say, "Children, eat your victuals, and say no more of it." To fill the hour,—that is happiness; to fill the hour and leave no crevice for a repentance or an approval. We live amid surfaces, and the true art of life is to skate well on them. Under the oldest mouldiest conventions a man of native force prospers just as well as in the newest world, and that by skill of handling and treatment. He can take hold anywhere. Life itself is a mixture of power and form, and will not bear the least excess of either. To finish the moment, to find the journey's end in every step of the road, to live the greatest number of good hours, is wisdom. It is not the part of men, but of fanatics, or of mathematicians if you will, to say that, the shortness of life considered, it is not worth caring whether for so short a duration we were sprawling in want or sitting high. Since our office is with moments, let us husband them. Five minutes of to-day are worth as much to me as five minutes in the next millennium. Let us be poised, and wise, and our own, to-day. Let us treat the men and women well; treat them as if they were real; perhaps they are. Men live in their fancy, like drunkards whose hands are too soft and tremulous for successful labor. It is a tempest of fancies, and the only ballast I know is a respect to the present hour. Without any shadow of doubt, amidst this vertigo of shows and politics, I settle myself ever the firmer in the creed that we should not postpone and refer and wish, but do broad justice where we are, by whomsoever we deal with, accepting our actual companions and circumstances, however humble or odious, as the mystic officials to whom the universe has delegated its whole pleasure for us. If these are mean and malignant, their contentment, which is the last victory of justice, is a more satisfying echo to the heart than the voice of poets and the casual sympathy of admirable persons. I think that however a thoughtful man may suffer from the defects and absurdities of his company, he cannot without affectation deny to any set of men and women a sensibility to extraordinary merit. The coarse and frivolous have an instinct of superiority, if they have not a sympathy, and honor it in their blind capricious way with sincere homage.

The fine young people despise life, but in me, and in such as with me are free from dyspepsia, and to whom a day is a sound and solid good, it is a great excess of politeness to look scornful and to cry for company. I am grown by sympathy a little eager and sentimental, but leave me alone and I should relish every hour and what it brought me, the potluck of the day, as heartily as the oldest gossip in the bar-room. I am thankful for small mercies. I compared notes with one of my friends who expects everything of the universe and is disappointed when anything is less than the best, and I found that I begin at the other extreme, expecting nothing, and am always full of thanks for moderate goods. I accept the clangor and jangle of contrary tendencies. I find my account in sots and bores also. They give a reality to the circumjacent picture which such a vanishing meteorous appearance can ill spare. In the morning I awake and find the old world, wife, babes and mother, Concord and Boston, the dear old spiritual world and even the dear old devil not far off. If we will take the good we find, asking no questions, we shall have heaping measures. The great gifts are not got by analysis. Everything good is on the highway. The middle region of our being is the temperate zone. We may climb into the thin and cold realm of pure geometry and lifeless science, or sink into that of sensation. Between these extremes is the equator of life, of thought, of spirit, of poetry,—a narrow belt. Moreover, in popular experience everything good is on the highway. A collector peeps into all the picture-shops of Europe for a landscape of Poussin, a crayon-sketch of Salvator; but the Transfiguration, the Last Judgment, the Communion of Saint Jerome, and what are as transcendent as these, are on the walls of the Vatican, the Uffizi, or the Louvre, where every footman may see them; to say nothing of Nature's pictures in every street, of sunsets and sunrises every day, and the sculpture of the human body never absent. A collector recently bought at public auction, in London, for one hundred and fifty-seven guineas, an autograph of Shakspeare; but for nothing a school-boy can read Hamlet and can detect secrets of highest concernment yet unpublished therein. I think I will never read any but the commonest books,—the Bible, Homer, Dante, Shakspeare and Milton. Then we are impatient of so public a life and planet, and run hither and thither for nooks and secrets. The imagination delights in the woodcraft of Indians, trappers and bee-hunters. We fancy that we are strangers, and not so intimately domesticated in the planet as the wild man and the wild beast and bird. But the exclusion reaches them also; reaches the climbing, flying, gliding, feathered and four-footed man. Fox and woodchuck, hawk and snipe and bittern, when nearly seen, have no more root in the deep world than man, and are just such superficial tenants of the globe. Then the new molecular philosophy shows astronomical interspaces betwixt atom and atom, shows that the world is all outside; it has no inside.

The mid-world is best. Nature, as we know her, is no saint. The lights of the church, the ascetics, Gentoos and corn-eaters, she does not distinguish by any favor. She comes eating and drinking and sinning. Her darlings, the great, the strong, the beautiful, are not children of our law; do not come out of the Sunday School, nor weigh their food, nor punctually keep the commandments. If we will be strong with her strength we must not harbor such disconsolate consciences, borrowed too from the consciences of other nations. We must set up the strong present tense against all the rumors of wrath, past or to come. So many things are unsettled which it is of the first importance to settle;—and, pending their settlement, we will do as we do. Whilst the debate goes forward on the equity of commerce, and will not be closed for a century or two, New and Old England may keep shop. Law of copyright and international copyright is to be discussed, and in the interim we will sell our books for the most we can. Expediency of literature, reason of literature, lawfulness of writing down a thought, is questioned; much is to say on both sides, and, while the fight waxes hot, thou, dearest scholar, stick to thy foolish task, add a line every hour, and between whiles add a line. Right to hold land, right of property, is disputed, and the conventions convene, and before the vote is taken, dig away in your garden, and spend your earnings as a waif or godsend to all serene and beautiful purposes. Life itself is a bubble and a scepticism, and a sleep within a sleep. Grant it, and as much more as they will,—but thou, God's darling! heed thy private dream; thou wilt not be missed in the scorning and scepticism; there are enough of them; stay there in thy closet and toil until the rest are agreed what to do about it. Thy sickness, they say, and thy puny habit require that thou do this or avoid that, but know that thy life is a flitting state, a tent for a night, and do thou, sick or well, finish that stint. Thou are sick, but shalt not be worse, and the universe, which holds thee dear, shall be the better.

Human life is made up of the two elements, power and form, and the proportion must be invariably kept if we would have it sweet and sound. Each of these elements in excess makes a mischief as hurtful as its defect. Everything runs to excess; every good quality is noxious if unmixed, and, to carry the danger to the edge of ruin, nature causes each man's peculiarity to superabound. Here, among the farms, we adduce the scholars as examples of this treachery. They are nature's victims of expression. You who see the artist, the orator, the poet, too near, and find their life no more excellent than that of mechanics or farmers, and themselves victims of partiality, very hollow and haggard, and pronounce them failures, not heroes, but quacks,—conclude very reasonably that these arts are not for man, but are disease. Yet nature will not bear you out. Irresistible nature made men such, and makes legions more of such, every day. You love the boy reading in a book, gazing at a drawing or a cast; yet what are these millions who read and behold, but incipient writers and sculptors? Add a little more of that quality which now reads and sees, and they will seize the pen and chisel. And if one remembers how innocently he began to be an artist, he perceives that nature joined with his enemy. A man is a golden impossibility. The line he must walk is a hair's breadth. The wise through excess of wisdom is made a fool.

How easily, if fate would suffer it, we might keep forever these beautiful limits, and adjust ourselves, once for all, to the perfect calculation of the kingdom of known cause and effect. In the street and in the newspapers, life appears so plain a business that manly resolution and adherence to the multiplication-table through all weathers will insure success. But ah! presently comes a day, or is it only a half-hour, with its angel-whispering,—which discomfits the conclusions of nations and of years! To-morrow again every thing looks real and angular, the habitual standards are reinstated, common-sense is as rare as genius,—is the basis of genius, and experience is hands and feet to every enterprise;—and yet, he who should do his business on this understanding would be quickly bankrupt. Power keeps quite another road than the turnpikes of choice and will; namely the subterranean and invisible tunnels and channels of life. It is ridiculous that we are diplomatists, and doctors, and considerate people; there are no dupes like these. Life is a series of surprises, and would not be worth taking or keeping if it were not.

God delights to isolate us every day, and hide from us the past and the future. We would look about us, but with grand politeness he draws down before us an impenetrable screen of purest sky, and another behind us of purest sky. 'You will not remember,' he seems to say, 'and you will not expect.' All good conversation, manners and action come from a spontaneity which forgets usages and makes the moment great. Nature hates calculators; her methods are saltatory and impulsive. Man lives by pulses; our organic movements are such; and the chemical and ethereal agents are undulatory and alternate; and the mind goes antagonizing on, and never prospers but by fits. We thrive by casualties. Our chief experiences have been casual. The most attractive class of people are those who are powerful obliquely and not by the direct stroke; men of genius, but not yet accredited; one gets the cheer of their light without paying too great a tax. Theirs is the beauty of the bird or the morning light, and not of art. In the thought of genius there is always a surprise; and the moral sentiment is well called "the newness," for it is never other; as new to the oldest intelligence as to the young child;—"the kingdom that cometh without observation." In like manner, for practical success, there must not be too much design. A man will not be observed in doing that which he can do best. There is a certain magic about his properest action which stupefies your powers of observation, so that though it is done before you, you wist not of it. The art of life has a pudency, and will not be exposed. Every man is an impossibility until he is born; every thing impossible until we see a success. The ardors of piety agree at last with the coldest scepticism,—that nothing is of us or our works,—that all is of God. Nature will not spare us the smallest leaf of laurel. All writing comes by the grace of God, and all doing and having. I would gladly be moral and keep due metes and bounds, which I dearly love, and allow the most to the will of man; but I have set my heart on honesty in this chapter, and I can see nothing at last, in success or failure, than more or less of vital force supplied from the Eternal. The results of life are uncalculated and uncalculable. The years teach much which the days never know. The persons who compose our company converse, and come and go, and design and execute many things, and somewhat comes of it all, but an unlooked-for result. The individual is always mistaken. He designed many things, and drew in other persons as coadjutors, quarrelled with some or all, blundered much, and something is done; all are a little advanced, but the individual is always mistaken. It turns out somewhat new and very unlike what he promised himself.

The ancients, struck with this irreducibleness of the elements of human life to calculation, exalted Chance into a divinity; but that is to stay too long at the spark, which glitters truly at one point, but the universe is warm with the latency of the same fire. The miracle of life which will not be expounded but will remain a miracle, introduces a new element. In the growth of the embryo, Sir Everard Home I think noticed that the evolution was not from one central point, but coactive from three or more points. Life has no memory. That which proceeds in succession might be remembered, but that which is coexistent, or ejaculated from a deeper cause, as yet far from being conscious, knows not its own tendency. So is it with us, now sceptical or without unity, because immersed in forms and effects all seeming to be of equal yet hostile value, and now religious, whilst in the reception of spiritual law. Bear with these distractions, with this coetaneous growth of the parts; they will one day be *members*, and obey one will. On that one will, on that secret cause, they nail our attention and hope. Life is hereby melted into an expectation or a religion. Underneath the inharmonious and trivial particulars, is a musical perfection; the Ideal journeying always with us, the heaven without rent or seam. Do but observe the mode of our illumination. When I converse with a profound mind, or if at any time being alone I have good thoughts, I do not at once arrive at satisfactions, as when, being thirsty, I drink water; or go to the fire, being cold; no! but I am at first apprised of my vicinity to a new and excellent region of life. By persisting to read or to think, this region gives further sign of itself, as it were in flashes of light, in sudden discoveries of its profound beauty and repose, as if the clouds that covered it parted at intervals and showed the approaching traveller the inland mountains, with the tranquil eternal meadows spread at their base, whereon flocks graze and shepherds pipe and dance. But every insight from this realm of thought is felt as initial, and promises a sequel. I do not make it; I arrive there, and behold what was there already. I make! O no! I clap my hands in infantine joy and amazement before the first opening to me of this august magnificence, old with the love and homage of innumerable ages, young with the life of life, the sunbright Mecca of the desert. And what a future it opens! I feel a new heart beating with the love of the new beauty. I am ready to die out of nature and be born again into this new yet unapproachable America I have found in the West:—

> "Since neither now nor yesterday began
>   These thoughts, which have been ever, nor yet can
>   A man be found who their first entrance knew."

If I have described life as a flux of moods, I must now add that there is that in us which changes not and which ranks all sensations and states of mind. The consciousness in each man is a sliding scale, which identifies him now with the First Cause, and now with the flesh of his body; life above life, in infinite degrees. The sentiment from which it sprung determines the dignity of any deed, and the question ever is, not what you have done or forborne, but at whose command you have done or forborne it.

Fortune, Minerva, Muse, Holy Ghost,—these are quaint names, too narrow to cover this unbounded substance. The baffled intellect must still kneel before this cause, which refuses to be named,—ineffable cause, which every fine genius has essayed to represent by some emphatic symbol, as, Thales by water, Anaximenes by air, Anaxagoras by *Nous*, thought, Zoroaster by fire, Jesus and the moderns by love; and the metaphor of each has become a national religion. The Chinese Mencius has not been the least successful in his generalization. "I fully understand language," he said, "and nourish well my vast-flowing vigor."—"I beg to ask what you call vast-flowing vigor?" said his companion. "The explanation," replied Mencius, "is difficult. This vigor is supremely great, and in the highest degree unbending. Nourish it correctly and do it no injury, and it will fill up the vacancy between heaven and earth. This vigor accords with and assists justice and reason, and leaves no hunger."—In our more correct writing we give to this generalization the name of Being, and thereby confess that we have arrived as far as we can go. Suffice it for the joy of the universe that we have not arrived at a wall, but at interminable oceans. Our life seems not present so much as prospective; not for the affairs on which it is wasted, but as a hint of this vast-flowing vigor. Most of life seems to be mere advertisement of faculty; information is given us not to sell ourselves cheap; that we are very great. So, in particulars, our greatness is always in a tendency or direction, not in an action. It is for us to believe in the rule, not in the exception. The noble are thus known from the ignoble. So in accepting the leading of the sentiments, it is not what we believe concerning the immortality of the soul or the like but *the universal impulse to believe*, that is the material circumstance and is the principal fact in the history of the globe. Shall we describe this cause as that which works directly? The spirit is not helpless or needful of mediate organs. It has plentiful powers and direct effects. I am explained without explaining, I am felt without acting, and where I am not. Therefore all just persons are satisfied with their own praise. They refuse to explain themselves, and are content that new actions should do them that office. They believe that we communicate without speech and above speech, and that no right action of ours is quite unaffecting to our friends, at whatever distance; for the influence of action is not to be measured by miles. Why should I fret myself because a circumstance has occurred which hinders my presence where I was expected? If I am not at the meeting, my presence where I am should be as useful to the commonwealth of friendship and wisdom, as would be my presence in that place. I exert the same quality of power in all places. Thus journeys the mighty Ideal before us; it never was known to fall into the rear. No man ever came to an experience which was satiating, but his good is tidings of a better. Onward and onward! In liberated moments we know that a new picture of life and duty is already possible; the elements already exist in many minds around you of a doctrine of life which shall transcend any written record we have. The new statement will comprise the scepticisms as well as the faiths of society, and out of unbeliefs a creed shall be formed. For scepticisms are not gratuitous or lawless, but are limitations of the affirmative statement, and the new philosophy must take them in and make affirmations outside of them, just as much as it must include the oldest beliefs.

It is very unhappy, but too late to be helped, the discovery we have made that we exist. That discovery is called the Fall of Man. Ever afterwards we suspect our instruments. We have learned that we do not see directly, but mediately, and that we have no means of correcting these colored and distorting lenses which we are, or of computing the amount of their errors. Perhaps these subject-lenses have a creative power; perhaps there are no objects. Once we lived in what we saw; now, the rapaciousness of this new power, which threatens to absorb all things, engages us. Nature, art, persons, letters, religions, objects, successively tumble in, and God is but one of its ideas. Nature and literature are subjective phenomena; every evil and every good thing is a shadow which we cast. The street is full of humiliations to the proud. As the fop con-

trived to dress his bailiffs in his livery and make them wait
on his guests at table, so the chagrins which the bad heart
gives off as bubbles, at once take form as ladies and gentlemen in the street, shopmen or bar-keepers in hotels, and
threaten or insult whatever is threatenable and insultable
in us. 'T is the same with our idolatries. People forget that
it is the eye which makes the horizon, and the rounding
mind's eye which makes this or that man a type or representative of humanity, with the name of hero or saint.
Jesus, the "providential man," is a good man on whom
many people are agreed that these optical laws shall take
effect. By love on one part and by forbearance to press
objection on the other part, it is for a time settled that we
will look at him in the centre of the horizon, and ascribe to
him the properties that will attach to any man so seen. But
the longest love or aversion has a speedy term. The great
and crescive self, rooted in absolute nature, supplants all
relative existence and ruins the kingdom of mortal friendship and love. Marriage (in what is called the spiritual
world) is impossible, because of the inequality between
every subject and every object. The subject is the receiver
of Godhead, and at every comparison must feel his being
enhanced by that cryptic might. Though not in energy,
yet by presence, this magazine of substance cannot be
otherwise than felt; nor can any force of intellect attribute
to the object the proper deity which sleeps or wakes forever in every subject. Never can love make consciousness
and ascription equal in force. There will be the same gulf
between every me and thee as between the original and
the picture. The universe is the bride of the soul. All private sympathy is partial. Two human beings are like
globes, which can touch only in a point, and whilst they
remain in contact all other points of each of the spheres
are inert; their turn must also come, and the longer a particular union lasts the more energy of appetency the parts
not in union acquire.

Life will be imaged, but cannot be divided nor doubled.
Any invasion of its unity would be chaos. The soul is not

twin-born but the only begotten, and though revealing itself as child in time, child in appearance, is of a fatal and universal power, admitting no co-life. Every day, every act betrays the ill-concealed deity. We believe in ourselves as we do not believe in others. We permit all things to ourselves, and that which we call sin in others is experiment for us. It is an instance of our faith in ourselves that men never speak of crime as lightly as they think; or every man thinks a latitude safe for himself which is nowise to be indulged to another. The act looks very differently on the inside and on the outside; in its quality and in its consequences. Murder in the murderer is no such ruinous thought as poets and romancers will have it; it does not unsettle him or fright him from his ordinary notice of trifles; it is an act quite easy to be contemplated; but in its sequel it turns out to be a horrible jangle and confounding of all relations. Especially the crimes that spring from love seem right and fair from the actor's point of view, but when acted are found destructive of society. No man at last believes that he can be lost, or that the crime in him is as black as in the felon. Because the intellect qualifies in our own case the moral judgments. For there is no crime to the intellect. That is antinomian or hypernomian, and judges law as well as fact. "It is worse than a crime, it is a blunder," said Napoleon, speaking the language of the intellect. To it, the world is a problem in mathematics or the science of quantity, and it leaves out praise and blame and all weak emotions. All stealing is comparative. If you come to absolutes, pray who does not steal? Saints are sad, because they behold sin (even when they speculate) from the point of view of the conscience, and not of the intellect; a confusion of thought. Sin, seen from the thought, is a diminution, or *less;* seen from the conscience or will, it is pravity or *bad.* The intellect names it shade, absence of light, and no essence. The conscience must feel it as essence, essential evil. This it is not; it has an objective existence, but no subjective.

Thus inevitably does the universe wear our color, and

every object fall successively into the subject itself. The subject exists, the subject enlarges; all things sooner or later fall into place. As I am, so I see; use what language we will, we can never say anything but what we are; Hermes, Cadmus, Columbus, Newton, Bonaparte, are the mind's ministers. Instead of feeling a poverty when we encounter a great man, let us treat the new-comer like a travelling geologist who passes through our estate and shows us good slate, or limestone, or anthracite, in our brush pasture. The partial action of each strong mind in one direction is a telescope for the objects on which it is pointed. But every other part of knowledge is to be pushed to the same extravagance, ere the soul attains her due sphericity. Do you see that kitten chasing so prettily her own tail? If you could look with her eyes you might see her surrounded with hundreds of figures performing complex dramas, with tragic and comic issues, long conversations, many characters, many ups and downs of fate,—and meantime it is only puss and her tail. How long before our masquerade will end its noise of tambourines, laughter and shouting, and we shall find it was a solitary performance? A subject and an object,—it takes so much to make the galvanic circuit complete, but magnitude adds nothing. What imports it whether it is Kepler and the sphere, Columbus and America, a reader and his book, or puss with her tail?

It is true that all the muses and love and religion hate these developments, and will find a way to punish the chemist who publishes in the parlor the secrets of the laboratory. And we cannot say too little of our constitutional necessity of seeing things under private aspects, or saturated with our humors. And yet is the God the native of these bleak rocks. That need makes in morals the capital virtue of self-trust. We must hold hard to this poverty, however scandalous, and by more vigorous self-recoveries, after the sallies of action, possess our axis more firmly. The life of truth is cold and so far mournful; but it is not the slave of tears, contritions and perturbations. It does not attempt another's work, nor adopt another's facts. It is a main lesson of wisdom to know your own from another's. I have learned that I cannot dispose of other people's facts; but I possess such a key to my own as persuades me, against all their denials, that they also have a key to theirs. A sympathetic person is placed in the dilemma of a swimmer among drowning men, who all catch at him, and if he give so much as a leg or a finger they will drown him. They wish to be saved from the mischiefs of their vices, but not from their vices. Charity would be wasted on this poor waiting on the symptoms. A wise and hardy physician will say, *Come out of that*, as the first condition of advice.

In this our talking America we are ruined by our good nature and listening on all sides. This compliance takes away the power of being greatly useful. A man should not be able to look other than directly and forthright. A preoccupied attention is the only answer to the importunate frivolity of other people; an attention, and to an aim which makes their wants frivolous. This is a divine answer, and leaves no appeal and no hard thoughts. In Flaxman's drawing of the Eumenides of Aeschylus, Orestes supplicates Apollo, whilst the Furies sleep on the threshold. The face of the god expresses a shade of regret and compassion, but is calm with the conviction of the irreconcilableness of the two spheres. He is born into other politics, into the eternal and beautiful. The man at his feet asks for his interest in turmoils of the earth, into which his nature cannot enter. And the Eumenides there lying express pictorially this disparity. The god is surcharged with his divine destiny.

Illusion, Temperament, Succession, Surface, Surprise, Reality, Subjectiveness,—these are threads on the loom of time, these are the lords of life. I dare not assume to give their order, but I name them as I find them in my way. I know better than to claim any completeness for my picture. I am a fragment, and this is a fragment of me. I can very confidently announce one or another law, which throws itself into relief and form, but I am too young yet by some ages to compile a code. I gossip for my hour concerning the eternal politics. I have seen many fair pictures not in vain. A wonderful time I have lived in. I am not the novice I was fourteen, nor yet seven years ago. Let who will ask, Where is the fruit? I find a private fruit sufficient. This is a fruit,—that I should not ask for a rash effect from meditations, counsels and the hiving of truths. I should feel it pitiful to demand a result on this town and country, an overt effect on the instant month and year. The effect is deep and secular as the cause. It works on periods in which mortal lifetime is lost. All I know is reception; I am and I have: but I do not get, and when I have fancied I had gotten anything, I found I did not. I worship with wonder the great Fortune. My reception has been so large, that I am not annoyed by receiving this or that superabundantly. I say to the Genius, if he will pardon the proverb, *In for a mill, in for a million.* When I receive a new gift, I do not macerate my body to make the account square, for if I should die I could not make the account square. The benefit overran the merit the first day, and has overrun the merit ever since. The merit itself, so-called, I reckon part of the receiving.

Also that hankering after an overt or practical effect seems to me an apostasy. In good earnest I am willing to spare this most unnecessary deal of doing. Life wears to me a visionary face. Hardest roughest action is visionary also. It is but a choice between soft and turbulent dreams. People disparage knowing and the intellectual life, and urge doing. I am very content with knowing, if only I could know. That is an august entertainment, and would suffice me a great while. To know a little would be worth the expense of this world. I hear always the law of Adrastia, "that every soul which had acquired any truth, should be safe from harm until another period."

I know that the world I converse with in the city and in the farms, is not the world I *think*. I observe that differ-

ence, and shall observe it. One day I shall know the value
and law of this discrepance. But I have not found that
much was gained by manipular attempts to realize the
world of thought. Many eager persons successively make
an experiment in this way, and make themselves ridiculous. They acquire democratic manners, they foam at the
mouth, they hate and deny. Worse, I observe that in the
history of mankind there is never a solitary example of
success,—taking their own tests of success. I say this po-
lemically, or in reply to the inquiry, Why not realize your
world? But far be from me the despair which prejudges
the law by a paltry empiricism;—since there never was a
right endeavor but it succeeded. Patience and patience, we
shall win at the last. We must be very suspicious of the
deceptions of the element of time. It takes a good deal of
time to eat or to sleep, or to earn a hundred dollars, and a
very little time to entertain a hope and an insight which
becomes the light of our life. We dress our garden, eat our
dinners, discuss the household with our wives, and these
things make no impression, are forgotten next week; but,
in the solitude to which every man is always returning, he
has a sanity and revelations which in his passage into new
worlds he will carry with him. Never mind the ridicule,
never mind the defeat; up again, old heart!—it seems to
say,—there is victory yet for all justice; and the true romance which the world exists to realize will be the transformation of genius into practical power.

Later Essays

Editor's Note

~~~~~~~~~~~~~~~~~~~~~~~~~~~~~~~~~~~

The Emerson of the first two volumes of essays is the most enduring. But his range was wider than they suggest, and some of the other essays within that range are distinguished indeed. They nearly all began as lectures intended from the outset to be printed as essays in a book. Emerson first read "Plato" as part of a series of lectures on notable men which he delivered to the Boston Lyceum in the winter of 1845–46. However, he had been thinking about Plato and enjoying him for two decades at least. If we are all either Platonists or Aristotelians, there is no doubt where Emerson stood. He responded enthusiastically both to Plato pure and Plato as interpreted by the Neoplatonists. When he published *Representative Men* in 1850, he put Plato first in the book. He chose five other representative figures, and four of these might have been expected from his way of thinking: Swedenborg, Montaigne, Shakespeare, and Goethe. One, though, was a surprise: Napoleon. To Emerson he exemplified the "man of the world," by which he meant that Napoleon was an ordinary man who possessed certain ordinary qualities to a superlative degree. Coolly and realistically he assessed Napoleon's career: it was a gigantic failure because it violated the laws of nature.

Emerson's essay "Fate" went through the usual refining process before he put it into *The Conduct of Life*, published in 1860. "Fate," the first chapter in the book, revealed the slow erosion of the years that had replaced Emerson the conspicuous optimist with the judicious observer who recognized the strength of circumstance in human affairs. The essay "Illusions" is the final chapter in *The Conduct of Life*. In it he examines our misconceptions with a combination of understanding and plain dealing. Now a man in his late fifties, he summons anecdotes and observations from the substantial store he has gathered. He affirms, with examples, that truth and rightness remain the favorites of the universe. Our illusions may lead us to deny this but during the rare times when we see with piercing clarity, we find the gods still sitting on their thrones.

In "Society and Solitude" we have another lecture purposefully developed into an essay. Emerson set it at the head of his book by the same title, issued in 1870. Like "Illusions" it has its anecdotes, and naturally more of them by now. This was a lecture that he honed for his growing Midwestern audiences. It could not be called folksy—nothing of his ever was—but it showed a practiced awareness of the people sitting before him. Though he maintained the same positions he had held a decade earlier, he now domesticated them. The main issue was still the individual's relation to the group, and Emerson stayed firmly on the side of the individual.

C.B.

PLATO;
OR, THE PHILOSOPHER

~~~~~~~~~~~~~~~~~

Among secular books, Plato only is entitled to Omar's fanatical compliment to the Koran, when he said, "Burn the libraries; for their value is in this book." These sentences contain the culture of nations; these are the corner-stone of schools; these are the fountain-head of literatures. A discipline it is in logic, arithmetic, taste, symmetry, poetry, language, rhetoric, ontology, morals or practical wisdom. There was never such range of speculation. Out of Plato come all things that are still written and debated among men of thought. Great havoc makes he among our originalities. We have reached the mountain from which all these drift boulders were detached. The Bible of the learned for twenty-two hundred years, every brisk young man who says in succession fine things to each reluctant generation,—Boethius, Rabelais, Erasmus, Bruno, Locke, Rousseau, Alfieri, Coleridge,—is some reader of Plato, translating into the vernacular, wittily, his good things. Even the men of grander proportion suffer some deduction from the misfortune (shall I say?) of coming after this exhausting generalizer. St. Augustine, Copernicus, Newton, Behmen, Swedenborg, Goethe, are likewise his debtors and must say after him. For it is fair to credit the broadest generalizer with all the particulars deducible from his thesis.

Plato is philosophy, and philosophy, Plato,—at once the glory and the shame of mankind, since neither Saxon nor Roman have availed to add any idea to his categories. No wife, no children had he, and the thinkers of all civilized nations are his posterity and are tinged with his mind. How many great men Nature is incessantly sending up out of night, to be *his men*,—Platonists! the Alexandrians, a constellation of genius; the Elizabethans, not less; Sir Thomas More, Henry More, John Hales, John Smith, Lord Bacon, Jeremy Taylor, Ralph Cudworth, Sydenham, Thomas Taylor; Marcilius Ficinus and Picus Mirandola. Calvinism is in his Phædo: Christianity is in it. Mahometanism draws all its philosophy, in its hand-book of morals, the Akhlak-y-Jalaly, from him. Mysticism finds in Plato all its texts. This citizen of a town in Greece is no villager nor patriot. An Englishman reads and says, 'how English!' a German,—'how Teutonic!' an Italian,—'how Roman and how Greek!' As they say that Helen of Argos had that universal beauty that every body felt related to her, so Plato seems to a reader in New England an American genius. His broad humanity transcends all sectional lines.

This range of Plato instructs us what to think of the vexed question concerning his reputed works,—what are genuine, what spurious. It is singular that wherever we find a man higher by a whole head than any of his contemporaries, it is sure to come into doubt what are his real works. Thus Homer, Plato, Raffaelle, Shakspeare. For these men magnetize their contemporaries, so that their companions can do for them what they can never do for themselves; and the great man does thus live in several bodies, and write, or paint or act, by many hands; and after some time it is not easy to say what is the authentic work of the master and what is only of his school.

Plato, too, like every great man, consumed his own times. What is a great man but one of great affinities, who takes up into himself all arts, sciences, all knowables, as his food? He can spare nothing; he can dispose of every thing. What is not good for virtue, is good for knowledge. Hence his contemporaries tax him with plagiarism. But the inventor only knows how to borrow; and society is glad to forget the innumerable laborers who ministered to this architect, and reserves all its gratitude for him. When we are praising Plato, it seems we are praising quotations from Solon and Sophron and Philolaus. Be it so. Every book is a quotation; and every house is a quotation out of all forests and mines and stone quarries; and every man is a quotation from all his ancestors. And this grasping inventor puts all nations under contribution.

Plato absorbed the learning of his times,—Philolaus, Timæus, Heraclitus, Parmenides, and what else; then his master, Socrates; and finding himself still capable of a larger synthesis,—beyond all example then or since,—he travelled into Italy, to gain what Pythagoras had for him; then into Egypt, and perhaps still farther East, to import the other element, which Europe wanted, into the European mind. This breadth entitles him to stand as the representative of philosophy. He says, in the Republic, "Such a genius as philosophers must of necessity have, is wont but seldom in all its parts to meet in one man, but its different parts generally spring up in different persons." Every man who would do anything well, must come to it from a higher ground. A philosopher must be more than a philosopher. Plato is clothed with the powers of a poet, stands upon the highest place of the poet, and (though I doubt he wanted the decisive gift of lyric expression), mainly is not a poet because he chose to use the poetic gift to an ulterior purpose.

Great geniuses have the shortest biographies. Their cousins can tell you nothing about them. They lived in their writings, and so their house and street life was trivial and commonplace. If you would know their tastes and complexions, the most admiring of their readers most resembles them. Plato especially has no external biography. If he had lover, wife, or children, we hear nothing of them. He ground them all into paint. As a good chimney burns its smoke, so a philosopher converts the value of all his fortunes into his intellectual performances.

He was born 427 A.C., about the time of the death of Pericles; was of patrician connection in his times and city, and is said to have had an early inclination for war, but, in his twentieth year, meeting with Socrates, was easily dissuaded from this pursuit and remained for ten years his scholar, until the death of Socrates. He then went to Megara, accepted the invitations of Dion and of Dionysius to the court of Sicily, and went thither three times, though very capriciously treated. He travelled into Italy; then into Egypt, where he stayed a long time; some say three,—some say thirteen years. It is said he went farther, into Babylonia: this is uncertain. Returning to Athens, he gave lessons in the Academy to those whom his fame drew thither; and died, as we have received it, in the act of writing, at eighty-one years.

But the biography of Plato is interior. We are to account for the supreme elevation of this man in the intellectual history of our race,—how it happens that in proportion to the culture of men they become his scholars; that, as our Jewish Bible has implanted itself in the table-talk and household life of every man and woman in the European and American nations, so the writings of Plato have preoccupied every school of learning, every lover of thought, every church, every poet,—making it impossible to think, on certain levels, except through him. He stands between the truth and every man's mind, and has almost impressed language and the primary forms of thought with his name and seal. I am struck, in reading him, with the extreme modernness of his style and spirit. Here is the germ of that Europe we know so well, in its long history of arts and arms; here are all its traits, already discernible in the mind of Plato,—and in none before him. It has spread itself since into a hundred histories, but has added no new element. This perpetual modernness is the measure of merit in every work of art; since the author of it was not misled by any thing short-lived or local, but abode by real and abiding traits. How Plato came thus to be Europe, and philosophy, and almost literature, is the problem for us to solve.

This could not have happened without a sound, sincere

and catholic man, able to honor, at the same time, the ideal, or laws of the mind, and fate, or the order of nature. The first period of a nation, as of an individual, is the period of unconscious strength. Children cry, scream and stamp with fury, unable to express their desires. As soon as they can speak and tell their want and the reason of it, they become gentle. In adult life, whilst the perceptions are obtuse, men and women talk vehemently and superlatively, blunder and quarrel: their manners are full of desperation; their speech is full of oaths. As soon as, with culture, things have cleared up a little, and they see them no longer in lumps and masses but accurately distributed, they desist from that weak vehemence and explain their meaning in detail. If the tongue had not been framed for articulation, man would still be a beast in the forest. The same weakness and want, on a higher plane, occurs daily in the education of ardent young men and women. 'Ah! you don't understand me; I have never met with any one who comprehends me:' and they sigh and weep, write verses and walk alone,—fault of power to express their precise meaning. In a month or two, through the favor of their good genius, they meet some one so related as to assist their volcanic estate, and good communication being once established, they are thenceforward good citizens. It is ever thus. The progress is to accuracy, to skill, to truth, from blind force.

There is a moment in the history of every nation, when, proceeding out of this brute youth, the perceptive powers reach their ripeness and have not yet become microscopic: so that man, at that instant, extends across the entire scale, and, with his feet still planted on the immense forces of night, converses by his eyes and brain with solar and stellar creation. That is the moment of adult health, the culmination of power.

Such is the history of Europe, in all points; and such in philosophy. Its early records, almost perished, are of the immigrations from Asia, bringing with them the dreams of barbarians; a confusion of crude notions of morals and of natural philosophy, gradually subsiding through the partial insight of single teachers.

Before Pericles came the Seven Wise Masters, and we have the beginnings of geometry, metaphysics and ethics: then the partialists,—deducing the origin of things from flux or water, or from air, or from fire, or from mind. All mix with these causes mythologic pictures. At last comes Plato, the distributor, who needs no barbaric paint, or tattoo, or whooping; for he can define. He leaves with Asia the vast and superlative; he is the arrival of accuracy and intelligence. "He shall be as a god to me, who can rightly divide and define."

This defining is philosophy. Philosophy is the account which the human mind gives to itself of the constitution of the world. Two cardinal facts lie forever at the base; the one, and the two.—1. Unity, or Identity; and, 2. Variety. We unite all things by perceiving the law which pervades them; by perceiving the superficial differences and the profound resemblances. But every mental act,—this very perception of identity or oneness, recognizes the difference of things. Oneness and otherness. It is impossible to speak or to think without embracing both.

The mind is urged to ask for one cause of many effects; then for the cause of that; and again the cause, diving still into the profound: self-assured that it shall arrive at an absolute and sufficient one,—a one that shall be all. "In the midst of the sun is the light, in the midst of the light is truth, and in the midst of truth is the imperishable being," say the Vedas. All philosophy, of East and West, has the same centripetence. Urged by an opposite necessity, the mind returns from the one to that which is not one, but other or many; from cause to effect; and affirms the necessary existence of variety, the self-existence of both, as each is involved in the other. These strictly-blended elements it is the problem of thought to separate and to reconcile. Their existence is mutually contradictory and exclusive; and each so fast slides into the other that we can never say what is one, and what it is not. The Proteus is as nimble in the highest as in the lowest grounds; when we contemplate the one, the true, the good,—as in the surfaces and extremities of matter.

In all nations there are minds which incline to dwell in the conception of the fundamental Unity. The raptures of prayer and ecstasy of devotion lose all being in one Being. This tendency finds its highest expression in the religious writings of the East, and chiefly in the Indian Scriptures, in the Vedas, the Bhagavat Geeta, and the Vishnu Purana. Those writings contain little else than this idea, and they rise to pure and sublime strains in celebrating it.

The Same, the Same: friend and foe are of one stuff; the ploughman, the plough and the furrow are of one stuff; and the stuff is such and so much that the variations of form are unimportant. "You are fit" (says the supreme Krishna to a sage) "to apprehend that you are not distinct from me. That which I am, thou art, and that also is this world, with its gods and heroes and mankind. Men contemplate distinctions, because they are stupefied with ignorance." "The words *I* and *mine* constitute ignorance. What is the great end of all, you shall now learn from me. It is soul,—one in all bodies, pervading, uniform, perfect, pre-eminent over nature, exempt from birth, growth and decay, omnipresent, made up of true knowledge, independent, unconnected with unrealities, with name, species and the rest, in time past, present and to come. The knowledge that this spirit, which is essentially one, is in one's own and in all other bodies, is the wisdom of one who knows the unity of things. As one diffusive air, passing through the perforations of a flute, is distinguished as the notes of a scale, so the nature of the Great Spirit is single, though its forms be manifold, arising from the consequences of acts. When the difference of the investing form, as that of god or the rest, is destroyed, there is no distinction." "The whole world is but a manifestation of Vishnu, who is identical with all things, and is to be regarded by the wise as not differing from, but as the same as themselves. I neither am going nor coming; nor is my dwelling in any one place; nor art thou, thou; nor are others, others; nor am I, I." As if he had said, 'All is for the soul, and the soul is Vishnu; and animals and stars are transient paintings; and light is whitewash; and durations are deceptive; and form is imprisonment; and heaven itself a decoy.' That which the soul seeks is resolution into being above form, out of Tartarus and out of heaven,—liberation from nature.

If speculation tends thus to a terrific unity, in which all things are absorbed, action tends directly backwards to diversity. The first is the course or gravitation of mind; the second is the power of nature. Nature is the manifold. The unity absorbs, and melts or reduces. Nature opens and creates. These two principles reappear and interpenetrate all things, all thought; the one, the many. One is being; the other, intellect: one is necessity; the other, freedom: one, rest; the other, motion: one, power; the other, distribution: one, strength; the other, pleasure: one, consciousness; the other, definition: one, genius; the other, talent: one, earnestness; the other, knowledge: one, possession; the other, trade: one, caste; the other, culture: one, king; the other, democracy: and, if we dare carry these generalizations a step higher, and name the last tendency of both, we might say, that the end of the one is escape from organization,—pure science; and the end of the other is the highest instrumentality, or use of means, or executive deity.

Each student adheres, by temperament and by habit, to the first or to the second of these gods of the mind. By religion, he tends to unity; by intellect, or by the senses, to the many. A too rapid unification, and an excessive appliance to parts and particulars, are the twin dangers of speculation.

To this partiality the history of nations corresponded. The country of unity, of immovable institutions, the seat of a philosophy delighting in abstractions, of men faithful in doctrine and in practice to the idea of a deaf, unimplorable, immense fate, is Asia; and it realizes this faith in the social institution of caste. On the other side, the genius of Europe is active and creative: it resists caste by culture; its philosophy was a discipline; it is a land of arts, inventions, trade, freedom. If the East loved infinity, the West delighted in boundaries.

European civility is the triumph of talent, the extension of system, the sharpened understanding, adaptive skill, delight in forms, delight in manifestation, in comprehensible results. Pericles, Athens, Greece, had been working in this element with the joy of genius not yet chilled by any foresight of the detriment of an excess. They saw before them no sinister political economy; no ominous Malthus; no Paris or London; no pitiless subdivision of classes,—the doom of the pin-makers, the doom of the weavers, of dressers, of stockingers, of carders, of spinners, of colliers; no Ireland; no Indian caste, superinduced by the efforts of Europe to throw it off. The understanding was in its health and prime. Art was in its splendid novelty. They cut the Pentelican marble as if it were snow, and their perfect works in architecture and sculpture seemed things of course, not more difficult than the completion of a new ship at the Medford yards, or new mills at Lowell. These things are in course, and may be taken for granted. The Roman legion, Byzantine legislation, English trade, the saloons of Versailles, the cafés of Paris, the steam-mill, steamboat, steam-coach, may all be seen in perspective; the town-meeting, the ballot-box, the newspaper and cheap press.

Meantime, Plato, in Egypt and in Eastern pilgrimages, imbibed the idea of one Deity, in which all things are absorbed. The unity of Asia and the detail of Europe; the infinitude of the Asiatic soul and the defining, result-loving, machine-making, surface-seeking, opera-going Europe,—Plato came to join, and, by contact, to enhance the energy of each. The excellence of Europe and Asia are in his brain. Metaphysics and natural philosophy expressed the genius of Europe; he substructs the religion of Asia, as the base.

In short, a balanced soul was born, perceptive of the two elements. It is as easy to be great as to be small. The reason why we do not at once believe in admirable souls is because they are not in our experience. In actual life, they are so rare as to be incredible; but primarily there is not only no presumption against them, but the strongest presumption in favor of their appearance. But whether voices were heard in the sky, or not; whether his mother or his father dreamed that the infant man-child was the son of Apollo; whether a swarm of bees settled on his lips, or not;—a man who could see two sides of a thing was born. The wonderful synthesis so familiar in nature; the upper and the under side of the medal of Jove; the union of impossibilities, which reappears in every object; its real and its ideal power,—was now also transferred entire to the consciousness of a man.

The balanced soul came. If he loved abstract truth, he saved himself by propounding the most popular of all principles, the absolute good, which rules rulers, and judges the judge. If he made transcendental distinctions, he fortified himself by drawing all his illustrations from sources disdained by orators and polite conversers; from mares and puppies; from pitchers and soup-ladles; from cooks and criers; the shops of potters, horse-doctors, butchers and fishmongers. He cannot forgive in himself a partiality, but is resolved that the two poles of thought shall appear in his statement. His argument and his sentence are self-poised and spherical. The two poles appear; yes, and become two hands, to grasp and appropriate their own.

Every great artist has been such by synthesis. Our strength is transitional, alternating; or, shall I say, a thread of two strands. The sea-shore, sea seen from shore, shore seen from sea; the taste of two metals in contact; and our enlarged powers at the approach and at the departure of a friend; the experience of poetic creativeness, which is not found in staying at home, nor yet in travelling, but in transitions from one to the other, which must therefore be adroitly managed to present as much transitional surface as possible; this command of two elements must explain the power and the charm of Plato. Art expresses the one or the same by the different. Thought seeks to know unity in unity; poetry to show it by variety; that is, always by an object or symbol. Plato keeps the two vases, one of æther and one of pigment, at his side, and invariably uses both. Things added to things, as statistics, civil history, are inventories. Things used as language are inexhaustibly attractive. Plato turns incessantly the obverse and the reverse of the medal of Jove.

To take an example:—The physical philosophers had sketched each his theory of the world; the theory of atoms, of fire, of flux, of spirit; theories mechanical and chemical in their genius. Plato, a master of mathematics, studious of all natural laws and causes, feels these, as second causes, to be no theories of the world but bare inventories and lists. To the study of nature he therefore prefixes the dogma,— "Let us declare the cause which led the Supreme Ordainer to produce and compose the universe. He was good; and he who is good has no kind of envy. Exempt from envy, he wished that all things should be as much as possible like himself. Whosoever, taught by wise men, shall admit this as the prime cause of the origin and foundation of the world, will be in the truth." "All things are for the sake of the good, and it is the cause of every thing beautiful." This dogma animates and impersonates his philosophy.

The synthesis which makes the character of his mind appears in all his talents. Where there is great compass of wit, we usually find excellencies that combine easily in the living man, but in description appear incompatible. The mind of Plato is not to be exhibited by a Chinese catalogue, but is to be apprehended by an original mind in the exercise of its original power. In him the freest abandonment is united with the precision of a geometer. His daring imagination gives him the more solid grasp of facts; as the birds of highest flight have the strongest alar bones. His patrician polish, his intrinsic elegance, edged by an irony so subtle that it stings and paralyzes, adorn the soundest health and strength of frame. According to the old sentence, "If Jove should descend to the earth, he would speak in the style of Plato."

With this palatial air there is, for the direct aim of several of his works and running through the tenor of them all, a certain earnestness, which mounts, in the Republic and in the Phædo, to piety. He has been charged with feigning sickness at the time of the death of Socrates. But the anecdotes that have come down from the times attest his manly interference before the people in his master's behalf, since even the savage cry of the assembly to Plato is preserved; and the indignation towards popular government, in many of his pieces, expresses a personal exasperation. He has a probity, a native reverence for justice and honor, and a humanity which makes him tender for the superstitions of the people. Add to this, he believes that poetry, prophecy and the high insight are from a wisdom of which man is not master; that the gods never philosophize, but by a celestial mania these miracles are accomplished. Horsed on these winged steeds, he sweeps the dim regions, visits worlds which flesh cannot enter; he saw the souls in pain, he hears the doom of the judge, he beholds the penal metempsychosis, the Fates, with the rock and shears, and hears the intoxicating hum of their spindle.

But his circumspection never forsook him. One would say he had read the inscription on the gates of Busyrane,—"Be bold;" and on the second gate,—"Be bold, be bold, and evermore be bold;" and then again had paused well at the third gate,—"Be not too bold." His strength is like the momentum of a falling planet, and his discretion the return of its due and perfect curve,—so excellent is his Greek love of boundary and his skill in definition. In reading logarithms one is not more secure than in following Plato in his flights. Nothing can be colder than his head, when the lightnings of his imagination are playing in the sky. He has finished his thinking before he brings it to the reader, and he abounds in the surprises of a literary master. He has that opulence which furnishes, at every turn, the precise weapon he needs. As the rich man wears no more garments, drives no more horses, sits in no more chambers than the poor,—but has that one dress, or equipage, or instrument, which is fit for the hour and the need; so Plato, in his plenty, is never restricted, but has the fit word. There is indeed no weapon in all the armory of wit which he did not possess and use,—epic, analysis, mania, intuition, music, satire and irony, down to the customary and polite. His illustrations are poetry and his jests illustrations. Socrates' profession of obstetric art is good philosophy; and his finding that word "cookery," and "adulatory art," for rhetoric, in the Gorgias, does us a substantial service still. No orator can measure in effect with him who can give good nicknames.

What moderation and understatement and checking his thunder in mid volley! He has good-naturedly furnished the courtier and citizen with all that can be said against the schools. "For philosophy is an elegant thing, if any one modestly meddles with it; but if he is conversant with it more than is becoming, it corrupts the man." He could well afford to be generous,—he, who from the sunlike centrality and reach of his vision, had a faith without cloud. Such as his perception, was his speech: he plays with the doubt and makes the most of it: he paints and quibbles; and by and by comes a sentence that moves the sea and land. The admirable earnest comes not only at intervals, in the perfect yes and no of the dialogue, but in bursts of light. "I, therefore, Callicles, am persuaded by these accounts, and consider how I may exhibit my soul before the judge in a healthy condition. Wherefore, disregarding the honors that most men value, and looking to the truth, I shall endeavor in reality to live as virtuously as I can; and when I die, to die so. And I invite all other men, to the utmost of my power; and you too I in turn invite to this contest, which, I affirm, surpasses all contests here."

He is a great average man; one who, to the best thinking, adds a proportion and equality in his faculties, so that men see in him their own dreams and glimpses made available and made to pass for what they are. A great common-sense is his warrant and qualification to be the world's interpreter. He has reason, as all the philosophic and poetic class have: but he has also what they have not,—this strong solving sense to reconcile his poetry with the appearances of the world, and build a bridge from the streets of cities to the Atlantis. He omits never this graduation, but slopes his thought, however picturesque the precipice on one side, to an access from the plain. He never writes in ecstasy, or catches us up into poetic raptures.

Plato apprehended the cardinal facts. He could prostrate himself on the earth and cover his eyes whilst he adored that which cannot be numbered, or gauged, or known, or named: that of which every thing can be affirmed and denied: that "which is entity and nonentity." He called it super-essential. He even stood ready, as in the Parmenides, to demonstrate that it was so,—that this Being exceeded the limits of intellect. No man ever more fully acknowledged the Ineffable. Having paid his homage, as for the human race, to the Illimitable, he then stood erect, and for the human race affirmed, 'And yet things are knowable!'—that is, the Asia in his mind was first heartily honored,—the ocean of love and power, before form, before will, before knowledge, the Same, the Good, the One; and now, refreshed and empowered by this worship, the instinct of Europe, namely, culture, returns; and he cries, 'Yet things are knowable!' They are knowable, because being from one, things correspond. There is a scale; and the correspondence of heaven to earth, of matter to mind, of the part to the whole, is our guide. As there is a science of stars, called astronomy; a science of quantities, called mathematics; a science of qualities, called chemistry; so there is a science of sciences,—I call it Dialectic,—which is the Intellect discriminating the false and the true. It rests on the observation of identity and diversity; for to judge is to unite to an object the notion which belongs to it. The sciences, even the best,—mathematics and astronomy,—are like sportsmen, who seize whatever prey offers, even without being able to make any use of it. Dialectic must teach the use of them. "This is of that rank that no intellectual man will enter on any study for its own sake, but only with a view to advance himself in that one sole science which embraces all."

"The essence or peculiarity of man is to comprehend a whole; or that which in the diversity of sensations can be comprised under a rational unity." "The soul which has never perceived the truth, cannot pass into the human form." I announce to men the Intellect. I announce the good of being interpenetrated by the mind that made nature: this benefit, namely, that it can understand nature, which it made and maketh. Nature is good, but intellect is better: as the law-giver is before the law-receiver. I give you joy, O sons of men! that truth is altogether wholesome; that we have hope to search out what might be the very self of everything. The misery of man is to be baulked of the sight of essence and to be stuffed with conjectures; but the supreme good is reality; the supreme beauty is reality; and all virtue and all felicity depend on this science of the real: for courage is nothing else than knowledge; the fairest fortune that can befall man is to be guided by his dæmon to that which is truly his own. This also is the essence of justice,—to attend every one his own: nay, the notion of virtue is not to be arrived at except through direct contemplation of the divine essence. Courage then! for "the persuasion that we must search that which we do not know, will render us, beyond comparison, better, braver and more industrious than if we thought it impossible to discover what we do not know, and useless to search for it." He secures a position not to be commanded, by his passion for reality; valuing philosophy only as it is the pleasure of conversing with real being.

Thus, full of the genius of Europe, he said, *Culture.* He
saw the institutions of Sparta and recognized, more genially one would say than any since, the hope of education. He delighted in every accomplishment, in every
graceful and useful and truthful performance; above all in
the splendors of genius and intellectual achievement.
"The whole of life, O Socrates," said Glauco, "is, with the
wise, the measure of hearing such discourses as these."
What a price he sets on the feats of talent, on the powers
of Pericles, of Isocrates, of Parmenides! What price above
price on the talents themselves! He called the several faculties, gods, in his beautiful personation. What value he
gives to the art of gymnastic in education; what to geometry; what to music; what to astronomy, whose appeasing
and medicinal power he celebrates! In the Timæus he indicates the highest employment of the eyes. "By us it is
asserted that God invented and bestowed sight on us for
this purpose,—that on surveying the circles of intelligence
in the heavens, we might properly employ those of our
own minds, which, though disturbed when compared
with the others that are uniform, are still allied to their
circulations; and that having thus learned, and being naturally possessed of a correct reasoning faculty, we might,
by imitating the uniform revolutions of divinity, set right
our own wanderings and blunders." And in the Republic,—"By each of these disciplines a certain organ of the
soul is both purified and reanimated which is blinded and
buried by studies of another kind; an organ better worth
saving than ten thousand eyes, since truth is perceived by
this alone."

He said, Culture; but he first admitted its basis, and
gave immeasurably the first place to advantages of nature.
His patrician tastes laid stress on the distinctions of birth.
In the doctrine of the organic character and disposition is
the origin of caste. "Such as were fit to govern, into their
composition the informing Deity mingled gold; into the
military, silver; iron and brass for husbandmen and artificers." The East confirms itself, in all ages, in this faith.

The Koran is explicit on this point of caste. "Men have their metal, as of gold and silver. Those of you who were the worthy ones in the state of ignorance, will be the worthy ones in the state of faith, as soon as you embrace it." Plato was not less firm. "Of the five orders of things, only four can be taught to the generality of men." In the Republic he insists on the temperaments of the youth, as first of the first.

A happier example of the stress laid on nature is in the dialogue with the young Theages, who wishes to receive lessons from Socrates. Socrates declares that if some have grown wise by associating with him, no thanks are due to him; but, simply, whilst they were with him they grew wise, not because of him; he pretends not to know the way of it. "It is adverse to many, nor can those be benefited by associating with me whom the Dæmon opposes; so that it is not possible for me to live with these. With many however he does not prevent me from conversing, who yet are not at all benefited by associating with me. Such, O Theages, is the association with me; for, if it pleases the God, you will make great and rapid proficiency: you will not, if he does not please. Judge whether it is not safer to be instructed by some one of those who have power over the benefit which they impart to men, than by me, who benefit or not, just as it may happen." As if he had said, 'I have no system. I cannot be answerable for you. You will be what you must. If there is love between us, inconceivably delicious and profitable will our intercourse be; if not, your time is lost and you will only annoy me. I shall seem to you stupid, and the reputation I have, false. Quite above us, beyond the will of you or me, is this secret affinity or repulsion laid. All my good is magnetic, and I educate, not by lessons, but by going about my business.'

He said, Culture; he said, Nature; and he failed not to add, 'There is also the divine.' There is no thought in any mind but it quickly tends to convert itself into a power and organizes a huge instrumentality of means. Plato, lover of limits, loved the illimitable, saw the enlargement and nobility which come from truth itself and good itself, and attempted as if on the part of the human intellect, once for all to do it adequate homage,—homage fit for the immense soul to receive, and yet homage becoming the intellect to render. He said then, 'Our faculties run out into infinity, and return to us thence. We can define but a little way; but here is a fact which will not be skipped, and which to shut our eyes upon is suicide. All things are in a scale; and, begin where we will, ascend and ascend. All things are symbolical; and what we call results are beginnings.'

A key to the method and completeness of Plato is his twice bisected line. After he has illustrated the relation between the absolute good and true and the forms of the intelligible world, he says: "Let there be a line cut in two unequal parts. Cut again each of these two main parts,— one representing the visible, the other the intelligible world,—and let these two new sections represent the bright part and the dark part of each of these worlds. You will have, for one of the sections of the visible world, images, that is, both shadows and reflections;—for the other section, the objects of these images, that is, plants, animals, and the works of art and nature. Then divide the intelligible world in like manner; the one section will be of opinions and hypotheses, and the other section of truths." To these four sections, the four operations of the soul correspond,—conjecture, faith, understanding, reason. As every pool reflects the image of the sun, so every thought and thing restores us an image and creature of the supreme Good. The universe is perforated by a million channels for his activity. All things mount and mount.

All his thought has this ascension; in Phædrus, teaching that beauty is the most lovely of all things, exciting hilarity and shedding desire and confidence through the universe wherever it enters, and it enters in some degree into all things:—but that there is another, which is as much more beautiful than beauty as beauty is than chaos; namely, wisdom, which our wonderful organ of sight cannot reach unto, but which, could it be seen, would ravish us with its perfect reality. He has the same regard to it as the source of excellence in works of art. When an artificer, he says, in the fabrication of any work, looks to that which always subsists according *to the same;* and, employing a model of this kind, expresses its idea and power in his work,—it must follow that his production should be beautiful. But when he beholds that which is born and dies, it will be far from beautiful.

Thus ever: the Banquet is a teaching in the same spirit, familiar now to all the poetry and to all the sermons of the world, that the love of the sexes is initial, and symbolizes at a distance the passion of the soul for that immense lake of beauty it exists to seek. This faith in the Divinity is never out of mind, and constitutes the ground of all his dogmas. Body cannot teach wisdom;—God only. In the same mind he constantly affirms that virtue cannot be taught; that it is not a science, but an inspiration; that the greatest goods are produced to us through mania and are assigned to us by a divine gift.

This leads me to that central figure which he has established in his Academy as the organ through which every considered opinion shall be announced, and whose biography he has likewise so labored that the historic facts are lost in the light of Plato's mind. Socrates and Plato are the double star which the most powerful instruments will not entirely separate. Socrates again, in his traits and genius, is the best example of that synthesis which constitutes Plato's extraordinary power. Socrates, a man of humble stem, but honest enough; of the commonest history; of a personal homeliness so remarkable as to be a cause of wit in others:—the rather that his broad good nature and exquisite taste for a joke invited the sally, which was sure to be paid. The players personated him on the stage; the potters copied his ugly face on their stone jugs. He was a cool fellow, adding to his humor a perfect temper and a knowledge of his man, be he who he might whom he talked with, which laid the companion open to certain defeat in any debate,—and in debate he immoderately delighted. The young men are prodigiously fond of him and invite him to their feasts, whither he goes for conversation. He can drink, too; has the strongest head in Athens; and after leaving the whole party under the table, goes away as if nothing had happened, to begin new dialogues with somebody that is sober. In short, he was what our country-people call *an old one*.

He affected a good many citizen-like tastes, was monstrously fond of Athens, hated trees, never willingly went beyond the walls, knew the old characters, valued the bores and philistines, thought every thing in Athens a little better than anything in any other place. He was plain as a Quaker in habit and speech, affected low phrases, and illustrations from cocks and quails, soup-pans and syca-more-spoons, grooms and farriers, and unnamable offices,—especially if he talked with any superfine person. He had a Franklin-like wisdom. Thus he showed one who was afraid to go on foot to Olympia, that it was no more than his daily walk within doors, if continuously extended, would easily reach.

Plain old uncle as he was, with his great ears, an immense talker,—the rumor ran that on one or two occasions, in the war with Bœotia, he had shown a determination which had covered the retreat of a troop; and there was some story that under cover of folly, he had, in the city government, when one day he chanced to hold a seat there, evinced a courage in opposing singly the popular voice, which had well-nigh ruined him. He is very poor; but then he is hardy as a soldier, and can live on a few olives; usually, in the strictest sense, on bread and water, except when entertained by his friends. His necessary expenses were exceedingly small, and no one could live as he did. He wore no under garment; his upper garment was the same for summer and winter, and he went barefooted; and it is said that to procure the pleasure, which he loves, of talking at his ease all day with the most elegant and cultivated young men, he will now and then return to his shop and carve statues, good or bad, for sale. However that be, it is certain that he had grown to delight in nothing else than this conversation; and that, under his hypocritical pretence of knowing nothing, he attacks and brings down all the fine speakers, all the fine philosophers of Athens, whether natives or strangers from Asia Minor and the islands. Nobody can refuse to talk with him, he is so honest and really curious to know; a man who was willingly confuted if he did not speak the truth, and who willingly confuted others asserting what was false; and not less pleased when confuted than when confuting; for he thought not any evil happened to men of such a magnitude as false opinion respecting the just and unjust. A pitiless disputant, who knows nothing, but the bounds of whose conquering intelligence no man had ever reached; whose temper was imperturbable; whose dreadful logic was always leisurely and sportive; so careless and ignorant as to disarm the wariest and draw them, in the pleasantest manner, into horrible doubts and confusion. But he always knew the way out; knew it, yet would not tell it. No escape; he drives them to terrible choices by his dilemmas, and tosses the Hippiases and Gorgiases with their grand reputations, as a boy tosses his balls. The tyrannous realist!—Meno has discoursed a thousand times, at length, on virtue, before many companies, and very well, as it appeared to him; but at this moment he cannot even tell what it is,—this cramp-fish of a Socrates has so bewitched him.

This hard-headed humorist, whose strange conceits, drollery and *bonhommie* diverted the young patricians, whilst the rumor of his sayings and quibbles gets abroad every day,—turns out, in the sequel, to have a probity as invincible as his logic, and to be either insane, or at least, under cover of this play, enthusiastic in his religion. When accused before the judges of subverting the popular creed, he affirms the immortality of the soul, the future reward and punishment; and refusing to recant, in a caprice of the popular government was condemned to die, and sent to the prison. Socrates entered the prison and took away all ignominy from the place, which could not be a prison whilst he was there. Crito bribed the jailer; but Socrates would not go out by treachery. "Whatever inconvenience ensue, nothing is to be preferred before justice. These things I hear like pipes and drums, whose sound makes me deaf to every thing you say." The fame of this prison, the fame of the discourses there and the drinking of the hemlock are one of the most precious passages in the history of the world.

The rare coincidence, in one ugly body, of the droll and the martyr, the keen street and market debater with the sweetest saint known to any history at that time, had forcibly struck the mind of Plato, so capacious of these contrasts; and the figure of Socrates by a necessity placed itself in the foreground of the scene, as the fittest dispenser of the intellectual treasures he had to communicate. It was a rare fortune that this AEsop of the mob and this robed scholar should meet, to make each other immortal in their mutual faculty. The strange synthesis in the character of Socrates capped the synthesis in the mind of Plato. Moreover by this means he was able, in the direct way and without envy to avail himself of the wit and weight of Socrates, to which unquestionably his own debt was great; and these derived again their principal advantage from the perfect art of Plato.

It remains to say that the defect of Plato in power is only that which results inevitably from his quality. He is intellectual in his aim; and therefore, in expression, literary. Mounting into heaven, diving into the pit, expounding the laws of the state, the passion of love, the remorse of crime, the hope of the parting soul,—he is literary, and never otherwise. It is almost the sole deduction from the merit of Plato that his writings have not,—what is no doubt incident to this regnancy of intellect in his work,— the vital authority which the screams of prophets and the sermons of unlettered Arabs and Jews possess. There is an interval; and to cohesion, contact is necessary.

I know not what can be said in reply to this criticism but that we have come to a fact in the nature of things: an oak is not an orange. The qualities of sugar remain with sugar, and those of salt with salt.

In the second place, he has not a system. The dearest defenders and disciples are at fault. He attempted a theory of the universe, and his theory is not complete or self-evident. One man thinks he means this, and another that; he has said one thing in one place, and the reverse of it in another place. He is charged with having failed to make the transition from ideas to matter. Here is the world, sound as a nut, perfect, not the smallest piece of chaos left, never a stitch nor an end, not a mark of haste, or botching, or second thought; but the theory of the world is a thing of shreds and patches.

The longest wave is quickly lost in the sea. Plato would willingly have a Platonism, a known and accurate expression for the world, and it should be accurate. It shall be the world passed through the mind of Plato,—nothing less. Every atom shall have the Platonic tinge; every atom, every relation or quality you knew before, you shall know again and find here, but now ordered; not nature, but art. And you shall feel that Alexander indeed overran, with men and horses, some countries of the planet; but countries, and things of which countries are made, elements, planet itself, laws of planet and of men, have passed through this man as bread into his body, and become no longer bread, but body: so all this mammoth morsel has become Plato. He has clapped copyright on the world. This is the ambition of individualism. But the mouthful proves too large. *Boa constrictor* has good will to eat it, but he is foiled. He falls abroad in the attempt; and biting, gets strangled: the bitten world holds the biter fast by his own teeth. There he perishes: unconquered nature lives on and forgets him. So it fares with all: so must it fare with Plato. In view of eternal nature, Plato turns out to be philosophical exercitations. He argues on this side and on that. The acutest German, the lovingest disciple, could never tell what Platonism was; indeed, admirable texts can be quoted on both sides of every great question from him.

These things we are forced to say if we must consider the effort of Plato or of any philosopher to dispose of nature,—which will not be disposed of. No power of genius has ever yet had the smallest success in explaining existence. The perfect enigma remains. But there is an injustice in assuming this ambition for Plato. Let us not seem to treat with flippancy his venerable name. Men, in proportion to their intellect, have admitted his transcendent claims. The way to know him is to compare him, not with nature, but with other men. How many ages have gone by, and he remains unapproached! A chief structure of human wit, like Karnac, or the mediæval cathedrals, or the Etrurian remains, it requires all the breath of human faculty to know it. I think it is trueliest seen when seen with the most respect. His sense deepens, his merits multiply, with study. When we say, Here is a fine collection of fables; or when we praise the style, or the common sense, or arithmetic, we speak as boys, and much of our impatient criticism of the dialectic, I suspect, is no better.

The criticism is like our impatience of miles, when we are in a hurry; but it is still best that a mile should have seventeen hundred and sixty yards. The great-eyed Plato proportioned the lights and shades after the genius of our life.

Plato:
New Readings

The publication, in Mr. Bohn's "Serial Library," of the excellent translations of Plato, which we esteem one of the chief benefits the cheap press has yielded, gives us an occasion to take hastily a few more notes of the elevation and bearings of this fixed star; or to add a bulletin, like the journals, of *Plato at the latest dates*.

Modern science, by the extent of its generalization, has learned to indemnify the student of man for the defects of individuals by tracing growth and ascent in races; and, by the simple expedient of lighting up the vast background, generates a feeling of complacency and hope. The human being has the saurian and the plant in his rear. His arts and sciences, the easy issue of his brain, look glorious when prospectively beheld from the distant brain of ox, crocodile and fish. It seems as if nature, in regarding the geologic night behind her, when, in five or six millenniums, she had turned out five or six men, as Homer, Phidias, Menu and Columbus, was no wise discontented with the result. These samples attested the virtue of the tree. These were a clear amelioration of trilobite and saurus, and a good basis for further proceeding. With this artist, time and space are cheap, and she is insensible to what you say of tedious preparation. She waited tranquilly the flowing periods of paleontology, for the hour to be struck when man should arrive. Then periods must pass before the motion of the earth can be suspected; then before the map of the instincts and the cultivable powers can be drawn. But as of races, so the succession of individual men is fatal and beautiful, and Plato has the fortune in the history of mankind to mark an epoch.

Plato's fame does not stand on a syllogism, or on any masterpieces of the Socratic reasoning, or on any thesis, as for example the immortality of the soul. He is more than an expert, or a schoolman, or a geometer, or the prophet of a peculiar message. He represents the privilege of the intellect, the power, namely, of carrying up every fact to successive platforms and so disclosing in every fact a germ of expansion. These expansions are in the essence of thought. The naturalist would never help us to them by any discoveries of the extent of the universe, but is as poor when cataloguing the resolved nebula of Orion, as when measuring the angles of an acre. But the Republic of Plato, by these expansions, may be said to require and so to anticipate the astronomy of Laplace. The expansions are organic. The mind does not create what it perceives, any more than the eye creates the rose. In ascribing to Plato the merit of announcing them, we only say, Here was a more complete man, who could apply to nature the whole scale of the senses, the understanding and the reason. These expansions or extensions consist in continuing the spiritual sight where the horizon falls on our natural vision, and by this second sight discovering the long lines of law which shoot in every direction. Everywhere he stands on a path which has no end, but runs continuously round the universe. Therefore every word becomes an exponent of nature. Whatever he looks upon discloses a second sense, and ulterior senses. His perception of the generation of contraries, of death out of life and life out of death,—that law by which, in nature, decomposition is recomposition, and putrefaction and cholera are only signals of a new creation; his discernment of the little in the large and the large in the small; studying the state in the citizen and the citizen in the state; and leaving it doubtful whether he exhibited the Republic as an allegory on the education of the private soul; his beautiful definitions of ideas, of time, of form, of figure, of the line, sometimes hypothetically given, as his defining of virtue, courage, justice, temperance; his love of the apologue, and his apologues themselves; the cave of Trophonius; the ring of Gyges; the charioteer and two horses; the golden, silver, brass and iron temperaments; Theuth and Thamus; and the vision of Hades and the Fates,—fables which have imprinted themselves in the human memory like the signs of the zodiac; his soliform eye and his boniform soul; his doctrine of assimilation; his doctrine of reminiscence; his clear vision of the laws of return, or reaction, which secure instant justice throughout the universe, instanced everywhere, but specially in the doctrine, "what comes from God to us, returns from us to God," and in Socrates' belief that the laws below are sisters of the laws above.

More striking examples are his moral conclusions. Plato

affirms the coincidence of science and virtue; for vice can never know itself and virtue, but virtue knows both itself and vice. The eye attested that justice was best, as long as it was profitable; Plato affirms that it is profitable throughout; that the profit is intrinsic, though the just conceal his justice from gods and men; that it is better to suffer injustice than to do it; that the sinner ought to covet punishment; that the lie was more hurtful than homicide; and that ignorance, or the involuntary lie, was more calamitous than involuntary homicide; that the soul is unwillingly deprived of true opinions, and that no man sins willingly; that the order or proceeding of nature was from the mind to the body, and, though a sound body cannot restore an unsound mind, yet a good soul can, by its virtue, render the body the best possible. The intelligent have a right over the ignorant, namely, the right of instructing them. The right punishment of one out of tune is to make him play in tune; the fine which the good, refusing to govern, ought to pay, is, to be governed by a worse man; that his guards shall not handle gold and silver, but shall be instructed that there is gold and silver in their souls, which will make men willing to give them every thing which they need.

This second sight explains the stress laid on geometry. He saw that the globe of earth was not more lawful and precise than was the supersensible; that a celestial geometry was in place there, as a logic of lines and angles here below; that the world was throughout mathematical; the proportions are constant of oxygen, azote and lime; there is just so much water and slate and magnesia; not less are the proportions constant of the moral elements.

This eldest Goethe, hating varnish and falsehood, delighted in revealing the real at the base of the accidental; in discovering connection, continuity and representation everywhere, hating insulation; and appears like the god of wealth among the cabins of vagabonds, opening power and capability in everything he touches. Ethical science was new and vacant when Plato could write thus:—"Of all whose arguments are left to the men of the present time, no one has ever yet condemned injustice, or praised justice, otherwise than as respects the repute, honors and emoluments arising therefrom; while, as respects either of them in itself, and subsisting by its own power in the soul of the possessor, and concealed both from gods and men, no one has yet sufficiently investigated, either in poetry or prose writings,—how, namely, that injustice is the greatest of all the evils that the soul has within it, and justice the greatest good."

His definition of ideas, as what is simple, permanent, uniform and self-existent, forever discriminating them from the notions of the understanding, marks an era in the world. He was born to behold the self-evolving power of spirit, endless, generator of new ends; a power which is the key at once to the centrality and the evanescence of things. Plato is so centred that he can well spare all his dogmas. Thus the fact of knowledge and ideas reveals to him the fact of eternity; and the doctrine of reminiscence he offers as the most probable particular explication. Call that fanciful,—it matters not: the connection between our knowledge and the abyss of being is still real, and the explication must be not less magnificent.

He has indicated every eminent point in speculation. He wrote on the scale of the mind itself, so that all things have symmetry in his tablet. He put in all the past, without weariness, and descended into detail with a courage like that he witnessed in nature. One would say that his forerunners had mapped out each a farm or a district or an island, in intellectual geography, but that Plato first drew the sphere. He domesticates the soul in nature: man is the microcosm. All the circles of the visible heaven represent as many circles in the rational soul. There is no lawless particle, and there is nothing casual in the action of the human mind. The names of things, too, are fatal, following the nature of things. All the gods of the Pantheon are, by their names, significant of a profound sense. The gods are the ideas. Pan is speech, or manifestation; Saturn, the contemplative; Jove, the regal soul; and Mars, passion. Venus is proportion; Calliope, the soul of the world; Aglaia, intellectual illustration.

These thoughts, in sparkles of light, had appeared often to pious and to poetic souls; but this well-bred, all-knowing Greek geometer comes with command, gathers them all up into rank and gradation, the Euclid of holiness, and marries the two parts of nature. Before all men, he saw the intellectual values of the moral sentiment. He describes his own ideal, when he paints, in Timæus, a god leading things from disorder into order. He kindled a fire so truly in the centre that we see the sphere illuminated, and can distinguish poles, equator and lines of latitude, every arc and node: a theory so averaged, so modulated, that you would say the winds of ages had swept through this rhythmic structure, and not that it was the brief extempore blotting of one short-lived scribe. Hence it has happened that a very well-marked class of souls, namely those who delight in giving a spiritual, that is, an ethico-intellectual expression to every truth, by exhibiting an ulterior end which is yet legitimate to it,—are said to Platonize. Thus, Michael Angelo is a Platonist in his sonnets: Shakspeare is a Platonist when he writes,—

> "Nature is made better by no mean,
> But nature makes that mean,"

or,—

> "He, that can endure
> To follow with allegiance a fallen lord,
> Does conquer him that did his master conquer,
> And earns a place in the story."

Hamlet is a pure Platonist, and 't is the magnitude only of Shakspeare's proper genius that hinders him from being classed as the most eminent of this school. Swedenborg, throughout his prose poem of "Conjugal Love," is a Platonist.

His subtlety commended him to men of thought. The secret of his popular success is the moral aim which endeared him to mankind. "Intellect," he said, "is king of heaven and of earth;" but in Plato, intellect is always moral. His writings have also the sempiternal youth of poetry. For their arguments, most of them, might have been couched in sonnets: and poetry has never soared higher than in the Timæus and the Phædrus. As the poet, too, he is only contemplative. He did not, like Pythagoras, break himself with an institution. All his painting in the Republic must be esteemed mythical, with intent to bring out, sometimes in violent colors, his thought. You cannot institute, without peril of charlatanism.

It was a high scheme, his absolute privilege for the best (which, to make emphatic, he expressed by community of women), as the premium which he would set on grandeur. There shall be exempts of two kinds: first, those who by demerit have put themselves below protection,—outlaws; and secondly, those who by eminence of nature and desert are out of the reach of your rewards. Let such be free of the city and above the law. We confide them to themselves; let them do with us as they will. Let none presume to measure the irregularities of Michael Angelo and Socrates by village scales.

In his eighth book of the Republic, he throws a little mathematical dust in our eyes. I am sorry to see him, after such noble superiorities, permitting the lie to governors. Plato plays Providence a little with the baser sort, as people allow themselves with their dogs and cats.

NAPOLEON;
OR, THE MAN OF THE WORLD

~~~~~~~~~~~~~~~~~~~~~~~~~~~~~~~~~~

Among the eminent persons of the nineteenth century, Bonaparte is far the best known and the most powerful; and owes his predominance to the fidelity with which he expresses the tone of thought and belief, the aims of the masses of active and cultivated men. It is Swedenborg's theory that every organ is made up of homogeneous particles; or as it is sometimes expressed, every whole is made of similars; that is, the lungs are composed of infinitely small lungs; the liver, of infinitely small livers; the kidney, of little kidneys, etc. Following this analogy, if any man is found to carry with him the power and affections of vast numbers, if Napoleon is France, if Napoleon is Europe, it is because the people whom he sways are little Napoleons.

In our society there is a standing antagonism between the conservative and the democratic classes; between those who have made their fortunes, and the young and the poor who have fortunes to make; between the interests of dead labor,—that is, the labor of hands long ago still in the grave, which labor is now entombed in money stocks, or in land and buildings owned by idle capitalists,—and the interests of living labor, which seeks to possess itself of land and buildings and money stocks. The first class is timid, selfish, illiberal, hating innovation, and continually losing numbers by death. The second class is selfish also, encroaching, bold, self-relying, always outnumbering the other and recruiting its numbers every hour by births. It desires to keep open every avenue to the competition of all, and to multiply avenues: the class of business men in

America, in England, in France and throughout Europe; the class of industry and skill. Napoleon is its representative. The instinct of active, brave, able men, throughout the middle class every where, has pointed out Napoleon as the incarnate Democrat. He had their virtues and their vices; above all, he had their spirit or aim. That tendency is material, pointing at a sensual success and employing the richest and most various means to that end; conversant with mechanical powers, highly intellectual, widely and accurately learned and skilful, but subordinating all intellectual and spiritual forces into means to a material success. To be the rich man, is the end. "God has granted," says the Koran, "to every people a prophet in its own tongue." Paris and London and New York, the spirit of commerce, of money and material power, were also to have their prophet; and Bonaparte was qualified and sent.

Every one of the million readers of anecdotes or memoirs or lives of Napoleon, delights in the page, because he studies in it his own history. Napoleon is thoroughly modern, and, at the highest point of his fortunes, has the very spirit of the newspapers. He is no saint,—to use his own word, "no capuchin," and he is no hero, in the high sense. The man in the street finds in him the qualities and powers of other men in the street. He finds him, like himself, by birth a citizen, who, by very intelligible merits, arrived at such a commanding position that he could indulge all those tastes which the common man possesses but is obliged to conceal and deny: good society, good books, fast travelling, dress, dinners, servants without number, personal weight, the execution of his ideas, the standing in the attitude of a benefactor to all persons about him, the refined enjoyments of pictures, statues, music, palaces and conventional honors,—precisely what is agreeable to the heart of every man in the nineteenth century, this powerful man possessed.

It is true that a man of Napoleon's truth of adaptation to the mind of the masses around him, becomes not merely representative but actually a monopolizer and usurper of other minds. Thus Mirabeau plagiarized every good thought, every good word that was spoken in France. Dumont relates that he sat in the gallery of the Convention and heard Mirabeau make a speech. It struck Dumont that he could fit it with a peroration, which he wrote in pencil immediately, and showed it to Lord Elgin, who sat by him. Lord Elgin approved it, and Dumont, in the evening, showed it to Mirabeau. Mirabeau read it, pronounced it admirable, and declared he would incorporate it into his harangue to-morrow, to the Assembly. "It is impossible," said Dumont, "as, unfortunately, I have shown it to Lord Elgin." "If you have shown it to Lord Elgin and to fifty persons beside, I shall still speak it to-morrow:" and he did speak it, with much effect, at the next day's session. For Mirabeau, with his overpowering personality, felt that these things which his presence inspired were as much his own as if he had said them, and that his adoption of them gave them their weight. Much more absolute and centralizing was the successor to Mirabeau's popularity and to much more than his predominance in France. Indeed, a man of Napoleon's stamp almost ceases to have a private speech and opinion. He is so largely receptive, and is so placed, that he comes to be a bureau for all the intelligence, wit and power of the age and country. He gains the battle; he makes the code; he makes the system of weights and measures; he levels the Alps; he builds the road. All distinguished engineers, savans, statists, report to him: so likewise do all good heads in every kind: he adopts the best measures, sets his stamp on them, and not these alone, but on every happy and memorable expression. Every sentence spoken by Napoleon and every line of his writing, deserves reading, as it is the sense of France.

Bonaparte was the idol of common men because he had in transcendent degree the qualities and powers of common men. There is a certain satisfaction in coming down to the lowest ground of politics, for we get rid of cant and hypocrisy. Bonaparte wrought, in common with that great class he represented, for power and wealth,—but Bonaparte, specially, without any scruple as to the means. All the sentiments which embarrass men's pursuit of these objects, he set aside. The sentiments were for women and children. Fontanes, in 1804, expressed Napoleon's own sense, when in behalf of the Senate he addressed him,—"Sire, the desire of perfection is the worst disease that ever afflicted the human mind." The advocates of liberty and of progress are "ideologists;"—a word of contempt often in his mouth;—"Necker is an ideologist:" "Lafayette is an ideologist."

An Italian proverb, too well known, declares that "if you would succeed, you must not be too good." It is an advantage, within certain limits, to have renounced the dominion of the sentiments of piety, gratitude and generosity; since what was an impassable bar to us, and still is to others, becomes a convenient weapon for our purposes; just as the river which was a formidable barrier, winter transforms into the smoothest of roads.

Napoleon renounced, once for all, sentiments and affections, and would help himself with his hands and his head. With him is no miracle and no magic. He is a worker in brass, in iron, in wood, in earth, in roads, in buildings, in money and in troops, and a very consistent and wise master-workman. He is never weak and literary, but acts with the solidity and the precision of natural agents. He has not lost his native sense and sympathy with things. Men give way before such a man, as before natural events. To be sure there are men enough who are immersed in things, as farmers, smiths, sailors and mechanics generally; and we know how real and solid such men appear in the presence of scholars and grammarians: but these men ordinarily lack the power of arrangement, and are like hands without a head. But Bonaparte superadded to this mineral and animal force, insight and generalization, so that men saw in him combined the natural and the intellectual power, as if the sea and land had taken flesh and begun to cipher. Therefore the land and sea seem to presuppose him. He came unto his own and they received him. This ciphering operative knows what he is working with and what is the product. He knew the properties of gold and iron, of wheels and ships, of troops and diplomatists, and required that each should do after its kind.

The art of war was the game in which he exerted his arithmetic. It consisted, according to him, in having always more forces than the enemy, on the point where the enemy is attacked, or where he attacks: and his whole talent is strained by endless manœuvre and evolution, to march always on the enemy at an angle, and destroy his forces in detail. It is obvious that a very small force, skilfully and rapidly manœuvring so as always to bring two men against one at the point of engagement, will be an overmatch for a much larger body of men.

The times, his constitution and his early circumstances combined to develop this pattern democrat. He had the virtues of his class and the conditions for their activity. That common-sense which no sooner respects any end than it finds the means to effect it; the delight in the use of means; in the choice, simplification and combining of means; the directness and thoroughness of his work; the prudence with which all was seen and the energy with which all was done, make him the natural organ and head of what I may almost call, from its extent, the *modern* party.

Nature must have far the greatest share in every success, and so in his. Such a man was wanted, and such a man was born; a man of stone and iron, capable of sitting on horseback sixteen or seventeen hours, of going many days together without rest or food except by snatches, and with the speed and spring of a tiger in action; a man not embarrassed by any scruples; compact, instant, selfish, prudent, and of a perception which did not suffer itself to be baulked or misled by any pretences of others, or any superstition or any heat or haste of his own. "My hand of iron," he said, "was not at the extremity of my arm, it was immediately connected with my head." He respected the power of nature and fortune, and ascribed to it his superiority, instead of valuing himself, like inferior men, on his opinionativeness, and waging war with nature. His favorite rhetoric lay in allusion to his star; and he pleased himself, as well as the people, when he styled himself the "Child of Destiny." "They charge me," he said, "with the commission of great crimes: men of my stamp do not commit crimes. Nothing has been more simple than my elevation, 't is in vain to ascribe it to intrigue or crime; it was owing to the peculiarity of the times and to my reputation of having fought well against the enemies of my country. I have always marched with the opinion of great masses and with events. Of what use then would crimes be to me?" Again he said, speaking of his son, "My son can not replace me; I could not replace myself. I am the creature of circumstances."

He had a directness of action never before combined with so much comprehension. He is a realist, terrific to all talkers and confused truth-obscuring persons. He sees where the matter hinges, throws himself on the precise point of resistance, and slights all other considerations. He is strong in the right manner, namely by insight. He never blundered into victory, but won his battles in his head before he won them on the field. His principal means are in himself. He asks counsel of no other. In 1796 he writes to the Directory: "I have conducted the campaign without consulting any one. I should have done no good if I had been under the necessity of conforming to the notions of another person. I have gained some advantages over superior forces and when totally destitute of every thing, because, in the persuasion that your confidence was reposed in me, my actions were as prompt as my thoughts."

History is full, down to this day, of the imbecility of kings and governors. They are a class of persons much to be pitied, for they know not what they should do. The weavers strike for bread, and the king and his ministers, knowing not what to do, meet them with bayonets. But Napoleon understood his business. Here was a man who in each moment and emergency knew what to do next. It is an immense comfort and refreshment to the spirits, not only of kings, but of citizens. Few men have any next; they live from hand to mouth, without plan, and are ever at the end of their line, and after each action wait for an impulse from abroad. Napoleon had been the first man of the world, if his ends had been purely public. As he is, he inspires confidence and vigor by the extraordinary unity of his action. He is firm, sure, self-denying, self-postponing, sacrificing every thing,—money, troops, generals, and his own safety also, to his aim; not misled, like common adventurers, by the splendor of his own means. "Incidents ought not to govern policy," he said, "but policy, incidents." "To be hurried away by every event is to have no political system at all." His victories were only so many doors, and he never for a moment lost sight of his way onward, in the dazzle and uproar of the present circumstance. He knew what to do, and he flew to his mark. He would shorten a straight line to come at his object. Horrible anecdotes may no doubt be collected from his history, of the price at which he bought his successes; but he must not therefore be set down as cruel, but only as one who knew no impediment to his will; not bloodthirsty, not cruel,—but woe to what thing or person stood in his way! Not bloodthirsty, but not sparing of blood,—and pitiless. He saw only the object: the obstacle must give way. "Sire, General Clarke can not combine with General Junot, for the dreadful fire of the Austrian battery."—"Let him carry the battery."—"Sire, every regiment that approaches the heavy artillery is sacrificed: Sire, what orders?"—"Forward, forward!" Seruzier, a colonel of artillery, gives, in his "Military Memoirs," the following sketch of a scene after the battle of Austerlitz.—"At the moment in which the Russian army was making its retreat, painfully, but in good order, on the ice of the lake, the Emperor Napoleon came riding at full speed toward the artillery. 'You are losing time,' he cried; 'fire upon those masses; they must be engulfed: fire upon the ice!' The order remained unexecuted for ten minutes. In vain several officers and myself were placed on the slope of a hill to produce the effect: their balls and mine rolled upon the ice without breaking it up. Seeing that, I tried a simple method of elevating light howitzers. The almost perpendicular fall of the heavy projectiles produced the desired effect. My method was immediately followed by the adjoining batteries, and in less than no time we buried" some "thousands of Russians and Austrians under the waters of the lake."

In the plenitude of his resources, every obstacle seemed to vanish. "There shall be no Alps," he said; and he built his perfect roads, climbing by graded galleries their steepest precipices, until Italy was as open to Paris as any town in France. He laid his bones to, and wrought for his crown. Having decided what was to be done, he did that with might and main. He put out all his strength. He risked every thing and spared nothing, neither ammunition, nor money, nor troops, nor generals, nor himself.

We like to see every thing do its office after its kind, whether it be a milch-cow or a rattle-snake; and if fighting be the best mode of adjusting national differences, (as large majorities of men seem to agree,) certainly Bonaparte was right in making it thorough. The grand principle of war, he said, was that an army ought always to be ready, by day and by night and at all hours, to make all the resistance it is capable of making. He never economized his ammunition, but, on a hostile position, rained a torrent of iron,—shells, balls, grape-shot,—to annihilate all defence. On any point of resistance he concentrated squadron on squadron in overwhelming numbers until it was swept out of existence. To a regiment of horse-chasseurs at Lobenstein, two days before the battle of Jena, Napoleon said, "My lads, you must not fear death; when soldiers brave death, they drive him into the enemy's ranks." In the fury of assault, he no more spared himself. He went to the edge of his possibility. It is plain that in Italy he did what he could, and all that he could. He came, several times, within an inch of ruin; and his own person was all but lost. He was flung into the marsh at Arcola. The Austrians were between him and his troops, in the *mêlée*, and he was brought off with desperate efforts. At Lonato, and at other places, he was on the point of being taken prisoner. He fought sixty battles. He had never enough. Each victory was a new weapon. "My power would fall, were I not to support it by new achievements. Conquest has made me what I am, and conquest must maintain me." He felt, with every wise man, that as much life is needed for conservation as for creation. We are always in peril, always in a bad plight, just on the edge of destruction and only to be saved by invention and courage.

This vigor was guarded and tempered by the coldest prudence and punctuality. A thunderbolt in the attack, he was found invulnerable in his intrenchments. His very attack was never the inspiration of courage, but the result of calculation. His idea of the best defence consists in being still the attacking party. "My ambition," he says, "was great, but was of a cold nature." In one of his conversations with Las Casas, he remarked, "As to moral courage, I have rarely met with the two-o'clock-in-the-morning kind: I mean unprepared courage; that which is necessary on an unexpected occasion, and which, in spite of the most unforeseen events, leaves full freedom of judgment and decision:" and he did not hesitate to declare that he was himself eminently endowed with this two-o'clock-in-the-morning courage, and that he had met with few persons equal to himself in this respect.

Every thing depended on the nicety of his combinations, and the stars were not more punctual than his arithmetic. His personal attention descended to the smallest particulars. "At Montebello, I ordered Kellermann to attack with eight hundred horse, and with these he separated the six thousand Hungarian grenadiers, before the very eyes of the Austrian cavalry. This cavalry was half a league off and required a quarter of an hour to arrive on the field of action, and I have observed that it is always these quarters of an hour that decide the fate of a battle." "Before he fought a battle, Bonaparte thought little about what he should do in case of success, but a great deal about what he should do in case of a reverse of fortune." The same prudence and good sense mark all his behavior. His instructions to his secretary at the Tuileries are worth remembering. "During the night, enter my chamber as seldom as possible. Do not awake me when you have any good news to communicate; with that there is no hurry. But when you bring bad news, rouse me instantly, for then there is not a moment to be lost." It was a whimsical economy of the same kind which dictated his practice, when general in Italy, in regard to his burdensome correspondence. He directed Bourrienne to leave all letters unopened for three weeks, and then observed with satisfaction how large a part of the correspondence had thus disposed of itself and no longer required an answer. His achievement of business was immense, and enlarges the known powers of man. There have been many working kings, from Ulysses to William of Orange, but none who accomplished a tithe of this man's performance.

To these gifts of nature, Napoleon added the advantage of having been born to a private and humble fortune. In his later days he had the weakness of wishing to add to his crowns and badges the prescription of aristocracy; but he knew his debt to his austere education, and made no secret of his contempt for the born kings, and for "the hereditary asses," as he coarsely styled the Bourbons. He said that "in their exile they had learned nothing, and forgot nothing." Bonaparte had passed through all the degrees of military service, but also was citizen before he was emperor, and so has the key to citizenship. His remarks and estimates discover the information and justness of measurement of the middle class. Those who had to deal with him found that he was not to be imposed upon, but could cipher as well as another man. This appears in all parts of his Memoirs, dictated at St. Helena. When the expenses of the empress, of his household, of his palaces, had accumu-

lated great debts, Napoleon examined the bills of the creditors himself, detected overcharges and errors, and reduced the claims by considerable sums.

His grand weapon, namely the millions whom he
directed, he owed to the representative character which
clothed him. He interests us as he stands for France and
for Europe; and he exists as captain and king only as far as
the Revolution, or the interest of the industrious masses,
found an organ and a leader in him. In the social interests,
he knew the meaning and value of labor, and threw himself naturally on that side. I like an incident mentioned by
one of his biographers at St. Helena. "When walking with
Mrs. Balcombe, some servants, carrying heavy boxes,
passed by on the road, and Mrs. Balcombe desired them,
in rather an angry tone, to keep back. Napoleon interfered, saying 'Respect the burden, Madam.'" In the time
of the empire he directed attention to the improvement
and embellishment of the markets of the capital. "The
market-place," he said, "is the Louvre of the common
people." The principal works that have survived him are
his magnificent roads. He filled the troops with his spirit,
and a sort of freedom and companionship grew up between him and them, which the forms of his court never
permitted between the officers and himself. They performed, under his eye, that which no others could do. The
best document of his relation to his troops is the order of
the day on the morning of the battle of Austerlitz, in
which Napoleon promises the troops that he will keep his
person out of reach of fire. This declaration, which is the
reverse of that ordinarily made by generals and sovereigns
on the eve of a battle, sufficiently explains the devotion of
the army to their leader.

But though there is in particulars this identity between
Napoleon and the mass of the people, his real strength lay
in their conviction that he was their representative in his
genius and aims, not only when he courted, but when he
controlled, and even when he decimated them by his conscriptions. He knew, as well as any Jacobin in France, how

to philosophize on liberty and equality; and when allusion was made to the precious blood of centuries, which was spilled by the killing of the Duc d'Enghien, he suggested, "Neither is my blood ditchwater." The people felt that no longer the throne was occupied and the land sucked of its nourishment, by a small class of legitimates, secluded from all community with the children of the soil, and holding the ideas and superstitions of a long-forgotten state of society. Instead of that vampyre, a man of themselves held, in the Tuileries, knowledge and ideas like their own, opening of course to them and their children all places of power and trust. The day of sleepy, selfish policy, ever narrowing the means and opportunities of young men, was ended, and a day of expansion and demand was come. A market for all the powers and productions of man was opened; brilliant prizes glittered in the eyes of youth and talent. The old, iron-bound, feudal France was changed into a young Ohio or New York; and those who smarted under the immediate rigors of the new monarch, pardoned them as the necessary severities of the military system which had driven out the oppressor. And even when the majority of the people had begun to ask whether they had really gained any thing under the exhausting levies of men and money of the new master, the whole talent of the country, in every rank and kindred, took his part and defended him as its natural patron. In 1814, when advised to rely on the higher classes, Napoleon said to those around him, "Gentlemen, in the situation in which I stand, my only nobility is the rabble of the Faubourgs."

Napoleon met this natural expectation. The necessity of his position required a hospitality to every sort of talent, and its appointment to trusts; and his feeling went along with this policy. Like every superior person, he undoubtedly felt a desire for men and compeers, and a wish to measure his power with other masters, and an impatience of fools and underlings. In Italy, he sought for men and found none. "Good God!" he said, "how rare men are! There are eighteen millions in Italy, and I have with diffi-

culty found two,—Dandolo and Melzi." In later years,
with larger experience, his respect for mankind was not
increased. In a moment of bitterness he said to one of his
oldest friends, "Men deserve the contempt with which
they inspire me. I have only to put some gold-lace on the
coat of my virtuous republicans and they immediately become just what I wish them." This impatience at levity
was, however, an oblique tribute of respect to those able
persons who commanded his regard not only when he
found them friends and coadjutors but also when they resisted his will. He could not confound Fox and Pitt, Car-
not, Lafayette and Bernadotte, with the danglers of his
court; and in spite of the detraction which his systematic
egotism dictated toward the great captains who conquered
with and for him, ample acknowledgments are made by
him to Lannes, Duroc, Kleber, Dessaix, Massena, Murat,
Ney and Augereau. If he felt himself their patron and the
founder of their fortunes, as when he said "I made my
generals out of mud,"—he could not hide his satisfaction
in receiving from them a seconding and support commensurate with the grandeur of his enterprise. In the Russian
campaign he was so much impressed by the courage and
resources of Marshal Ney, that he said, "I have two hundred millions in my coffers, and I would give them all for
Ney." The characters which he has drawn of several of his
marshals are discriminating, and though they did not content the insatiable vanity of French officers, are no doubt
substantially just. And in fact every species of merit was
sought and advanced under his government. "I know," he
said, "the depth and draught of water of every one of my
generals." Natural power was sure to be well received at
his court. Seventeen men in his time were raised from
common soldiers to the rank of king, marshal, duke, or
general; and the crosses of his Legion of Honor were given
to personal valor, and not to family connexion. "When
soldiers have been baptized in the fire of a battlefield, they
have all one rank in my eyes."

When a natural king becomes a titular king, every body

is pleased and satisfied. The Revolution entitled the strong populace of the Faubourg St. Antoine, and every horse-boy and powder-monkey in the army, to look on Napoleon as flesh of his flesh and the creature of *his* party: but there is something in the success of grand talent which enlists an universal sympathy. For in the prevalence of sense and spirit over stupidity and malversation, all reasonable men have an interest; and as intellectual beings we feel the air purified by the electric shock, when material force is overthrown by intellectual energies. As soon as we are removed out of the reach of local and accidental partialities, Man feels that Napoleon fights for him; these are honest victories; this strong steam-engine does our work. Whatever appeals to the imagination, by transcending the ordinary limits of human ability, wonderfully encourages and liberates us. This capacious head, revolving and disposing sovereignly trains of affairs, and animating such multitudes of agents; this eye, which looked through Europe; this prompt invention; this inexhaustible resource:—what events! what romantic pictures! what strange situations!—when spying the Alps, by a sunset in the Sicilian sea; drawing up his army for battle in sight of the Pyramids, and saying to his troops, "From the tops of those pyramids, forty centuries look down on you;" fording the Red Sea; wading in the gulf of the Isthmus of Suez. On the shore of Ptolemais, gigantic projects agitated him. "Had Acre fallen, I should have changed the face of the world." His army, on the night of the battle of Austerlitz, which was the anniversary of his inauguration as Emperor, presented him with a bouquet of forty standards taken in the fight. Perhaps it is a little puerile, the pleasure he took in making these contrasts glaring; as when he pleased himself with making kings wait in his antechambers, at Tilsit, at Paris and at Erfurt.

We can not, in the universal imbecility, indecision and indolence of men, sufficiently congratulate ourselves on this strong and ready actor, who took occasion by the beard, and showed us how much may be accomplished by the mere force of such virtues as all men possess in less degrees; namely, by punctuality, by personal attention, by courage and thoroughness. "The Austrians," he said, "do not know the value of time." I should cite him, in his earlier years, as a model of prudence. His power does not consist in any wild or extravagant force; in any enthusiasm like Mahomet's, or singular power of persuasion; but in the exercise of common-sense on each emergency, instead of abiding by rules and customs. The lesson he teaches is that which vigor always teaches;—that there is always room for it. To what heaps of cowardly doubts is not that man's life an answer. When he appeared it was the belief of all military men that there could be nothing new in war; as it is the belief of men to-day that nothing new can be undertaken in politics, or in church, or in letters, or in trade, or in farming, or in our social manners and customs; and as it is at all times the belief of society that the world is used up. But Bonaparte knew better than society; and moreover knew that he knew better. I think all men know better than they do; know that the institutions we so volubly commend are go-carts and baubles; but they dare not trust their presentiments. Bonaparte relied on his own sense, and did not care a bean for other people's. The world treated his novelties just as it treats everybody's novelties,—made infinite objection, mustered all the impediments; but he snapped his finger at their objections. "What creates great difficulty," he remarks, "in the profession of the land-commander, is the necessity of feeding so many men and animals. If he allows himself to be guided by the commissaries he will never stir, and all his expeditions will fail." An example of his common-sense is what he says of the passage of the Alps in winter, which all writers, one repeating after the other, had described as impracticable. "The winter," says Napoleon, "is not the most unfavorable season for the passage of lofty mountains. The snow is then firm, the weather settled, and there is nothing to fear from avalanches, the real and only danger to be apprehended in the Alps. On these high mountains there are often very fine days in December, of a dry cold, with extreme calmness in the air." Read his account, too, of the way in which battles are gained. "In all battles a moment occurs when the bravest troops, after having made the greatest efforts, feel inclined to run. That terror proceeds from a want of confidence in their own courage, and it only requires a slight opportunity, a pretence, to restore confidence to them. The art is, to give rise to the opportunity and to invent the pretence. At Arcola I won the battle with twenty-five horsemen. I seized that moment of lassitude, gave every man a trumpet, and gained the day with this handful. You see that two armies are two bodies which meet and endeavor to frighten each other; a moment of panic occurs, and that moment must be turned to advantage. When a man has been present in many actions, he distinguishes that moment without difficulty: it is as easy as casting up an addition."

This deputy of the nineteenth century added to his gifts a capacity for speculation on general topics. He delighted in running through the range of practical, of literary and of abstract questions. His opinion is always original and to the purpose. On the voyage to Egypt he liked, after dinner, to fix on three or four persons to support a proposition, and as many to oppose it. He gave a subject, and the discussions turned on questions of religion, the different kinds of government, and the art of war. One day he asked whether the planets were inhabited? On another, what was the age of the world? Then he proposed to consider the probability of the destruction of the globe, either by water or by fire: at another time, the truth or fallacy of presentiments, and the interpretation of dreams. He was very fond of talking of religion. In 1806 he conversed with Fournier, bishop of Montpellier, on matters of theology. There were two points on which they could not agree, viz. that of hell, and that of salvation out of the pale of the church. The Emperor told Josephine that he disputed like a devil on these two points, on which the bishop was inexorable. To the philosophers he readily yielded all that was proved against religion as the work of men and time, but he would not hear of materialism. One fine night, on deck, amid a clatter of materialism, Bonaparte pointed to the stars, and said, "You may talk as long as you please, gentlemen, but who made all that?" He delighted in the conversation of men of science, particularly of Monge and Berthollet; but the men of letters he slighted; they were "manufacturers of phrases." Of medicine too he was fond of talking, and with those of its practitioners whom he most esteemed,—with Corvisart at Paris, and with Antonomarchi at St. Helena. "Believe me," he said to the last, "we had better leave off all these remedies: life is a fortress which neither you nor I know any thing about. Why throw obstacles in the way of its defence? Its own means are superior to all the apparatus of your laboratories. Corvisart candidly agreed with me that all your filthy mixtures are good for nothing. Medicine is a collection of uncertain prescriptions, the results of which, taken collectively, are more fatal than useful to mankind. Water, air and cleanliness are the chief articles in my pharmacopœia."

His memoirs, dictated to Count Montholon and General Gourgaud at St. Helena, have great value, after all the deduction that it seems is to be made from them on account of his known disingenuousness. He has the good-nature of strength and conscious superiority. I admire his simple, clear narrative of his battles;—good as Cæsar's; his good-natured and sufficiently respectful account of Marshal Wurmser and his other antagonists; and his own equality as a writer to his varying subject. The most agreeable portion is the Campaign in Egypt.

He had hours of thought and wisdom. In intervals of leisure, either in the camp or the palace, Napoleon appears as a man of genius directing on abstract questions the native appetite for truth and the impatience of words he was wont to show in war. He could enjoy every play of invention, a romance, a *bon mot*, as well as a strategem in a campaign. He delighted to fascinate Josephine and her ladies, in a dim-lighted apartment, by the terrors of a fiction to which his voice and dramatic power lent every addition.

I call Napoleon the agent or attorney of the middle class of modern society; of the throng who fill the markets, shops, counting-houses, manufactories, ships, of the modern world, aiming to be rich. He was the agitator, the destroyer of prescription, the internal improver, the liberal, the radical, the inventor of means, the opener of doors and markets, the subverter of monopoly and abuse. Of course the rich and aristocratic did not like him. England, the centre of capital, and Rome and Austria, centres of tradition and genealogy, opposed him. The consternation of the dull and conservative classes, the terror of the foolish old men and old women of the Roman conclave, who in their despair took hold of any thing, and would cling to red-hot iron,—the vain attempts of statists to amuse and deceive him, of the emperor of Austria to bribe him; and the instinct of the young, ardent and active men every where, which pointed him out as the giant of the middle class, make his history bright and commanding. He had the virtues of the masses of his constituents: he had also their vices. I am sorry that the brilliant picture has its reverse. But that is the fatal quality which we discover in our pursuit of wealth, that it is treacherous, and is bought by the breaking or weakening of the sentiments; and it is inevitable that we should find the same fact in the history of this champion, who proposed to himself simply a brilliant career, without any stipulation or scruple concerning the means.

Bonaparte was singularly destitute of generous sentiments. The highest-placed individual in the most cultivated age and population of the world,—he has not the merit of common truth and honesty. He is unjust to his generals; egotistic and monopolizing; meanly stealing the credit of their great actions from Kellermann, from Bernadotte; intriguing to involve his faithful Junot in hopeless bankruptcy, in order to drive him to a distance from Paris, because the familiarity of his manners offends the new pride of his throne. He is a boundless liar. The official paper, his "Moniteur," and all his bulletins, are proverbs for saying what he wished to be believed; and worse,—he sat, in his premature old age, in his lonely island, coldly falsifying facts and dates and characters, and giving to history a theatrical *éclat*. Like all Frenchmen he has a passion for stage effect. Every action that breathes of generosity is poisoned by this calculation. His star, his love of glory, his doctrine of the immortality of the soul, are all French. "I must dazzle and astonish. If I were to give the liberty of the press, my power could not last three days." To make a great noise is his favorite design. "A great reputation is a great noise: the more there is made, the farther off it is heard. Laws, institutions, monuments, nations, all fall; but the noise continues, and resounds in after ages." His doctrine of immortality is simply fame. His theory of influence is not flattering. "There are two levers for moving men,—interest and fear. Love is a silly infatuation, depend upon it. Friendship is but a name. I love nobody. I do not even love my brothers: perhaps Joseph a little, from habit, and because he is my elder; and Duroc, I love him too; but why?—because his character pleases me: he is stern and resolute, and I believe the fellow never shed a tear. For my part I know very well that I have no true friends. As long as I continue to be what I am, I may have as many pretended friends as I please. Leave sensibility to women; but men should be firm in heart and purpose, or they should have nothing to do with war and government." He was thoroughly unscrupulous. He would steal, slander, assassinate, drown and poison, as his interest dictated. He had no generosity, but mere vulgar hatred; he was intensely selfish; he was perfidious; he cheated at cards; he was a prodigious gossip, and opened letters, and delighted in his infamous police, and rubbed his hands with joy when he had intercepted some morsel of intelligence concerning the men and women about him, boasting that "he knew every thing;" and interfered with the cutting the dresses of the women; and listened after the hurrahs and the compliments of the street, incognito. His manners were coarse. He treated women with low familiarity. He had the habit of pulling their ears and pinching their cheeks when he was in good humor, and of pulling the ears and whiskers of men, and of striking and horseplay with them, to his last days. It does not appear that he listened at key-holes, or at least that he was caught at it. In short, when you have penetrated through all the circles of power and splendor, you were not dealing with a gentleman, at last; but with an impostor and a rogue; and he fully deserves the epithet of *Jupiter Scapin*, or a sort of Scamp Jupiter.

In describing the two parties into which modern society divides itself,—the democrat and the conservative,—I said, Bonaparte represents the democrat, or the party of men of business, against the stationary or conservative party. I omitted then to say, what is material to the statement, namely that these two parties differ only as young and old. The democrat is a young conservative; the conservative is an old democrat. The aristocrat is the democrat ripe and gone to seed;—because both parties stand on the one ground of the supreme value of property, which one endeavors to get, and the other to keep. Bonaparte may be said to represent the whole history of this party, its youth and its age; yes, and with poetic justice its fate, in his own. The counter-revolution, the counter-party, still waits for its organ and representative, in a lover and a man of truly public and universal aims.

Here was an experiment, under the most favorable conditions, of the powers of intellect without conscience. Never was such a leader so endowed and so weaponed; never leader found such aids and followers. And what was the result of this vast talent and power, of these immense armies, burned cities, squandered treasures, immolated millions of men, of this demoralized Europe? It came to no result. All passed away like the smoke of his artillery, and left no trace. He left France smaller, poorer, feebler, than he found it; and the whole contest for freedom was to be begun again. The attempt was in principle suicidal. France served him with life and limb and estate, as long as it could identify its interest with him; but when men saw that after victory was another war; after the destruction of armies, new conscriptions; and they who had toiled so desperately were never nearer to the reward,—they could not spend what they had earned, nor repose on their down-beds, nor strut in their châteaux,—they deserted him. Men found that his absorbing egotism was deadly to all other men. It resembled the torpedo, which inflicts a succession of shocks on any one who takes hold of it, producing spasms which contract the muscles of the hand, so that the man can not open his fingers; and the animal inflicts new and more violent shocks, until he paralyzes and kills his victim. So this exorbitant egotist narrowed, impoverished and absorbed the power and existence of those who served him; and the universal cry of France and of Europe in 1814 was, "Enough of him;" *"Assez de Bonaparte."*

It was not Bonaparte's fault. He did all that in him lay to live and thrive without moral principle. It was the nature of things, the eternal law of man and of the world which baulked and ruined him; and the result, in a million experiments, will be the same. Every experiment, by multitudes or by individuals, that has a sensual and selfish aim, will fail. The pacific Fourier will be as inefficient as the pernicious Napoleon. As long as our civilization is essentially one of property, of fences, of exclusiveness, it will be mocked by delusions. Our riches will leave us sick; there will be bitterness in our laughter, and our wine will burn our mouth. Only that good profits which we can taste with all doors open, and which serves all men.

FATE

Delicate omens traced in air,
To the lone bard true witness bare;
Birds with auguries on their wings
Chanted undeceiving things,
Him to beckon, him to warn;
Well might then the poet scorn
To learn of scribe or courier
Hints writ in vaster character;
And on his mind, at dawn of day,
Soft shadows of the evening lay.
For the prevision is allied
Unto the thing so signified;
Or say, the foresight that awaits
Is the same Genius that creates.

It chanced during one winter a few years ago, that our cities were bent on discussing the theory of the Age. By an odd coincidence, four or five noted men were each reading a discourse to the citizens of Boston or New York, on the Spirit of the Times. It so happened that the subject had the same prominence in some remarkable pamphlets and journals issued in London in the same season. To me, however, the question of the times resolved itself into a practical question of the conduct of life. How shall I live? We are incompetent to solve the times. Our geometry cannot span the huge orbits of the prevailing ideas, behold their return and reconcile their opposition. We can only obey our own polarity. 'T is fine for us to speculate and elect our course, if we must accept an irresistible dictation.

In our first steps to gain our wishes we come upon immovable limitations. We are fired with the hope to reform men. After many experiments we find that we must begin earlier,—at school. But the boys and girls are not docile; we can make nothing of them. We decide that they are not of good stock. We must begin our reform earlier still,—at generation: that is to say, there is Fate, or laws of the world.

But if there be irresistible dictation, this dictation understands itself. If we must accept Fate, we are not less compelled to affirm liberty, the significance of the individual, the grandeur of duty, the power of character. This is true, and that other is true. But our geometry cannot span these extreme points and reconcile them. What to do? By obeying each thought frankly, by harping, or, if you will, pounding on each string, we learn at last its power. By the same obedience to other thoughts we learn theirs, and then comes some reasonable hope of harmonizing them. We are sure that, though we know not how, necessity does comport with liberty, the individual with the world, my popularity with the spirit of the times. The riddle of the age has for each a private solution. If one would study his own time, it must be by this method of taking up in turn each of the leading topics which belong to our scheme of human life, and by firmly stating all that is agreeable to experience on one, and doing the same justice to the opposing facts in the others, the true limitations will appear. Any excess of emphasis on one part would be corrected, and a just balance would be made.

But let us honestly state the facts. Our America has a bad name for superficialness. Great men, great nations, have not been boasters and buffoons, but perceivers of the terror of life, and have manned themselves to face it. The Spartan, embodying his religion in his country, dies before its majesty without a question. The Turk, who believes his doom is written on the iron leaf in the moment when he entered the world, rushes on the enemy's sabre with undivided will. The Turk, the Arab, the Persian, accepts the foreordained fate:—

> "On two days, it steads not to run from thy grave,
>   The appointed, and the unappointed day;
> On the first, neither balm nor physician can save,
>   Nor thee, on the second, the Universe slay."

The Hindoo under the wheel is as firm. Our Calvinists in the last generation had something of the same dignity. They felt that the weight of the Universe held them down to their place. What could *they* do? Wise men feel that there is something which cannot be talked or voted away,—a strap or belt which girds the world:—

> "The Destinee, ministre general,
>   That executeth in the world over al,
>   The purveiance that God hath seen beforne,
>   So strong it is, that though the world had sworne
>   The contrary of a thing by yea or nay,
>   Yet sometime it shall fallen on a day
>   That falleth not oft in a thousand yeer;
>   For certainly, our appetités here,
>   Be it of warre, or pees, or hate, or love,
>   All this is ruled by the sight above."
>   CHAUCER: *The Knighte's Tale.*

The Greek Tragedy expressed the same sense. "Whatever is fated that will take place. The great immense mind of Jove is not to be transgressed."

Savages cling to a local god of one tribe or town. The broad ethics of Jesus were quickly narrowed to village theologies, which preach an election or favoritism. And now and then an amiable parson, like Jung Stilling or Robert Huntington, believes in a pistareen-Providence, which, whenever the good man wants a dinner, makes that somebody shall knock at his door and leave a half-dollar.

But Nature is no sentimentalist,—does not cosset or pamper us. We must see that the world is rough and surly, and will not mind drowning a man or a woman, but swallows your ship like a grain of dust. The cold, inconsiderate of persons, tingles your blood, benumbs your feet, freezes a man like an apple. The diseases, the elements, fortune, gravity, lightning, respect no persons. The way of Providence is a little rude. The habit of snake and spider, the snap of the tiger and other leapers and bloody jumpers, the crackle of the bones of his prey in the coil of the anaconda,—these are in the system, and our habits are like theirs. You have just dined, and however scrupulously the slaughter-house is concealed in the graceful distance of miles, there is complicity, expensive races,—race living at the expense of race. The planet is liable to shocks from comets, perturbations from planets, rendings from earthquake and volcano, alterations of climate, precessions of equinoxes. Rivers dry up by opening of the forest. The sea changes its bed. Towns and counties fall into it. At Lisbon an earthquake killed men like flies. At Naples three years ago ten thousand persons were crushed in a few minutes. The scurvy at sea, the sword of the climate in the west of Africa, at Cayenne, at Panama, at New Orleans, cut off men like a massacre. Our western prairie shakes with fever and ague. The cholera, the small-pox, have proved as mortal to some tribes as a frost to the crickets, which, having filled the summer with noise, are silenced by a fall of the temperature of one night. Without uncovering what does not concern us, or counting how many species of parasites hang on a bombyx, or groping after intestinal parasites or infusory biters, or the obscurities of alternate generation,—the forms of the shark, the *labrus*, the jaw of the sea-wolf paved with crushing teeth, the weapons of the grampus, and other warriors hidden in the sea, are hints of ferocity in the interiors of nature. Let us not deny it up and down. Providence has a wild, rough, incalculable road to its end, and it is of no use to try to whitewash its huge, mixed instrumentalities, or to dress up that terrific benefactor in a clean shirt and white neckcloth of a student in divinity.

Will you say, the disasters which threaten mankind are exceptional, and one need not lay his account for cataclysms every day? Aye, but what happens once may happen again, and so long as these strokes are not to be parried by us they must be feared.

But these shocks and ruins are less destructive to us than the stealthy power of other laws which act on us daily. An expense of ends to means is fate;—organization tyrannizing over character. The menagerie, or forms and powers of the spine, is a book of fate; the bill of the bird, the skull of the snake, determines tyrannically its limits. So is the scale of races, of temperaments; so is sex; so is climate; so is the reaction of talents imprisoning the vital power in certain directions. Every spirit makes its house; but afterwards the house confines the spirit.

The gross lines are legible to the dull; the cabman is phrenologist so far, he looks in your face to see if his shilling is sure. A dome of brow denotes one thing, a pot-belly another; a squint, a pug-nose, mats of hair, the pigment of the epidermis, betray character. People seem sheathed in their tough organization. Ask Spurzheim, ask the doctors, ask Quetelet if temperaments decide nothing?—or if there be anything they do not decide? Read the description in medical books of the four temperaments and you will think you are reading your own thoughts which you had not yet told. Find the part which black eyes and which blue eyes play severally in the company. How shall a man escape from his ancestors, or draw off from his veins the black drop which he drew from his father's or his mother's life? It often appears in a family as if all the qualities of the progenitors were potted in several jars,—some ruling quality in each son or daughter of the house; and sometimes the unmixed temperament, the rank unmitigated elixir, the family vice is drawn off in a separate individual and the others are proportionally relieved. We sometimes see a change of expression in our companion and say his father or his mother comes to the windows of his eyes, and sometimes a remote relative. In different hours a man represents each of several of his ancestors, as if there were seven or eight of us rolled up in each man's skin,—seven or eight ancestors at least; and they constitute the variety of notes for that new piece of music which his life is. At the corner of the street you read the possibility of each passenger in the facial angle, in the complexion, in the depth of his eye. His parentage determines it. Men are what their mothers made them. You may as well ask a loom which weaves huckabuck why it does not make cashmere, as expect poetry from this engineer, or a chemical discovery from that jobber. Ask the digger in the ditch to explain Newton's laws; the fine organs of his brain have been pinched by overwork and squalid poverty from father to son for a hundred years. When each comes forth from his mother's womb, the gate of gifts closes behind him. Let him value his hands and feet, he has but one pair. So he has but one future, and that is already predetermined in his lobes and described in that little fatty face, pig-eye, and squat form. All the privilege and all the legislation of the world cannot meddle or help to make a poet or a prince of him.

Jesus said, "When he looketh on her, he hath committed adultery." But he is an adulterer before he has yet looked on the woman, by the superfluity of animal and the defect of thought in his constitution. Who meets him, or who meets her, in the street, sees that they are ripe to be each other's victim.

In certain men digestion and sex absorb the vital force, and the stronger these are, the individual is so much weaker. The more of these drones perish, the better for the hive. If, later, they give birth to some superior individual, with force enough to add to this animal a new aim and a complete apparatus to work it out, all the ancestors are gladly forgotten. Most men and most women are merely one couple more. Now and then one has a new cell or camarilla opened in his brain,—an architectural, a musical, or a philological knack; some stray taste or talent for flowers, or chemistry, or pigments, or story-telling; a good hand for drawing, a good foot for dancing, an athletic frame for wide journeying, etc.—which skill nowise alters rank in the scale of nature, but serves to pass the time; the life of sensation going on as before. At last these hints and tendencies are fixed in one or in a succession. Each absorbs so much food and force as to become itself a new centre. The new talent draws off so rapidly the vital force that not enough remains for the animal functions, hardly enough for health; so that in the second generation, if the like genius appear, the health is visibly deteriorated and the generative force impaired.

People are born with the moral or with the material bias;—uterine brothers with this diverging destination; and I suppose, with high magnifiers, Mr. Frauenhofer or Dr. Carpenter might come to distinguish in the embryo, at the fourth day,—this is a Whig, and that a Free-soiler.

It was a poetic attempt to lift this mountain of Fate, to reconcile this despotism of race with liberty, which led the Hindoos to say, "Fate is nothing but the deeds committed in a prior state of existence." I find the coincidence of the extremes of Eastern and Western speculation in the daring statement of Schelling, "There is in every man a certain feeling that he has been what he is from all eternity, and by no means became such in time." To say it less sublimely,—in the history of the individual is always an account of his condition, and he knows himself to be a party to his present estate.

A good deal of our politics is physiological. Now and then a man of wealth in the heyday of youth adopts the tenet of broadest freedom. In England there is always some man of wealth and large connection, planting himself, during all his years of health, on the side of progress, who, as soon as he begins to die, checks his forward play, calls in his troops and becomes conservative. All conservatives are such from personal defects. They have been effeminated by position or nature, born halt and blind, through luxury of their parents, and can only, like invalids, act on the defensive. But strong natures, backwoodsmen, New Hampshire giants, Napoleons, Burkes, Broughams, Websters, Kossuths, are inevitable patriots, until their life ebbs and their defects and gout, palsy and money, warp them.

The strongest idea incarnates itself in majorities and nations, in the healthiest and strongest. Probably the election goes by avoirdupois weight, and if you could weigh bodily the tonnage of any hundred of the Whig and the Democratic party in a town on the Dearborn balance, as they passed the hay-scales, you could predict with certainty which party would carry it. On the whole it would be rather the speediest way of deciding the vote, to put the selectmen or the mayor and aldermen at the hay-scales.

In science we have to consider two things: power and circumstance. All we know of the egg, from each successive discovery, is, *another vesicle;* and if, after five hundred years you get a better observer or a better glass, he finds, within the last observed, another. In vegetable and animal tissue it is just alike, and all that the primary power or spasm operates is still vesicles, vesicles. Yes,—but the tyrannical Circumstance! A vesicle in new circumstances, a vesicle lodged in darkness, Oken thought, became animal; in light, a plant. Lodged in the parent animal, it suffers changes which end in unsheathing miraculous capability in the unaltered vesicle, and it unlocks itself to fish, bird, or quadruped, head and foot, eye and claw. The Circumstance is Nature. Nature is what you may do. There is much you may not. We have two things,—the circumstance, and the life. Once we thought positive power was all. Now we learn that negative power, or circumstance, is half. Nature is the tyrannous circumstance, the thick skull, the sheathed snake, the ponderous, rock-like jaw; necessitated activity; violent direction; the conditions of a tool, like the locomotive, strong enough on its track, but which can do nothing but mischief off of it; or skates, which are wings on the ice but fetters on the ground.

The book of Nature is the book of Fate. She turns the gigantic pages,—leaf after leaf,—never re-turning one. One leaf she lays down, a floor of granite; then a thousand ages, and a bed of slate; a thousand ages, and a measure of coal; a thousand ages, and a layer of marl and mud: vegetable forms appear; her first misshapen animals, zoöphyte, trilobium, fish; then, saurians,—rude forms, in which she has only blocked her future statue, concealing under these unwieldy monsters the fine type of her coming king. The face of the planet cools and dries, the races meliorate, and man is born. But when a race has lived its term, it comes no more again.

The population of the world is a conditional population; not the best, but the best that could live now; and the scale of tribes, and the steadiness with which victory adheres to one tribe and defeat to another, is as uniform as the superposition of strata. We know in history what weight belongs to race. We see the English, French, and Germans planting themselves on every shore and market of America and Australia, and monopolizing the commerce of these countries. We like the nervous and victorious habit of our own branch of the family. We follow the step of the Jew, of the Indian, of the Negro. We see how much will has been expended to extinguish the Jew, in vain. Look at the unpalatable conclusions of Knox, in his Fragment of Races;—a rash and unsatisfactory writer, but charged with pungent and unforgetable truths. "Nature respects race, and not hybrids." "Every race has its own *habitat.*" "Detach a colony from the race, and it deteriorates to the crab." See the shades of the picture. The German and Irish millions, like the Negro, have a great deal of guano in their destiny. They are ferried over the Atlantic and carted over America, to ditch and to drudge, to make corn cheap and then to lie down prematurely to make a spot of green grass on the prairie.

One more fagot of these adamantine bandages is the

new science of Statistics. It is a rule that the most casual
and extraordinary events, if the basis of population is
broad enough, become matter of fixed calculation. It
would not be safe to say when a captain like Bonaparte, a
singer like Jenny Lind, or a navigator like Bowditch would
be born in Boston; but, on a population of twenty or two
hundred millions, something like accuracy may be had.

'T is frivolous to fix pedantically the date of particular
inventions. They have all been invented over and over
fifty times. Man is the arch machine of which all these
shifts drawn from himself are toy models. He helps himself on each emergency by copying or duplicating his own
structure, just so far as the need is. 'T is hard to find the
right Homer, Zoroaster, or Menu; harder still to find the
Tubal Cain, or Vulcan, or Cadmus, or Copernicus, or
Fust, or Fulton; the indisputable inventor. There are
scores and centuries of them. "The air is full of men."
This kind of talent so abounds, this constructive tool-
making efficiency, as if it adhered to the chemic atoms; as
if the air he breathes were made of Vaucansons, Franklins,
and Watts.

Doubtless in every million there will be an astronomer,
a mathematician, a comic poet, a mystic. No one can read
the history of astronomy without perceiving that Copernicus, Newton, Laplace, are not new men, or a new kind
of men, but that Thales, Anaximenes, Hipparchus, Empedocles, Aristarchus, Pythagoras, Œnipodes, had an-
ticipated them; each had the same tense geometrical brain,
apt for the same vigorous computation and logic; a mind
parallel to the movement of the world. The Roman mile
probably rested on a measure of a degree of the meridian.
Mahometan and Chinese know what we know of leap-
year, of the Gregorian calendar, and of the precession of
the equinoxes. As in every barrel of cowries brought to
New Bedford there shall be one *orangia*, so there will, in a
dozen millions of Malays and Mahometans, be one or two
astronomical skulls. In a large city, the most casual things,
and things whose beauty lies in their casualty, are pro-

duced as punctually and to order as the baker's muffin for breakfast. Punch makes exactly one capital joke a week; and the journals contrive to furnish one good piece of news every day.

And not less work the laws of repression, the penalties of violated functions. Famine, typhus, frost, war, suicide and effete races must be reckoned calculable parts of the system of the world.

These are pebbles from the mountain, hints of the terms by which our life is walled up, and which show a kind of mechanical exactness, as of a loom or mill in what we call casual or fortuitous events.

The force with which we resist these torrents of tendency looks so ridiculously inadequate that it amounts to little more than a criticism or protest made by a minority of one, under compulsion of millions. I seemed in the height of a tempest to see men overboard struggling in the waves, and driven about here and there. They glanced intelligently at each other, but 't was little they could do for one another; 't was much if each could keep afloat alone. Well, they had a right to their eye-beams, and all the rest was Fate.

We cannot trifle with this reality, this cropping-out in our planted gardens of the core of the world. No picture of life can have any veracity that does not admit the odious facts. A man's power is hooped in by a necessity which, by many experiments, he touches on every side until he learns its arc.

The element running through entire nature, which we popularly call Fate, is known to us as limitation. Whatever limits us we call Fate. If we are brute and barbarous, the fate takes a brute and dreadful shape. As we refine, our checks become finer. If we rise to spiritual culture, the antagonism takes a spiritual form. In the Hindoo fables, Vishnu follows Maya through all her ascending changes, from insect and crawfish up to elephant; whatever form she took, he took the male form of that kind, until she became at last woman and goddess, and he a man and a god. The limitations refine as the soul purifies, but the ring of necessity is always perched at the top.

When the gods in the Norse heaven were unable to bind the Fenris Wolf with steel or with weight of mountains,—the one he snapped and the other he spurned with his heel,—they put round his foot a limp band softer than silk or cobweb, and this held him; the more he spurned it the stiffer it drew. So soft and so stanch is the ring of Fate. Neither brandy, nor nectar, nor sulphuric ether, nor hell-fire, nor ichor, nor poetry, nor genius, can get rid of this limp band. For if we give it the high sense in which the poets use it, even thought itself is not above Fate; that too must act according to eternal laws, and all that is wilful and fantastic in it is in opposition to its fundamental essence.

And last of all, high over thought, in the world of morals, Fate appears as vindicator, levelling the high, lifting the low, requiring justice in man, and always striking soon or late when justice is not done. What is useful will last, what is hurtful will sink. "The doer must suffer," said the Greeks; "you would soothe a Deity not to be soothed." "God himself cannot procure good for the wicked," said the Welsh triad. "God may consent, but only for a time," said the bard of Spain. The limitation is impassable by any insight of man. In its last and loftiest ascensions, insight itself and the freedom of the will is one of its obedient members. But we must not run into generalizations too large, but show the natural bounds or essential distinctions, and seek to do justice to the other elements as well.

Thus we trace Fate in matter, mind, and morals; in race, in retardations of strata, and in thought and character as well. It is everywhere bound or limitation. But Fate has its lord; limitation its limits,—is different seen from above and from below, from within and from without. For though Fate is immense, so is Power, which is the other fact in the dual world, immense. If Fate follows and limits Power, Power attends and antagonizes Fate. We must respect Fate as natural history, but there is more than natural history. For who and what is this criticism that pries into the matter? Man is not order of nature, sack and sack, belly and members, link in a chain, nor any ignominious baggage; but a stupendous antagonism, a dragging together of the poles of the Universe. He betrays his relation to what is below him,—thick-skulled, small-brained, fishy, quadrumanous, quadruped ill-disguised, hardly escaped into biped,—and has paid for the new powers by loss of some of the old ones. But the lightning which explodes and fashions planets, maker of planets and suns, is in him. On one side elemental order, sandstone and granite, rock-ledges, peat-bog, forest, sea and shore; and on the other part thought, the spirit which composes and decomposes nature,—here they are, side by side, god and devil, mind and matter, king and conspirator, belt and spasm, riding peacefully together in the eye and brain of every man.

Nor can he blink the freewill. To hazard the contradiction,—freedom is necessary. If you please to plant yourself on the side of Fate, and say, Fate is all; then we say, a part of Fate is the freedom of man. Forever wells up the impulse of choosing and acting in the soul. Intellect annuls Fate. So far as a man thinks, he is free. And though nothing is more disgusting than the crowing about liberty by slaves, as most men are, and the flippant mistaking for freedom of some paper preamble like a Declaration of Independence or the statute right to vote, by those who have never dared to think or to act,—yet it is wholesome to man to look not at Fate, but the other way: the practical view is the other. His sound relation to these facts is to use and command, not to cringe to them. "Look not on Nature, for her name is fatal," said the oracle. The too much contemplation of these limits induces meanness. They who talk much of destiny, their birth-star, etc., are in a lower dangerous plane, and invite the evils they fear.

I cited the instinctive and heroic races as proud believers in Destiny. They conspire with it; a loving resignation is with the event. But the dogma makes a different impression when it is held by the weak and lazy. 'T is weak and vicious people who cast the blame on Fate. The right use of Fate is to bring up our conduct to the loftiness of nature. Rude and invincible except by themselves are the elements. So let man be. Let him empty his breast of his windy conceits, and show his lordship by manners and deeds on the scale of nature. Let him hold his purpose as with the tug of gravitation. No power, no persuasion, no bribe shall make him give up this point. A man ought to compare advantageously with a river, an oak, or a mountain. He shall have not less the flow, the expansion, and the resistance of these.

'T is the best use of Fate to teach a fatal courage. Go face the fire at sea, or the cholera in your friend's house, or the burglar in your own, or what danger lies in the way of duty,—knowing you are guarded by the cherubim of Destiny. If you believe in Fate to your harm, believe it at least for your good.

For if Fate is so prevailing, man also is part of it, and can confront fate with fate. If the Universe have these savage accidents, our atoms are as savage in resistance. We should be crushed by the atmosphere, but for the reaction of the air within the body. A tube made of a film of glass can resist the shock of the ocean if filled with the same water. If there be omnipotence in the stroke, there is omnipotence of recoil.

1. But Fate against Fate is only parrying and defence: there are also the noble creative forces. The revelation of Thought takes man out of servitude into freedom. We rightly say of ourselves, we were born and afterward we were born again, and many times. We have successive experiences so important that the new forgets the old, and hence the mythology of the seven or the nine heavens. The day of days, the great day of the feast of life, is that in which the inward eye opens to the Unity in things, to the

omnipresence of law:—sees that what is must be and
ought to be, or is the best. This beatitude dips from on
high down on us and we see. It is not in us so much as we
are in it. If the air come to our lungs, we breathe and live;
if not, we die. If the light come to our eyes, we see; else
not. And if truth come to our mind we suddenly expand
to its dimensions, as if we grew to worlds. We are as law-
givers; we speak for Nature; we prophesy and divine.

This insight throws us on the party and interest of the
Universe, against all and sundry; against ourselves as
much as others. A man speaking from insight affirms of
himself what is true of the mind: seeing its immortality, he
says, I am immortal; seeing its invincibility, he says, I am
strong. It is not in us, but we are in it. It is of the maker,
not of what is made. All things are touched and changed
by it. This uses and is not used. It distances those who
share it from those who share it not. Those who share it
not are flocks and herds. It dates from itself; not from former men or better men, gospel, or constitution, or college,
or custom. Where it shines, Nature is no longer intrusive,
but all things make a musical or pictorial impression. The
world of men show like a comedy without laughter: popu-
lations, interests, government, history; 't is all toy figures
in a toy house. It does not overvalue particular truths. We
hear eagerly every thought and word quoted from an intellectual man. But in his presence our own mind is roused
to activity, and we forget very fast what he says, much
more interested in the new play of our own thought than
in any thought of his. 'T is the majesty into which we
have suddenly mounted, the impersonality, the scorn of
egotisms, the sphere of laws, that engage us. Once we
were stepping a little this way and a little that way; now
we are as men in a balloon, and do not think so much of
the point we have left, or the point we would make, as of
the liberty and glory of the way.

Just as much intellect as you add, so much organic
power. He who sees through the design, presides over it,
and must will that which must be. We sit and rule, and,

though we sleep, our dream will come to pass. Our thought, though it were only an hour old, affirms an oldest necessity, not to be separated from thought, and not to be separated from will. They must always have coexisted. It apprises us of its sovereignty and godhead, which refuse to be severed from it. It is not mine or thine, but the will of all mind. It is poured into the souls of all men, as the soul itself which constitutes them men. I know not whether there be, as is alleged, in the upper region of our atmosphere, a permanent westerly current which carries with it all atoms which rise to that height, but I see that when souls reach a certain clearness of perception they accept a knowledge and motive above selfishness. A breath of will blows eternally through the universe of souls in the direction of the Right and Necessary. It is the air which all intellects inhale and exhale, and it is the wind which blows the worlds into order and orbit.

Thought dissolves the material universe by carrying the mind up into a sphere where all is plastic. Of two men, each obeying his own thought, he whose thought is deepest will be the strongest character. Always one man more than another represents the will of Divine Providence to the period.

2. If thought makes free, so does the moral sentiment. The mixtures of spiritual chemistry refuse to be analyzed. Yet we can see that with the perception of truth is joined the desire that it shall prevail; that affection is essential to will. Moreover, when a strong will appears, it usually results from a certain unity of organization, as if the whole energy of body and mind flowed in one direction. All great force is real and elemental. There is no manufacturing a strong will. There must be a pound to balance a pound. Where power is shown in will, it must rest on the universal force. Alaric and Bonaparte must believe they rest on a truth, or their will can be bought or bent. There is a bribe possible for any finite will. But the pure sympathy with universal ends is an infinite force, and cannot be bribed or bent. Whoever has had experience of the

moral sentiment cannot choose but believe in unlimited power. Each pulse from that heart is an oath from the Most High. I know not what the word *sublime* means, if it be not the intimations, in this infant, of a terrific force. A text of heroism, a name and anecdote of courage, are not arguments but sallies of freedom. One of these is the verse of the Persian Hafiz, " 'T is written on the gate of Heaven, 'Woe unto him who suffers himself to be betrayed by Fate!' " Does the reading of history make us fatalists? What courage does not the opposite opinion show! A little whim of will to be free gallantly contending against the universe of chemistry.

But insight is not will, nor is affection will. Perception is cold, and goodness dies in wishes. As Voltaire said, 't is the misfortune of worthy people that they are cowards; "un des plus grands malheurs des honnêtes gens c'est qu'ils sont des lâches." There must be a fusion of these two to generate the energy of will. There can be no driving force except through the conversion of the man into his will, making him the will, and the will him. And one may say boldly that no man has a right perception of any truth who has not been reacted on by it so as to be ready to be its martyr.

The one serious and formidable thing in nature is a will. Society is servile from want of will, and therefore the world wants saviours and religions. One way is right to go; the hero sees it, and moves on that aim, and has the world under him for root and support. He is to others as the world. His approbation is honor; his dissent, infamy. The glance of his eye has the force of sunbeams. A personal influence towers up in memory only worthy, and we gladly forget numbers, money, climate, gravitation, and the rest of Fate.

We can afford to allow the limitation, if we know it is the meter of the growing man. We stand against Fate, as children stand up against the wall in their father's house and notch their height from year to year. But when the boy grows to man, and is master of the house, he pulls down that wall and builds a new and bigger. 'T is only a question of time. Every brave youth is in training to ride and rule this dragon. His science is to make weapons and wings of these passions and retarding forces. Now whether, seeing these two things, fate and power, we are permitted to believe in unity? The bulk of mankind believe in two gods. They are under one dominion here in the house, as friend and parent, in social circles, in letters, in art, in love, in religion; but in mechanics, in dealing with steam and climate, in trade, in politics, they think they come under another; and that it would be a practical blunder to transfer the method and way of working of one sphere into the other. What good, honest, generous men at home, will be wolves and foxes on 'Change! What pious men in the parlor will vote for what reprobates at the polls! To a certain point, they believe themselves the care of a Providence. But in a steamboat, in an epidemic, in war, they believe a malignant energy rules.

But relation and connection are not somewhere and sometimes, but everywhere and always. The divine order does not stop where their sight stops. The friendly power works on the same rules in the next farm and the next planet. But where they have not experience they run against it and hurt themselves. Fate then is a name for facts not yet passed under the fire of thought; for causes which are unpenetrated.

But every jet of chaos which threatens to exterminate us is convertible by intellect into wholesome force. Fate is unpenetrated causes. The water drowns ship and sailor like a grain of dust. But learn to swim, trim your bark, and the wave which drowned it will be cloven by it and carry it like its own foam, a plume and a power. The cold is inconsiderate of persons, tingles your blood, freezes a man like a dew-drop. But learn to skate, and the ice will give you a graceful, sweet, and poetic motion. The cold will brace your limbs and brain to genius, and make you foremost men of time. Cold and sea will train an imperial

Saxon race, which nature cannot bear to lose, and after cooping it up for a thousand years in yonder England, gives a hundred Englands, a hundred Mexicos. All the bloods it shall absorb and domineer: and more than Mexicos, the secrets of water and steam, the spasms of electricity, the ductility of metals, the chariot of the air, the ruddered balloon are awaiting you.

The annual slaughter from typhus far exceeds that of war; but right drainage destroys typhus. The plague in the sea-service from scurvy is healed by lemon juice and other diets portable or procurable; the depopulation by cholera and small-pox is ended by drainage and vaccination; and every other pest is not less in the chain of cause and effect, and may be fought off. And whilst art draws out the venom, it commonly extorts some benefit from the vanquished enemy. The mischievous torrent is taught to drudge for man; the wild beasts he makes useful for food, or dress, or labor; the chemic explosions are controlled like his watch. These are now the steeds on which he rides. Man moves in all modes, by legs of horses, by wings of wind, by steam, by gas of balloon, by electricity, and stands on tiptoe threatening to hunt the eagle in his own element. There's nothing he will not make his carrier.

Steam was till the other day the devil which we dreaded. Every pot made by any human potter or brazier had a hole in its cover, to let off the enemy, lest he should lift pot and roof and carry the house away. But the Marquis of Worcester, Watt, and Fulton bethought themselves that where was power was not devil, but was God; that it must be availed of, and not by any means let off and wasted. Could he lift pots and roofs and houses so handily? He was the workman they were in search of. He could be used to lift away, chain and compel other devils far more reluctant and dangerous, namely, cubic miles of earth, mountains, weight or resistance of water, machinery, and the labors of all men in the world; and time he shall lengthen, and shorten space.

It has not fared much otherwise with higher kinds of

steam. The opinion of the million was the terror of the world, and it was attempted either to dissipate it, by amusing nations, or to pile it over with strata of society,— a layer of soldiers, over that a layer of lords, and a king on the top; with clamps and hoops of castles, garrisons, and police. But sometimes the religious principle would get in and burst the hoops and rive every mountain laid on top of it. The Fultons and Watts of politics, believing in unity, saw that it was a power, and by satisfying it (as justice satisfies everybody), through a different disposition of society,—grouping it on a level instead of piling it into a mountain,—they have contrived to make of this terror the most harmless and energetic form of a State.

Very odious, I confess, are the lessons of Fate. Who likes to have a dapper phrenologist pronouncing on his fortunes? Who likes to believe that he has, hidden in his skull, spine, and pelvis, all the vices of a Saxon or Celtic race, which will be sure to pull him down,—with what grandeur of hope and resolve he is fired,—into a selfish, huckstering, servile, dodging animal? A learned physician tells us the fact is invariable with the Neapolitan, that when mature he assumes the forms of the unmistakable scoundrel. That is a little overstated,—but may pass.

But these are magazines and arsenals. A man must thank his defects, and stand in some terror of his talents. A transcendent talent draws so largely on his forces as to lame him; a defect pays him revenues on the other side. The sufferance which is the badge of the Jew, has made him, in these days, the ruler of the rulers of the earth. If Fate is ore and quarry, if evil is good in the making, if limitation is power that shall be, if calamities, oppositions, and weights are wings and means,—we are reconciled.

Fate involves the melioration. No statement of the Universe can have any soundness which does not admit its ascending effort. The direction of the whole and of the parts is toward benefit, and in proportion to the health. Behind every individual closes organization; before him opens liberty,—the Better, the Best. The first and worse races are

dead. The second and imperfect races are dying out, or
remain for the maturing of higher. In the latest race, in
man, every generosity, every new perception, the love and
praise he extorts from his fellows, are certificates of advance out of fate into freedom. Liberation of the will from
the sheaths and clogs of organization which he has outgrown, is the end and aim of this world. Every calamity is
a spur and valuable hint; and where his endeavors do not
yet fully avail, they tell as tendency. The whole circle of
animal life—tooth against tooth, devouring war, war for
food, a yelp of pain and a grunt of triumph, until at last
the whole menagerie, the whole chemical mass is mellowed and refined for higher use—pleases at a sufficient
perspective.

But to see how fate slides into freedom and freedom
into fate, observe how far the roots of every creature run,
or find if you can a point where there is no thread of connection. Our life is consentaneous and far-related. This
knot of nature is so well tied that nobody was ever cunning enough to find the two ends. Nature is intricate,
overlapped, interweaved and endless. Christopher Wren
said of the beautiful King's College chapel, that "if anybody would tell him where to lay the first stone, he would
build such another." But where shall we find the first
atom in this house of man, which is all consent, inoscula-
tion and balance of parts?

The web of relation is shown in *habitat*, shown in hibernation. When hibernation was observed, it was found
that whilst some animals became torpid in winter, others
were torpid in summer: hibernation then was a false name.
The *long sleep* is not an effect of cold, but is regulated by
the supply of food proper to the animal. It becomes torpid
when the fruit or prey it lives on is not in season, and re-
gains its activity when its food is ready.

Eyes are found in light; ears in auricular air; feet on
land; fins in water; wings in air; and each creature where it
was meant to be, with a mutual fitness. Every zone has its
own *Fauna*. There is adjustment between the animal and

its food, its parasite, its enemy. Balances are kept. It is not
allowed to diminish in numbers, nor to exceed. The like
adjustments exist for man. His food is cooked when he arrives; his coal in the pit; the house ventilated; the mud of
the deluge dried; his companions arrived at the same hour,
and awaiting him with love, concert, laughter and tears.
These are coarse adjustments, but the invisible are not
less. There are more belongings to every creature than his
air and his food. His instincts must be met, and he has
predisposing power that bends and fits what is near him to
his use. He is not possible until the invisible things are
right for him, as well as the visible. Of what changes then
in sky and earth, and in finer skies and earths, does the appearance of some Dante or Columbus apprise us!

How is this effected? Nature is no spend-thrift, but
takes the shortest way to her ends. As the general says to
his soldiers, "If you want a fort, build a fort," so nature
makes every creature do its own work and get its living,—
is it planet, animal or tree. The planet makes itself. The
animal cell makes itself;—then, what it wants. Every creature, wren or dragon, shall make its own lair. As soon as
there is life, there is self-direction and absorbing and using
of material. Life is freedom,—life in the direct ratio of its
amount. You may be sure the new-born man is not inert.
Life works both voluntarily and supernaturally in its
neighborhood. Do you suppose he can be estimated by his
weight in pounds, or that he is contained in his skin,—this
reaching, radiating, jaculating fellow? The smallest candle
fills a mile with its rays, and the papillæ of a man run out
to every star.

When there is something to be done, the world knows
how to get it done. The vegetable eye makes leaf, pericarp,
root, bark, or thorn, as the need is; the first cell converts
itself into stomach, mouth, nose, or nail, according to the
want; the world throws its life into a hero or a shepherd,
and puts him where he is wanted. Dante and Columbus
were Italians, in their time; they would be Russians or
Americans to-day. Things ripen, new men come. The ad-

aptation is not capricious. The ulterior aim, the purpose beyond itself, the correlation by which planets subside and crystallize, then animate beasts and men,—will not stop but will work into finer particulars, and from finer to finest.

The secret of the world is the tie between person and event. Person makes event, and event person. The "times," "the age," what is that but a few profound persons and a few active persons who epitomize the times?— Goethe, Hegel, Metternich, Adams, Calhoun, Guizot, Peel, Cobden, Kossuth, Rothschild, Astor, Brunel, and the rest. The same fitness must be presumed between a man and the time and event, as between the sexes, or between a race of animals and the food it eats, or the inferior races it uses. He thinks his fate alien, because the copula is hidden. But the soul contains the event that shall befall it; for the event is only the actualization of its thoughts, and what we pray to ourselves for is always granted. The event is the print of your form. It fits you like your skin. What each does is proper to him. Events are the children of his body and mind. We learn that the soul of Fate is the soul of us, as Hafiz sings,—

> "Alas! till now I had not known,
> My guide and fortune's guide are one."

All the toys that infatuate men and which they play for,—houses, land, money, luxury, power, fame, are the selfsame thing, with a new gauze or two of illusion overlaid. And of all the drums and rattles by which men are made willing to have their heads broke, and are led out solemnly every morning to parade,—the most admirable is this by which we are brought to believe that events are arbitrary and independent of actions. At the conjuror's, we detect the hair by which he moves his puppet, but we have not eyes sharp enough to descry the thread that ties cause and effect.

Nature magically suits the man to his fortunes, by

making these the fruit of his character. Ducks take to the water, eagles to the sky, waders to the sea margin, hunters to the forest, clerks to counting-rooms, soldiers to the frontier. Thus events grow on the same stem with persons; are sub-persons. The pleasure of life is according to the man that lives it, and not according to the work or the place. Life is an ecstasy. We know what madness belongs to love,—what power to paint a vile object in hues of heaven. As insane persons are indifferent to their dress, diet, and other accommodations, and as we do in dreams, with equanimity, the most absurd acts, so a drop more of wine in our cup of life will reconcile us to strange company and work. Each creature puts forth from itself its own condition and sphere, as the slug sweats out its slimy house on the pear-leaf, and the woolly aphides on the apple perspire their own bed, and the fish its shell. In youth we clothe ourselves with rainbows and go as brave as the zodiac. In age we put out another sort of perspiration,—gout, fever, rheumatism, caprice, doubt, fretting and avarice.

A man's fortunes are the fruit of his character. A man's friends are his magnetisms. We go to Herodotus and Plutarch for examples of Fate; but we are examples. *"Quisque suos patimur manes."* The tendency of every man to enact all that is in his constitution is expressed in the old belief that the efforts which we make to escape from our destiny only serve to lead us into it: and I have noticed a man likes better to be complimented on his position, as the proof of the last or total excellence, than on his merits.

A man will see his character emitted in the events that seem to meet, but which exude from and accompany him. Events expand with the character. As once he found himself among toys, so now he plays a part in colossal systems, and his growth is declared in his ambition, his companions and his performance. He looks like a piece of luck, but is a piece of causation; the mosaic, angulated and ground to fit into the gap he fills. Hence in each town there is some man who is, in his brain and performance, an explanation of the tillage, production, factories, banks, churches, ways of living and society of that town. If you do not chance to meet him, all that you see will leave you a little puzzled; if you see him it will become plain. We know in Massachusetts who built New Bedford, who built Lynn, Lowell, Lawrence, Clinton, Fitchburg, Holyoke, Portland, and many another noisy mart. Each of these men, if they were transparent, would seem to you not so much men as walking cities, and wherever you put them they would build one.

History is the action and reaction of these two,—Nature and Thought; two boys pushing each other on the curbstone of the pavement. Everything is pusher or pushed; and matter and mind are in perpetual tilt and balance, so. Whilst the man is weak, the earth takes up him. He plants his brain and affections. By and by he will take up the earth, and have his gardens and vineyards in the beautiful order and productiveness of his thought. Every solid in the universe is ready to become fluid on the approach of the mind, and the power to flux it is the measure of the mind. If the wall remain adamant, it accuses the want of thought. To a subtle force it will stream into new forms, expressive of the character of the mind. What is the city in which we sit here, but an aggregate of incongruous materials which have obeyed the will of some man? The granite was reluctant, but his hands were stronger, and it came. Iron was deep in the ground and well combined with stone, but could not hide from his fires. Wood, lime, stuffs, fruits, gums, were dispersed over the earth and sea, in vain. Here they are, within reach of every man's day-labor,—what he wants of them. The whole world is the flux of matter over the wires of thought to the poles or points where it would build. The races of men rise out of the ground preoccupied with a thought which rules them, and divided into parties ready armed and angry to fight for this metaphysical abstraction. The quality of the thought differences the Egyptian and the Roman, the Austrian and the American. The men who come on the stage at one period are all found to be related to each other. Certain ideas are in the air. We are all impressionable, for we are made of them; all impressionable, but some more than others, and these first express them. This explains the curious contemporaneousness of inventions and discoveries. The truth is in the air, and the most impressionable brain will announce it first, but all will announce it a few minutes later. So women, as most susceptible, are the best index of the coming hour. So the great man, that is, the man most imbued with the spirit of the time, is the impressionable man;—of a fibre irritable and delicate, like iodine to light. He feels the infinitesimal attractions. His mind is righter than others because he yields to a current so feeble as can be felt only by a needle delicately poised.

The correlation is shown in defects. Möller, in his Essay on Architecture, taught that the building which was fitted accurately to answer its end would turn out to be beautiful though beauty had not been intended. I find the like unity in human structures rather virulent and pervasive; that a crudity in the blood will appear in the argument; a hump in the shoulder will appear in the speech and handiwork. If his mind could be seen, the hump would be seen. If a man has a see-saw in his voice, it will run into his sentences, into his poem, into the structure of his fable, into his speculation, into his charity. And as every man is hunted by his own dæmon, vexed by his own disease, this checks all his activity.

So each man, like each plant, has his parasites. A strong, astringent, bilious nature has more truculent enemies than the slugs and moths that fret my leaves. Such an one has curculios, borers, knife-worms; a swindler ate him first, then a client, then a quack, then smooth, plausible gentlemen, bitter and selfish as Moloch.

This correlation really existing can be divined. If the threads are there, thought can follow and show them. Especially when a soul is quick and docile, as Chaucer sings:—

> "Or if the soule of proper kind
> Be so parfite as men find,
> That it wot what is to come,
> And that he warneth all and some
> Of everiche of hir aventures,
> By avisions or figures;
> But that our flesh hath no might
> To understand it aright
> For it is warned too derkely."

Some people are made up of rhyme, coincidence, omen, periodicity, and presage: they meet the person they seek; what their companion prepares to say to them, they first say to him; and a hundred signs apprise them of what is about to befall.

Wonderful intricacy in the web, wonderful constancy in the design this vagabond life admits. We wonder how the fly finds its mate, and yet year after year, we find two men, two women, without legal or carnal tie, spend a great part of their best time within a few feet of each other. And the moral is that what we seek we shall find; what we flee from flees from us; as Goethe said, "what we wish for in youth, comes in heaps on us in old age," too often cursed with the granting of our prayer: and hence the high caution, that since we are sure of having what we wish, we beware to ask only for high things.

One key, one solution to the mysteries of human condition, one solution to the old knots of fate, freedom, and foreknowledge, exists; the propounding, namely, of the double consciousness. A man must ride alternately on the horses of his private and his public nature, as the equestrians in the circus throw themselves nimbly from horse to horse, or plant one foot on the back of one and the other foot on the back of the other. So when a man is the victim of his fate, has sciatica in his loins and cramp in his mind; a club-foot and a club in his wit; a sour face and a selfish temper; a strut in his gait and a conceit in his affection; or is ground to powder by the vice of his race;—he is to rally on his relation to the Universe, which his ruin benefits. Leaving the dæmon who suffers, he is to take sides with the Deity who secures universal benefit by his pain.

To offset the drag of temperament and race, which pulls down, learn this lesson, namely, that by the cunning copresence of two elements, which is throughout nature, whatever lames or paralyzes you draws in with it the divinity, in some form, to repay. A good intention clothes itself with sudden power. When a god wishes to ride, any chip or pebble will bud and shoot out winged feet and serve him for a horse.

Let us build altars to the Blessed Unity which holds nature and souls in perfect solution, and compels every atom to serve an universal end. I do not wonder at a snow-flake, a shell, a summer landscape, or the glory of the stars; but at the necessity of beauty under which the universe lies; that all is and must be pictorial; that the rainbow and the curve of the horizon and the arch of the blue vault are only results from the organism of the eye. There is no need for foolish amateurs to fetch me to admire a garden of flowers, or a sun-gilt cloud, or a waterfall, when I cannot look without seeing splendor and grace. How idle to choose a random sparkle here or there, when the indwelling necessity plants the rose of beauty on the brow of chaos, and discloses the central intention of Nature to be harmony and joy.

Let us build altars to the Beautiful Necessity. If we thought men were free in the sense that in a single exception one fantastical will could prevail over the law of things, it were all one as if a child's hand could pull down the sun. If in the least particular one could derange the order of nature,—who would accept the gift of life?

Let us build altars to the Beautiful Necessity, which secures that all is made of one piece; that plaintiff and defendant, friend and enemy, animal and plant, food and eater are of one kind. In astronomy is vast space but no foreign system; in geology, vast time but the same laws as to-day. Why should we be afraid of Nature, which is no other than "philosophy and theology embodied"? Why should we fear to be crushed by savage elements, we who are made up of the same elements? Let us build to the Beautiful Necessity, which makes man brave in believing that he cannot shun a danger that is appointed, nor incur one that is not; to the Necessity which rudely or softly educates him to the perception that there are no contingencies; that Law rules throughout existence; a Law which is not intelligent but intelligence;—not personal nor impersonal—it disdains words and passes understanding; it dissolves persons; it vivifies nature; yet solicits the pure in heart to draw on all its omnipotence.

ILLUSIONS

Flow, flow the waves hated,
Accursed, adored,
The waves of mutation:
No anchorage is.
Sleep is not, death is not;
Who seem to die live.
House you were born in,
Friends of your spring-time,
Old man and young maid,
Day's toil and its guerdon,
They are all vanishing,
Fleeing to fables,
Cannot be moored.
See the stars through them,
Through treacherous marbles.
Know, the stars yonder,
The stars everlasting,
Are fugitive also,
And emulate, vaulted,
The lambent heat-lightning,
And fire-fly's flight.

When thou dost return
On the wave's circulation,
Beholding the shimmer,
The wild dissipation,
And, out of endeavor
To change and to flow,
The gas become solid,
And phantoms and nothings
Return to be things,

And endless imbroglio
Is law and the world,—
Then first shalt thou know,
That in the wild turmoil,
Horsed on the Proteus,
Thou ridest to power,
And to endurance.

Some years ago, in company with an agreeable party, I
spent a long summer day in exploring the Mammoth Cave
in Kentucky. We traversed, through spacious galleries af-
fording a solid masonry foundation for the town and
county overhead, the six or eight black miles from the
mouth of the cavern to the innermost recess which tour-
ists visit,—a niche or grotto made of one seamless stalac-
tite, and called, I believe, Serena's Bower. I lost the light
of one day. I saw high domes and bottomless pits; heard
the voice of unseen waterfalls; paddled three quarters of a
mile in the deep Echo River, whose waters are peopled
with the blind fish; crossed the streams "Lethe" and
"Styx;" plied with music and guns the echoes in these
alarming galleries; saw every form of stalagmite and sta-
lactite in the sculptured and fretted chambers;—icicle,
orange-flower, acanthus, grapes and snowball. We shot
Bengal lights into the vaults and groins of the sparry
cathedrals and examined all the masterpieces which the
four combined engineers, water, limestone, gravitation
and time, could make in the dark.

The mysteries and scenery of the cave had the same
dignity that belongs to all natural objects, and which
shames the fine things to which we foppishly compare
them. I remarked especially the mimetic habit with which
nature, on new instruments, hums her old tunes, making
night to mimic day, and chemistry to ape vegetation. But I
then took notice and still chiefly remember that the best
thing which the cave had to offer was an illusion. On arriving at what is called the "Star-Chamber," our lamps

were taken from us by the guide and extinguished or put aside, and, on looking upwards, I saw or seemed to see the night heaven thick with stars glimmering more or less brightly over our heads, and even what seemed a comet flaming among them. All the party were touched with astonishment and pleasure. Our musical friends sung with much feeling a pretty song, "The stars are in the quiet sky," etc., and I sat down on the rocky floor to enjoy the serene picture. Some crystal specks in the black ceiling high overhead, reflecting the light of a half-hid lamp, yielded this magnificent effect.

I own I did not like the cave so well for eking out its sublimities with this theatrical trick. But I have had many experiences like it, before and since; and we must be content to be pleased without too curiously analyzing the occasions. Our conversation with nature is not just what it seems. The cloud-rack, the sunrise and sunset glories, rainbows and Northern Lights are not quite so spheral as our childhood thought them, and the part our organization plays in them is too large. The senses interfere everywhere and mix their own structure with all they report of. Once we fancied the earth a plane, and stationary. In admiring the sunset we do not yet deduct the rounding, coördinating, pictorial powers of the eye.

The same interference from our organization creates the most of our pleasure and pain. Our first mistake is the belief that the circumstance gives the joy which we give to the circumstance. Life is an ecstasy. Life is sweet as nitrous oxide; and the fisherman dripping all day over a cold pond, the switchman at the railway intersection, the farmer in the field, the negro in the rice-swamp, the fop in the street, the hunter in the woods, the barrister with the jury, the belle at the ball, all ascribe a certain pleasure to their employment, which they themselves give it. Health and appetite impart the sweetness to sugar, bread and meat. We fancy that our civilization has got on far, but we still come back to our primers.

We live by our imaginations, by our admirations, by

our sentiments. The child walks amid heaps of illusions, which he does not like to have disturbed. The boy, how sweet to him is his fancy! how dear the story of barons and battles! What a hero he is, whilst he feeds on his heroes! What a debt is his to imaginative books! He has no better friend or influence than Scott, Shakspeare, Plutarch and Homer. The man lives to other objects, but who dare affirm that they are more real? Even the prose of the streets is full of refractions. In the life of the dreariest alderman, fancy enters into all details and colors them with rosy hue. He imitates the air and actions of people whom he admires, and is raised in his own eyes. He pays a debt quicker to a rich man than to a poor man. He wishes the bow and compliment of some leader in the state or in society; weighs what he says; perhaps he never comes nearer to him for that, but dies at last better contented for this amusement of his eyes and his fancy.

The world rolls, the din of life is never hushed. In London, in Paris, in Boston, in San Francisco, the carnival, the masquerade is at its height. Nobody drops his domino. The unities, the fictions of the piece it would be an impertinence to break. The chapter of fascinations is very long. Great is paint; nay, God is the painter; and we rightly accuse the critic who destroys too many illusions. Society does not love its unmaskers. It was wittily if somewhat bitterly said by D'Alembert, "*qu'un état de vapeur était un état très fâcheux, parcequ'il nous faisait voir les choses comme elles sont*"[that a fit of melancholy was a very unpleasant state, because it made us see things as they are]. I find men victims of illusion in all parts of life. Children, youths, adults and old men, all are led by one bawble or another. Yoganidra, the goddess of illusion, Proteus, or Momus, or Gylfi's Mocking,—for the Power has many names,—is stronger than the Titans, stronger that Apollo. Few have overheard the gods or surprised their secret. Life is a succession of lessons which must be lived to be understood. All is riddle, and the key to a riddle is another riddle. There are as many pillows of illusion as flakes in a snow-storm. We wake from one dream into another dream. The toys to be sure are various, and are graduated in refinement to the quality of the dupe. The intellectual man requires a fine bait; the sots are easily amused. But everybody is drugged with his own frenzy, and the pageant marches at all hours, with music and banner and badge.

Amid the joyous troop who give in to the charivari, comes now and then a sad-eyed boy whose eyes lack the requisite refractions to clothe the show in due glory, and who is afflicted with a tendency to trace home the glittering miscellany of fruits and flowers to one root. Science is a search after identity, and the scientific whim is lurking in all corners. At the State Fair a friend of mine complained that all the varieties of fancy pears in our orchards seem to have been selected by somebody who had a whim for a particular kind of pear, and only cultivated such as had that perfume; they were all alike. And I remember the quarrel of another youth with the confectioners, that when he racked his wit to choose the best comfits in the shops, in all the endless varieties of sweetmeat he could find only three flavors, or two. What then? Pears and cakes are good for something; and because you unluckily have an eye or nose too keen, why need you spoil the comfort which the rest of us find in them? I knew a humorist who in a good deal of rattle had a grain or two of sense. He shocked the company by maintaining that the attributes of God were two,—power and risibility, and that it was the duty of every pious man to keep up the comedy. And I have known gentlemen of great stake in the community, but whose sympathies were cold,—presidents of colleges and governors and senators,—who held themselves bound to sign every temperance pledge, and act with Bible societies and missions and peace-makers, and cry *Hist-a-boy!* to every good dog. We must not carry comity too far, but we all have kind impulses in this direction. When the boys come into my yard for leave to gather horse-chestnuts, I own I enter into nature's game, and affect to grant the permission reluctantly, fearing that any moment they will find out the imposture of that showy chaff. But this tenderness is quite unnecessary; the enchantments are laid on very thick. Their young life is thatched with them. Bare and grim to tears is the lot of the children in the hovel I saw yesterday; yet not the less they hung it round with frippery romance, like the children of the happiest fortune, and talked of "the dear cottage where so many joyful hours had flown." Well, this thatching of hovels is the custom of the country. Women, more than all, are the element and kingdom of illusion. Being fascinated, they fascinate. They see through Claude-Lorraines. And how dare any one, if he could, pluck away the *coulisses*, stage effects and ceremonies, by which they live? Too pathetic, too pitiable, is the region of affection, and its atmosphere always liable to *mirage*.

We are not very much to blame for our bad marriages. We live amid hallucinations; and this especial trap is laid to trip up our feet with, and all are tripped up first or last. But the mighty Mother who had been so sly with us, as if she felt that she owed us some indemnity, insinuates into the Pandora-box of marriage some deep and serious benefits and some great joys. We find a delight in the beauty and happiness of children that makes the heart too big for the body. In the worst-assorted connections there is ever some mixture of true marriage. Teague and his jade get some just relations of mutual respect, kindly observation, and fostering of each other; learn something, and would carry themselves wiselier if they were now to begin.

'T is fine for us to point at one or another fine madman, as if there were any exempts. The scholar in his library is none. I, who have all my life heard any number of orations and debates, read poems and miscellaneous books, conversed with many geniuses, am still the victim of any new page; and if Marmaduke, or Hugh, or Moosehead, or any other, invent a new style or mythology, I fancy that the world will be all brave and right if dressed in these colors, which I had not thought of. Then at once I will daub with this new paint; but it will not stick. 'T is like the cement which the peddler sells at the door; he makes broken crockery hold with it, but you can never buy of him a bit of the cement which will make it hold when he is gone.

Men who make themselves felt in the world avail themselves of a certain fate in their constitution which they know how to use. But they never deeply interest us unless they lift a corner of the curtain, or betray, never so slightly, their penetration of what is behind it. 'T is the charm of practical men that outside of their practicality are a certain poetry and play, as if they led the good horse Power by the bridle, and preferred to walk, though they can ride so fiercely. Bonaparte is intellectual, as well as Cæsar; and the best soldiers, sea-captains and railway men have a gentleness when off duty, a good-natured admission that there are illusions, and who shall say that he is not their sport? We stigmatize the cast-iron fellows who cannot so detach themselves, as "dragon-ridden," "thunder-stricken," and fools of fate, with whatever powers endowed.

Since our tuition is through emblems and indirections, it is well to know that there is method in it, a fixed scale and rank above rank in the phantasms. We begin low with coarse masks and rise to the most subtle and beautiful. The red men told Columbus "they had an herb which took away fatigue;" but he found the illusion of "arriving from the east at the Indies" more composing to his lofty spirit than any tobacco. Is not our faith in the impenetrability of matter more sedative than narcotics? You play with jackstraws, balls, bowls, horse and gun, estates and politics; but there are finer games before you. Is not time a pretty toy? Life will show you masks that are worth all your carnivals. Yonder mountain must migrate into your mind. The fine star-dust and nebulous blur in Orion, "the portentous year of Mizar and Alcor," must come down and be dealt with in your household thought. What if you shall come to discern that the play and playground of all this pompous history are radiations from yourself, and

that the sun borrows his beams? What terrible questions
we are learning to ask! The former men believed in magic,
by which temples, cities and men were swallowed up, and
all trace of them gone. We are coming on the secret of a
magic which sweeps out of men's minds all vestige of theism and beliefs which they and their fathers held and were
framed upon.

There are deceptions of the senses, deceptions of the
passions, and the structural, beneficent illusions of sentiment and of the intellect. There is the illusion of love,
which attributes to the beloved person all which that person shares with his or her family, sex, age or condition,
nay, with the human mind itself. 'T is these which the
lover loves, and Anna Matilda gets the credit of them. As
if one shut up always in a tower, with one window
through which the face of heaven and earth could be seen,
should fancy that all the marvels he beheld belonged to
that window. There is the illusion of time, which is very
deep; who has disposed of it?—or come to the conviction
that what seems the *succession* of thought is only the distribution of wholes into causal series? The intellect sees
that every atom carries the whole of nature; that the mind
opens to omnipotence; that, in the endless striving and as-
cents, the metamorphosis is entire, so that the soul doth
not know itself in its own act when that act is perfected.
There is illusion that shall deceive even the elect. There is
illusion that shall deceive even the performer of the miracle. Though he make his body, he denies that he makes it.
Though the world exist from thought, thought is daunted
in presence of the world. One after the other we accept the
mental laws, still resisting those which follow, which
however must be accepted. But all our concessions only
compel us to new profusion. And what avails it that science has come to treat space and time as simply forms of
thought, and the material world as hypothetical, and
withal our pretension of *property* and even of self-hood
are fading with the rest, if, at last, even our thoughts are
not finalities, but the incessant flowing and ascension

reach these also, and each thought which yesterday was a finality, to-day is yielding to a larger generalization?

With such volatile elements to work in, 't is no wonder if our estimates are loose and floating. We must work and affirm, but we have no guess of the value of what we say or do. The cloud is now as big as your hand, and now it covers a county. That story of Thor, who was set to drain the drinking-horn in Asgard and to wrestle with the old woman and to run with the runner Lok, and presently found that he had been drinking up the sea, and wrestling with Time, and racing with Thought,—describes us, who are contending, amid these seeming trifles, with the supreme energies of nature. We fancy we have fallen into bad company and squalid condition, low debts, shoe-bills, broken glass to pay for, pots to buy, butcher's meat, sugar, milk and coal. 'Set me some great task, ye gods! and I will show my spirit.' 'Not so,' says the good Heaven; 'plod and plough, vamp your old coats and hats, weave a shoestring; great affairs and the best wine by and by.' Well, 't is all phantasm; and if we weave a yard of tape in all humility and as well as we can, long hereafter we shall see it was no cotton tape at all but some galaxy which we braided, and that the threads were Time and Nature.

We cannot write the order of the variable winds. How can we penetrate the law of our shifting moods and susceptibility? Yet they differ as all and nothing. Instead of the firmament of yesterday, which our eyes require, it is to-day an egg-shell which coops us in; we cannot even see what or where our stars of destiny are. From day to day the capital facts of human life are hidden from our eyes. Suddenly the mist rolls up and reveals them, and we think how much good time is gone that might have been saved had any hint of these things been shown. A sudden rise in the road shows us the system of mountains, and all the summits, which have been just as near us all the year, but quite out of mind. But these alternations are not without their order, and we are parties to our various fortune. If life seem a succession of dreams, yet poetic justice is done

in dreams also. The visions of good men are good; it is the
undisciplined will that is whipped with bad thoughts and
bad fortunes. When we break the laws, we lose our hold
on the central reality. Like sick men in hospitals, we
change only from bed to bed, from one folly to another;
and it cannot signify much what becomes of such
castaways, wailing, stupid, comatose creatures, lifted from
bed to bed, from the nothing of life to the nothing of
death.

In this kingdom of illusions we grope eagerly for stays
and foundations. There is none but a strict and faithful
dealing at home and a severe barring out of all duplicity or
illusion there. Whatever games are played with us, we
must play no games with ourselves, but deal in our privacy with the last honesty and truth. I look upon the simple and childish virtues of veracity and honesty as the root
of all that is sublime in character. Speak as you think, be
what you are, pay your debts of all kinds. I prefer to be
owned as sound and solvent, and my word as good as my
bond, and to be what cannot be skipped, or dissipated, or
undermined, to all the *éclat* in the universe. This reality is
the foundation of friendship, religion, poetry and art. At
the top or at the bottom of all illusions, I set the cheat
which still leads us to work and live for appearances; in
spite of our conviction, in all sane hours, that it is what we
really are that avails with friends, with strangers, and with
fate or fortune.

One would think from the talk of men that riches and
poverty were a great matter; and our civilization mainly
respects it. But the Indians say that they do not think the
white man, with his brow of care, always toiling, afraid of
heat and cold, and keeping within doors, has any advantage of them. The permanent interest of every man is
never to be in a false position, but to have the weight of
nature to back him in all that he does. Riches and poverty
are a thick or thin costume; and our life—the life of all of
us—identical. For we transcend the circumstance continually and taste the real quality of existence; as in our

employments, which only differ in the manifestations but express the same laws; or in our thoughts, which wear no silks and taste no ice-creams. We see God face to face every hour, and know the savor of nature.

The early Greek philosophers Heraclitus and Xenophanes measured their force on this problem of identity. Diogenes of Apollonia said that unless the atoms were made of one stuff, they could never blend and act with one another. But the Hindoos, in their sacred writings, express the liveliest feeling, both of the essential identity and of that illusion which they conceive variety to be. "The notion, '*I am,*' and '*This is mine,*' which influence mankind, are but delusions of the mother of the world. Dispel, O Lord of all creatures! the conceit of knowledge which proceeds from ignorance." And the beatitude of man they hold to lie in being freed from fascination.

The intellect is stimulated by the statement of truth in a trope, and the will by clothing the laws of life in illusions. But the unities of Truth and of Right are not broken by the disguise. There need never be any confusion in these. In a crowded life of many parts and performers, on a stage of nations, or in the obscurest hamlet in Maine or California, the same elements offer the same choices to each new comer, and, according to his election, he fixes his fortune in absolute Nature. It would be hard to put more mental and moral philosophy than the Persians have thrown into a sentence,—

"Fooled thou must be, though wisest of the wise:
    Then be the fool of virtue, not of vice."

There is no chance and no anarchy in the universe. All is system and gradation. Every god is there sitting in his sphere. The young mortal enters the hall of the firmament; there is he alone with them alone, they pouring on him benedictions and gifts, and beckoning him up to their thrones. On the instant, and incessantly, fall snow-storms of illusions. He fancies himself in a vast crowd which sways this way and that and whose movement and doings he must obey: he fancies himself poor, orphaned, insignificant. The mad crowd drives hither and thither, now furiously commanding this thing to be done, now that. What is he that he should resist their will, and think or act for himself? Every moment new changes and new showers of deceptions to baffle and distract him. And when, by and by, for an instant, the air clears and the cloud lifts a little, there are the gods still sitting around him on their thrones,—they alone with him alone.

SOCIETY AND SOLITUDE

~~~~~~~~~~~~~~~~~~~~

I fell in with a humorist on my travels, who had in his chamber a cast of the Rondanini Medusa, and who assured me that the name which that fine work of art bore in the catalogues was a misnomer, as he was convinced that the sculptor who carved it intended it for Memory, the mother of the Muses. In the conversation that followed, my new friend made some extraordinary confessions. "Do you not see," he said, "the penalty of learning, and that each of these scholars whom you have met at S——, though he were to be the last man, would, like the executioner in Hood's poem, guillotine the last but one?" He added many lively remarks, but his evident earnestness engaged my attention, and in the weeks that followed we became better acquainted. He had good abilities, a genial temper and no vices; but he had one defect,—he could not speak in the tone of the people. There was some paralysis on his will, such that when he met men on common terms he spoke weakly and from the point, like a flighty girl. His consciousness of the fault made it worse. He envied every drover and lumberman in the tavern their manly speech. He coveted Mirabeau's *don terrible de la familiarité*, believing that he whose sympathy goes lowest is the man from whom kings have the most to fear. For himself he declared that he could not get enough alone to write a letter to a friend. He left the city; he hid himself in pastures. The solitary river was not solitary enough; the sun and moon put him out. When he bought a house, the first thing he did was to plant trees. He could not enough conceal himself. Set a hedge here; set oaks there,—trees behind trees; above all, set evergreens, for they will keep a secret all the year round. The most agreeable compliment you could pay him was to imply that you had not observed him in a house or a street where you had met him. Whilst he suffered at being seen where he was, he consoled himself with the delicious thought of the inconceivable number of places where he was not. All he wished of his tailor was to provide that sober mean of color and cut which would never detain the eye for a moment. He went to Vienna, to Smyrna, to London. In all the variety of costumes, a carnival, a kaleidoscope of clothes, to his horror he could never discover a man in the street who wore anything like his own dress. He would have given his soul for the ring of Gyges. His dismay at his visibility had blunted the fears of mortality. "Do you think," he said, "I am in such great terror of being shot,—I, who am only waiting to shuffle off my corporeal jacket to slip away into the back stars, and put diameters of the solar system and sidereal orbits between me and all souls,—there to wear out ages in solitude, and forget memory itself, if it be possible?" He had a remorse running to despair of his social *gaucheries*, and walked miles and miles to get the twitchings out of his face, the starts and shrugs out of his arms and shoulders. God may forgive sins, he said, but awkwardness has no forgiveness in heaven or earth. He admired in Newton not so much his theory of the moon as his letter to Collins, in which he forbade him to insert his name with the solution of the problem in the Philosophical Transactions: "It would perhaps increase my acquaintance, the thing which I chiefly study to decline."

These conversations led me somewhat later to the knowledge of similar cases, and to the discovery that they are not of very infrequent occurrence. Few substances are found pure in nature. Those constitutions which can bear in open day the rough dealing of the world must be of that mean and average structure such as iron and salt, atmospheric air and water. But there are metals, like potassium and sodium, which, to be kept pure, must be kept under naphtha. Such are the talents determined on some specialty, which a culminating civilization fosters in the heart of great cities and in royal chambers. Nature protects her own work. To the culture of the world an Archimedes, a Newton is indispensable; so she guards them by a certain aridity. If these had been good fellows, fond of dancing, port and clubs, we should have had no Theory of the Sphere and no Principia. They had that necessity of isolation which genius feels. Each must stand on his glass tripod if he would keep his electricity. Even Swedenborg, whose theory of the universe is based on affection, and who reprobates to weariness the danger and vice of pure intellect, is constrained to make an extraordinary exception: "There are also angels who do not live consociated, but separate, house and house; these dwell in the midst of heaven, because they are the best of angels."

We have known many fine geniuses with that imperfection that they cannot do anything useful, not so much as write one clean sentence. 'T is worse, and tragic, that no man is fit for society who has fine traits. At a distance he is admired, but bring him hand to hand, he is a cripple. One protects himself by solitude, and one by courtesy, and one by an acid, worldly manner,—each concealing how he can the thinness of his skin and his incapacity for strict association. But there is no remedy that can reach the heart of the disease but either habits of self-reliance that should go in practice to making the man independent of the human race, or else a religion of love. Now he hardly seems entitled to marry; for how can he protect a woman, who cannot protect himself?

We pray to be conventional. But the wary Heaven takes care you shall not be, if there is anything good in you. Dante was very bad company, and was never invited to dinner. Michel Angelo had a sad, sour time of it. The ministers of beauty are rarely beautiful in coaches and saloons. Columbus discovered no isle or key so lonely as himself. Yet each of these potentates saw well the reason of his exclusion. Solitary was he? Why, yes; but his society was limited only by the amount of brain nature appropriated in that age to carry on the government of the world. "If I stay," said Dante, when there was question of going to Rome, "who will go? and if I go, who will stay?"

But the necessity of solitude is deeper than we have said, and is organic. I have seen many a philosopher whose world is large enough for only one person. He affects to be a good companion; but we are still surprising his secret, that he means and needs to impose his system on all the rest. The determination of each is *from* all the others, like that of each tree up into free space. 'T is no wonder, when each has his whole head, our societies should be so small. Like President Tyler, our party falls from us every day, and we must ride in a sulky at last. Dear heart! take it sadly home to thee,—there is no coöperation. We begin with friendships, and all our youth is a reconnoitring and recruiting of the holy fraternity they shall combine for the salvation of men. But so the remoter stars seem a nebula of united light, yet there is no group which a telescope will not resolve; and the dearest friends are separated by impassable gulfs. The coöperation is involuntary, and is put upon us by the Genius of Life, who reserves this as a part of his prerogative. 'T is fine for us to talk; we sit and muse and are serene and complete; but the moment we meet with anybody, each becomes a fraction.

Though the stuff of tragedy and of romances is in a moral union of two superior persons whose confidence in each other for long years, out of sight and in sight, and against all appearances, is at last justified by victorious proof of probity to gods and men, causing joyful emotions, tears and glory,—though there be for heroes this *moral union*, yet they too are as far off as ever from an intellectual union, and the moral union is for comparatively low and external purposes, like the coöperation of a ship's company or of a fire-club. But how insular and pathetically solitary are all the people we know! Nor dare they tell what they think of each other when they meet in the street. We have a fine right, to be sure, to taunt men of the world with superficial and treacherous courtesies!

Such is the tragic necessity which strict science finds underneath our domestic and neighborly life, irresistibly driving each adult soul as with whips into the desert, and making our warm covenants sentimental and momentary. We must infer that the ends of thought were peremptory, if they were to be secured at such ruinous cost.

They are deeper than can be told, and belong to the immensities and eternities. They reach down to that depth where society itself originates and disappears; where the question is, Which is first, man or men? where the individual is lost in his source.

But this banishment to the rocks and echoes no metaphysics can make right or tolerable. This result is so against nature, such a half-view, that it must be corrected by a common sense and experience. "A man is born by the side of his father, and there he remains." A man must be clothed with society, or we shall feel a certain bareness and poverty, as of a displaced and unfurnished member. He is to be dressed in arts and institutions, as well as in body garments. Now and then a man exquisitely made can live alone, and must; but coop up most men and you undo them. "The king lived and ate in his hall with men, and understood men," said Selden. When a young barrister said to the late Mr. Mason, "I keep my chamber to read law,"—"Read law!" replied the veteran, "'t is in the court-room you must read law." Nor is the rule otherwise for literature. If you would learn to write, 't is in the street you must learn it. Both for the vehicle and for the aims of fine arts you must frequent the public square. The people, and not the college, is the writer's home. A scholar is a candle which the love and desire of all men will light. Never his lands or his rents, but the power to charm the disguised soul that sits veiled under this bearded and that rosy visage is his rent and ration. His products are as needful as those of the baker or the weaver. Society cannot do without cultivated men. As soon as the first wants are satisfied, the higher wants become imperative.

'T is hard to mesmerize ourselves, to whip our own top; but through sympathy we are capable of energy and endurance. Concert fires people to a certain fury of performance they can rarely reach alone. Here is the use of society: it is so easy with the great to be great; so easy to come up to an existing standard;—as easy as it is to the lover to swim to his maiden through waves so grim before. The benefits of affection are immense; and the one event which never loses its romance is the encounter with superior persons on terms allowing the happiest intercourse.

It by no means follows that we are not fit for society, because *soirées* are tedious and because the *soirée* finds us tedious. A backwoodsman, who had been sent to the university, told me that when he heard the best-bred young men at the law-school talk together, he reckoned himself a boor; but whenever he caught them apart, and had one to himself alone, then they were the boors and he the better man. And if we recall the rare hours when we encountered the best persons, we then found ourselves, and then first society seemed to exist. That was society, though in the transom of a brig or on the Florida Keys.

A cold sluggish blood thinks it has not facts enough to the purpose, and must decline its turn in the conversation. But they who speak have no more,—have less. 'T is not new facts that avail, but the heat to dissolve everybody's facts. Heat puts you in right relation with magazines of facts. The capital defect of cold, arid natures is the want of animal spirits. They seem a power incredible, as if God should raise the dead. The recluse witnesses what others perform by their aid, with a kind of fear. It is as much out of his possibility as the prowess of Cœur-de-Lion, or an Irishman's day's work on the railroad. 'T is said the present and the future are always rivals. Animal spirits constitute the power of the present, and their feats are like the structure of a pyramid. Their result is a lord, a general, or a boon companion. Before these what a base mendicant is

Memory with his leathern badge! But this genial heat is latent in all constitutions, and is disengaged only by the friction of society. As Bacon said of manners, "To obtain them, it only needs not to despise them," so we say of animal spirits that they are the spontaneous product of health and of a social habit. "For behavior, men learn it, as they take diseases, one of another."

But the people are to be taken in very small doses. If solitude is proud, so is society vulgar. In society, high advantages are set down to the individual as disqualifications. We sink as easily as we rise, through sympathy. So many men whom I know are degraded by their sympathies; their native aims being high enough, but their relation all too tender to the gross people about them. Men cannot afford to live together on their merits, and they adjust themselves by their demerits,—by their love of gossip, or by sheer tolerance and animal good nature. They untune and dissipate the brave aspirant.

The remedy is to reinforce each of these moods from the other. Conversation will not corrupt us if we come to the assembly in our own garb and speech and with the energy of health to select what is ours and reject what is not. Society we must have; but let it be society, and not exchanging news or eating from the same dish. Is it society to sit in one of your chairs? I cannot go to the houses of my nearest relatives, because I do not wish to be alone. Society exists by chemical affinity, and not otherwise.

Put any company of people together with freedom for conversation, and a rapid self-distribution takes place into sets and pairs. The best are accused of exclusiveness. It would be more true to say they separate as oil from water, as children from old people, without love or hatred in the matter, each seeking his like; and any interference with the affinities would produce constraint and suffocation. All conversation is a magnetic experiment. I know that my friend can talk eloquently; you know that he cannot articulate a sentence: we have seen him in different company. Assort your party, or invite none. Put Stubbs and Coleridge, Quintilian and Aunt Miriam, into pairs, and you make them all wretched. 'T is an extempore Sing-Sing built in a parlor. Leave them to seek their own mates, and they will be as merry as sparrows.

A higher civility will reëstablish in our customs a certain reverence which we have lost. What to do with these brisk young men who break through all fences, and make themselves at home in every house? I find out in an instant if my companion does not want me, and ropes cannot hold me when my welcome is gone. One would think that the affinities would pronounce themselves with a surer reciprocity.

Here again, as so often, nature delights to put us between extreme antagonisms, and our safety is in the skill with which we keep the diagonal line. Solitude is impracticable, and society fatal. We must keep our head in the one and our hands in the other. The conditions are met, if we keep our independence, yet do not lose our sympathy. These wonderful horses need to be driven by fine hands. We require such a solitude as shall hold us to its revelations when we are in the street and in palaces; for most men are cowed in society, and say good things to you in private, but will not stand to them in public. But let us not be the victims of words. Society and solitude are deceptive names. It is not the circumstance of seeing more or fewer people, but the readiness of sympathy, that imports; and a sound mind will derive its principles from insight, with ever a purer ascent to the sufficient and absolute right, and will accept society as the natural element in which they are to be applied.

A Yankee Abroad
English Traits

Editor's Note

Emerson had been lecturing about the English for twenty years, and thinking about them for longer than that, when he published *English Traits* in August 1856. By the late 1840s the topic had become one of his favorites for the lecture platform on both sides of the Atlantic. He shared the assumption, so firm in the nineteenth century, that national character exists; so he asked himself what kind of people the English were. Today we would ask the question a bit reluctantly, for we see more exceptions than the nineteenth century did to any generalizations about collective character. Yet the reply that Emerson perfected over the years still makes illuminating and often delightful reading.

He showed himself to be a shrewd as well as a sympathetic observer. Often he crisped his observations with a nice wit. When he composed *English Traits* he laid aside his usual Transcendentalism as inappropriate to his subject. Gone was his cloudy mystical creed; in its place came common sense. And wisdom, too, from a traveler in his prime.

This was a side of Emerson's work with which Mark Van Doren was completely in sympathy (as he wasn't with the Neoplatonic side). Here, in somewhat abbreviating the book, we have followed his wise selections, thus omitting the first two chapters as being of less interest today. It is to be noted that those two omitted chapters set the tone of the book, as openings often do with Emerson. The first sentence is simple: "I have been twice to England," and from there the author goes on to state his credentials. He is never flat. By the third sentence he begins to build atmosphere; "It was a dark Sunday morning; there were few people in the streets." By the fourth he is letting wit emerge: "For the first time for many months we were forced to check the saucy habit of travellers' criticism, as we could no longer speak in the streets without being understood."

The third chapter, "Land," with which our selections begin, reveals Emerson's talent for brief aphorisms: "England is a garden. Under an ash-colored sky, the fields have been combed and rolled until they appear to have been finished with a pencil instead of a plough." Today *English Traits* can still be a book to carry with us when we cross the ocean. Though the winds of change have swept away much of the England that Emerson vividly presented, a surprising amount remains and can be appreciated with his help.

C.B.

ENGLISH TRAITS

~~~~~~~~~~~~~~~~~~~~~~~~~~~~~~~~~~~~~

Land

Alfieri thought Italy and England the only countries worth living in; the former because there Nature vindicates her rights and triumphs over the evils inflicted by the governments; the latter because art conquers nature and transforms a rude, ungenial land into a paradise of comfort and plenty. England is a garden. Under an ash-colored sky, the fields have been combed and rolled till they appear to have been finished with a pencil instead of a plough. The solidity of the structures that compose the towns speaks the industry of ages. Nothing is left as it was made. Rivers, hills, valleys, the sea itself, feel the hand of a master. The long habitation of a powerful and ingenious race has turned every rood of land to its best use, has found all the capabilities, the arable soil, the quarriable rock, the highways, the byways, the fords, the navigable waters; and the new arts of intercourse meet you every where; so that England is a huge phalanstery, where all that man wants is provided within the precinct. Cushioned and comforted in every manner, the traveller rides as on a cannon-ball, high and low, over rivers and towns, through mountains in tunnels of three or four miles, at near twice the speed of our trains; and reads quietly the Times newspaper, which, by its immense correspondence and reporting seems to have machinized the rest of the world for his occasion.

The problem of the traveller landing at Liverpool is, Why England is England? What are the elements of that power which the English hold over other nations? If there be one test of national genius universally accepted, it is success; and if there be one successful country in the universe for the last millennium, that country is England.

A wise traveller will naturally choose to visit the best of actual nations; and an American has more reasons than another to draw him to Britain. In all that is done or begun by the Americans towards right thinking or practice, we are met by a civilization already settled and overpowering. The culture of the day, the thoughts and aims of men, are English thoughts and aims. A nation considerable for a thousand years since Egbert, it has, in the last centuries, obtained the ascendent, and stamped the knowledge, activity and power of mankind with its impress. Those who resist it do not feel it or obey it less. The Russian in his snows is aiming to be English. The Turk and Chinese also are making awkward efforts to be English. The practical common-sense of modern society, the utilitarian direction which labor, laws, opinion, religion take, is the natural genius of the British mind. The influence of France is a constituent of modern civility, but not enough opposed to the English for the most wholesome effect. The American is only the continuation of the English genius into new conditions, more or less propitious.

See what books fill our libraries. Every book we read, every biography, play, romance, in whatever form, is still English history and manners. So that a sensible Englishman once said to me, "As long as you do not grant us copyright, we shall have the teaching of you."

But we have the same difficulty in making a social or moral estimate of England, that the sheriff finds in drawing a jury to try some cause which has agitated the whole community and on which every body finds himself an interested party. Officers, jurors, judges have all taken sides. England has inoculated all nations with her civilization, intelligence and tastes; and to resist the tyranny and prepossession of the British element, a serious man must aid himself by comparing with it the civilizations of the farthest east and west, the old Greek, the Oriental, and, much more, the ideal standard; if only by means of the very impatience which English forms are sure to awaken in independent minds.

Besides, if we will visit London, the present time is the best time, as some signs portend that it has reached its highest point. It is observed tht the English interest us a little less within a few years; and hence the impression that the British power has culminated, is in solstice, or already declining.

As soon as you enter England, which, with Wales, is no larger than the State of Georgia, this little land stretches by an illusion to the dimensions of an empire. Add South Carolina, and you have more than an equivalent for the area of Scotland. The innumerable details, the crowded succession of towns, cities, cathedrals, castles and great and decorated estates, the number and power of the trades and guilds, the military strength and splendor, the multitudes of rich and of remarkable people, the servants and equipages,—all these catching the eye and never allowing it to pause, hide all boundaries by the impression of magnificence and endless wealth.

I reply to all the urgencies that refer me to this and that object indispensably to be seen,—Yes, to see England well needs a hundred years; for what they told me was the merit of Sir John Soane's Museum, in London,—that it was well packed and well saved,—is the merit of England;—it is stuffed full, in all corners and crevices, with towns, towers, churches, villas, palaces, hospitals and charity-houses. In the history of art it is a long way from a cromlech to York minster; yet all the intermediate steps may still be traced in this all-preserving island.

The territory has a singular perfection. The climate is warmer by many degrees than it is entitled to by latitude. Neither hot nor cold, there is no hour in the whole year when one cannot work. Here is no winter, but such days as we have in Massachusetts in November, a temperature which makes no exhausting demand on human strength, but allows the attainment of the largest stature. Charles the Second said, "It invited men abroad more days in the year and more hours in the day than another country." Then England has all the materials of a working country except wood. The constant rain—a rain with every tide, in some parts of the island—keeps its multitude of rivers full and brings agricultural production up to the highest point. It has plenty of water, of stone, of potter's clay, of coal, of salt and of iron. The land naturally abounds with game; immense heaths and downs are paved with quails, grouse and woodcock, and the shores are animated by water-birds. The rivers and the surrounding sea spawn with fish; there are salmon for the rich and sprats and herrings for the poor. In the northern lochs, the herring are in innumerable shoals; at one season, the country people say, the lakes contain one part water and two parts fish.

The only drawback on this industrial conveniency is the darkness of its sky. The night and day are too nearly of a color. It strains the eyes to read and to write. Add the coal smoke. In the manufacturing towns, the fine soot or *blacks* darken the day, give white sheep the color of black sheep, discolor the human saliva, contaminate the air, poison many plants and corrode the monuments and buildings.

The London fog aggravates the distempers of the sky, and sometimes justifies the epigram on the climate by an English wit, "in a fine day, looking up a chimney; in a foul day, looking down one." A gentleman in Liverpool told me that he found he could do without a fire in his parlor about one day in the year. It is however pretended that the enormous consumption of coal in the island is also felt in modifying the general climate.

Factitious climate, factitious position. England resembles a ship in its shape, and if it were one, its best admiral could not have worked it or anchored it in a more judicious or effective position. Sir John Herschel said, "London is the centre of the terrene globe." The shop-keeping nation, to use a shop word, has a *good stand.* The old

Venetians pleased themselves with the flattery that Venice was in 45°, midway between the poles and the line; as if that were an imperial centrality. Long of old, the Greeks fancied Delphi the navel of the earth, in their favorite mode of fabling the earth to be an animal. The Jews believed Jerusalem to be the centre. I have seen a kratometric chart designed to show that the city of Philadelphia was in the same thermic belt, and by inference in the same belt of empire, as the cities of Athens, Rome and London. It was drawn by a patriotic Philadelphian, and was examined with pleasure, under his showing, by the inhabitants of Chestnut Street. But when carried to Charleston, to New Orleans and to Boston, it somehow failed to convince the ingenious scholars of all those capitals.

But England is anchored at the side of Europe, and right in the heart of the modern world. The sea, which, according to Virgil's famous line, divided the poor Britons utterly from the world, proved to be the ring of marriage with all nations. It is not down in the books,—it is written only in the geologic strata,—that fortunate day when a wave of the German Ocean burst the old isthmus which joined Kent and Cornwall to France, and gave to this fragment of Europe its impregnable sea-wall, cutting off an island of eight hundred miles in length, with an irregular breadth reaching to three hundred miles; a territory large enough for independence, enriched with every seed of national power, so near that it can see the harvests of the continent, and so far that who would cross the strait must be an expert mariner, ready for tempests. As America, Europe and Asia lie, these Britons have precisely the best commercial position in the whole planet, and are sure of a market for all the goods they can manufacture. And to make these advantages avail, the river Thames must dig its spacious outlet to the sea from the heart of the kingdom, giving road and landing to innumerable ships, and all the conveniency to trade that a people so skilful and sufficient in economizing water-front by docks, warehouses and lighters required. When James the

First declared his purpose of punishing London by removing his Court, the Lord Mayor replied that "in removing his royal presence from his lieges, they hoped he would leave them the Thames."

In the variety of surface, Britain is a miniature of Europe, having plain, forest, marsh, river, seashore, mines in Cornwall; caves in Matlock and Derbyshire; delicious landscape in Dovedale, delicious sea-view at Tor Bay, Highlands in Scotland, Snowdon in Wales, and in Westmoreland and Cumberland a pocket Switzerland, in which the lakes and mountains are on a sufficient scale to fill the eye and touch the imagination. It is a nation conveniently small. Fontenelle thought that nature had sometimes a little affectation; and there is such an artificial completeness in this nation of artificers as if there were a design from the beginning to elaborate a bigger Birmingham. Nature held counsel with herself and said, 'My Romans are gone. To build my new empire, I will choose a rude race, all masculine, with brutish strength. I will not grudge a competition of the roughest males. Let buffalo gore buffalo, and the pasture to the strongest! For I have work that requires the best will and sinew. Sharp and temperate northern breezes shall blow, to keep that will alive and alert. The sea shall disjoin the people from others, and knit them to a fierce nationality. It shall give them markets on every side. Long time I will keep them on their feet, by poverty, border-wars, seafaring, sea-risks and the stimulus of gain. An island,—but not so large, the people not so many as to glut the great markets and depress one another, but proportioned to the size of Europe and the continents.'

With its fruits, and wares, and money, must its civil influence radiate. It is a singular coincidence to this geographic centrality, the spiritual centrality which Emanuel Swedenborg ascribes to the people. "For the English nation, the best of them are in the centre of all Christians, because they have interior intellectual light. This appears conspicuously in the spiritual world. This light they derive from the liberty of speaking and writing, and thereby of thinking."

Race

An ingenious anatomist has written a book to prove that races are imperishable, but nations are pliant political constructions, easily changed or destroyed. But this writer did not found his assumed races on any necessary law, disclosing their ideal or metaphysical necessity; nor did he on the other hand count with precision the existing races and settle the true bounds; a point of nicety, and the popular test of the theory. The individuals at the extremes of divergence in one race of men are as unlike as the wolf to the lapdog. Yet each variety shades down imperceptibly into the next, and you cannot draw the line where a race begins or ends. Hence every writer makes a different count. Blumenbach reckons five races; Humboldt three; and Mr. Pickering, who lately in our Exploring Expedition thinks he saw all the kinds of men that can be on the planet, makes eleven.

The British Empire is reckoned to contain (in 1848) 222,000,000 souls—perhaps a fifth of the population of the globe; and to comprise a territory of 5,000,000 square miles. So far have British people predominated. Perhaps forty of these millions are of British stock. Add the United States of America, which reckon (in the same year), exclusive of slaves, 20,000,000 of people, on a territory of 3,000,000 square miles, and in which the foreign element, however considerable, is rapidly assimilated, and you have a population of English descent and language of 60,000,000, and governing a population of 245,000,000 souls.

The British census proper reckons twenty-seven and a half millions in the home countries. What makes this census important is the quality of the units that compose it. They are free forcible men, in a country where life is safe and has reached the greatest value. They give the bias to the current age; and that, not by chance or by mass, but by their character and by the number of individuals among them of personal ability. It has been denied that the English have genius. Be it as it may, men of vast intellect have been born on their soil, and they have made or applied the principal inventions. They have sound bodies and supreme endurance in war and in labor. The spawning force of the race has sufficed to the colonization of great parts of the world; yet it remains to be seen whether they can make good the exodus of millions from Great Britain, amounting in 1852 to more than a thousand a day. They have assimilating force, since they are imitated by their foreign subjects; and they are still aggressive and propagandist, enlarging the dominion of their arts and liberty. Their laws are hospitable, and slavery does not exist under them. What oppression exists is incidental and temporary; their success is not sudden or fortunate, but they have maintained constancy and self-equality for many ages.

Is this power due to their race, or to some other cause? Men hear gladly of the power of blood or race. Every body likes to know that his advantages cannot be attributed to air, soil, sea, or to local wealth, as mines and quarries, nor to laws and traditions, nor to fortune; but to superior brain, as it makes the praise more personal to him.

We anticipate in the doctrine of race something like that law of physiology that whatever bone, muscle, or essential organ is found in one healthy individual, the same part or organ may be found in or near the same place in its congener; and we look to find in the son every mental and moral property that existed in the ancestor. In race, it is not the broad shoulders, or litheness, or stature that give advantage, but a symmetry that reaches as far as to the wit. Then the miracle and renown begin. Then first we care to examine the pedigree, and copy heedfully the training,—what food they ate, what nursing, school, and exercises they had, which resulted in this mother-wit, delicacy of thought and robust wisdom. How came such men as King Alfred, and Roger Bacon, William of Wykeham, Walter Raleigh, Philip Sidney, Isaac Newton, William Shakspeare, George Chapman, Francis Bacon, George Herbert, Henry Vane, to exist here? What made these delicate natures? was it the air? was it the sea? was it the parentage? For it is certain that these men are samples of their contemporaries. The hearing ear is always found close to the speaking tongue, and no genius can long or often utter any thing which is not invited and gladly entertained by men around him.

It is race, is it not, that puts the hundred millions of India under the dominion of a remote island in the north of Europe? Race avails much, if that be true which is alleged, that all Celts are Catholics and all Saxons are Protestants; that Celts love unity of power, and Saxons the representative principle. Race is a controlling influence in the Jew, who, for two millenniums, under every climate, has preserved the same character and employments. Race in the negro is of appalling importance. The French in Canada, cut off from all intercourse with the parent people, have held their national traits. I chanced to read Tacitus On the Manners of the Germans, not long since, in Missouri and the heart of Illinois, and I found abundant points of resemblance between the Germans of the Hercynian forest, and our *Hoosiers, Suckers* and *Badgers* of the American woods.

But whilst race works immortally to keep its own, it is resisted by other forces. Civilization is a re-agent, and eats away the old traits. The Arabs of to-day are the Arabs of Pharaoh; but the Briton of to-day is a very different person from Cassibelaunus or Ossian. Each religious sect has its physiognomy. The Methodists have acquired a face; the Quakers, a face; the nuns, a face. An Englishman will pick out a dissenter by his manners. Trades and professions carve their own lines on face and form. Certain circumstances of English life are not less effective; as personal liberty; plenty of food; good ale and mutton;

open market, or good wages for every kind of labor; high bribes to talent and skill; the island life, or the million opportunities and outlets for expanding and misplaced talent; readiness of combination among themselves for politics or for business; strikes; and sense of superiority founded on habit of victory in labor and in war: and the appetite for superiority grows by feeding.

It is easy to add to the counteracting forces to race. Credence is a main element. 'T is said that the views of nature held by any people determine all their institutions. Whatever influences add to mental or moral faculty, take men out of nationality as out of other conditions, and make the national life a culpable compromise.

These limitations of the formidable doctrine of race suggest others which threaten to undermine it, as not sufficiently based. The fixity or inconvertibleness of races as we see them is a weak argument for the eternity of these frail boundaries, since all our historical period is a point to the duration in which nature has wrought. Any the least and solitariest fact in our natural history, such as the melioration of fruits and of animal stocks, has the worth of a *power* in the opportunity of geologic periods. Moreover, though we flatter the self-love of men and nations by the legend of pure races, all our experience is of the gradation and resolution of races, and strange resemblances meet us everywhere. It need not puzzle us that Malay and Papuan, Celt and Roman, Saxon and Tartar should mix, when we see the rudiments of tiger and baboon in our human form, and know that the barriers of races are not so firm but that some spray sprinkles us from the antediluvian seas.

The low organizations are simplest; a mere mouth, a jelly, or a straight worm. As the scale mounts, the organizations become complex. We are piqued with pure descent, but nature loves inoculation. A child blends in his face the faces of both parents and some feature from every ancestor whose face hangs on the wall. The best nations are those most widely related; and navigation, as effecting a world-wide mixture, is the most potent advancer of nations.

The English composite character betrays a mixed origin. Everything English is a fusion of distant and antagonistic elements. The language is mixed; the names of men are of different nations,—three languages, three or four nations;—the currents of thought are counter: contemplation and practical skill; active intellect and dead conservatism; world-wide enterprise and devoted use and wont; aggressive freedom and hospitable law with bitter class-legislation; a people scattered by their wars and affairs over the face of the whole earth, and homesick to a man; a country of extremes,—dukes and chartists, Bishops of Durham and naked heathen colliers;—nothing can be praised in it without damning exceptions, and nothing denounced without salvos of cordial praise.

Neither do this people appear to be of one stem, but collectively a better race than any from which they are derived. Nor is it easy to trace it home to its original seats. Who can call by right names what races are in Britain? Who can trace them historically? Who can discriminate them anatomically, or metaphysically?

In the impossibility of arriving at satisfaction on the historical question of race, and—come of whatever disputable ancestry—the indisputable Englishman before me, himself very well marked, and nowhere else to be found,—I fancied I could leave quite aside the choice of a tribe as his lineal progenitors. Defoe said in his wrath, "the Englishman was the mud of all races." I incline to the belief that, as water, lime and sand make mortar, so certain temperaments marry well, and, by well-managed contrarieties, develop as drastic a character as the English. On the whole it is not so much a history of one or of certain tribes of Saxons, Jutes, or Frisians, coming from one place and genetically identical, as it is an anthology of temperaments out of them all. Certain temperaments suit the sky and soil of England, say eight or ten or twenty varieties, as, out of a hundred pear-trees, eight or ten suit the soil of an orchard and thrive,—whilst all the unadapted temperaments die out.

The English derive their pedigree from such a range of nationalities that there needs sea-room and land-room to unfold the varieties of talent and character. Perhaps the ocean serves as a galvanic battery, to distribute acids at one pole and alkalies at the other. So England tends to accumulate her liberals in America, and her conservatives at London. The Scandinavians in her race still hear in every age the murmurs of their mother, the ocean; the Briton in the blood hugs the homestead still.

Again, as if to intensate the influences that are not of race, what we think of when we talk of English traits really narrows itself to a small district. It excludes Ireland and Scotland and Wales, and reduces itself at last to London, that is, to those who come and go thither. The portraits that hang on the walls in the Academy Exhibition at London, the figures in Punch's drawings of the public men or of the club-houses, the prints in the shop-windows, are distinctive English, and not American, no, nor Scotch, nor Irish: but 't is a very restricted nationality. As you go north into the manufacturing and agricultural districts, and to the population that never travels; as you go into Yorkshire, as you enter Scotland, the world's Englishman is no longer found. In Scotland there is a rapid loss of all grandeur of mien and manners; a provincial eagerness and acuteness appear; the poverty of the country makes itself remarked, and a coarseness of manners; and, among the intellectual, is the insanity of dialectics. In Ireland are the same climate and soil as in England, but less food, no right relation to the land, political dependence, small tenantry and an inferior or misplaced race.

These queries concerning ancestry and blood may be well allowed, for there is no prosperity that seems more to depend on the kind of man than British prosperity. Only a hardy and wise people could have made this small territory great. We say, in a regatta or yacht-race, that if the boats are anywhere nearly matched, it is the man that wins. Put the best sailing-master into either boat, and he will win.

Yet it is fine for us to speculate in face of unbroken traditions, though vague and losing themselves in fable. The traditions have got footing, and refuse to be disturbed. The kitchen-clock is more convenient than sidereal time. We must use the popular category, as we do the Linnæan classification, for convenience, and not as exact and final. Otherwise we are presently confounded when the best-settled traits of one race are claimed by some new ethnologist as precisely characteristic of the rival tribe.

I found plenty of well-marked English types, the ruddy complexion fair and plump, robust men, with faces cut like a die, and a strong island speech and accent; a Norman type, with the complacency that belongs to that constitution. Others who might be Americans, for any thing that appeared in their complexion or form; and their speech was much less marked and their thought much less bound. We will call them Saxons. Then the Roman has implanted his dark complexion in the trinity or quaternity of bloods.

1. The sources from which tradition derives their stock are mainly three. And first they are of the oldest blood of the world,—the Celtic. Some peoples are deciduous or transitory. Where are the Greeks? Where the Etrurians? Where the Romans? But the Celts or Sidonides are an old family, of whose beginning there is no memory, and their end is likely to be still more remote in the future; for they have endurance and productiveness. They planted Britain, and gave to the seas and mountains names which are poems and imitate the pure voices of nature. They are favorably remembered in the oldest records of Europe. They had no violent feudal tenure, but the husbandman owned the land. They had an alphabet, astronomy, priestly culture and a sublime creed. They have a hidden

and precarious genius. They made the best popular literature of the Middle Ages in the songs of Merlin and the tender and delicious mythology of Arthur.

2. The English come mainly from the Germans, whom the Romans found hard to conquer in two hundred and ten years,—say impossible to conquer, when one remembers the long sequel;—a people about whom in the old empire the rumor ran there was never any that meddled with them that repented it not.

3. Charlemagne, halting one day in a town of Narbonnese Gaul, looked out of a window and saw a fleet of Northmen cruising in the Mediterranean. They even entered the port of the town where he was, causing no small alarm and sudden manning and arming of his galleys. As they put out to sea again, the emperor gazed long after them, his eyes bathed in tears. "I am tormented with sorrow," he said, "when I foresee the evils they will bring on my posterity." There was reason for these Xerxes' tears. The men who have built a ship and invented the rig, cordage, sail, compass and pump; the working in and out of port, have acquired much more than a ship. Now arm them and every shore is at their mercy. For if they have not numerical superiority where they anchor, they have only to sail a mile or two to find it. Bonaparte's art of war, namely of concentrating force on the point of attack, must always be theirs who have the choice of the battle-ground. Of course they come into the fight from a higher ground of power than the land-nations; and can engage them on shore with a victorious advantage in the retreat. As soon as the shores are sufficiently peopled to make piracy a losing business, the same skill and courage are ready for the service of trade.

The Heimskringla, or Sagas of the Kings of Norway, collected by Snorro Sturleson, is the Iliad and Odyssey of English history. Its portraits, like Homer's, are strongly individualized. The Sagas describe a monarchical republic like Sparta. The government disappears before the importance of citizens. In Norway, no Persian masses fight and perish to aggrandize a king, but the actors are bonders or landholders, every one of whom is named and personally and patronymically described, as the king's friend and companion. A sparse population gives this high worth to every man. Individuals are often noticed as very handsome persons, which trait only brings the story nearer to the English race. Then the solid material interest predominates, so dear to English understanding, wherein the association is logical, between merit and land. The heroes of the Sagas are not the knights of South Europe. No vaporing of France and Spain has corrupted them. They are substantial farmers whom the rough times have forced to defend their properties. They have weapons which they use in a determined manner, by no means for chivalry, but for their acres. They are people considerably advanced in rural arts, living amphibiously on a rough coast, and drawing half their food from the sea and half from the land. They have herds of cows, and malt, wheat, bacon, butter and cheese. They fish in the fiord and hunt the deer. A king among these farmers has a varying power, sometimes not exceeding the authority of a sheriff. A king was maintained, much as in some of our country districts a winter-schoolmaster is quartered, a week here, a week there, and a fortnight on the next farm,—on all the farms in rotation. This the king calls going into guest-quarters; and it was the only way in which, in a poor country, a poor king with many retainers could be kept alive when he leaves his own farm to collect his dues through the kingdom.

These Norsemen are excellent persons in the main, with good sense, steadiness, wise speech and prompt action. But they have a singular turn for homicide; their chief end of man is to murder or to be murdered; oars, scythes, harpoons, crowbars, peat-knives and hay-forks are tools valued by them all the more for their charming aptitude for assassinations. A pair of kings, after dinner, will divert themselves by thrusting each his sword through the other's body, as did Yngve and Alf. Another pair ride out on a morning for a frolic, and finding no weapon near, will take the bits out of their horses' mouths and crush each other's heads with them, as did Alric and Eric. The sight of a tent-cord or a cloak-string puts them on hanging somebody, a wife, or a husband, or, best of all, a king. If a farmer has so much as a hay-fork, he sticks it into a King Dag. King Ingiald finds it vastly amusing to burn up half a dozen kings in a hall, after getting them drunk. Never was poor gentleman so surfeited with life, so furious to be rid of it, as the Northman. If he cannot pick any other quarrel, he will get himself comfortably gored by a bull's horns, like Egil, or slain by a land-slide, like the agricultural King Onund. Odin died in his bed, in Sweden; but it was a proverb of ill condition to die the death of old age. King Hake of Sweden cuts and slashes in battle, as long as he can stand, then orders his war-ship, loaded with his dead men and their weapons, to be taken out to sea, the tiller shipped and the sails spread; being left alone he sets fire to some tar-wood and lies down contented on deck. The wind blew off the land, the ship flew, burning in clear flame, out between the islets into the ocean, and there was the right end of King Hake.

The early Sagas are sanguinary and piratical; the later are of a noble strain. History rarely yields us better passages than the conversation between King Sigurd the Crusader and King Eystein his brother, on their respective merits,—one the soldier, and the other a lover of the arts of peace.

But the reader of the Norman history must steel himself by holding fast the remote compensations which result from animal vigor. As the old fossil world shows that the first steps of reducing the chaos were confided to saurians and other huge and horrible animals, so the foundations of the new civility were to be laid by the most savage men.

The Normans came out of France into England worse men than they went into it one hundred and sixty years before. They had lost their own language and learned the

Romance or barbarous Latin of the Gauls, and had acquired, with the language, all the vices it had names for. The conquest has obtained in the chronicles the name of the "memory of sorrow." Twenty thousand thieves landed at Hastings. These founders of the House of Lords were greedy and ferocious dragoons, sons of greedy and ferocious pirates. They were all alike, they took everything they could carry, they burned, harried, violated, tortured and killed, until everything English was brought to the verge of ruin. Such however is the illusion of antiquity and wealth, that decent and dignified men now existing boast their descent from these filthy thieves, who showed a far juster conviction of their own merits, by assuming for their types the swine, goat, jackal, leopard, wolf and snake, which they severally resembled.

England yielded to the Danes and Northmen in the tenth and eleventh centuries, and was the receptacle into which all the mettle of that strenuous population was poured. The continued draught of the best men in Norway, Sweden and Denmark to these piratical expeditions exhausted those countries, like a tree which bears much fruit when young, and these have been second-rate powers ever since. The power of the race migrated and left Norway void. King Olaf said, "When King Harold, my father, went westward to England, the chosen men in Norway followed him; but Norway was so emptied then, that such men have not since been to find in the country, nor especially such a leader as King Harold was for wisdom and bravery."

It was a tardy recoil of these invasions, when, in 1801, the British government sent Nelson to bombard the Danish forts in the Sound, and, in 1807, Lord Cathcart, at Copenhagen, took the entire Danish fleet, as it lay in the basins, and all the equipments from the Arsenal, and carried them to England. Konghelle, the town where the kings of Norway, Sweden and Denmark were wont to meet, is now rented to a private English gentleman for a hunting ground.

It took many generations to trim and comb and perfume the first boat-load of Norse pirates into royal highnesses and most noble Knights of the Garter; but every sparkle of ornament dates back to the Norse boat. There will be time enough to mellow this strength into civility and religion. It is a medical fact that the children of the blind see; the children of felons have a healthy conscience. Many a mean, dastardly boy is, at the age of puberty, transformed into a serious and generous youth.

The mildness of the following ages has not quite effaced these traits of Odin; as the rudiment of a structure matured in the tiger is said to be still found unabsorbed in the Caucasian man. The nation has a tough, acrid, animal nature, which centuries of churching and civilizing have not been able to sweeten. Alfieri said "the crimes of Italy were the proof of the superiority of the stock;" and one may say of England that this watch moves on a splinter of adamant. The English uncultured are a brutal nation. The crimes recorded in their calendars leave nothing to be desired in the way of cold malignity. Dear to the English heart is a fair stand-up fight. The brutality of the manners in the lower class appears in the boxing, bear-baiting, cock-fighting, love of executions, and in the readiness for a set-to in the streets, delightful to the English of all classes. The coster-mongers of London streets hold cowardice in loathing:—"we must work our fists well; we are all handy with our fists." The public schools are charged with being bear-gardens of brutal strength, and are liked by the people for that cause. The fagging is a trait of the same quality. Medwin, in the Life of Shelley, relates that at a military school they rolled up a young man in a snowball, and left him so in his room while the other cadets went to church;—and crippled him for life. They have retained impressment, deck-flogging, army-flogging and school-flogging. Such is the ferocity of the army discipline that a soldier, sentenced to flogging, sometimes prays that his sentence may be commuted to death. Flogging, banished from the armies of Western Europe, remains here by the sanction of the Duke of Wellington. The right of the husband to sell the wife has been retained down to our times. The Jews have been the favorite victims of royal and popular persecution. Henry III. mortgaged all the Jews in the kingdom to his brother the Earl of Cornwall, as security for money which he borrowed. The torture of criminals, and the rack for extorting evidence, were slowly disused. Of the criminal statutes, Sir Samuel Romilly said, "I have examined the codes of all nations, and ours is the worst, and worthy of the Anthropophagi." In the last session (1848), the House of Commons was listening to the details of flogging and torture practised in the jails.

As soon as this land, thus geographically posted, got a hardy people into it, they could not help becoming the sailors and factors of the globe. From childhood, they dabbled in water, they swam like fishes, their playthings were boats. In the case of the ship-money, the judges delivered it for law, that "England being an island, the very midland shires therein are all to be accounted maritime;" and Fuller adds, "the genius even of landlocked counties driving the natives with a maritime dexterity." As early as the conquest it is remarked, in explanation of the wealth of England, that its merchants trade to all countries.

The English at the present day have great vigor of body and endurance. Other countrymen look slight and undersized beside them, and invalids. They are bigger men than the Americans. I suppose a hundred English taken at random out of the street would weigh a fourth more than so many Americans. Yet, I am told, the skeleton is not larger. They are round, ruddy and handsome; at least the whole bust is well formed, and there is a tendency to stout and powerful frames. I remarked the stoutness on my first landing at Liverpool; porter, drayman, coachman, guard,—what substantial, respectable, grandfatherly figures, with costume and manners to suit. The American has arrived at the old mansion-house and finds himself among uncles, aunts and grandsires. The pictures on the chimney-tiles of his nursery were pictures of these people.

Here they are in the identical costumes and air which so took him.

It is the fault of their forms that they grow stocky, and the women have that disadvantage,—few tall, slender figures of flowing shape, but stunted and thickset persons. The French say that the Englishwomen have two left hands. But in all ages they are a handsome race. The bronze monuments of crusaders lying cross-legged in the Temple Church at London, and those in Worcester and in Salisbury cathedrals, which are seven hundred years old, are of the same type as the best youthful heads of men now in England;—please by beauty of the same character, an expression blending good-nature, valor and refinement, and mainly by that uncorrupt youth in the face of manhood, which is daily seen in the streets of London.

Both branches of the Scandinavian race are distinguished for beauty. The anecdote of the handsome captives which Saint Gregory found at Rome, A.D. 600, is matched by the testimony of the Norman chroniclers, five centuries later, who wondered at the beauty and long flowing hair of the young English captives. Meantime the Heimskringla has frequent occasion to speak of the personal beauty of its heroes. When it is considered what humanity, what resources of mental and moral power the traits of the blonde race betoken, its accession to empire marks a new and finer epoch, wherein the old mineral force shall be subjugated at last by humanity and shall plough in its furrow henceforward. It is not a final race, once a crab always crab,—but a race with a future.

On the English face are combined decision and nerve with the fair complexion, blue eyes and open and florid aspect. Hence the love of truth, hence the sensibility, the fine perception and poetic construction. The fair Saxon man, with open front and honest meaning, domestic, affectionate, is not the wood out of which cannibal, or inquisitor, or assassin is made, but he is moulded for law, lawful trade, civility, marriage, the nurture of children, for colleges, churches, charities and colonies.

They are rather manly than warlike. When the war is over, the mask falls from the affectionate and domestic tastes, which make them women in kindness. This union of qualities is fabled in their national legend of "Beauty and the Beast," or, long before, in the Greek legend of Hermaphrodite. The two sexes are co-present in the English mind. I apply to Britannia, queen of seas and colonies, the words in which her latest novelist portrays his heroine; "She is as mild as she is game, and as game as she is mild." The English delight in the antagonism which combines in one person the extremes of courage and tenderness. Nelson, dying at Trafalgar, sends his love to Lord Collingwood, and like an innocent schoolboy that goes to bed, says "Kiss me, Hardy," and turns to sleep. Lord Collingwood, his comrade, was of a nature the most affectionate and domestic. Admiral Rodney's figure approached to delicacy and effeminacy, and he declared himself very sensible to fear, which he surmounted only by considerations of honor and public duty. Clarendon says the Duke of Buckingham was so modest and gentle, that some courtiers attempted to put affronts on him, until they found that this modesty and effeminacy was only a mask for the most terrible determination. And Sir Edward Parry said of Sir John Franklin, that "if he found Wellington Sound open, he explored it; for he was a man who never turned his back on a danger, yet of that tenderness that he would not brush away a mosquito." Even for their highwaymen the same virtue is claimed, and Robin Hood comes described to us as *mitissimus prædonum;* the gentlest thief. But they know where their war-dogs lie. Cromwell, Blake, Marlborough, Chatham, Nelson and Wellington are not to be trifled with, and the brutal strength which lies at the bottom of society, the animal ferocity of the quays and cockpits, the bullies of the costermongers of Shoreditch, Seven Dials and Spitalfields, they know how to wake up.

They have a vigorous health and last well into middle and old age. The old men are as red as roses, and still handsome. A clear skin, a peach-bloom complexion and good teeth are found all over the island. They use a plentiful and nutritious diet. The operative cannot subsist on water-cresses. Beef, mutton, wheat-bread and malt-liquors are universal among the first-class laborers. Good feeding is a chief point of national pride among the vulgar, and in their caricatures they represent the Frenchman as a poor, starved body. It is curious that Tacitus found the English beer already in use among the Germans: "They make from barley or wheat a drink corrupted into some resemblance to wine." Lord Chief Justice Fortescue, in Henry VI.'s time, says, "The inhabitants of England drink no water, unless at certain times on a religious score and by way of penance." The extremes of poverty and ascetic penance, it would seem, never reach cold water in England. Wood the antiquary, in describing the poverty and maceration of Father Lacey, an English Jesuit, does not deny him beer. He says, "His bed was under a thatching, and the way to it up a ladder; his fare was coarse; his drink, of a penny a gawn, or gallon."

They have more constitutional energy than any other people. They think, with Henri Quatre, that manly exercises are the foundation of that elevation of mind which gives one nature ascendant over another; or with the Arabs, that the days spent in the chase are not counted in the length of life. They box, run, shoot, ride, row, and sail from pole to pole. They eat and drink, and live jolly in the open air, putting a bar of solid sleep between day and day. They walk and ride as fast as they can, their head bent forward, as if urged on some pressing affair. The French say that Englishmen in the street always walk straight before them like mad dogs. Men and women walk with infatuation. As soon as he can handle a gun, hunting is the fine art of every Englishman of condition. They are the most voracious people of prey that ever existed. Every season turns out the aristocracy into the country to shoot and fish. The more vigorous run out of the island to America, to Asia, to Africa and Australia, to hunt with fury by gun, by trap, by harpoon, by lasso, with dog, with horse, with elephant or with dromedary, all the game that is in nature. These men have written the game-books of all countries, as Hawker, Scrope, Murray, Herbert, Maxwell, Cumming and a host of travellers. The people at home are addicted to boxing, running, leaping and rowing matches.

I suppose the dogs and horses must be thanked for the fact that the men have muscles almost as tough and supple as their own. If in every efficient man there is first a fine animal, in the English race it is of the best breed, a wealthy, juicy, broad-chested creature, steeped in ale and good cheer and a little overloaded by his flesh. Men of animal nature rely, like animals, on their instincts. The Englishman associates well with dogs and horses. His attachment to the horse arises from the courage and address required to manage it. The horse finds out who is afraid of it, and does not disguise its opinion. Their young boiling clerks and lusty collegians like the company of horses better than the company of professors. I suppose the horses are better company for them. The horse has more uses than Buffon noted. If you go into the streets, every driver in 'bus or dray is a bully, and if I wanted a good troop of soldiers, I should recruit among the stables. Add a certain degree of refinement to the vivacity of these riders, and you obtain the precise quality which makes the men and women of polite society formidable.

They come honestly by their horsemanship, with *Hengst* and *Horsa* for their Saxon founders. The other branch of their race had been Tartar nomads. The horse was all their wealth. The children were fed on mares' milk. The pastures of Tartary were still remembered by the tenacious practice of the Norsemen to eat horseflesh at religious feasts. In the Danish invasions the marauders seized upon horses where they landed, and were at once converted into a body of expert cavalry.

At one time this skill seems to have declined. Two centuries ago the English horse never performed any eminent service beyond the seas; and the reason assigned was that the genius of the English hath always more inclined them to foot-service, as pure and proper manhood, without any mixture; whilst in a victory on horseback, the credit ought to be divided betwixt the man and his horse. But in two hundred years a change has taken place. Now, they boast that they understand horses better than any other people in the world, and that their horses are become their second selves.

"William the Conqueror being," says Camden, "better affected to beasts than to men, imposed heavy fines and punishments on those that should meddle with his game." The Saxon Chronicle says "he loved the tall deer as if he were their father." And rich Englishmen have followed his example, according to their ability, ever since, in encroaching on the tillage and commons with their game-preserves. It is a proverb in England that it is safer to shoot a man than a hare. The severity of the game-laws certainly indicates an extravagant sympathy of the nation with horses and hunters. The gentlemen are always on horseback, and have brought horses to an ideal perfection; the English racer is a factitious breed. A score or two of mounted gentlemen may frequently be seen running like centaurs down a hill nearly as steep as the roof of a house. Every inn-room is lined with pictures of races; telegraphs communicate, every hour, tidings of the heats from Newmarket and Ascot; and the House of Commons adjourns over the "Derby Day."

Ability

The Saxon and the Northman are both Scandinavians. History does not allow us to fix the limits of the application of these names with any accuracy, but from the residence of a portion of these people in France, and from some effect of that powerful soil on their blood and manners, the Norman has come popularly to represent in England the aristocratic, and the Saxon the democratic principle. And though, I doubt not, the nobles are of both tribes, and the workers of both, yet we are forced to use the names a little mythically, one to represent the worker and the other the enjoyer.

The island was a prize for the best race. Each of the dominant races tried its fortune in turn. The Phœnician, the Celt and the Goth had already got in. The Roman came, but in the very day when his fortune culminated. He looked in the eyes of a new people that was to supplant his own. He disembarked his legions, erected his camps and towers,—presently he heard bad news from Italy, and worse and worse, every year; at last, he made a handsome compliment of roads and walls, and departed. But the Saxon seriously settled in the land, builded, tilled, fished and traded, with German truth and adhesiveness. The Dane came and divided with him. Last of all the Norman or French-Dane arrived, and formally conquered, harried and ruled the kingdom. A century later it came out that the Saxon had the most bottom and longevity, had managed to make the victor speak the language and accept the law and usage of the victim; forced the baron to dictate Saxon terms to Norman kings; and, step by step, got all the essential securities of civil liberty invented and confirmed. The genius of the race and the genius of the place conspired to this effect. The island is lucrative to free labor, but not worth possession on other terms. The race was so intellectual that a feudal or military tenure could not last longer than the war. The power of the Saxon-Danes, so thoroughly beaten in the war that the name of English and villein were synonymous, yet so vivacious as to extort charters from the kings, stood on the strong personality of these people. Sense and economy must rule in a world which is made of sense and economy, and the banker, with his seven per cent., drives the earl out of his castle. A nobility of soldiers cannot keep down a commonalty of shrewd scientific persons. What signifies a pedigree of a hundred links, against a cotton-spinner with steam in his mill; or against a company of broad-shouldered Liverpool merchants, for whom Stephenson and

Brunel are contriving locomotives and a tubular bridge?

These Saxons are the hands of mankind. They have the taste for toil, a distaste for pleasure or repose, and the telescopic appreciation of distant gain. They are the wealth-makers,—and by dint of mental faculty which has its own conditions. The Saxon works after liking, or only for himself; and to set him at work and to begin to draw his monstrous values out of barren Britain, all dishonor, fret and barrier must be removed, and then his energies begin to play.

The Scandinavian fancied himself surrounded by Trolls,—a kind of goblin men with vast power of work and skilful production,—divine stevedores, carpenters, reapers, smiths and masons, swift to reward every kindness done them, with gifts of gold and silver. In all English history this dream comes to pass. Certain Trolls or working brains, under the names of Alfred, Bede, Caxton, Bracton, Camden, Drake, Selden, Dugdale, Newton, Gibbon, Brindley, Watt, Wedgwood, dwell in the troll-mounts of Britain and turn the sweat of their face to power and renown.

If the race is good, so is the place. Nobody landed on this spellbound island with impunity. The enchantments of barren shingle and rough weather transformed every adventurer into a laborer. Each vagabond that arrived bent his neck to the yoke of gain, or found the air too tense for him. The strong survived, the weaker went to the ground. Even the pleasure-hunters and sots of England are of a tougher texture. A hard temperament had been formed by Saxon and Saxon-Dane, and such of these French or Normans as could reach it were naturalized in every sense.

All the admirable expedients or means hit upon in England must be looked at as growths or irresistible off-shoots of the expanding mind of the race. A man of that brain thinks and acts thus; and his neighbor, being afflicted with the same kind of brain, though he is rich and called a baron or a duke, thinks the same thing, and is

ready to allow the justice of the thought and act in his re-
tainer or tenant, though sorely against his baronial or
ducal will.

The island was renowned in antiquity for its breed of
mastiffs, so fierce that when their teeth were set you must
cut their heads off to part them. The man was like his dog.
The people have that nervous bilious temperament which
is known by medical men to resist every means employed
to make its possessor subservient to the will of others. The
English game is main force to main force, the planting of
foot to foot, fair play and open field,—a rough tug without
trick or dodging, till one or both come to pieces. King
Ethelwald spoke the language of his race when he planted
himself at Wimborne and said he "would do one of two
things, or there live, or there lie." They hate craft and subtlety. They neither poison, nor waylay, nor assassinate;
and when they have pounded each other to a poultice,
they will shake hands and be friends for the remainder of
their lives.

You shall trace these Gothic touches at school, at country fairs, at the hustings and in parliament. No artifice, no
breach of truth and plain dealing,—not so much as secret
ballot, is suffered in the island. In parliament, the tactics of
the opposition is to resist every step of the government by
a pitiless attack: and in a bargain, no prospect of advantage
is so dear to the merchant as the thought of being tricked
is mortifying.

Sir Kenelm Digby, a courtier of Charles and James,
who won the sea-fight of Scanderoon, was a model
Englishman in his day. "His person was handsome and
gigantic, he had so graceful elocution and noble address,
that, had he been dropt out of the clouds in any part of the
world, he would have made himself respected: he was
skilled in six tongues, and master of arts and arms." Sir
Kenelm wrote a book, *Of Bodies and of Souls*, in which he
propounds, that "syllogisms do breed, or rather are all the
variety of man's life. They are the steps by which we walk
in all our businesses. Man, as he is man, doth nothing else

but weave such chains. Whatsoever he doth, swarving from this work, he doth as deficient from the nature of man: and, if he do aught beyond this, by breaking out into divers sorts of exterior actions, he findeth, nevertheless, in this linked sequel of simple discourses, the art, the cause, the rule, the bounds and the model of it."

There spoke the genius of the English people. There is a necessity on them to be logical. They would hardly greet the good that did not logically fall,—as if it excluded their own merit, or shook their understandings. They are jealous of minds that have much facility of association, from an instinctive fear that the seeing many relations to their thought might impair this serial continuity and lucrative concentration. They are impatient of genius, or of minds addicted to contemplation, and cannot conceal their contempt for sallies of thought, however lawful, whose steps they cannot count by their wonted rule. Neither do they reckon better a syllogism that ends in syllogism. For they have a supreme eye to facts, and theirs is a logic that brings salt to soup, hammer to nail, oar to boat; the logic of cooks, carpenters and chemists, following the sequence of nature, and one on which words make no impression. Their mind is not dazzled by its own means, but locked and bolted to results. They love men who, like Samuel Johnson, a doctor in the schools, would jump out of his syllogism the instant his major proposition was in danger, to save that at all hazards. Their practical vision is spacious, and they can hold many threads without entangling them. All the steps they orderly take; but with the high logic of never confounding the minor and major proposition; keeping their eye on their aim, in all the complicity and delay incident to the several series of means they employ. There is room in their minds for this and that,—a science of degrees. In the courts the independence of the judges and the loyalty of the suitors are equally excellent. In parliament they have hit on that capital invention of freedom, a constitutional opposition. And when courts and parliament are both deaf, the plaintiff is not silenced.

Calm, patient, his weapon of defence from year to year is the obstinate reproduction of the grievance, with calculations and estimates. But, meantime, he is drawing numbers and money to his opinion, resolved that if all remedy fails, right of revolution is at the bottom of his charter-box. They are bound to see their measure carried, and stick to it through ages of defeat.

Into this English logic, however, an infusion of justice enters, not so apparent in other races;—a belief in the existence of two sides, and the resolution to see fair play. There is on every question an appeal from the assertion of the parties to the proof of what is asserted. They kiss the dust before a fact. Is it a machine, is it a charter, is it a boxer in the ring, is it a candidate on the hustings,—the universe of Englishmen will suspend their judgment until the trial can be had. They are not to be led by a phrase, they want a working plan, a working machine, a working constitution, and will sit out the trial and abide by the issue and reject all preconceived theories. In politics they put blunt questions, which must be answered; Who is to pay the taxes? What will you do for trade? What for corn? What for the spinner?

This singular fairness and its results strike the French with surprise. Philip de Commines says, "Now, in my opinion, among all the sovereignties I know in the world, that in which the public good is best attended to, and the least violence exercised on the people, is that of England." Life is safe, and personal rights; and what is freedom without security? whilst, in France, "fraternity," "equality," and "indivisible unity" are names for assassination. Montesquieu said, "England is the freest country in the world. If a man in England had as many enemies as hairs on his head, no harm would happen to him."

Their self-respect, their faith in causation, and their realistic logic or coupling of means to ends, have given them the leadership of the modern world. Montesquieu said, "No people have true common-sense but those who are born in England." This common-sense is a perception of all the conditions of our earthly existence; of laws that can be stated, and of laws that cannot be stated, or that are learned only by practice, in which allowance for friction is made. They are impious in their skepticism of theory, and in high departments they are cramped and sterile. But the unconditional surrender to facts, and the choice of means to reach their ends, are as admirable as with ants and bees.

The bias of the nation is a passion for utility. They love the lever, the screw and pulley, the Flanders draught-horse, the waterfall, wind-mills, tide-mills; the sea and the wind to bear their freight ships. More than the diamond Koh-i-noor, which glitters among their crown jewels, they prize that dull pebble which is wiser than a man, whose poles turn themselves to the poles of the world, and whose axis is parallel to the axis of the world. Now, their toys are steam and galvanism. They are heavy at the fine arts, but adroit at the coarse; not good in jewelry or mosaics, but the best iron-masters, colliers, wool-combers and tanners in Europe. They apply themselves to agriculture, to draining, to resisting encroachments of sea, wind, travel-ling sands, cold and wet sub-soil; to fishery, to manufac-ture of indispensable staples,—salt, plumbago, leather, wool, glass, pottery and brick,—to bees and silkworms;—and by their steady combinations they succeed. A manu-facturer sits down to dinner in a suit of clothes which was wool on a sheep's back at sunrise. You dine with a gentle-man on venison, pheasant, quail, pigeons, poultry, mush-rooms and pine-apples, all the growth of his estate. They are neat husbands for ordering all their tools pertaining to house and field. All are well kept. There is no want and no waste. They study use and fitness in their building, in the order of their dwellings and in their dress. The French-man invented the ruffle; the Englishman added the shirt. The Englishman wears a sensible coat buttoned to the chin, of rough but solid and lasting texture. If he is a lord, he dresses a little worse than a commoner. They have dif-fused the taste for plain substantial hats, shoes and coats through Europe. They think him the best dressed man whose dress is so fit for his use that you cannot notice or remember to describe it.

They secure the essentials in their diet, in their arts and manufactures. Every article of cutlery shows, in its shape, thought and long experience of workmen. They put the expense in the right place, as, in their sea-steamers, in the solidity of the machinery and the strength of the boat. The admirable equipment of their arctic ships carries London to the pole. They build roads, aqueducts; warm and ventilate houses. And they have impressed their directness and practical habit on modern civilization.

In trade, the Englishman believes that nobody breaks who ought not to break; and that if he do not make trade everything, it will make him nothing; and acts on this belief. The spirit of system, attention to details, and the subordination of details, or the not driving things too finely (which is charged on the Germans), constitute that dispatch of business which makes the mercantile power of England.

In war, the Englishman looks to his means. He is of the opinion of Civilis, his German ancestor, whom Tacitus reports as holding that "the gods are on the side of the strongest;"—a sentence which Bonaparte unconsciously translated, when he said that "he had noticed that Providence always favored the heaviest battalion." Their military science propounds that if the weight of the advancing column is greater than that of the resisting, the latter is destroyed. Therefore Wellington, when he came to the army in Spain, had every man weighed, first with accoutrements, and then without; believing that the force of an army depended on the weight and power of the individual soldiers, in spite of cannon. Lord Palmerston told the House of Commons that more care is taken of the health and comfort of English troops than of any other troops in the world; and that hence the English can put more men into the rank, on the day of action, on the field of battle, than any other army. Before the bombardment of the Danish forts in the Baltic, Nelson spent day after day, himself, in the boats, on the exhausting service of sounding the channel. Clerk of Eldin's celebrated manoeuvre of breaking the line of sea-battle, and Nelson's feat of *doubling*, or stationing his ships one on the outer bow, and another on the outer quarter of each of the enemy's, were only translations into naval tactics of Bonaparte's rule of concentration. Lord Collingwood was accustomed to tell his men that if they could fire three well-directed broadsides in five minutes, no vessel could resist them; and from constant practice they came to do it in three minutes and a half.

But conscious that no race of better men exists, they rely most on the simplest means, and do not like ponderous and difficult tactics, but delight to bring the affair hand to hand; where the victory lies with the strength, courage and endurance of the individual combatants. They adopt every improvement in rig, in motor, in weapons, but they fundamentally believe that the best stratagem in naval war is to lay your ship close alongside of the enemy's ship and bring all your guns to bear on him, until you or he go to the bottom. This is the old fashion, which never goes out of fashion, neither in nor out of England.

It is not usually a point of honor, nor a religious sentiment, and never any whim, that they will shed their blood for; but usually property, and right measured by property, that breeds revolution. They have no Indian taste for a tomahawk-dance, no French taste for a badge or a proclamation. The Englishman is peaceably minding his business and earning his day's wages. But if you offer to lay hand on his day's wages, on his cow, or his right in common, or his shop, he will fight to the Judgment. Magna-charta, jury-trial, *habeas-corpus*, star-chamber, ship-money, Popery, Plymouth colony, American Revolution, are all questions involving a yeoman's right to his dinner, and except as touching that, would not have lashed the British nation to rage and revolt.

Whilst they are thus instinct with a spirit of order and

of calculation, it must be owned they are capable of larger views; but the indulgence is expensive to them, costs great crises, or accumulations of mental power. In common, the horse works best with blinders. Nothing is more in the line of English thought than our unvarnished Connecticut question, "Pray, sir, how do you get your living when you are at home?" The questions of freedom, of taxation, of privilege, are money questions. Heavy fellows, steeped in beer and fleshpots, they are hard of hearing and dim of sight. Their drowsy minds need to be flagellated by war and trade and politics and persecution. They cannot well read a principle, except by the light of fagots and of burning towns.

Tacitus says of the Germans, "Powerful only in sudden efforts, they are impatient of toil and labor." This highly destined race, if it had not somewhere added the chamber of patience to its brain, would not have built London. I know not from which of the tribes and temperaments that went to the composition of the people this tenacity was supplied, but they clinch every nail they drive. They have no running for luck, and no immoderate speed. They spend largely on their fabric, and await the slow return. Their leather lies tanning seven years in the vat. At Rogers's mills, in Sheffield, where I was shown the process of making a razor and a penknife, I was told there is no luck in making good steel; that they make no mistakes, every blade in the hundred and in the thousand is good. And that is characteristic of all their work,—no more is attempted than is done.

When Thor and his companions arrive at Utgard, he is told that "nobody is permitted to remain here, unless he understand some art, and excel in it all other men." The same question is still put to the posterity of Thor. A nation of laborers, every man is trained to some one art or detail and aims at perfection in that; not content unless he has something in which he thinks he surpasses all other men. He would rather not do anything at all than not do it well. I suppose no people have such thoroughness;—from the highest to the lowest, every man meaning to be master of his art.

"To show capacity," a Frenchman described as the end of a speech in debate: "No," said an Englishman, "but to set your shoulder at the wheel,—to advance the business." Sir Samuel Romilly refused to speak in popular assemblies, confining himself to the House of Commons, where a measure can be carried by a speech. The business of the House of Commons is conducted by a few persons, but these are hard-worked. Sir Robert Peel "knew the Blue Books by heart." His colleagues and rivals carry Hansard in their heads. The high civil and legal offices are not beds of ease, but posts which exact frightful amounts of mental labor. Many of the great leaders, like Pitt, Canning, Castlereagh, Romilly, are soon worked to death. They are excellent judges in England of a good worker, and when they find one, like Clarendon, Sir Philip Warwick, Sir William Coventry, Ashley, Burke, Thurlow, Mansfield, Pitt, Eldon, Peel, or Russell, there is nothing too good or too high for him.

They have a wonderful heat in the pursuit of a public aim. Private persons exhibit, in scientific and antiquarian researches, the same pertinacity as the nation showed in the coalitions in which it yoked Europe against the empire of Bonaparte, one after the other defeated, and still renewed, until the sixth hurled him from his seat.

Sir John Herschel, in completion of the work of his father, who had made the catalogue of the stars of the northern hemisphere, expatriated himself for years at the Cape of Good Hope, finished his inventory of the southern heaven, came home, and redacted it in eight years more;—a work whose value does not begin until thirty years have elapsed, and thenceforward a record to all ages of the highest import. The Admiralty sent out the Arctic expeditions year after year, in search of Sir John Franklin, until at last they have threaded their way through polar pack and Behring's Straits and solved the geographical problem. Lord Elgin, at Athens, saw the imminent ruin of the Greek remains, set up his scaffoldings, in spite of epigrams, and, after five years' labor to collect them, got his marbles on ship-board. The ship struck a rock and went to the bottom. He had them all fished up by divers, at a vast expense, and brought to London; not knowing that Haydon, Fuseli and Canova, and all good heads in all the world, were to be his applauders. In the same spirit, were the excavation and research by Sir Charles Fellowes for the Xanthian monument, and of Layard for his Nineveh sculptures.

The nation sits in the immense city they have builded, a London extended into every man's mind, though he live in Van Dieman's Land or Capetown. Faithful performance of what is undertaken to be performed, they honor in themselves, and exact in others, as certificate of equality with themselves. The modern world is theirs. They have made and make it day by day. The commercial relations of the world are so intimately drawn to London, that every dollar on earth contributes to the strength of the English government. And if all the wealth in the planet should perish by war or deluge, they know themselves competent to replace it.

They have approved their Saxon blood, by their seagoing qualities; their descent from Odin's smiths, by their hereditary skill in working in iron; their British birth, by husbandry and immense wheat harvests; and justified their occupancy of the centre of habitable land, by their supreme ability and cosmopolitan spirit. They have tilled, builded, forged, spun and woven. They have made the island a thoroughfare, and London a shop, a law-court, a record-office and scientific bureau, inviting to strangers; a sanctuary to refugees of every political and religious opinion; and such a city that almost every active man, in any nation, finds himself at one time or other forced to visit it.

In every path of practical activity they have gone even with the best. There is no secret of war in which they have not shown mastery. The steam-chamber of Watt, the locomotive of Stephenson, the cotton-mule of Roberts, perform the labor of the world. There is no department of literature, of science, or of useful art, in which they have not produced a first-rate book. It is England whose opinion is waited for on the merit of a new invention, an improved science. And in the complications of the trade and politics of their vast empire, they have been equal to every exigency, with counsel and with conduct. Is it their luck, or is it in the chambers of their brain,—it is their commercial advantage that whatever light appears in better method or happy invention, breaks out *in their race*. They are a family to which a destiny attaches, and the Banshee has sworn that a male heir shall never be wanting. They have a wealth of men to fill important posts, and the vigilance of party criticism insures the selection of a competent person.

A proof of the energy of the British people is the highly artificial construction of the whole fabric. The climate and geography, I said, were factitious, as if the hands of man had arranged the conditions. The same character pervades the whole kingdom. Bacon said, "Rome was a state not subject to paradoxes;" but England subsists by antagonisms and contradictions. The foundations of its greatness are the rolling waves; and from first to last it is a museum of anomalies. This foggy and rainy country furnishes the world with astronomical observations. Its short rivers do not afford water-power, but the land shakes under the thunder of the mills. There is no gold-mine of any importance, but there is more gold in England than in all other countries. It is too far north for the culture of the vine, but the wines of all countries are in its docks. The French Comte de Lauraguais said, "No fruit ripens in England but a baked apple;" but oranges and pine-apples are as cheap in London as in the Mediterranean. The Mark-Lane Express, or the Custom House Returns, bear out to the letter the vaunt of Pope,—

"Let India boast her palms, nor envy we
    The weeping amber, nor the spicy tree,
While, by our oaks, those precious loads are borne,
    And realms commanded which those trees adorn."

The native cattle are extinct, but the island is full of artificial breeds. The agriculturist Bakewell created sheep and
cows and horses to order, and breeds in which every thing
was omitted but what is economical. The cow is sacrificed
to her bag, the ox to his sirloin. Stall-feeding makes
sperm-mills of the cattle, and converts the stable to a
chemical factory. The rivers, lakes and ponds, too much
fished, or obstructed by factories, are artificially filled
with the eggs of salmon, turbot and herring.

Chat Moss and the fens of Lincolnshire and Cambridge-
shire are unhealthy and too barren to pay rent. By cylin-
drical tiles and gutta-percha tubes, five millions of acres of
bad land have been drained and put on equality with the
best, for rape-culture and grass. The climate too, which
was already believed to have become milder and drier by
the enormous consumption of coal, is so far reached by
this new action, that fogs and storms are said to disappear.
In due course, all England will be drained and rise a second time out of the waters. The latest step was to call in
the aid of stream to agriculture. Steam is almost an Englishman. I do not know but they will send him to Parliament next, to make laws. He weaves, forges, saws, pounds,
fans, and now he must pump, grind, dig and plough for
the farmer. The markets created by the manufacturing
population have erected agriculture into a great thriving
and spending industry. The value of the houses in Britain
is equal to the value of the soil. Artificial aids of all kinds
are cheaper than the natural resources. No man can afford
to walk, when the parliamentary-train carries him for a
penny a mile. Gas-burners are cheaper than daylight in
numberless floors in the cities. All the houses in London
buy their water. The English trade does not exist for the

exportation of native products, but on its manufactures, or the making well every thing which is ill-made elsewhere. They make ponchos for the Mexican, bandannas for the Hindoo, ginseng for the Chinese, beads for the Indian, laces for the Flemings, telescopes for astronomers, cannons for kings.

The Board of Trade caused the best models of Greece and Italy to be placed within the reach of every manufacturing population. They caused to be translated from foreign languages and illustrated by elaborate drawings, the most approved works of Munich, Berlin and Paris. They have ransacked Italy to find new forms, to add a grace to the products of their looms, their potteries and their foundries.

The nearer we look, the more artificial is their social system. Their law is a network of fictions. Their property, a scrip or certificate of right to interest on money that no man ever saw. Their social classes are made by statute. Their ratios of power and representation are historical and legal. The last Reform-bill took away political power from a mound, a ruin and a stone wall, whilst Birmingham and Manchester, whose mills paid for the wars of Europe, had no representative. Purity in the elective Parliament is secured by the purchase of seats. Foreign power is kept by armed colonies; power at home, by a standing army of police. The pauper lives better than the free laborer, the thief better than the pauper, and the transported felon better than the one under imprisonment. The crimes are factitious; as smuggling, poaching, nonconformity, heresy and treason. The sovereignty of the seas is maintained by the impressment of seamen. "The impressment of seamen," said Lord Eldon, "is the life of our navy." Solvency is maintained by means of a national debt, on the principle, "If you will not lend me the money, how can I pay you?" For the administration of justice, Sir Samuel Romilly's expedient for clearing the arrears of business in Chancery was, the Chancellor's staying away entirely from his court. Their system of education is factitious. The Universities galvanize dead languages into a semblance of life. Their church is artificial. The manners and customs of society are artificial;—made-up men with made-up manners;—and thus the whole is Birminghamized, and we have a nation whose existence is a work of art;—a cold, barren, almost arctic isle being made the most fruitful, luxurious and imperial land in the whole earth.

Man in England submits to be a product of political economy. On a bleak moor a mill is built, a banking-house is opened, and men come in as water in a sluice-way, and towns and cities rise. Man is made as a Birmingham button. The rapid doubling of the population dates from Watt's steam-engine. A landlord who owns a province says, "The tenantry are unprofitable; let me have sheep." He unroofs the houses and ships the population to America. The nation is accustomed to the instantaneous creation of wealth. It is the maxim of their economists, "that the greater part in value of the wealth now existing in England has been produced by human hands within the last twelve months." Meantime, three or four days' rain will reduce hundreds to starving in London.

One secret of their power is their mutual good understanding. Not only good minds are born among them, but all the people have good minds. Every nation has yielded some good wit, if, as has chanced to many tribes, only one. But the intellectual organization of the English admits a communicableness of knowledge and ideas among them all. An electric touch by any of their national ideas, melts them into one family and brings the hoards of power which their individuality is always hiving, into use and play for all. Is it the smallness of the country, or is it the pride and affection of race,—they have solidarity, or responsibleness, and trust in each other.

Their minds, like wool, admit of a dye which is more lasting than the cloth. They embrace their cause with more tenacity than their life. Though not military, yet every common subject by the poll is fit to make a soldier of. These private, reserved, mute family-men can adopt a public end with all their heat, and this strength of affection makes the romance of their heroes. The difference of rank does not divide the national heart. The Danish poet Oehlenschläger complains that who writes in Danish writes to two hundred readers. In Germany there is one speech for the learned, and another for the masses, to that extent that, it is said, no sentiment or phrase from the works of any great German writer is ever heard among the lower classes. But in England, the language of the noble is the language of the poor. In Parliament, in pulpits, in theatres, when the speakers rise to thought and passion, the language becomes idiomatic; the people in the street best understand the best words. And their language seems drawn from the Bible, the Common Law and the works of Shakspeare, Bacon, Milton, Pope, Young, Cowper, Burns and Scott. The island has produced two or three of the greatest men that ever existed, but they were not solitary in their own time. Men quickly embodied what Newton found out, in Greenwich observatories and practical navigation. The boys know all that Hutton knew of strata, or Dalton of atoms, or Harvey of blood-vessels; and these studies, once dangerous, are in fashion. So what is invented or known in agriculture, or in trade, or in war, or in art, or in literature and antiquities. A great ability, not amassed on a few giants, but poured into the general mind, so that each of them could at a pinch stand in the shoes of the other; and they are more bound in character than differenced in ability or in rank. The laborer is a possible lord. The lord is a possible basket-maker. Every man carries the English system in his brain, knows what is confided to him and does therein the best he can. The chancellor carries England on his mace, the midshipman at the point of his dirk, the smith on his hammer, the cook in the bowl of his spoon; the postilion cracks his whip for England, and the sailor times his oars to "God save the King!" The very felons have their pride in each other's English stanchness. In politics and in war they hold together as by hooks of steel. The charm in Nelson's history is the unselfish greatness, the assurance of being supported to the uttermost by those whom he supports to the uttermost. Whilst they are some ages ahead of the rest of the world in the art of living; whilst in some directions they do not represent the modern spirit but constitute it;—this vanguard of civility and power they coldly hold, marching in phalanx, lockstep, foot after foot, file after file of heroes, ten thousand deep.

Manners

I find the Englishman to be him of all men who stands firmest in his shoes. They have in themselves what they value in their horses,—mettle and bottom. On the day of my arrival at Liverpool, a gentleman, in describing to me the Lord Lieutenant of Ireland, happened to say, "Lord Clarendon has pluck like a cock and will fight till he dies;" and what I heard first I heard last, and the one thing the English value is *pluck*. The word is not beautiful, but on the quality they signify by it the nation is unanimous. The cabmen have it; the merchants have it; the bishops have it; the women have it; the journals have it;—the Times newspaper they say is the pluckiest thing in England, and Sydney Smith had made it a proverb that little Lord John Russell, the minister, would take the command of the Channel fleet to-morrow.

They require you to dare to be of your own opinion, and they hate the practical cowards who cannot in affairs answer directly yes or no. They dare to displease, nay, they will let you break all the commandments, if you do it natively and with spirit. You must be somebody; then you may do this or that, as you will.

Machinery has been applied to all work, and carried to such perfection that little is left for the men but to mind the engines and feed the furnaces. But the machines require punctual service, and as they never tire, they prove too much for their tenders. Mines, forges, mills, breweries, railroads, steam-pump, steam-plough, drill of regiments, drill of police, rule of court and shop-rule have operated to give a mechanical regularity to all the habit and action of men. A terrible machine has possessed itself of the ground, the air, the men and women, and hardly even thought is free.

The mechanical might and organization requires in the people constitution and answering spirits; and he who goes among them must have some weight of metal. At last, you take your hint from the fury of life you find, and say, one thing is plain, this is no country for fainthearted people: don't creep about diffidently; make up your mind; take your own course, and you shall find respect and furtherance.

It requires, men say, a good constitution to travel in Spain. I say as much of England, for other cause, simply on account of the vigor and brawn of the people. Nothing but the most serious business could give one any counterweight to these Baresarks, though they were only to order eggs and muffins for their breakfast. The Englishman speaks with all his body. His elocution is stomachic,—as the American's is labial. The Englishman is very petulant and precise about his accommodation at inns and on the roads; a quiddle about his toast and his chop and every species of convenience, and loud and pungent in his expressions of impatience at any neglect. His vivacity betrays itself at all points, in his manners, in his respiration, and the inarticulate noises he makes in clearing the throat;—all significant of burly strength. He has stamina; he can take the initiative in emergencies. He has that *aplomb* which results from a good adjustment of the moral and physical nature and the obedience of all the powers to the will; as if the axes of his eyes were united to his backbone, and only moved with the trunk.

This vigor appears in the incuriosity and stony neglect, each of every other. Each man walks, eats, drinks, shaves, dresses, gesticulates, and, in every manner acts and suffers without reference to the bystanders, in his own fashion, only careful not to interfere with them or annoy them; not that he is trained to neglect the eyes of his neighbors,—he is really occupied with his own affair and does not think of them. Every man in this polished country consults only his convenience, as much as a solitary pioneer in Wisconsin. I know not where any personal eccentricity is so freely allowed, and no man gives himself any concern with it. An Englishman walks in a pouring rain, swinging his closed umbrella like a walking-stick; wears a wig, or a shawl, or a saddle, or stands on his head, and no remark is made. And as he has been doing this for several generations, it is now in the blood.

In short, every one of these islanders is an island himself, safe, tranquil, incommunicable. In a company of strangers you would think him deaf; his eyes never wander from his table and newspaper. He is never betrayed into any curiosity or unbecoming emotion. They have all been trained in one severe school of manners, and never put off the harness. He does not give his hand. He does not let you meet his eye. It is almost an affront to look a man in the face without being introduced. In mixed or in select companies they do not introduce persons; so that a presentation is a circumstance as valid as a contract. Introductions are sacraments. He withholds his name. At the hotel, he is hardly willing to whisper it to the clerk at the book-office. If he give you his private address on a card, it is like an avowal of friendship; and his bearing, on being introduced, is cold, even though he is seeking your acquaintance and is studying how he shall serve you.

It was an odd proof of this impressive energy, that in my lectures I hesitated to read and threw out for its impertinence many a disparaging phrase which I had been accustomed to spin, about poor, thin, unable mortals;—so much had the fine physique and the personal vigor of this robust race worked on my imagination.

I happened to arrive in England at the moment of a commercial crisis. But it was evident that let who will fail, England will not. These people have sat here a thousand years, and here will continue to sit. They will not break up, or arrive at any desperate revolution, like their neighbors; for they have as much energy, as much continence of character as they ever had. The power and possession which surround them are their own creation, and they exert the same commanding industry at this moment.

They are positive, methodical, cleanly and formal, loving routine and conventional ways; loving truth and religion, to be sure, but inexorable on points of form. All the world praises the comfort and private appointments of an English inn, and of English households. You are sure of neatness and of personal decorum. A Frenchman may possibly be clean; an Englishman is conscientiously clean. A certain order and complete propriety is found in his dress and in his belongings.

Born in a harsh and wet climate, which keeps him in doors whenever he is at rest, and being of an affectionate and loyal temper, he dearly loves his house. If he is rich, he buys a demesne and builds a hall; if he is in middle condition, he spares no expense on his house. Without, it is all planted; within, it is wainscoted, carved, curtained, hung with pictures and filled with good furniture. 'T is a passion which survives all others, to deck and improve it. Hither he brings all that is rare and costly, and with the national tendency to sit fast in the same spot for many generations, it comes to be, in the course of time, a museum of heirlooms, gifts and trophies of the adventures and exploits of the family. He is very fond of silver plate, and though he have no gallery of portraits of his ancestors, he has of their punch-bowls and porringers. Incredible amounts of plate are found in good houses, and the poorest have some spoon or saucepan, gift of a godmother, saved out of better times.

An English family consists of a few persons, who, from youth to age, are found revolving within a few feet of each other, as if tied by some invisible ligature, tense as that cartilage which we have seen attaching the two Siamese. England produces under favorable conditions of ease and culture the finest women in the world. And as the men are affectionate and true-hearted, the women inspire and re-fine them. Nothing can be more delicate without being fantastical, nothing more firm and based in nature and sentiment than the courtship and mutual carriage of the sexes. The song of 1596 says, "The wife of every Englishman is counted blest." The sentiment of Imogen in Cymbeline is copied from English nature; and not less the Portia of Brutus, the Kate Percy and the Desdemona. The romance does not exceed the height of noble passion in Mrs. Lucy Hutchinson, or in Lady Russell, or even as one discerns through the plain prose of Pepys's Diary, the sacred habit of an English wife. Sir Samuel Romilly could not bear the death of his wife. Every class has its noble and tender examples.

Domesticity is the taproot which enables the nation to branch wide and high. The motive and end of their trade and empire is to guard the independence and privacy of their homes. Nothing so much marks their manners as the concentration on their household ties. This domesticity is carried into court and camp. Wellington governed India and Spain and his own troops, and fought battles, like a good family-man, paid his debts, and though general of an army in Spain, could not stir abroad for fear of public creditors. This taste for house and parish merits has of course its doting and foolish side. Mr. Cobbett attributes the huge popularity of Perceval, prime minister in 1810, to the fact that he was wont to go to church every Sunday, with a large quarto gilt prayer-book under one arm, his wife hanging on the other, and followed by a long brood of children.

They keep their old customs, costumes, and pomps, their wig and mace, sceptre and crown. The Middle Ages still lurk in the streets of London. The Knights of the Bath take oath to defend injured ladies; the gold-stick-in-wait-ing survives. They repeated the ceremonies of the elev-enth century in the coronation of the present Queen. A hereditary tenure is natural to them. Offices, farms, trades and traditions descend so. Their leases run for a hundred and a thousand years. Terms of service and partnership are life-long, or are inherited. "Holdship has been with me," said Lord Eldon, "eight-and-twenty years, knows all my business and books." Antiquity of usage is sanction enough. Wordsworth says of the small freeholders of Westmoreland, "Many of these humble sons of the hills had a consciousness that the land which they tilled had for more than five hundred years been possessed by men of the same name and blood." The ship-carpenter in the public yards, my lord's gardener and porter, have been there for more than a hundred years, grandfather, father, and son.

The English power resides also in their dislike of change. They have difficulty in bringing their reason to act, and on all occasions use their memory first. As soon as they have rid themselves of some grievance and settled the better practice, they make haste to fix it as a finality, and never wish to hear of alteration more.

Every Englishman is an embryonic chancellor: his instinct is to search for a precedent. The favorite phrase of their law is, "a custom whereof the memory of man runneth not back to the contrary." The barons say, *"Nolumus mutari;"* and the cockneys stifle the curiosity of the foreigner on the reason of any practice with "Lord, sir, it was always so." They hate innovation. Bacon told them, Time was the right reformer; Chatham, that "confidence was a plant of slow growth;" Canning, to "advance with the times;" and Wellington, that "habit was ten times nature." All their statesmen learn the irresistibility of the tide of custom, and have invented many fine phrases to cover this slowness of perception and prehensility of tail.

A sea-shell should be the crest of England, not only because it represents a power built on the waves, but also the hard finish of the men. The Englishman is finished like a cowry or a murex. After the spire and the spines are formed, or with the formation, a juice exudes and a hard enamel varnishes every part. The keeping of the proprieties is an indispensable as clean linen. No merit quite countervails the want of this whilst this sometimes stands in lieu of all. " 'T is in bad taste," is the most formidable word an Englishman can pronounce. But this japan costs them dear. There is a prose in certain Englishmen which exceeds in wooden deadness all rivalry with other countrymen. There is a knell in the conceit and externality of their voice, which seems to say, *Leave all hope behind.* In this Gibraltar of propriety, mediocrity gets intrenched and consolidated and founded in adamant. An Englishman of fashion is like one of those souvenirs, bound in gold vellum, enriched with delicate engravings on thick hot-pressed paper, fit for the hands of ladies and princes, but with nothing in it worth reading or remembering.

A severe decorum rules the court and the cottage. When Thalberg the pianist was one evening performing before the Queen at Windsor, in a private party, the Queen accompanied him with her voice. The circumstance took air, and all England shuddered from sea to sea. The indecorum was never repeated. Cold, repressive manners prevail. No enthusiasm is permitted except at the opera. They avoid every thing marked. They require a tone of voice that excites no attention in the room. Sir Philip Sidney is one of the patron saints of England, of whom Wotton said, "His wit was the measure of congruity."

Pretension and vaporing are once for all distasteful. They keep to the other extreme of low tone in dress and manners. They avoid pretension and go right to the heart of the thing. They hate nonsense, sentimentalism and high-flown expression; they use a studied plainness. Even Brummel, their fop, was marked by the severest simplicity in dress. They value themselves on the absence of every thing theatrical in the public business, and on conciseness and going to the point, in private affairs.

In an aristocratical country like England, not the Trial by Jury, but the dinner, is the capital institution. It is the mode of doing honor to a stranger, to invite him to eat,— and has been for many hundred years. "And they think," says the Venetian traveller of 1500, "no greater honor can be conferred or received, than to invite others to eat with them, or to be invited themselves, and they would sooner give five or six ducats to provide an entertainment for a person, than a groat to assist him in any distress." It is reserved to the end of the day, the family-hour being generally six, in London, and if any company is expected, one or two hours later. Every one dresses for dinner, in his own house, or in another man's. The guests are expected to arrive within half an hour of the time fixed by card of invitation, and nothing but death or mutilation is permitted to detain them. The English dinner is precisely the model on which our own are constructed in the Atlantic cities. The company sit one or two hours before the ladies leave the table. The gentlemen remain over their wine an hour longer, and rejoin the ladies in the drawing-room and take coffee. The dress-dinner generates a talent of table-talk which reaches great perfection: the stories are so good that one is sure they must have been often told before, to have got such happy turns. Hither come all manner of clever projects, bits of popular science, of practical intervention, of miscellaneous humor; political, literary and personal news; railroads, horses, diamonds, agriculture, horticulture, pisciculture and wine.

English stories, *bon-mots* and the recorded table-talk of their wits, are as good as the best of the French. In America, we are apt scholars, but have not yet attained the same perfection: for the range of nations from which London draws, and the steep contrasts of condition, create the picturesque in society, as broken country makes picturesque landscape; whilst our prevailing equality makes a prairie tameness: and secondly, because the usage of a dress-dinner every day at dark has a tendency to hive and produce to advantage every thing good. Much attrition has worn every sentence into a bullet. Also one meets now and then with polished men who know every thing, have tried every thing, and can do every thing, and are quite superior to letters and science. What could they not, if only they would?

Truth

The Teutonic tribes have a national singleness of heart, which contrasts with the Latin races. The German name has a proverbial significance of sincerity and honest meaning. The arts bear testimony to it. The faces of clergy and laity in old sculptures and illuminated missals are charged with earnest belief. Add to this hereditary rectitude the punctuality and precise dealing which commerce creates, and you have the English truth and credit. The government strictly performs its engagements. The subjects do not understand trifling on its part. When any breach of promise occurred, in the old days of prerogative, it was resented by the people as an intolerable grievance. And in modern times, any slipperiness in the government of political faith, or any repudiation or crookedness in matters of finance, would bring the whole nation to a committee of inquiry and reform. Private men keep their promises, never so trivial. Down goes the flying word on the tablets, and is indelible as Domesday Book.

Their practical power rests on their national sincerity. Veracity derives from instinct, and marks superiority in organization. Nature has endowed some animals with cunning, as a compensation for strength withheld; but it has provoked the malice of all others, as if avengers of public wrong. In the nobler kinds, where strength could be afforded, her races are loyal to truth, as truth is the foundation of the social state. Beasts that make no truce with man, do not break faith with each other. 'T is said that the wolf, who makes a *cache* of his prey and brings his fellows with him to the spot, if, on digging, it is not found, is instantly and unresistingly torn in pieces. English veracity seems to result on a sounder animal structure, as if they could afford it. They are blunt in saying what they think, sparing of promises, and they require plain dealing of others. We will not have to do with a man in a mask. Let us know the truth. Draw a straight line, hit whom and where it will. Alfred, whom the affection of the nation makes the type of their race, is called by a writer at the Norman Conquest, the *truth-speaker; Alueredus veridicus.* Geoffrey of Monmouth says of King Aurelius, uncle of Arthur, that "above all things he hated a lie." The Northman Guttorm said to King Olaf, "It is royal work to fulfil royal words." The mottoes of their families are monitory proverbs, as, *Fare fac,*—Say, do,—of the Fairfaxes; *Say and seal,* of the house of Fiennes; *Vero nil verius,* of the DeVeres. To be king of their word is their pride. When they unmask cant, they say, "The English of this is," etc.; and to give the lie is the extreme insult. The phrase of the lowest of the people is "honor-bright," and their vulgar praise, "His word is as good as his bond." They hate shuffling and equivocation, and the cause is damaged in the public opinion, on which any paltering can be fixed. Even Lord Chesterfield, with his French breeding, when he came to define a gentleman, declared that truth made his distinction; and nothing ever spoken by him would find so hearty a suffrage from his nation. The Duke of Wellington, who had the best right to say so, advises the French General Kellermann that he may rely on the parole of an English officer. The English, of all classes, value themselves on this trait, as distinguishing them from the French, who, in the popular belief, are more polite than true. An Englishman understates, avoids the superlative, checks himself in compliments, alleging that in the French language one cannot speak without lying.

They love reality in wealth, power, hospitality, and do not easily learn to make a show, and take the world as it goes. They are not fond of ornaments, and if they wear them, they must be gems. They read gladly in old Fuller that a lady in the reign of Elizabeth "would have as patiently digested a lie, as the wearing of false stones or pendants of counterfeit pearl." They have the earth-hunger, or preference for property in land, which is said to mark the Teutonic nations. They build of stone: public and private buildings are massive and durable. In comparing their ships' houses and public offices with the American, it is commonly said that they spend a pound where we spend a dollar. Plain rich clothes, plain rich equipage, plain rich finish throughout their house and belongings mark the English truth.

They confide in each other,—English believes in English. The French feel the superiority of this probity. The Englishman is not springing a trap for his admiration, but is honestly minding his business. The Frenchman is vain. Madame De Staël says that the English irritated Napoleon, mainly because they have found out how to unite success with honesty. She was not aware how wide an application her foreign readers would give to the remark. Wellington discovered the ruin of Bonaparte's affairs, by his own probity. He augured ill of the empire as soon as he saw that it was mendacious and lived by war. If war do not bring in its sequel new trade, better agriculture and manufactures, but only games, fireworks and spectacles,—no prosperity could support it; much less a nation decimated for conscripts and out of pocket, like France. So he drudged for years on his military works at Lisbon, and from this base at last extended his gigantic lines to Waterloo, believing in his countrymen and their syllogisms above all the rhodomontade of Europe.

At a St. George's festival, in Montreal, where I happened to be a guest since my return home, I observed that the chairman complimented his compatriots, by saying, "they confided that wherever they met an Englishman, they found a man who would speak the truth." And one cannot think this festival fruitless, if, all over the world, on the 23d of April, wherever two or three English are found, they meet to encourage each other in the nationality of veracity.

In the power of saying rude truth, sometimes in the lion's mouth, no men surpass them. On the king's birthday, when each bishop was expected to offer the king a

purse of gold, Latimer gave Henry VIII. a copy of the
Vulgate, with a mark at the passage, "Whoremongers and
adulterers God will judge;" and they so honor stoutness in
each other that the king passed it over. They are tenacious
of their belief and cannot easily change their opinions to
suit the hour. They are like ships with too much head on
to come quickly about, nor will prosperity or even adversity be allowed to shake their habitual view of conduct.
Whilst I was in London, M. Guizot arrived there on his escape from Paris, in February, 1848. Many private friends
called on him. His name was immediately proposed as an
honorary member of the Athenæum. M. Guizot was
blackballed. Certainly they knew the distinction of his
name. But the Englishman is not fickle. He had really
made up his mind now for years as he read his newspaper,
to hate and despise M. Guizot; and the altered position of
the man as an illustrious exile and a guest in the country,
makes no difference to him, as it would instantly to an
American.

They require the same adherence, thorough conviction
and reality, in public men. It is the want of character
which makes the low reputation of the Irish members.
"See them," they said, "one hundred and twenty-seven all
voting like sheep, never proposing any thing, and all but
four voting the income tax,"—which was an ill-judged
concession of the government, relieving Irish property
from the burdens charged on English.

They have a horror of adventurers in or out of Parliament. The ruling passion of Englishmen in these days is a
terror of humbug. In the same proportion they value honesty, stoutness, and adherence to your own. They like a
man committed to his objects. They hate the French, as
frivolous; they hate the Irish, as aimless; they hate the
Germans, as professors. In February, 1848, they said,
Look, the French king and his party fell for want of a shot;
they had not conscience to shoot, so entirely was the pith
and heart of monarchy eaten out.

They attack their own politicians every day, on the same grounds, as adventurers. They love stoutness in standing for your right, in declining money or promotion that costs any concession. The barrister refuses the silk gown of Queen's Counsel, if his junior have it one day earlier. Lord Collingwood would not accept his medal for victory on 14 February, 1797, if he did not receive one for victory on 1st June, 1794; and the long withholden medal was accorded. When Castlereagh dissuaded Lord Wellington from going to the king's levee until the unpopular Cintra business had been explained, he replied, "You furnish me a reason for going. I will go to this, or I will never go to a king's levee." The radical mob at Oxford cried after the tory Lord Eldon, "There's old Eldon; cheer him; he never ratted." They have given the parliamentary nickname of *Trimmers* to the timeservers, whom English character does not love.

They are very liable in their politics to extraordinary delusions; thus to believe what stands recorded in the gravest books, that the movement of 10 April, 1848, was urged or assisted by foreigners: which, to be sure, is paralleled by the democratic whimsy in this country which I have noticed to be shared by men sane on other points, that the English are at the bottom of the agitation of slavery, in American politics: and then again by the French popular legends on the subject of *perfidious Albion*. But suspicion will make fools of nations as of citizens.

A slow temperament makes them less rapid and ready than other countrymen, and has given occasion to the observation that English wit comes afterwards,—which the French denote as *esprit d'escalier*. This dulness makes their attachment to home and their adherence in all foreign countries to home habits. The Englishman who visits Mount Etna will carry his tea-kettle to the top. The old Italian author of the "Relation of England" (in 1500), says, "I have it on the best information, that, when the war is actually raging most furiously, they will seek for good eating and all their other comforts, without thinking what harm might befall them." Then their eyes seem to be set at the bottom of a tunnel, and they affirm the one small fact they know, with the best faith in the world that nothing else exists. And as their own belief in guineas is perfect, they readily, on all occasions, apply the pecuniary argument as final. Thus when the Rochester rappings began to be heard of in England, a man deposited £100 in a sealed box in the Dublin Bank, and then advertised in the newspapers to all somnambulists, mesmerizers and others, that whoever could tell him the number of his note should have the money. He let it lie there six months, the newspapers now and then, at his instance, stimulating the attention of the adepts; but none could ever tell him; and he said, "Now let me never be bothered more with this proven lie." It is told of a good Sir John that he heard a case stated by counsel, and made up his mind; then the counsel for the other side taking their turn to speak, he found himself so unsettled and perplexed that he exclaimed, "So help me God! I will never listen to evidence again." Any number of delightful examples of this English stolidity are the anecdotes of Europe. I knew a very worthy man,—a magistrate, I believe he was, in the town of Derby,—who went to the opera to see Malibran. In one scene, the heroine was to rush across a ruined bridge. Mr. B. arose and mildly yet firmly called the attention of the audience and the performers to the fact that, in his judgment, the bridge was unsafe! This English stolidity contrasts with French wit and tact. The French, it is commonly said, have greatly more influence in Europe than the English. What influence the English have is by brute force of wealth and power; that of the French by affinity and talent. The Italian is subtle, the Spaniard treacherous: tortures, it is said, could never wrest from an Egyptian the confession of a secret. None of these traits belong to the Englishman. His choler and conceit force everything out. Defoe, who knew his countrymen well, says of them,—

> "In close intrigue, their faculty's but weak,
>   For generally whate'er they know, they speak,
>   And often their own counsels undermine
>   By mere infirmity without design;
>   From whence, the learned say, it doth proceed,
>   That English treasons never can succeed;
>   For they're so open-hearted, you may know
>   Their own most secret thoughts, and others' too."

Character

The English race are reputed morose. I do not know that they have sadder brows than their neighbors of northern climates. They are sad by comparison with the singing and dancing nations: not sadder, but slow and staid, as finding their joys at home. They, too, believe that where there is no enjoyment of life there can be no vigor and art in speech or thought; that your merry heart goes all the way, your sad one tires in a mile. This trait of gloom has been fixed on them by French travellers, who, from Froissart, Voltaire, Le Sage, Mirabeau, down to the lively journalists of the *feuilletons*, have spent their wit on the solemnity of their neighbors. The French say, gay conversation is unknown in their island. The Englishman finds no relief from reflection, except in reflection. When he wishes for amusement, he goes to work. His hilarity is like an attack of fever. Religion, the theatre and the reading the books of his country all feed and increase his natural melancholy. The police does not interfere with public diversions. It thinks itself bound in duty to respect the pleasures and rare gayety of this inconsolable nation; and their well-known courage is entirely attributable to their disgust of life.

I suppose their gravity of demeanor and their few

words have obtained this reputation. As compared with the Americans, I think them cheerful and contented. Young people in this country are much more prone to melancholy. The English have a mild aspect and a ringing cheerful voice. They are large-natured and not so easily amused as the southerners, and are among them as grown people among children, requiring war, or trade, or engineering, or science, instead of frivolous games. They are proud and private, and even if disposed to recreation, will avoid an open garden. They sported sadly; *ils s'amusaient tristement, selon la coutume de leur pays,* said Froissart; and I suppose never nation built their party-walls so thick, or their garden-fences so high. Meat and wine produce no effect on them. They are just as cold, quiet and composed, at the end, as at the beginning of dinner.

The reputation of taciturnity they have enjoyed for six or seven hundred years; and a kind of pride in bad public speaking is noted in the House of Commons, as if they were willing to show that they did not live by their tongues, or thought they spoke well enough if they had the tone of gentlemen. In mixed company they shut their mouths. A Yorkshire mill-owner told me he had ridden more than once all the way from London to Leeds, in the first-class carriage, with the same persons, and no word exchanged. The club-houses were established to cultivate social habits, and it is rare that more than two eat together, and oftenest one eats alone. Was it then a stroke of humor in the serious Swedenborg, or was it only his pitiless logic, that made him shut up the English souls in a heaven by themselves?

They are contradictorily described as sour, splenetic and stubborn,—and as mild, sweet and sensible. The truth is they have great range and variety of character. Commerce sends abroad multitudes of different classes. The choleric Welshman, the fervid Scot, the bilious resident in the East or West Indies, are wide of the perfect behavior of the educated and dignified man of family. So is the burly farmer; so is the country squire, with his narrow and violent life. In every inn is the Commercial-Room, in which 'travellers,' or bagmen who carry patterns and solicit orders for the manufacturers, are wont to be entertained. It easily happens that this class should characterize England to the foreigner, who meets them on the road and at every public house, whilst the gentry avoid the taverns, or seclude themselves whilst in them.

But these classes are the right English stock, and may fairly show the national qualities, before yet art and education have dealt with them. They are good lovers, good haters, slow but obstinate admirers, and in all things very much steeped in their temperament, like men hardly awaked from deep sleep, which they enjoy. Their habits and instincts cleave to nature. They are of the earth, earthy; and of the sea, as the sea-kinds, attached to it for what it yields them, and not from any sentiment. They are full of coarse strength, rude exercise, butcher's meat and sound sleep; and suspect any poetic insinuation or any hint for the conduct of life which reflects on this animal existence, as if somebody were fumbling at the umbilical cord and might stop their supplies. They doubt a man's sound judgment if he does not eat with appetite, and shake their heads if he is particularly chaste. Take them as they come, you shall find in the common people a surly indifference, sometimes gruffness and ill temper; and in minds of more power, magazines of inexhaustible war, challenging

"The ruggedest hour that time and spite dare bring
To frown upon the enraged Northumberland."

They are headstrong believers and defenders of their opinion, and not less resolute in maintaining their whim and perversity. Hezekiah Woodward wrote a book against the Lord's Prayer. And one can believe that Burton, the Anatomist of Melancholy, having predicted from the stars the hour of his death, slipped the knot himself round his own neck, not to falsify his horoscope.

Their looks bespeak an invincible stoutness: they have extreme difficulty to run away, and will die game. Wellington said of the young coxcombs of the Life-Guards, delicately brought up, "But the puppies fight well;" and Nelson said of his sailors, "They really mind shot no more than peas." Of absolute stoutness no nation has more or better examples. They are good at storming redoubts, at boarding frigates, at dying in the last ditch, or any desperate service which has daylight and honor in it; but not, I think, at enduring the rack, or any passive obedience, like jumping off a castle-roof at the word of a czar. Being both vascular and highly organized, so as to be very sensible of pain; and intellectual, so as to see reason and glory in a matter.

Of that constitutional force which yields the supplies of the day, they have the more than enough; the excess which creates courage on fortitude, genius in poetry, invention in mechanics, enterprise in trade, magnificence in wealth, splendor in ceremonies, petulance and projects in youth. The young men have a rude health which runs into peccant humors. They drink brandy like water, cannot expend their quantities of waste strength on riding, hunting, swimming and fencing, and run into absurd frolics with the gravity of the Eumenides. They stoutly carry into every nook and corner of the earth their turbulent sense; leaving no lie uncontradicted, no pretension unexamined. They chew hasheesh; cut themselves with poisoned creases; swing their hammock in the boughs of the Bohon Upas; taste every poison; buy every secret; at Naples they put St. Januarius's blood in an alembic; they saw a hole into the head of the "winking Virgin," to know why she winks; measure with an English footrule every cell of the Inquisition, every Turkish caaba, every Holy of holies; translate and send to Bentley the arcanum bribed and bullied away from shuddering Bramins; and measure their own strength by the terror they cause. These travellers are of every class, the best and the worst; and it may easily happen that those of rudest behavior are taken notice of and remembered. The Saxon melancholy in the vulgar rich and poor appears as gushes of ill-humor, which every check exasperates into sarcasm and vituperation. There are multitudes of rude young English who have the self-sufficiency and bluntness of their nation, and who, with their disdain of the rest of mankind and with this indigestion and choler, have made the English traveller a proverb for uncomfortable and offensive manners. It was no bad description of the Briton generically, what was said two hundred years ago of one particular Oxford scholar: "He was a very bold man, uttered any thing that came into his mind, not only among his companions, but in public coffee-houses, and would often speak his mind of particular persons then accidentally present, without examining the company he was in; for which he was often reprimanded and several times threatened to be kicked and beaten."

The common Englishman is prone to forget a cardinal article in the bill of social rights, that every man has a right to his own ears. No man can claim to usurp more than a few cubic feet of the audibilities of a public room, or to put upon the company with the loud statement of his crotchets or personalities.

But it is in the deep traits of race that the fortunes of nations are written, and however derived,—whether a happier tribe or mixture of tribes, the air, or what circumstance that mixed for them the golden mean of temperament,—here exists the best stock in the world, broad-fronted, broad-bottomed, best for depth, range and equability; men of aplomb and reserves, great range and many moods, strong instincts, yet apt for culture; war-class as well as clerks; earls and tradesmen; wise minority, as well as foolish majority; abysmal temperament, hiding wells of wrath, and glooms on which no sunshine settles, alternated with a common sense and humanity which hold them fast to every piece of cheerful duty; making this temperament a sea to which all storms are superficial; a race to which their fortunes flow, as if they alone had the elastic organization at once fine and robust enough for dominion; as if the burly inexpressive, now mute and contumacious, now fierce and sharp-tongued dragon, which once made the island light with his fiery breath, had bequeathed his ferocity to his conqueror. They hide virtues under vices, or the semblance of them. It is the misshapen hairy Scandinavian troll again, who lifts the cart out of the mire, or threshes,

> "The corn
> That ten day-laborers could not end,"

but it is done in the dark and with muttered maledictions. He is a churl with a soft place in his heart, whose speech is a brash of bitter waters, but who loves to help you at a pinch. He says no, and serves you, and your thanks disgust him. Here was lately a cross-grained miser, odd and ugly, resembling in countenance the portrait of Punch with the laugh left out; rich by his own industry; sulking in a lonely house; who never gave a dinner to any man and disdained all courtesies: yet as true a worshipper of beauty in form and color as ever existed, and profusely pouring over the cold mind of his countrymen creations of grace and truth, removing the reproach of sterility from English art, catching from their savage climate every fine hint, and importing into their galleries every tint and trait of sunnier cities and skies; making an era in painting; and when he saw that the splendor of one of his pictures in the Exhibition dimmed his rival's that hung next it, secretly took a brush and blackened his own.

They do not wear their heart in their sleeve for daws to peck at. They have that phlegm or staidness which it is a compliment to disturb. "Great men," said Aristotle, "are always of a nature originally melancholy." 'T is the habit of a mind which attaches to abstractions with a passion which gives vast results. They dare to displease, they do not speak to expectation. They like the sayers of No, better than the sayers of Yes. Each of them has an opinion which he feels it becomes him to express all the more that it differs from yours. They are meditating opposition. This gravity is inseparable from minds of great resources.

There is an English hero superior to the French, the German, the Italian, or the Greek. When he is brought to the strife with fate, he sacrifices a richer material possession, and on more purely metaphysical grounds. He is there with his own consent, face to face with fortune, which he defies. On deliberate choice and from grounds of character, he has elected his part to live and die for, and dies with grandeur. This face has added new elements to humanity and has a deeper root in the world.

They have great range of scale, from ferocity to exquisite refinement. With larger scale, they have great retrieving power. After running each tendency to an extreme, they try another tack with equal heat. More intellectual than other races, when they live with other races they do not take their language, but bestow their own. They subsidize other nations, and are not subsidized. They proselyte, and are not proselyted. They assimilate other races to themselves, and are not assimilated. The English did not calculate the conquest of the Indies. It fell to their character. So they administer, in different parts of the world, the codes of every empire and race; in Canada, old French law; in the Mauritius, the Code Napoléon; in the West Indies, the edicts of the Spanish Cortes; in the East Indies, the Laws of Menu; in the Isle of Man, of the Scandinavian Thing; at the Cape of Good Hope, of the old Netherlands; and in the Ionian Islands, the Pandects of Justinian.

They are very conscious of their advantageous position in history. England is the lawgiver, the patron, the instructor, the ally. Compare the tone of the French and of the English press: the first querulous, captious, sensitive about English opinion; the English press never timorous about French opinion, but arrogant and contemptuous.

They are testy and headstrong through an excess of will and bias; churlish as men sometimes please to be who do not forget a debt, who ask no favors and who will do what they like with their own. With education and intercourse, these asperities wear off and leave the good-will pure. If anatomy is reformed according to national tendencies, I suppose the spleen will hereafter be found in the Englishman, not found in the American, and differencing the one from the other. I anticipate another anatomical discovery, that this organ will be found to be cortical and caducous; that they are superficially morose, but at last tender-hearted, herein differing from Rome and the Latin nations. Nothing savage, nothing mean resides in the English heart. They are subject to panics of credulity and of rage, but the temper of the nation, however disturbed, settles itself soon and easily, as, in this temperate zone, the sky after whatever storms clears again, and serenity is its normal condition.

A saving stupidity masks and protects their perception, as the curtain of the eagle's eye. Our swifter Americans, when they first deal with English, pronounce them stupid; but, later, do them justice as people who wear well, or hide their strength. To understand the power of performance that is in their finest wits, in the patient Newton, or in the versatile transcendent poets, or in the Dugdales, Gibbons, Hallams, Eldons and Peels, one should see how English day-laborers hold out. High and low, they are of an unctuous texture. There is an adipocere in their constitution, as if they had oil also for their mental wheels and could perform vast amounts of work without damaging themselves.

Even the scale of expense on which people live, and to which scholars and professional men conform, proves the tension of their muscle, when vast numbers are found who can each lift this enormous load. I might even add, their daily feasts argue a savage vigor of body.

No nation was ever so rich in able men; "Gentlemen," as Charles I. said of Strafford, "whose abilities might make a prince rather afraid than ashamed in the greatest affairs of state;" men of such temper, that, like Baron Vere, "had one seen him returning from a victory, he would by his silence have suspected that he had lost the day; and, had he beheld him in a retreat, he would have collected him a conqueror by the cheerfulness of his spirit."

The following passage from the "Heimskringla" might almost stand as a portrait of the modern Englishman:— "Haldor was very stout and strong and remarkably handsome in appearances. King Harold gave him this testimony, that he, among all his men, cared least about doubtful circumstances, whether they betokened danger or pleasure; for whatever turned up, he was never in higher nor in lower spirits, never slept less nor more on account of them, nor ate nor drank but according to his custom. Haldor was not a man of many words, but short in conversation, told his opinion bluntly and was obstinate and hard: and this could not please the king, who had many clever people about him, zealous in his service. Haldor remained a short time with the king, and then came to Iceland, where he took up his abode in Hiardaholt and dwelt in that farm to a very advanced age."

The national temper, in the civil history, is not flashy or whiffling. The slow, deep English mass smoulders with fire, which at last sets all its borders in flame. The wrath of London is not French wrath, but has a long memory, and, in its hottest heat, a register and rule.

Half their strength they put not forth. They are capable of a sublime resolution, and if hereafter the war of races, often predicted, and making itself a war of opinions also (a question of despotism and liberty coming from Eastern Europe), should menace the English civilization, these sea-kings may take once again to their floating castles and find a new home and a second millennium of power in their colonies.

The stability of England is the security of the modern world. If the English race were as mutable as the French, what reliance? But the English stand for liberty. The conservative, money-loving, lord-loving English are yet liberty-loving; and so freedom is safe: for they have more personal force than any other people. The nation always resist the immoral action of their government. They think humanely on the affairs of France, of Turkey, of Poland, of Hungary, of Schleswig Holstein, though overborne by the statecraft of the rulers at last.

Does the early history of each tribe show the permanent bias, which, though not less potent, is masked as the tribe spreads its activity into colonies, commerce, codes, arts, letters? The early history shows it, as the musician plays the air which he proceeds to conceal in a tempest of variations. In Alfred, in the Northmen, one may read the genius of the English society, namely that private life is the place of honor. Glory, a career, and ambition, words familiar to the longitude of Paris, are seldom heard in English speech. Nelson wrote from their hearts his homely telegraph, "England expects every man to do his duty."

For actual service, for the dignity of a profession, or to appease diseased or inflamed talent, the army and navy may be entered (the worst boys doing well in the navy); and the civil service in departments where serious official work is done; and they hold in esteem the barrister engaged in the severer studies of the law. But the calm, sound and most British Briton shrinks from public life as charlatanism, and respects an economy founded on agriculture, coal-mines, manufactures or trade, which secures an independence through the creation of real values.

They wish neither to command nor obey, but to be kings in their own houses. They are intellectual and deeply enjoy literature; they like well to have the world served up to them in books, maps, models, and every mode of exact information, and, though not creators in art, they value its refinement. They are ready for leisure, can direct and fill their own day, nor need so much as others the constraint of a necessity. But the history of the nation discloses, at every turn, this original predilection for private independence, and however this inclination may have been disturbed by the bribes with which their vast colonial power has warped men out of orbit, the inclination endures, and forms and reforms the laws, letters, manners and occupations. They choose that welfare which is compatible with the commonwealth, knowing that such alone is stable; as wise merchants prefer investments in the three per cents.

Cockayne

The English are a nation of humorists. Individual right is pushed to the uttermost bound compatible with public order. Property is so perfect that it seems the craft of that race, and not to exist elsewhere. The king cannot step on an acre which the peasant refuses to sell. A testator endows a dog or a rookery, and Europe cannot interfere with his absurdity. Every individual has his particular way of living, which he pushes to folly, and the decided sympathy of his compatriots is engaged to back up Mr. Crump's whim by statutes and chancellors and horse-guards. There is no freak so ridiculous but some Englishman has attempted to immortalize by money and law. British citizenship is as omnipotent as Roman was. Mr. Cockayne is very sensible of this. The pursy man means by freedom the right to do as he pleases, and does wrong in order to feel his freedom, and makes a conscience of persisting in it.

He is intensely patriotic, for his country is so small. His confidence in the power and performance of his nation makes him provokingly incurious about other nations. He dislikes foreigners. Swedenborg, who lived much in England, notes "the similitude of minds among the English, in consequence of which they contract familiarity with friends who are of that nation, and seldom with others; and they regard foreigners as one looking through a telescope from the top of a palace regards those who dwell or wander about out of the city." A much older traveller, the Venetian who wrote the "Relation of England," in 1500, says:—"The English are great lovers of themselves and of every thing belonging to them. They think that there are no other men than themselves and no other world but England; and whenever they see a handsome foreigner, they say that he looks like an Englishman and it is a great pity he should not be an Englishman; and whenever they partake of any delicacy with a foreigner, they ask him whether such a thing is made in his country." When he adds epithets of praise, his climax is, "So English;" and when he wishes to pay you the highest compliment, he says, "I should not know you from an Englishman." France is, by its natural contrast, a kind of blackboard on which English character draws its own traits in chalk. This arrogance habitually exhibits itself in allusions to the French. I suppose that all men of English blood in America, Europe or Asia, have a secret feeling of joy that they are not French natives. Mr. Coleridge is said to have given public thanks to God, at the close of a lecture, that he had defended him from being able to utter a single sentence in the French language. I have found that Englishmen have such a good opinion of England, that the ordinary phrases in all good society, of postponing or disparaging one's own things in talking with a stranger, are seriously mistaken by them for an insuppressible homage to the merits of their nation; and the New Yorker or Pennsylvanian who modestly laments the disadvantage of a new country, loghuts and savages, is surprised by the instant and unfeigned commiseration of the whole company, who plainly account all the world out of England a heap of rubbish.

The same insular limitation pinches his foreign politics. He sticks to his traditions and usages, and, so help him God! he will force his island by-laws down the throat of great countries, like India, China, Canada, Australia, and not only so, but impose Wapping on the Congress of Vienna and trample down all nationalities with his taxed boots. Lord Chatham goes for liberty and no taxation without representation;—for that is British law; but not a hobnail shall they dare make in America, but buy their nails in England;—for that also is British law; and the fact that British commerce was to be re-created by the independence of America, took them all by surprise.

In short, I am afraid that English nature is so rank and aggressive as to be a little incompatible with every other. The world is not wide enough for two.

But beyond this nationality, it must be admitted, the island offers a daily worship to the old Norse god Brage, celebrated among our Scandinavian forefathers for his eloquence and majestic air. The English have a steady courage that fits them for great attempts and endurance: they have also a petty courage, through which every man delights in showing himself for what he is and in doing what he can; so that in all companies, each of them has too good an opinion of himself to imitate anybody. He hides no defect of his form, features, dress, connection, or birthplace, for he thinks every circumstance belonging to him comes recommended to you. If one of them have a bald, or a red, or a green head, or bow legs, or a scar, or mark, or a paunch, or a squeaking or a raven voice, he has persuaded himself that there is something modish and becoming in it, and that it sits well on him.

But nature makes nothing in vain, and this little superfluity of self-regard in the English brain is one of the secrets of their power and history. It sets every man on being and doing what he really is and can. It takes away a dodging, skulking, secondary air, and encourages a frank and manly bearing, so that each man makes the most of himself and loses no opportunity for want of pushing. A man's personal defects will commonly have, with the rest of the world, precisely that importance which they have to himself. If he makes light of them, so will other men. We all find in these a convenient metre of character, since a little man would be ruined by the vexation. I remember a shrewd politician, in one of our western cities, told me that "he had known several successful statesmen made by their foible." And another, an ex-governor of Illinois, said to me, "If the man knew anything, he would sit in a corner and be modest; but he is such an ignorant peacock that he goes bustling up and down and hits on extraordinary discoveries."

There is also this benefit in brag, that the speaker is unconsciously expressing his own ideal. Humor him by all means, draw it all out and hold him to it. Their culture generally enables the travelled English to avoid any ridiculous extremes of this self-pleasing, and to give it an agreeable air. Then the natural disposition is fostered by the respect which they find entertained in the world for English ability. It was said of Louis XIV., that his gait and air were becoming enough in so great a monarch, yet would have been ridiculous in another man; so the prestige of the English name warrants a certain confident bearing, which a Frenchman or Belgian could not carry. At all events, they feel themselves at liberty to assume the most extraordinary tone on the subject of English merits.

An English lady on the Rhine hearing a German speaking of her party as foreigners, exclaimed, "No, we are not foreigners; we are English; it is you that are foreigners." They tell you daily in London the story of the Frenchman and Englishman who quarrelled. Both were unwilling to fight, but their companions put them up to it; at last it was agreed that they should fight alone, in the dark, and with pistols: the candles were put out, and the Englishman, to make sure not to hit any body, fired up the chimney,—and brought down the Frenchman. They have no curiosity about foreigners, and answer any information you may volunteer with "Oh, Oh!" until the informant makes up his mind that they shall die in their ignorance, for any help he will offer. There are really no limits to this conceit, though brighter men among them make painful efforts to be candid.

The habit of brag runs through all classes, from the "Times" newspaper through politicians and poets, through Wordsworth, Carlyle, Mill and Sydney Smith, down to the boys of Eton. In the gravest treatise on political economy, in a philosophical essay, in books of science, one is surprised by the most innocent exhibition of unflinching nationality. In a tract on Corn, a most amiable and accomplished gentleman writes thus:—"Though Britain, according to Bishop Berkeley's idea, were surrounded by a wall of brass ten thousand cubits in height, still she would as far excel the rest of the globe in riches, as she now does both in this secondary quality and in the more important ones of freedom, virtue and science."

The English dislike the American structure of society, whilst yet trade, mills, public education and Chartism are doing what they can to create in England the same social condition. America is the paradise of the economists; is the favorable exception invariably quoted to the rules of ruin; but when he speaks directly of the Americans the islander forgets his philosophy and remembers his disparaging anecdotes.

But this childish patriotism costs something, like all narrowness. The English sway of their colonies has no root of kindness. They govern by their arts and ability; they are more just than kind; and whenever an abatement of their power is felt, they have not conciliated the affection on which to rely.

Coarse local distinctions, as those of nation, province or town, are useful in the absence of real ones; but we must not insist on these accidental lines. Individual traits are always triumphing over national ones. There is no fence in metaphysics discriminating Greek, or English, or Spanish science. Æsop and Montaigne, Cervantes and Saadi are men of the world; and to wave our own flag at the dinner table or in the University is to carry the boisterous dulness of a fire-club into a polite circle. Nature and destiny are always on the watch for our follies. Nature trips us up when we strut; and there are curious examples in history on this very point of national pride.

George of Cappadocia, born at Epiphania in Cilicia, was a low parasite who got a lucrative contract to supply the army with bacon. A rogue and informer, he got rich and was forced to run from justice. He saved his money, embraced Arianism, collected a library, and got promoted by a faction to the episcopal throne of Alexandria. When Julian came, A.D. 361, George was dragged to prison; the prison was burst open by the mob and George was lynched, as he deserved. And this precious knave became, in good time, Saint George of England, patron of chivalry, emblem of victory and civility and the pride of the best blood of the modern world.

Strange, that the solid truth-speaking Briton should derive from an impostor. Strange, that the New World should have no better luck,—that broad America must wear the name of a thief. Amerigo Vespucci, the pickle-dealer at Seville, who went out, in 1499, a subaltern with Hojeda, and whose highest naval rank was boatswain's mate in an expedition that never sailed, managed in this lying world to supplant Columbus and baptize half the earth with his own dishonest name. Thus nobody can throw stones. We are equally badly off in our founders; and the false pickle-dealer is an offset to the false bacon-seller.

Wealth

There is no country in which so absolute a homage is paid to wealth. In America there is a touch of shame when a man exhibits the evidences of large property, as if after all it needed apology. But the Englishman has pure pride in his wealth, and esteems it a final certificate. A coarse logic rules throughout all English souls;—if you have merit, can you not show it by your good clothes and coach and horses? How can a man be a gentleman without a pipe of wine? Haydon says, "There is a fierce resolution to make every man live according to the means he possesses." There is a mixture of religion in it. They are under the Jewish law, and read with sonorous emphasis that their days shall be long in the land, they shall have sons and daughters, flocks and herds, wine and oil. In exact proportion is the reproach of poverty. They do not wish to be represented except by opulent men. An Englishman who has lost his fortune is said to have died of a broken heart. The last term of insult is, "a beggar." Nelson said, "The want of fortune is a crime which I can never get over." Sydney Smith said, "Poverty is infamous in England." And one of their recent writers speaks, in reference to a private and scholastic life, of "the grave moral deterioration which follows an empty exchequer." You shall find this sentiment, if not so frankly put, yet deeply implied in the novels and romances of the present century, and not only in these, but in biography and in the votes of public assemblies, in the tone of the preaching and in the table-talk.

I was lately turning over Wood's *Athenæ Oxonienses*, and looking naturally for another standard in a chronicle of the scholars of Oxford for two hundred years. But I found the two disgraces in that, as in most English books, are, first, disloyalty to Church and State, and second, to be born poor, or to come to poverty. A natural fruit of England is the brutal political economy. Malthus finds no cover laid at Nature's table for the laborer's son. In 1809, the majority in Parliament expressed itself by the language of Mr. Fuller in the House of Commons, "If you do not like the country, damn you, you can leave it." When Sir S. Romilly proposed his bill forbidding parish officers to bind children apprentices at a greater distance than forty miles from their home, Peel opposed, and Mr. Wortley said, "though, in the higher ranks, to cultivate family affections was a good thing, it was not so among the lower orders. Better take them away from those who might deprave them. And it was highly injurious to trade to stop binding to manufacturers, as it must raise the price of labor and of manufactured goods."

The respect for truth of facts in England is equalled only by the respect for wealth. It is at once the pride of art of the Saxon, as he is a wealth-maker, and his passion for independence. The Englishman believes that every man must take care of himself, and has himself to thank if he do not mend his condition. To pay their debts is their national point of honor. From the Exchequer and the East India House to the huckster's shop, every thing prospers because it is solvent. The British armies are solvent and pay for what they take. The British empire is solvent; for in spite of the huge national debt, the valuation mounts. During the war from 1789 to 1815, whilst they complained that they were taxed within an inch of their lives, and by dint of enormous taxes were subsidizing all the continent against France, the English were growing rich every year faster than any people ever grew before. It is their maxim that the weight of taxes must be calculated, not by what is taken, but by what is left. Solvency is in the ideas and mechanism of an Englishman. The Crystal Palace is not considered honest until it pays; no matter how much convenience, beauty, or *éclat*, it must be self-supporting. They are contented with slower steamers, as long as they know that swifter boats lose money. They proceed logically by the double method of labor and thrift. Every household exhibits an exact economy, and nothing of that uncalculated headlong expenditure which families use in America. If they cannot pay, they do not buy; for they have no presumption of better fortunes next year, as our people have; and they say without shame, I cannot afford it. Gentlemen do not hesitate to ride in the second-class cars, or in the second cabin. An economist, or a man who can proportion his means and his ambition, or bring the year round with expenditure which expresses his character without embarrassing one day of his future, is already a master of life, and a freeman. Lord Burleigh writes to his son that "one ought never to devote more than two thirds of his income to the ordinary expenses of life, since the extraordinary will be certain to absorb the other third."

The ambition to create value evokes every kind of ability; government becomes a manufacturing corporation, and every house a mill. The headlong bias to utility will let no talent lie in a napkin,—if possible will teach spiders to weave silk stockings. An Englishman, while he eats and drinks no more or not much more than another man, labors three times as many hours in the course of a year as another European; or, his life as a workman is three lives. He works fast. Everything in England is at a quick pace. They have reinforced their own productivity by the creation of that marvellous machinery which differences this age from any other age.

It is a curious chapter in modern history, the growth of the machine-shop. Six hundred years ago, Roger Bacon explained the precession of the equinoxes, the consequent necessity of the reform of the calendar; measured the length of the year; invented gunpowder; and announced (as if looking from his lofty cell, over five centuries, into ours) that "machines can be constructed to drive ships more rapidly than a whole galley of rowers could do; nor would they need anything but a pilot to steer them. Carriages also might be constructed to move with an incredible speed, without the aid of any animal. Finally, it would not be impossible to make machines which by means of a suit of wings should fly in the air in the manner of birds." But the secret slept with Bacon. The six hundred years have not yet fulfilled his words. Two centuries ago the sawing of timber was done by hand; the carriage wheels ran on wooden axles; the land was tilled by wooden ploughs. And it was to little purpose that they had pit-coal, or that looms were improved, unless Watt and Stephenson had taught them to work force-pumps and power-looms by steam. The great strides were all taken within the last hundred years. The Life of Sir Robert Peel, in his day the model Englishman, very properly has, for a frontispiece, a drawing of the spinning-jenny, which wove the web of his fortunes. Hargreaves invented the spinning-jenny, and died in a work-house. Arkwright improved the invention, and the machine dispensed with the work of ninety-nine men; that is, one spinner could do as much work as one hundred had done before. The loom was improved further. But the men would sometimes strike for wages and combine against the masters, and, about 1829-30, much fear was felt lest the trade would be drawn away by these interruptions and the emigration of the spinners to Belgium and the United States. Iron and steel are very obedient. Whether it were not possible to make a spinner that would not rebel, nor mutter, nor scowl, nor strike for wages, nor emigrate? At the solicitation of the masters, after a mob and riot at Staley Bridge, Mr. Roberts of Manchester undertook to create this peaceful fellow, instead of the quarrelsome fellow God had made. After a few trials, he succeeded, and in 1830 procured a patent for his self-acting mule; a creation, the delight of mill-owners, and "destined," they said, "to restore order among the industrious classes;" a machine requiring only a child's hand to piece the broken yarns. As Arkwright had destroyed domestic spinning, so Roberts destroyed the factory spinner. The power of machinery in Great Britain, in mills, has been computed to be equal to 600,000,000 men, one man being able by the aid of steam to do the work which required two hundred and fifty men to accomplish fifty years ago. The production has been commensurate. England already had this laborious race, rich soil, water, wood, coal, iron and favorable climate. Eight hundred years ago commerce had made it rich, and it was recorded, "England is the richest of all the northern nations." The Norman historians recite that "in 1067, William carried with him into Normandy, from England, more gold and silver than had ever before been seen in Gaul." But when, to this labor and trade and these native resources was added this goblin of steam, with his myriad arms, never tired, working night and day everlastingly, the amassing of property has run out of all figures. It makes the motor of the last ninety years. The steam-pipe has added to her population and wealth the equivalent of four or five Englands. Forty thousand ships are entered in Lloyd's lists. The yield of wheat has gone on from 2,000,-000 quarters in the time of the Stuarts, to 13,000,000 in 1854. A thousand million of pounds sterling are said to compose the floating money of commerce. In 1848,

Lord John Russell stated that the people of this country had laid out £300,000,000 of capital in railways, in the last four years. But a better measure than these sounding figures is the estimate that there is wealth enough in England to support the entire population in idleness for one year.

The wise, versatile, all-giving machinery makes chisels, roads, locomotives, telegraphs. Whitworth divides a bar to a millionth of an inch. Steam twines huge cannon into wreaths, as easily as it braids straw, and vies with the volcanic forces which twisted the strata. It can clothe shingle mountains with ship-oaks, make sword-blades that will cut gun-barrels in two. In Egypt, it can plant forests, and bring rain after three thousand years. Already it is ruddering the balloon, and the next war will be fought in the air. But another machine more potent in England than steam is the Bank. It votes an issue of bills, population is stimulated and cities rise; it refuses loans, and emigration empties the country; trade sinks; revolutions break out; kings are dethroned. By these new agents our social system is moulded. By dint of steam and of money, war and commerce are changed. Nations have lost their old omnipotence; the patriotic tie does not hold. Nations are getting obsolete, we go and live where we will. Steam has enabled men to choose what law they will live under. Money makes place for them. The telegraph is a limp band that will hold the Fenris-wolf of war. For now that a telegraph line runs through France and Europe from London, every message it transmits makes stronger by one thread the band which war will have to cut.

The introduction of these elements gives new resources to existing proprietors. A sporting duke may fancy that the state depends on the House of Lords, but the engineer sees that every stroke of the steam-piston gives value to the duke's land, fills it with tenants; doubles, quadruples, centuples the duke's capital, and creates new measures and new necessities for the culture of his children. Of course it draws the nobility into the competition, as stockholders in the mine, the canal, the railway, in the application of steam to agriculture, and sometimes into trade. But it also introduces large classes into the same competition; the old energy of the Norse race arms itself with these magnificent powers; new men prove an overmatch for the land-owner, and the mill buys out the castle. Scandinavian Thor, who once forged his bolts in icy Hecla and built galleys by lonely fiords, in England has advanced with the times, has shorn his beard, enters Parliament, sits down at a desk in the India House and lends Miöllnir to Birmingham for a steam-hammer.

The creation of wealth in England in the last ninety years is a main fact in modern history. The wealth of London determines prices all over the globe. All things precious, or useful, or amusing, or intoxicating, are sucked into this commerce and floated to London. Some English private fortunes reach, and some exceed a million of dollars a year. A hundred thousand palaces adorn the island. All that can feed the senses and passions, all that can succor the talent or arm the hands of the intelligent middle class, who never spare in what they buy for their own consumption; all that can aid science, gratify taste, or soothe comfort, is in open market. Whatever is excellent and beautiful in civil, rural, or ecclesiastic architecture, in fountain, garden, or grounds,—the English noble crosses sea and land to see and to copy at home. The taste and science of thirty peaceful generations; the gardens which Evelyn planted; the temples and pleasure-houses which Inigo Jones and Christopher Wren built; the wood that Gibbons carved; the taste of foreign and domestic artists, Shenstone, Pope, Brown, Loudon, Paxton,—are in the vast auction, and the hereditary principle heaps on the owner of to-day the benefit of ages of owners. The present possessors are to the full as absolute as any of their fathers in choosing and procuring what they like. This comfort and splendor, the breadth of lake and mountain, tillage, pasture and park, sumptuous castle and modern villa,—all consist with perfect order. They have no revolutions; no horse-guards dictating to the crown; no Parisian *pois-sardes* and barricades; no mob: but drowsy habitude, daily dress-dinners, wine and ale and beer and gin and sleep.

With this power of creation and this passion for independence, property has reached an ideal perfection. It is felt and treated as the national life-blood. The laws are framed to give property the securest possible basis, and the provisions to lock and transmit it have exercised the cunningest heads in a profession which never admits a fool. The rights of property nothing but felony and treason can override. The house is a castle which the king cannot enter. The Bank is a strong box to which the king has no key. Whatever surly sweetness possession can give, is tasted in England to the dregs. Vested rights are awful things, and absolute possession gives the smallest freeholder identity of interest with the duke. High stone fences and padlocked garden-gates announce the absolute will of the owner to be alone. Every whim of exaggerated egotism is put into stone and iron, into silver and gold, with costly deliberation and detail.

An Englishman hears that the Queen Dowager wishes to establish some claim to put her park paling a rod forward into his grounds, so as to get a coachway and save her a mile to the avenue. Instantly he transforms his paling into stone-masonry, solid as the walls of Cuma, and all Europe cannot prevail on him to sell or compound for an inch of the land. They delight in a freak as the proof of their sovereign freedom. Sir Edward Boynton, at Spic Park at Cadenham, on a precipice of incomparable prospect, built a house like a long barn, which had not a window on the prospect side. Strawberry Hill of Horace Walpole, Fonthill Abbey of Mr. Beckford, were freaks; and Newstead Abbey became one in the hands of Lord Byron.

But the proudest result of this creation has been the great and refined forces it has put at the disposal of the private citizen. In the social world an Englishman to-day has the best lot. He is a king in a plain coat. He goes with the most powerful protection, keeps the best company, is armed by the best education, is seconded by wealth; and his English name and accidents are like a flourish of trumpets announcing him. This, with his quiet style of manners, gives him the power of a sovereign without the inconveniences which belong to that rank. I much prefer the condition of an English gentleman of the better class to that of any potentate in Europe,—whether for travel, or for opportunity of society, or for access to means of science or study, or for mere comfort and easy healthy relation to people at home.

Such as we have seen is the wealth of England; a mighty mass, and made good in whatever details we care to explore. The cause and spring of it is the wealth of temperament in the people. The wonder of Britain is this plenteous nature. Her worthies are ever surrounded by as good men as themselves; each is a captain a hundred strong, and that wealth of men is represented again in the faculty of each individual,—that he has waste strength, power to spare. The English are so rich and seem to have established a tap-root in the bowels of the planet, because they are constitutionally fertile and creative.

But a man must keep an eye on his servants, if he would not have them rule him. Man is a shrewd inventor and is ever taking the hint of a new machine from his own structure, adapting some secret of his own anatomy in iron, wood and leather to some required function in the work of the world. But it is found that the machine unmans the user. What he gains in making cloth, he loses in general power. There should be temperance in making cloth, as well as in eating. A man should not be a silkworm, nor a nation a tent of caterpillars. The robust rural Saxon degenerates in the mills to the Leicester stockinger, to the imbecile Manchester spinner,—far on the way to be spiders and needles. The incessant repetition of the same hand-work dwarfs the man, robs him of his strength, wit and versatility, to make a pin-polisher, a bucklemaker, or any other specialty; and presently, in a change of industry, whole towns are sacrificed like ant-hills, when the fashion of shoe-strings supersedes buckles, when cotton takes the place of linen, or railways of turnpikes, or when commons are enclosed by landlords. Then society is admonished of the mischief of the division of labor, and that the best political economy is care and culture of men; for in these crises all are ruined except such as are proper individuals, capable of thought and of new choice and the application of their talent to new labor. Then again come in new calamities. England is aghast at the disclosure of her fraud in the adulteration of food, of drugs and of almost every fabric in her mills and shops; finding that milk will not nourish, nor sugar sweeten, nor bread satisfy, nor pepper bite the tongue, nor glue stick. In true England all is false and forged. This too is the reaction of machinery, but of the larger machinery of commerce. 'T is not, I suppose, want of probity, so much as the tyranny of trade, which necessitates a perpetual competition of underselling, and that again a perpetual deterioration of the fabric.

The machinery has proved, like the balloon, unmanageable, and flies away with the aeronaut. Steam from the first hissed and screamed to warn him; it was dreadful with its explosion, and crushed the engineer. The machinist has wrought and watched, engineers and firemen without number have been sacrificed in learning to tame and guide the monster. But harder still it has proved to resist and rule the dragon Money, with his paper wings. Chancellors and Boards of Trade, Pitt, Peel and Robinson and their Parliaments and their whole generation adopted false principles, and went to their graves in the belief that they were enriching the country which they were impoverishing. They congratulated each other on ruinous expedients. It is rare to find a merchant who knows why a crisis occurs in trade, why prices rise or fall, or who knows the mischief of paper-money. In the culmination of national prosperity, in the annexation of countries; building of ships, depots, towns; in the influx of tons of gold and silver; amid the chuckle of chancellors and financiers, it was found that bread rose to famine prices, that the yeoman was forced to sell his cow and pig, his tools and his acre of land; and the dreadful barometer of the poor-rates was touching the point of ruin. The poor-rate was sucking in the solvent classes and forcing an exodus of farmers and mechanics. What befalls from the violence of financial crises, befalls daily in the violence of artificial legislation.

Such a wealth has England earned, ever new, bounteous and augmenting. But the question recurs, does she take the step beyond, namely to the wise use, in view of the supreme wealth of nations? We estimate the wisdom of nations by seeing what they did with their surplus capital. And, in view of these injuries, some compensation has been attempted in England. A part of the money earned returns to the brain to buy schools, libraries, bishops, astronomers, chemists and artists with; and a part to repair the wrongs of this intemperate weaving, by hospitals, savings-banks, Mechanics' Institutes, public grounds and other charities and amenities. But the antidotes are frightfully inadequate, and the evil requires a deeper cure, which time and a simpler social organization must supply. At present she does not rule her wealth. She is simply a good England, but no divinity, or wise and instructed soul. She too is in the stream of fate, one victim more in a common catastrophe.

But being in the fault, she has the misfortune of greatness to be held as the chief offender. England must be held responsible for the despotism of expense. Her prosperity, the splendor which so much manhood and talent and perseverance has thrown upon vulgar aims, is the very argument of materialism. Her success strengthens the hands of base wealth. Who can propose to youth poverty and wisdom, when mean gain has arrived at the conquest of letters and arts; when English success has grown out of the very renunciation of principles, and the dedication to outsides? A civility of trifles, of money and expense, an erudition of sensation takes place, and the putting as many impediments as we can between the man and his objects. Hardly the bravest among them have the manliness to resist it successfully. Hence it has come that not the aims of a manly life, but the means of meeting a certain ponderous expense, is that which is to be considered by a youth in England emerging from his minority. A large family is reckoned a misfortune. And it is a consolation in the death of the young, that a source of expense is closed.

Aristocracy

The feudal character of the English state, now that it is getting obsolete, glares a little, in contrast with the democratic tendencies. The inequality of power and property shocks republican nerves. Palaces, halls, villas, walled parks, all over England, rival the splendor of royal seats. Many of the halls, like Haddon or Kedleston, are beautiful desolations. The proprietor never saw them; or never lived in them. Primogeniture built these sumptuous piles, and I suppose it is the sentiment of every traveller, as it was mine, It was well to come ere these were gone. Primogeniture is a cardinal rule of English property and institutions. Laws, customs, manners, the very persons and faces, affirm it.

The frame of society is aristocratic, the taste of the people is loyal. The estates, names and manners of the nobles flatter the fancy of the people and conciliate the necessary support. In spite of broken faith, stolen charters and the devastation of society by the profligacy of the court, we take sides as we read for the loyal England and King Charles's "return to his right" with his Cavaliers,—knowing what a heartless trifler he is, and what a crew of God-forsaken robbers they are. The people of England knew as much. But the fair idea of a settled government connecting itself with heraldic names, with the written and oral history of Europe, and, at last, with the Hebrew religion and the oldest traditions of the world, was too pleasing a vision to be shattered by a few offensive realities and the politics of shoe-makers and costermongers. The hopes of the commoners take the same direction with the interest of the patricians. Every man who becomes rich buys land and does what he can to fortify the nobility, into which he hopes to rise. The Anglican clergy are identified with the aristocracy. Time and law have made the joining and moulding perfect in every part. The Cathedrals, the Universities, the national music, the popular romances, conspire to uphold the heraldry which the current politics of the day are sapping. The taste of the people is conservative. They are proud of the castles, and of the language and symbol of chivalry. Even the word *lord* is the luckiest style that is used in any language to designate a patrician. The superior education and manners of the nobles recommend them to the country.

The Norwegian pirate got what he could and held it for his eldest son. The Norman noble, who was the Norwegian pirate baptized, did likewise. There was this advantage of Western over Oriental nobility, that this was recruited from below. English history is aristocracy with the doors open. Who has courage and faculty, let him come in. Of course the terms of admission to this club are hard and high. The selfishness of the nobles comes in aid of the interest of the nation to require signal merit. Piracy and war gave place to trade, politics and letters; the war-lord to the law-lord; the law-lord to the merchant and the mill-owner; but the privilege was kept, whilst the means of obtaining it were changed.

The foundations of these families lie deep in Norwegian exploits by sea and Saxon sturdiness on land. All nobility in its beginnings was somebody's natural superiority. The things these English have done were not done without peril of life, nor without wisdom and conduct; and the first hands, it may be presumed, were often challenged to show their right to their honors, or yield them to better men. "He that will be a head, let him be a bridge," said the Welsh chief Benegridran, when he carried all his men over the river on his back. "He shall have the book," said the mother of Alfred, "who can read it;" and Alfred won it by that title: and I make no doubt that feudal tenure was no sinecure, but baron, knight and tenant often had their memories refreshed, in regard to the service by which they held their lands. The De Veres, Bohuns, Mowbrays and Plantagenets were not addicted to contemplation. The Middle Age adorned itself with proofs of manhood and devotion. Of Richard Beauchamp, Earl of Warwick, the Emperor told Henry V. that no Christian king had such another knight for wisdom, nurture and manhood, and caused him to be named, "Father of curtesie." "Our success in France," says the historian, "lived and died with him."

The war-lord earned his honors, and no donation of land was large, as long as it brought the duty of protecting it, hour by hour, against a terrible enemy. In France and in England, the nobles were, down to a late day, born and bred to war: and the duel, which in peace still held them to the risks of war, diminished the envy that in trading and studious nations would else have pried into their title. They were looked on as men who played high for a great stake.

Great estates are not sinecures, if they are to be kept great. A creative economy is the fuel of magnificence. In the same line of Warwick, the successor next but one to Beauchamp was the stout earl of Henry VI. and Edward IV. Few esteemed themselves in the mode, whose heads were not adorned with the black ragged staff, his badge. At his house in London, six oxen were daily eaten at a breakfast, and every tavern was full of his meat, and who had any acquaintance in his family should have as much boiled and roast as he could carry on a long dagger.

The new age brings new qualities into request; the virtues of pirates gave way to those of planters, merchants, senators and scholars. Comity, social talent and fine manners, no doubt, have had their part also. I have met somewhere with a historiette, which, whether more or less true in its particulars, carries a general truth. "How came the Duke of Bedford by his great landed estates? His ancestor having travelled on the continent, a lively, pleasant man, became the companion of a foreign prince wrecked on the Dorsetshire coast, where Mr. Russell lived. The prince recommended him to Henry VIII., who, liking his company, gave him a large share of the plundered church lands."

The pretence is that the noble is of unbroken descent from the Norman, and has never worked for eight hundred years. But the fact is otherwise. Where is Bohun? where is De Vere? The lawyer, the farmer, the silk-mercer lies *perdu* under the coronet, and winks to the antiquary to say nothing; especially skilful lawyers, nobody's sons, who did some piece of work at a nice moment for government and were rewarded with ermine.

The national tastes of the English do not lead them to the life of the courtier, but to secure the comfort and independence of their homes. The aristocracy are marked by their predilection for country-life. They are called the county-families. They have often no residence in London and only go thither a short time, during the season, to see the opera; but they concentrate the love and labor of many generations on the building, planting and decoration of their homesteads. Some of them are too old and too proud to wear titles, or, as Sheridan said of Coke, "disdain to hide their head in a coronet;" and some curious examples are cited to show the stability of English families. Their proverb is, that fifty miles from London, a family will last a hundred years; at a hundred miles, two hundred years; and so on; but I doubt that steam, the enemy of time as well as of space, will disturb these ancient rules. Sir Henry Wotton says of the first Duke of Buckingham, "He was born at Brookeby in Leicestershire, where his ancestors had chiefly continued about the space of four hundred years, rather without obscurity, than with any great lustre." Wraxall says that in 1781, Lord Surrey, afterwards Duke of Norfolk, told him that when the year 1783 should arrive, he meant to give a grand festival to all the descendants of the body of Jockey of Norfolk, to mark the day when the dukedom should have remained three hundred years in their house, since its creation by Richard III. Pepys tells us, in writing of an Earl Oxford, in 1666, that the honor had now remained in that name and blood six hundred years.

This long descent of families and this cleaving through ages to the same spot of ground, captivates the imagination. It has too a connection with the names of the towns and districts of the country.

The names are excellent,—an atmosphere of legendary melody spread over the land. Older than all epics and histories which clothe a nation, this undershirt sits close to the body. What history too, and what stores of primitive and savage observation it infolds! Cambridge is the bridge of the Cam; Sheffield the field of the river Sheaf; Leicester the *castra*, or camp, of the Lear, or Leir (now Soar); Rochdale, of the Roch; Exeter or Excester, the *castra* of the Ex; Exmouth, Dartmouth, Sidmouth, Teignmouth, the mouths of the Ex, Dart, Sid and Teign rivers. Waltham is strong town; Radcliffe is red cliff; and so on:—a sincerity and use in naming very striking to an American, whose country is whitewashed all over by unmeaning names, the cast-off clothes of the country from which its emigrants came; or named at a pinch from a psalm-tune. But the English are those "barbarians" of Jamblichus, who "are stable in their manners, and firmly continue to employ the same words, which also are dear to the gods."

'T is an old sneer that the Irish peerage drew their names from playbooks. The English lords do not call their lands after their own names, but call themselves after their lands, as if the man represented the country that bred him; and they rightly wear the token of the glebe that gave them birth, suggesting that the tie is not cut, but that there in London,—the crags of Argyle, the kail of Cornwall, the downs of Devon, the iron of Wales, the clays of Stafford are neither forgetting nor forgotten, but know the man who was born by them and who, like the long line of his fathers, has carried that crag, that shore, dale, fen, or woodland, in his blood and manners. It has, too, the advantage of suggesting responsibleness. A susceptible man could not wear a name which represented in a strict sense a city or a county of England, without hearing in it a challenge to duty and honor.

The predilection of the patricians for residence in the country, combined with the degree of liberty possessed by the peasant, makes the safety of the English hall. Mirabeau wrote prophetically from England, in 1784, "If revolution break out in France, I tremble for the aristocracy: their châteaux will be reduced to ashes and their blood be spilt in torrents. The English tenant would defend his lord to the last extremity." The English go to their estates for grandeur. The French live at court, and exile themselves to their estates for economy. As they do not mean to live with their tenants, they do not conciliate them, but wring from them the last *sous*. Evelyn writes from Blois, in 1644: "The wolves are here in such numbers, that they often come and take children out of the streets; yet will not the Duke, who is sovereign here, permit them to be destroyed."

In evidence of the wealth amassed by ancient families, the traveller is shown the palaces in Piccadilly, Burlington House, Devonshire House, Lansdowne House in Berkshire Square, and lower down in the city, a few noble houses which still withstand in all their amplitude the encroachment of streets. The Duke of Bedford includes or included a mile square in the heart of London, where the British Museum, once Montague House, now stands, and the land occupied by Woburn Square, Bedford Square, Russell Square. The Marquis of Westminster built within a few years the series of squares called Belgravia. Stafford House is the noblest palace in London. Northumberland House holds its place by Charing Cross. Chesterfield House remains in Audley Street. Sion House and Holland House are in the suburbs. But most of the historical houses are masked or lost in the modern uses to which trade or charity has converted them. A multitude of town palaces contain inestimable galleries of art.

In the country, the size of private estates is more impressive. From Barnard Castle I rode on the highway twenty-three miles from High Force, a fall of the Tees, towards Darlington, past Raby Castle, through the estate of the Duke of Cleveland. The Marquis of Breadalbane rides out of his house a hundred miles in a straight line to the sea, on his own property. The Duke of Sutherland owns the County of Sutherland, stretching across Scotland from sea to sea. The Duke of Devonshire, besides his other estates, owns 96,000 acres in the County of Derby. The Duke of Richmond has 40,000 acres at Goodwood and 300,000 at Gordon Castle. The Duke of Norfolk's park in Sussex is fifteen miles in circuit. An agriculturist bought lately the island of Lewes, in Hebrides, containing 500,000 acres. The possessions of the Earl of Lonsdale gave him eight seats in Parliament. This is the Heptarchy again; and before the Reform of 1832, one hundred and fifty-four persons sent three hundred and seven members to Parliament. The borough-mongers governed England.

These large domains are growing larger. The great estates are absorbing the small freeholds. In 1786 the soil of England was owned by 250,000 corporations and proprietors; and in 1822, by 32,000. These broad estates find room in this narrow island. All over England, scattered at short intervals among ship-yards, mills, mines and forges, are the paradises of the nobles, where the livelong repose and refinement are heightened by the contrast with the roar of industry and necessity, out of which you have stepped aside.

I was surprised to observe the very small attendance usually in the House of Lords. Out of five hundred and seventy-three peers, on ordinary days only twenty or thirty. Where are they? I asked. "At home on their estates, devoured by *ennui*, or in the Alps, or up the Rhine, in the Harz Mountains, or in Egypt, or in India, on the Ghauts." But, with such interests at stake, how can these men afford to neglect them? "O," replied my friend, "why should they work for themselves, when every man in England works for them and will suffer before they come to harm?" The hardest radical instantly uncovers and changes his tone to a lord. It was remarked, on the 10th April, 1848 (the day of the Chartist demonstration), that the upper classes were for the first time actively interesting themselves in their own defence, and men of rank were sworn special constables with the rest. "Besides, why need they sit out the debate? Has not the Duke of Wellington, at this moment, their proxies—the proxies of fifty peers—in his pocket, to vote for them if there be an emergency?"

It is however true that the existence of the House of Peers as a branch of the government entitles them to fill half the Cabinet; and their weight of property and station gives them a virtual nomination of the other half; whilst they have their share in the subordinate offices, as a school of training. This monopoly of political power has given them their intellectual and social eminence in Europe. A few law lords and a few political lords take the brunt of public business. In the army, the nobility fill a large part of the high commissions, and give to these a tone of expense and splendor and also of exclusiveness. They have borne their full share of duty and danger in this service, and there are few noble families which have not paid, in some of their members, the debt of life or limb in the sacrifices of the Russian war. For the rest, the nobility have the lead in matters of state and of expense; in questions of taste, in social usages, in convival and domestic hospitalities. In general, all that is required of them is to sit securely, to preside at public meetings, to countenance charities and to give the example of that decorum so dear to the British heart.

If one asks, in the critical spirit of the day, what service this class have rendered?—uses appear, or they would have perished long ago. Some of these are easily enumerated, others more subtle make a part of unconscious history. Their institution is one step in the progress of society. For a race yields a nobility in some form, however we name the lords, as surely as it yields women.

The English nobles are high-spirited, active, educated men, born to wealth and power, who have run through every country and kept in every country the best company, have seen every secret of art and nature, and, when men of any ability or ambition, have been consulted in the conduct of every important action. You cannot wield great agencies without lending yourself to them, and when it happens that the spirit of the earl meets his rank and duties, we have the best examples of behavior. Power of any kind readily appears in the manners; and beneficent power, *le talent de bien faire*, gives a majesty which cannot be concealed or resisted.

These people seem to gain as much as they lose by their position. They survey society as from the top of St. Paul's, and if they never hear plain truth from men, they see the best of everything, in every kind, and they see things so grouped and amassed as to infer easily the sum and genius, instead of tedious particularities. Their good behavior deserves all its fame, and they have that simplicity and that air of repose which are the finest ornament of greatness.

The upper classes have only birth, say the people here, and not thoughts. Yes, but they have manners, and it is wonderful how much talent runs into manners:—nowhere and never so much as in England. They have the sense of superiority, the absence of all the ambitious effort which disgusts in the aspiring classes, a pure tone of thought and feeling, and the power to command, among their other luxuries, the presence of the most accomplished men in their festive meetings.

Loyalty is in the English a sub-religion. They wear the laws as ornaments, and walk by their faith in their painted

May-Fair as if among the forms of gods. The economist of 1855 who asks, Of what use are the lords? may learn of Franklin to ask, Of what use is a baby? They have been a social church proper to inspire sentiments mutually honoring the lover and the loved. Politeness is the ritual of society, as prayers are of the church, a school of manners, and a gentle blessing to the age in which it grew. 'T is a romance adorning English life with a larger horizon; a midway heaven, fulfilling to their sense their fairy tales and poetry. This, just as far as the breeding of the nobleman really made him brave, handsome, accomplished and great-hearted.

On general grounds, whatever tends to form manners or to finish men, has a great value. Every one who has tasted the delight of friendship will respect every social guard which our manners can establish, tending to secure from the intrusion of frivolous and distasteful people. The jealousy of every class to guard itself is a testimony to the reality they have found in life. When a man once knows that he has done justice to himself, let him dismiss all terrors of aristocracy as superstitions, so far as he is concerned. He who keeps the door of a mine, whether of cobalt, or mercury, or nickel, or plumbago, securely knows that the world cannot do without him. Everybody who is real is open and ready for that which is also real.

Besides, these are they who make England that strong-box and museum it is; who gather and protect works of art, dragged from amidst burning cities and revolutionary countries, and brought hither out of all the world. I look with respect at houses six, seven, eight hundred, or, like Warwick Castle, nine hundred years old. I pardoned high park-fences, when I saw that besides does and pheasants, these have preserved Arundel marbles, Townley galleries, Howard and Spenserian libraries, Warwick and Portland vases, Saxon manuscripts, monastic architectures, millennial trees, and breeds of cattle elsewhere extinct. In these manors, after the frenzy of war and destruction subsides a little, the antiquary finds the frailest Roman jar or crumbling Egyptian mummy-case, without so much as a new layer of dust, keeping the series of history unbroken and waiting for its interpreter, who is sure to arrive. These lords are the treasurers and librarians of mankind, engaged by their pride and wealth to this function.

Yet there were other works for British dukes to do. George Loudon, Quintinye, Evelyn, had taught them to make gardens. Arthur Young, Bakewell and Mechi have made them agricultural. Scotland was a camp until the day of Culloden. The Dukes of Athol, Sutherland, Buccleugh and the Marquis of Breadalbane have introduced the rape-culture, the sheep-farm, wheat, drainage, the plantation of forests, the artificial replenishment of lakes and ponds with fish, the renting of game-preserves. Against the cry of the old tenantry and the sympathetic cry of the English press, they have rooted out and planted anew, and now six millions of people live, and live better, on the same land that fed three millions.

The English barons, in every period, have been brave and great, after the estimate and opinion of their times. The grand old halls scattered up and down in England, are dumb vouchers to the state and broad hospitality of their ancient lords. Shakspeare's portraits of good Duke Humphrey, of Warwick, of Northumberland, of Talbot, were drawn in strict consonance with the traditions. A sketch of the Earl of Shrewsbury, from the pen of Queen Elizabeth's archbishop Parker; Lord Herbert of Cherbury's autobiography; the letters and essays of Sir Philip Sidney; the anecdotes preserved by the antiquaries Fuller and Collins; some glimpses at the interiors of noble houses, which we owe to Pepys and Evelyn; the details which Ben Jonson's masques (performed at Kenilworth, Althorpe, Belvoir and other noble houses), record or suggest; down to Aubrey's passages of the life of Hobbes in the house of the Earl of Devon, are favorable pictures of a romantic style of manners. Penshurst still shines for us, and its Christmas revels, "where logs not burn, but men."

At Wilton House the "Arcadia" was written, amidst conversations with Fulke Greville, Lord Brooke, a man of no vulgar mind, as his own poems declare him. I must hold Ludlow Castle an honest house, for which Milton's "Comus" was written, and the company nobly bred which performed it with knowledge and sympathy. In the roll of nobles are found poets, philosophers, chemists, astronomers, also men of solid virtues and of lofty sentiments; often they have been the friends and patrons of genius and learning, and especially of the fine arts; and at this moment, almost every great house has its sumptuous picture-gallery.

Of course there is another side to this gorgeous show. Every victory was the defeat of a party only less worthy. Castles are proud things, but 't is safest to be outside of them. War is a foul game, and yet war is not the worst part of aristocratic history. In later times, when the baron, educated only for war, with his brains paralyzed by his stomach, found himself idle at home, he grew fat and wanton and a sorry brute. Grammont, Pepys and Evelyn show the kennels to which the king and court went in quest of pleasure. Prostitutes taken from the theatres were made duchesses, their bastards dukes and earls. "The young men sat uppermost, the old serious lords were out of favor." The discourse that the king's companions had with him was "poor and frothy." No man who valued his head might do what these pot-companions familiarly did with the king. In logical sequence of these dignified revels, Pepys can tell the beggarly shifts to which the king was reduced, who could not find paper at his council table, and "no handkerchers" in his wardrobe, "and but three bands to his neck," and the linen-draper and the stationer were out of pocket and refusing to trust him, and the baker will not bring bread any longer. Meantime the English Channel was swept and London threatened by the Dutch fleet, manned too by English sailors, who, having been cheated of their pay for years by the king, enlisted with the enemy.

The Selwyn correspondence, in the reign of George III., discloses a rottenness in the aristocracy which threatened to decompose the state. The sycophancy and sale of votes and honor, for place and title; lewdness, gaming, smuggling, bribery and cheating; the sneer at the childish indiscretion of quarrelling with ten thousand a year; the want of ideas; the splendor of the titles, and the apathy of the nation, are instructive, and make the reader pause and explore the firm bounds which confined these vices to a handful of rich men. In the reign of the Fourth George, things do not seem to have mended, and the rotten debauchee let down from a window by an inclined plane into his coach to take the air, was a scandal to Europe which the ill fame of his queen and of his family did nothing to retrieve.

Under the present reign the perfect decorum of the Court is thought to have put a check on the gross vices of the aristocracy; yet gaming, racing, drinking and mistresses bring them down, and the democrat can still gather scandals, if he will. Dismal anecdotes abound, verifying the gossip of the last generation, of dukes served by bailiffs, with all their plate in pawn; of great lords living by the showing of their houses, and of an old man wheeled in his chair from room to room, whilst his chambers are exhibited to the visitor for money; of ruined dukes and earls living in exile for debt. The historic names of the Buckinghams, Beauforts, Marlboroughs and Hertfords have gained no new lustre, and now and then darker scandals break out, ominous as the new chapters added under the Orleans dynasty to the "Causes Célèbres" in France. Even peers who are men of worth and public spirit are overtaken and embarrassed by their vast expense. The respectable Duke of Devonshire, willing to be the Mæcenas and Lucullus of his island, is reported to have said that he cannot live at Chatsworth but one month in the year. Their many houses eat them up. They cannot sell them, because they are entailed. They will not let them, for pride's sake, but keep them empty, aired, and the grounds mown and dressed, at a cost of four or five thousand pounds a year. The spending is for a great part in servants, in many houses exceeding a hundred.

Most of them are only chargeable with idleness, which, because it squanders such vast power of benefit, has the mischief of crime. "They might be little Providences on earth," said my friend, "and they are, for the most part, jockeys and fops." Campbell says, "Acquaintance with the nobility, I could never keep up. It requires a life of idleness, dressing and attendance on their parties." I suppose too that a feeling of self-respect is driving cultivated men out of this society, as if the noble were slow to receive the lessons of the times and had not learned to disguise his pride of place. A man of wit, who is also one of the celebrities of wealth and fashion, confessed to his friend that he could not enter their houses without being made to feel that they were great lords, and he a low plebeian. With the tribe of *artistes*, including the musical tribe, the patrician morgue keeps no terms, but excludes them. When Julia Grisi and Mario sang at the houses of the Duke of Wellington and other grandees, a cord was stretched between the singer and the company.

When every noble was a soldier, they were carefully bred to great personal prowess. The education of a soldier is a simpler affair than that of an earl in the nineteenth century. And this was very seriously pursued; they were expert in every species of equitation, to the most dangerous practices, and this down to the accession of William of Orange. But graver men appear to have trained their sons for civil affairs. Elizabeth extended her thought to the future; and Sir Philip Sidney in his letter to his brother, and Milton and Evelyn, gave plain and hearty counsel. Already too the English noble and squire were preparing for the career of the country-gentleman and his peaceable expense. They went from city to city, learning receipts to make perfumes, sweet powders, pomanders, antidotes, gathering seeds, gems, coins and divers curiosities, preparing for a private life thereafter, in which they should take pleasure in these recreations.

All advantages given to absolve the young patrician from intellectual labor are of course mistaken. "In the university, noblemen are exempted from the public exercises for the degree, etc. by which they attain a degree called *honorary.* At the same time, the fees they have to pay for matriculation, and on all other occasions, are much higher." Fuller records "the observation of foreigners, that Englishmen, by making their children gentlemen before they are men, cause they are so seldom wise men." This cockering justifies Dr. Johnson's bitter apology for primogeniture, that "it makes but one fool in a family."

The revolution in society has reached this class. The great powers of industrial art have no exclusion of name or blood. The tools of our time, namely steam, ships, printing, money and popular education, belong to those who can handle them; and their effect has been that advantages once confined to men of family are now open to the whole middle class. The road that grandeur levels for his coach, toil can travel in his cart.

This is more manifest every day, but I think it is true throughout English history. English history, wisely read, is the vindication of the brain of that people. Here at last were climate and condition friendly to the working faculty. Who now will work and dare, shall rule. This is the charter, or the chartism, which fogs and seas and rains proclaimed,—that intellect and personal force should make the law; that industry and administrative talent should administer; that work should wear the crown. I know that not this, but something else is pretended. The fiction with which the noble and the bystander equally please themselves is that the former is of unbroken descent from the Norman, and so has never worked for eight hundred years. All the families are new, but the name is old, and they have made a covenant with their memories not to disturb it. But the analysis of the peerage and gentry shows the rapid decay and extinction of old families, the continual recruiting of these from new blood. The doors, though ostentatiously guarded, are really open, and hence the power of the bribe. All the barriers to rank only whet the thirst and enhance the prize. "Now," said Nelson, when clearing for battle, "a peerage, or Westminster Abbey!" "I have no illusion left," said Sidney Smith, "but the Archbishop of Canterbury." "The lawyers," said Burke, "are only birds of passage in this House of Commons," and then added, with a new figure, "they have their best bower anchor in the House of Lords."

Another stride that has been taken appears in the perishing of heraldry. Whilst the privileges of nobility are passing to the middle class, the badge is discredited and the titles of lordship are getting musty and cumbersome. I wonder that sensible men have not been already impatient of them. They belong, with wigs, powder and scarlet coats, to an earlier age and may be advantageously consigned, with paint and tattoo, to the dignitaries of Australia and Polynesia.

A multitude of English, educated at the universities, bred into their society with manners, ability and the gifts of fortune, are every day confronting the peers on a footing of equality, and outstripping them, as often, in the race of honor and influence. That cultivated class is large and ever enlarging. It is computed that, with titles and without, there are seventy thousand of these people coming and going in London, who make up what is called high society. They cannot shut their eyes to the fact that an untitled nobility possess all the power without the inconveniences that belong to rank, and the rich Englishman goes over the world at the present day, drawing more than all the advantages which the strongest of his kings could command.

Universities

Of British universities, Cambridge has the most illustrious names on its list. At the present day too, it has the advantage of Oxford, counting in its *alumni* a greater number of distinguished scholars. I regret that I had but a single day wherein to see King's College Chapel, the beautiful lawns and gardens of the colleges, and a few of its gownsmen.

But I availed myself of some repeated invitations to Oxford, where I had introductions to Dr. Daubeny, Professor of Botany, and to the Regius Professor of Divinity, as well as to a valued friend, a Fellow of Oriel, and went thither on the last day of March, 1848. I was the guest of my friend in Oriel, was housed close upon that college, and I lived on college hospitalities.

My new friends showed me their cloisters, the Bodleian Library, the Randolph Gallery, Merton Hall and the rest. I saw several faithful, high-minded young men, some of them in the mood of making sacrifices for peace of mind,—a topic, of course, on which I had no counsel to offer. Their affectionate and gregarious ways reminded me at once of the habits of *our* Cambridge men, though I imputed to these English an advantage in their secure and polished manners. The halls are rich with oaken wainscoting and ceiling. The pictures of the founders hang from the walls; the tables glitter with plate. A youth came forward to the upper table and pronounced the ancient form of grace before meals, which, I suppose, has been in use here for ages, *Benedictus, benedicat; benedicitur, benedicatur.*

It is a curious proof of the English use and wont, or of their good nature, that these young men are locked up every night at nine o'clock, and the porter at each hall is required to give the name of any belated student who is admitted after that hour. Still more descriptive is the fact that out of twelve hundred young men, comprising the most spirited of the aristocracy, a duel has never occurred.

Oxford is old, even in England, and conservative. Its foundations date from Alfred and even from Arthur, if, as is alleged, the Pheryllt of the Druids had a seminary here. In the reign of Edward I., it is pretended, here were thirty thousand students; and nineteen most noble foundations were then established. Chaucer found it as firm as if it had always stood; and it is, in British story, rich with great names, the school of the island and the link of England to the learned of Europe. Hither came Erasmus, with delight, in 1497. Albericus Gentilis, in 1580, was relieved and maintained by the university. Albert Alaskie, a noble Polonian, Prince of Sirad, who visited England to admire the wisdom of Queen Elizabeth, was entertained with stage-plays in the Refectory of Christ-Church in 1583. Isaac Casaubon, coming from Henri Quatre of France by invitation of James I., was admitted to Christ-Church, in July, 1613. I saw the Ashmolean Museum, whither Elias Ashmole in 1682 sent twelve cart-loads of rarities. Here indeed was the Olympia of all Antony Wood's and Aubrey's games and heroes, and every inch of ground has its lustre. For Wood's *Athenæ Oxonienses,* or calendar of the writers of Oxford for two hundred years, is a lively record of English manners and merits, and as much a national monument as Purchas's Pilgrims or Hansard's Register. On every side, Oxford is redolent of age and authority. Its gates shut of themselves against modern innovation. It is still governed by the statutes of Archbishop Laud. The books in Merton Library are still chained to the wall. Here, on August 27, 1660, John Milton's *Pro Populo Anglicano Defensio* and *Iconoclastes* were committed to the flames. I saw the school-court or quadrangle where, in 1683, the Convocation caused the Leviathan of Thomas Hobbes to be publicly burnt. I do not know whether this learned body have yet heard of the Declaration of American Independence, or whether the Ptolemaic astronomy does not still hold its ground against the novelties of Copernicus.

As many sons, almost so many benefactors. It is usual for a nobleman, or indeed for almost every wealthy student, on quitting college to leave behind him some article of plate; and gifts of all values, from a hall or a fellowship or a library, down to a picture or a spoon, are continually accruing, in the course of a century. My friend Doctor J. gave me the following anecdote. In Sir Thomas Lawrence's collection at London were the cartoons of Raphael and Michael Angelo. This inestimable prize was offered to Oxford University for seven thousand pounds. The offer was accepted, and the committee charged with the affair had collected three thousand pounds, when, among other friends, they called on Lord Eldon. Instead of a hundred pounds, he surprised them by putting down his name for three thousand pounds. They told him they should now very easily raise the remainder. "No," he said, "your men have probably already contributed all they can spare; I can as well give the rest:" and he withdrew his cheque for three thousand, and wrote four thousand pounds. I saw the whole collection in April, 1848.

In the Bodleian Library, Dr. Bandinel showed me the manuscript Plato, of the date of A.D. 896, brought by Dr. Clarke from Egypt; a manuscript Virgil of the same century; the first Bible printed at Mentz (I believe in 1450); and a duplicate of the same, which had been deficient in about twenty leaves at the end. But one day, being in Venice, he bought a room full of books and manuscripts,—every scrap and fragment,—for four thousand louis d'ors, and had the doors locked and sealed by the consul. On proceeding afterwards to examine his purchase, he found the twenty deficient pages of his Mentz Bible, in perfect order; brought them to Oxford with the rest of his purchase, and placed them in the volume; but has too much awe for the Providence that appears in bibliography also, to suffer the reunited parts to be re-bound. The oldest building here is two hundred years younger than the frail manuscript brought by Dr. Clarke from Egypt. No candle or fire is ever lighted in the Bodleian. Its catalogue is the standard catalogue on the desk of every library in Oxford. In each several college they underscore in red ink on this catalogue the titles of books contained in the library of that college,—the theory being that the Bodleian has all books. This rich library spent during the last year (1847), for the purchase of books, £1668.

The logical English train a scholar as they train an engineer. Oxford is a Greek factory, as Wilton mills weave carpet and Sheffield grinds steel. They know the use of a tutor, as they know the use of a horse; and they draw the greatest amount of benefit out of both. The reading men are kept, by hard walking, hard riding and measured eating and drinking, at the top of their condition, and two days before the examination, do no work, but lounge, ride, or run, to be fresh on the college doomsday. Seven years' residence is the theoretic period for a master's degree. In point of fact, it has long been three years' residence, and four years more of standing. This "three years" is about twenty-one months in all.

"The whole expense," says Professor Sewel, "of ordinary college tuition at Oxford, is about sixteen guineas a year." But this plausible statement may deceive a reader unacquainted with the fact that the principal teaching relied on is private tuition. And the expenses of private tuition are reckoned at from £50 to £70 a year, or $1000 for the whole course of three years and a half. At Cambridge, $750 a year is economical, and $1500 not extravagant.

The number of students and of residents, the dignity of the authorities, the value of the foundations, the history and the architecture, the known sympathy of entire Britain in what is done there, justify a dedication to study in the undergraduate such as cannot easily be in America, where his college is half suspected by the Freshman to be insignificant in the scale beside trade and politics. Oxford is a little aristocracy in itself, numerous and dignified enough to rank with other estates in the realm; and where fame and secular promotion are to be had for study, and in a direction which has the unanimous respect of all cultivated nations.

This aristocracy, of course, repairs its own losses; fills places, as they fall vacant, from the body of students. The number of fellowships at Oxford is 540, averaging £200 a year, with lodging and diet at the college. If a young American, loving learning and hindered by poverty, were offered a home, a table, the walks and the library in one of these academical palaces, and a thousand dollars a year, as long as he chose to remain a bachelor, he would dance for joy. Yet these young men thus happily placed, and paid to read, are impatient of their few checks, and many of them preparing to resign their fellowships. They shuddered at the prospect of dying a Fellow, and they pointed out to me a paralytic old man, who was assisted into the hall. As the number of undergraduates at Oxford is only about 1200 or 1300, and many of these are never competitors, the chance of a fellowship is very great. The income of the nineteen colleges is conjectured at £150,000 a year.

The effect of this drill is the radical knowledge of Greek and Latin and of mathematics, and the solidity and taste of English criticism. Whatever luck there may be in this or that award, an Eton captain can write Latin longs and shorts, can turn the Court-Guide into hexameters, and it is certain that a Senior Classic can quote correctly from the *Corpus Poetarum* and is critically learned in all the humanities. Greek erudition exists on the Isis and Cam, whether the Maud man or the Brasenose man be properly ranked or not; the atmosphere is loaded with Greek learning; the whole river has reached a certain height, and kills all that growth of weeds which this Castalian water kills. The English nature takes culture kindly. So Milton thought. It refines the Norseman. Access to the Greek mind lifts his standard of taste. He has enough to think of, and, unless of an impulsive nature, is indisposed from writing or speaking, by the fulness of his mind and the new severity of his taste. The great silent crowd of thoroughbred Grecians always known to be around him, the English writer cannot ignore. They prune his orations and point his pen. Hence the style and tone of English journalism. The men have learned accuracy and comprehension, logic, and pace, or speed of working. They have bottom, endurance, wind. When born with good constitutions, they make those eupeptic studying-mills, the cast-iron men, the *dura ilia*, whose powers of performance compare with ours as the steam-hammer with the music-box;—Cokes, Mansfields, Seldens and Bentleys, and when it happens that a superior brain puts a rider on this admirable horse, we obtain those masters of the world who combine the highest energy in affairs with a supreme culture.

It is contended by those who have been bred at Eton, Harrow, Rugby and Westminster, that the public sentiment within each of those schools is high-toned and manly; that, in their playgrounds, courage is universally admired, meanness despised, manly feelings and generous conduct are encouraged: that an unwritten code of honor deals to the spoiled child of rank and to the child of upstart wealth, an even-handed justice, purges their nonsense out of both and does all that can be done to make them gentlemen.

Again, at the universities, it is urged that all goes to form what England values as the flower of its national life,—a well-educated gentleman. The German Huber, in describing to his countrymen the attributes of an English gentleman, frankly admits that "in Germany, we have nothing of the kind. A gentleman must possess a political character, an independent and public position, or at least the right of assuming it. He must have average opulence, either of his own, or in his family. He should also have bodily activity and strength, unattainable by our sedentary life in public offices. The race of English gentlemen presents an appearance of manly vigor and form not elsewhere to be found among an equal number of persons. No other nation produces the stock. And in England, it has deteriorated. The university is a decided presumption in any man's favor. And so eminent are the members that a glance at the calendars will show that in all the world one cannot be in better company than on the books of one of the larger Oxford or Cambridge colleges."

These seminaries are finishing schools for the upper classes, and not for the poor. The useful is exploded. The definition of a public school is "a school which excludes all that could fit a man for standing behind a counter."

No doubt, the foundations have been perverted. Oxford, which equals in wealth several of the smaller European states, shuts up the lectureships which were made "public for all men thereunto to have concourse;" misspends the revenues bestowed for such youths "as should be most meet for towardness, poverty and painfulness;" there is gross favoritism; many chairs and many fellowships are made beds of ease; and it is likely that the university will know how to resist and make inoperative the terrors of parliamentary inquiry; no doubt their learning is grown obsolete;—but Oxford also has its merits, and I found here also proof of the national fidelity and thoroughness. Such knowledge as they prize they possess and impart. Whether in course or by indirection, whether by a cramming tutor or by examiners with prizes and foundational scholarships, education, according to the English notion of it, is arrived at. I looked over the Examination Papers of the year 1848, for the various scholarships and fellowships, the Lusby, the Hertford, the Dean-Ireland and the University (copies of which were kindly given me by a Greek professor), containing the tasks which many competitors had victoriously performed, and I believed they would prove too severe tests for the candidates for a Bachelor's degree in Yale or Harvard. And in general, here was proof of a more searching study in the appointed directions, and the knowledge pretended to be conveyed was conveyed. Oxford sends out yearly twenty or thirty very able men and three or four hundred well-educated men.

The diet and rough exercise secure a certain amount of old Norse power. A fop will fight, and in exigent circumstances will play the manly part. In seeing these youths I believed I saw already an advantage in vigor and color and general habit, over their contemporaries in the American colleges. No doubt much of the power and brilliancy of the reading-men is merely constitutional or hygienic. With a hardier habit and resolute gymnastics, with five miles more walking, or five ounces less eating, or with a saddle and gallop of twenty miles a day, with skating and rowing-matches, the American would arrive at as robust exegesis and cheery and hilarious tone. I should readily concede these advantages, which it would be easy to acquire, if I did not find also that they read better than we, and write better.

English wealth falling on their school and university training, makes a systematic reading of the best authors, and to the end of a knowledge how the things whereof they treat really stand: whilst pamphleteer or journalist, reading for an argument for a party, or reading to write, or at all events for some by-end imposed on them, must read meanly and fragmentarily. Charles I. said that he understood English law as well as a gentleman ought to understand it.

Then they have access to books; the rich libraries collected at every one of many thousands of houses, give an advantage not to be attained by a youth in this country, when one thinks how much more and better may be learned by a scholar who, immediately on hearing of a book, can consult it, than by one who is on the quest, for years, and reads inferior books because he cannot find the best.

Again, the great number of cultivated men keep each other up to a high standard. The habit of meeting well-read and knowing men teaches the art of omission and selection.

Universities are of course hostile to geniuses, which, seeing and using ways of their own, discredit the routine: as churches and monasteries persecute youthful saints. Yet we all send our sons to college, and though he be a genius, the youth must take his chance. The university must be retrospective. The gale that gives direction to the vanes on all its towers blows out of antiquity. Oxford is a library, and the professors must be librarians. And I should as soon think of quarrelling with the janitor for not magnifying his office by hostile sallies into the street, like the Governor of Kertch or Kinburn, as of quarrelling with the professors for not admiring the young neologists who pluck the beards of Euclid and Aristotle, or for not attempting themselves to fill their vacant shelves as original writers.

It is easy to carp at colleges, and the college, if we will wait for it, will have its own turn. Genius exists there also, but will not answer a call of a committee of the House of Commons. It is rare, precarious, eccentric and darkling. England is the land of mixture and surprise, and when you have settled it that the universities are moribund, out comes a poetic influence from the heart of Oxford, to mould the opinions of cities, to build their houses as simply as birds their nests, to give veracity to art and charm mankind, as an appeal to moral order always must. But besides this restorative genius, the best poetry of England of this age, in the old forms, comes from two graduates at Cambridge.

Religion

No people at the present day can be explained by their national religion. They do not feel responsible for it; it lies far outside of them. Their loyalty to truth and their labor and expenditure rest on real foundations, and not on a national church. And English life, it is evident, does not grow out of the Athanasian creed, or the Articles, or the Eucharist. It is with religion as with marriage. A youth marries in haste; afterwards, when his mind is opened to the reason of the conduct of life, he is asked what he thinks of the institution of marriage and of the right relations of the sexes? 'I should have much to say,' he might reply, 'if the question were open, but I have a wife and children, and all question is closed for me.' In the barbarous days of a nation, some *cultus* is formed or imported; altars are built, tithes are paid, priests ordained. The education and expenditure of the country take that direction, and when wealth, refinement, great men, and ties to the world supervene, its prudent men say, Why fight against Fate, or life these absurdities which are now mountainous? Better find some niche or crevice in this mountain of stone which religious ages have quarried and carved, wherein to bestow yourself, than attempt anything ridiculously and dangerously above your strength, like removing it.

In seeing old castles and cathedrals, I sometimes say, as to-day in front of Dundee Church tower, which is eight hundred years old, 'This was built by another and a better race than any that now look on it.' And plainly there has been great power of sentiment at work in this island, of which these buildings are the proofs; as volcanic basalts show the work of fire which has been extinguished for ages. England felt the full heat of the Christianity which fermented Europe, and drew, like the chemistry of fire, a firm line between barbarism and culture. The power of the religious sentiment put an end to human sacrifices, checked appetite, inspired the crusades, inspired resistance to tyrants, inspired self-respect, set bounds to serfdom and slavery, founded liberty, created the religious architecture,—York, Newstead, Westminster, Fountains Abbey, Ripon, Beverley and Dundee,—works to which the key is lost, with the sentiment which created them; inspired the English Bible, the liturgy, the monkish histories, the chronicle of Richard of Devizes. The priest translated the Vulgate, and translated the sanctities of old hagiology into English virtues on English ground. It was a certain affirmative or aggressive state of the Caucasian races. Man awoke refreshed by the sleep of ages. The violence of the northern savages exasperated Christianity into power. It lived by the love of the people. Bishop Wilfrid manumitted two hundred and fifty serfs, whom he found attached to the soil. The clergy obtained respite from labor for the boor on the Sabbath and on church festivals. "The lord who compelled his boor to labor between sunset on Saturday and sunset on Sunday, forfeited him altogether." The priest came out of the people and sympathized with his class. The church was the mediator, check and democratic principle, in Europe. Latimer, Wicliffe, Arundel, Cobham, Antony Parsons, Sir Harry

Vane, George Fox, Penn, Bunyan are the democrats, as well as the saints of their times. The Catholic Church, thrown on this toiling, serious people, has made in fourteen centuries a massive system, close fitted to the manners and genius of the country, at once domestical and stately. In the long time, it has blended with everything in heaven above and the earth beneath. It moves through a zodiac of feasts and fasts, names every day of the year, every town and market and headland and monument, and has coupled itself with the almanac, that no court can be held, no field ploughed, no horse shod, without some leave from the church. All maxims of prudence or shop or farm are fixed and dated by the church. Hence its strength in the agricultural districts. The distribution of land into parishes enforces a church sanction to every civil privilege; and the gradation of the clergy,—prelates for the rich and curates for the poor,—with the fact that a classical education has been secured to the clergyman, makes them "the link which unites the sequestered peasantry with the intellectual advancement of the age."

The English Church has many certificates to show of humble effective service in humanizing the people, in cheering and refining men, feeding, healing and educating. It has the seal of martyrs and confessors; the noblest books; a sublime architecture; a ritual marked by the same secular merits, nothing cheap or purchasable.

From this slow-grown church important reactions proceed; much for culture, much for giving a direction to the nation's affection and will to-day. The carved and pictured chapel—its entire surface animated with image and emblem—made the parish-church a sort of book and Bible to the people's eye.

Then, when the Saxon instinct had secured a service in the vernacular tongue, it was the tutor and university of the people. In York minster, on the day of the enthronization of the new archbishop, I heard the service of evening prayer read and chanted in the choir. It was strange to hear the pretty pastoral of the betrothal of Rebecca and

Isaac, in the morning of the world, read with circumstantiality in York minster, on the 13th January, 1848, to the decorous English audience, just fresh from the Times newspaper and their wine, and listening with all the devotion of national pride. That was binding old and new to some purpose. The reverence for the Scriptures is an element of civilization, for thus has the history of the world been preserved and is preserved. Here in England every day a chapter of Genesis, and a leader in the Times.

Another part of the same service on this occasion was not insignificant. Handel's coronation anthem, *God save the King*, was played by Dr. Camidge on the organ, with sublime effect. The minster and the music were made for each other. It was a hint of the part the church plays as a political engine. From his infancy, every Englishman is accustomed to hear daily prayers for the Queen, for the royal family and the Parliament, by name; and this lifelong consecration cannot be without influence on his opinions.

The universities also are parcel of the ecclesiastical system, and their first design is to form the clergy. Thus the clergy for a thousand years have been the scholars of the nation.

The national temperament deeply enjoys the unbroken order and tradition of its church; the liturgy, ceremony, architecture; the sober grace, the good company, the connection with the throne and with history, which adorn it. And whilst it endears itself thus to men of more taste than activity, the stability of the English nation is passionately enlisted to its support, from its inextricable connection with the cause of public order, with politics and with the funds.

Good churches are not built by bad men; at least there must be probity and enthusiasm somewhere in the society. These minsters were neither built nor filled by atheists. No church has had more learned, industrious or devoted men; plenty of "clerks and bishops, who, out of their gowns, would turn their backs on no man." Their architecture still glows with faith in immortality. Heats and genial periods arrive in history, or, shall we say, plenitudes of Divine Presence, by which high tides are caused in the human spirit, and great virtues and talents appear, as in the eleventh, twelfth, thirteenth, and again in the sixteenth and seventeenth centuries, when the nation was full of genius and piety.

But the age of the Wicliffes, Cobhams, Arundels, Beckets; of the Latimers, Mores, Cranmers; of the Taylors, Leightons, Herberts; of the Sherlocks and Butlers, is gone. Silent revolutions in opinion have made it impossible that men like these should return, or find a place in their once sacred stalls. The spirit that dwelt in this church has glided away to animate other activities, and they who come to the old shrines find apes and players rustling the old garments.

The religion of England is part of good-breeding. When you see on the continent the well-dressed Englishman come into his ambassador's chapel and put his face for silent prayer into his smooth-brushed hat, you cannot help feeling how much national pride prays with him, and the religion of a gentleman. So far is he from attaching any meaning to the words, that he believes himself to have done almost the generous thing, and that it is very condescending in him to pray to God. A great duke said on the occasion of a victory, in the House of Lords, that he thought the Almighty God had not been well used by them, and that it would become their magnanimity, after so great successes, to take order that a proper acknowledgment be made. It is the church of the gentry, but it is not the church of the poor. The operatives do not own it, and gentlemen lately testified in the House of Commons that in their lives they never saw a poor man in a ragged coat inside a church.

The torpidity on the side of religion of the vigorous English understanding shows how much wit and folly can agree in one brain. Their religion is a quotation; their church is a doll; and any examination is interdicted with screams of terror. In good company you expect them to laugh at the fanaticism of the vulgar; but they do not; they are the vulgar.

The English, in common perhaps with Christendom in the nineteenth century, do not respect power, but only performance; value ideas only for an economic result. Wellington esteems a saint only as far as he can be an army chaplain: "Mr. Briscoll, by his admirable conduct and good sense, got the better of Methodism, which had appeared among the soldiers and once among the officers." They value a philosopher as they value an apothecary who brings bark or a drench; and inspiration is only some blow-pipe, or a finer mechanical aid.

I suspect that there is in an Englishman's brain a valve that can be closed at pleasure, as an engineer shuts off steam. The most sensible and well-informed men possess the power of thinking just so far as the bishop in religious matters, and as the chancellor of the exchequer in politics. They talk with courage and logic, and show you magnificent results, but the same men who have brought free trade or geology to their present standing, look grave and lofty and shut down their valve as soon as the conversation approaches the English Church. After that, you talk with a box-turtle.

The action of the university, both in what is taught and in the spirit of the place, is directed more on producing an English gentleman, than a saint or a psychologist. It ripens a bishop, and extrudes a philosopher. I do not know that there is more cabalism in the Anglican than in other churches, but the Anglican clergy are identified with the aristocracy. They say here, that if you talk with a clergyman, you are sure to find him well-bred, informed and candid: he entertains your thought or your project with sympathy and praise. But if a second clergyman come in, the sympathy is at an end: two together are inaccessible to your thought, and whenever it comes to action, the clergyman invariably sides with his church.

The Anglican Church is marked by the grace and good sense of its forms, by the manly grace of its clergy. The gospel it preaches is 'By taste are ye saved.' It keeps the old structures in repair, spends a world of money in music and building, and in buying Pugin and architectural literature. It has a general good name for amenity and mildness. It is not in ordinary a persecuting church; it is not inquisitorial, not even inquisitive; is perfectly well-bred, and can shut its eyes on all proper occasions. If you let it alone, it will let you alone. But its instinct is hostile to all change in politics, literature, or social arts. The church has not been the founder of the London University, of the Mechanics' Institutes, of the Free School, of whatever aims at diffusion of knowledge. The Platonists of Oxford are as bitter against this heresy, as Thomas Taylor.

The doctrine of the Old Testament is the religion of England. The first leaf of the New Testament it does not open. It believes in a Providence which does not treat with levity a pound sterling. They are neither transcendentalists nor Christians. They put up no Socratic prayer, much less any saintly prayer for the Queen's mind; ask neither for light nor right, but say bluntly, "Grant her in health and wealth long to live." And one traces this Jewish prayer in all English private history, from the prayers of King Richard, in Richard of Devizes' Chronicle, to those in the diaries of Sir Samuel Romilly and of Haydon the painter. "Abroad with my wife," writes Pepys piously, "the first time that ever I rode in my own coach; which do make my heart rejoice and praise God, and pray him to bless it to me, and continue it." The bill for the naturalization of the Jews (in 1753) was resisted by petitions from all parts of the kingdom, and by petition from the city of London, reprobating this bill, as "tending extremely to the dishonor of the Christian religion, and extremely injurious to the interests and commerce of the kingdom in general, and of the city of London in particular."

But they have not been able to congeal humanity by act of Parliament. "The heavens journey still and sojourn not," and arts, wars, discoveries and opinion go onward at their own pace. The new age has new desires, new enemies, new trades, new charities, and reads the Scriptures with new eyes. The chatter of French politics, the steam-whistle, the hum of the mill and the noise of embarking emigrants had quite put most of the old legends out of mind; so that when you came to read the liturgy to a modern congregation, it was almost absurd in its unfitness, and suggested a masquerade of old costumes.

No chemist has prospered in the attempt to crystallize a religion. It is endogenous, like the skin and other vital organs. A new statement every day. The prophet and apostle knew this, and the nonconformist confutes the conformists, by quoting the texts they must allow. It is the condition of a religion to require religion for its expositor. Prophet and apostle can only be rightly understood by prophet and apostle. The statesman knows that the religious element will not fail, any more than the supply of fibrine and chyle; but it is in its nature constructive, and will organize such a church as it wants. The wise legislator will spend on temples, schools, libraries, colleges, but will shun the enriching of priests. If in any manner he can leave the election and paying of the priest to the people, he will do well. Like the Quakers, he may resist the separation of a class of priests, and create opportunity and expectation in the society to run to meet natural endowment in this kind. But when wealth accrues to a chaplaincy, a bishopric, or rectorship, it requires moneyed men for its stewards, who will give it another direction than to the mystics of their day. Of course, money will do after its kind, and will steadily work to unspiritualize and unchurch the people to whom it was bequeathed. The class certain to be excluded from all preferment are the religious,—and driven to other churches; which is nature's *vis medicatrix*.

The curates are ill paid, and the prelates are overpaid. This abuse draws into the church the children of the nobility and other unfit persons who have a taste for expense. Thus a bishop is only a surpliced merchant. Through his lawn I can see the bright buttons of the shopman's coat glitter. A wealth like that of Durham makes almost a premium on felony. Brougham, in a speech in the House of Commons on the Irish elective franchise, said, "How will the reverend bishops of the other house be able to express their due abhorrence of the crime of perjury, who solemnly declare in the presence of God that when they are called upon to accept a living, perhaps of £4000 a year, at that very instant they are moved by the Holy Ghost to accept the office and administration thereof, and for no other reason whatever?" The modes of initiation are more damaging than custom-house oaths. The Bishop is elected by the Dean and Prebends of the cathedral. The Queen sends these gentlemen a *congé d'élire*, or leave to elect; but also sends them the name of the person whom they are to elect. They go into the cathedral, chant and pray and beseech the Holy Ghost to assist them in their choice; and, after these invocations, invariably find that the dictates of the Holy Ghost agree with the recommendations of the Queen.

But you must pay for conformity. All goes well as long as you run with conformists. But you, who are an honest man in other particulars, know that there is alive somewhere a man whose honesty reaches to this point also that he shall not kneel to false gods, and on the day when you meet him, you sink into the class of counterfeits. Besides, this succumbing has grave penalties. If you take in a lie, you must take in all that belongs to it. England accepts this ornamented national church, and it glazes the eyes, bloats the flesh, gives the voice a stertorous clang, and clouds the understanding of the receivers.

The English Church, undermined by German criticism, had nothing left but tradition; and was led logically back to Romanism. But that was an element which only hot heads could breathe: in view of the educated class, generally, it was not a fact to front the sun; and the alienation of such men from the church became complete.

Nature, to be sure, had her remedy. Religious persons are driven out of the Established Church into sects, which instantly rise to credit and hold the Establishment in check. Nature has sharper remedies, also. The English, abhorring change in all things, abhorring it most in matters of religion, cling to the last rag of form, and are dreadfully given to cant. The English (and I wish it were confined to them, but 't is a taint in the Anglo-Saxon blood in both hemispheres),—the English and the Americans cant beyond all other nations. The French relinquish all that industry to them. What is so odious as the polite bows to God, in our books and newspapers? The popular press is flagitious in the exact measure of its sanctimony, and the religion of the day is a theatrical Sinai, where the thunders are supplied by the property-man. The fanaticism and hypocrisy create satire. Punch finds an inexhaustible material. Dickens writes novels on Exeter-Hall humanity. Thackeray exposes the heartless high life. Nature revenges herself more summarily by the heathenism of the lower classes. Lord Shaftesbury calls the poor thieves together and reads sermons to them, and they call it 'gas.' George Borrow summons the Gypsies to hear his discourse on the Hebrews in Egypt, and reads to them the Apostles' Creed in Romany. "When I had concluded," he says, "I looked around me. The features of the assembly were twisted, and the eyes of all turned upon me with a frightful squint; not an individual present but squinted; the genteel Pepa, the good-humored Chicharona, the Cosdami, all squinted; the Gypsy jockey squinted worst of all."

The church at this moment is much to be pitied. She has nothing left but possession. If a bishop meets an intelligent gentleman and reads fatal interrogations in his eyes, he has no resource but to take wine with him. False position introduces cant, perjury, simony and ever a lower class of mind and character into the clergy: and, when the hierarchy is afraid of science and education, afraid of piety, afraid of tradition and afraid of theology, there is nothing left but to quit a church which is no longer one.

But the religion of England,—is it the Established Church? no; is it the sects? no; they are only perpetuations of some private man's dissent, and are to the Established Church as cabs are to a coach, cheaper and more convenient, but really the same thing. Where dwells the religion? Tell me first where dwells electricity, or motion, or thought, or gesture. They do not dwell or stay at all. Electricity cannot be made fast, mortared up and ended, like London Monument or the Tower, so that you shall know where to find it, and keep it fixed, as the English do with their things, forevermore; it is passing, glancing, gesticular; it is a traveller, a newness, a surprise, a secret, which perplexes them and puts them out. Yet, if religion be the doing of all good, and for its sake the suffering of all evil, *souffrir de tout le monde, et ne faire souffrir personne*, that divine secret has existed in England from the days of Alfred to those of Romilly, of Clarkson and of Florence Nightingale, and in thousands who have no fame.

Result

England is the best of actual nations. It is no ideal framework, it is an old pile built in different ages, with repairs, additions and makeshifts; but you see the poor best you have got. London is the epitome of our times, and the Rome of to-day. Broad-fronted, broad-bottomed Teutons, they stand in solid phalanx foursquare to the points of compass; they constitute the modern world, they have earned their vantage ground and held it through ages of adverse possession. They are well marked and differing from other leading races. England is tender-hearted. Rome was not. England is not so public in its bias; private life is its place of honor. Truth in private life, untruth in public, marks these home-loving men. Their political conduct is not decided by general views, but by internal intrigues and personal and family interest. They cannot readily see beyond England. The history of Rome and Greece, when written by their scholars, degenerates into English party pamphlets. They cannot see beyond England, nor in England can they transcend the interests of the governing classes. "English principles" mean a primary regard to the interests of property. England, Scotland and Ireland combine to check the colonies. England and Scotland combine to check Irish manufactures and trade. England rallies at home to check Scotland. In England, the strong classes check the weaker. In the home population of near thirty millions, there are but one million voters. The Church punishes dissent, punishes education. Down to a late day, marriages performed by dissenters were illegal. A bitter class-legislation gives power to those who are rich enough to buy a law. The game-laws are a proverb of oppression. Pauperism incrusts and clogs the state, and in hard times becomes hideous. In bad seasons, the porridge was diluted. Multitudes lived miserably by shell-fish and sea-ware. In cities, the children are trained to beg, until they shall be old enough to rob. Men and women were convicted of poisoning scores of children for burial-fees. In Irish districts, men deteriorated in size and shape, the nose sunk, the gums were exposed, with diminished brain and brutal form. During the Australian emigration, multitudes were rejected by the commissioners as being too emaciated for useful colonists. During the Russian war, few of those that offered as recruits were found up to the medical standard, though it had been reduced.

The foreign policy of England, though ambitious and lavish of money, has not often been generous or just. It has a principal regard to the interest of trade, checked however by the aristocratic bias of the ambassador, which usually puts him in sympathy with the continental Courts. It sanctioned the partition of Poland, it betrayed Genoa, Sicily, Parma, Greece, Turkey, Rome and Hungary.

Some public regards they have. They have abolished slavery in the West Indies and put an end to human sacrifices in the East. At home they have a certain statute hospitality. England keeps open doors, as a trading country must, to all nations. It is one of their fixed ideas, and wrathfully supported by their laws in unbroken sequence for a thousand years. In *Magna Charta* it was ordained that all "merchants shall have safe and secure conduct to go out and come into England, and to stay there, and to pass as well by land as by water, to buy and sell by the ancient allowed customs, without any evil toll, except in time of war, or when they shall be of any nation at war with us." It is a statute and obliged hospitality and peremptorily maintained. But this shop-rule had one magnificent effect. It extends its cold unalterable courtesy to political exiles of every opinion, and is a fact which might give additional light to that portion of the planet seen from the farthest star. But this perfunctory hospitality puts no sweetness into their unaccommodating manners, no check on that puissant nationality which makes their existence incompatible with all that is not English.

What we must say about a nation is a superficial dealing with symptoms. We cannot go deep enough into the biography of the spirit who never throws himself entire into one hero, but delegates his energy in parts or spasms to vicious and defective individuals. But the wealth of the source is seen in the plenitude of English nature. What variety of power and talent; what facility and plenteousness of knighthood, lordship, ladyship, royalty, loyalty; what a proud chivalry is indicated in "Collins's Peerage," through eight hundred years! What dignity resting on what reality and stoutness! What courage in war, what sinew in labor, what cunning workmen, what inventors and engineers, what seamen and pilots, what clerks and scholars! No one man and no few men can represent them. It is a people of myriad personalities. Their many-headedness is owing to the advantageous position of the middle class, who are always the source of letters and science. Hence the vast plenty of their æsthetic production. As they are many-headed, so they are many-nationed: their colonization annexes archipelagoes and continents, and their speech seems destined to be the universal language of men. I have noted the reserve of power in the English temperament. In the island, they never let out all the length of all the reins, there is no Berserker rage, no abandonment or ecstasy of will or intellect, like that of the Arabs in the time of Mahomet, or like that which intoxicated France in 1789. But who would see the uncoiling of that tremendous spring, the explosion of their well-husbanded forces, must follow the swarms which pouring now for two hundred years from the British islands, have sailed and rode and traded and planted through all climates, mainly following the belt of empire, the temperate zones, carrying the Saxon seed, with its instinct for liberty and law, for arts and for thought,—acquiring under some skies a more electric energy than the native air allows,—to the conquest of the globe. Their colonial policy, obeying the necessities of a vast empire, has become liberal. Canada and Australia have been contented with substantial independence. They are expiating the wrongs of India by benefits; first, in works for the irrigation of the peninsula, and roads, and telegraphs; and secondly, in the instruction of the people, to qualify them for self-government, when the British power shall be finally called home.

Their mind is in a state of arrested development,—a divine cripple like Vulcan; a blind *savant* like Huber and Sanderson. They do not occupy themselves on matters of general and lasting import, but on a corporeal civilization, on goods that perish in the using. But they read with good intent, and what they learn they incarnate. The English mind turns every abstraction it can receive into a portable utensil, or a working institution. Such is their tenacity and such their practical turn, that they hold all they gain. Hence we say that only the English race can be trusted with freedom,—freedom which is double-edged and dangerous to any but the wise and robust. The English designate the kingdoms emulous of free institutions, as the sentimental nations. Their culture is not an outside varnish, but is thorough and secular in families and the race.

They are oppressive with their temperament, and all the more that they are refined. I have sometimes seen them walk with my countrymen when I was forced to allow them every advantage, and their companions seemed bags of bones.

There is cramp limitation in their habit of thought, sleepy routine, and a tortoise's instinct to hold hard to the ground with his claws, lest he should be thrown on his back. There is a drag of inertia which resists reform in every shape;—law-reform, army-reform, extension of suffrage, Jewish franchise, Catholic emancipation,—the abolition of slavery, of impressment, penal code and entails. They praise this drag, under the formula that it is the excellence of the British constitution that no law can anticipate the public opinion. These poor tortoises must hold hard, for they feel no wings sprouting at their shoulders. Yet somewhat divine warms at their heart and waits a happier hour. It hides in their sturdy will. "Will," said the old philosophy, "is the measure of power," and personality is the token of this race. *Quid vult valde vult.* What they do they do with a will. You cannot account for their success by their Christianity, commerce, charter, common law, Parliament, or letters, but by the contumacious sharp-tongued energy of English *naturel*, with a poise impossible to disturb, which makes all these its instruments. They are slow and reticent, and are like a dull good horse which lets every nag pass him, but with whip and spur will run down every racer in the field. They are right in their feeling, though wrong in their speculation.

The feudal system survives in the steep inequality of property and privilege, in the limited franchise, in the social barriers which confine patronage and promotion to a caste, and still more in the submissive ideas pervading these people. The fagging of the schools is repeated in the social classes. An Englishman shows no mercy to those below him in the social scale, as he looks for none from those above him; any forbearance from his superiors surprises him, and they suffer in his good opinion. But the feudal system can be seen with less pain on large historical grounds. It was pleaded in mitigation of the rotten borough, that it worked well, that substantial justice was done. Fox, Burke, Pitt, Erskine, Wilberforce, Sheridan, Romilly, or whatever national man, were by this means sent to Parliament, when their return by large constituencies would have been doubtful. So now we say that the right measures of England are the men it bred; that it has yielded more able men in five hundred years than any other nation; and, though we must not play Providence and balance the chances of producing ten great men against the comfort of ten thousand mean men, yet retrospectively, we may strike the balance and prefer one Alfred, one Shakspeare, one Milton, one Sidney, one Raleigh, one Wellington, to a million foolish democrats.

The American system is more democratic, more humane; yet the American people do not yield better or more able men, or more inventions or books or benefits than the English. Congress is not wiser or better than Parliament. France has abolished its suffocating old *régime*, but is not recently marked by any more wisdom or virtue.

The power of performance has not been exceeded,—the creation of value. The English have given importance to individuals, a principal end and fruit of every society. Every man is allowed and encouraged to be what he is, and is guarded in the indulgence of his whim. "Magna Charta," said Rushworth, "is such a fellow that he will have no sovereign." By this general activity and by this sacredness of individuals, they have in seven hundred years evolved the principles of freedom. It is the land of patriots, martyrs, sages and bards, and if the ocean out of which it emerged should wash it away, it will be remembered as an island famous for immortal laws, for the announcements of original right which make the stone tables of liberty.

The Yankee Sage

Editor's Note

~~~~~~~~~~~~~~~~~~~~~~~~~~~~~~~~~~~~~~

Here we see still further Emerson's range as a writer, as evidenced in several political statements, some essays in biography, a sketch of a character type, and a mellow piece of personalized history.

Emerson made his most noteworthy statement on any public issue aside from slavery in an open letter he addressed to President Martin Van Buren in April 1838. The letter urged the president not to let the Cherokee Indians be thrust out of their territory. The tone was the rare one of cold anger, reflecting not only Emerson's indignation at the outrage but his discomfort at taking a public position in a controversy. In consequence of his rising reputation, a number of newspapers printed the letter. However, it did not enter the Emerson canon, so to speak, till his son Edward published it in his 1904 edition of the *Miscellanies*.

Emerson's New York lecture, "The Fugitive Slave Law," was a noteworthy statement on slavery itself. The driving power came from his abhorrence of the idea that one human being could own another. Delivered on the fourth anniversary of Daniel Webster's weighty speech in favor of the law, Emerson's lecture deals in its first half with Webster. Well aware that he had been almost a myth figure, Emerson grants him every virtue except rectitude—and thus demolishes him. In the second half Emerson attacks slavery itself. He makes his words measured and judicious but they hit like hammer blows; they are filled with moral force. Given on March 7, 1854, the lecture did not appear in print until it was included in the *Miscellanies* volume of the collected works of 1884.

Of all the foes of slavery before the Civil War, John Brown was the most fanatical. On someone as basically gentle as Emerson his fanaticism made a profound impression. When Brown visited Concord and the two men met, he almost awed Emerson. A month after Brown was hanged for leading the raid on Harpers Ferry, Emerson made a short speech about him to a meeting in Salem. He saw Brown as a saint, a man endowed with "a romantic character absolutely without any vulgar trait; living to ideal ends." The speech, given on January 6, 1860, was his second about Brown. It was not printed till 1869, in a book called *Echoes of Harper's Ferry* that was put together by James Redpath. It was reprinted in 1884 in the *Miscellanies* volume of the collected works.

The three biographical essays take us to another world. Ezra Ripley, Henry Thoreau, and Thomas Carlyle were eons distant from John Brown. Yet each in his way was a strong, determined man; and Emerson appreciated the fact.

Though his sense of humor was not always apparent, it could appear in the most unlikely places, for instance, in an obituary. After his old friend and step-grandfather Ripley died, Emerson was asked to prepare an obituary for a Concord club they had both belonged to. For sixty-three years the pastor of Concord's foremost flock, at the First Parish Church, Dr. Ripley had lived so exemplary a life that any obituary could have been excused for being unctuous. Emerson's is not. He views the good doctor with a delightful blend of affection, admiration, and humor. In a dozen perceptive anecdotes he shows us what Dr. Ripley was like. We see him, for example, haying in his field when rain threatens and he looks up pleadingly at the Lord's sky, to remind Him that the hay in danger of ruin belongs to His servant Ezra. We also see that he relished kissing the ladies and gave them no dry pecks. Beneath the anecdotes and amiable judgments we feel the fundamental fact that Dr. Ripley had been a completely dedicated minister. Following its initial appearance after Dr. Ripley's death, the obituary appeared in expanded form in the *Atlantic Monthly* for November 1883. In 1884 it came to rest in *Lectures and Biographical Sketches*.

At Henry Thoreau's graveside Emerson was inevitably the person to offer the eulogy. Thoreau had risen from being his disciple to being his peer, but Emerson had never altered his appreciation of the younger man, this in spite of the fact that no one could be more contrary than Thoreau. We have no finer portrait in American literature of one great writer by another. The obituary first saw print in *The Boston Daily Advertiser* of May 8, 1862. Emerson expanded it for the *Atlantic Monthly* of August 1862, and Professor Joel Myerson has transcribed the manuscript Emerson prepared for the printer; it is the text followed in this volume. "Thoreau" was afterward included in *Lectures and Biographical Sketches*, in the 1884 edition of the collected works.

Emerson's profile of his famous Scottish friend Thomas Carlyle is written in the present tense. This gives it an immediacy that suits Carlyle's renowned extravagance of expression, but the tense is deceptive. Most of the material, taken from letters and journals, was more than thirty years old when Emerson read the piece to the Massachusetts Historical Society in 1881, shortly after Carlyle's death and a year before his own; it was the last time he spoke from a public platform. The tone of the piece, exactly right, is as important as the tense. The Carlyle he depicts is not merely conservative but reactionary. Yet Emerson makes him look like Punch in a Punch-and-Judy show: no matter how he flails about him, no one actually gets hurt. Thanks to Emerson's tone we accept the most tendentious opinions from Carlyle without resentment. He opposes freedom of speech and representative government with such gusto that we enjoy it. Emerson concludes by hailing him as the manliest person of his time. The Massachusetts Historical Society printed the "Carlyle" in

1881; so did *Scribner's Magazine* in its May issue. In 1884 it was collected in *Lectures and Biographical Sketches.*

Nothing could be further from Emerson's social polemics than his charming profile of what he presented as the typical Massachusetts farmer. In "Farming" he followed the English tradition of character writing—that is, sketching a type, say of an actor or a clerk. The piece was first read as an address to his neighbors at the Middlesex Cattle Show, in 1858. It is a hymn to nature as well as a celebration of those who tilled the Massachusetts soil. Plainly, his farmer seldom had a mean thought or stepped in cow manure. Some of Emerson's acquaintances complained that he revealed his lack of realism. He also demonstrated, however, that he saw the significance of ecology long before the word was in vogue. "Farming" was printed in *The Transactions of the Middlesex Agricultural Society* for 1858 and was then revised as a chapter in *Society and Solitude* in 1870.

In "Historic Notes of Life and Letters in New England" we have vintage Emerson. Here, as he looks back on his young manhood and his prime, he shows the wisdom which comes not only from an inner light but from decades of experience. He begins with the year 1820, the dawn of a new era as he sees it, and to us an era rather like our own. It was marked by a widespread resistance to social responsibility, especially among the young, who were "stiff, heady, and rebellious." Institutions and even groups meant little to them; the individual was their world. Luckily Emerson and his fellow students at Harvard found an outstanding individual to give them a model. Emerson's portrait of Edward Everett, professor of Greek, captures the enthusiasm that students felt about his lectures. The essay goes on to describe the emergence of Transcendentalism in the 1840s and then of other movements, including the pre-Marxist socialisms imported from England and France. The most influential French social thinker was Charles Fourier, whose enticing watchword was "Indulge!"

Emerson wrote the "Historic Notes" when he was sixty-four, and it was possibly the last essay that, as his family reported, he took real pleasure in writing. "I believe I must put in Brook Farm," he told them; and he put it in. Throughout the essay he surveyed the past with a serenity that carries with it the conviction of truth. The *Atlantic Monthly* published these rich reminiscences in its October 1883 issue, and they were included the following year in *Lectures and Biographical Sketches*.

C.B.

LETTER

~~~~~~~~~~~~~~~~~~~~~~~~~~~~~~~~~~

TO MARTIN VAN BUREN, PRESIDENT
OF THE UNITED STATES

Concord, Mass., April 23, 1838.

Sir: The seat you fill places you in a relation of credit and
nearness to every citizen. By right and natural position,
every citizen is your friend. Before any acts contrary to
his own judgment or interest have repelled the affections
of any man, each may look with trust and living anticipa-
tion to your government. Each has the highest right to call
your attention to such subjects as are of a public nature,
and properly belong to the chief magistrate; and the good
magistrate will feel a joy in meeting such confidence. In
this belief and at the instance of a few of my friends and
neighbors, I crave of your patience a short hearing for
their sentiments and my own: and the circumstance that
my name will be utterly unknown to you will only give
the fairer chance to your equitable construction of what I
have to say.

Sir, my communication respects the sinister rumors
that fill this part of the country concerning the Cherokee
people. The interest always felt in the aboriginal population—an interest naturally growing as that decays—has
been heightened in regard to this tribe. Even in our distant
State some good rumor of their worth and civility has arrived. We have learned with joy their improvement in the
social arts. We have read their newspapers. We have seen
some of them in our schools and colleges. In common with
the great body of the American people, we have witnessed

with sympathy the painful labors of these red men to redeem their own race from the doom of eternal inferiority, and to borrow and domesticate in the tribe the arts and customs of the Caucasian race. And notwithstanding the unaccountable apathy with which of late years the Indians have been sometimes abandoned to their enemies, it is not to be doubted that it is the good pleasure and the understanding of all humane persons in the Republic, of the men and the matrons sitting in the thriving independent families all over the land, that they shall be duly cared for; that they shall taste justice and love from all to whom we have delegated the office of dealing with them.

The newspapers now inform us that, in December, 1835, a treaty contracting for the exchange of all the Cherokee territory was pretended to be made by an agent on the part of the United States with some persons appearing on the part of the Cherokees; that the fact afterwards transpired that these deputies did by no means represent the will of the nation; and that, out of eighteen thousand souls composing the nation, fifteen thousand six hundred and sixty-eight have protested against the so-called treaty. It now appears that the government of the United States choose to hold the Cherokees to this sham treaty, and are proceeding to execute the same. Almost the entire Cherokee Nation stand up and say, "This is not our act. Behold us. Here are we. Do not mistake that handful of deserters for us;" and the American President and the Cabinet, the Senate and the House of Representatives, neither hear these men nor see them, and are contracting to put this active nation into carts and boats, and to drag them over mountains and rivers to a wilderness at a vast distance beyond the Mississippi. And a paper purporting to be an army order fixes a month from this day as the hour for this doleful removal.

In the name of God, sir, we ask you if this be so. Do the newspapers rightly inform us? Men and women with pale and perplexed faces meet one another in the streets and churches here, and ask if this be so. We have inquired if this be a gross misrepresentation from the party opposed to the government and anxious to blacken it with the people. We have looked in the newspapers of different parties and find a horrid confirmation of the tale. We are slow to believe it. We hoped the Indians were misinformed, and that their remonstrance was premature, and will turn out to be a needless act of terror.

The piety, the principle that is left in the United States, if only in its coarsest form, a regard to the speech of men,—forbid us to entertain it as a fact. Such a dereliction of all faith and virtue, such a denial of justice, and such deafness to screams for mercy were never heard of in times of peace and in the dealing of a nation with its own allies and wards, since the earth was made. Sir, does this government think that the people of the United States are become savage and mad? From their mind are the sentiments of love and a good nature wiped clean out? The soul of man, the justice, the mercy that is the heart's heart in all men, from Maine to Georgia, does abhor this business.

In speaking thus the sentiments of my neighbors and my own, perhaps I overstep the bounds of decorum. But would it not be a higher indecorum coldly to argue a matter like this? We only state the fact that a crime is projected that confounds our understandings by its magnitude,—a crime that really deprives us as well as the Cherokees of a country? for how could we call the conspiracy that should crush these poor Indians our government, or the land that was cursed by their parting and dying imprecations our country, any more? You, sir, will bring down that renowned chair in which you sit into infamy if your seal is set to this instrument of perfidy; and the name of this nation, hitherto the sweet omen of religion and liberty, will stink to the world.

You will not do us the injustice of connecting this remonstrance with any sectional and party feeling. It is in our hearts the simplest commandment of brotherly love. We will not have this great and solemn claim upon national and human justice huddled aside under the flimsy plea of its being a party act. Sir, to us the questions upon which the government and the people have been agitated during the past year, touching the prostration of the currency and of trade, seem but motes in comparison. These hard times, it is true, have brought the discussion home to every farmhouse and poor man's house in this town; but it is the chirping of grasshoppers beside the immortal question whether justice shall be done by the race of civilized to the race of savage man,—whether all the attributes of reason, of civility, of justice, and even of mercy, shall be put off by the American people, and so vast an outrage upon the Cherokee Nation and upon human nature shall be consummated.

One circumstance lessens the reluctance with which I intrude at this time on your attention my conviction that the government ought to be admonished of a new historical fact, which the discussion of this question has disclosed, namely, that there exists in a great part of the Northern people a gloomy diffidence in the *moral* character of the government.

On the broaching of this question, a general expression of despondency, of disbelief that any good will accrue from a remonstrance on an act of fraud and robbery, appeared in those men to whom we naturally turn for aid and counsel. Will the American government steal? Will it lie? Will it kill?—We ask triumphantly. Our counsellors and old statesmen here say that ten years ago they would have staked their lives on the affirmation that the proposed Indian measures could not be executed; that the unanimous country would put them down. And now the steps of this crime follow each other so fast, at such fatally quick time, that the millions of virtuous citizens, whose agents the government are, have no place to interpose, and must shut their eyes until the last howl and wailing of these tormented villages and tribes shall afflict the ear of the world.

I will not hide from you, as an indication of the alarming distrust, that a letter addressed as mine is, and suggesting to the mind of the Executive the plain obligations of man, has a burlesque character in the apprehensions of some of my friends. I, sir, will not beforehand treat you with the contumely of this distrust. I will at least state to you this fact, and show you how plain and humane people, whose love would be honor, regard the policy of the government, and what injurious inferences they draw as to the minds of the governors. A man with your experience in affairs must have seen cause to appreciate the futility of opposition to the moral sentiment. However feeble the sufferer and however great the oppressor, it is in the nature of things that the blow should recoil upon the aggressor. For God is in the sentiment, and it cannot be withstood. The potentate and the people perish before it; but with it, and as its executor, they are omnipotent.

I write thus, sir, to inform you of the state of mind these Indian tidings have awakened here, and to pray with one voice more that you, whose hands are strong with the delegated power of fifteen millions of men, will avert with that might the terrific injury which threatens the Cherokee tribe.

With great respect, sir, I am your fellow citizen,

RALPH WALDO EMERSON.

EZRA RIPLEY, D.D.

~~~~~~~~~~~~~~~~~~~~~~~~~~~~~~~~

Ezra Ripley was born May 1, 1751 (old style), at Woodstock, Connecticut. He was the fifth of the nineteen children of Noah and Lydia (Kent) Ripley. Seventeen of these nineteen children married, and it is stated that the mother died leaving nineteen children, one hundred and two grandchildren and ninety-six great-grandchildren. The father was born at Hingham, on the farm purchased by his ancestor, William Ripley, of England, at the first settlement of the town; which farm has been occupied by seven or eight generations. Ezra Ripley followed the business of farming till sixteen years of age, when his father wished him to be qualified to teach a grammar school, not thinking himself able to send one son to college without injury to his other children. With this view, the father agreed with the late Rev. Dr. Forbes of Gloucester, then minister of North Brookfield, to fit Ezra for college by the time he should be twenty-one years of age, and to have him labor during the time sufficiently to pay for his instruction, clothing and books.

But, when fitted for college, the son could not be contented with teaching, which he had tried the preceding winter. He had early manifested a desire for learning, and could not be satisfied without a public education. Always inclined to notice ministers, and frequently attempting, when only five or six years old, to imitate them by preaching, now that he had become a professor of religion he had an ardent desire to be a preacher of the gospel. He had to encounter great difficulties, but, through a kind providence and the patronage of Dr. Forbes, he entered

Harvard University, July, 1772. The commencement of the Revolutionary War greatly interrupted his education at college. In 1775, in his senior year, the college was removed from Cambridge to this town. The studies were much broken up. Many of the students entered the army, and the class never returned to Cambridge. There were an unusually large number of distinguished men in this class of 1776: Christopher Gore, Governor of Massachusetts and Senator in Congress; Samuel Sewall, Chief Justice of Massachusetts; George Thacher, Judge of the Supreme Court; Royall Tyler, Chief Justice of Vermont; and the late learned Dr. Prince, of Salem.

Mr. Ripley was ordained minister of Concord November 7, 1778. He married, November 16, 1780, Mrs. Phebe (Bliss) Emerson, then a widow of thirty-nine, with five children. They had three children: Sarah, born August 18, 1781; Samuel, born May 11, 1783; Daniel Bliss, born August 1, 1784. He died September 21, 1841.

To these facts, gathered chiefly from his own diary, and stated nearly in his own words, I can only add a few traits from memory.

He was identified with the ideas and forms of the New England Church, which expired about the same time with him, so that he and his coevals seemed the rear guard of the great camp and army of the Puritans, which, however in its last days declining into formalism, in the heyday of its strength had planted and liberated America. It was a pity that his old meeting-house should have been modernized in his time. I am sure all who remember both will associate his form with whatever was grave and droll in the old, cold, unpainted, uncarpeted, square-pewed meeting-house, with its four iron-gray deacons in their little box under the pulpit,—with Watts's hymns, with long prayers, rich with the diction of ages; and not less with the report like musketry from the movable seats. He and his contemporaries, the old New England clergy, were believers in what is called a particular providence,—certainly, as they held it, a very particular providence,—

following the narrowness of King David and the Jews, who thought the universe existed only or mainly for their church and congregation. Perhaps I cannot better illustrate this tendency than by citing a record from the diary of the father of his predecessor, the minister of Malden, written in the blank leaves of the almanac for the year 1735. The minister writes against January 31st: "Bought a shay for 27 pounds, 10 shillings. The Lord grant it may be a comfort and blessing to my family." In March following he notes: "Had a safe and comfortable journey to York." But April 24th, we find: "Shay overturned, with my wife and I in it, yet neither of us much hurt. Blessed be our gracious Preserver. Part of the shay, as it lay upon one side, went over my wife, and yet she was scarcely anything hurt. How wonderful the preservation." Then again, May 5th: "Went to the beach with three of the children. The beast, being frightened when we were all out of the shay, overturned and broke it. I desire (I hope I desire it) that the Lord would teach me suitably to resent this Providence, to make suitable remarks on it, and to be suitably affected with it. Have I done well to get me a shay? Have I not been proud or too fond of this convenience? Do I exercise the faith in the Divine care and protection which I ought to do? Should I not be more in my study and less fond of diversion? Do I not withhold more than is meet from pious and charitable uses?" Well, on 15th May we have this: "Shay brought home; mending cost thirty shillings. Favored in this respect beyond expectation." 16th May: "My wife and I rode together to Rumney Marsh. The beast frighted several times." And at last we have this record, June 4th: "Disposed of my shay to Rev. Mr. White."

The same faith made what was strong and what was weak in Dr. Ripley and his associates. He was a perfectly sincere man, punctual, severe, but just and charitable, and if he made his forms a strait-jacket to others, he wore the same himself all his years. Trained in this church, and very well qualified by his natural talent to work in it, it was never out of his mind. He looked at every person and thing from the parochial point of view. I remember, when a boy, driving about Concord with him, and in passing each house he told the story of the family that lived in it, and especially he gave me anecdotes of the nine church members who had made a division in the church in the time of his predecessor, and showed me how every one of the nine had come to bad fortune or to a bad end. His prayers for rain and against the lightning, "that it may not lick up our spirits;" and for good weather; and against sickness and insanity; "that we have not been tossed to and fro until the dawning of the day; that we have not been a terror to ourselves and others,"—are well remembered, and his own entire faith that these petitions were not to be overlooked, and were entitled to a favorable answer. Some of those around me will remember one occasion of severe drought in this vicinity, when the late Rev. Mr. Goodwin offered to relieve the Doctor of the duty of leading in prayer; but the Doctor suddenly remembering the season, rejected his offer with some humor, as with an air that said to all the congregation, "This is no time for you young Cambridge men; the affair, sir, is getting serious. I will pray myself." One August afternoon, when I was in his hayfield helping him with his man to rake up his hay, I well remember his pleading, almost reproachful looks at the sky, when the thunder-gust was coming up to spoil his hay. He raked very fast, then looked at the cloud, and said, "We are in the Lord's hand; mind your rake, George! We are in the Lord's hand;" and seemed to say, "You know me; this field is mine,—Dr Ripley's,—thine own servant!"

He used to tell the story of one of his old friends, the minister of Sudbury, who, being at the Thursday lecture in Boston, heard the officiating clergyman praying for rain. As soon as the service was over, he went to the petitioner, and said, "You Boston ministers, as soon as a tulip wilts under your windows, go to church and pray for rain, until all Concord and Sudbury are under water." I once rode with him to a house at Nine Acre Corner to attend the funeral of the father of a family. He mentioned to me on the way his fears that the oldest son, who was now to succeed to the farm, was becoming intemperate. We presently arrived, and the Doctor addressed each of the mourners separately: "Sir, I condole with you." "Madam, I condole with you." "Sir, I knew your great-grandfather. When I came to this town, your great-grandfather was a substantial farmer in this very place, a member of the church, and an excellent citizen. Your grandfather followed him, and was a virtuous man. Now your father is to be carried to his grave, full of labors and virtues. There is none of that large family left but you, and it rests with you to bear up the good name and usefulness of your ancestors. If you fail,—'Ichabod, the glory is departed.' Let us pray." Right manly he was, and the manly thing he could always say. I can remember a little speech he made to me, when the last tie of blood which held me and my brothers to his house was broken by the death of his daughter. He said, on parting, "I wish you and your brothers to come to this house as you have always done. You will not like to be excluded; I shall not like to be neglected."

When "Put" Merriam, after his release from the state prison, had the effrontery to call on the Doctor as an old acquaintance, in the midst of general conversation Mr. Frost came in, and the Doctor presently said, "Mr. Merriam, my brother and colleague, Mr. Frost, has come to take tea with me. I regret very much the causes (which you know very well) which make it impossible for me to ask you to stay and break bread with us." With the Doctor's views it was a matter of religion to say thus much. He had a reverence and love of society, and the patient, continuing courtesy, carrying out every respectful attention to the end, which marks what is called the manners of the old school. His hospitality obeyed Charles Lamb's rule, and "ran fine to the last." His partiality for ladies was always strong, and was by no means abated by time. He claimed privilege of years, was much addicted to kissing;

spared neither maid, wife nor widow, and, as a lady thus favored remarked to me, "seemed as if he was going to make a meal of you."

He was very credulous, and as he was no reader of books or journals, he knew nothing beyond the columns of his weekly religious newspaper, the tracts of his sect, and perhaps the Middlesex Yeoman. He was the easy dupe of any tonguey agent, whether colonizationist or anti-papist, or charlatan of iron combs, or tractors, or phrenology, or magnetism, who went by. At the time when Jack Downing's letters were in every paper, he repeated to me at table some of the particulars of that gentleman's intimacy with General Jackson, in a manner that betrayed to me at once that he took the whole for fact. To undeceive him, I hastened to recall some particulars to show the absurdity of the thing, as the Major and the President going out skating on the Potomac, etc. "Why," said the Doctor with perfect faith, "it was a bright moonlight night;" and I am not sure that he did not die in the belief in the reality of Major Downing. Like other credulous men, he was opinionative, and, as I well remember, a great browbeater of the poor old fathers who still survived from the 19th of April, to the end that they should testify to his history as he had written it.

He was a man so kind and sympathetic, his character was so transparent, and his merits so intelligible to all observers, that he was very justly appreciated in this community. He was a natural gentleman, no dandy, but courtly, hospitable, manly and public-spirited; his nature social, his house open to all men. We remember the remark made by the old farmer who used to travel hither from Maine, that no horse from the Eastern country would go by the Doctor's gate. Travellers from the West and North and South bear the like testimony. His brow was serene and open to his visitor, for he loved men, and he had no studies, no occupations, which company could interrupt. His friends were his study, and to see them loosened his talents and his tongue. In his house dwelt

order and prudence and plenty. There was no waste and
no stint. He was open-handed and just and generous. In-
gratitude and meanness in his beneficiaries did not wear
out his compassion; he bore the insult, and the next day
his basket for the beggar, his horse and chaise for the cripple, were at their door. Though he knew the value of a
dollar as well as another man, yet he loved to buy dearer
and sell cheaper than others. He subscribed to all charities, and it is no reflection on others to say that he was the
most public-spirited man in the town. The late Dr. Gar-
diner, in a funeral sermon on some parishioner whose virtues did not readily come to mind, honestly said, "He was
good at fires." Dr. Ripley had many virtues, and yet all
will remember that even in his old age, if the firebell was
rung, he was instantly on horseback with his buckets, and
bag.

He showed even in his fireside discourse traits of that
pertinency and judgment, softening ever and anon into
elegancy, which make the distinction of the scholar, and
which, under better discipline, might have ripened into a
Bentley or a Porson. He had a foresight, when he opened
his mouth, of all that he would say, and he marched
straight to the conclusion. In debate, in the vestry of the
Lyceum, the structure of his sentences was admirable; so
neat, so natural, so terse, his words fell like stones; and
often, though quite unconscious of it, his speech was a satire on the loose, voluminous, draggle-tail periods of other
speakers. He sat down when he had done. A man of anecdote, his talk in the parlor was chiefly narrative. We remember the remark of a gentleman who listened with
much delight to his conversation at the time when the
Doctor was preparing to go to Baltimore and Washington,
that "a man who could tell a story so well was company
for kings and John Quincy Adams."

Sage and savage strove harder in him than in any of my
acquaintances, each getting the mastery by turns, and
pretty sudden turns: "Save us from the extremity of cold
and these violent sudden changes." "The society will meet

after the Lyceum, as it is difficult to bring people together in the evening,—and no moon." "Mr. N. F. is dead, and I expect to hear of the death of Mr. B. It is cruel to separate old people from their wives in this cold weather."

With a very limited acquaintance with books, his knowledge was an external experience, an Indian wisdom, the observation of such facts as country life for nearly a century could supply. He watched with interest the garden, the field, the orchard, the house and the barn, horse, cow, sheep and dog, and all the common objects that engage the thought of the farmer. He kept his eye on the horizon, and knew the weather like a sea-captain. The usual experiences of men, birth, marriage, sickness, death, burial; the common temptations; the common ambitions;—he studied them all, and sympathized so well in these that he was excellent company and counsel to all, even the most humble and ignorant. With extraordinary states of mind, with states of enthusiasm or enlarged speculation, he had no sympathy, and pretended to none. He was sincere, and kept to his point, and his mark was never remote. His conversation was strictly personal and apt to the party and the occasion. An eminent skill he had in saying difficult and unspeakable things; in delivering to a man or a woman that which all their other friends had abstained from saying, in uncovering the bandage from a sore place, and applying the surgeon's knife with a truly surgical spirit. Was a man a sot, or a spendthrift, or too long time a bachelor, or suspected of some hidden crime, or had he quarrelled with his wife, or collared his father, or was there any cloud or suspicious circumstances in his behavior, the good pastor knew his way straight to that point, believing himself entitled to a full explanation, and whatever relief to the conscience of both parties plain speech could effect was sure to be procured. In all such passages he justified himself to the conscience, and commonly to the love, of the persons concerned. He was the more competent to these searching discourses from his knowledge of family history. He knew everybody's grandfather, and seemed to address each person rather as the representative of his house and name, than as an individual. In him have perished more local and personal anecdotes of this village and vicinity than are possessed by any survivor. This intimate knowledge of families, and this skill of speech, and still more, his sympathy, made him incomparable in his parochial visits, and in his exhortations and prayers. He gave himself up to his feelings, and said on the instant the best things in the world. Many and many a felicity he had in his prayer, now forever lost, which defied all the rules of all the rhetoricians. He did not know when he was good in prayer or sermon, for he had no literature and no art; but he believed, and therefore spoke. He was eminently loyal in his nature, and not fond of adventure or innovation. By education, and still more by temperament, he was engaged to the old forms of the New England Church. Not speculative, but affectionate; devout, but with an extreme love of order, he adopted heartily, though in its mildest form, the creed and catechism of the fathers, and appeared a modern Israelite in his attachment to the Hebrew history and faith. He was a man very easy to read, for his whole life and conversation were consistent. All his opinions and actions might be securely predicted by a good observer on short acquaintance. My classmate at Cambridge, Frederick King, told me from Governor Gore, who was the Doctor's classmate, that in college he was called Holy Ripley.

And now, in his old age, when all the antique Hebraism and its customs are passing away, it is fit that he too should depart,—most fit that in the fall of laws a loyal man should die.

THE FUGITIVE
SLAVE LAW

I do not often speak to public questions;—they are odious and hurtful, and it seems like meddling or leaving your work. I have my own spirits in prison;—spirits in deeper prisons, whom no man visits if I do not. And then I see what havoc it makes with any good mind, a dissipated philanthropy. The one thing not to be forgiven to intellectual persons is, not to know their own task, or to take their ideas from others. From this want of manly rest in their own and rash acceptance of other people's watchwords come the imbecility and fatigue of their conversation. For they cannot affirm these from any original experience, and of course not with the natural movement and total strength of their nature and talent, but only from their memory, only from their cramped position of standing for their teacher. They say what they would have you believe, but what they do not quite know.

My own habitual view is to the well-being of students or scholars. And it is only when the public event affects them, that it very seriously touches me. And what I have to say is to them. For every man speaks mainly to a class whom he works with and more or less fully represents. It is to these I am beforehand related and engaged, in this audience or out of it—to them and not to others. And yet, when I say the class of scholars or students,—that is a class which comprises in some sort all mankind, comprises every man in the best hours of his life; and in these days not only virtually but actually. For who are the readers and thinkers of 1854? Owing to the silent revolution which the newspaper has wrought, this class has come in this country to take in all classes. Look into the morning trains which, from every suburb, carry the business men into the city to their shops, counting-rooms, work-yards and warehouses. With them enters the car—the newsboy, that humble priest of politics, finance, philosophy, and religion. He unfolds his magical sheets,—twopence a head his bread of knowledge costs—and instantly the entire rectangular assembly, fresh from their breakfast, are bending as one man to their second breakfast. There is, no doubt, chaff enough in what he brings; but there is fact, thought, and wisdom in the crude mass, from all regions of the world.

I have lived all my life without suffering any known inconvenience from American Slavery. I never saw it; I never heard the whip; I never felt the check on my free speech and action, until, the other day, when Mr. Webster, by his personal influence, brought the Fugitive Slave Law on the country. I say Mr. Webster, for though the Bill was not his, it is yet notorious that he was the life and soul of it, that he gave it all he had: it cost him his life, and under the shadow of his great name inferior men sheltered themselves, threw their ballots for it and made the law. I say inferior men. There were all sorts of what are called brilliant men, accomplished men, men of high station, a President of the United States, Senators, men of eloquent speech, but men without self-respect, without character, and it was strange to see that office, age, fame, talent, even a repute for honesty, all count for nothing. They had no opinions, they had no memory for what they had been saying like the Lord's Prayer all their lifetime: they were only looking to what their great Captain did: if he jumped, they jumped, if he stood on his head, they did. In ordinary, the supposed sense of their district and State is their guide, and that holds them to the part of liberty and justice. But it is always a little difficult to decipher what this public sense is; and when a great man comes who knots up into himself the opinions and wishes of the people, it is so much easier to follow him as an exponent of this. He too is responsible; they will not be. It will always suffice to say,—"I followed him."

I saw plainly that the great show their legitimate power in nothing more than in their power to misguide us. I saw that a great man, deservedly admired for his powers and their general right direction, was able,—fault of the total want of stamina in public men,—when he failed, to break them all with him, to carry parties with him.

In what I have to say of Mr. Webster I do not confound him with vulgar politicians before or since. There is always base ambition enough, men who calculate on the immense ignorance of the masses; that is their quarry and farm: they use the constituencies at home only for their shoes. And, of course, they can drive out from the contest any honorable man. The low can best win the low, and all men like to be made much of. There are those too who have power and inspiration only to do ill. Their talent or their faculty deserts them when they undertake anything right. Mr. Webster had a natural ascendancy of aspect and carriage which distinguished him over all his contemporaries. His countenance, his figure, and his manners were all in so grand a style, that he was, without effort, as superior to his most eminent rivals as they were to the humblest; so that his arrival in any place was an event which drew crowds of people, who went to satisfy their eyes, and could not see him enough. I think they looked at him as the representative of the American Continent. He was there in his Adamitic capacity, as if he alone of all men did not disappoint the eye and the ear, but was a fit figure in the landscape.

I remember his appearance at Bunker's Hill. There was the Monument, and here was Webster. He knew well that a little more or less of rhetoric signified nothing: he was only to say plain and equal things,—grand things if he had them, and, if he had them not, only to abstain from saying unfit things,—and the whole occasion was answered by his presence. It was a place for behavior more than for speech, and Mr. Webster walked through his part with entire success. His excellent organization, the perfection of his elocution and all that thereto belongs,—voice, accent, intonation, attitude, manner,—we shall not soon find again. Then he was so thoroughly simple and wise in his rhetoric; he saw through his matter, hugged his fact so close, went to the principle or essential, and never indulged in a weak flourish, though he knew perfectly well how to make such exordiums, episodes and perorations as might give perspective to his harangues without in the least embarrassing his march or confounding his transitions. In his statement things lay in daylight; we saw them in order as they were. Though he knew very well how to present his own personal claims, yet in his argument he was intellectual,—stated his fact pure of all personality, so that his splendid wrath, when his eyes became lamps, was the wrath of the fact and the cause he stood for.

His power, like that of all great masters, was not in excellent parts, but was total. He had a great and everywhere equal propriety. He worked with that closeness of adhesion to the matter in hand which a joiner or a chemist uses, and the same quiet and sure feeling of right to his place that an oak or a mountain have to theirs. After all his talents have been described, there remains that perfect propriety which animated all the details of the action or speech with the character of the whole, so that his beauties of detail are endless. He seemed born for the bar, born for the senate, and took very naturally a leading part in large private and in public affairs; for his head distributed things in their right places, and what he saw so well he compelled other people to see also. Great is the privilege of eloquence. What gratitude does every man feel to him who speaks well for the right,—who translates truth into language entirely plain and clear!

The history of this country has given a disastrous importance to the defects of this great man's mind. Whether evil influences and the corruption of politics, or whether original infirmity, it was the misfortune of his country that with this large understanding he had not what is better than intellect, and the source of its health. It is a law of our nature that great thoughts come from the heart. If his moral sensibility had been proportioned to the force of his understanding, what limits could have been set to his genius and beneficent power? But he wanted that deep source of inspiration. Hence a sterility of thought, the want of generalization in his speeches, and the curious fact that, with a general ability which impresses all the world, there is not a single general remark, not an observation on life and manners, not an aphorism that can pass into literature from his writings.

Four years ago to-night, on one of those high critical moments in history when great issues are determined, when the powers of right and wrong are mustered for conflict, and it lies with one man to give a casting vote,—Mr. Webster, most unexpectedly, threw his whole weight on the side of Slavery, and caused by his personal and official authority the passage of the Fugitive Slave Bill.

It is remarked of the Americans that they value dexterity too much, and honor too little; that they think they praise a man more by saying that he is "smart" than by saying that he is right. Whether the defect be national or not, it is the defect and calamity of Mr. Webster; and it is so far true of his countrymen, namely, that the appeal is sure to be made to his physical and mental ability when his character is assailed. His speeches on the seventh of March, and at Albany, at Buffalo, at Syracuse and Boston are cited in justification. And Mr. Webster's literary editor believes that it was his wish to rest his fame on the speech of the seventh of March. Now, though I have my own opinions on this seventh of March discourse and those others, and think them very transparent and very open to criticism,—yet the secondary merits of a speech, namely, its logic, its illustrations, its points, etc., are not here in question. Nobody doubts that Daniel Webster could make a good speech. Nobody doubts that there were good and plausible things to be said on the part of the South.

But this is not a question of ingenuity, not a question of syllogisms, but of sides. *How came he there?*

There are always texts and thoughts and arguments. But it is the genius and temper of the man which decides whether he will stand for right or for might. Who doubts the power of any fluent debater to defend either of our political parties, or any client in our courts? There was the same law in England for Jeffries and Talbot and Yorke to read slavery out of, and for Lord Mansfield to read freedom. And in this country one sees that there is always margin enough in the statute for a liberal judge to read one way and a servile judge another.

But the question which History will ask is broader. In the final hour, when he was forced by the peremptory necessity of the closing armies to take a side,—did he take the part of great principles, the side of humanity and justice, or the side of abuse and oppression and chaos?

Mr. Webster decided for Slavery, and that, when the aspect of the institution was no longer doubtful, no longer feeble and apologetic and proposing soon to end itself, but when it was strong, aggressive, and threatening an illimitable increase. He listened to State reasons and hopes, and left, with much complacency we are told, the testament of his speech to the astonished State of Massachusetts, *vera pro gratis;* a ghastly result of all those years of experience in affairs, this, that there was nothing better for the foremost American man to tell his countrymen than that Slavery was now at that strength that they must beat down their conscience and become kidnappers for it.

This was like the doleful speech falsely ascribed to the patriot Brutus: "Virtue, I have followed thee through life, and I find thee but a shadow." Here was a question of an immoral law; a question agitated for ages, and settled always in the same way by every great jurist, that an immoral law cannot be valid. Cicero, Grotius, Coke, Blackstone, Burlamaqui, Vattel, Burke, Jefferson, do all affirm this, and I cite them, not that they can give evidence to what is indisputable, but because, though lawyers and practical statesmen, the habit of their profession did not hide from them that this truth was the foundation of States.

Here was the question, Are you for man and for the good of man; or are you for the hurt and harm of man? It was the question whether man shall be treated as leather? whether the Negro shall be, as the Indians were in Spanish America, a piece of money? Whether this system, which is a kind of mill or factory for converting men into monkeys, shall be upheld and enlarged? And Mr. Webster and the country went for the application to these poor men of quadruped law.

People were expecting a totally different course from Mr. Webster. If any man had in that hour possessed the weight with the country which he had acquired, he could have brought the whole country to its senses. But not a moment's pause was allowed. Angry parties went from bad to worse, and the decision of Webster was accompanied with everything offensive to freedom and good morals. There was something like an attempt to debauch the moral sentiment of the clergy and of the youth. Burke said he "would pardon something to the spirit of liberty." But by Mr. Webster the opposition to the law was sharply called treason, and prosecuted so. He told the people at Boston "they must conquer their prejudices;" that "agitation of the subject of Slavery must be suppressed." He did as immoral men usually do, made very low bows to the Christian Church, and went through all the Sunday decorums; but when allusion was made to the question of duty and the sanctions of morality, he very frankly said, at Albany, "Some higher law, something existing somewhere between here and the third heaven,—I do not know where." And if the reporters say true, this wretched atheism found some laughter in the company.

I said I had never in my life up to this time suffered from the Slave Institution. Slavery in Virginia or Carolina was like Slavery in Africa or the Feejees, for me. There was an old fugitive law, but it had become, or was fast becoming, a dead letter, and, by the genius and laws of Massachusetts, inoperative. The new Bill made it operative, required me to hunt slaves, and it found citizens in Massachusetts willing to act as judges and captors. Moreover, it discloses the secret of the new times, that Slavery was no longer mendicant, but was become aggressive and dangerous.

The way in which the country was dragged to consent to this, and the disastrous defection (on the miserable cry of Union) of the men of letters, of the colleges, of educated men, nay, of some preachers of religion,—was the darkest passage in the history. It showed that our prosperity had hurt us, and that we could not be shocked by crime. It showed that the old religion and the sense of the right had faded and gone out; that while we reckoned ourselves a highly cultivated nation, our bellies had run away with our brains, and the principles of culture and progress did not exist.

For I suppose that liberty is an accurate index, in men and nations, of general progress. The theory of personal liberty must always appeal to the most refined communities and to the men of the rarest perception and of delicate moral sense. For there are rights which rest on the finest sense of justice, and, with every degree of civility, it will be more truly felt and defined. A barbarous tribe of good stock will, by means of their best heads, secure substantial liberty. But where there is any weakness in a race, and it becomes in a degree matter of concession and protection from their stronger neighbors, the incompatibility and offensiveness of the wrong will of course be most evident to the most cultivated. For it is,—is it not?—the essence of courtesy, of politeness, of religion, of love, to prefer another, to postpone oneself, to protect another from oneself. That is the distinction of the gentleman, to defend the weak and redress the injured, as it is of the savage and the brutal to usurp and use others.

In Massachusetts, as we all know, there has always existed a predominant conservative spirit. We have more money and value of every kind than other people, and wish to keep them. The plea on which freedom was resisted was Union. I went to certain serious men, who had a little more reason than the rest, and inquired why they took this part? They answered that they had no confidence in their strength to resist the Democratic party; that they saw plainly that all was going to the utmost verge of license; each was vying with his neighbor to lead the party, by proposing the worst measure, and they threw themselves on the extreme conservatism, as a drag on the wheel: that they knew Cuba would be had, and Mexico would be had, and they stood stiffly on conservatism, and as near to monarchy as they could, only to moderate the velocity with which the car was running down the precipice. In short, their theory was despair; the Whig wisdom was only reprieve, a waiting to be last devoured. They side with Carolina, or with Arkansas, only to make a show of Whig strength, wherewith to resist a little longer this general ruin.

I have a respect for conservatism. I know how deeply founded it is in our nature, and how idle are all attempts to shake ourselves free from it. We are all conservatives, half Whig, half Democrat, in our essences: and might as well try to jump out of our skins as to escape from our Whiggery. There are two forces in Nature, by whose antagonism we exist; the power of Fate, Fortune, the laws of the world, the order of things, or however else we choose to phrase it, the material necessities, on the one hand,—and Will or Duty or Freedom on the other.

May and Must, and the sense of right and duty, on the one hand, and the material necessities on the other: May and Must. In vulgar politics the Whig goes for what has been, for the old necessities,—the Musts. The reformer goes for the Better, for the ideal good, for the Mays. But each of these parties must of necessity take in, in some measure, the principles of the other. Each wishes to cover the whole ground; to hold fast *and* to advance. Only, one lays the emphasis on keeping, and the other on advancing. I too think the *musts* are a safe company to follow, and even agreeable. But if we are Whigs, let us be Whigs of nature and science, and so for all the necessities. Let us know that, over and above all the *musts* of poverty and appetite, is the instinct of man to rise, and the instinct to love and help his brother.

Now, Gentlemen, I think we have in this hour instruction again in the simplest lesson. Events roll, millions of men are engaged, and the result is the enforcing of some of those first commandments which we heard in the nursery. We never get beyond our first lesson, for, really, the world exists, as I understand it, to teach the science of liberty, which begins with liberty from fear.

The events of this month are teaching one thing plain and clear, the worthlessness of good tools to bad workmen; that official papers are of no use; resolutions of public meetings, platforms of conventions, no, nor laws, nor constitutions, any more. These are all declaratory of the will of the moment, and are passed with more levity and on grounds far less honorable than ordinary business transactions of the street.

You relied on the constitution. It has not the word *slave* in it; and very good argument has shown that it would not warrant the crimes that are done under it; that, with provisions so vague for an object not named, and which could not be availed of to claim a barrel of sugar or a barrel of corn, the robbing of a man and of all his posterity is effected. You relied on the Supreme Court. The law was right, excellent law for the lambs. But what if unhappily the judges were chosen from the wolves, and give to all the law a wolfish interpretation? You relied on the Missouri Compromise. That is ridden over. You relied on State sovereignty in the Free States to protect their citizens. They are driven with contempt out of the courts and out of the territory of the Slave States,—if they are so happy as to get out with their lives,—and now you relied on these dismal guaranties infamously made in 1850; and, before the body of Webster is yet crumbled, it is found that they have crumbled. This eternal monument of his fame and of the Union is rotten in four years. They are no guaranty to the free states. They are a guaranty to the slave states that, as they have hitherto met with no repulse, they shall meet with none.

I fear there is no reliance to be put on any kind or form of covenant, no, not on sacred forms, none on churches, none on bibles. For one would have said that a Christian would not keep slaves;—but the Christians keep slaves. Of course they will not dare to read the Bible? Won't they? They quote the Bible, quote Paul, quote Christ, to justify slavery. If slavery is good, then is lying, theft, arson, homicide, each and all good, and to be maintained by Union societies.

These things show that no forms, neither constitutions, nor laws, nor covenants, nor churches, nor bibles, are of any use in themselves. The Devil nestles comfortably into them all. There is no help but in the head and heart and hamstrings of a man. Covenants are of no use without honest men to keep them; laws of none but with loyal citizens to obey them. To interpret Christ it needs Christ in the heart. The teachings of the Spirit can be apprehended only by the same spirit that gave them forth. To make good the cause of Freedom, you must draw off from all foolish trust in others. You must be citadels and warriors yourselves, declarations of Independence, the charter, the battle and the victory. Cromwell said, "We can only resist the superior training of the King's soldiers, by enlisting godly men." And no man has a right to hope that the laws of New York will defend him from the contamination of slaves another day until he has made up his mind that he will not owe his protection to the laws of New York, but to his own sense and spirit. Then he protects New York. He only who is able to stand alone is qualified for society.

And that I understand to be the end for which a soul exists in this world,—to be himself the counterbalance of all falsehood and all wrong. "The army of unright is encamped from pole to pole, but the road of victory is known to the just." Everything may be taken away; he may be poor, he may be houseless, yet he will know out of his arms to make a pillow, and out of his breast a bolster. Why have the minority no influence? Because they have not a real minority of one.

I conceive that thus to detach a man and make him feel that he is to owe all to himself, is the way to make him strong and rich; and here the optimist must find, if anywhere, the benefit of Slavery. We have many teachers; we are in this world for culture, to be instructed in realities, in the laws of moral and intelligent nature; and our education is not conducted by toys and luxuries, but by austere and rugged masters, by poverty, solitude, passions, War, Slavery; to know that Paradise is under the shadow of swords; that divine sentiments which are always soliciting us are breathed into us from on high, and are an offset to a Universe of suffering and crime; that self-reliance, the height and perfection of man, is reliance on God. The insight of the religious sentiment will disclose to him unexpected aids in the nature of things. The Persian Saadi said, "Beware of hurting the orphan. When the orphan sets a-crying, the throne of the Almighty is rocked from side to side."

Whenever a man has come to this mind, that there is no Church for him but his believing prayer; no Constitution but his dealing well and justly with his neighbor; no liberty but his invincible will to do right,—then certain aids and allies will promptly appear: for the constitution of the Universe is on his side. It is of no use to vote down gravitation of morals. What is useful will last, whilst that which is hurtful to the world will sink beneath all the opposing forces which it must exasperate. The terror which the Marseillaise struck into oppression, it thunders again to-day,—

"Tout est soldat pour vous combattre."

Everything turns soldier to fight you down. The end for which man was made is not crime in any form, and a man cannot steal without incurring the penalties of the thief, though all the legislatures vote that it is virtuous, and though there be a general conspiracy among scholars and official persons to hold him up, and to say, *"Nothing is good but stealing."* A man who commits a crime defeats the end of his existence. He was created for benefit, and he exists for harm; and as well-doing makes power and wisdom, ill-doing takes them away. A man who steals another man's labor steals away his own faculties; his integrity, his humanity is flowing away from him. The habit of oppression cuts out the moral eyes, and, though the intellect goes on simulating the moral as before, its sanity is gradually destroyed. It takes away the presentiments.

I suppose in general this is allowed, that if you have a nice question of right and wrong, you would not go with it to Louis Napoleon, or to a political hack, or to a slave-driver. The habit of mind of traders in power would not be esteemed favorable to delicate moral perception. American slavery affords no exception to this rule. No excess of good nature or of tenderness in individuals has been able to give a new character to the system, to tear down the whipping-house. The plea in the mouth of a slave-holder that the negro is an inferior race sounds very oddly in my ear. "The masters of slaves seem generally anxious to prove that they are not of a race superior in any noble quality to the meanest of their bondmen." And indeed when the Southerner points to the anatomy of the negro, and talks of chimpanzee,—I recall Montesquieu's remark, "It will not do to say that negroes are men, lest it should turn out that whites are not."

Slavery is disheartening; but Nature is not so helpless but it can rid itself at last of every wrong. But the spasms of Nature are centuries and ages, and will tax the faith of short-lived men. Slowly, slowly the Avenger comes, but comes surely. The proverbs of the nations affirm these delays, but affirm the arrival. They say, "God may consent, but not forever." The delay of the Divine Justice—this was the meaning and soul of the Greek Tragedy; this the soul of their religion. "There has come, too, one to whom lurking warfare is dear, Retribution, with a soul full of wiles; a violator of hospitality; guileful without the guilt of guile; limping, late in her arrival." They said of the happiness of the unjust, that "at its close it begets itself an offspring and does not die childless, and instead of good fortune, there sprouts forth for posterity ever-ravening calamity:"—

> "For evil word shall evil word be said,
>   For murder-stroke a murder-stroke be paid.
>   Who smites must smart."

These delays, you see them now in the temper of the times. The national spirit in this country is so drowsy, preoccupied with interest, deaf to principle. The Anglo-Saxon race is proud and strong and selfish. They believe only in Anglo-Saxons. In 1825 Greece found America deaf, Poland found America deaf, Italy and Hungary found her deaf. England maintains trade, not liberty; stands against Greece; against Hungary; against Schleswig-Holstein; against the French Republic whilst it was a republic.

To faint hearts the times offer no invitation, and torpor exists here throughout the active classes on the subject of domestic slavery and its appalling aggressions. Yes, that is the stern edict of Providence, that liberty shall be no hasty fruit, but that event on event, population on population, age on age, shall cast itself into the opposite scale, and not until liberty has slowly accumulated weight enough to countervail and preponderate against all this, can the sufficient recoil come. All the great cities, all the refined circles, all the statesmen, Guizot, Palmerston, Webster, Calhoun, are sure to be found befriending liberty with their words, and crushing it with their votes. Liberty is never cheap. It is made difficult, because freedom is the accomplishment and perfectness of man. He is a finished man; earning and bestowing good; equal to the world; at home in Nature and dignifying that; the sun does not see anything nobler, and has nothing to teach him. Therefore mountains of difficulty must be surmounted, stern trials met, wiles of seduction, dangers, healed by a quarantine of calamities to measure his strength before he dare say, I am free.

Whilst the inconsistency of slavery with the principles on which the world is built guarantees its downfall, I own that the patience it requires is almost too sublime for mortals, and seems to demand of us more than mere hoping. And when one sees how fast the rot spreads,—it is growing serious,—I think we demand of superior men that they be superior in this,—that the mind and the virtue shall give their verdict in their day, and accelerate so far the progress of civilization. Possession is sure to throw its stupid strength for existing power, and appetite and ambition will go for that. Let the aid of virtue, intelligence and education be cast where they rightfully belong. They are organically ours. Let them be loyal to their own. I wish to see the instructed class here know their own flag, and not fire on their comrades. We should not forgive the clergy for taking on every issue the immoral side; nor the Bench, if it put itself on the side of the culprit; nor the Government, if it sustain the mob against the laws.

It is a potent support and ally to a brave man standing single, or with a few, for the right, and out-voted and ostracized, to know that better men in other parts of the country appreciate the service and will rightly report him to his own and the next age. Without this assurance, he will sooner sink. He may well say, 'If my countrymen do not care to be defended, I too will decline the controversy, from which I only reap invectives and hatred.' Yet the lovers of liberty may with reason tax the coldness and indifferentism of scholars and literary men. They are lovers of liberty in Greece and Rome and in the English Commonwealth, but they are lukewarm lovers of the liberty of America in 1854. The universities are not, as in Hobbes's time, "the core of rebellion," no, but the seat of inertness. They have forgotten their allegiance to the Muse, and grown worldly and political. I listened, lately, on one of those occasions when the university chooses one of its distinguished sons returning from the political arena, believing that senators and statesmen would be glad to throw off the harness and to dip again in the Castalian pools. But if audiences forget themselves, statesmen do not. The low bows to all the crockery gods of the day were duly made:—only in one part of the discourse the orator allowed to transpire, rather against his will, a little sober sense. It was this: 'I am, as you see, a man virtuously inclined, and only corrupted by my profession of politics. I should prefer the right side. You, gentlemen of these literary and scientific schools, and the important class you represent, have the power to make your verdict clear and prevailing. Had you done so, you would have found me its glad organ and champion. Abstractly, I should have preferred that side. But you have not done it. You have not spoken out. You have failed to arm me. I can only deal with masses as I find them. Abstractions are not for me. I go then for such parties and opinions as have provided me with a working apparatus. I give you my word, not without regret, that I was first for you; and though I am now to deny and condemn you, you see it is not my will but the party necessity.' Having made this manifesto and professed his adoration for liberty in the time of his grandfathers, he proceeded with his work of denouncing freedom and freemen at the present day, much in the tone and spirit in which Lord Bacon prosecuted his benefactor Essex. He denounced every name and aspect under which liberty and progress dare show themselves in this age and country, but with a lingering conscience which qualified each sentence with a recommendation to mercy.

But I put it to every noble and generous spirit, to every

poetic, every heroic, every religious heart, that not so is our learning, our education, our poetry, our worship to be declared. Liberty is aggressive, Liberty is the Crusade of all brave and conscientious men, the Epic Poetry, the new religion, the chivalry of all gentlemen. This is the oppressed Lady whom true knights on their oath and honor must rescue and save.

Now at last we are disenchanted and shall have no more false hopes. I respect the Anti-Slavery Society. It is the Cassandra that has foretold all that has befallen, fact for fact, years ago; foretold all, and no man laid it to heart. It seemed, as the Turks say, "Fate makes that a man should not believe his own eyes." But the Fugitive Law did much to unglue the eyes of men, and now the Nebraska Bill leaves us staring. The Anti-Slavery Society will add many members this year. The Whig Party will join it; the Democrats will join it. The population of the free states will join it. I doubt not, at last, the slave states will join it. But be that sooner or later, and whoever comes or stays away, I hope we have reached the end of our unbelief, have come to a belief that there is a divine Providence in the world, which will not save us but through our own coöperation.

FARMING

The glory of the farmer is that, in the division of labors, it is his part to create. All trade rests at last on his primitive activity. He stands close to Nature; he obtains from the earth the bread and the meat. The food which was not, he causes to be. The first farmer was the first man, and all historic nobility rests on possession and use of land. Men do not like hard work, but every man has an exceptional respect for tillage, and a feeling that this is the original calling of his race, that he himself is only excused from it by some circumstance which made him delegate it for a time to other hands. If he have not some skill which recommends him to the farmer, some product for which the farmer will give him corn, he must himself return into his due place among the planters. And the profession has in all eyes its ancient charm, as standing nearest to God, the first cause.

Then the beauty of Nature, the tranquillity and innocence of the countryman, his independence and his pleasing arts,—the care of bees, of poultry, of sheep, of cows, the dairy, the care of hay, of fruits, of orchards and forests, and the reaction of these on the workman, in giving him a strength and plain dignity like the face and manners of Nature,—all men acknowledge. All men keep the farm in reserve as an asylum where, in case of mischance, to hide their poverty,—or a solitude, if they do not succeed in society. And who knows how many glances of remorse are turned this way from the bankrupts of trade, from mortified pleaders in courts and senates, or from the victims of idleness and pleasure? Poisoned by town life and town

vices, the sufferer resolves: 'Well, my children, whom I
have injured, shall go back to the land, to be recruited and
cured by that which should have been my nursery, and
now shall be their hospital.'

The farmer's office is precise and important, but you
must not try to paint him in rose-color; you cannot make
pretty compliments to fate and gravitation, whose minister he is. He represents the necessities. It is the beauty of
the great economy of the world that makes his comeliness.
He bends to the order of the seasons, the weather, the soils
and crops, as the sails of a ship bend to the wind. He represents continuous hard labor, year in, year out, and small
gains. He is a slow person, timed to Nature, and not to
city watches. He takes the pace of seasons, plants and
chemistry. Nature never hurries: atom by atom, little by
little, she achieves her work. The lesson one learns in fish-
ing, yachting, hunting or planting is the manners of Nature; patience with the delays of wind and sun, delays of
the seasons, bad weather, excess or lack of water,—patience with the slowness of our feet, with the parsimony of
our strength, with the largeness of sea and land we must
traverse, etc. The farmer times himself to Nature, and acquires that livelong patience which belongs to her. Slow,
narrow man, his rule is that the earth shall feed and clothe
him; and he must wait for his crop to grow. His entertainments, his liberties and his spending must be on a farmer's
scale, and not on a merchant's. It were as false for farmers
to use a wholesale and massy expense, as for states to use a
minute economy. But if thus pinched on one side, he has
compensatory advantages. He is permanent, clings to his
land as the rocks do. In the town where I live, farms remain in the same families for seven and eight generations;
and most of the first settlers (in 1635), should they reappear on the farms to-day, would find their own blood and
names still in possession. And the like fact holds in the
surrounding towns.

This hard work will always be done by one kind of
man; not by scheming speculators, nor by soldiers, nor

professors, nor readers of Tennyson; but by men of endurance—deep-chested, long-winded, tough, slow and sure, and timely. The farmer has a great health, and the appetite of health, and means to his end; he has broad lands for his home, wood to burn great fires, plenty of plain food; his milk at least is unwatered; and for sleep, he has cheaper and better and more of it than citizens.

He has grave trusts confided to him. In the great household of Nature, the farmer stands at the door of the bread-room, and weighs to each his loaf. It is for him to say whether men shall marry or not. Early marriages and the number of births are indissolubly connected with abundance of food; or, as Burke said, "Man breeds at the mouth." Then he is the Board of Quarantine. The farmer is a hoarded capital of health, as the farm is the capital of wealth; and it is from him that the health and power, moral and intellectual, of the cities came. The city is always recruited from the country. The men in cities who are the centres of energy, the driving-wheels of trade, politics or practical arts, and the women of beauty and genius, are the children or grandchildren of farmers, and are spending the energies which their father's hardy, silent life accumulated in frosty furrows, in poverty, necessity and darkness.

He is the continuous benefactor. He who digs a well, constructs a stone fountain, plants a grove of trees by the roadside, plants an orchard, builds a durable house, reclaims a swamp, or so much as puts a stone seat by the wayside, makes the land so far lovely and desirable, makes a fortune which he cannot carry away with him, but which is useful to his country long afterwards. The man that works at home helps society at large with somewhat more of certainty than he who devotes himself to charities. If it be true that, not by votes of political parties but by the eternal laws of political economy, slaves are driven out of a slave state as fast as it is surrounded by free states, then the true abolitionist is the farmer, who, heedless of laws and constitutions, stands all day in the field, investing his labor in the land, and making a product with which no forced labor can compete.

We commonly say that the rich man can speak the truth, can afford honesty, can afford independence of opinion and action;—and that is the theory of nobility. But it is the rich man in a true sense, that is to say, not the man of large income and large expenditure, but solely the man whose outlay is less than his income and is steadily kept so.

In English factories, the boy that watches the loom, to tie the thread when the wheel stops to indicate that a thread is broken, is called a *minder*. And in this great factory of our Copernican globe, shifting its slides, rotating its constellations, times and tides, bringing now the day of planting, then of watering, then of weeding, then of reaping, then of curing and storing,—the farmer is the *minder*. His machine is of colossal proportions; the diameter of the water-wheel, the arms of the levers, the power of the battery, are out of all mechanic measure; and it takes him long to understand its parts and its working. This pump never "sucks;" these screws are never loose; this machine is never out of gear; the vat and piston, wheels and tires, never wear out, but are self-repairing.

Who are the farmer's servants? Not the Irish, nor the coolies, but Geology and Chemistry, the quarry of the air, the water of the brook, the lightning of the cloud, the castings of the worm, the plough of the frost. Long before he was born, the sun of ages decomposed the rocks, mellowed his land, soaked it with light and heat, covered it with vegetable film, then with forests, and accumulated the sphagnum whose decays made the peat of his meadow.

Science has shown the great circles in which Nature works; the manner in which marine plants balance the marine animals, as the land plants supply the oxygen which the animals consume, and the animals the carbon which the plants absorb. These activities are incessant. Nature works on a method of *all for each and each for all*. The strain that is made on one point bears on every arch and foundation of the structure. There is a perfect solidarity. You cannot detach an atom from its holdings, or strip off from it the electricity, gravitation, chemic affinity or the relation to light and heat and leave the atom bare. No, it brings with it its universal ties.

Nature, like a cautious testator, ties up her estate so as not to bestow it all on one generation, but has a forelooking tenderness and equal regard to the next and the next, and the fourth and the fortieth age. There lie the inexhaustible magazines. The eternal rocks, as we call them, have held their oxygen or lime undiminished, entire, as it was. No particle of oxygen can rust or wear, but has the same energy as on the first morning. The good rocks, those patient waiters, say to him: 'We have the sacred power as we received it. We have not failed of our trust, and now—when in our immense day the hour is at last struck—take the gas we have hoarded, mingle it with water, and let it be free to grow in plants and animals and obey the thought of man.'

The earth works for him; the earth is a machine which yields almost gratuitous service to every application of intellect. Every plant is a manufacturer of soil. In the stomach of the plant development begins. The tree can draw on the whole air, the whole earth, on all the rolling main. The plant is all suction-pipe,—imbibing from the ground by its root, from the air by its leaves, with all its might.

The air works for him. The atmosphere, a sharp solvent, drinks the essence and spirit of every solid on the globe,—a menstruum which melts the mountains into it. Air is matter subdued by heat. As the sea is the grand receptacle of all rivers, so the air is the receptacle from which all things spring, and into which they all return. The invisible and creeping air takes form and solid mass. Our senses are skeptics, and believe only the impression of the moment, and do not believe the chemical fact that these huge mountain chains are made up of gases and rolling wind. But Nature is as subtle as she is strong. She turns her capital day by day; deals never with dead, but ever with quick subjects. All things are flowing, even those that seem immovable. The adamant is always passing into smoke. The plants imbibe the materials which they want from the air and the ground. They burn, that is, exhale and decompose their own bodies into the air and earth again. The animal burns, or undergoes the like perpetual consumption. The earth burns, the mountains burn and decompose, slower, but incessantly. It is almost inevitable to push the generalization up into higher parts of Nature, rank over rank into sentient beings. Nations burn with internal fire of thought and affection, which wastes while it works. We shall find finer combustion and finer fuel. Intellect is a fire: rash and pitiless it melts this wonderful bone-house which is called man. Genius even, as it is the greatest good, is the greatest harm. Whilst all thus burns,—the universe in a blaze kindled from the torch of the sun,—it needs a perpetual tempering, a phlegm, a sleep, atmospheres of azote, deluges of water, to check the fury of the conflagration; a hoarding to check the spending, a centripetence equal to the centrifugence; and this is invariably supplied.

The railroad dirt-cars are good excavators, but there is no porter like Gravitation, who will bring down any weights which man cannot carry, and if he wants aid, knows where to find his fellow laborers. Water works in masses, and sets its irresistible shoulder to your mills or your ships, or transports vast boulders of rock in its iceberg a thousand miles. But its far greater power depends on its talent of becoming little, and entering the smallest holes and pores. By this agency, carrying in solution elements needful to every plant, the vegetable world exists.

But as I said, we must not paint the farmer in rosecolor. Whilst these grand energies have wrought for him and made his task possible, he is habitually engaged in small economies, and is taught the power that lurks in petty things. Great is the force of a few simple arrangements; for instance, the powers of a fence. On the prairie you wander a hundred miles and hardly find a stick or a stone. At rare intervals a thin oak-opening has been spared, and every such section has been long occupied. But the farmer manages to procure wood from far, puts up a rail-fence, and at once the seeds sprout and the oaks rise. It was only browsing and fire which had kept them down. Plant fruit-trees by the roadside, and their fruit will never be allowed to ripen. Draw a pine fence about them, and for fifty years they mature for the owner their delicate fruit. There is a great deal of enchantment in a chestnut rail or picketed pine boards.

Nature suggests every economical expedient somewhere on a great scale. Set out a pine-tree, and it dies in the first year, or lives a poor spindle. But Nature drops a pine-cone in Mariposa, and it lives fifteen centuries, grows three or four hundred feet high, and thirty in diameter,— grows in a grove of giants, like a colonnade of Thebes. Ask the tree how it was done. It did not grow on a ridge, but in a basin, where it found deep soil, cold enough and dry enough for the pine; defended itself from the sun by growing in groves, and from the wind by the walls of the mountain. The roots that shot deepest, and the stems of happiest exposure, drew the nourishment from the rest, until the less thrifty perished and manured the soil for the stronger, and the mammoth Sequoias rose to their enormous proportions. The traveller who saw them remembered his orchard at home, where every year, in the destroying wind, his forlorn trees pined like suffering virtue. In September, when the pears hang heaviest and are taking from the sun their gay colors, comes usually a gusty day which shakes the whole garden and throws down the heaviest fruit in bruised heaps. The planter took the hint of the Sequoias, built a high wall, or—better— surrounded the orchard with a nursery of birches and evergreens. Thus he had the mountain basin in miniature; and his pears grew to the size of melons, and the vines beneath them ran an eighth of a mile. But this shelter creates a new climate. The wall that keeps off the strong wind keeps off the cold wind. The high wall reflecting the heat back on the soil gives that acre a quadruple share of sunshine,—

> "Enclosing in the garden square
> A dead and standing pool of air,"

and makes a little Cuba within it, whilst all without is Labrador.

The chemist comes to his aid every year by following out some new hint drawn from Nature, and now affirms that this dreary space occupied by the farmer is needless; he will concentrate his kitchen-garden into a box of one or two rods square, will take the roots into his laboratory; the vines and stalks and stems may go sprawling about in the fields outside, he will attend to the roots in his tub, gorge them with food that is good for them. The smaller his garden, the better he can feed it, and the larger the crop. As he nursed his Thanksgiving turkeys on bread and milk, so he will pamper his peaches and grapes on the viands they like best. If they have an appetite for potash, or salt, or iron, or ground bones, or even now and then for a dead hog, he will indulge them. They keep the secret well, and never tell on your table whence they drew their sunset complexion or their delicate flavors.

See what the farmer accomplishes by a cart-load of tiles: he alters the climate by letting off water which kept the land cold through constant evaporation, and allows the warm rain to bring down into the roots the temperature of the air and of the surface soil; and he deepens the soil, since the discharge of this standing water allows the roots of his plants to penetrate below the surface to the subsoil, and accelerates the ripening of the crop. The town of Concord is one of the oldest towns in this country, far on now in its third century. The selectmen have once in every five years perambulated the boundaries, and yet, in this very year, a large quantity of land has been discovered and added to the town without a murmur of complaint from any quarter. By drainage we went down to a subsoil we did not know, and have found there is a Concord under old Concord, which we are now getting the best crops from; a Middlesex under Middlesex; and, in fine, that Massachusetts has a basement story more valuable and that promises to pay a better rent than all the superstructure. But these tiles have acquired by association a new interest. These tiles are political economists, confuters of Malthus and Ricardo; they are so many Young Americans announcing a better era,—more bread. They drain the land, make it sweet and friable; have made English Chat Moss a garden, and will now do as much for the Dismal Swamp. But beyond this benefit they are the text of better opinions and better auguries for mankind.

There has been a nightmare bred in England of indigestion and spleen among landlords and loom-lords, namely, the dogma that men breed too fast for the powers of the soil; that men multiply in a geometrical ratio, whilst corn multiplies only in an arithmetical; and hence that, the more prosperous we are, the faster we approach these frightful limits: nay, the plight of every new generation is worse than of the foregoing, because the first comers take up the best lands; the next, the second best; and each succeeding wave of population is driven to poorer, so that the land is ever yielding less returns to enlarging hosts of eaters. Henry Carey of Philadelphia replied: "Not so, Mr. Malthus, but just the opposite of so is the fact."

The first planter, the savage, without helpers, without tools, looking chiefly to safety from his enemy,—man or beast,—takes poor land. The better lands are loaded with timber, which he cannot clear; they need drainage, which he cannot attempt. He cannot plough, or fell trees, or drain the rich swamp. He is a poor creature; he scratches with a sharp stick, lives in a cave or a hutch, has no road but the trail of the moose or bear; he lives on their flesh when he can kill one, on roots and fruits when he cannot. He falls, and is lame; he coughs, he has a stitch in his side, he has a fever and chills; when he is hungry, he cannot always kill and eat a bear,—chances of war,—sometimes the bear eats him. 'T is long before he digs or plants at all, and then only a patch. Later he learns that his planting is better than hunting; that the earth works faster for him than he can work for himself,—works for him when he is asleep, when it rains, when heat overcomes him. The sunstroke which knocks him down brings his corn up. As his family thrive, and other planters come up around him, he begins to fell trees and clear good land; and when, by and by, there is more skill, and tools and roads, the new generations are strong enough to open the lowlands, where the wash of mountains has accumulated the best soil, which yield a hundred-fold the former crops. The last lands are the best lands. It needs science and great numbers to cultivate the best lands, and in the best manner. Thus true political economy is not mean, but liberal, and on the pattern of the sun and sky. Population increases in the ratio of morality; credit exists in the ratio of morality.

Meantime we cannot enumerate the incidents and agents of the farm without reverting to their influence on the farmer. He carries out this cumulative preparation of means to their last effect. This crust of soil which ages have refined he refines again for the feeding of a civil and instructed people. The great elements with which he deals cannot leave him unaffected, or unconscious of his ministry; but their influence somewhat resembles that which the same Nature has on the child,—of subduing and silencing him. We see the farmer with pleasure and respect when we think what powers and utilities are so meekly worn. He knows every secret of labor; he changes the face of the landscape. Put him on a new planet and he would know where to begin; yet there is no arrogance in his bearing, but a perfect gentleness. The farmer stands well on the world. Plain in manners as in dress, he would not shine in palaces; he is absolutely unknown and inadmissible therein; living or dying, he never shall be heard of in them; yet the drawing-room heroes put down beside him would shrivel in his presence; he solid and unexpressive, they expressed to gold-leaf. But he stands well on the world,—as Adam did, as an Indian does, as Homer's heroes, Agamemnon or Achilles, do. He is a person whom a poet of any clime—Milton, Firdusi, or Cervantes— would appreciate as being really a piece of the old Nature, comparable to sun and moon, rainbow and flood; because he is, as all natural persons are, representative of Nature as much as these.

That uncorrupted behavior which we admire in animals and in young children belongs to him, to the hunter, the sailor,—the man who lives in the presence of Nature. Cities force growth and make men talkative and entertaining, but they make them artificial. What possesses interest for us is the *naturel* of each, his constitutional excellence. This is forever a surprise, engaging and lovely; we cannot be satiated with knowing it, and about it; and it is this which the conversation with Nature cherishes and guards.

JOHN BROWN

~~~~~~

Speech at Salem, January 6, 1860

Mr. Chairman: I have been struck with one fact, that the best orators who have added their praise to his fame,—and I need not go out of this house to find the purest eloquence in the country,—have one rival who comes off a little better, and that is JOHN BROWN. Everything that is said of him leaves people a little dissatisfied; but as soon as they read his own speeches and letters they are heartily contented,—such is the singleness of purpose which justifies him to the head and the heart of all. Taught by this experience, I mean, in the few remarks I have to make, to cling to his history, or let him speak for himself.

John Brown, the founder of liberty in Kansas, was born in Torrington, Litchfield County, Connecticut, in 1800. When he was five years old his father emigrated to Ohio, and the boy was there set to keep sheep and to look after cattle and dress skins; he went bareheaded and barefooted, and clothed in buckskin. He said that he loved rough play, could never have rough play enough; could not see a seedy hat without wishing to pull it off. But for this it needed that the playmates should be equal; not one in fine clothes and the other in buckskin; not one his own master, hale and hearty, and the other watched and whipped. But it chanced that in Pennsylvania, where he was sent by his father to collect cattle, he fell in with a boy whom he heartily liked and whom he looked upon as his superior. This boy was a slave; he saw him beaten with an iron shovel, and otherwise maltreated; he saw that this boy had nothing better to look forward to in life, whilst he himself was

petted and made much of; for he was much considered in
the family where he then stayed, from the circumstance
that this boy of twelve years had conducted alone a drove
of cattle a hundred miles. But the colored boy had no
friend, and no future. This worked such indignation in
him that he swore an oath of resistance to slavery as long
as he lived. And thus his enterprise to go into Virginia and
run off five hundred or a thousand slaves was not a piece
of spite or revenge, a plot of two years or of twenty years,
but the keeping of an oath made to heaven and earth
forty-seven years before. Forty-seven years at least,
though I incline to accept his own account of the matter at
Charlestown, which makes the date a little older, when he
said, "This was all settled millions of years before the
world was made."

He grew up a religious and manly person, in severe
poverty; a fair specimen of the best stock of New England;
having that force of thought and that sense of right which
are the warp and woof of greatness. Our farmers were Or-
thodox Calvinists, mighty in the Scriptures; had learned
that life was a preparation, a "probation," to use their
word, for a higher world, and was to be spent in loving
and serving mankind.

Thus was formed a romantic character absolutely without any vulgar trait; living to ideal ends, without any mixture of self-indulgence or compromise, such as lowers the
value of benevolent and thoughtful men we know; abste-
mious, refusing luxuries, not sourly and reproachfully,
but simply as unfit for his habit; quiet and gentle as a child
in the house. And, as happens usually to men of romantic
character, his fortunes were romantic. Walter Scott would
have delighted to draw his picture and trace his adventurous career. A shepherd and herdsman, he learned the
manners of animals, and knew the secret signals by which
animals communicate. He made his hard bed on the
mountains with them; he learned to drive his flock
through thickets all but impassable; he had all the skill of a

shepherd by choice of breed and by wise husbandry to obtain the best wool, and that for a course of years. And the anecdotes preserved show a far-seeing skill and conduct which, in spite of adverse accidents, should secure, one year with another, an honest reward, first to the farmer, and afterwards to the dealer. If he kept sheep, it was with a royal mind; and if he traded in wool, he was a merchant prince, not in the amount of wealth, but in the protection of the interests confided to him.

I am not a little surprised at the easy effrontery with which political gentlemen, in and out of Congress, take it upon them to say that there are not a thousand men in the North who sympathize with John Brown. It would be far safer and nearer the truth to say that all people, in proportion to their sensibility and self-respect, sympathize with him. For it is impossible to see courage, and disinterestedness, and the love that casts out fear, without sympathy. All women are drawn to him by their predominance of sentiment. All gentlemen, of course, are on his side. I do not mean by "gentlemen," people of scented hair and perfumed handkerchiefs, but men of gentle blood and generosity, "fulfilled with all nobleness," who, like the Cid, give the outcast leper a share of their bed; like the dying Sidney, pass the cup of cold water to the dying soldier who needs it more. For what is the oath of gentle blood and knighthood? What but to protect the weak and lowly against the strong oppressor?

Nothing is more absurd than to complain of this sympathy, or to complain of a party of men united in opposition to slavery. As well complain of gravity, or the ebb of the tide. Who makes the abolitionist? The slave-holder. The sentiment of mercy is the natural recoil which the laws of the universe provide to protect mankind from destruction by savage passions. And our blind statesmen go up and down, with committees of vigilance and safety, hunting for the origin of this new heresy. They will need a very vigilant committee indeed to find its birthplace, and a very strong force to root it out. For the arch-abolitionist, older than Brown, and older than the Shenandoah Mountains, is Love, whose other name is Justice, which was before Alfred, before Lycurgus, before slavery, and will be after it.

THOREAU[1]

~~~~~~

Henry D. Thoreau was the last male descendant of a French ancestor who came to this country from the isle of Guernsey. His character exhibited occasional traits drawn from this blood in singular combination with a very strong Saxon genius.

He was born in Concord, Massachusetts, on the 12th of July, 1817. He was graduated at Harvard College, in 1837, but without any literary distinction. An iconoclast in literature, he seldom thanked colleges for their service to him, holding them in small esteem, whilst yet his debt to them was important. After leaving the University, he joined his brother in teaching a private school, which he soon renounced. His father was a manufacturer of lead pencils, and Henry applied himself for a time to this craft, believing he could make a better pencil than was then in use. After completing his experiments, he exhibited his work to chemists and artists in Boston, and having obtained their certificates to its excellence and to its equality with the best London manufacture, he returned home contented. His friends congratulated him that he had now opened his way to fortune. But he replied, that he should never make another pencil. "Why should I? I would not do again what I have done once." He resumed his endless walks, and miscellaneous studies, making every day some new acquaintance with Nature, though as yet never speak-

[1] Thanks are owed to Joel Myerson of the University of South Carolina for permission to use his accurate text of the tribute to Thoreau. Professor Myerson edited the text from the manuscript, in Emerson's hand, that carries his revisions for the printer.—M.C.

ing of zoology or botany, since, though very studious of natural facts, he was incurious of technical and textual science.

At this time, a strong, healthy youth fresh from college, whilst all his companions were choosing their profession, or eager to begin some lucrative employment, it was inevitable that his thoughts should be exercised on the same question, and it required rare decision to refuse all the accustomed paths, and keep his solitary freedom at the cost of disappointing the natural expectations of his family and friends. All the more difficult that he had a perfect probity, was exact in securing his own independence, and in holding every man to the like duty. But Thoreau never faltered. He was a born protestant. He declined to give up his large ambition of knowledge and action for any narrow craft or profession, aiming at a much more comprehensive calling, the art of living well. If he slighted and defied the opinions of others, it was only that he was more intent to reconcile his practice with his own belief. Never idle or self-indulgent, he preferred when he wanted money, earning it by some piece of manual labor agreeable to him, as building a boat or a fence, planting, grafting, surveying, or other short work, to any long engagements. With his hardy habits and few wants, his skill in wood-craft, and his powerful arithmetic, he was very competent to live in any part of the world. It would cost him less time to supply his wants than another. He was therefore secure of his leisure.

A natural skill for mensuration, growing out of his mathematical knowledge, and his habit of ascertaining the measures and distances of objects which interested him, the size of trees, the depth and extent of ponds and rivers, the height of mountains and the air-line distance of his favorite summits,—this, and his intimate knowledge of the territory about Concord, made him drift into the profession of land-surveyor. It had the advantage for him that it led him continually into new and secluded grounds, and helped his studies of nature. His accuracy and skill in this work were readily appreciated, and he found all the employment he wanted.

He could easily solve the problems of the surveyor, but he was daily beset with graver questions which he manfully confronted. He interrogated every custom, and wished to settle all his practice on an ideal foundation. He was a protestant *à l'outrance* and few lives contain so many renunciations. He was bred to no profession; he never married; he lived alone; he never went to church; he never voted; he refused to pay a tax to the state; he ate no flesh, he drank no wine, he never knew the use of tobacco; and, though a naturalist, he used neither trap nor gun. He chose wisely, no doubt, for himself to be the bachelor of thought and nature. He had no talent for wealth, and knew how to be poor without the least hint of squalor or inelegance. Perhaps he fell into his way of living, without forecasting it much, but approved it with later wisdom. "I am often reminded," he wrote in his journal, "that, if I had bestowed on me the wealth of Crœsus, my aims must be still the same, and my means essentially the same." He had no temptations to fight against; no appetites, no passions, no taste for elegant trifles. A fine house, dress, the manners and talk of highly cultivated people were all thrown away on him. He much preferred a good Indian, and considered these refinements as impediments to conversation, wishing to meet his companion on the simplest terms. He declined invitations to dinner-parties, because there each was in every one's way, and he could not meet the individuals to any purpose. "They make their pride," he said, "in making their dinner cost much: I make my pride in making my dinner cost little." When asked at table, what dish he preferred, he answered, "the nearest." He did not like the taste of wine, and never had a vice in his life. He said, "I have a faint recollection of pleasure derived from smoking dried lily stems, before I was a man. I had commonly a supply of these. I have never smoked any thing more noxious."

He chose to be rich by making his wants few, and supplying them himself. In his travels, he used the railroad only to get over so much country as was unimportant to the present purpose, walking hundreds of miles, avoiding taverns, buying a lodging in farmers' and fishermen's houses, as cheaper, and more agreeable to him, and because there he could better find the men and the information he wanted.

There was somewhat military in his nature not to be subdued, always manly and able, but rarely tender, as if he did not feel himself except in opposition. He wanted a fallacy to expose, a blunder to pillory, I may say, required a little sense of victory, a roll of the drum, to call his powers into full exercise. It cost him nothing to say No; indeed he found it much easier than to say Yes. It seemed as if his first instinct on hearing a proposition was to controvert it, so impatient was he of the limitations of our daily thought. This habit of course is a little chilling to the social affections; and though the companion would in the end acquit him of any malice or untruth, yet it mars conversation. Hence no equal companion stood in affectionate relations with one so pure and guileless. "I love Henry," said one of his friends, "but I cannot like him: and as for taking his arm, I should as soon think of taking the arm of an elm-tree."

Yet hermit and stoic as he was, he was really fond of sympathy, and threw himself heartily and childlike into the company of young people whom he loved, and whom he delighted to entertain, as he only could, with the varied and endless anecdotes of his experiences by field and river. And he was always ready to lead a huckleberry party or a search for chestnuts or grapes. Talking one day of a public discourse, Henry remarked, that whatever succeeded with the audience, was bad. I said, "Who would not like to write something which all can read, like 'Robinson Crusoe'; and who does not see with regret that his page is not solid with a right materialistic treatment, which delights everybody." Henry objected, of course, and vaunted the better lectures which reached only a few persons. But, at supper, a young girl, understanding that he was to lecture at the Lyceum, sharply asked him, "whether his lecture would be a nice, interesting story such as she wished to hear, or whether it was one of those old philosophical things that she did not care about?" Henry turned to her, and bethought himself, and, I saw, was trying to believe that he had matter that might fit her and her brother, who were to sit up and go to the lecture, if it was a good one for them.

He was a speaker and actor of the truth,—born such,— and was ever running into dramatic situations from this cause. In any circumstance, it interested all bystanders to know what part Henry would take, and what he would say: and he did not disappoint expectation, but used an original judgment on each emergency. In 1845, he built himself a small framed house on the shores of Walden Pond, and lived there two years alone, a life of labor and study. This action was quite native and fit for him. No one who knew him would tax him with affectation. He was more unlike his neighbors in his thought, than in his action. As soon as he had exhausted the advantages of that solitude, he abandoned it. In 1847, not approving some uses to which the public expenditure was applied, he refused to pay his town-tax, and was put in jail. A friend paid the tax for him, and he was released. The like annoyance was threatened the next year. But, as his friends paid the tax, notwithstanding his protest, I believe he ceased to resist. No opposition or ridicule had any weight with him. He coldly and fully stated his opinion without affecting to believe that it was the opinion of the company. It was of no consequence if every one present held the opposite opinion. On one occasion he went to the University Library to procure some books. The Librarian refused to lend them. Mr. Thoreau repaired to the President, who stated to him the rules and usages which permitted the loan of books to resident graduates, to clergymen who were alumni, and to some others resident within a circle of ten miles' radius from the College. Mr. Thoreau explained to the President that the railroad had destroyed the old scale of distances,—that the library was useless, yes, and President and College useless, on the terms of his rules,—that the one benefit he owed to the College was its library,—that at this moment, not only his want of books was imperative, but he wanted a large number of books, and assured him that he Thoreau, and not the Librarian, was the proper custodian of these. In short, the President found the petitioner so formidable and the rules getting to look so ridiculous, that he ended by giving him a privilege which in his hands proved unlimited thereafter.

No truer American existed than Thoreau. His preference of his country and condition was genuine, and his aversation from English and European manners and tastes almost reached contempt. He listened impatiently to news or bon mots gleaned from London circles; and, though he tried to be civil, these anecdotes fatigued him. The men were all imitating each other, and on a small mould. Why can they not live as far apart as possible, and each be a man by himself? What he sought was the most energetic nature, and he wished to go to Oregon, not to London. "In every part of Great Britain," he wrote in his diary, "are discovered traces of the Romans, their funereal urns, their camps, their roads, their dwellings. But New England, at least, is not based on any Roman ruins. We have not to lay the foundations of our houses on the ashes of a former civilization."

But idealist as he was, standing for abolition of slavery, abolition of tariffs, almost for abolition of government, it is needless to say he found himself not only unrepresented in actual politics, but almost equally opposed to every class of reformers. Yet he paid the tribute of his uniform respect to the anti-slavery party. One man, whose personal acquaintance he had formed, he honored with exceptional regard. Before the first friendly word had been spoken for Captain John Brown, after the arrest, he sent notices to most houses in Concord, that he would speak in a public hall on the condition and character of John

Brown, on Sunday Evening, and invited all people to come. The Republican committee, the abolitionist committee, sent him word that it was premature and not advisable. He replied, "I did not send to you for advice but to announce that I am to speak." The hall was filled at an early hour by people of all parties, and his earnest eulogy of the hero was heard by all respectfully, by many with a sympathy that surprised themselves.

It was said of Plotinus, that he was ashamed of his body, and 'tis very likely he had good reason for it; that his body was a bad servant, and he had not skill in dealing with the material world, as happens often to men of abstract intellect. But Mr. Thoreau was equipped with a most adapted and serviceable body. He was of short stature, firmly built, of light complexion, with strong, serious blue eyes, and a grave aspect; his face covered in the late years with a becoming beard. His senses were acute, his frame well-knit and hardy, his hands strong and skilful in the use of tools. And there was a wonderful fitness of body and mind. He would pace sixteen rods more accurately than another man could measure them with rod and chain. He could find his path in the woods at night, he said, better by his feet than his eyes. He could estimate the measure of a tree very well by his eye; he could estimate the weight of a calf or a pig, like a dealer. From a box containing a bushel or more of loose pencils, he could take up with his hands fast enough just a dozen pencils at every grasp. He was a good swimmer, runner, skater, boatman, and would probably out-walk most countrymen in a day's journey. And the relation of body to mind was still finer than we have indicated. He said, he wanted every stride his legs made. The length of his walk uniformly made the length of his writing. If shut up in the house, he did not write at all.

He had a strong common sense, like that which Rose Flammock, the weaver's daughter, in Scott's romance, commends in her father, as resembling a yardstick, which, whilst it measures dowlas and diaper, can equally well measure tapestry and cloth of gold. He had always a new resource. When I was planting forest trees, and had procured half a peck of acorns, he said, that only a small portion of them would be sound, and proceeded to examine them, and select the sound ones. But finding this took time, he said, "I think, if you put them all into water, the good ones will sink," which experiment we tried with success. He could plan a garden, or a house, or a barn; would have been competent to lead a "Pacific Exploring Expedition"; could give judicious counsel in the gravest private or public affairs. He lived for the day, not cumbered and mortified by his memory. If he brought you yesterday a new proposition, he would bring you today another not less revolutionary. A very industrious man, and setting, like all highly organized men, a high value on his time, he seemed the only man of leisure in town, always ready for any excursion that promised well, or for conversation prolonged into late hours. His trenchant sense was never stopped by his rules of daily prudence, but was always up to the new occasion. He liked and used the simplest food, yet, when some one urged a vegetable diet, Thoreau thought all diets a very small matter; saying, that "the man who shoots the buffalo lives better than the man who boards at the Graham house." He said, "You can sleep near the railroad, and never be disturbed. Nature knows very well what sounds are worth attending to, and has made up her mind not to hear the railroad-whistle. But things respect the devout mind, and a mental ecstacy was never interrupted."

He noted what repeatedly befel him, that, after receiving from a distance a rare plant, he would presently find the same in his own haunts. And those pieces of luck which happen only to good players happened to him. One day walking with a stranger who inquired, where Indian arrowheads could be found, he replied, "Every where," and stooping forward, picked one on the instant from the ground. At Mount Washington, in Tuckerman's Ravine, Thoreau had a bad fall, and sprained his foot. As he was in the act of getting up from his fall, he saw for the first time, the leaves of the *Arnica mollis*.

His robust common sense, armed with stout hands, keen perceptions, and strong will, cannot yet account for the superiority which shone in his simple and hidden life. I must add the cardinal fact that there was an excellent wisdom in him, proper to a rare class of men, which showed him the material world as a means and symbol. This discovery, which sometimes yields to poets a certain casual and interrupted light serving for the ornament of their writing, was in him an unsleeping insight; and, whatever faults or obstructions of temperament might cloud it, he was not disobedient to the heavenly vision. In his youth, he said, one day, "The other world is all my art: my pencils will draw no other; my jack-knife will cut nothing else; I do not use it as a means." This was the muse and genius that ruled his opinions, conversation, studies, work, and course of life. This made him a searching judge of men. At first glance, he measured his companion, and, though insensible to some fine traits of culture, could very well report his weight and calibre. And this made the impression of genius which his conversation often gave.

He understood the matter in hand at a glance, and saw the limitations and poverty of those he talked with, so that nothing seemed concealed from such terrible eyes. I have repeatedly known young men of sensibility converted in a moment to the belief that this was the man they were in search of, the man of men, who could tell them all they should do. His own dealing with them was never affectionate, but superior, didactic; scorning their petty ways; very slowly conceding or not conceding at all the promise of his society at their houses or even at his own. "Would he not walk with them?"—He did not know. There was nothing so important to him as his walk; he had no walks to throw away on company. Visits were offered him from respectful parties, but he declined them. Admiring friends offered to carry him at their own cost to the Yellow Stone

River; to the West Indies; to South America. But though
nothing could be more grave or considered than his refus-
als, they remind one in quite new relations of that fop
Brummel's reply to the gentleman who offered him his
carriage in a shower, "But where will *you* ride then?" And
what accusing silences, and what searching and irresistible
speeches battering down all defences, his companions can
remember!

Mr. Thoreau dedicated his genius with such entire love
to the fields, hills, and waters of his native town, that he
made them known and interesting to all reading Americans, and to people over the sea. The river on whose banks
he was born and died, he knew from its springs to its con-
fluence with the Merrimack. He had made summer and
winter observations on it for many years, and at every
hour of the day and the night. The result of the recent
survey of the Water Commissioners appointed by the
State of Massachusetts, he had reached by his private experiments, several years earlier. Every fact which occurs
in the bed, on the banks, or in the air over it; the fishes,
and their spawning and nests, their manners, their food;
the shad-flies which fill the air on a certain evening once a
year, and which are snapped at by the fishes so raven-
ously, that many of these die of repletion; the conical
heaps of small stones on the river shallows, one of which
heaps will sometimes overfill a cart,—these heaps the huge
nests of small fishes; the birds which frequent the stream,
heron, duck, sheldrake, loon, osprey; the snake, muskrat,
otter, woodchuck, and fox, on the banks; the turtle, frog,
hyla, and cricket, which make the banks vocal,—were all
known to him, and, as it were, townsmen and fellow-crea-
tures: so that he felt an absurdity or violence in any narrative of one of these by itself apart, and still more of its
dimensions on an inch-rule, or in the exhibition of its skeleton, or the specimen of a squirrel or a bird in brandy. He
liked to speak of the manners of the river, as itself a lawful
creature, yet with exactness, and always to an observed
fact. As he knew the river, so the ponds in this region.

One of the weapons he used, more important than microscope or alcohol receiver, to other investigators, was a whim which grew on him by indulgence, yet appeared in gravest statement, namely, of extolling his own town and neighborhood as the most favored centre for natural observation. He remarked that the Flora of Massachusetts embraced almost all the important plants of America,— most of the oaks, most of the willows, the best pines, the ash, the maple, the beech, the nuts. He returned Kane's "Arctic Voyage" to a friend of whom he had borrowed it with the remark, that "most of the phenomena noted might be observed in Concord." He seemed a little envious of the Pole, for the coincident sunrise and sunset, or five minutes' day after six months. A splendid fact which Annursnuc had never afforded him. He found red snow in one of his walks; and told me that he expected to find yet the *Victoria regia* in Concord. He was the attorney of the indigenous plants, and owned to a preference of the weeds to the imported plants, as of the Indian to the civilized man: and noticed with pleasure that the willow bean-poles of his neighbor had grown more than his beans. "See these weeds," he said, "which have been hoed at by a million farmers all spring and summer, and yet have prevailed, and just now come out triumphant over all lanes, pastures, fields, and gardens, such is their vigor. We have insulted them with low names too, as pigweed, wormwood, chickweed, shad blossom." He says they have brave names too, abrosia, stellaria, amelanchier, amaranth, etc.

I think his fancy for referring every thing to the meridian of Concord, did not grow out of any ignorance or depreciation of other longitudes or latitudes, but was rather a playful expression of his conviction of the indifferency of all places, and that the best place for each is where he stands. He expressed it once in this wise: "I think nothing is to be hoped from you, if this bit of mould under your feet is not sweeter to you to eat, than any other in this world, or in any world."

The other weapon with which he conquered all obsta-

cles in science was patience. He knew how to sit immove-
able, a part of the rock he rested on, until the bird, the
reptile, the fish, which had retired from him, should come
back, and resume its habits, nay, moved by curiosity
should come to him and watch him.

It was a pleasure and a privilege to walk with him. He
knew the country like a fox or a bird, and passed through
it as freely by paths of his own. He knew every track in
the snow, or on the ground, and what creature had taken
this path before him. One must submit abjectly to such a
guide, and the reward was great. Under his arm he carried
an old music book to press plants; in his pocket, his diary
and pencil, a spy-glass for birds, microscope, jack-knife,
and twine. He wore straw hat, stout shoes, strong gray
trowsers, to brave shrub-oaks and smilax, and to climb a
tree for a hawk's or a squirrel's nest. He waded into the
pool for the water-plants, and his strong legs were no insignificant part of his armour. On the day I speak of he
looked for the menyanthes, detected it across the wide
pool, and, on examination of the florets, decided that it had
been in flower five days. He drew out of his breast-pocket
his diary, and read the names of all the plants that should
bloom on this day, whereof he kept account as a banker
when his notes fall due. The cypripedium not due till to-
morrow. He thought, that, if waked up from a trance, in
this swamp, he could tell by the plants what time of the
year it was within two days. The redstart was flying about
and presently the fine grosbeaks, whose brilliant scarlet
makes the rash gazer wipe his eye, and whose fine clear
note Thoreau compared to that of a tanager which has got
rid of its hoarseness. Presently he heard a note which he
called that of the night-warbler, a bird he had never identified, had been in search of twelve years, which always,
when he saw it, was in the act of diving down into a tree or
bush, and which it was vain to seek; the only bird that
sings indifferently by night and by day. I told him he
must beware of finding and booking it, lest life should
have nothing more to show him. He said, "What you seek

in vain for, half your life, one day you come full upon all
the family at dinner. You seek it like a dream, and, as soon
as you find it, you become its prey."

His interest in the flower or the bird lay very deep in
his mind, was connected with Nature,—and the meaning
of Nature was never attempted to be defined by him. He
would not offer a memoir of his observations to the Natural History Society. "Why should I? To detach the description from its connections in my mind, would make it
no longer true or valuable to me: and they do not wish
what belongs to it." His power of observation seems to
indicate additional senses. He saw as with microscope,
heard as with ear-trumpet, and his memory was a photo-
graphic register of all he saw and heard. And yet none
knew better than he that it is not the fact that imports, but
the impression or effect of the fact on your mind. Every
fact lay in glory in his mind, a type of the order and
beauty of the whole.

His determination on Natural History was organic. He
confessed that he sometimes felt like a hound or a panther,
and, if born among Indians, would have been a fell hunter.
But, restrained by his Massachusetts culture, he played
out the game in this mild form of botany and ichthyology.
His intimacy with animals suggested what Thomas Fuller
records of Butler the apiologist, that "either he had told
the bees things or the bees had told him." Snakes coiled
round his leg; the fishes swam into his hand, and he took
them out of the water; he pulled the woodchuck out of its
hole by the tail, and took the foxes under his protection
from the hunters. Our naturalist had perfect magnanimity; he had no secrets: he would carry you to the heron's
haunt, or, even to his most prized botanical swamp;—possibly knowing that you could never find it again,—yet
willing to take his risks.

No college ever offered him a diploma, or a professor's
chair; no academy made him its corresponding secretary,
its discoverer, or even its member. Whether these learned
bodies feared the satire of his presence. Yet so much

knowledge of nature's secret and genius few others possessed, none in a more large and religious synthesis. For
not a particle of respect had he to the opinions of any man
or body of men, but homage solely to the truth itself. And
as he discovered everywhere among doctors some leaning
of courtesy, it discredited them. He grew to be revered
and admired by his townsmen, who had at first known
him only as an oddity. The farmers who employed him as
a surveyor soon discovered his rare accuracy and skill, his
knowledge of their lands, of trees, of birds, of Indian remains, and the like, which enabled him to tell every
farmer more than he knew before of his own farm. So that
he began to feel as if Mr. Thoreau had better rights in his
land than he. They felt, too, the superiority of character
which addressed all men with a native authority.

Indian relics abound in Concord, arrowheads, stone
chisels, pestles, and fragments of pottery; and, on the river
bank, large heaps of clam-shells and ashes mark spots
which the savages frequented. These, and every circumstance touching the Indian, were important in his eyes.
His visits to Maine were chiefly for love of the Indian. He
had the satisfaction of seeing the manufacture of the bark-
canoe, as well as of trying his hand in its management on
the rapids. He was inquisitive about the making of the
stone arrowhead, and, in his last days, charged a youth
setting out for the Rocky Mountains, to find an Indian
who could tell him that: "It was well worth a visit to California, to learn it." Occasionally, a small party of Penob-
scot Indians would visit Concord, and pitch their tents for
a few weeks in summer on the river bank. He failed not to
make acquaintance with the best of them, though he well
knew that asking questions of Indians is like catechizing
beavers and rabbits. In his last visit to Maine, he had great
satisfaction from Joseph Polis, an intelligent Indian of
Oldtown, who was his guide for some weeks.

He was equally interested in every natural fact. The
depth of his perception found likeness of law throughout
nature, and, I know not any genius who so swiftly in-

ferred universal law from the single fact. He was no pedant of a department. His eye was open to beauty, and his
ear to music. He found these, not in rare conditions, but
wheresoever he went. He thought the best of music was in
single strains; and he found poetic suggestion in the hum-
ming of the telegraph wire.

His poetry might be bad or good; he no doubt wanted a
lyric facility, and technical skill; but he had the source of
poetry in his spiritual perception. He was a good reader
and critic, and his judgment on poetry was to the ground
of it. He could not be deceived as to the presence or absence of the poetic element in any composition, and his
thirst for this made him negligent and perhaps scornful of
superficial graces. He would pass by many delicate
rhythms, but he would have detected every live stanza or
line in a volume, and knew very well where to find an
equal poetic charm in prose. He was so enamoured of the
spiritual beauty, that he held all actual written poems in
very light esteem in the comparison. He admired Æschylus and Pindar, but when some one was commending
them, he said, that, "Æschylus and the Greeks, in describing Apollo and Orpheus, had given no song, or no
good one. They ought not to have moved trees, but to
have chaunted to the gods such a hymn as would have
sung all their old ideas out of their heads, and new ones
in." His own verses are often rude and defective. The gold
does not yet run pure, is drossy and crude. The thyme and
marjoram are not yet honey. But if he want lyric fineness,
and technical merits, if he have not the poetic temperament, he never lacks the causal thought, showing that his
genius was better than his talent. He knew the worth of
the Imagination for the uplifting and consolation of
human life, and liked to throw every thought into a symbol. The fact you tell is of no value, but only the impression. For this reason his presence was poetic, always
piqued the curiosity to know more deeply the secrets of
his mind. He had many reserves,—an unwillingness to exhibit to profane eyes what was still sacred in his own, and

knew well how to throw a poetic veil over his experience.
All readers of "Walden" will remember his mythical
record of his disappointments:—

> "I long ago lost a hound, a bay horse, and a turtle-dove,
> and am still on their trail. Many are the travellers I
> have spoken concerning them, describing their tracks,
> and what calls they answered to. I have met one or
> two who had heard the hound, and the tramp of the
> horse, and even seen the dove disappear behind a
> cloud, and they seemed as anxious to recover them as
> if they had lost them themselves."

His riddles were worth the reading, and I confide that, if
at any time I do not understand the expression, it is yet
just. Such was the wealth of his truth, that it was not
worth his while to use words in vain.

His poem entitled "Sympathy" reveals the tenderness
under that triple steel of stoicism, and the intellectual subtlety it could animate. His classic poem on "Smoke" suggests Simonides, but is better than any poem of
Simonides. His biography is in his verses. His habitual
thought makes all his poetry a hymn to the Cause of
causes, the spirit which vivifies and controls his own.

> "I hearing get, who had but ears,
>   And sight, who had but eyes before;
> I moments live, who lived but years,
>   And truth discern, who knew but learning's lore."

And still more in these religious lines:—

> "Now chiefly is my natal hour,
>   And only now my prime of life;
> I will not doubt the love untold
> Which not my worth or want hath bought,
> Which wooed me young, and wooes me old,
>   And to this evening hath me brought."

Whilst he used in his writings a certain petulance of remark in reference to churches or churchmen, he was a person of a rare, tender, and absolute religion, a person incapable of any profanation, by act or by thought. Of course, the same isolation which belonged to his original thinking and living detached him from the social religious forms. This is neither to be censured nor regretted. Aristotle long ago explained it, when he said, "One who surpasses his fellow citizens in virtue, is no longer a part of the city. Their law is not for him, since he is a law to himself."

Thoreau was sincerity itself, and might fortify the convictions of prophets in the ethical laws, by his holy living. It was an affirmative experience which refused to be set aside. A truth-speaker he, capable of the most deep and strict conversation; a physician to the wounds of any soul; a friend knowing not only the secret of friendship, but almost worshipped by those few persons who resorted to him as their confessor and prophet, and knew the deep value of his mind and great heart. He thought that without religion or devotion of some kind, nothing great was ever accomplished: and he thought that the bigoted sectarian had better bear this in mind.

His virtues of course sometimes ran into extremes. It was easy to trace to the inexorable demand on all for exact truth that austerity which made this willing hermit more solitary even than he wished. Himself of a perfect probity, he required not less of others. He had a disgust at crime, and no worldly success could cover it. He detected paltering as readily in dignified and prosperous persons as in beggars, and with equal scorn. Such dangerous frankness was in his dealing, that his admirers called him "that terrible Thoreau," as if he spoke, when silent, and was still present when he had departed. I think the severity of his ideal interfered to deprive him of a healthy sufficiency of human society.

The habit of a realist to find things the reverse of their appearance inclined him to put every statement in a paradox. A certain habit of antagonism defaced his earlier writings, a trick of rhetoric not quite outgrown in his later, of substituting for the obvious word and thought its diametrical opposite. He praised wild mountains and winter forests for their domestic air; in snow and ice, he would find sultriness; and commended the wilderness for resembling Rome and Paris. "It was so dry, that you might call it wet."

The tendency to magnify the moment, to read all the laws of nature in the one object or one combination under your eye, is of course comic to those who do not share the philosopher's perception of identity. To him there was no such thing as size. The pond was a small ocean; the Atlantic, a large Walden Pond. He referred every minute fact to cosmical laws. Though he meant to be just, he seemed haunted by a certain chronic assumption that the science of the day pretended completeness and he had just found out that the savans had neglected to discriminate a particular botanical variety, had failed to describe the seeds, or count the sepals. "That is to say," we replied, "the blockheads were not born in Concord, but who said they were? It was their unspeakable misfortune to be born in London, or Paris, or Rome; but, poor fellows, they did what they could, considering that they never saw Bateman Pond, or Nine-Acre-Corner, or Becky Stow's Swamp. Besides, what were you sent into the world for, but to add this observation?"

Had his genius been only contemplative, he had been fitted to his life, but with his energy and practical ability he seemed born for great enterprise and for command: and I so much regret the loss of his rare powers of action, that I cannot help counting it a fault in him that he had no ambition. Wanting this, instead of engineering for all America, he was the captain of a huckleberry party. Pounding beans is good to the end of pounding empires one of these days, but if, at the end of years, it is still only beans!—

But these foibles, real or apparent, were fast vanishing

in the incessant growth of a spirit so robust and wise, and which effaced its defects with new triumphs. His study of nature was a perpetual ornament to him, and inspired his friends with curiosity to see the world through his eyes, and to hear his adventures. They possessed every kind of interest. He had many elegances of his own, whilst he scoffed at conventional elegance. Thus he could not bear to hear the sound of his own steps, the grit of gravel; and therefore never willingly walked in the road, but in the grass, on mountains, and in woods. His senses were acute, and he remarked that by night every dwelling-house gives out bad air, like a slaughter-house. He liked the pure fragrance of melilot. He honored certain plants with special regard, and over all the pond-lily,—then the gentian, and the *Mikania scandens*, and "Life Everlasting," and a bass tree which he visited every year when it bloomed in the middle of July. He thought the scent a more oracular inquisition than the sight,—more oracular and trustworthy. The scent, of course reveals what is concealed from the other senses. By it he detected earthiness. He delighted in echoes, and said, they were almost the only kind of kindred voices that he heard. He loved nature so well, was so happy in her solitude, that he became very jealous of cities, and the sad work which their refinements and artifices made with man and his dwelling. The axe was always destroying his forest—"Thank God," he said, "they cannot cut down the clouds. All kinds of figures are drawn on the blue ground, with this fibrous white paint."

I subjoin a few sentences taken from his unpublished manuscripts not only as records of his thought and feeling, but for their power of description and literary excellence.

"Some circumstantial evidence is very strong, as when you find a trout in the milk."

"The chub is a soft fish, and tastes like boiled brown paper salted."

"The youth gets together his materials to build a bridge to the moon, or, perchance, a palace or temple on the earth, and, at length, the middle-aged man concludes to build a woodshed with them."

"The locust z---ing."

"Devil's-needles zig-zagging along the Nut-Meadow brook."

"Sugar is not so sweet to the palate, as sound to the healthy ear."

"I put on some hemlock boughs, and the rich salt crackling of their leaves was like mustard to the ear, the crackling of uncountable regiments. Dead trees love the fire."

"The blue-bird carries the sky on his back."

"The tanager flies through the green foliage, as if it would ignite the leaves."

"If I wish for a horse-hair for my compass-sight, I must go to the stable; but the hair-bird with her sharp eyes goes to the road."

"Immortal water, alive even to the superficies."

"Fire is the most tolerable third party."

"Nature made ferns for pure leaves, to show what she could do in that line."

"No tree has so fair a bole, and so handsome an instep as the beech."

"How did these beautiful rainbow tints get into the shell of the fresh-water clam, buried in the mud at the bottom of our dark river?"

"Hard are the times when the infant's shoes are second-foot."

"We are strictly confined to our men to whom we give liberty."

"Nothing is so much to be feared as fear. Atheism may comparatively be popular with God himself."

"Of what significance the things you can forget? A little thought is sexton to all the world."

"How can we expect a harvest of thought, who have not had a seed-time of character?"

"Only he can be trusted with gifts, who can present a face of bronze to expectations."

"I ask to be melted. You can only ask of the metals that they be tender to the fire that melts them. To nought else can they be tender."

There is a flower known to botanists, one of the same genus with our summer plant called "Life Everlasting," a *Gnaphalium* like that, which grows on the most inaccessible cliffs of the Tyrolese mountains, where the chamois dare hardly venture, and which the hunter, tempted by its beauty, and by his love, (for it is immensely valued by the Swiss maidens,) climbs the cliffs to gather, and is sometimes found dead at the foot, with the flower in his hand. It is called by botanists the *Gnaphalium leontopodium*, but by the Swiss, *Edelweisse*, which signifies, *Noble Purity*. Thoreau seemed to me living in the hope to gather this plant, which belonged to him of right. The scale on which his studies proceeded was so large as to require longevity, and we were the less prepared for his sudden disappearance. The country knows not yet, or in the least part, how great a son it has lost. It seems an injury that he should leave in the midst his broken task, which none else can finish,—a kind of indignity to so noble a soul, that it should depart out of nature before yet he has been really shown to his peers for what he is. But he, at least, is content. His soul was made for the noblest society; he had in a short life exhausted the capabilities of this world; wherever there is knowledge, wherever there is virtue, wherever there is beauty, he will find a home.

HISTORIC NOTES OF
LIFE AND LETTERS
IN NEW ENGLAND

~~~~~~~~~~~~~~~~~~~~~~~~~~~~~~~~~~~~

The ancient manners were giving way. There grew a certain tenderness on the people, not before remarked. Children had been repressed and kept in the background; now they were considered, cosseted and pampered. I recall the remark of a witty physician who remembered the hardships of his own youth; he said, "It was a misfortune to have been born when children were nothing, and to live till men were nothing."

There are always two parties, the party of the Past and the party of the Future; the Establishment and the Movement. At times the resistance is reanimated, the schism runs under the world and appears in Literature, Philosophy, Church, State and social customs. It is not easy to date these eras of activity with any precision, but in this region one made itself remarked, say in 1820 and the twenty years following.

It seemed a war between intellect and affection; a crack in Nature, which split every church in Christendom into Papal and Protestant; Calvinism into Old and New schools; Quakerism into Old and New; brought new divisions in politics; as the new conscience touching temperance and slavery. The key to the period appeared to be that the mind had become aware of itself. Men grew reflective and intellectual. There was a new consciousness. The former generations acted under the belief that a shining social prosperity was the beatitude of man, and sacrificed uniformly the citizen to the State. The modern mind believed that the nation existed for the individual, for the guardianship and education of every man. This idea, roughly written in revolutions and national movements, in the mind of the philosopher had far more precision; the individual is the world.

This perception is a sword such as was never drawn before. It divides and detaches bone and marrow, soul and body, yea, almost the man from himself. It is the age of severance, of dissociation, of freedom, of analysis, of detachment. Every man for himself. The public speaker disclaims speaking for any other; he answers only for himself. The social sentiments are weak; the sentiment of patriotism is weak; veneration is low; the natural affections feebler than they were. People grow philosophical about native land and parents and relations. There is an universal resistance to ties and ligaments once supposed essential to civil society. The new race is stiff, heady and rebellious; they are fanatics in freedom; they hate tolls, taxes, turnpikes, banks, hierarchies, governors, yea, almost laws. They have a neck of unspeakable tenderness; it winces at a hair. They rebel against theological as against political dogmas; against mediation, or saints, or any nobility in the unseen.

The age tends to solitude. The association of the time is accidental and momentary and hypocritical, the detachment intrinsic and progressive. The association is for power, merely,—for means; the end being the enlargement and independency of the individual. Anciently, society was in the course of things. There was a Sacred Band, a Theban Phalanx. There can be none now. College classes, military corps, or trades-unions may fancy themselves indissoluble for a moment, over their wine; but it is a painted hoop, and has no girth. The age of arithmetic and of criticism has set in. The structures of old faith in every department of society a few centuries have sufficed to destroy. Astrology, magic, palmistry, are long gone. The very last ghost is laid. Demonology is on its last legs. Prerogative, government, goes to pieces day by day. Europe is strewn with wrecks; a constitution once a week. In

social manners and morals the revolution is just as evident.
In the law courts, crimes of fraud have taken the place of
crimes of force. The stockholder has stepped into the
place of the warlike baron. The nobles shall not any
longer, as feudal lords, have power of life and death over
the churls, but now, in another shape, as capitalists, shall
in all love and peace eat them up as before. Nay, government itself becomes the resort of those whom government
was invented to restrain. "Are there any brigands on the
road?" inquired the traveller in France. "Oh, no, set your
heart at rest on that point," said the landlord; "what
should these fellows keep the highway for, when they can
rob just as effectually, and much more at their ease, in the
bureaus of office?"

In literature the effect appeared in the decided tendency
of criticism. The most remarkable literary work of the age
has for its hero and subject precisely this introversion: I
mean the poem of Faust. In philosophy, Immanuel Kant
has made the best catalogue of the human faculties and the
best analysis of the mind. Hegel also, especially. In science
the French *savant*, exact, pitiless, with barometer, cruci-
ble, chemic test and calculus in hand, travels into all nooks
and islands, to weigh, to analyze and report. And chemistry, which is the analysis of matter, has taught us that we
eat gas, drink gas, tread on gas, and are gas. The same decomposition has changed the whole face of physics; the
like in all arts, modes. Authority falls, in Church, College,
Courts of Law, Faculties, Medicine. Experiment is credible; antiquity is grown ridiculous.

It marked itself by a certain predominance of the intellect in the balance of powers. The warm swart Earth-
spirit which made the strength of past ages, mightier than
it knew, with instincts instead of science, like a mother
yielding food from her own breast instead of preparing it
through chemic and culinary skill,—warm negro ages of
sentiment and vegetation,—all gone; another hour had
struck and other forms arose. Instead of the social existence which all shared, was now separation. Every one for

himself; driven to find all his resources, hopes, rewards, society and deity within himself.

The young men were born with knives in their brain, a tendency to introversion, self-dissection, anatomizing of motives. The popular religion of our fathers had received many severe shocks from the new times; from the Arminians, which was the current name of the backsliders from Calvinism, sixty years ago; then from the English philosophic theologians, Hartley and Priestley and Belsham, the followers of Locke; and then I should say much later from the slow but extraordinary influence of Swedenborg; a man of prodigious mind, though as I think tainted with a certain suspicion of insanity, and therefore generally disowned, but exerting a singular power over an important intellectual class; then the powerful influence of the genius and character of Dr. Channing.

Germany had created criticism in vain for us until 1820, when Edward Everett returned from his five years in Europe, and brought to Cambridge his rich results, which no one was so fitted by natural grace and the splendor of his rhetoric to introduce and recommend. He made us for the first time acquainted with Wolff's theory of the Homeric writings, with the criticism of Heyne. The novelty of the learning lost nothing in the skill and genius of his relation, and the rudest undergraduate found a new morning opened to him in the lecture-room of Harvard Hall.

There was an influence on the young people from the genius of Everett which was almost comparable to that of Pericles in Athens. He had an inspiration which did not go beyond his head, but which made him the master of elegance. If any of my readers were at that period in Boston or Cambridge, they will easily remember his radiant beauty of person, of a classic style, his heavy large eye, marble lids, which gave the impression of mass which the slightness of his form needed; sculptured lips; a voice of such rich tones, such precise and perfect utterance, that, although slightly nasal, it was the most mellow and beautiful and correct of all the instruments of the time. The

word that he spoke, in the manner in which he spoke it,
became current and classical in New England. He had a
great talent for collecting facts, and for bringing those he
had to bear with ingenious felicity on the topic of the moment. Let him rise to speak on what occasion soever, a fact
had always just transpired which composed, with some
other fact well known to the audience, the most pregnant
and happy coincidence. It was remarked that for a man
who threw out so many facts he was seldom convicted of a
blunder. He had a good deal of special learning, and all his
learning was available for purposes of the hour. It was all
new learning, that wonderfully took and stimulated the
young men. It was so coldly and weightily communicated
from so commanding a platform, as if in the consciousness
and consideration of all history and all learning,—adorned
with so many simple and austere beauties of expression,
and enriched with so many excellent digressions and significant quotations, that, though nothing could be conceived beforehand less attractive or indeed less fit for
green boys from Connecticut, New Hampshire and Massachusetts, with their unripe Latin and Greek reading,
than exegetical discourses in the style of Voss and Wolff
and Ruhnken, on the Orphic and Ante-Homeric remains,—yet this learning instantly took the highest place
to our imagination in our unoccupied American Par-
nassus. All his auditors felt the extreme beauty and dignity of the manner, and even the coarsest were contented
to go punctually to listen, for the manner, when they had
found out that the subject-matter was not for them. In the
lecture-room, he abstained from all ornament, and pleased
himself with the play of detailing erudition in a style of
perfect simplicity. In the pulpit (for he was then a clergyman) he made amends to himself and his auditor for the
self-denial of the professor's chair, and, with an infantine
simplicity still, of manner, he gave the reins to his florid,
quaint and affluent fancy.

Then was exhibited all the richness of a rhetoric which
we have never seen rivalled in this country. Wonderful

how memorable were words made which were only pleasing pictures, and covered no new or valid thoughts. He abounded in sentences, in wit, in satire, in splendid allusion, in quotation impossible to forget, in daring imagery, in parable and even in a sort of defying experiment of his own wit and skill in giving an oracular weight to Hebrew or Rabbinical words;—feats which no man could better accomplish, such was his self-command and the security of his manner. All his speech was music, and with such variety and invention that the ear was never tired. Especially beautiful were his poetic quotations. He delighted in quoting Milton, and with such sweet modulation that he seemed to give as much beauty as he borrowed; and whatever he has quoted will be remembered by any who heard him, with inseparable association with his voice and genius. He had nothing in common with vulgarity and infirmity, but, speaking, walking, sitting, was as much aloof and uncommon as a star. The smallest anecdote of his behavior or conversation was eagerly caught and repeated, and every young scholar could recite brilliant sentences from his sermons, with mimicry, good or bad, of his voice. This influence went much farther, for he who was heard with such throbbing hearts and sparkling eyes in the lighted and crowded churches, did not let go his hearers when the church was dismissed, but the bright image of that eloquent form followed the boy home to his bedchamber; and not a sentence was written in academic exercises, not a declamation attempted in the college chapel, but showed the omnipresence of his genius to youthful heads. This made every youth his defender, and boys filled their mouths with arguments to prove that the orator had a heart. This was a triumph of Rhetoric. It was not the intellectual or the moral principles which he had to teach. It was not thoughts. When Massachusetts was full of his fame it was not contended that he had thrown any truths into circulation. But his power lay in the magic of form; it was in the graces of manner; in a new perception of Grecian beauty, to which he had opened our eyes.

There was that finish about this person which is about women, and which distinguishes every piece of genius from the works of talent,—that these last are more or less matured in every degree of completeness according to the time bestowed on them, but works of genius in their first and slightest form are still wholes. In every public discourse there was nothing left for the indulgence of his hearer, no marks of late hours and anxious, unfinished study, but the goddess of grace had breathed on the work a last fragrancy and glitter.

By a series of lectures largely and fashionably attended for two winters in Boston he made a beginning of popular literary and miscellaneous lecturing, which in that region at least had important results. It is acquiring greater importance every day, and becoming a national institution. I am quite certain that this purely literary influence was of the first importance to the American mind.

In the pulpit Dr. Frothingham, an excellent classical and German scholar, had already made us acquainted, if prudently, with the genius of Eichhorn's theologic criticism. And Professor Norton a little later gave form and method to the like studies in the then infant Divinity School. But I think the paramount source of the religious revolution was Modern Science; beginning with Copernicus, who destroyed the pagan fictions of the Church, by showing mankind that the earth on which we live was not the centre of the Universe, around which the sun and stars revolved every day, and thus fitted to be the platform on which the Drama of the Divine Judgment was played before the assembled Angels of Heaven,—"the scaffold of the divine vengeance" Saurin called it,—but a little scrap of a planet, rushing around the sun in our system, which in turn was too minute to be seen at the distance of many stars which we behold. Astronomy taught us our insignificance in Nature; showed that our sacred as our profane history had been written in gross ignorance of the laws, which were far grander than we knew; and compelled a certain extension and uplifting of our views of the Deity and his Providence. This correction of our superstitions was confirmed by the new science of Geology, and the whole train of discoveries in every department. But we presently saw also that the religious nature in man was not affected by these errors in his understanding. The religious sentiment made nothing of bulk or size, or far or near; triumphed over time as well as space; and every lesson of humility, or justice, or charity, which the old ignorant saints had taught him, was still forever true.

Whether from these influences, or whether by a reaction of the general mind against the too formal science, religion and social life of the earlier period,—there was, in the first quarter of our nineteenth century, a certain sharpness of criticism, an eagerness for reform, which showed itself in every quarter. It appeared in the popularity of Lavater's Physiognomy, now almost forgotten. Gall and Spurzheim's Phrenology laid a rough hand on the mysteries of animal and spiritual nature, dragging down every sacred secret to a street show. The attempt was coarse and odious to scientific men, but had a certain truth in it; it felt connection where the professors denied it, and was a leading to a truth which had not yet been announced. On the heels of this intruder came Mesmerism, which broke into the inmost shrines, attempted the explanation of miracle and prophecy, as well as of creation. What could be more revolting to the contemplative philosopher! But a certain success attended it, against all expectation. It was human, it was genial, it affirmed unity and connection between remote points, and as such was excellent criticism on the narrow and dead classification of what passed for science; and the joy with which it was greeted was an instinct of the people which no true philosopher would fail to profit by. But while society remained in doubt between the indignation of the old school and the audacity of the new, a higher note sounded. Unexpected aid from high quarters came to iconoclasts. The German poet Goethe revolted against the science of the day, against French and English science, declared war against the great name of Newton, proposed his own new and simple optics; in Botany, his simple theory of metamorphosis;—the eye of a leaf is all; every part of the plant from root to fruit is only a modified leaf, the branch of a tree is nothing but a leaf whose serratures have become twigs. He extended this into anatomy and animal life, and his views were accepted. The revolt became a revolution. Schelling and Oken introduced their ideal natural philosophy, Hegel his metaphysics, and extended it to Civil History.

The result in literature and the general mind was a return to law; in science, in politics, in social life; as distinguished from the profligate manners and politics of earlier times. The age was moral. Every immorality is a departure from nature, and is punished by natural loss and deformity. The popularity of Combe's Constitution of Man; the humanity which was the aim of all the multitudinous works of Dickens; the tendency even of Punch's caricature, was all on the side of the people. There was a breath of new air, much vague expectation, a consciousness of power not yet finding its determinate aim.

I attribute much importance to two papers of Dr. Channing, one on Milton and one on Napoleon, which were the first specimens in this country of that large criticism which in England had given power and fame to the Edinburgh Review. They were widely read, and of course immediately fruitful in provoking emulation which lifted the style of Journalism. Dr. Channing, whilst he lived, was the star of the American Church, and we then thought, if we do not still think, that he left no successor in the pulpit. He could never be reported, for his eye and voice could not be printed, and his discourses lose their best in losing them. He was made for the public; his cold temperament made him the most unprofitable private companion; but all America would have been impoverished in wanting him. We could not then spare a single word he uttered in public, not so much as the reading a lesson in Scripture, or a hymn, and it is curious that his printed writings are almost a history of the times; as there was no great public interest, political, literary or even economical (for he wrote on the Tariff), on which he did not leave some printed record of his brave and thoughtful opinion. A poor little invalid all his life, he is yet one of those men who vindicate the power of the American race to produce greatness.

Dr. Channing took counsel in 1840 with George Ripley, to the point whether it were possible to bring cultivated, thoughtful people together, and make society that deserved the name. He had earlier talked with Dr. John Collins Warren on the like purpose, who admitted the wisdom of the design and undertook to aid him in making the experiment. Dr. Channing repaired to Dr. Warren's house on the appointed evening, with large thoughts which he wished to open. He found a well-chosen assembly of gentlemen variously distinguished; there was mutual greeting and introduction, and they were chatting agreeably on indifferent matters and drawing gently towards their great expectation, when a side-door opened, the whole company streamed in to an oyster supper, crowned by excellent wines; and so ended the first attempt to establish æsthetic society in Boston.

Some time afterwards Dr. Channing opened his mind to Mr. and Mrs. Ripley, and with some care they invited a limited party of ladies and gentlemen. I had the honor to be present. Though I recall the fact, I do not retain any instant consequence of this attempt, or any connection between it and the new zeal of the friends who at that time began to be drawn together by sympathy of studies and of aspiration. Margaret Fuller, George Ripley, Dr. Convers Francis, Theodore Parker, Dr. Hedge, Mr. Brownson, James Freeman Clarke, William H. Channing and many others, gradually drew together and from time to time spent an afternoon at each other's houses in a serious conversation. With them was always one well-known form, a pure idealist, not at all a man of letters, nor of any practical talent, nor a writer of books; a man quite too cold and contemplative for the alliances of friendship, with rare simplicity and grandeur of perception, who read Plato as an equal, and inspired his companions only in proportion as they were intellectual,—whilst the men of talent complained of the want of point and precision in this abstract and religious thinker.

These fine conversations, of course, were incomprehensible to some in the company, and they had their revenge in their little joke. One declared that "It seemed to him like going to heaven in a swing;" another reported that, at a knotty point in the discourse, a sympathizing Englishman with a squeaking voice interrupted with the question, "Mr. Alcott, a lady near me desires to inquire whether omnipotence abnegates attribute?"

I think there prevailed at that time a general belief in Boston that there was some concert of *doctrinaires* to establish certain opinions and inaugurate some movement in literature, philosophy and religion, of which design the supposed conspirators were quite innocent; for there was no concert, and only here and there two or three men or women who read and wrote, each alone, with unusual vivacity. Perhaps they only agreed in having fallen upon Coleridge and Wordsworth and Goethe, then on Carlyle, with pleasure and sympathy. Otherwise, their education and reading were not marked, but had the American superficialness, and their studies were solitary. I suppose all of them were surprised at this rumor of a school or sect, and certainly at the name of Transcendentalism, given nobody knows by whom, or when it was first applied. As these persons became in the common chances of society acquainted with each other, there resulted certainly strong friendships, which of course were exclusive in proportion to their heat: and perhaps those persons who were mutually the best friends were the most private and had no ambition of publishing their letters, diaries or conversation.

From that time meetings were held for conversation, with very little form, from house to house, of people engaged in studies, fond of books, and watchful of all the intellectual light from whatever quarter it flowed. Nothing could be less formal, yet the intelligence and character and varied ability of the company gave it some notoriety and perhaps waked curiosity as to its aims and results.

Nothing more serious came of it than the modest quarterly journal called The Dial, which, under the editorship of Margaret Fuller, and later of some other, enjoyed its obscurity for four years. All its papers were unpaid contributions, and it was rather a work of friendship among the narrow circle of students than the organ of any party. Perhaps its writers were its chief readers: yet it contained some noble papers by Margaret Fuller, and some numbers had an instant exhausting sale, because of papers by Theodore Parker.

Theodore Parker was our Savonarola, an excellent scholar, in frank and affectionate communication with the best minds of his day, yet the tribune of the people, and the stout Reformer to urge and defend every cause of humanity with and for the humblest of mankind. He was no artist. Highly refined persons might easily miss in him the element of beauty. What he said was mere fact, almost offended you, so bald and detached; little cared he. He stood altogether for practical truth; and so to the last. He used every day and hour of his short life, and his character appeared in the last moments with the same firm control as in the midday of strength. I habitually apply to him the words of a French philosopher who speaks of "the man of Nature who abominates the steam-engine and the factory. His vast lungs breathe independence with the air of the mountains and the woods."

The vulgar politician disposed of this circle cheaply as "the sentimental class." State Street had an instinct that they invalidated contracts and threatened the stability of stocks; and it did not fancy brusque manners. Society always values, even in its teachers, inoffensive people, susceptible of conventional polish. The clergyman who would live in the city *may* have piety, but *must* have taste, whilst there was often coming, among these, some John the Baptist, wild from the woods, rude, hairy, careless of dress and quite scornful of the etiquette of cities. There was a pilgrim in those days walking in the country who stopped at every door where he hoped to find hearing for his doctrine, which was, Never to give or receive money. He was a poor printer, and explained with simple warmth the belief of himself and five or six young men with whom he agreed in opinion, of the vast mischief of our insidious coin. He thought every one should labor at some necessary product, and as soon as he had made more than enough for himself, were it corn, or paper, or cloth, or boot-jacks, he should give of the commodity to any applicant, and in turn go to his neighbor for any article which he had to spare. Of course we were curious to know how he sped in his experiments on the neighbor, and his anecdotes were interesting, and often highly creditable. But he had the courage which so stern a return to Arcadian manners required, and had learned to sleep, in cold nights, when the farmer at whose door he knocked declined to give him a bed, on a wagon covered with the buffalo-robe under the shed,—or under the stars, when the farmer denied the shed and the buffalo-robe. I think he persisted for two years in his brave practice, but did not enlarge his church of believers.

These reformers were a new class. Instead of the fiery souls of the Puritans, bent on hanging the Quaker, burning the witch and banishing the Romanist, these were gentle souls, with peaceful and even with genial dispositions, casting sheep's-eyes even on Fourier and his houris. It was a time when the air was full of reform. Robert Owen of Lanark came hither from England in 1845, and read lectures or held conversations wherever he found listeners; the most amiable, sanguine and candid of men. He had not the least doubt that he had hit on a right and perfect socialism, or that all mankind would adopt it. He was then seventy years old, and being asked, "Well, Mr. Owen, who is your disciple? How many men are there possessed of your views who will remain after you are gone, to put them in practice?" "Not one," was his reply. Robert Owen knew Fourier in his old age. He said that Fourier learned of him all the truth he had; the rest of his system was imagination, and the imagination of a banker. Owen made the best impression by his rare benevolence. His love of men made us forget his "Three Errors." His charitable construction of men and their actions was invariable. He was the better Christian in his controversy with Christians, and he interpreted with great generosity the acts of the "Holy Alliance," and Prince Metternich, with whom the persevering *doctrinaire* had obtained interviews; "Ah," he said, "you may depend on it there are as tender hearts and as much good will to serve men, in palaces, as in colleges."

And truly I honor the generous ideas of the Socialists, the magnificence of their theories and the enthusiasm with which they have been urged. They appeared the inspired men of their time. Mr. Owen preached his doctrine of labor and reward, with the fidelity and devotion of a saint, to the slow ears of his generation. Fourier, almost as wonderful an example of the mathematical mind of France as La Place or Napoleon, turned a truly vast arithmetic to the question of social misery, and has put men under the obligation which a generous mind always confers, of conceiving magnificent hopes and making great demands as the right of man. He took his measure of that which all should and might enjoy, from no soup-society or charity-concert, but from the refinements of palaces, the wealth of universities and the triumphs of artists. He thought nobly. A man is entitled to pure air, and to the air of good conversation in his bringing up, and not, as we or so many of us, to the poor-smell and musty chambers, cats and fools. Fourier carried a whole French Revolution in his head, and much more. Here was arithmetic on a huge scale. His ciphering goes where ciphering never went before, namely, into stars, atmospheres and animals, and men and women, and classes of every character. It was the most entertaining of French romances, and could not but suggest vast possibilities of reform to the coldest and least sanguine.

We had an opportunity of learning something of these Socialists and their theory, from the indefatigable apostle of the sect in New York, Albert Brisbane. Mr. Brisbane pushed his doctrine with all the force of memory, talent, honest faith and importunacy. As we listened to his exposition it appeared to us the sublime of mechanical philosophy; for the system was the perfection of arrangement and contrivance. The force of arrangement could no farther go. The merit of the plan was that it was a system; that it had not the partiality and hint-and-fragment character of most popular schemes, but was coherent and comprehensive of facts to a wonderful degree. It was not daunted by distance, or magnitude, or remoteness of any sort, but strode about nature with a giant's step, and skipped no fact, but wove its large Ptolemaic web of cycle and epicycle, of phalanx and phalanstery, with laudable assiduity. Mechanics were pushed so far as fairly to meet spiritualism. One could not but be struck with strange coincidences betwixt Fourier and Swedenborg. Genius hitherto has been shamefully misapplied, a mere trifler. It must now set itself to raise the social condition of man and to redress the disorders of the planet he inhabits. The Desert of Sahara, the Campagna di Roma, the frozen Polar circles, which by their pestilential or hot or cold airs poison the temperate regions, accuse man. Society, concert, coöperation, is the secret of the coming Paradise. By reason of the isolation of men at the present day, all work is drudgery. By concert and the allowing each laborer to choose his own work, it becomes pleasure. "Attractive Industry" would speedily subdue, by adventurous scientific and persistent tillage, the pestilential tracts; would equalize temperature, give health to the globe and cause the earth to yield "healthy imponderable fluids" to the solar system, as now it yields noxious fluids. The hyæna, the jackal, the gnat, the bug, the flea, were all beneficent parts of the system; the good Fourier knew what those creatures should have been, had not the mould slipped, through the bad state of the atmosphere; caused no doubt by the same vicious imponderable fluids. All these shall be redressed by human culture, and the useful goat and dog and innocent poetical moth, or the wood-tick to consume decomposing wood, shall take their place. It takes sixteen hundred and eighty men to make one Man, complete in all the faculties; that is, to be sure that you have got a good joiner, a good cook, a barber, a poet, a judge, an umbrella-maker, a mayor and alderman, and so on. Your community should consist of two thousand persons, to prevent accidents of omission; and each community should take up six thousand acres of land. Now fancy the earth planted with fifties and hundreds of these phalanxes side by side,—what tillage, what architecture, what refectories, what dormitories, what reading-rooms, what concerts, what lectures, what gardens, what baths! What is not in one will be in another, and many will be within easy distance. Then know you one and all, that Constantinople is the natural capital of the globe. There, in the Golden Horn, will the ArchPhalanx be established; there will the Omniarch reside. Aladdin and his magician, or the beautiful Scheherezade can alone, in these prosaic times before the sight, describe the material splendors collected there. Poverty shall be abolished; deformity, stupidity and crime shall be no more. Genius, grace, art, shall abound, and it is not to be doubted but that in the reign of "Attractive Industry" all men will speak in blank verse.

Certainly we listened with great pleasure to such gay and magnificent pictures. The ability and earnestness of the advocate and his friends, the comprehensiveness of their theory, its apparent directness of proceeding to the end they would secure, the indignation they felt and uttered in the presence of so much social misery, commanded our attention and respect. It contained so much truth, and promised in the attempts that shall be made to realize it so much valuable instruction, that we are engaged to observe every step of its progress. Yet in spite of the assurances of its friends that it was new and widely discriminated from all other plans for the regeneration of society, we could not exempt it from the criticism which we apply to so many projects for reform with which the brain of the age teems. Our feeling was that Fourier had skipped no fact but one, namely Life. He treats man as a plastic thing, something that may be put up or down, ripened or retarded, moulded, polished, made into solid or fluid or gas, at the will of the leader; or perhaps as a vegetable, from which, though now a poor crab, a very good peach can by manure and exposure be in time produced,—but skips the faculty of life, which spawns and scorns system and system-makers; which eludes all conditions; which makes or supplants a thousand phalanxes and New Harmonies with each pulsation. There is an order in which in a sound mind the faculties always appear, and which, according to the strength of the individual, they seek to realize in the surrounding world. The value of Fourier's system is that it is a statement of such an order externized, or carried outward into its correspondence in facts. The mistake is that this particular order and series is to be imposed, by force or preaching and votes, on all men, and carried into rigid execution. But what is true and good must not only be begun by life, but must be conducted to its issues by life. Could not the conceiver of this design have also believed that a similar model lay in every mind, and that the method of each associate might be trusted, as well as that of his particular Committee and General Office, No. 200 Broadway? Nay, that it would be better to say, Let us be lovers and servants of that which is just, and straightway every man becomes a centre of a holy and beneficent republic, which he sees to include all men in its law, like that of Plato, and of Christ. Before such a man the whole world becomes Fourierized or Christized or humanized, and in obedience to his most private being he finds himself, according to his presentiment, though against all sensuous probability, acting in strict concert with all others who followed their private light.

Yet, in a day of small, sour and fierce schemes, one is admonished and cheered by a project of such friendly aims and of such bold and generous proportion; there is an intellectual courage and strength in it which is superior and commanding; it certifies the presence of so much truth in the theory, and in so far is destined to be fact.

It argued singular courage, the adoption of Fourier's system, to even a limited extent, with his books lying before the world only defended by the thin veil of the French language. The Stoic said, Forbear, Fourier said, Indulge. Fourier was of the opinion of Saint-Evremond; abstinence from pleasure appeared to him a great sin. Fourier was very French indeed. He labored under a misapprehension of the nature of women. The Fourier marriage was a calculation how to secure the greatest amount of kissing that the infirmity of human constitution admitted. It was false and prurient, full of absurd French superstitions about women; ignorant how serious and how moral their nature always is; how chaste is their organization; how lawful a class.

It is the worst of community that it must inevitably transform into charlatans the leaders, by the endeavor continually to meet the expectation and admiration of this eager crowd of men and women seeking they know not what. Unless he have a Cossack roughness of clearing himself of what belongs not, charlatan he must be.

It was easy to see what must be the fate of this fine system in any serious and comprehensive attempt to set it on foot in this country. As soon as our people got wind of the doctrine of Marriage held by this master, it would fall at once into the hands of a lawless crew who would flock in troops to so fair a game, and, like the dreams of poetic people on the first outbreak of the old French Revolution, so theirs would disappear in a slime of mire and blood.

There is of course to every theory a tendency to run to

an extreme, and to forget the limitations. In our free institutions, where every man is at liberty to choose his home and his trade, and all possible modes of working and gaining are open to him, fortunes are easily made by thousands, as in no other country. Then property proves too much for the man, and the men of science, art, intellect, are pretty sure to degenerate into selfish housekeepers, dependent on wine, coffee, furnace-heat, gas-light and fine furniture. Then instantly things swing the other way, and we suddenly find that civilization crowed too soon; that what we bragged as triumphs were treacheries: that we have opened the wrong door and let the enemy into the castle; that civilization was a mistake; that nothing is so vulgar as a great warehouse of rooms full of furniture and trumpery; that, in the circumstances, the best wisdom were an auction or a fire. Since the foxes and the birds have the right of it, with a warm hole to keep out the weather, and no more,—a pent-house to fend the sun and rain is the house which lays no tax on the owner's time and thoughts, and which he can leave, when the sun is warm, and defy the robber. This was Thoreau's doctrine, who said that the Fourierists had a sense of duty which led them to devote themselves to their second-best. And Thoreau gave in flesh and blood and pertinacious Saxon belief the purest ethics. He was more real and practically believing in them than any of his company, and fortified you at all times with an affirmative experience which refused to be set aside. Thoreau was in his own person a practical answer, almost a refutation, to the theories of the socialists. He required no Phalanx, no Government, no society, almost no memory. He lived extempore from hour to hour, like the birds and the angels; brought every day a new proposition, as revolutionary as that of yesterday, but different: the only man of leisure in his town; and his independence made all others look like slaves. He was a good Abbot Samson, and carried a counsel in his breast. "Again and again I congratulate myself on my so-called poverty, I could not overstate this advantage." "What you call bareness and poverty, is to me simplicity. God could not be unkind to me if he should try. I love best to have each thing in its season only, and enjoy doing without it at all other times. It is the greatest of all advantages to enjoy no advantage at all. I have never got over my surprise that I should have been born into the most estimable place in all the world, and in the very nick of time too." There's an optimist for you.

I regard these philanthropists as themselves the effects of the age in which we live, and, in common with so many other good facts, the efflorescence of the period, and predicting a good fruit that ripens. They were not the creators they believed themselves, but they were unconscious prophets of a true state of society; one which the tendencies of nature lead unto, one which always establishes itself for the sane soul, though not in that manner in which they paint it; but they were describers of that which is really being done. The large cities are phalansteries; and the theorists drew all their argument from facts already taking place in our experience. The cheap way is to make every man do what he was born for. One merchant to whom I described the Fourier project, thought it must not only succeed, but that agricultural association must presently fix the price of bread, and drive single farmers into association in self-defence, as the great commercial and manufacturing companies had done. Society in England and in America is trying the experiment again in small pieces, in coöperative associations, in cheap eating-houses, as well as in the economies of club-houses and in cheap reading-rooms.

It chanced that here in one family were two brothers, one a brilliant and fertile inventor, and close by him his own brother, a man of business, who knew how to direct his faculty and make it instantly and permanently lucrative. Why could not the like partnership be formed between the inventor and the man of executive talent everywhere? Each man of thought is surrounded by wiser men than he, if they cannot write as well. Cannot he and they combine? Talents supplement each other. Beaumont and Fletcher and many French novelists have known how to utilize such partnerships. Why not have a larger one, and with more various members?

Housekeepers say, "There are a thousand things to everything," and if one must study all the strokes to be laid, all the faults to be shunned in a building or work of art, of its keeping, its composition, its site, its color, there would be no end. But the architect, acting under a necessity to build the house for its purpose, finds himself helped, he knows not how, into all these merits of detail, and steering clear, though in the dark, of those dangers which might have shipwrecked him.

BROOK FARM

The West Roxbury Association was formed in 1841, by a society of members, men and women, who bought a farm in West Roxbury, of about two hundred acres, and took possession of the place in April. Mr. George Ripley was the President, and I think Mr. Charles Dana (afterwards well known as one of the editors of the New York Tribune) was the Secretary. Many members took shares by paying money, others held shares by their labor. An old house on the place was enlarged, and three new houses built. William Allen was at first and for some time the head farmer, and the work was distributed in orderly committees to the men and women. There were many employments more or less lucrative found for, or brought hither by these members,—shoemakers, joiners, sempstresses. They had good scholars among them, and so received pupils for their education. The parents of the children in some instances wished to live there, and were received as boarders. Many persons, attracted by the beauty of the place and the culture and ambition of the community, joined them as boarders, and lived there for years. I think the numbers of this mixed community soon reached eighty or ninety souls.

It was a noble and generous movement in the projectors, to try an experiment of better living. They had the feeling that our ways of living were too conventional and expensive, not allowing each to do what he had a talent for, and not permitting men to combine cultivation of mind and heart with a reasonable amount of daily labor. At the same time, it was an attempt to lift others with themselves, and to share the advantages they should attain, with others now deprived of them.

There was no doubt great variety of character and purpose in the members of the community. It consisted in the main of young people,—few of middle age, and none old. Those who inspired and organized it were of course persons impatient of the routine, the uniformity, perhaps they would say the squalid contentment of society around them, which was so timid and skeptical of any progress. One would say then that impulse was the rule in the society, without centripetal balance; perhaps it would not be severe to say, intellectual sans-culottism, an impatience of the formal, routinary character of our educational, religious, social and economical life in Massachusetts. Yet there was immense hope in these young people. There was nobleness; there were self-sacrificing victims who compensated for the levity and rashness of their companions. The young people lived a great deal in a short time, and came forth some of them perhaps with shattered constitutions. And a few grave sanitary influences of character were happily there, which, I was assured, were always felt.

George W. Curtis of New York, and his brother, of English Oxford, were members of the family from the first. Theodore Parker, the near neighbor of the farm and the most intimate friend of Mr. Ripley, was a frequent visitor. Mr. Ichabod Morton of Plymouth, a plain man formerly engaged through many years in the fisheries with success, eccentric,—with a persevering interest in education, and of a very democratic religion, came and built a house on the farm, and he, or members of his family, continued there to the end. Margaret Fuller, with her joyful conversation and large sympathy, was often a guest, and always in correspondence with her friends. Many ladies, whom to name were to praise, gave character and varied attraction to the place.

In and around Brook Farm, whether as members, boarders or visitors, were many remarkable persons, for character, intellect or accomplishments. I recall one youth of the subtlest mind, I believe I must say the subtlest observer and diviner of character I ever met, living, reading, writing, talking there, perhaps as long as the colony held together; his mind fed and overfed by whatever is exalted in genius, whether in Poetry or Art, in Drama or Music, or in social accomplishment and elegancy; a man of no employment or practical aims, a student and philosopher, who found his daily enjoyment not with the elders or his exact contemporaries so much as with the fine boys who were skating and playing ball or bird-hunting; forming the closest friendships with such, and finding his delight in the petulant heroism of boys; yet was he the chosen counsellor to whom the guardians would repair on any hitch or difficulty that occurred, and draw from him a wise counsel. A fine, subtle, inward genius, puny in body and habit as a girl, yet with an *aplomb* like a general, never disconcerted. He lived and thought, in 1842, such worlds of life; all hinging on the thought of Being or Reality as opposed to consciousness; hating intellect with the ferocity of a Swedenborg. He was the Abbé or spiritual father, from his religious bias. His reading lay in Æschylus, Plato, Dante, Calderon, Shakspeare, and in modern novels and romances of merit. There too was Hawthorne, with his cold yet gentle genius, if he failed to do justice to this temporary home. There was the accomplished Doctor of Music, who has presided over its literature ever since in our metropolis. Rev. William Henry Channing, now of London, was from the first a student of Socialism in France and England, and in perfect sympathy with this experiment. An English baronet, Sir John Caldwell, was a frequent visitor, and more or less directly interested in the leaders and the success.

Hawthorne drew some sketches, not happily, as I think; I should rather say, quite unworthy of his genius. No friend who knew Margaret Fuller could recognize her rich and brilliant genius under the dismal mask which the public fancied was meant for her in that disagreeable story.

The Founders of Brook Farm should have this praise, that they made what all people try to make, an agreeable place to live in. All comers, even the most fastidious, found it the pleasantest of residences. It is certain that freedom from household routine, variety of character and talent, variety of work, variety of means of thought and instruction, art, music, poetry, reading, masquerade, did not permit sluggishness or despondency; broke up routine. There is agreement in the testimony that it was, to most of the associates, education; to many, the most important period of their life, the birth of valued friendships, their first acquaintance with the riches of conversation, their training in behavior. The art of letter-writing, it is said, was immensely cultivated. Letters were always flying not only from house to house, but from room to room. It was a perpetual picnic, a French Revolution in small, an Age of Reason in a patty-pan.

In the American social communities, the gossip found such vent and sway as to become despotic. The institutions were whispering-galleries, in which the adored Saxon privacy was lost. Married women I believe uniformly decided against the community. It was to them like the brassy and lacquered life in hotels. The common school was well enough, but to the common nursery they had grave objections. Eggs might be hatched in ovens, but the hen on her own account much preferred the old way. A hen without her chickens was but half a hen.

It was a curious experience of the patrons and leaders of this noted community, in which the agreement with many parties was that they should give so many hours of instruction in mathematics, in music, in moral and intellectual philosophy, and so forth,—that in every instance the newcomers showed themselves keenly alive to the advantages of the society, and were sure to avail themselves of every means of instruction; their knowledge was increased, their manners refined,—but they became in that proportion averse to labor, and were charged by the heads of the departments with a certain indolence and selfishness.

In practice it is always found that virtue is occasional, spotty, and not linear or cubic. Good people are as bad as rogues if steady performance is claimed; the conscience of the conscientious runs in veins, and the most punctilious in some particulars are latitudinarian in others. It was very gently said that people on whom beforehand all persons would put the utmost reliance were not responsible. They saw the necessity that the work must be done, and did it not, and it of course fell to be done by the few religious workers. No doubt there was in many a certain strength drawn from the fury of dissent. Thus Mr. Ripley told Theodore Parker, "There is your accomplished friend ———: he would hoe corn all Sunday if I would let him, but all Massachusetts could not make him do it on Monday."

Of course every visitor found that there was a comic side to this Paradise of shepherds and shepherdesses. There was a stove in every chamber, and every one might burn as much wood as he or she would saw. The ladies took cold on washing-day; so it was ordained that the gentlemen-shepherds should wring and hang out clothes; which they punctually did. And it would sometimes occur that when they danced in the evening, clothespins dropped plentifully from their pockets. The country members naturally were surprised to observe that one man ploughed all day and one looked out of the window all day, and perhaps drew his picture, and both received at night the same wages. One would meet also some modest pride in their advanced condition, signified by a frequent phrase, "Before we came out of civilization."

The question which occurs to you had occurred much earlier to Fourier: "How in this charming Elysium is the dirty work to be done?" And long ago Fourier had exclaimed, "Ah! I have it," and jumped with joy. "Don't you see," he cried, "that nothing so delights the young Caucasian child as dirt? See the mud-pies that all children will make if you will let them. See how much more joy they find in pouring their pudding on the table-cloth than into their beautiful mouths. The children from six to eight, organized into companies with flags and uniforms, shall do this last function of civilization."

In Brook Farm was this peculiarity, that there was no head. In every family is the father; in every factory, a foreman; in a shop, a master; in a boat, the skipper; but in this Farm, no authority; each was master or mistress of his or her actions; happy, hapless anarchists. They expressed, after much perilous exience, the conviction that plain dealing was the best defence of manners and moral between the sexes. People cannot live together in any but necessary ways. The only candidates who will present themselves will be those who have tried the experiment of independence and ambition, and have failed; and none others will barter for the most comfortble equality the chance of superiority. Then all communities have quarrelled. Few people can live together on their merits. There must be kindred, or mutual economy, or a common interest in their business, or other external tie.

The society at Brook Farm existed, I think, about six or seven years, and then broke up, the Farm was sold, and I believe all the partners came out with pecuniary loss. Some of them had spent on it the accumulations of years. I suppose they all, at the moment, regarded it as a failure. I do not think they can so regard it now, but probably as an important chapter in their experience which has been of lifelong value. What knowledge of themselves and of each other, what various practical wisdom, what personal power, what studies of character, what accumulated culture many of the members owed to it! What mutual measure they took of each other! It was a close union, like that in a ship's cabin, of clergymen, young collegians, merchants, mechanics, farmers' sons and daughters, with men and women of rare opportunities and delicate culture, yet assembled there by a sentiment which all shared, some of them hotly shared, of the honesty of a life of labor and of the beauty of a life of humanity. The yeoman saw refined manners in persons who were his friends; and the lady or the romantic scholar saw the continuous strength and faculty in people who would have disgusted them but that these powers were now spent in the direction of their own theory of life.

I recall these few selected facts, none of them of much independent interest, but symptomatic of the times and country. I please myself with the thought that our American mind is not now eccentric or rude in its strength, but is beginning to show a quiet power, drawn from wide and abundant sources, proper to a Continent and to an educated people. If I have owed much to the special influences I have indicated, I am not less aware of that excellent and increasing circle of masters in arts and in song and in science, who cheer the intellect of our cities and this country to-day,—whose genius is not a lucky accident, but normal, and with broad foundation of culture, and so inspires the hope of steady strength advancing on itself, and a day without night.

CARLYLE

~~~~~~~~~~~~~~~~~~~~~~~~~~~~~~~~~~~

THOMAS CARLYLE is an immense talker, as extraordinary in his conversation as in his writing,—I think even more so.

He is not mainly a scholar, like the most of my acquaintances, but a practical Scotchman, such as you would find in any saddler's or iron-dealer's shop, and then only accidentally and by a surprising addition, the admirable scholar and writer he is. If you would know precisely how he talks, just suppose Hugh Whelan (the gardener) had found leisure enough in addition to all his daily work to read Plato and Shakspeare, Augustine and Calvin, and, remaining Hugh Whelan all the time, should talk scornfully of all this nonsense of books that he had been bothered with, and you shall have just the tone and talk and laughter of Carlyle. I called him a trip-hammer with "an Æolian attachment." He has, too, the strong religious tinge you sometimes find in burly people. That, and all his qualities, have a certain virulence, coupled though it be in his case with the utmost impatience of Christendom and Jewdom and all existing presentments of the good old story. He talks like a very unhappy man,—profoundly solitary, displeased and hindered by all men and things about him, and, biding his time, meditating how to undermine and explode the whole world of nonsense which torments him. He is obviously greatly respected by all sorts of people, understands his own value quite as well as (Daniel) Webster, of whom his behavior sometimes reminds me, and can see society on his own terms.

And, though no mortal in America could pretend to talk with Carlyle, who is also as remarkable in England as the Tower of London, yet neither would he in any manner satisfy us (Americans), or begin to answer the questions which we ask. He is a very national figure, and would by no means bear transplantation. They keep Carlyle as a sort of portable cathedral-bell, which they like to produce in companies where he is unknown, and set a-swinging, to the surprise and consternation of all persons,—bishops, courtiers, scholars, writers,—and, as in companies here (in England) no man is named or introduced, great is the effect and great the inquiry. Forster of Rawdon described to me a dinner at the *table d'hôte* of some provincial hotel where he carried Carlyle, and where an Irish canon had uttered something. Carlyle began to talk, first to the waiters, and then to the walls, and then, lastly, unmistakably to the priest, in a manner that frightened the whole company.

Young men, especially those holding liberal opinions, press to see him, but it strikes me like being hot to see the mathematical or Greek professor before they have got their lesson. It needs something more than a clean shirt and reading German to visit him. He treats them with contempt; they profess freedom and he stands for slavery; they praise republics and he likes the Russian Czar; they admire Cobden and free trade and he is a protectionist in political economy; they will eat vegetables and drink water, and he is a Scotchman who thinks English national character has a pure enthusiasm for beef and mutton,—describes with gusto the crowds of people who gaze at the sirloins in the dealer's shop-window, and even likes the Scotch night-cap; they praise moral suasion, he goes for murder, money, capital punishment and other pretty abominations of English law. They wish freedom of the press, and he thinks the first thing he would do, if he got into Parliament, would be to turn out the reporters, and stop all manner of mischievous speaking to Buncombe, and wind-bags. "In the Long Parliament," he says, "the only great Parliament, they sat secret and silent, grave as an ecumenical council, and I know not what they would have done to anybody that had got in there and attempted to tell out of doors what they did." They go for free institutions, for letting things alone, and only giving opportunity and motive to every man; he for a stringent government, that shows people what they must do, and makes them do it. "Here," he says, "the Parliament gathers up six millions of pounds every year to give to the poor, and yet the people starve. I think if they would give it to me, to provide the poor with labor, and with authority to make them work or shoot them,—and I to be hanged if I did not do it,—I could find them in plenty of Indian meal."

He throws himself readily on the other side. If you urge free trade, he remembers that every laborer is a monopolist. The navigation laws of England made its commerce. "St. John was insulted by the Dutch; he came home, got the law passed that foreign vessels should pay high fees, and it cut the throat of the Dutch, and made the English trade." If you boast of the growth of the country, and show him the wonderful results of the census, he finds nothing so depressing as the sight of a great mob. He saw once, as he told me, three or four miles of human beings, and fancied that "the airth was some great cheese, and these were mites." If a tory takes heart at his hatred of stump-oratory and model republics, he replies, "Yes, the idea of a pig-headed soldier who will obey orders, and fire on his own father at the command of his officer, is a great comfort to the aristocratic mind." It is not so much that Carlyle cares for this or that dogma, as that he likes genuineness (the source of all strength) in his companions.

If a scholar goes into a camp of lumbermen or a gang of riggers, those men will quickly detect any fault of character. Nothing will pass with them but what is real and sound. So this man is a hammer that crushes mediocrity and pretension. He detects weakness on the instant, and touches it. He has a vivacious, aggressive temperament, and unimpressionable. The literary, the fashionable, the

political man, each fresh from triumphs in his own sphere,
comes eagerly to see this man, whose fun they have heartily enjoyed, sure of a welcome, and are struck with despair
at the first onset. His firm, victorious, scoffing vituperation
strikes them with chill and hesitation. His talk often reminds you of what was said of Johnson: "If his pistol
missed fire, he would knock you down with the butt-end."

Mere intellectual partisanship wearies him; he detects
in an instant if a man stands for any cause to which he is
not born and organically committed. A natural defender
of anything, a lover who will live and die for that which he
speaks for, and who does not care for him or for anything
but his own business, he respects; and the nobler this object, of course, the better. He hates a literary trifler, and if,
after Guizot had been a tool of Louis Philippe for years, he
is now to come and write essays on the character of Washington, on "The Beautiful" and on "Philosophy of History," he thinks that nothing.

Great is his reverence for realities,—for all such traits as
spring from the intrinsic nature of the actor. He humors
this into the idolatry of strength. A strong nature has a
charm for him, previous, it would seem, to all inquiry
whether the force be divine or diabolic. He preaches, as
by cannonade, the doctrine that every noble nature was
made by God, and contains, if savage passions, also fit
checks and grand impulses, and, however extravagant, will
keep its orbit and return from far.

Nor can that decorum which is the idol of the
Englishman, and in attaining which the Englishman exceeds all nations, win from him any obeisance. He is eaten
up with indignation against such as desire to make a fair
show in the flesh.

Combined with this warfare on respectabilities, and, indeed, pointing all his satire, is the severity of his moral
sentiment. In proportion to the peals of laughter amid
which he strips the plumes of a pretender and shows the
lean hypocrisy to every vantage of ridicule, does he wor-

ship whatever enthusiasm, fortitude, love or other sign of a good nature is in a man.

There is nothing deeper in his constitution than his humor, than the considerate, condescending good nature with which he looks at every object in existence, as a man might look at a mouse. He feels that the perfection of health is sportiveness, and will not look grave even at dulness or tragedy.

His guiding genius is his moral sense, his perception of the sole importance of truth and justice; but that is a truth of character, not of catechisms. He says, "There is properly no religion in England. These idle nobles at Tattersall's—there is no work or word of serious purpose in them; they have this great lying Church; and life is a humbug." He prefers Cambridge to Oxford, but he thinks Oxford and Cambridge education indurates the young men, as the Styx hardened Achilles, so that when they come forth of them, they say, "Now we are proof; we have gone through all the degrees, and are case-hardened against the veracities of the Universe; nor man nor God can penetrate us."

Wellington he respects as real and honest, and as having made up his mind, once for all, that he will not have to do with any kind of a lie. Edwin Chadwick is one of his heroes,—who proposes to provide every house in London with pure water, sixty gallons to every head, at a penny a week; and in the decay and downfall of all religions, Carlyle thinks that the only religious act which a man nowadays can securely perform is to wash himself well.

Of course the new French revolution of 1848 was the best thing he had seen, and the teaching this great swindler, Louis Philippe, that there is a God's justice in the Universe, after all, was a great satisfaction. Czar Nicholas was his hero; for in the ignominy of Europe, when all thrones fell like card-houses, and no man was found with conscience enough to fire a gun for his crown, but every one ran away in a *coucou*, with his head shaved, through the Barrière de Passy, one man remained who believed he was put there by God Almighty to govern his empire, and, by the help of God, had resolved to stand there.

He was very serious about the bad times; he had seen this evil coming, but thought it would not come in his time. But now 't is coming, and the only good he sees in it is the visible appearance of the gods. He thinks it the only question for wise men, instead of art and fine fancies and poetry and such things, to address themselves to the problem of society. This confusion is the inevitable end of such falsehoods and nonsense as they have been embroiled with.

Carlyle has, best of all men in England, kept the manly attitude in his time. He has stood for scholars, asking no scholar what he should say. Holding an honored place in the best society, he has stood for the people, for the Chartist, for the pauper, intrepidly and scornfully, teaching the nobles their peremptory duties.

His errors of opinion are as nothing in comparison with this merit, in my judgment. This *aplomb* cannot be mimicked; it is the speaking to the heart of the thing. And in England, where the *morgue* of aristocracy has very slowly admitted scholars into society,—a very few houses only in the high circles being ever opened to them,—he has carried himself erect, made himself a power confessed by all men, and taught scholars their lofty duty. He never feared the face of man.

The Bard

~~~~~~~~~~~~~~~~~~~~~~~~~~~~~~~

Because we are accustomed to the irregular rhythms and intentional discords of much modern poetry, we scarcely realize how far Emerson's rough-hewn verses departed from the nineteenth-century norm. He could do the conventional thing if and when he wished. The middle decades of the century were dominated by Henry Wadsworth Longfellow. When Emerson so desired, as he did in "Concord Hymn" and "Brahma," he could match the smooth regularity of Longfellow's lyrics. But the terrain that Emerson made his own lay between Longfellow's and the "organic" poetry sometimes written by Thoreau, which, like twentieth-century free verse, had its form dictated from within by its content. Emerson cast his usual work into brisk couplets with jogging rhythms and offhand rhymes. Vigorous examples are poems such as "Each and All" and "The Problem," which begins:

> I like a church; I like a cowl;
> I love a prophet of the soul;
> And on my heart monastic aisles
> Fall like sweet strains, or pensive smiles;
> Yet not for all his faith can see
> Would I that cowlèd churchman be.

Emerson's gift for metaphor distinguished both his poetry and his prose. Metaphor is everything in that splendid short poem "Days":

> Daughters of Time, the hypocritic Days,
> Muffled and dumb like barefoot dervishes,

as it is in several other of his best lyrics. Still, many of his poems are direct, rather than metaphorical, statements of his insights. We might say that he both felt and thought as a poet; Longfellow rightly termed him "a singer of ideas." "It is not metres," Emerson said, "but a metre-making argument that makes a poem."

Labeling his first collection simply *Poems*, Emerson had the book published in December 1846. It included many of his enduring lyrics. Critics found a few of them baffling but, whatever their reservations, recognized that they were hearing a fresh, strong voice. Two decades later Emerson published *May-Day and Other Pieces*. He had worked over the pieces partly in the effort to make their meaning clearer. His work had more polish now, but his poetic energy was waning, and not many of the later poems had the force or the rawboned beauty of the best in his first collection. Emerson's *Selected Poems* came out in 1876, but by then he needed help from his family and friends in making the selection. Unfortunately their taste was more conventional than Emerson's had been. For the 1884 edition of the collected works his friend James Elliot Cabot brought together the poems from the three previous volumes, plus a few new ones, to make the posthumously published *Poems*. Now the reader could see the rich and eccentric amplitude of Emerson's poetry.

C.B.

EACH AND ALL

Little thinks, in the field, yon red-cloaked clown
Of thee from the hill-top looking down;
The heifer that lows in the upland farm,
Far-heard, lows not thine ear to charm;
The sexton, tolling his bell at noon,
Deems not that great Napoleon
Stops his horse, and lists with delight,
Whilst his files sweep round yon Alpine height;
Nor knowest thou what argument
Thy life to thy neighbor's creed hath lent.
All are needed by each one;
Nothing is good or fair alone.
I thought the sparrow's note from heaven,
Singing at dawn on the alder bough;
I brought him home, in his nest, at even;
He sings the song, but it cheers not now,
For I did not bring home the river and sky;—
He sang to my ear,—they sang to my eye.
The delicate shells lay on the shore;
The bubbles of the latest wave
Fresh pearls to their enamel gave,
And the bellowing of the savage sea
Greeted their safe escape to me.
I wiped away the weeds and foam,
I fetched my sea-born treasures home;
But the poor, unsightly, noisome things
Had left their beauty on the shore
With the sun and the sand and the wild uproar.
The lover watched his graceful maid,
As 'mid the virgin train she strayed,
Nor knew her beauty's best attire
Was woven still by the snow-white choir.
At last she came to his hermitage,
Like the bird from the woodlands to the cage;—
The gay enchantment was undone,

A gentle wife, but fairy none.
Then I said, 'I covet truth;
Beauty is unripe childhood's cheat;
I leave it behind with the games of youth:'—
As I spoke, beneath my feet
The ground-pine curled its pretty wreath,
Running over the club-moss burrs;
I inhaled the violet's breath;
Around me stood the oaks and firs;
Pine-cones and acorns lay on the ground;
Over me soared the eternal sky,
Full of light and of deity;
Again I saw, again I heard,
The rolling river, the morning bird;—
Beauty through my senses stole;
I yielded myself to the perfect whole.

THE PROBLEM

I like a church; I like a cowl;
I love a prophet of the soul;
And on my heart monastic aisles
Fall like sweet strains, or pensive smiles;
Yet not for all his faith can see
Would I that cowlèd churchman be.

Why should the vest on him allure,
Which I could not on me endure?

Not from a vain or shallow thought
His awful Jove young Phidias brought;
Never from lips of cunning fell
The thrilling Delphic oracle;
Out from the heart of nature rolled
The burdens of the Bible old;
The litanies of nations came,
Like the volcano's tongue of flame,
Up from the burning core below,—
The canticles of love and woe:

The hand that rounded Peter's dome
And groined the aisles of Christian Rome
Wrought in a sad sincerity;
Himself from God he could not free;
He builded better than he knew;—
The conscious stone to beauty grew.

Know'st thou what wove yon woodbird's nest
Of leaves, and feathers from her breast?
Or how the fish outbuilt her shell,
Painting with morn each annual cell?
Or how the sacred pine-tree adds
To her old leaves new myriads?
Such and so grew these holy piles,
Whilst love and terror laid the tiles.
Earth proudly wears the Parthenon,
As the best gem upon her zone,
And Morning opes with haste her lids
To gaze upon the Pyramids;
O'er England's abbeys bends the sky,
As on its friends, with kindred eye;
For out of Thought's interior sphere
These wonders rose to upper air;
And Nature gladly gave them place,
Adopted them into her race,
And granted them an equal date
With Andes and with Ararat.

These temples grew as grows the grass;
Art might obey, but not surpass.
The passive Master lent his hand
To the vast soul that o'er him planned;
And the same power that reared the shrine
Bestrode the tribes that knelt within.
Ever the fiery Pentecost
Girds with one flame the countless host,
Trances the heart through chanting choirs,
And through the priest the mind inspires.
The word unto the prophet spoken
Was writ on tables yet unbroken;

The word by seers or sibyls told,
In groves of oak, or fanes of gold,
Still floats upon the morning wind,
Still whispers to the willing mind.
One accent of the Holy Ghost
The heedless world hath never lost.
I know what say the fathers wise,—
The Book itself before me lies,
Old *Chrysostom*, best Augustine,
And he who blent both in his line,
The younger *Golden Lips* or mines,
Taylor, the Shakspeare of divines.
His words are music in my ear,
I see his crowlèd portrait dear;
And yet, for all his faith could see,
I would not the good bishop be.

URIEL

It fell in the ancient periods
    Which the brooding soul surveys,
Or ever the wild Time coined itself
    Into calendar months and days.

This was the lapse of Uriel,
Which in Paradise befell.
Once, among the Pleiads walking,
Seyd overheard the young gods talking;
And the treason, too long pent,
To his ears was evident.
The young deities discussed
Laws of form, and metre just,
Orb, quintessence, and sunbeams,
What subsisteth, and what seems.
One, with low tones that decide,
And doubt and reverend use defied,
With a look that solved the sphere,
And stirred the devils everywhere,

Gave his sentiment divine
Against the being of a line.
'Line in nature is not found;
Unit and universe are round;
In vain produced, all rays return;
Evil will bless, and ice will burn.'
As Uriel spoke with piercing eye,
A shudder ran around the sky;
The stern old war-gods shook their heads,
The seraphs frowned from myrtle-beds;
Seemed to the holy festival
The rash word boded ill to all;
The balance-beam of Fate was bent;
The bounds of good and ill were rent;
Strong Hades could not keep his own,
But all slid to confusion.

A sad self-knowledge, withering, fell
On the beauty of Uriel;
In heaven once eminent, the god
Withdrew, that hour, into his cloud;
Whether doomed to long gyration
In the sea of generation,
Or by knowledge grown too bright
To hit the nerve of feebler sight.
Straightway, a forgetting wind
Stole over the celestial kind,
And their lips the secret kept,
If in ashes the fire-seed slept.
But now and then, truth-speaking things
Shamed the angels' veiling wings;
And, shrilling from the solar course,
Or from fruit of chemic force,
Procession of a soul in matter,
Or the speeding change of water,
Or out of the good of evil born,
Came Uriel's voice of cherub scorn,
And a blush tinged the upper sky,
And the gods shook, they knew not why.

MITHRIDATES

I cannot spare water or wine,
    Tobacco-leaf, or poppy, or rose;
From the earth-poles to the Line,
    All between that works or grows,
Every thing is kin of mine.

Give me agates for my meat;
Give me cantharids to eat;
From air and ocean bring me foods,
From all zones and altitudes;—

From all natures, sharp and slimy,
    Salt and basalt, wild and tame:
Tree and lichen, ape, sea-lion,
    Bird, and reptile, be my game.

Ivy for my fillet band;
Blinding dog-wood in my hand;
Hemlock for my sherbet cull me,
And the prussic juice to lull me;
Swing me in the upas boughs,
Vampyre-fanned, when I carouse.

Too long shut in strait and few,
Thinly dieted on dew,
I will use the world, and sift it,
To a thousand humors shift it,
As you spin a cherry.
O doleful ghosts, and goblins merry!
O all you virtues, methods, mights,
Means, appliances, delights,
Reputed wrongs and braggart rights,
Smug routine, and things allowed,
Minorities, things under cloud!
Hither! take me, use me, fill me,
Vein and artery, though ye kill me!

HAMATREYA

Bulkeley, Hunt, Willard, Hosmer, Meriam, Flint,
Possessed the land which rendered to their toil
Hay, corn, roots, hemp, flax, apples, wool and wood.
Each of these landlords walked amidst his farm,
Saying, ' 'T is mine, my children's and my name's.
How sweet the west wind sounds in my own trees!
How graceful climb those shadows on my hill!
I fancy these pure waters and the flags
Know me, as does my dog: we sympathize;
And, I affirm, my actions smack of the soil.'

Where are these men? Asleep beneath their grounds:
And strangers, fond as they, their furrows plough.
Earth laughs in flowers, to see her boastful boys
Earth-proud, proud of the earth which is not theirs;
Who steer the plough, but cannot steer their feet
Clear of the grave.
They added ridge to valley, brook to pond,
And sighed for all that bounded their domain;
'This suits me for a pasture; that's my park;
We must have clay, lime, gravel, granite-ledge,
And misty lowland, where to go for peat.
The land is well,—lies fairly to the south.
'T is good, when you have crossed the sea and back,
To find the sitfast acres where you left them.'
Ah! the hot owner sees not Death, who adds
Him to his land, a lump of mould the more.
Hear what the Earth says:—

EARTH-SONG

'Mine and yours;
Mine, not yours.
Earth endures;
Stars abide—
Shine down in the old sea;
Old are the shores;
But where are old men?

I who have seen much,
Such have I never seen.

'The lawyer's deed
Ran sure,
In tail,
To them, and to their heirs
Who shall succeed,
Without fail,
Forevermore.

'Here is the land,
Shaggy with wood,
With its old valley,
Mound and flood.
But the heritors?—
Fled like the flood's foam.
The lawyer, and the laws,
And the kingdom,
Clean swept herefrom.

'They called me theirs,
Who so controlled me;
Yet every one
Wished to stay, and is gone,
How am I theirs,
If they cannot hold me,
But I hold them?'

When I heard the Earth-song
I was no longer brave;
My avarice cooled
Like lust in the chill of the grave.

THE RHODORA:

ON BEING ASKED, WHENCE IS THE FLOWER?

In May, when sea-winds pierced our solitudes,
I found the fresh Rhodora in the woods,
Spreading its leafless blooms in a damp nook,

To please the desert and the sluggish brook.
The purple petals, fallen in the pool,
Made the black water with their beauty gay;
Here might the red-bird come his plumes to cool,
And court the flower that cheapens his array.
Rhodora! if the sages ask thee why
This charm is wasted on the earth and sky,
Tell them, dear, that if eyes were made for seeing,
Then Beauty is its own excuse for being:
Why thou wert there, O rival of the rose!
I never thought to ask, I never knew:
But, in my simple ignorance, suppose
The self-same Power that brought me there brought you.

THE HUMBLE-BEE

Burly, dozing humble-bee,
Where thou art is clime for me.
Let them sail for Porto Rique,
Far-off heats through seas to seek;
I will follow thee alone,
Thou animated torrid-zone!
Zigzag steerer, desert cheerer,
Let me chase thy waving lines;
Keep me nearer, me thy hearer,
Singing over shrubs and vines.

Insect lover of the sun,
Joy of thy dominion!
Sailor of the atmosphere;
Swimmer through the waves of air;
Voyager of light and noon;
Epicurean of June;
Wait, I prithee, till I come
Within earshot of thy hum,—
All without is martyrdom.

When the south wind, in May days,
With a net of shining haze

Silvers the horizon wall,
And with softness touching all,
Tints the human countenance
With a color of romance,
And infusing subtle heats,
Turns the sod to violets,
Thou, in sunny solitudes,
Rover of the underwoods,
The green silence dost displace
With thy mellow, breezy bass.

Hot midsummer's petted crone,
Sweet to me thy drowsy tone
Tells of countless sunny hours,
Long days, and solid banks of flowers;
Of gulfs of sweetness without bound
In Indian wildernesses found;
Of Syrian peace, immortal leisure,
Firmest cheer, and bird-like pleasure.

Aught unsavory or unclean
Hath my insect never seen;
But violets and bilberry bells,
Maple-sap and daffodels,
Grass with green flag half-mast high,
Succory to match the sky,
Columbine with horn of honey,
Scented fern, and agrimony,
Clover, catchfly, adder's-tongue
And brier-roses, dwelt among;
All beside was unknown waste,
All was picture as he passed.

Wiser far than human seer,
Yellow-breeched philosopher!
Seeing only what is fair,
Sipping only what is sweet,
Thou dost mock at fate and care,
Leave the chaff, and take the wheat.
When the fierce northwestern blast
Cools sea and land so far and fast,

Thou already slumberest deep;
Woe and want thou canst outsleep;
Want and woe, which torture us,
Thy sleep makes ridiculous.

THE SNOW-STORM

Announced by all the trumpets of the sky,
Arrives the snow, and, driving o'er the fields,
Seems nowhere to alight: the whited air
Hides hills and woods, the river, and the heaven,
And veils the farm-house at the garden's end.
The sled and traveller stopped, the courier's feet
Delayed, all friends shut out, the housemates sit
Around the radiant fireplace, enclosed
In a tumultuous privacy of storm.

Come see the north wind's masonry.
Out of an unseen quarry evermore
Furnished with tile, the fierce artificer
Curves his white bastions with projected roof
Round every windward stake, or tree, or door.
Speeding, the myriad-handed, his wild work
So fanciful, so savage, nought cares he
For number or proportion. Mockingly,
On coop or kennel he hangs Parian wreaths;
A swan-like form invests the hidden thorn;
Fills up the farmer's lane from wall to wall,
Maugre the farmer's sighs; and at the gate
A tapering turret overtops the work.
And when his hours are numbered, and the world
Is all his own, retiring, as he were not,
Leaves, when the sun appears, astonished Art
To mimic in slow structures, stone by stone,
Built in an age, the mad wind's night-work,
The frolic architecture of the snow.

WOODNOTES: I

1

When the pine tosses its cones
To the song of its waterfall tones,
Who speeds to the woodland walks?
To birds and trees who talks?
Cæsar of his leafy Rome,
There the poet is at home.
He goes to the river-side,—
Not hook nor line hath he;
He stands in the meadows wide,—
Nor gun nor scythe to see.
Sure some god his eye enchants:
What he knows nobody wants.
In the wood he travels glad,
Without better fortune had,
Melancholy without bad.
Knowledge this man prizes best
Seems fantastic to the rest:
Pondering shadows, colors, clouds,
Grass-buds and caterpillar-shrouds,
Boughs on which the wild bees settle,
Tints that spot the violet's petal,
Why Nature loves the number five,
And why the star-form she repeats:
Lover of all things alive,
Wonderer at all he meets,
Wonderer chiefly at himself,
Who can tell him what he is?
Or how meet in human elf
Coming and past eternities?

2

And such I knew, a forest seer,
A minstrel of the natural year,
Foreteller of the vernal ides,

Wise harbinger of spheres and tides,
A lover true, who knew by heart
Each joy the mountain dales impart;
It seemed that Nature could not raise
A plant in any secret place,
In quaking bog, on snowy hill,
Beneath the grass that shades the rill,
Under the snow, between the rocks,
In damp fields known to bird and fox.
But he would come in the very hour
It opened in its virgin bower,
As if a sunbeam showed the place,
And tell its long-descended race.
It seemed as if the breezes brought him,
It seemed as if the sparrows taught him;
As if by secret sight he knew
Where, in far fields, the orchis grew.
Many haps fall in the field
Seldom seen by wishful eyes,
But all her shows did Nature yield,
To please and win this pilgrim wise.
He saw the partridge drum in the woods;
He heard the woodcock's evening hymn;
He found the tawny thrushes' broods;
And the shy hawk did wait for him;
What others did at distance hear,
And guessed within the thicket's gloom,
Was shown to this philosopher,
And at his bidding seemed to come.

3

In unploughed Maine he sought the lumberers' gang
Where from a hundred lakes young rivers sprang;
He trode the unplanted forest floor, whereon
The all-seeing sun for ages hath not shone;
Where feeds the moose, and walks the surly bear,
And up the tall mast runs the woodpecker.
He saw beneath dim aisles, in odorous beds,

The slight Linnæa hang its twin-born heads,
And blessed the monument of the man of flowers,
Which breathes his sweet fame through the northern
    bowers.
He heard, when in the grove, at intervals,
With sudden roar the aged pine-tree falls,—
One crash, the death-hymn of the perfect tree,
Declares the close of its green century.
Low lies the plant to whose creation went
Sweet influence from every element;
Whose living towers the years conspired to build,
Whose giddy top the morning loved to gild.
Through these green tents, by eldest Nature dressed,
He roamed, content alike with man and beast.
Where darkness found him he lay glad at night;
There the red morning touched him with its light.
Three moons his great heart him a hermit made,
So long he roved at will the boundless shade.
The timid it concerns to ask their way,
And fear what foe in caves and swamps can stray,
To make no step until the event is known,
And ills to come as evils past bemoan.
Not so the wise; no coward watch he keeps
To spy what danger on his pathway creeps;
Go where he will, the wise man is at home,
His hearth the earth,—his hall the azure dome;
Where his clear spirit leads him, there's his road
By God's own light illumined and foreshowed.

4

'T was one of the charmed days
When the genius of God doth flow;
The wind may alter twenty ways,
A tempest cannot blow;
It may blow north, it still is warm;
Or south, it still is clear;
Or east, it smells like a clover-farm;
Or west, no thunder fear.
The musing peasant, lowly great,

Beside the forest water sate;
The rope-like pine-roots crosswise grown
Composed the network of his throne;
The wide lake, edged with sand and grass,
Was burnished to a floor of glass,
Painted with shadows green and proud
Of the tree and of the cloud.
He was the heart of all the scene;
On him the sun looked more serene;
To hill and cloud his face was known,—
It seemed the likeness of their own;
They knew by secret sympathy
The public child of earth and sky.
'You ask,' he said, 'what guide
Me through trackless thickets led,
Through thick-stemmed woodlands rough and wide.
I found the water's bed.
The watercourses were my guide;
I travelled grateful by their side,
Or through their channel dry;
They led me through the thicket damp,
Through brake and fern, the beavers' camp,
Through beds of granite cut my road,
And their resistless friendship showed.
The falling waters led me,
The foodful waters fed me,
And brought me to the lowest land,
Unerring to the ocean sand.
The moss upon the forest bark
Was pole-star when the night was dark;
The purple berries in the wood
Supplied me necessary food;
For Nature ever faithful is
To such as trust her faithfulness.
When the forest shall mislead me,
When the night and morning lie,
When sea and land refuse to feed me,
'T will be time enough to die;
Then will yet my mother yield

A pillow in her greenest field,
Nor the June flowers scorn to cover
The clay of their departed lover.'

FABLE

The mountain and the squirrel
Had a quarrel,
And the former called the latter 'Little Prig;'
Bun replied,
'You are doubtless very big;
But all sorts of things and weather
Must be taken in together,
To make up a year
And a sphere.
And I think it no disgrace
To occupy my place.
If I'm not so large as you,
You are not so small as I,
And not half so spry.
I'll not deny you make
A very pretty squirrel track;
Talents differ; all is well and wisely put;
If I cannot carry forests on my back,
Neither can you crack a nut.'

ODE

INSCRIBED TO W. H. CHANNING

Though loath to grieve
The evil time's sole patriot,
I cannot leave
My honied thought
For the priest's cant,
Or statesman's rant.

If I refuse
My study for their politique,
Which at the best is trick,
The angry Muse
Puts confusion in my brain.

But who is he that prates
Of the culture of mankind,
Of better arts and life?
Go, blindworm, go,
Behold the famous States
Harrying Mexico
With rifle and with knife!

Or who, with accent bolder,
Dare praise the freedom-loving mountaineer?
I found by thee, O rushing Contoocook!
And in thy valleys, Agiochook!
The jackals of the negro-holder.

The God who made New Hampshire
Taunted the lofty land
With little men;—
Small bat and wren
House in the oak:—
If earth-fire cleave
The upheaved land, and bury the folk,
The southern crocodile would grieve.
Virtue palters; Right is hence;
Freedom praised, but hid;
Funeral eloquence
Rattles the coffin-lid.

What boots thy zeal,
O glowing friend,
That would indignant rend
The northland from the south?
Wherefore? to what good end?
Boston Bay and Bunker Hill
Would serve things still;—
Things are of the snake.

The horseman serves the horse,
The neatherd serves the neat,
The merchant serves the purse,
The eater serves his meat;
'T is the day of the chattel,
Web to weave, and corn to grind;
Things are in the saddle,
And ride mankind.

There are two laws discrete,
Not reconciled,—
Law for man, and law for thing;
The last builds town and fleet,
But it runs wild,
And doth the man unking.

'T is fit the forest fall,
The steep be graded,
The mountain tunnelled,
The sand shaded,
The orchard planted,
The glebe tilled,
The prairie granted,
The steamer built.

Let man serve law for man;
Live for friendship, live for love,
For truth's and harmony's behoof;
The state may follow how it can,
As Olympus follows Jove.

Yet do not I implore
The wrinkled shopman to my sounding woods,
Nor bid the unwilling senator
Ask votes of thrushes in the solitudes.
Every one to his chosen work;—
Foolish hands may mix and mar;
Wise and sure the issues are.
Round they roll till dark is light,
Sex to sex, and even to odd;—
The over-god
Who marries Right to Might,

Who peoples, unpeoples,—
He who exterminates
Races by stronger races,
Black by white faces,—
Knows to bring honey
Out of the lion;
Grafts gentlest scion
On pirate and Turk.

The Cossack eats Poland,
Like stolen fruit;
Her last noble is ruined,
Her last poet mute:
Straight, into double band
The victors divide;
Half for freedom strike and stand;—
The astonished Muse finds thousands at her side.

COMPENSATION

Why should I keep holiday
  When other men have none?
Why but because, when these are gay,
  I sit and mourn alone?

And why, when mirth unseals all tongues,
  Should mine alone be dumb?
Ah! late I spoke to silent throngs,
  And now their hour is come.

GIVE ALL TO LOVE

Give all to love;
Obey thy heart;
Friends, kindred, days,
Estate, good-fame,
Plans, credit and the Muse,—
Nothing refuse.

'T is a brave master;
Let it have scope:
Follow it utterly,
Hope beyond hope:
High and more high
It dives into noon,
With wing unspent,
Untold intent;
But it is a god,
Knows its own path
And the outlets of the sky.

It was never for the mean;
It requireth courage stout.
Souls above doubt,
Valor unbending,
It will reward,—
They shall return
More than they were,
And ever ascending.

Leave all for love;
Yet, hear me, yet,
One word more thy heart behoved,
One pulse more of firm endeavor,—
Keep thee to-day,
To-morrow, forever,
Free as an Arab
Of thy beloved.

Cling with life to the maid;
But when the surprise,
First vague shadow of surmise
Flits across her bosom young,
Of a joy apart from thee,
Free be she, fancy-free;
Nor thou detain her vesture's hem,
Nor the palest rose she flung
From her summer diadem.

Though thou loved her as thyself,
As a self of purer clay,

Though her parting dims the day,
Stealing grace from all alive;
Heartily know,
When half-gods go,
The gods arrive.

MERLIN

I

Thy trivial harp will never please
Or fill my craving ear;
Its chords should ring as blows the breeze,
Free, peremptory, clear.
No jingling serenader's art,
Nor tinkle of piano strings,
Can make the wild blood start
In its mystic springs.
The kingly bard
Must smite the chords rudely and hard,
As with hammer or with mace;
That they may render back
Artful thunder, which conveys
Secrets of the solar track,
Sparks of the supersolar blaze.
Merlin's blows are strokes of fate,
Chiming with the forest tone,
When boughs buffet boughs in the wood;
Chiming with the gasp and moan
Of the ice-imprisoned flood;
With the pulse of manly hearts;
With the voice of orators;
With the din of city arts;
With the cannonade of wars;
With the marches of the brave;
And prayers of might from martyrs' cave.

Great is the art,
Great be the manners, of the bard.

He shall not his brain encumber
With the coil of rhythm and number;
But, leaving rule and pale forethought,
He shall aye climb
For his rhyme,
'Pass in, pass in,' the angels say,
'In to the upper doors,
Nor count compartments of the floors,
But mount to paradise
By the stairway of surprise.'

Blameless master of the games,
King of sport that never shames,
He shall daily joy dispense
Hid in song's sweet influence.
Forms more cheerly live and go,
What time the subtle mind
Sings aloud the tune whereto
Their pulses beat,
And march their feet,
And their members are combined.

By Sybarites beguiled,
He shall no task decline;
Merlin's mighty line
Extremes of nature reconciled,—
Bereaved a tyrant of his will,
And made the lion mild.
Songs can the tempest still,
Scattered on the stormy air,
Mould the year to fair increase,
And bring in poetic peace.

He shall not seek to weave,
In weak, unhappy times,
Efficacious rhymes;
Wait his returning strength.
Bird that from the nadir's floor
To the zenith's top can soar,—

The soaring orbit of the muse exceeds that journey's
      length.
Nor profane affect to hit
Or compass that, by meddling wit,
Which only the propitious mind
Publishes when 't is inclined.
There are open hours
When the God's will sallies free,
And the dull idiot might see
The flowing fortunes of a thousand years;—
Sudden, at unawares,
Self-moved, fly-to the doors,
Nor sword of angels could reveal
What they conceal.

II

The rhyme of the poet
Modulates the king's affairs;
Balance-loving Nature
Made all things in pairs.
To every foot its antipode;
Each color with its counter glowed;
To every tone beat answering tones,
Higher or graver;
Flavor gladly blends with flavor;
Leaf answers leaf upon the bough;
And match the paired cotyledons.
Hands to hands, and feet to feet,
In one body grooms and brides;
Eldest rite, two married sides
In every mortal meet.
Light's far furnace shines,
Smelting balls and bars,
Forging double stars,
Glittering twins and trines.
The animals are sick with love,
Lovesick with rhyme;

Each with all propitious Time
Into chorus wove.
Like the dancers' ordered band,
Thoughts come also hand in hand;
In equal couples mated,
Or else alternated;
Adding by their mutual gage,
One to other, health and age.
Solitary fancies go
Short-lived wandering to and fro,
Most like to bachelors,
Or an ungiven maid,
Not ancestors,
With no posterity to make the lie afraid,
Or keep truth undecayed.
Perfect-paired as eagle's wings,
Justice is the rhyme of things;
Trade and counting use
The self-same tuneful muse;
And Nemesis,
Who with even matches odd,
Who athwart space redresses
The partial wrong,
Fills the just period,
And finishes the song.
Subtle rhymes, with ruin rife,
Murmur in the house of life,
Sung by the Sisters as they spin;
In perfect time and measure they
Build and unbuild our echoing clay.
As the two twilights of the day
Fold us music-drunken in.

BACCHUS

Bring me wine, but wine which never grew
In the belly of the grape,
Or grew on vine whose tap-roots, reaching through

Under the Andes to the Cape,
Suffer no savor of the earth to scape.

Let its grapes the morn salute
From a nocturnal root,
Which feels the acrid juice
Of Styx and Erebus;
And turns the woe of Night,
By its own craft, to a more rich delight.

We buy ashes for bread;
We buy diluted wine;
Give me of the true,—
Whose ample leaves and tendrils curled
Among the silver hills of heaven
Draw everlasting dew;
Wine of wine,
Blood of the world,
Form of forms, and mould of statures,
That I intoxicated,
And by the draught assimilated,
May float at pleasure through all natures;
The bird-language rightly spell,
And that which roses say so well.

Wine that is shed
Like the torrents of the sun
Up the horizon walls,
Or like the Atlantic streams, which run
When the South Sea calls.

Water and bread,
Food which needs no transmuting,
Rainbow-flowering, wisdom-fruiting,
Wine which is already man,
Food which teach and reason can.

Wine which Music is,—
Music and wine are one,—
That I, drinking this,
Shall hear far Chaos talk with me;
Kings unborn shall walk with me;

And the poor grass shall plot and plan
What it will do when it is man.
Quickened so, will I unlock
Every crypt of every rock.

I thank the joyful juice
For all I know;—
Winds of remembering
Of the ancient being blow,
And seeming-solid walls of use
Open and flow.

Pour, Bacchus! the remembering wine;
Retrieve the loss of me and mine!
Vine for vine be antidote,
And the grape requite the lote!
Haste to cure the old despair,—
Reason in Nature's lotus drenched,
The memory of ages quenched;
Give them again to shine;
Let wine repair what this undid;
And where the infection slid,
A dazzling memory revive;
Refresh the faded tints,
Recut the aged prints,
And write my old adventures with the pen
Which on the first day drew,
Upon the tablets blue,
The dancing Pleiads and eternal men.

THRENODY

The South-wind brings
Life, sunshine and desire,
And on every mount and meadow
Breathes aromatic fire;
But over the dead he has no power,
The lost, the lost, he cannot restore;

And, looking over the hills, I mourn
The darling who shall not return.

I see my empty house,
I see my trees repair their boughs;
And he, the wondrous child,
Whose silver warble wild
Outvalued every pulsing sound
Within the air's cerulean round,—
The hyacinthine boy, for whom
Morn well might break and April bloom,
The gracious boy, who did adorn
The world whereinto he was born,
And by his countenance repay
The favor of the loving Day,—
Has disappeared from the Day's eye;
Far and wide she cannot find him;
My hopes pursue, they cannot bind him.
Returned this day, the South-wind searches,
And finds young pines and budding birches;
But finds not the budding man;
Nature, who lost, cannot remake him;
Fate let him fall, Fate can't retake him;
Nature, Fate, men, him seek in vain.

And whither now, my truant wise and sweet,
O, whither tend thy feet?
I had the right, few days ago,
Thy steps to watch, thy place to know:
How have I forfeited the right?
Hast thou forgot me in a new delight?
I hearken for thy household cheer,
O eloquent child!
Whose voice, an equal messenger,
Conveyed thy meaning mild.
What though the pains and joys
Whereof it spoke were toys
Fitting his age and ken,
Yet fairest dames and bearded men,
Who heard the sweet request,

So gentle, wise and grave,
Bended with joy to his behest
And let the world's affairs go by,
A while to share his cordial game,
Or mend his wicker wagon-frame,
Still plotting how their hungry ear
That winsome voice again might hear;
For his lips could well pronounce
Words that were persuasions.

Gentlest guardians marked serene
His early hope, his liberal mien;
Took counsel from his guiding eyes
To make this wisdom earthly wise.
Ah, vainly do these eyes recall
The school-march, each day's festival,
When every morn my bosom glowed
To watch the convoy on the road;
The babe in willow wagon closed,
With rolling eyes and face composed;
With children forward and behind,
Like Cupids studiously inclined;
And he the chieftain paced beside,
The centre of the troop allied,
With sunny face of sweet repose,
To guard the babe from fancied foes.
The little captain innocent
Took the eye with him as he went;
Each village senior paused to scan
And speak the lovely caravan.
From the window I look out
To mark thy beautiful parade,
Stately marching in cap and coat
To some tune by fairies played;—
A music heard by thee alone
To works as noble led thee on.

Now Love and Pride, alas! in vain,
Up and down their glances strain.
The painted sled stands where it stood;

The kennel by the corded wood;
His gathered sticks to stanch the wall
Of the snow-tower, when snow should fall;
The ominous hole he dug in the sand,
And childhood's castles built or planned;
His daily haunts I well discern,—
The poultry-yard, the shed, the barn,—
And every inch of garden ground
Paced by the blessed feet around,
From the roadside to the brook
Whereinto he loved to look.
Step the meek fowls where erst they ranged;
The wintry garden lies unchanged;
The brook into the stream runs on;
But the deep-eyed boy is gone.

On that shaded day,
Dark with more clouds than tempests are,
When thou didst yield thy innocent breath
In birdlike heavings unto death,
Night came, and Nature had not thee;
I said, 'We are mates in misery.'
The morrow dawned with needless glow;
Each snowbird chirped, each fowl must crow;
Each tramper started; but the feet
Of the most beautiful and sweet
Of human youth had left the hill
And garden,—they were bound and still.
There's not a sparrow or a wren,
There's not a blade of autumn grain,
Which the four seasons do not tend
And tides of life and increase lend;
And every chick of every bird,
And weed and rock-moss is preferred.
O ostrich-like forgetfulness!
O loss of larger in the less!
Was there no star that could be sent,
No watcher in the firmament,
No angel from the countless host
That loiters round the crystal coast,

Could stoop to heal that only child,
Nature's sweet marvel undefiled,
And keep the blossom of the earth,
Which all her harvests were not worth?
Not mine,—I never called thee mine,
But Nature's heir,—if I repine,
And seeing rashly torn and moved
Not what I made, but what I loved,
Grow early old with grief that thou
Must to the wastes of Nature go,—
'T is because a general hope
Was quenched, and all must doubt and grope.
For flattering planets seemed to say
This child should ills of ages stay,
By wondrous tongue, and guided pen,
Bring the flown Muses back to men.
Perchance not he but Nature ailed,
The world and not the infant failed.
It was not ripe yet to sustain
A genius of so fine a strain,
Who gazed upon the sun and moon
As if he came unto his own,
And, pregnant with his grander thought,
Brought the old order into doubt.
His beauty once their beauty tried;
They could not feed him, and he died,
And wandered backward as in scorn,
To wait an æon to be born.
Ill day which made this beauty waste,
Plight broken, this high face defaced!
Some went and came about the dead;
And some in books of solace read;
Some to their friends the tidings say;
Some went to write, some went to pray;
One tarried here, there hurried one;
But their heart abode with none.
Covetous death bereaved us all,
To aggrandize one funeral.
The eager fate which carried thee
Took the largest part of me:

For this losing is true dying;
This is lordly man's down-lying,
This his slow but sure reclining,
Star by star his world resigning.

O child of paradise,
Boy who made dear his father's home,
In whose deep eyes
Men read the welfare of the times to come,
I am too much bereft.
The world dishonored thou hast left.
O truth's and nature's costly lie!
O trusted broken prophecy!
O richest fortune sourly crossed!
Born for the future, to the future lost!

The deep Heart answered, 'Weepest thou?
Worthier cause for passion wild
If I had not taken the child.
And deemest thou as those who pore,
With aged eyes, short way before,—
Think'st Beauty vanished from the coast
Of matter, and thy darling lost?
Taught he not thee—the man of eld,
Whose eyes within his eyes beheld
Heaven's numerous hierarchy span
The mystic gulf from God to man?
To be alone wilt thou begin
When worlds of lovers hem thee in?
To-morrow, when the masks shall fall
That dizen Nature's carnival,
The pure shall see by their own will,
Which overflowing Love shall fill,
'T is not within the force of fate
The fate-conjoined to separate.
But thou, my votary, weepest thou?
I gave thee sight—where is it now?
I taught thy heart beyond the reach
Of ritual, bible, or of speech;
Wrote in thy mind's transparent table,
As far as the incommunicable

Taught thee each private sign to raise
Lit by the supersolar blaze.
Past utterance, and past belief,
And past the blasphemy of grief,
The mysteries of Nature's heart;
And though no Muse can these impart,
Throb thine with Nature's throbbing breast,
And all is clear from east to west.

'I came to thee as to a friend;
Dearest, to thee I did not send
Tutors, but a joyful eye,
Innocence that matched the sky,
Lovely locks, a form of wonder,
Laughter rich as woodland thunder,
That thou might'st entertain apart
The richest flowering of all art:
And, as the great all-loving Day
Through smallest chambers takes its way,
That thou might'st break thy daily bread
With prophet, savior and head;
That thou might'st cherish for thine own
The riches of sweet Mary's Son,
Boy-Rabbi, Israel's paragon.
And thoughtest thou such guest
Would in thy hall take up his rest?
Would rushing life forget her laws,
Fate's flowing revolution pause?
High omens ask diviner guess;
Not to be conned to tediousness
And know my higher gifts unbind
The zone that girds the incarnate mind.
When the scanty shores are full
With Thought's perilous, whirling pool;
When frail Nature can no more,
Then the Spirit strikes the hour:
My servant Death, with solving rite,
Pours finite into infinite.
Wilt thou freeze love's tidal flow,

Whose streams through Nature circling go?
Nail the wild star to its track
On the half-climbed zodiac?
Light is light which radiates,
Blood is blood which circulates,
Life is life which generates,
And many-seeming life is one,—
Wilt thou transfix and make it none?
Its onward force too starkly pent
In figure, bone and lineament?
Wilt thou, uncalled, interrogate,
Talker! the unreplying Fate?
Nor see the genius of the whole
Ascendant in the private soul,
Beckon it when to go and come,
Self-announced its hour of doom?
Fair the soul's recess and shrine,
Magic-built to last a season;
Masterpiece of love benign,
Fairer that expansive reason
Whose omen 't is, and sign.
Wilt thou not ope thy heart to know
What rainbows teach, and sunsets show?
Verdict which accumulates
From lengthening scroll of human fates,
Voice of earth to earth returned,
Prayers of saints that inly burned,—
Saying, *What is excellent,*
As God lives, is permanent;
Hearts are dust, hearts' loves remain;
Heart's love will meet thee again.
Revere the Maker; fetch thine eye
Up to his style, and manners of the sky.
Not of adamant and gold
Built he heaven stark and cold;
No, but a nest of bending reeds,
Flowering grass and scented weeds;
Or like a traveller's fleeing tent,
Or bow above the tempest bent;

Built of tears and sacred flames,
And virtue reaching to its aims;
Built of furtherance and pursuing,
Not of spent deeds, but of doing.
Silent rushes the swift Lord
Through ruined systems still restored,
Broadsowing, bleak and void to bless,
Plants with worlds the wilderness;
Waters with tears of ancient sorrow
Apples of Eden ripe to-morrow.
House and tenant go to ground,
Lost in God, in Godhead found.'

CONCORD HYMN

SUNG AT THE COMPLETION OF THE BATTLE MONUMENT, JULY 4, 1837

By the rude bridge that arched the flood,
    Their flag to April's breeze unfurled,
Here once the embattled farmers stood
    And fired the shot heard round the world.

The foe long since in silence slept;
    Alike the conqueror silent sleeps;
And Time the ruined bridge has swept
    Down the dark stream which seaward creeps.

On this green bank, by this soft stream,
    We set to-day a votive stone;
That memory may their deed redeem,
    When, like our sires, our sons are gone.

Spirit, that made those heroes dare
    To die, and leave their children free,
Bid Time and Nature gently spare
    The shaft we raise to them and thee.

BRAHMA

If the red slayer think he slays,
   Or if the slain think he is slain,
They know not well the subtle ways
   I keep, and pass, and turn again.

Far or forgot to me is near;
   Shadow and sunlight are the same;
The vanished gods to me appear;
   And one to me are shame and fame.

They reckon ill who leave me out;
   When me they fly, I am the wings;
I am the doubter and the doubt,
   And I the hymn the Brahmin sings.

The strong gods pine for my abode,
   And pine in vain the sacred Seven;
But thou, meek lover of the good!
   Find me, and turn thy back on heaven.

DAYS

Daughters of Time, the hypocritic Days,
Muffled and dumb like barefoot dervishes,
And marching single in an endless file,
Bring diadems and fagots in their hands.
To each they offer gifts after his will,
Bread, kingdoms, stars, and sky that holds them all.
I, in my pleached garden, watched the pomp,
Forgot my morning wishes, hastily
Took a few herbs and apples, and the Day
Turned and departed silent. I, too late,
Under her solemn fillet saw the scorn.

TWO RIVERS

Thy summer voice, Musketaquit,
Repeats the music of the rain;
But sweeter rivers pulsing flit
Through thee, as thou through Concord Plain.

Thou in thy narrow banks art pent:
The stream I love unbounded goes
Through flood and sea and firmament;
Through light, through life, it forward flows.

I see the inundation sweet,
I hear the spending of the stream
Through years, through men, through Nature fleet,
Through love and thought, through power and dream.

Musketaquit, a goblin strong,
Of shard and flint makes jewels gay;
They lose their grief who hear his song,
And where he winds is the day of day.

So forth and brighter fares my stream,—
Who drink it shall not thirst again;
No darkness stains its equal gleam,
And ages drop in it like rain.

MUSIC

Let me go where'er I will,
I hear a sky-born music still:
It sounds from all things old,
It sounds from all things young,
From all that's fair, from all that's foul,
Peals out a cheerful song.

It is not only in the rose,
It is not only in the bird,
Not only where the rainbow glows,
Nor in the song of woman heard,

But in the darkest, meanest things
There alway, alway something sings.

'T is not in the high stars alone,
Nor in the cup of budding flowers,
Nor in the redbreast's mellow tone,
Nor in the bow that smiles in showers,
But in the mud and scum of things
There alway, alway something sings.

TERMINUS

It is time to be old,
To take in sail:—
The god of bounds,
Who sets to seas a shore,
Came to me in his fatal rounds,
And said: 'No more!
No farther shoot
Thy broad ambitious branches, and thy root.
Fancy departs: no more invent;
Contract thy firmament
To compass of a tent.
There's not enough for this and that,
Make thy option which of two;
Economize the failing river,
Not the less revere the Giver,
Leave the many and hold the few.
Timely wise accept the terms,
Soften the fall with wary foot;
A little while
Still plan and smile,
And,—fault of novel germs,—
Mature the unfallen fruit.
Curse, if thou wilt, thy sires,
Bad husbands of their fires,
Who, when they gave thee breath,
Failed to bequeath
The needful sinew stark as once,

The Baresark marrow to thy bones,
But left a legacy of ebbing veins,
Inconstant heat and nerveless reins,—
Amid the Muses, left thee deaf and dumb,
Amid the gladiators, halt and numb.'

As the bird trims her to the gale,
I trim myself to the storm of time,
I man the rudder, reef the sail,
Obey the voice at eve obeyed at prime:
'Lowly faithful, banish fear,
Right onward drive unharmed;
The port, well worth the cruise, is near,
And every wave is charmed.'

FURTHER READING*

Background Studies

Matthiessen, F. O. *American Renaissance: Art and Expression in the Age of Emerson and Whitman.* Oxford, 1941. (A classic in cultural criticism.)

Miller, Perry. *The Transcendentalists: An Anthology.* Harvard, 1950. (A generous sample of the writings of the movement.)

Buell, Lawrence. *Literary Transcendentalism: Style and Vision in the American Renaissance.* Cornell, 1973. (Transcendental forms and styles.)

Boller, Paul F. *American Transcendentalism, 1830–1860: An Intellectual Inquiry.* Putnam, 1974. (Development of Transcendental ideas.)

Buell, Lawrence. *New England Literary Culture.* Cambridge, 1986. (Lucid, encyclopedic study of popular culture affecting high culture.)

Emerson's Biography

Cabot, James Elliot. *A Memoir of Ralph Waldo Emerson.* Houghton Mifflin, 1887. (Recollections of a friend of nearly forty years.)

Rusk, Ralph L. *The Life of Ralph Waldo Emerson.* Columbia, 1940. (The standard biography before Gay Wilson Allen's.)

Whicher, Stephen. *Freedom and Fate: An Inner Life of Ralph Waldo Emerson.* Pennsylvania, 1953. (Emerson's gradual acceptance of the belief that our freedom of soul and body is limited by fate.)

Allen, Gay Wilson. *Waldo Emerson.* Viking, 1981. (New information, fresh insights.)

McAleer, John. *Ralph Waldo Emerson: Days of Encounter.* Little, Brown, 1984. (Emerson illuminated through his relationships with others.)

Emerson en famille

Emerson, Ellen Tucker. *The Life of Lidian Jackson Emerson.* Ed. Delores Bird Carpenter. Twayne, 1980. (Emerson observed by his daughter while she is writing about her mother.)

The Letters of Ellen Tucker Emerson. Ed. Edith E. W. Gregg. Kent State, 1982. (The sprightly, observant correspondence of the daughter of a great man.)

Aspects of Emerson

Robinson, David. *Apostle of Culture: Emerson as Preacher and Lecturer.* Pennsylvania, 1982. (Emerson in the pulpit and on the platform.)

Rosenwald, Lawrence. *Emerson and the Art of the Diary.* Oxford, 1988. (Emerson as our foremost diarist; his journal as his highest art.)

Emerson's Attitudes

Paul, Sherman. *Emerson's Angle of Vision: Man and Nature in American Experience.* Harvard, 1952. (The angle is Emerson's important idea of Correspondence.)

Porte, Joel. *Representative Man: Ralph Waldo Emerson in His Time.* Oxford, 1979. (Stimulating study of Emerson's psychology and of some of his relationships to his milieu.)

Emerson's Writing

The Complete Works of Ralph Waldo Emerson, Centenary Edition, 12 vols. Ed. Edward Waldo Emerson. Houghton Mifflin, 1903–4.

The Letters of Ralph Waldo Emerson, 6 vols. Ed. Ralph L. Rusk. Columbia, 1939.

The Early Lectures of Ralph Waldo Emerson, 3 vols. Ed. Robert E. Spiller and others. Harvard, 1959–72.

The Journals and Miscellaneous Notebooks of Ralph Waldo Emerson, 16 vols. Ed. William H. Gilman and others. Harvard, 1960–82. (Definitive edition.)

Emerson's Nature—Origin, Growth, Meaning. Ed. Merton M. Sealts, Jr., and Alfred R. Ferguson. Dodd, Mead, 1969. (The text of the "Bible of New England Transcendentalism" plus all the apparatus.)

The Collected Works of Ralph Waldo Emerson, 4 vols. Ed. Alfred R. Ferguson and others. Harvard, 1971–9. (Definitive edition: vol. 1, *Nature, Addresses, and Lectures*; vol. 2, *Essays, First Series*; vol 3, *Essays, Second Series*; vol. 4, *Representative Men.*)

Bibliography

Myerson, Joel, comp. *Ralph Waldo Emerson: A Descriptive Bibliography.* Pittsburgh, 1982.

*Entries are arranged by the date of first publication.

THE BOOK AND THE BROTHERHOOD
Iris Murdoch

any years ago Gerard Hernshaw and his friends banded together to finance a
litical and philosophical book by a monomaniacal Marxist genius. Now opin-
ns have changed, and support for the book comes at the price of moral indigna-
n; the resulting disagreements lead to passion, hatred, a duel, murder, and a
icide pact.   *602 pages   ISBN: 0-14-010470-4*   **$8.95**

GRAVITY'S RAINBOW
Thomas Pynchon

nomas Pynchon's classic antihero is Tyrone Slothrop, an American lieutenant in
ondon whose body anticipates German rocket launchings. Surely one of the
ost important works of fiction produced in the twentieth century, *Gravity's
ainbow* is a complex and awesome novel in the great tradition of James Joyce's
ysses.   *768 pages   ISBN: 0-14-010661-8*   **$10.95**

FIFTH BUSINESS
Robertson Davies

ne first novel in the celebrated "Deptford Trilogy," which also includes *The
anticore* and *World of Wonders*, *Fifth Business* stands alone as the story of a
tional man who discovers that the marvelous is only another aspect of the
al.   *266 pages   ISBN: 0-14-004387-X*   **$4.95**

WHITE NOISE
Don DeLillo

ck Gladney, a professor of Hitler Studies in Middle America, and his fourth
ife, Babette, navigate the usual rocky passages of family life in the television
;e. Then, their lives are threatened by an "airborne toxic event"—a more urgent
d menacing version of the "white noise" of transmissions that typically engulfs
em.   *326 pages   ISBN: 0-14-007702-2*   **$7.95**

FOR THE BEST LITERATURE, LOOK FOR THE 🐧

☐ **A SPORT OF NATURE**
Nadine Gordimer

Hillela, Nadine Gordimer's "sport of nature," is seductive and intuitively gifted at life. Casting herself adrift from her family at seventeen, she lives among political exiles on an East African beach, marries a black revolutionary, and ultimately plays a heroic role in the overthrow of apartheid.

354 pages   ISBN: 0-14-008470-3   **$7.95**

☐ **THE COUNTERLIFE**
Philip Roth

By far Philip Roth's most radical work of fiction, *The Counterlife* is a book of conflicting perspectives and points of view about people living out dreams of renewal and escape. Illuminating these lives is the skeptical, enveloping intelligence of the novelist Nathan Zuckerman, who calculates the price and examines the results of his characters' struggles for a change of personal fortune.

372 pages   ISBN: 0-14-009769-4   **$4.95**

☐ **THE MONKEY'S WRENCH**
Primo Levi

Through the mesmerizing tales told by two characters—one, a construction worker/philosopher who has built towers and bridges in India and Alaska; the other, a writer/chemist, rigger of words and molecules—Primo Levi celebrates the joys of work and the art of storytelling.

174 pages   ISBN: 0-14-010357-0   **$6.95**

☐ **IRONWEED**
William Kennedy

"Riding up the winding road of Saint Agnes Cemetery in the back of the rattling old truck, Francis Phelan became aware that the dead, even more than the living, settled down in neighborhoods." So begins William Kennedy's Pulitzer-Prize winning novel about an ex-ballplayer, part-time gravedigger, and full-time drunk, whose return to the haunts of his youth arouses the ghosts of his past and present.

228 pages   ISBN: 0-14-007020-6   **$6.95**

☐ **THE COMEDIANS**
Graham Greene

Set in Haiti under Duvalier's dictatorship, *The Comedians* is a story about the committed and the uncommitted. Actors with no control over their destiny, they play their parts in the foreground; experience love affairs rather than love; have enthusiasms but not faith; and if they die, they die like Mr. Jones, by accident.

288 pages   ISBN: 0-14-002766-1   **$4.95**

FOR THE BEST LITERATURE, LOOK FOR THE 🐧

☐ **THE LAST SONG OF MANUEL SENDERO**
Ariel Dorfman

In an unnamed country, in a time that might be now, the son of Manuel Sendero refuses to be born, beginning a revolution where generations of the future wait for a world without victims or oppressors.

464 pages   *ISBN: 0-14-008896-2*   **$7.95**

☐ **THE BOOK OF LAUGHTER AND FORGETTING**
Milan Kundera

In this collection of stories and sketches, Kundera addresses themes including sex and love, poetry and music, sadness and the power of laughter. "*The Book of Laughter and Forgetting* calls itself a novel," writes John Leonard of *The New York Times*, "although it is part fairly tale, part literary criticism, part political tract, part musicology, part autobiography. It can call itself whatever it wants to, because the whole is genius."

240 pages   *ISBN: 0-14-009693-0*   **$6.95**

☐ **TIRRA LIRRA BY THE RIVER**
Jessica Anderson

Winner of the Miles Franklin Award, Australia's most prestigious literary prize, *Tirra Lirra by the River* is the story of a woman's seventy-year search for the place where she truly belongs. Nora Porteous's series of escapes takes her from a small Australia town to the suburbs of Sydney to London, where she seems finally to become the woman she always wanted to be.

142 pages   *ISBN: 0-14-006945-3*   **$4.95**

☐ **LOVE UNKNOWN**
A. N. Wilson

In their sweetly wild youth, Monica, Belinda, and Richeldis shared a bachelor-girl flat and became friends for life. Now, twenty years later, A. N. Wilson charts the intersecting lives of the three women through the perilous waters of love, marriage, and adultery in this wry and moving modern comedy of manners.

202 pages   *ISBN: 0-14-010190-X*   **$6.95**

☐ **THE WELL**
Elizabeth Jolley

Against the stark beauty of the Australian farmlands, Elizabeth Jolley portrays an eccentric, affectionate relationship between the two women—Hester, a lonely spinster, and Katherine, a young orphan. Their pleasant, satisfyingly simple life is nearly perfect until a dark stranger invades their world in a most horrifying way.

176 pages   *ISBN: 0-14-008901-2*   **$6.95**

FOR THE BEST LITERATURE, LOOK FOR THE ⓟ

☐ **VOSS**
Patrick White

Set in nineteenth-century Australia, *Voss* is the story of the secret passion between an explorer and a young orphan. From the careful delineation of Victorian society to the stark narrative of adventure in the Australian desert, Patrick White's novel is one of extraordinary power and virtuosity. White won the Nobel Prize for Literature in 1973.

448 pages   *ISBN: 0-14-001438-1*   **$7.95**

☐ **STONES FOR IBARRA**
Harriet Doerr

An American couple, the only foreigners in the Mexican village of Ibarra, have come to reopen a long-dormant copper mine. Their plan is to live out their lives here, connected to the place and to each other. Along the way, they learn much about life, death, and the tide of fate from the Mexican people around them.

214 pages   *ISBN: 0-14-007562-3*   **$6.95**

You can find all these books at your local bookstore, or use this handy coupon for ordering:

Penguin Books By Mail
Dept. BA Box 999
Bergenfield, NJ 07621-0999

Please send me the above title(s). I am enclosing _____ (please add sales tax if appropriate and $1.50 to cover postage and handling). Send check or money order—no CODs. Please allow four weeks for shipping. We cannot ship to post office boxes or addresses outside the USA. *Prices subject to change without notice.*

Ms./Mrs./Mr. _____

Address _____

City/State _____ Zip _____

Sales tax: CA: 6.5%   NY: 8.25%   NJ: 6%   PA: 6%   TN: 5.5%